H. P. LOVECRAFT

SELECTS

CLASSIC HORROR STORIES

H. P. LOVECRAFT

SELECTS

CLASSIC HORROR STORIES

FALL RIVER PRESS

New York

FALL RIVER PRESS

New York

An Imprint of Sterling Publishing Co., Inc.
1166 Avenue of the Americas
New York, NY 10036

ISBN 978-1-4351-6281-5

Manufactured in the United States of America

2 4 6 8 10 9 7 5 3

www.sterlingpublishing.com

Contents

Introduction

———◆———

THE OLDEST AND STRONGEST EMOTION OF MANKIND IS FEAR." SO WROTE
horror master H. P. Lovecraft in his landmark essay "Supernatural Horror
in Literature," a historical survey that has long served as a required reading
list for tales of horror and the supernatural. At the time Lovecraft wrote his essay—he
began work on it in 1925, and continued revising it as he read more, nearly up until
his death in 1937—virtually no work of this sort existed. Studies of gothic fiction and
ghost stories had been published but there was no comprehensive survey of the weird
tale in its many forms as it had been produced from antiquity to modern times and
across different cultures. One other attribute distinguished Lovecraft's essay: it was
not written by an academic or scholar, but by a working writer of supernatural fiction
with an encyclopedic knowledge of the literature. Lovecraft made his first professional
fiction sale to the pulp fiction magazine *Weird Tales* in 1923, after several years of writing for the amateur press, and by the time he made his last revisions to his essay he was
considered a groundbreaking writer of weird fiction who had produced an impressive body of work. The canonization of Lovecraft by the literary establishment in the
years since his death only further validates the unique perspective he brought to his
appraisal of the supernatural horror fiction tradition.

    H. P. Lovecraft Selects: Classic Horror Stories pays tribute to Lovecraft and his
essay by gathering into one volume the work of thirty-seven authors whose stories
Lovecraft singled out for their excellence. Most of the stories selected Lovecraft named
by title. Some appeared in short-fiction collections that he praised or are among the
most representative works of authors whom he singled out for distinction. That all of
the writers who appear in the book are looked on today as masters of the weird tale is

a testament to Lovecraft's critical acumen, and quite possibly to the attention that his essay focused on their work.

The earliest-published selections were written in the twilight of the gothic novel era, which spanned the decades of the late-eighteenth and early-nineteenth centuries. Lovecraft rightly criticized the book that is considered the first gothic novel, Horace Walpole's *The Castle of Otranto*, as "tedious, artificial, and melodramatic," but he noted that it created "a novel type of scene, puppet-characters, and incidents; which, handled to better advantage by writers more naturally adapted to weird creation, stimulated the growth of an imitative Gothic school which in turn inspired the real weavers of cosmic terror—the line of actual artists beginning with Poe."

Prussian author E. T. A. Hoffmann was one of those "better writers." Lovecraft praised Hoffmann's stories as "a byword for mellowness of background and maturity of form," adding that "generally they convey the grotesque rather than the terrible." "The Sandman," reprinted here, is one of several tales that Hoffmann based on European folklore—in this case the legend of the Sandman, who dispenses pleasant dreams through the agency of magical sand sprinkled on the eyes of sleepers. For this story Hoffmann twisted the legend into nightmare, making the Sandman a horrifying incarnation of the protagonist Nathanael's neuroses and childish fears. Hoffmann's tale would go on to have a life beyond the printed page when it was later adapted by Arthur Saint-Léon for his ballet *Coppélia*, and by Jacques Offenbach for his opera *Tales of Hoffmann*.

Sir Walter Scott was best-known in his day as a writer of historical novels but, as Lovecraft noted, "Scott frequently concerned himself with the weird, weaving it into many of his novels and poems, and sometimes producing such independent bits of narration as 'The Tapestried Chamber.'" Scott's tale is one of the most reprinted ghost stories in the English language, and its basic premise is one that shaped much ghost fiction written in the wake of its publication.

American author Charles Brockden Brown wrote during the high-gothic era, and Lovecraft praised his writing for "an uncanny atmospheric power which gives his horrors a frightful vitality as long as they remained unexplained." Although he took exception to the rationalized horrors of Brown's best-known novel *Wieland; or, The Transformation*, Lovecraft identified its villain, the biloquist (i.e., ventriloquist) Carwin, as "a typical villain of the Manfred Montoni type" (a reference to the gothic fiction of Walpole and Ann Radcliffe, respectively). Written in the years after the publication of *Wieland*, "Carwin, The Biloquist" is an incomplete fragment in which

Brown attempted to show how its title character mastered as a young man the skills that he later put to sinister use in the novel.

Like many critics after him, Lovecraft referenced John Polidori's *The Vampyre* as part of his discussion of Mary Shelley's *Frankenstein; or, The Modern Prometheus*, a novel for which he had the highest regard. As history has it, both Shelley's and Polidori's stories came about as the result of a contest involving Polidori (then serving as physician to Lord Byron), Byron, Percy Bysshe Shelley, and Mary Shelley to write the best horror story during their summer holiday in Switzerland in 1816. *The Vampyre* is regarded as the first story to work the vampire theme into a literary narrative that transcended its usual treatment in folk legends, and Lovecraft praised it for "some excellent passages of stark fright, including a terrible nocturnal experience in a shunned Grecian wood." Although Lovecraft could not have known how popular a character the vampire would eventually become in supernatural fiction, he surely knew that Polidori's tale had struck a chord with both writers and their readers, if only because of the number of vampire stories written after it that he singled out in his essay. These include "Clarimonde" by French author Théophile Gautier, which Lovecraft felt displayed "glimpses of forbidden visits that allure, tantalise, and sometimes horrify"; "For the Blood Is the Life" by American writer F. Marion Crawford, which, he wrote, "touches powerfully on a case of moon-cursed vampirism near an ancient tower on the rocks of the lonely South Italian sea-coast"; and "Seaton's Aunt" by British writer Walter de la Mare, which Lovecraft considered one of several stories by the author that were "unforgettable for their command of fear's and sorcery's darkest ramifications."

But on to Poe, whom Lovecraft considered the paragon of excellence in the weird fiction canon. To Lovecraft, Poe's fiction was the turning point for the modern weird tale, for reasons that he outlined at length:

> Before Poe the bulk of weird writers had worked largely in the dark; without an understanding of the psychological basis of the horror appeal, and hampered by more or less of conformity to certain empty literary conventions such as the happy ending, virtue rewarded, and in general a hollow moral didacticism, acceptance of popular standards and values, and striving of the author to obtrude his own emotions into the story and take sides with the partisans of the majority's artificial ideas. Poe, on the other hand, perceived the essential impersonality of the real artist; and knew that the

function of creative fiction is merely to express and interpret events and sensations as they are, regardless of how they tend or what they prove— good or evil, attractive or repulsive, stimulating or depressing—with the author always acting as a vivid and detached chronicler rather than as a teacher, sympathiser, or vendor of opinion. He saw clearly that all phases of life and thought are equally eligible as subject-matter for the artist, and being inclined by temperament to strangeness and gloom, decided to be the interpreter of those powerful feelings, and frequent happenings which attend pain rather than pleasure, decay rather than growth, terror rather than tranquillity, and which are fundamentally either adverse or indifferent to the tastes and traditional outward sentiments of mankind, and to the health, sanity, and normal expansive welfare of the species.

Poe's approach, in Lovecraft's opinion, established a new standard for realism in literary horror that all writers who followed him were compelled to conform to. Lovecraft paired Poe's tale "Ligeia," reprinted here, with his equally well-known tale "The Fall of the House of Usher," observing how "both of these tales owe their supreme magic to the cunning development which appears in the selection and collocation of every least incident." Describing its account of a deceased wife who, through sheer force of will from beyond the grave takes possession of her successor, and even imposes her physical features upon her, Lovecraft noted how "the narrative reaches its terrific climax with relentless power."

Although Poe served as his barometer for literary perfection in horror fiction, Lovecraft was aware that the tale of supernatural horror had a pedigree in Great Britain and the European continent that predated Poe's emergence, and that the literary tradition of the horror tale as it evolved there was still being shaped by contemporary writers. Looking to France, Lovecraft grouped the fiction of Prosper Mérimée with that of the French decadents, and noted how the author's "The Venus of Ille" "presents in terse and convincing prose the same ancient statue-bride theme which Thomas Moore cast in ballad form in 'The Ring.' " Of the French collaborators who signed themselves Erckmann-Chatrian, he wrote, "their power of creating a shuddering midnight atmosphere was tremendous despite a tendency toward natural explanations and scientific wonders," singling out their story "The Waters of Death" as one "full of engulfing darkness and mystery." "On the River" was one of the "potently dark creations" of Guy de Maupassant, a writer whose work Lovecraft felt demonstrated "with marvellous force the imminence of nameless terrors, and the relentless dogging of an ill-starred individual by hideous and menacing representatives of the outer blackness." Lovecraft also called attention to the macabre fiction of Maurice Level, a leading exponent of the non-supernatural *conte cruel*. Of Level's "The Last Kiss," he wrote that "the wrenching of the emotions is accomplished through dramatic tantalisations, frustrations, and gruesome physical horrors" redolent of the Grand Guignol. In fact, Level's tale was adapted for performance at France's Grand Guignol theatre, many of whose productions took their cues from the *conte cruel*.

Turning his eye on England, Lovecraft called attention to Captain H. B. Marryatt's short tale "The Were-wolf" (also reprinted as "The White Wolf of the Hartz Mountains"), a chapter from his novel *The Phantom Ship* that is frequently reprinted as a self-contained story. He praised Rudyard Kipling's "indubitable mastery" of the weird in "The Phantom 'Rickshaw," among other stories, and he remarked that Lafcadio Hearn's volume *Fantastics*, from which "The Ghostly Kiss" is reprinted, featured "some of the most impressive ghoulishness in all literature." A number of M. P. Shiel's works caught Lovecraft's fancy, including "The House of Sounds," which Lovecraft dubbed Shiel's "undoubted masterpiece," and which, likening it to Poe's "The Fall of the House of Usher," he described as "floridly written in the 'yellow 'nineties,' and recast with more artistic restraint in the early twentieth century." Lovecraft also praised Clemence Housman's novella *The Were-Wolf*, noting that it "attains a high degree of gruesome tension and achieves to some extent the atmosphere of authentic folklore."

Among more contemporary contributions to England's weird fiction legacy, Lovecraft cited E. F. Benson's "The Man Who Went Too Far," which "breathes whisperingly of a house at the edge of a dark wood, and of Pan's hoof-mark on the breast of a dead man," and the occasional weird fiction of H. G. Wells, whose tale "The Red Room" (a.k.a. "The Ghost of Fear") "reaches a very high level." He praised Arthur Conan Doyle's "Lot No. 249," "wherein the reanimated mummy theme is used with more than ordinary skill," and he showered accolades on John Metcalfe's "The Bad Lands" for "containing graduations of horror that strongly savour of genius." Gauging the "tenacious vigour" of the literature of cosmic fear by the number of non-horror writers who had tried their hand at it, Lovecraft cited "The Monkey's Paw," an "able melodramatic bit" by a writer best known for his humorous fiction. Likewise E. M. Forster's "The Story of a Panic," which Lovecraft felt "may be said to hold the true element of cosmic horror," even though it was written by an author associated with the literary mainstream. Although he was of the opinion that

Mrs. H. D. Everett worked with very old and conventional models for her weird fiction, he observed that she "occasionally reaches singular heights of spiritual terror in her collection of short stories," of which "The Death-Mask" is the title tale. He further called out the tales in May Sinclair's collection *Uncanny Stories*, whose contents included "Where Their Fire Is Not Quenched," although he felt that Sinclair's stories "are inclined to lay more stress on human emotions and psychological delving than upon the stark phenomena of a cosmos utterly unreal."

At the time when he wrote his essay, Lovecraft was relatively new to the work of British writer William Hope Hodgson, but he was impressed by Hodgson's forays into weird fiction. As he wrote, "few can equal him in adumbrating the nearness of nameless forces and monstrous besieging entities through casual hints and insignificant details, or in conveying feelings of the spectral and the abnormal in connexion with regions or buildings." Lovecraft was especially drawn to Hodgson's novel *The House on the Borderland*, which he considered the greatest of his works. "The wanderings of the narrator's spirit through limitless light-years of cosmic space and kalpas of eternity, and its witnessing of the solar system's final destruction, constitute something almost unique in standard literature" he observed.

Perhaps Lovecraft's greatest achievement in his essay was to identify the literary tradition of supernatural horror fiction as it evolved in America. Hitherto, weird fiction of the nineteenth and early twentieth century had been viewed as the inevitable extension of the British and continental gothic traditions. With his identification of Poe as the turning point for the modern weird tales, Lovecraft turned his sights on other American practitioners who followed in Poe's footsteps. Of Nathaniel Hawthorne, he observed that many of his shorter tales "exhibit weirdness, either of atmosphere or of incident, to a remarkable degree." The unfinished but self-contained fragment "Ethan Brand" he felt "rises to genuine heights of cosmic fear with its vignette of the wild hill country and the blazing, desolate lime-kilns, and its delineation of the Byronic 'unpardonable sinner,' whose troubled life ends with a peal of fearful laughter in the night as he seeks rest amidst the flames of the furnace." Lovecraft was among the first critics to call attention to the work of Irish-American writer Fitz-James O'Brien, citing his "What Was It?" as "the first well-shaped short story of a tangible but invisible being." He admired the grimly realistic stories of Ambrose Bierce, among them "The Death of Halpin Frayser," noting that, although "many of them treat only of the physical and psychological horrors within Nature, a substantial proportion admit the malignly supernatural and form a leading element in America's fund of weird literature." Assessing the fiction of New England realist Mary E. Wilkins Freeman, Lovecraft wrote that "horror material of authentic force" could be found in her collection *The Wind in the Rose-Bush*, from which "The Southwest Chamber" is taken. And he felt that "The Dead Valley" from Ralph Adams Cram's sole collection of weird fiction, *Black Spirits and White*, achieved "a memorably potent degree of vague regional horror through subtleties of atmosphere and description." Noting that many of Edward Lucas White's tales of horror were based on actual dreams, Lovecraft called out "The Snout" as one of a handful of stories that "rouse darker apprehensions" than simple strangeness.

In the section of his essay entitled "Modern Masters," Lovecraft devoted considerable attention to writers whose work he felt had evolved far beyond weird tales struck from the gothic prototype. He acknowledged them as writers of serious weird stories, which he defined as follows: "Serious weird stories are either made realistically intense by close consistency and perfect fidelity to Nature except in the one supernatural direction which the author allows himself, or else cast altogether in the realm of phantasy, with atmosphere cunningly adapted to the visualisation of a delicately exotic world of unreality beyond space and time, in which almost anything may happen if it but happen in true accord with certain types of imagination and illusion normal to the sensitive human brain." Among these writers he included Arthur Machen, whose tale "The White People" is often cited as one of the greatest weird tales in the English language. Summarizing its account of an innocent young girl's indoctrination into a witch-cult, Lovecraft writes that "the details of this journey are given with marvellous vividness, and form to the keen critic a masterpiece of fantastic writing, with almost unlimited power in the intimation of potent hideousness and cosmic aberration." Lovecraft regarded British writer Algernon Blackwood as "less intense than Mr. Machen in delineating the extremes of stark fear," but nevertheless praised him as "the one absolute and unquestioned master of weird atmosphere." He described "Ancient Sorceries," which he considered the best of the five stories collected in Blackwood's *John Silence—Physician Extraordinary*, as "hypnotically vivid." Lovecraft also had high praise for the work of Morton Drax Plunkett, better known as Lord Dunsany. "The Hoard of the Gibbelins," from Dunsany's collection *The Book of Wonder*, is one of the stories that bore out Lovecraft's estimation of Dunsany as "unexcelled in the sorcery of crystalline singing prose, and supreme in the creation of a gorgeous and languorous world of iridescently exotic vision." Lovecraft considered ghost story writer M. R. James to be "at the opposite pole of genius from Lord Dunsany," but thought him "gifted with an almost diabolic power of calling horror by gentle steps from the midst of prosaic daily life." James's "The Treasure of Abbot Thomas" is one of several stories that Lovecraft praised for its deployment of what he considered one of the author's greatest creations—what he referred to as "a new type of ghost": "In inventing a new type of ghost, he has departed considerably from the conventional Gothic tradition; for where the older stock ghosts were pale and stately, and apprehended chiefly through the sense of sight, the average James ghost is lean, dwarfish, and hairy—a sluggish, hellish night-abomination midway betwixt beast and man—and usually touched before it is seen." Lovecraft also considered the tale representative of James's storytelling style, in which "the laconic unfolding of abnormal events in adroit order is amply sufficient to produce the desired effect of cumulative horror."

At the end of his essay's section on the weird tradition in America, Lovecraft called attention to the fiction of fellow *Weird Tales* contributor Clark Ashton Smith, noting that some of Smith's best work could be found in the recently published collection *The Double Shadow and Other Fantasies*. "A Night in Malnéant," first published in that collection, bears out Lovecraft's contention that, "in sheer daemonic strangeness and fertility of conception, Mr. Smith is perhaps unexcelled by any other writer dead or living." Lovecraft's estimation of Smith also bears out the acuity of his own critical perceptions with regard to the history of weird fiction. Lovecraft understood that the tradition of supernatural horror fiction was not static but rather an organic process that was still evolving, even as he, Smith, and other living writers extended it. It is interesting to speculate what other writers and works Lovecraft might have worked into his essay had he lived longer and read more, for there are some glaring absences from it. Nevertheless, few would argue that Lovecraft failed to convey the full scope of his subject in "Supernatural Horror in Literature." Nearly a century after he wrote it, it remains one of the greatest efforts in the English language to map the *terra incognita* of the weird fiction tradition.

—Stefan Dziemianowicz
New York, 2016

The Sandman

E. T. A. Hoffmann

---◆---

NATHANIEL TO LOTHAIRE

Certainly you must all be uneasy that I have not written for so long—so very long. My mother, I am sure, is angry, and Clara will believe that I am passing my time in dissipation, entirely forgetful of the fair angel-image that is so deeply imprinted in my heart and mind. Such, however, is not the case. Daily and hourly I think of you all, and in my sweet dreams the kindly form of my lovely Clara passes before me, and smiles upon me with her bright eyes as she was wont when I appeared among you. Alas, how could I write to you in the distracted mood which has hitherto disturbed my every thought! Something horrible has crossed my path of life. Dark forebodings of a cruel, threatening, fate spread themselves over me like dark clouds, which no friendly sunbeam can penetrate. Now will I tell you what has befallen me. I must do so, that I plainly see—but if I only think of it, it will laugh out of me like mad. Ah, my dear Lothaire, how shall I begin it? How shall I make you in any way sensible that that which occurred to me a few days ago could really have such a fatal effect on my life? If you were here you could see for yourself, but now you will certainly take me for a crazy ghost-seer. In a word, the horrible thing which happened to me, and the painful impression of which I in vain endeavour to escape, is nothing more than this; that some days ago, namely on the 30th of October, at twelve o'clock at noon, a barometer-dealer came into my room and offered me his wares. I bought nothing, and threatened to throw him down stairs, upon which he took himself off of his own accord.

You suspect that only relations of the most peculiar kind, and exerting the greatest influence over my life can give any import to this occurrence, nay, that the person of that unlucky dealer must have a hostile effect upon me. So it is, indeed. I collect myself with all my might, that patiently and quietly I may tell you so much of my early youth as will bring all plainly and clearly in bright images before your active mind. As I am about to begin I fancy that I hear you laughing and Clara saying: "Childish stories indeed!" Laugh at me I beseech you, laugh with all your heart. But, heavens, my hair stands on end, and it seems as if I am asking you to laugh at me, in mad despair, as Franz Moor asked Daniel. But to my story.

Excepting at dinner time I and my brothers and sisters saw my father very little during the day. He was, perhaps, busily engaged at his ordinary occupation. After supper, which, according to the old custom was served up at seven o'clock, we all went with my mother into my father's work-room, and seated ourselves at the round table. My father smoked tobacco and drank a large glass of beer. Often he told us a number of wonderful stories, and grew so warm over them that his pipe continually went out. I had to light it again, with burning paper, which I thought great sport. Often, too, he would give us picture-books, and sit in his arm-chair silent and thoughtful, puffing out such thick clouds of smoke that we all seemed to be swimming in the clouds. On such evenings as these my mother was very melancholy, and immediately the clock struck nine, she would say: "Now children, to bed—to bed! The Sandman is coming, I can see." And certainly on all these occasions I heard something with a heavy, slow step go bouncing up the stairs. That I thought must be the Sandman. Once that dull noise and footstep were particularly fearful, and I asked my mother, while she took us away: "Eh, mamma, who is this naughty Sandman, who always drives us away from papa? What does he look like?" "There is no Sandman, dear child," replied my mother. "When I say the Sandman comes, I only mean that you are sleepy and cannot keep your eyes open,—just as if sand had been sprinkled into them." This answer of my mother's did not satisfy me—nay, in my childish mind the thought soon matured itself that she only denied the existence of the Sandman to hinder us from being terrified at him. Certainly I always heard him coming up the stairs. Full of curiosity to hear more of this Sandman, and his particular connection with children, I at last asked the old woman who tended my youngest sister what sort of man he was. "Eh, Natty," said she, "do you not know that yet? He is a wicked man, who comes to children when they will not go to bed, and throws a handful of sand into their eyes, so that they start out bleeding from their heads. These eyes he puts in a bag and carries them to the half-moon to feed his own children, who sit in the nest up yonder, and have crooked beaks like owls with which they may pick up the eyes of the naughty human children."

A most frightful image of the cruel Sandman was horribly depicted in my mind, and when in the evening I heard the noise on the stairs, I trembled with agony and alarm. My mother could get nothing out of me, but the cry of "The Sandman, the Sandman!" which was stuttered forth through my tears. I then ran into the bed-room, where the frightful apparition of the Sandman terrified me during the whole night. I had already grown old enough to perceive that the nurse's tale about the Sandman and the nest of children in the half-moon could not be quite true, but, nevertheless, this Sandman remained a fearful spectre, and I was seized with the utmost horror, when I heard him not only come up the stairs, but violently force open my father's room-door and enter. Sometimes he staid away for a long period, but oftener his visits were in close succession. This lasted for years, and I could not accustom myself to the terrible goblin; the image of the dreadful Sandman did not become more faint. His intercourse with my father began more and more to occupy my fancy. An unconquerable fear prevented me from asking my father about it, but if I—I myself could penetrate the mystery, and behold the wondrous Sandman—that was the wish which grew upon me with years. The Sandman had brought me into the path of the marvellous and wonderful, which so readily finds a domicile in the mind of a child. Nothing was to me more delightful than to read or hear horrible stories of goblins, witches, pigmies, &c.; but above them all stood the Sandman, whom, in the oddest and most frightful shapes, I was always drawing with chalk or charcoal on the tables, cupboards, and walls. When I was ten years old, my mother removed me from the children's room into a little chamber, situated in a corridor near my father's room. Still, as before, we were obliged speedily to take our departure as soon as, on the stroke of nine, the unknown was heard in the house. I could hear in my little chamber how he entered my father's room, and then it soon appeared to me that a thin vapor of a singular odor diffused itself about the house. Stronger and stronger with my curiosity grew my resolution to form in some manner the Sandman's acquaintance. Often I sneaked from my room to the corridor, when my mother had passed, but never could I discover any thing, for the Sandman had always gone in at the door when I reached the place where I might have seen him. At last, urged by an irresistible impulse, I resolved to hide myself in my father's room and await the appearance of the Sandman.

By the silence of my father, and the melancholy of my mother, I perceived one evening that the Sandman was coming. I, therefore, feigned great weariness, left the room before nine o'clock, and hid myself in a corner close to the door. The house-door creaked, and the heavy, slow, groaning step went through the passage and towards the stairs. My mother passed me with the rest of the children. Softly—very softly, I opened the door of my father's room. He sat as usually, stiff and silent, with his back turned to the door. He did not perceive me, and I swiftly darted into the room and behind the curtain, drawn before an open press, which stood close to the door, and in which my father's clothes were hanging. The steps sounded nearer and nearer—there was a strange coughing and scraping and murmuring without. My heart trembled with anxiety and expectation. A sharp step close—very close to the door,—a smart stroke on the latch, and the door was open with a rattling noise. Screwing up my courage with all my might, I cautiously peeped out. The Sandman was standing before my father in the middle of the room, the light of the candles shone full upon his face. The Sandman, the fearful Sandman, was the old advocate Coppelius, who had often dined with us.

But the most hideous form could not have inspired me with deeper horror than this very Coppelius. Imagine a large broad-shouldered man, with a head disproportionately big, a face the colour of yellow ochre, a pair of gray bushy eyebrows, from beneath which a pair of green cat's eyes sparkled with the most penetrating lustre, and with a large nose curved over his upper lip. His wry mouth was often twisted into a malicious laugh, when a couple of dark red spots appeared upon his cheeks, and a strange hissing sound was heard through his compressed teeth. Coppelius always appeared in an ashen-gray coat, cut in old-fashioned style, with waistcoat and breeches of the same colour, while his stockings were black, and his shoes adorned with buckles set with precious stones. The little peruke scarcely reached further than the crown of his head, the curls stood high above his large red ears, and a broad hair-bag projected stiffly from his neck, so that the silver buckle which fastened his folded cravat might be plainly seen. The whole figure was hideous and repulsive, but most disgusting to us children were his coarse brown hairy fists; indeed, we did not like to eat what he had touched with them. This he had remarked, and it was his delight, under some pretext or other, to touch a piece of cake, or some nice fruit, that our kind mother might privately have put in our plate, in order that we, with tears in our eyes, might, from disgust and abhorrence, no longer be able to enjoy the treat intended for us. He acted in the same manner on holidays, when my father gave us a little glass of sweet wine. Then would he swiftly draw his fist over it, or perhaps he would even raise the glass to his blue lips, and laugh most devilishly, when we could only express our indignation by soft sobs. He always called us the little beasts, we dared not utter a sound when he was present, and we heartily cursed the ugly, unkind man, who deliberately marred our slightest pleasures. My mother seemed to hate the repulsive Coppelius as much as we did, since as soon as he showed himself her liveliness, her free and cheerful mind was changed into a gloomy solemnity. My father conducted himself towards him, as though he was a superior being, whose bad manners were to be tolerated, and who was to be kept in good humour at any rate. He need only give the slightest hint, and the favourite dishes were cooked, and the choicest wines served.

When I now saw this Coppelius, the frightful and terrific thought took possession of my soul, that indeed no one but he could be the Sandman. But the Sandman was no longer that bugbear of a nurse's tale, who provided the owl's nest in the half-moon with children's eyes,—no, he was a hideous spectral monster, who, wherever he appeared, brought with him grief, want, and destruction—temporal and eternal.

I was rivetted to the spot as if enchanted. At the risk of being discovered, and as I plainly foresaw, of being severely punished, I remained with my head peeping through the curtain. My father received Coppelius with solemnity. "Now to our work!" cried the latter with a harsh, grating voice, as he flung off his coat. My father silently and gloomily drew off his night-gown, and both attired themselves in long black frocks. Whence they took these, I did not see. My father opened the door of what I had always thought to be a cupboard, but I now saw that it was no cupboard, but rather a black hollow, in which there was a little hearth. Coppelius entered, and a blue flame began to crackle up on the hearth. All sorts of strange utensils lay around. Heavens!—As my old father now stooped down to the fire, he looked quite another man. A frightful convulsive pain seemed to have distorted his mild reverend features into a hideous repulsive diabolical countenance. He looked like Coppelius: the latter was brandishing red hot tongs, and with them taking shining masses busily out of the thick smoke, which he afterwards hammered. It seemed to me, as if I saw human faces around without any eyes—but with deep holes instead. "Eyes here, eyes!" said Coppelius in a dull roaring voice. Overcome by the wildest terror, I shrieked out, and fell from my hiding place upon the floor. Coppelius seized me, and showing his teeth, bleated out, "Ah—little wretch,—little wretch!"—then dragging me up, he flung me on the hearth, where the fire began to singe my hair. "Now we have eyes enough—a pretty pair of child's eyes." Thus whispered Coppelius and taking out of the flame some red-hot grains with his fists, he was about to sprinkle them in my eyes. My father upon this raised his hands in supplication, and cried: "Master, master, leave my Nathaniel his eyes!" Coppelius uttered a yelling laugh, and said: "Well let the lad have his eyes and cry his share in the world, but we will examine the mechanism of his hands and feet." And then he seized me so forcibly that my joints cracked, and screwed off my hands and feet, and then put them on again, one here and the other there. "Every thing is not right here!—As good as it was—the old one has understood it!" So did Coppelius say, in a hissing, lisping tone, but all around me became black and dark, a sudden cramp darted through my bones and nerves—and I lost all feeling. A gentle warm breath passed over my face; I woke as out of a sleep of death. My mother had been stooping over me. "Is the Sandman yet there?" I stammered. "No, no, my dear child, he has gone away long ago,—he will not hurt you!"—So said my mother, and she kissed and embraced her recovered darling.

Why should I weary you, my dear Lothaire! Why should I be so diffuse with details, when I have so much more to tell. Suffice it to say, that I had been discovered while watching, and ill-used by Coppelius. Agony and terror had brought on delirium and fever, of which I lay sick for several weeks. "Is the sandman still there?" That was my first sensible word and the sign of my amendment—my recovery. I can now only tell you, the most frightful moment in my juvenile years. Then you will be convinced that it is no fault of my eyes, that all to me seems colourless, but that a dark fatality has actually suspended over my life a gloomy veil of clouds, which I shall perhaps only tear away in death.

Coppelius was no more to be seen; it was said he had left the town.

About a year might have elapsed, when, according to the old custom, we sat at the round table. My father was very cheerful, and told much that was entertaining, about his travels in his youth; when, as the clock struck nine, we heard the house-door creak on the hinges, and slow steps, heavy as iron, groaned through the passage and up the stairs. "That is Coppelius," said my mother, turning pale. "Yes!—that is Coppelius!" repeated my father, with a faint broken voice. The tears started from my mother's eyes. "But father—father!" she cried, "must it be so?" "He comes to me for the last time, I promise you," was the answer. "Only go now—go with the children—go—go to bed. Good night!"

I felt as if I were pressed into cold, heavy stone,—my breath was stopped. My mother caught me by the arm as I stood immoveable. "Come, come, Nathaniel!" I allowed myself to be led, and entered my chamber! "Be quiet—be quiet—go to bed—go to sleep!" cried my mother after me; but tormented by restlessness, and an inward anguish perfectly indescribable, I could not close my eyes. The hateful, abominable Coppelius stood before me with fiery eyes, and laughed at me maliciously. It was in vain that I endeavoured to get rid of his image. About midnight there was a frightful noise, like the firing of a gun. The whole house resounded. There was a rattling and a rustling by my door, and the house-door was closed with a violent sound. "That

is Coppelius!" I cried, and I sprang out of bed in terror. There was then a shriek as
if of acute inconsolable grief. I darted into my father's room; the door was open, a
suffocating smoke rolled towards me, and the servant girl cried: "Ah, my master, my
master!" On the floor of the smoking hearth lay my father dead, with his face burned
and blackened, and hideously distorted,—my sisters were shrieking and moaning
around him,—and my mother had fainted. "Coppelius!—cursed Satan, thou hast slain
my father!" I cried, and lost my senses. When, two days afterwards, my father was laid
in his coffin, his features were again as mild and gentle as they had been in his life. My
soul was comforted by the thought that his compact with the devilish Coppelius could
not have plunged him into eternal perdition.

The explosion had awakened the neighbours, the occurrence had become the common talk, and had reached the ears of the magistracy, who wished to make Coppelius
answerable. He had, however, vanished from the spot, without leaving a trace.

If I tell you, my dear friend, that the barometer-dealer was the accursed Coppelius
himself, you will not blame me for regarding a phenomenon so unpropitious as bod-
ing some heavy calamity. He was dressed differently, but the figure and features of
Coppelius are too deeply imprinted in my mind, for an error in this respect to be possible. Besides, Coppelius has not even altered his name. As I hear he gives himself out
as a Piedmontese optician, and calls himself Giuseppe Coppola.

I am determined to cope with him, and to avenge my father's death, be the issue
what it may.

Tell my mother nothing of the hideous monster's appearance. Remember me to
my dear sweet Clara, to whom I will write in a calmer mood.—Farewell.

CLARA TO NATHANIEL

It is true that you have not written to me for a long time, but nevertheless I believe
that I am still in your mind and thoughts. For assuredly you were thinking of me most
intently, when designing to send your last letter to my brother Lothaire, you directed
it to me, instead of him. I joyfully opened the letter, and did not perceive my error
till I came to the words: "Ah, my dear Lothaire." Now, by rights I should have read
no farther, but should have handed over the letter to my brother. Although you have
often in your childish teasing mood, charged me with having such a quiet, womanish,
steady disposition, that like the lady, even if the house were about to fall in, I should
smooth down a wrong fold in the window curtain before I ran away, I can hardly tell

you how your letter shocked me. I could scarcely breathe,——my eyes became dizzy. Ah, my dear Nathaniel, how could such a horrible event have crossed your life? To be parted from you, never to see you again,——the thought darted through my breast like a burning dagger. I read and read. Your description of the repulsive Coppelius is terrific. For the first time I learned, how your good old father died a shocking violent death. My brother Lothaire, to whom I gave up the letter as his property, sought to calm me, but in vain. The fatal barometer-maker, Giuseppe Coppola followed me at every step, and I am almost ashamed to confess that he disturbed my healthy and generally peaceful sleep with all sorts of horrible visions. Yet soon,——even the next day, I was quite changed again. Do not be offended, dearest one, if Lothaire tells you, that in spite of your strange misgiving, that Coppelius will in some manner injure you, I am in the same cheerful unembarrassed frame of mind as ever.

I will honestly confess to you that, according to my opinion, all the terrible things of which you speak, merely occurred in your own mind, and that the actual external world had little to do with them. Old Coppelius may have been repulsive enough, but his hatred of children was what really caused the abhorrence of your children towards him.

In your childish mind the frightful sandman in the nurse's tale was naturally associated with old Coppelius, who, even if you had not believed in the sandman, would still have been a spectral monster, especially dangerous to children. The awful nightly occupation with your father, was no more than this, that both secretly made alchemical experiments, and with these your mother was constantly dissatisfied, since besides a great deal of money being uselessly wasted, your father's mind being filled with a fallacious desire after higher wisdom was alienated from his family—as they say, is always the case with such experimentalists. Your father no doubt, by some act of carelessness, occasioned his own death, of which Coppelius was completely guiltless. Would you believe it, that I yesterday asked our neighbour, the clever apothecary, whether such a sudden and fatal explosion was possible in such chemical experiments? "Certainly," he replied, and in his way told me at great length and very circumstantially how such an event might take place, uttering a number of strange-sounding names, which I am unable to recollect. Now, I know you will be angry with your Clara; you will say that her cold disposition is impenetrable to every ray of the mysterious, which often embraces man with invisible arms, that she only sees the varigated surface of the world, and has the delight of a silly child, at some gold-glittering fruit, which contains within it a deadly poison.

Ah! my dear Nathaniel! Do you not then believe that even in free, cheerful, careless minds, here may dwell the suspicion of some dread power, which endeavours to destroy us in our own selves? Forgive me, if I, a silly girl, presume in any manner to indicate, what I really think of such an internal struggle; I shall not find out the right words after all, and you will laugh at me, not because my thoughts are foolish, but because I set about so clumsily to express them.

If there is a dark power, which with such enmity and treachery lays a thread within us, by which it holds us fast, and draws us along a path of peril and destruction, which we should not otherwise have trod; if, I say, there is such a power, it must form itself within us, or from ourselves; indeed, become identical with ourselves, for it is only in this condition that we can believe in it, and grant it the room which it requires, to accomplish its secret work. Now, if we have a mind, which is sufficiently firm, sufficiently strengthened by cheerful life, always to recognise this strange hostile operation as such, and calmly to follow the path which belongs to our inclination and calling, then will the dark power fail in its attempt to gain a power, that shall be a reflection of ourselves. Lothaire adds that it is certain, that the dark physical power, if of our own accord, we have yielded ourselves up to it, often draws within us some strange form, which the external world has thrown in our way, so that we ourselves kindle the spirit, which, as we in our strange delusion believe, speaks to us in that form. It is the phantom of our own selves, the close relationship with which, and its deep operation on our mind casts us into hell, or transports us into heaven. You see, dear Nathaniel, that I and my brother Lothaire have freely given our opinion on the subject of dark powers, which subject, now I find I have not been able to write down the chief part without trouble, appears to me somewhat deep. Lothaire's last words I do not quite comprehend. I can only suspect what he means, and yet I feel as if it were all very true. I beg of you, get the ugly advocate, Coppelius, and the barometer-seller, Giuseppe Coppola, quite out of your head. Be convinced that these strange fears have no power over you, and that it is only a belief in their hostile influence that can make them hostile in reality. If the great excitement of your mind did not speak from every line of your letter, if your situation did not give me the deepest pain, I could joke about the Sandman-Advocate, and the barometer-seller, Coppelius. Be cheerful, I have determined to appear before you as your guardian-spirit, and if the ugly Coppelius takes it in his head to annoy you in your dreams, to scare him away with loud peals of laughter. I am not a bit afraid of him nor of his disgusting hands; he shall neither spoil my sweetmeats as an advocate, nor my eyes as a sandman. Ever yours, my dear Nathaniel.

NATHANIEL TO LOTHAIRE

I am very sorry that in consequence of the error occasioned by my wandering state of mind, Clara broke open the letter intended for you, and read it. She has written me a very profound philosophical epistle, in which she proves, at great length, that Coppelius and Coppola only exist in my own mind, and are phantoms of myself, which will be dissipated directly I recognise them as such. Indeed, one could not believe that the mind which often peers out of those bright, smiling, childish eyes, like a sweet charming dream, could define with such intelligence, in such a professor-like manner. She appeals to you—you, it seems have been talking about me. I suppose you read her logical lectures, that she may learn to divide and sift every thing acutely. Pray leave it off. Besides it is quite certain that the barometer-dealer, Guiseppe Coppola, is not the advocate Coppelius. I attend the lectures of the professor of physics, who has lately arrived. His name is the same as that of the famous natural philosopher, Spalanzani, and he is of Italian origin. He has known Coppola for years, and moreover it is clear from his accent that he is really a Piedmontese. Coppelius was a German, but I think no honest one. Calmed I am not, and though you and Clara may consider me a gloomy visionary, I cannot get rid of the impression, which the accursed face of Coppelius makes upon me. I am glad that Coppola has left the town, as Spalanzani says. This professor is a strange fellow—a little round man, with high cheek bones, sharp nose, pouting lips, and little piercing eyes. Yet you will get a better notion of him than by this description, if you look at the portrait of Cagliostro, designed by Chodowiecki, in one of the Berlin annuals, Spalanzani looks like that exactly. I lately went up stairs, and perceived that the curtain, which was generally drawn completely over a glass door, left a little opening on one side. I know not what curiosity impelled me to look through, a tall and very slender lady most symmetrically formed, and most splendidly attired, sat in the room by a little table on which she had laid her arms, her hands being folded together. She sat opposite to the door, so that I could completely see her angelic countenance. She did not appear to see me, and indeed there was something fixed about her eyes as if, I might almost say, she had no power of sight. It seemed to me that she was sleeping with her eyes open. I felt very uncomfortable, and therefore I slunk away into the auditorium, which was close at hand. Afterwards I learned that the form I had seen was that of Spalanzani's daughter Olympia, whom he kept confined in a very strange and improper manner, so that no one could approach her. After all, there may be something the matter with her; she is silly perhaps, or something of the

kind. But why should I write you all this? I could have conveyed it better and more circumstantially by word of mouth. Know that I shall see you in a fortnight. I must again
behold my dear; sweet, angelic Clara. The ill-humour will then be dispersed, which,
I must confess, has endeavoured to get the mastery over me, since that fatal, sensible
letter. Therefore I do not write to her to-day. A thousand greetings, &c.

Nothing more strange and chimerical can be imagined than that which occurred to my
poor friend, the young student Nathaniel, and which I, gracious reader, have undertaken to tell you. Have you, kind reader, ever known a something that has completely
filled your heart, thoughts, and senses, so as to exclude every thing else? There was
in you a fermentation and a boiling, and your blood inflamed to the hottest glow
bounded through your veins, and gave a higher colour to your cheeks. Your glance
was so strange, as if you wished to perceive, in empty space, forms which to no other
eyes are visible, and your speech flowed away into dark sighs. Then your friends asked
you: "What is it, revered one?" "What is the matter, dear one." And now you wished
to express the internal picture with all its glowing tints, with all its light and shade,
and laboured hard to find words only to begin. You thought that in the very first word
you ought to crowd together all the wonderful, noble, horrible, comical, frightful,
that had happened, so that it might strike all the hearers at once like an electric shock.
But every word, every thing that is in the form of speech, appeared to you colourless,
cold and dead. You hunt and hunt, and stutter and stammer, and the sober questions
of your friends dart like icy breezes upon your internal fire until it is ready to go out;
whereas if, like a bold painter, you had first with a few daring strokes drawn an outline
of the internal picture, you might with small trouble have laid on the colours brighter
and brighter, and the living throng of various forms would have carried your friends
along with it, and they, like you, would have seen themselves in the picture that had
proceeded from your mind. Now I must confess to you, kind reader, that no one has
really asked me for the history of the young Nathaniel, but you know well enough that
I belong to the queer race of authors, who, if they have any thing in their mind, such
as I have just described, feel as if every one who comes near them, and indeed perhaps
the whole world besides, is asking them: "What is it then—tell it, my dear friend?"
Thus was I forcibly compelled to tell you of the momentous life of Nathaniel. The singularity and marvellousness of the story filled my entire soul, but for that very reason
and because, my reader, I had to make you equally inclined to endure oddity, which is
no small matter, I tormented myself to begin the history of Nathaniel in a manner as

inspiring, original and striking as possible. "Once upon a time," the beautiful beginning of every tale, was too tame. "In the little provincial town of S—— lived"—was somewhat better, as it at least prepared for the climax. Or should I dart at once *medias in res*, with "Go to the devil, cried the student Nathaniel with rage and horror in his wild looks, when the barometer-seller, Guiseppe Coppola?"—I had indeed already written this down, when I fancied that in the wild looks of the student Nathaniel, I could detect something ludicrous, whereas the story is not comical at all. No form of language suggested itself to my mind, which even in the slightest degree seemed to reflect the colouring of the internal picture. I resolved that I would not begin it at all. So take, gentle reader, the three letters, which friend Lothaire was good enough to give me, as the sketch of the picture which I shall endeavour to colour more and more as I proceed in my narrative. Perhaps, like a good portrait-painter, I may succeed in catching many a form in such a manner, that you will find it is a likeness without having the original, and feel as if you had often seen the person with your own corporeal eyes. Perchance, dear reader, you will then believe that nothing is stranger and madder than actual life, and that this is all that the poet can conceive, as it were in the dull reflection of a dimly polished mirror.

In order that that which it is necessary in the first place to know, may be made clearer, we must add to these letters the circumstance, that shortly after the death of Nathaniel's father, Clara and Lothaire, the children of a distant relative, who had likewise died, and left them orphans, were taken by Nathaniel's mother to her own home. Clara and Nathaniel formed a strong attachment for each other, and no one in the world having any objection to make, they were betrothed, when Nathaniel left the place to pursue his studies in G——. He is, according to the date of his last letter, hearing the lectures of the celebrated professor of physics, Spalanzani.

Now I could proceed in my story with confidence, but at this moment Clara's image stands so plainly before me, that I cannot look another way, as indeed was always the case when she gazed at me, with one of her lively smiles. Clara could not by any means be reckoned beautiful; that was the opinion of all who are competent judges of beauty, by their calling. Nevertheless, the architects praised the exact symmetry of her frame, and the painters considered her neck, shoulders, and bosom almost too chastely formed, but then they all fell in love with her wondrous Magdalen-hair, and above every thing prated about *battonisch* colouring. One of them, a most fantastical fellow, singularly compared Clara's eyes to a lake by Ruysdael, in which the pure azure of a cloudless sky, the wood and flowery field, the whole cheerful life of the rich landscape are reflected. Poets and composers went still further. "What is a lake—what is a mirror!" said they, "can we look upon the girl without wondrous, heavenly songs and tunes flashing towards us from her glances, and penetrating our inmost soul, so that all there is awakened and stirred. If even then we sing nothing that is really sensible, there is not much in us, and that we can feelingly read in the delicate smile which plays on Clara's lips, when we presume to tinkle something before her, which is to pass for a song, although it is only a confused jumble of tones." So it was. Clara had the vivid fancy of a cheerful, unembarrassed child, a deep, tender, feminine disposition, an acute, clever understanding. The misty dreams had but a bad chance with her, since, though she did not talk,—as indeed talking would have been altogether repugnant to her tacit nature, her bright glance and her firm ironical smile would say to them: "Good friends, how can you imagine that I shall take your fleeting shadowy images for real forms with life and motion?" On this account Clara was censured by many as cold, unfeeling and prosaic; while others, who conceived life in its clear depth, greatly loved the feeling, acute, childlike girl, but none so much as Nathaniel, whose perception in art and science was clear and strong. Clara was attached to her lover with all her soul, and when he parted from her, the first cloud passed over her life. With what transport did she rush into his arms when, as he had promised in his last letter to Lothaire, he had actually returned to his native town and entered his mother's room. Nathaniel's expectations were completely fulfilled; for directly he saw Clara he thought neither of the Advocate Coppelius, nor of her "sensible" letter. All gloomy forebodings had gone.

However, Nathaniel was quite right, when he wrote to his friend Lothaire that the form of the repulsive barometer-seller, Coppola, had had a most hostile effect on his life. All felt, even in the first days, that Nathaniel had undergone a thorough change in his whole temperament. He sank into a gloomy reverie, and conducted himself in a strange manner, that had never been known in him before. Every thing, his whole life, had become to him a dream and a foreboding, and he was always saying that every man, although he might think himself free, only served for the cruel sport of dark powers. These he said it was vain to resist, and man must patiently resign himself to his fate. He went even so far as to say, that it is foolish to think that we do any thing in art and science according to our own self-acting will, for the inspiration which alone enables us to produce any thing, does not proceed from within ourselves, but is the effect of a higher principle without.

To the clear-headed Clara this mysticism was in the highest degree repugnant, but contradiction appeared to be useless. Only when Nathaniel proved that Coppelius was the evil principle, which had seized him at the moment when he was listening behind the curtain, and that this repugnant principle would in some horrible manner disturb the happiness of their life, Clara grew very serious, and said: "Yes, Nathaniel, you are right. Coppelius is an evil, hostile principle; he can produce terrible effects, like a diabolical power that has come invisibly into life; but only then, when you will not banish him from your mind and thoughts. So long as you believe in him he really exists, and exerts his influence; only your belief is his power."

Nathaniel, quite indignant that Clara established the demon's existence only in his own mind, would then come out with all the mystical doctrine of devils and fearful powers. But Clara would break off peevishly, by introducing some indifferent matter, to the no small annoyance of Nathaniel. He thought that such deep secrets were closed to cold, unsusceptible minds, without being clearly aware that he reckoned Clara among these subordinate natures, and therefore he constantly endeavoured to initiate her into the mysteries. In the morning, when Clara was getting breakfast ready, he stood by her, and read out of all sorts of mystical books, till she cried: "But, dear Nathaniel, suppose I blame you as the evil principle, that has a hostile effect upon my coffee? For if to please you, I leave every thing standing still, and look in your eyes, while you read, my coffee will run into the fire, and none of you will get any breakfast."

Nathaniel closed the book at once, and hurried indignantly to his chamber. Once he had a remarkable *forte* for graceful, lively tales, which he wrote down, and to which Clara listened with the greatest delight; now, his creations were gloomy, incomprehensible, formless, so that although Clara, out of compassion, did not say so, he plainly felt how little she was interested. Nothing was more insupportable to Clara than tediousness; in her looks and in her words a mental drowsiness, not to be conquered, was expressed. Nathaniel's productions were, indeed, very tedious. His indignation at Clara's cold, prosaic disposition, constantly increased, and Clara could not overcome her dislike of Nathaniel's dark, gloomy, tedious mysticism, so that they became more and more estranged from each other in mind, without perceiving it. The form of the ugly Coppelius, as Nathaniel himself was forced to confess, grew more dim in his fancy, and it often cost him trouble to colour with sufficient liveliness in his pictures, when he appeared as a ghastly bugbear of fate. At last it struck him that he would make the gloomy foreboding, that Coppelius would destroy his happiness in love, the subject of a poem. He represented himself and Clara as united by true love; but occasionally it seemed as though a black hand darted into their life, and tore away some newly-springing joy. At last, while they were standing at the altar, the hideous Coppelius appeared, and touched Clara's lively eyes. They flashed into Nathaniel's heart, like bleeding sparks, scorching and burning, when Coppelius caught him, and flung him into a flaming, fiery circle, which flew round with the swiftness of the stream, and carried him along with it, amid its roaring. The roar is like that of the hurricane, when it fiercely lashes the foaming waves, which, like black giants with white heads, rise up for the furious combat. But through the wild tumult he hears Clara's voice: "Can you not, then, see me? Coppelius has deceived you. Those, indeed, were not my eyes, which so burned in your breast—they were glowing drops of your own heart's blood. I have my eyes still—only look at them!" Nathaniel reflects: "That is Clara, and I am hers for ever!" Then it seems to him as though thought forcibly entered the fiery circle, which stands still, while the noise dully ceases in the dark abyss. Nathaniel looks into Clara's eyes, but it is only death that, with Clara's eyes, kindly looks on him.

While Nathaniel composed this poem he was very calm and collected; he polished and improved every line, and having subjected himself to the fetters of metre, he did not rest till all was correct and melodious. When at last he had finished and read the poem aloud to himself, a wild horror seized him, and he cried out: "Whose horrible voice is that?" Soon, however, the whole appeared to him a very successful work, and he felt that it must inflame Clara's cold temperament, although he did not clearly consider for what Clara was to be excited, nor what purpose it would answer to torment her with the frightful images which threatened a horrible destiny, destructive to their love. Both of them—that is to say Nathaniel and Clara—were sitting in their mother's little garden, Clara very cheerful, because Nathaniel, during the three days in which he had been writing his poem, had not teased her with his dreams and his forebodings. Even Nathaniel spoke livelily and joyfully about pleasant matters, as he used to do formerly, so that Clara said: "Now for the first time I have you again! Do you not see that we have driven away the ugly Coppelius?" Then it first struck Nathaniel that he had in his pocket the poem, which he had intended to read. He at once drew the sheets out and began, while Clara, expecting something tedious as usual, resigned herself and began quietly to knit. But as the dark cloud rose ever blacker and blacker, she let the stocking fall and looked full into his face. He was carried along unceasingly by his poem, an internal fire deeply reddened his cheeks, tears flowed from his eyes. At last when he had concluded, he groaned in a state of utter exhaustion, and catching Clara's hand, sighed forth, as if melted into the most inconsolable grief: "Oh Clara!—Clara!" Clara pressed him gently to her bosom, and said softly, but very solemnly and sincerely: "Nathaniel, dearest Nathaniel, do throw that mad, senseless, insane stuff into the fire!" Upon this Nathaniel sprang up enraged, and thrusting Clara from him, cried: "Thou inanimate, accursed automaton!" He ran off; Clara, deeply offended, shed bitter tears, and sobbed aloud: "Ah, he has never loved me, for he does not understand me." Lothaire entered the arbour; Clara was obliged to tell him all that had occurred. He loved his sister with all his soul, and every word of her complaint fell like a spark of fire into his heart, so that the indignation which he had long harboured against the visionary Nathaniel, now broke out into the wildest rage. He ran to Nathaniel and reproached him for his senseless conduct towards his beloved sister in hard words, which the infuriated Nathaniel retorted in the same style. The appellation of "fantastical, mad fool," was answered by that of "miserable common-place fellow." A duel was inevitable. They agreed on the following morning, according to the academical custom of the place, to fight with sharp rapiers behind the garden. Silently and gloomily they slunk about. Clara had overheard the violent dispute, and seeing the fencing-master bring the rapiers at dawn, guessed what was to occur. Having reached the place of combat, Lothaire and Nathaniel had in gloomy silence flung off their coats, and with the fierce desire of fighting in their flaming eyes, were about to fall upon one another, when Clara rushed through the garden door. Sobbing, she cried aloud, "Ye wild cruel men! Strike me down before you attack each other, for how shall I live longer in the world if my lover murders my brother, or my brother murders my lover." Lothaire lowered his weapon, and looked in silence on the ground; but in Nathaniel's heart, amid the most poignant sorrow, revived all the love for the beautiful Clara, which he had felt in the best days of his happy youth. The weapon fell from his hand, he threw himself at Clara's feet. "Can you ever forgive me, my only—my beloved Clara? Can you forgive me, my dear brother, Lothaire?"

Lothaire was touched by the deep contrition of his friend; all three embraced in reconciliation amid a thousand tears, and vowed eternal love and fidelity.

Nathaniel felt as though a heavy burden, which pressed him to the ground, had been rolled away, as though by resisting the dark power, which held him fast, he had saved his whole being, which had been threatened with annihilation. Three happy days he passed with his dear friends, and then went to G——, where he intended to stay a year, and then to return to his native town for ever.

All that referred to Coppelius was kept a secret from the mother, for it was well known that she could not think of him without terror, as she, as well as Nathaniel, accused him of causing her husband's death.

* * *

How surprised was Nathaniel, when proceeding to his lodging, he saw that the whole house was burned down, and that only the bare walls stood up amid the ashes. However, notwithstanding the fire had broken out in the laboratory of the apothecary who lived on the ground-floor, and had therefore consumed the house from bottom to top, some bold active friends had succeeded in entering Nathaniel's room in the upper story, in time to save the books, manuscripts, and instruments. They carried all safe and sound into another house, where they took a room, which Nathaniel entered at once. He did not think it at all remarkable that he lodged opposite to Professor Spalanzani; neither did it appear singular when he perceived that his window looked straight into the room where Olympia often sat alone, so that he could plainly recognise her figure, although the features of her face were indistinct and confused. At last it struck him, that Olympia often remained for hours in this attitude, in which he had once seen her through the glass-door, sitting at a little table without any occupation, and that she plainly enough looked over at him with an unvarying glance. He was forced to confess that he had never seen a more lovely form, but with Clara in his heart, the stiff Olympia was perfectly indifferent to him. Occasionally, to be sure, he gave a transient look over his compendium, at the beautiful statue, but that was all. He was just writing to Clara, when he heard a light tap at the door; it paused at his words, and the repulsive face of Coppola peeped in. Nathaniel's heart trembled within him, but remembering what Spalanzani had told him about the countryman, Coppola, and also the sacred promises he had made to Clara with respect to the Sandman Coppelius, he felt ashamed of his childish fear, and collecting himself with all his might, said as softly and civily as possible: "I do not want a barometer, my good friend; pray, go." Upon this, Coppola advanced a good way into the room, and said in a hoarse voice, while his wide mouth distorted itself into a hideous laugh, and his little eyes under their long gray lashes sparkled forth piercingly: "Eh, eh—no barometer—no barometer? I have besides pretty eyes—pretty eyes!"—"Madman!" cried Nathaniel with horror, "how can you have eyes?—Eyes?" But Coppola had already put his barometer aside, and plunged his hand into his wide coat-pocket, whence he drew lunettes and spectacles, which he placed upon the table. "There—there—spectacles on the nose, those are my eyes—pretty eyes!" And so saying he drew out more and more spectacles so that the whole table began to glisten and sparkle in the most extraordinary manner. A thousand eyes glanced, and quivered convulsively, and stared at Nathaniel; yet he could not look away from the table, and Coppola kept still laying down more and more spectacles, while flaming glances were intermingled more and more wildly, and shot their blood-red rays into Nathaniel's breast. Overcome with horror, he shrieked out: "Hold, hold, frightful man!" He seized fast by the arm Coppola, who was searching his pockets to bring out still more spectacles, although the whole table was already covered. Coppola had greatly extricated himself with a hoarse repulsive laugh, and with the words: "Ah, nothing for you—but here are pretty glasses"; he had collected all the spectacles, put them up, and from the breast-pocket of his coat had drawn forth a number of telescopes large and small. As soon as the spectacles were removed Nathaniel felt quite easy, and thinking of Clara, perceived that the hideous phantom was but the creature of his own mind, and that Coppola was an honest optician, and could by no means be the accursed double of Coppelius. Moreover, in all the glasses which Coppola now placed on the table, there was nothing remarkable, or at least nothing so ghost-like as the spectacles, and to make matters right Nathaniel resolved to buy something of Coppola. He took up a little and very neatly worked pocket-telescope, and looked through the window to try it. Never in his life had he met a glass which brought the objects so sharply, plainly, and clearly before his eyes. Involuntarily he looked into Spalanzani's room; Olympia was sitting as usual before the little table, with her arms laid upon it, and her hands folded. For the first time could he see the wondrous beauty in the form of her face;—only the eyes seemed to him singularly stiff and dead. Nevertheless, as he looked more sharply through the glass, it seemed to him as if moist morn-beams were rising in the eyes of Olympia. It was as if the power of seeing was kindled for the first time; the glances flashed with constantly increasing liveliness. As if spell-bound, Nathaniel reclined against the window, meditating on the charming Olympia. A hemming and scraping aroused him as if from a dream. Coppola was standing behind him: "*Tre ʒecchini*—three ducats!" Nathaniel, who had quite forgotten the optician, quickly paid him what he asked. "Is it not so? A pretty glass—a pretty glass?" asked Coppola, in his hoarse, repulsive voice, and with his malicious smile. "Yes—yes," replied Nathaniel, peevishly; "good bye, friend." Coppola left the room, not without casting many strange glances at Nathaniel. He heard him laugh loudly on the stairs. "Ah," thought Nathaniel, "he is laughing at me because no doubt, I have paid him too much for this little glass." While he softly uttered these words, it seemed as if a deep deadly sigh was sounding fearfully through the room, and his breath was stopped by inward anguish. He perceived, however, that it was himself that had sighed. "Clara," he said to himself, "is right in taking me for a senseless dreamer, but it is pure madness—nay, more than madness, that the stupid thought, that I have paid Coppola too much for the glass, pains me even so strangely. I cannot see the cause." He now sat down to finish his letter to Clara; but a glance through the window convinced him that Olympia was still sitting there, and he instantly sprang out, as if impelled by an irresistible power, seized Coppola's glass, and could not tear himself from the seductive view of Olympia, till his friend and brother Sigismund called him to go to Professor Spalanzani's lecture. The curtain was drawn close before the fatal room, and he could neither perceive Olympia now nor during the two following days, although he scarcely ever left the window, and constantly looked through Coppola's glass. On the third day the windows were completely covered. Quite in despair, and impelled by a burning wish, he ran out of the town-gate. Olympia's form floated before him in the air, stepped forth from the bushes, and peeped at him with large beaming eyes from the clear brook. Clara's image had completely vanished from his mind; he thought of nothing but Olympia, and complained aloud and in a murmuring tone: "Ah, thou noble, sublime star of my love, hast thou only risen upon me, to vanish immediately, and leave me in dark hopeless night?"

When he was retiring to his lodging, he perceived that there was a great bustle in Spalanzani's house. The doors were wide open, all sorts of utensils were being carried in, the windows of the first floor were being taken out, maid servants were going about sweeping and dusting with great hair-brooms, and carpenters and upholsterers were knocking and hammering within. Nathaniel remained standing in the street in a state of perfect wonder, when Sigismund came up to him, laughing, and said: "Now, what do you say to our old Spalanzani?" Nathaniel assured him that he could say nothing because he knew nothing about the professor, but on the contrary perceived with astonishment the mad proceedings in a house otherwise so quiet and gloomy. He then learnt from Sigismund that Spalanzani intended to give a grand festival on the following day,—a concert and ball—and that half the university was invited. It was generally reported that Spalanzani, who had so long kept his daughter most painfully from every human eye, would now let her appear for the first time.

Nathaniel found a card of invitation, and with heart beating highly went at the appointed hour to the professor's, where the coaches were already rolling, and the lights were shining in the decorated saloons. The company was numerous and brilliant. Olympia appeared dressed with great richness and taste. Her beautifully turned face, her figure called for admiration. The somewhat strange bend of her back inwards, the wasp-like thinness of her waist, seemed to be produced by too tight lacing. In her step and deportment there was something measured and stiff, which struck many as unpleasant, but it was ascribed to the constraint produced by the company. The concert began.

Olympia played the piano with great dexterity, and executed a bravura, with a voice, like the sound of a glass bell, clear, and almost cutting. Nathaniel was quite enraptured; he stood in the hindermost row, and could not perfectly recognise Olympia's features in the dazzling light. He, therefore, quite unperceived, took out Coppola's glass, and looked towards the fair Olympia. Ah! then he saw, with what a longing glance she looked towards him, how every tone first resolved itself plainly in the glance of love, which penetrated, in its glowing career, his inmost soul. The artistical *roulades* seemed to Nathaniel the exultation of a mind illuminated with love, and when, at last, after the cadence, the long trill sounded shrilly through the saloon, he felt as if grasped by glowing arms; he could no longer restrain himself, but with mingled pain and rapture shouted out, "Olympia!" All looked at him, and many laughed. The organist of the cathedral made a more gloomy face than usual, and simply said: "Well, well." The concert had finished, the ball began. "To dance with her—with her!" That was the aim of all Nathaniel's wishes, of all his efforts; but how to gain courage to ask her, the queen of the festival? Nevertheless—he himself did not know how it happened—no sooner had the dancing begun, than he was standing close to Olympia, who had not yet been asked to dance, and, scarcely able to stammer out a few words, had seized her hand. The hand of Olympia was as cold as ice; he felt a horrible deadly frost thrilling through him. He looked into her eye—that was beaming full of love and desire, and at the same time it seemed as though the pulse began to beat, and the stream of life to glow in the cold hand. And in the soul of Nathaniel the joy of love rose still higher; he clasped the beautiful Olympia, and with her flew through the dance. He thought that his dancing was usually correct as to time, but the peculiar rhythmical steadiness with which Olympia moved, and which often put him completely out, soon showed him, that his time was very defective. However, he would dance with no other lady, and would have liked to murder any one who approached Olympia for the purpose of asking her. But this only happened twice, and to his astonishment Olympia remained seated after every dance, when he lost no time in making her rise again. Had he been able to see any other object besides the fair Olympia, all sorts of unfortunate quarrels would have been inevitable, for the half-soft, scarcely-suppressed laughter, which arose among the young people in every corner, was manifestly directed to Olympia, whom they pursued with very curious glances—one could not tell why. Heated by the dance, and by the wine, of which he had freely partaken, Nathaniel had laid aside all his ordinary reserve. He sat by Olympia, with her hand in his, and, highly inflamed and inspired, told his passion, in words which no one understood—neither himself nor Olympia. Yet, perhaps, *she* did; for she looked immoveably in his face, and sighed several times, "Ah, ah!" Upon this, Nathaniel said, "Oh, thou splendid, heavenly lady! Thou ray from the promised land of love—thou deep soul, in winch all my being is reflected!" with much more stuff of the like kind; but Olympia merely went on sighing, "Ah—ah!" Professor Spalanzani occasionally passed the happy pair, and smiled on them, with a look of singular satisfaction. To Nathaniel, although he felt in quite another region, it seemed all at once as though Professor Spalanzani was growing considerably darker; he looked around, and, to his no small horror, perceived that the two last candles in the empty saloon had burned down to their sockets, and were just going out. Music and dancing had ceased long ago. "Separation—separation!" he cried, wildly, and in despair; he kissed Olympia's hand, he bent towards her mouth, when his glowing lips were met by lips cold as ice! Just as when he touched Olympia's cold hand, he felt himself overcome by horror; the legend of the dead bride darted suddenly through his mind, but Olympia pressed him fast, and her lips seemed to recover to life at his kiss. Professor Spalanzani strode through the empty hall, his steps caused a hollow echo, and his figure, round which a flickering shadow played, had a fearful, spectral appearance. "Dost thou love me, dost thou love me, Olympia? Only this word!—Dost thou love me?" So whispered Nathaniel; but Olympia, as she rose, only sighed, "Ah—ah!" "Yes, my gracious, my beautiful star of love," said Nathaniel, "thou hast risen upon me, and thou wilt shine, ever illuminating my inmost soul." "Ah—ah!" replied Olympia, going. Nathaniel followed her; they both stood before the professor.

"You have had a very animated conversation with my daughter," said he, smiling; "so, dear Herr Nathaniel, if you have any taste for talking with a silly girl, your visits shall be welcome."

Nathaniel departed, with a whole heaven beaming in his bosom. The next day Spalanzani's festival was the subject of conversation. Notwithstanding the professor had done every thing to appear splendid, the wags had all sorts of incongruities and oddities to talk about, and were particularly hard upon the dumb, stiff Olympia, to whom, in spite of her beautiful exterior, they ascribed absolute stupidity, and were pleased to find therein the cause why Spalanzani kept her so long concealed. Nathaniel did not hear this without increased rage; but, nevertheless, he held his peace, for, thought he, "Is it worth while to convince these fellows that it is their own stupidity that prevents them from recognising Olympia's deep, noble mind?"

One day Sigismund said to him: "Be kind enough, brother, to tell me how it was possible for a sensible fellow like you to fall in love with that wax face, that wooden doll up there?"

Nathaniel was about to fly out in a passion, but he quickly recollected himself, and retorted: "Tell me, Sigismund, how it is that Olympia's heavenly charms could escape your glance, which generally perceives every thing so clearly—your active senses? But, for that very reason, Heaven be thanked, I have not you for my rival; otherwise, one of us must have fallen a bleeding corpse!"

Sigismund plainly perceived his friend's condition, so he skilfully gave the conversation a turn, and added, after observing that in love-affairs there was no disputing about the object: "Nevertheless it is strange, that many of us think much the same about Olympia. To us—pray do not take it ill, brother,—she appears singularly stiff and soulless. Her shape is symmetrical—so is her face—that is true! She might pass for beautiful, if her glance were not so utterly without a ray of life—without the power of seeing. Her pace is strangely measured, every movement seems to depend on some wound-up clockwork. Her playing—her singing has the unpleasantly correct and spiritless measure of a singing machine, and the same may be said of her dancing. To us, this Olympia has been quite unpleasant; we wished to have nothing to do with her; it seems as if she acts like a living being, and yet has some strange peculiarity of her own." Nathaniel did not completely yield to the bitter feeling, which was coming over him at these words of Sigismund; he mastered his indignation, and merely said, with great earnestness, "Well may Olympia appear awful to you, cold prosaic man. Only to the poetical mind does the similarly organised develop itself. To me alone was her glance of love revealed, beaming through mind and thought; only in the love of Olympia do I find myself again. It may not suit you, that she does not indulge in idle chit-chat like other shallow minds. She utters few words, it is true, but these few words appear as genuine hieroglyphics of the inner world, full of love and deep knowledge of the spiritual life in contemplation of the eternal *yonder*. But you have no sense for all this, and my words are wasted on you." "God preserve you, brother," said Sigismund very mildly, almost sorrowfully; "but it seems to me, that you are in an evil way. You may depend upon me, if all—no, no, I will not say any thing further." All of a sudden it seemed to Nathaniel as if the cold prosaic Sigismund meant very well towards him, and, therefore, he shook the proffered hand very heartily.

Nathaniel had totally forgotten, that there was in the world a Clara, whom he had once loved;—his mother—Lothaire—all had vanished from his memory; he lived only for Olympia, with whom he sat for hours every day, uttering strange fantastical stuff about his love, about the sympathy that glowed to life, about the affinity of souls, to all of which Olympia listened with great devotion. From the very bottom of his desk, he drew out all that he had ever written. Poems, fantasies, visions, romances, tales—this stock was daily increased with all sorts of extravagant sonnets, stanzas, and *canzone*, and he read all to Olympia for hours in succession without fatigue. Never had he known such an admirable listener. She neither embroidered nor knitted, she never looked out of window, she fed no favourite bird, she played neither with lap-dog nor pet cat, she did not twist a slip of paper nor any thing else in her hand, she was not obliged to suppress a yawn by a gentle forced cough. In short, she sat for hours, looking straight into her lover's eyes, without stirring, and her glance became more and more lively and animated. Only when Nathaniel rose at last, and kissed her hand and also her lips, she said "Ah, ah!" adding "good night, dearest!" "Oh deep, noble mind!" cried Nathaniel in his own room, "by thee, by thee, dear one, am I fully comprehended." He trembled with inward transport, when he considered the wonderful accordance that was revealed more and more every day in his own mind, and that of Olympia, for it seemed to him as if Olympia had spoken concerning him and his poetical talent out of the depths of his own mind;—as if the voice had actually sounded from within himself. That must indeed have been the case, for Olympia never uttered any words whatever beyond those which have been already mentioned. Even when Nathaniel, in clear and sober moments, as for instance, when he had just woke in the morning, remembered Olympia's utter passivity, and her paucity and scarcity of words, he said: "Words, words! The glance of her heavenly eye speaks more than any language here below. Can a child of heaven adapt herself to the narrow circle which a miserable earthly necessity has drawn?" Professor Spalanzani appeared highly delighted at the intimacy of his daughter with Nathaniel. To the latter he gave the most unequivocal signs of approbation, and when Nathaniel ventured at last to hint at an union with Olympia, he smiled with his white face, and thought "he would leave his daughter a free choice in the matter." Encouraged by these words, and with burning passion in his heart, Nathaniel resolved to implore Olympia on the very next day, that she would say directly, in plain words, that which her kind glance had told him long ago; namely, that she loved him. He sought the ring which his mother had given him at parting, that he might give it to Olympia as a symbol of his devotion, of his life which budded forth and bloomed with her alone. Clara's letters and Lothaire's came into his hands during the search; but he flung them aside indifferently, found the ring, put it up and hastened over to Olympia. Already on the steps, in the hall he heard a strange noise, which seemed to proceed from Spalanzani's room. There was a stamping, a clattering, a pushing, a hurling against the door, intermingled with curses and imprecations. "Let go, let go, rascal!—scoundrel! Body and soul ventured in it? Ha, ha, ha! that I never will consent to—I, I made the eyes, I the clockwork—stupid blockhead with your clockwork—accursed dog of a bungling watch-maker—off with you—Satan—stop, pipe-maker—infernal beast—hold—begone—let go!" These words were uttered by the voices of Spalanzani, and the hideous Coppelius, who was thus raging and clamoring. Nathaniel rushed in, overcome by the most inexpressible anguish. The professor held a female figure fast by the shoulders, the Italian Coppola grasped it by the feet, and thus they were tugging and pulling, this way and that, contending for the possession of it, with the utmost fury. Nathaniel started back with horror, when in the figure he recognised Olympia. Boiling with the wildest indignation, he was about to rescue his beloved from these infuriated men, but at that moment, Coppola, turning himself with the force of a giant, wrenched the figure from the professor's hand, and then with the figure itself gave him a tremendous blow, which made him reel and fall backwards over the table, where vials, retorts, bottles, and glass cylinders were standing. All these were dashed to a thousand shivers. Now Coppola flung the figure across his shoulders, and, with frightful, yelling laughter, dashed down the stairs, so that the feet of the figure, which dangled in the ugliest manner, rattled with a wooden sound on every step. Nathaniel stood paralysed; he had seen but too plainly that Olympia's waxen, deadly pale countenance had no eyes, but black holes instead—she was, indeed, a lifeless doll. Spalanzani was writhing on the floor; the pieces of glass had cut his head, heart, and arms, and the blood was spirting up, as from so many fountains. But he soon collected all his strength. "After him—after him—why do you pause? Coppelius, Coppelius, has robbed me of my best automaton—a work of twenty years—body and soul set upon it—the clock-work—the speech—the walk, mine; the eyes stolen from you. The infernal rascal—after him; fetch Olympia—there you have the eyes!"

And now Nathaniel saw how a pair of eyes, which lay upon the ground, were staring at him; these Spalanzani caught up, with the unwounded hand, and flung against his heart. At this, madness seized him with its burning claws, and clutched into his soul, tearing to pieces all his thoughts and senses. "Ho—ho—ho—a circle of fire! of fire!—turn thyself round, circle! merrily, merrily, ho, thou wooden doll—turn thyself, pretty doll!" With these words he flew at the professor and pressed in his throat. He would have strangled him, had not the noise attracted many people, who rushed in, forced open Nathaniel's grasp, and thus saved the professor, whose wounds were bound immediately. Sigismund, strong as he was, was not able to master the mad Nathaniel, who with frightful voice kept crying out: "Turn thyself, wooden doll!" and struck around him with clenched fists. At last the combined force of many succeeded in overcoming him, in flinging him to the ground, and binding him. His words were merged into a hideous roar, like that of a brute, and raging in this insane condition he was taken to the mad-house.

Before, gentle reader, I proceed to tell thee what more befel the unfortunate Nathaniel, I can tell thee, in case thou takest an interest in the skilful optician and automaton-maker, Spalanzani, that he was completely healed of his wounds. He was, however, obliged to leave the university, because Nathaniel's story had created a sensation, and it was universally deemed an unpardonable imposition to smuggle wooden dolls instead of living persons into respectable tea-parties—for such Olympia had visited with success. The lawyers called it a most subtle deception, and the more culpable, inasmuch as he had planned it so artfully against the public, that not a single soul—a few cunning students excepted—had detected it, although all now wished to play the acute, and referred to various facts, which appeared to them suspicious. Nothing very clever was revealed in this way. For instance, could it strike any one as so very suspicious, that Olympia, according to the expression of an elegant tea-ite, had, contrary to all usage, sneezed oftener than she had yawned? "The *former*," remarked this elegant person, "was the self-winding-up of the concealed clockwork, which had, moreover, creaked audibly"—and so on. The professor of poetry and eloquence took a pinch of snuff, clapped first the lid of his box, cleared his throat, and said, solemnly, "Ladies and gentlemen, do you not perceive how the whole affair lies? It is all an allegory—a continued metaphor—you understand me—*Sapienti sat*." But many were not satisfied with this; the story of the automaton had struck deep root into their souls, and, in fact, an abominable mistrust against human figures in general, began to creep in. Many lovers, to be quite convinced that they were not enamoured of wooden dolls, would request their mistress to sing and dance a little out of time, to embroider and knit, and play with their lap-dogs, while listening to reading, &c.; and, above all, not to listen merely, but also sometimes to talk, in such a manner as presupposed actual thought and feeling. With many did the bond of love become firmer, and more chaining, while others, on the contrary, slipped gently out of the noose. "One cannot really answer for this," said some. At tea-parties, yawning prevailed to an incredible extent, and there was no sneezing at all, that all suspicion might be avoided. Spalanzani, as already stated, was obliged to decamp, to escape the criminal prosecution for fraudulently introducing an automaton into human society. Coppola had vanished also.

Nathaniel awakened as from a heavy, frightful dream; he opened his eyes, and felt an indescribable sensation of pleasure streaming through him, with soft heavenly warmth. He was in bed in his own room, in his father's house, Clara was stooping over him, and Lothaire and his mother were standing near. "At last, at last, oh beloved Nathaniel, hast thou recovered from thy serious illness—now thou art again mine!" So spoke Clara, from the very depth of her soul, and clasped Nathaniel in her arms. But with mingled sorrow and delight did the brightly glowing tears fall from his eyes, and he deeply groaned forth: "My own—my own Clara!" Sigismund, who had faithfully remained with his friend in the hour of trouble, now entered. Nathaniel stretched out his hand to him. "And thou, faithful brother, hast not deserted me?" Every trace of Nathaniel's madness had vanished, and he soon gained strength amid the care of his mother, his beloved, and his friends. Good fortune also had visited the house, for an old penurious uncle, of whom nothing had been expected, had died, and had left the mother, besides considerable property, an estate in a pleasant spot near the town. Thither Nathaniel, with his Clara, whom he now thought of marrying, his mother, and Lothaire, desired to go. Nathaniel had now grown milder and more docile than he had ever been, and he now understood, for the first time, the heavenly purity and the greatness of Clara's mind. No one, by the slightest hint, reminded him of the past. Only, when Sigismund took leave of him, Nathaniel said: "Heavens, brother, I was in an evil way, but a good angel led me betimes to the path of light! Ah, that was Clara!" Sigismund did not let him carry the discourse further for fear that deeply wounding recollections might burst forth bright and flaming. It was about this time that the four happy persons thought of going to the estate. They were crossing, at noon, the streets of the city, where they had made several purchases, and the high steeple of the town-house already cast its gigantic shadow over the market-place. "Oh," said Clara, "let us ascend it once more, and look at the distant mountains!" No sooner said than done. Nathaniel and Clara both ascended the steps, the mother returned home with the servant, and Lothaire, not inclined to clamber up so many steps, chose to remain below. The two lovers stood arm in arm in the highest gallery of the tower, and looked down upon the misty forests, behind which the blue mountains were rising like a gigantic city.

"Look there at that curious little gray bush, which actually seems as if it were striding towards us," said Clara. Nathaniel mechanically put his hand into his breast pocket—he found Coppola's telescope, and he looked on one side. Clara was before the glass. There was a convulsive movement in his pulse and veins,—pale as death, he stared at Clara, but soon streams of fire flashed and glared from his rolling eyes, and he roared frightfully, like a hunted beast. Then he sprang high into the air, and, in the intervals of a horrible laughter, shrieked out, in a piercing tone, "Wooden doll— turn thyself!" Seizing Clara with immense force he wished to hurl her down, but with the energy of a desperate death-struggle she clutched the railings. Lothaire heard the raging of the madman—he heard Clara's shriek of agony—fearful forebodings darted through his mind, he ran up, the door of the second flight was fastened, and the shrieks of Clara became louder and louder. Frantic with rage and anxiety, he dashed against the door, which, at last, burst open. Clara's voice became fainter and fainter. "Help—help—save me!"—with these words the voice seemed to die in the air. "She is gone—murdered by the madman!" cried Lothaire. The door of the gallery was also closed, but despair gave him a giant's strength, and he burst it from the hinges. Heavens—Clara, grasped by the mad Nathaniel, was hanging in the air over the gallery,—only with one hand she still held one of the iron railings. Quick as lightning Lothaire caught his sister, drew her in, and, at the same moment, struck the madman in the face with his clenched fist, so that he reeled and let go his prey.

Lothaire ran down with his fainting sister in his arms. She was saved. Nathaniel went raging about the gallery and bounded high in the air, crying, "Fire circle turn thyself—turn thyself!" The people collected at the sound of the wild shriek, and among them, prominent by his gigantic stature, was the advocate Coppelius, who had just come to the town, and was proceeding straight to the market-place. Some wished to ascend and secure the madman, but Coppelius laughed, saying, "Ha, ha,— only wait—he will soon come down of his own accord," and looked up like the rest. Nathaniel suddenly stood still as if petrified; he stooped down, perceived Coppelius, and yelling out, "Ah, pretty eyes—pretty eyes!"—he sprang over the railing.

When Nathaniel lay on the stone pavement, with his head shattered, Coppelius had disappeared in the crowd.

Many years afterwards it is said that Clara was seen in a remote spot, sitting hand in hand with a kind-looking man before the door of a country house, while two lively boys played before her. From this it may be inferred that she at last found that quiet domestic happiness which suited her serene and cheerful mind, and which the morbid Nathaniel would never have given her.

J. O.

The Vampyre

John Polidori

———◆———

I T HAPPENED THAT IN THE MIDST OF THE DISSIPATIONS ATTENDANT UPON A London winter, there appeared at the various parties of the leaders of the *ton* a nobleman, more remarkable for his singularities, than his rank. He gazed upon the mirth around him, as if he could not participate therein. Apparently, the light laughter of the fair only attracted his attention, that he might by a look quell it, and throw fear into those breasts where thoughtlessness reigned. Those who felt this sensation of awe, could not explain whence it arose: some attributed it to the dead grey eye, which, fixing upon the object's face, did not seem to penetrate, and at one glance to pierce through to the inward workings of the heart; but fell upon the cheek with a leaden ray that weighed upon the skin it could not pass. His peculiarities caused him to be invited to every house; all wished to see him, and those who had been accustomed to violent excitement, and now felt the weight of *ennui*, were pleased at having something in their presence capable of engaging their attention. In spite of the deadly hue of his face, which never gained a warmer tint, either from the blush of modesty, or from the strong emotion of passion, though its form and outline were beautiful, many of the female hunters after notoriety attempted to win his attentions, and gain, at least, some marks of what they might term affection: Lady Mercer, who had been the mockery of every monster shewn in drawing-rooms since her marriage, threw herself in his way, and did all but put on the dress of a mountebank, to attract his notice:—though in vain:—when she stood before him, though his eyes were apparently fixed upon hers, still it seemed as if they were unperceived;—even her unappalled impudence was baffled, and she left, the field. But though the common adultress could not influence even the guidance of his eyes, it was not that the female sex was indifferent to him: yet such was the apparent caution with which he spoke to the virtuous wife and innocent daughter, that few knew he ever addressed himself to females. He had, however, the reputation of a winning tongue; and whether it was that it even overcame the dread of his singular character, or that they were moved by his apparent hatred of vice, he was as often among those females who form the boast of their sex from their domestic virtues, as among those who sully it by their vices.

About the same time, there came to London a young gentleman of the name of Aubrey: he was an orphan left with an only sister in the possession of great wealth, by parents who died while he was yet in childhood. Left also to himself by guardians, who thought it their duty merely to take care of his fortune, while they relinquished the more important charge of his mind to the care of mercenary subalterns, he cultivated more his imagination than his judgment. He had, hence, that high romantic feeling of honour and candour, which daily ruins so many milliners' apprentices. He believed all to sympathise with virtue, and thought that vice was thrown in by Providence merely for the picturesque effect of the scene, as we see in romances: he thought that the misery of a cottage merely consisted in the vesting of clothes, which were as warm, but which were better adapted to the painter's eye by their irregular folds and various coloured patches. He thought, in fine, that the dreams of poets were the realities of life. He was handsome, frank, and rich: for these reasons, upon his entering into the gay circles, many mothers surrounded him, striving which should describe with least truth their languishing or romping favourites: the daughters at the same time, by their brightening countenances when he approached, and by their sparkling eyes, when he opened his lips, soon led him into false notions of his talents and his merit. Attached as lie was to the romance of his solitary hours, he was startled at finding, that, except in the tallow and wax candles that flickered, not from the presence of a ghost, but from want of snuffing, there was no foundation in real life for any of that congeries of pleasing pictures and descriptions contained in those volumes, from which he had formed his study. Finding, however, some compensation in his gratified vanity, he was about to relinquish his dreams, when the extraordinary being we have above described, crossed him in his career.

He watched him; and the very impossibility of forming an idea of the character of a man entirely absorbed in himself, who gave few other signs of his observation of external objects, than the tacit assent to their existence, implied by the avoidance of their contact: allowing his imagination to picture every thing that flattered its propensity to extravagant ideas, he soon formed this object into the hero of a romance, and determined to observe the offspring of his fancy, rather than the person before him. He became acquainted with him, paid him attentions, and so far advanced upon his notice, that his presence was always recognised. He gradually learnt that Lord Ruthven's affairs were embarrassed, and soon found, from the notes of preparation in —— Street, that he was about to travel. Desirous of gaining some information respecting this singular character, who, till now, had only whetted his curiosity, he hinted to his guardians, that it was time for him to perform the tour, which for many generations has been thought necessary to enable the young to take some rapid steps in the career of vice towards putting themselves upon an equality with the aged, and not allowing them to appear as if fallen from the skies, whenever scandalous intrigues are mentioned as the subjects of pleasantry or of praise, according to the degree of skill shewn in carrying them on. They consented: and Aubrey immediately mentioning his intentions to Lord Ruthven, was surprised to receive from him a proposal to join him. Flattered by such a mark of esteem from him, who, apparently, had nothing in common with other men, he gladly accepted it, and in a few days they had passed the circling waters.

Hitherto, Aubrey had had no opportunity of studying Lord Ruthven's character, and now he found, that, though many more of his actions were exposed to his view, the results offered different conclusions from the apparent motives to his conduct. His companion was profuse in his liberality;—the idle, the vagabond, and the beggar, received from his hand more than enough to relieve their immediate wants. But Aubrey could not avoid remarking, that it was not upon the virtuous, reduced to indigence by the misfortunes attendant even upon virtue, that he bestowed his alms;— these were sent from the door with hardly suppressed sneers; but when the profligate came to ask something, not to relieve his wants, but to allow him to wallow in his lust, or to sink him still deeper in his iniquity, he was sent away with rich charity. This was, however, attributed by him to the greater importunity of the vicious, which generally prevails over the retiring bashfulness of the virtuous indigent. There was one circumstance about the charity of his Lordship, which was still more impressed upon his mind: all those upon whom it was bestowed, inevitably found that there was a curse upon it, for they were all either led to the scaffold, or sunk to the lowest and the most abject misery. At Brussels and other towns through which they passed, Aubrey was surprized at the apparent eagerness with which his companion sought for the centres of all fashionable vice; there he entered into all the spirit of the faro table: he betted, and always gambled with success, except where the known sharper was his antagonist, and then he lost even more than he gained; but it was always with the same unchanging face, with which he generally watched the society around: it was not, however, so when he encountered the rash youthful novice, or the luckless father of a numerous family; then his very wish seemed fortune's law—this apparent abstractedness of

mind was laid aside, and his eyes sparkled with more fire than that of the cat whilst
dallying with the half-dead mouse. In every town, he left the formerly affluent youth,
torn from the circle he adorned, cursing, in the solitude of a dungeon, the fate that had
drawn him within the reach of this fiend; whilst many a father sat frantic, amidst the
speaking looks of mute hungry children, without a single farthing of his late immense
wealth, wherewith to buy even sufficient to satisfy their present craving. Yet he took
no money from the gambling table; but immediately lost, to the ruiner of many, the
last gilder he had just snatched from the convulsive grasp of the innocent: this might
but be the result of a certain degree of knowledge, which was not, however, capable
of combating the cunning of the more experienced. Aubrey often wished to represent
this to his friend, and beg him to resign that charity and pleasure which proved the ruin
of all, and did not tend to his own profit;—but he delayed it—for each day he hoped
his friend would give him some opportunity of speaking frankly and openly to him;
however, this never occurred. Lord Ruthven in his carriage, and amidst the various
wild and rich scenes of nature, was always the same: his eye spoke less than his lip; and
though Aubrey was near the object of his curiosity, he obtained no greater gratification
from it than the constant excitement of vainly wishing to break that mystery, which to
his exalted imagination began to assume the appearance of something supernatural.

They soon arrived at Rome, and Aubrey for a time lost sight of his companion;
he left him in daily attendance upon the morning circle of an Italian countess, whilst
he went in search of the memorials of another almost deserted city. Whilst he was
thus engaged, letters arrived from England, which he opened with eager impatience;
the first was from his sister, breathing nothing but affection; the others were from his
guardians, the latter astonished him; if it had before entered into his imagination that
there was an evil power resident in his companion, these seemed to give him sufficient
reason for the belief. His guardians insisted upon his immediately leaving his friend,
and urged, that his character was dreadfully vicious, for that the possession of irresistible powers of seduction, rendered his licentious habits more dangerous to society. It
had been discovered, that his contempt for the adultress had not originated in hatred
of her character; but that he had required, to enhance his gratification, that his victim,
the partner of his guilt, should be hurled from the pinnacle of unsullied virtue, down
to the lowest abyss of infamy and degradation: in fine, that all those females whom he
had sought, apparently on account of their virtue, had, since his departure, thrown
even the mask aside, and had not scrupled to expose the whole deformity of their vices
to the public gaze.

Aubrey determined upon leaving one, whose character had not yet shown a single bright point on which to rest the eye. He resolved to invent some plausible pretext for abandoning him altogether, purposing, in the mean while, to watch him more closely, and to let no slight circumstances pass by unnoticed. He entered into the same circle, and soon perceived, that his Lordship was endeavouring to work upon the inexperience of the daughter of the lady whose house he chiefly frequented. In Italy, it is seldom that an unmarried female is met with in society; he was therefore obliged to carry on his plans in secret; but Aubrey's eye followed him in all his windings, and soon discovered that an assignation had been appointed, which would most likely end in the ruin of an innocent, though thoughtless girl. Losing no time, he entered the apartment of Lord Ruthven, and abruptly asked him his intentions with respect to the lady, informing him at the same time that he was aware of his being about to meet her that very night. Lord Ruthven answered, that his intentions were such as he supposed all would have upon such an occasion; and upon being pressed whether he intended to marry her, merely laughed. Aubrey retired; and, immediately writing a note, to say, that from that moment he must decline accompanying his Lordship in the remainder of their proposed tour, he ordered his servant to seek other apartments, and calling upon the mother of the lady, informed her of all he knew, not only with regard to her daughter, but also concerning the character of his Lordship. The assignation was prevented. Lord Ruthven next day merely sent his servant to notify his complete assent to a separation; but did not hint any suspicion of his plans having been foiled by Aubrey's interposition.

Having left Rome, Aubrey directed his steps towards Greece, and crossing the Peninsula, soon found himself at Athens. He then fixed his residence in the house of a Greek; and soon occupied himself in tracing the faded records of ancient glory upon monuments that apparently, ashamed of chronicling the deeds of freemen only before slaves, had hidden themselves beneath the sheltering soil or many coloured lichen. Under the same roof as himself, existed a being, so beautiful and delicate, that she might have formed the model for a painter, wishing to pourtray on canvass the promised hope of the faithful in Mahomet's paradise, save that her eyes spoke too much mind for any one to think she could belong to those who had no souls. As she danced upon the plain, or tripped along the mountain's side, one would have thought the gazelle a poor type of her beauties; for who would have exchanged her eye, apparently the eye of animated nature, for that sleepy luxurious look of the animal suited but to the taste of an epicure. The light step of Ianthe often accompanied Aubrey in his search after antiquities, and often would the unconscious girl, engaged in the pursuit of a Kashmere butterfly, show the whole beauty of her form, floating as it were upon the wind, to the eager gaze of him, who forgot the letters he had just decyphered upon an almost effaced tablet, in the contemplation of her sylph-like figure. Often would her tresses falling, as she flitted around, exhibit in the sun's ray such delicately brilliant and swiftly fading hues, as might well excuse the forgetfulness of the antiquary, who let escape from his mind the very object he had before thought of vital importance to the proper interpretation of a passage in Pausanias. But why attempt to describe charms which all feel, but none can appreciate?—It was innocence, youth, and beauty, unaffected by crowded drawing-rooms and stifling balls. Whilst he drew those remains of which lie wished to preserve a memorial for his future hours, she would stand by, and watch the magic effects of his pencil, in tracing the scenes of her native place; she would then describe to him the circling dance upon the open plain, would paint, to him in all the glowing colours of youthful memory, the marriage pomp she remembered viewing in her infancy; and then, turning to subjects that had evidently made a greater impression upon her mind, would tell him all the supernatural tales of her nurse. Her earnestness and apparent belief of what she narrated, excited the interest even of Aubrey; and often as she told him the tale of the living vampyre, who had passed years amidst his friends, and dearest ties, forced every year, by feeding upon the life of a lovely female to prolong his existence for the ensuing months, his blood would run cold, whilst he attempted to laugh her out of such idle and horrible fantasies; but Ianthe cited to him the names of old men, who had at last detected one living among themselves, after several of their near relatives and children had been found marked with the stamp of the fiend's appetite; and when she found him so incredulous, she begged of him to believe her, for it had been, remarked, that those who had dared to question their existence, always had some proof given, which obliged them, with grief and heartbreaking, to confess it was true. She detailed to him the traditional appearance of these monsters, and his horror was increased, by hearing a pretty accurate description of Lord Ruthven; he, however, still persisted in persuading her, that there could be no truth in her fears, though at the same time he wondered at the many coincidences which had all tended to excite a belief in the supernatural power of Lord Ruthven.

Aubrey began to attach himself more and more to Ianthe; her innocence, so contrasted with all the affected virtues of the women among whom he had sought for his vision of romance, won his heart; and while he ridiculed the idea of a young man of English habits, marrying an uneducated Greek girl, still he found himself more and more attached to the almost fairy form before him. He would tear himself at times from her, and, forming a plan for some antiquarian research, he would depart, determined not to return until his object was attained; but he always found it impossible to fix his attention upon the ruins around him, whilst in his mind he retained an image that seemed alone the rightful possessor of his thoughts. Ianthe was unconscious of his love, and was ever the same frank infantile being he had first known. She always seemed to part from him with reluctance; but it was because she had no longer any one with whom she could visit her favourite haunts, whilst her guardian was occupied in sketching or uncovering some fragment which had yet escaped the destructive hand of time. She had appealed to her parents on the subject of Vampyres, and they both, with several present, affirmed their existence, pale with horror at the very name. Soon after, Aubrey determined to proceed upon one of his excursions, which was to detain him for a few hours; when they heard the name of the place, they all at once begged of him not to return at night, as he must necessarily pass through a wood, where no Greek would ever remain, after the day had closed, upon any consideration. They described it as the resort of the vampyres in their nocturnal orgies, and denounced the most heavy evils as impending upon him who dared to cross their path. Aubrey made light of their representations, and tried to laugh them out of the idea; but when he saw them shudder at his daring thus to mock a superior, infernal power, the very name of which apparently made their blood freeze, he was silent.

Next morning Aubrey set off upon his excursion unattended; he was surprised to observe the melancholy face of his host, and was concerned to find that his words, mocking the belief of those horrible fiends, had inspired them with such terror. When he was about to depart, Ianthe came to the side of his horse, and earnestly begged of him to return, ere night allowed the power of these beings to be put in action;—he promised. He was, however, so occupied in his research, that he did not perceive that day-light would soon end, and that in the horizon there was one of those specks which, in the warmer climates, so rapidly gather into a tremendous mass, and pour all their rage upon the devoted country.—He at last, however, mounted his horse, determined to make up by speed for his delay: but it was too late. Twilight, in these southern climates, is almost unknown; immediately the sun sets, night begins: and ere he had advanced far, the power of the storm was above—its echoing thunders had scarcely an interval of rest—its thick heavy rain forced its way through the canopying foliage, whilst the blue forked lightning seemed to fall and radiate at his very feet. Suddenly his horse took fright, and he was carried with dreadful rapidity through the entangled forest. The animal at last, through fatigue, stopped, and he found, by the glare of lightning, that he was in the neighbourhood of a hovel that hardly lifted itself up from the masses of dead leaves and brushwood which surrounded it. Dismounting, he approached, hoping to find some one to guide him to the town, or at least trusting to obtain shelter from the pelting of the storm. As he approached, the thunders, for a moment silent, allowed him to hear the dreadful shrieks of a woman mingling with the stifled, exultant mockery of a laugh, continued in one almost unbroken sound;—he was startled: but, roused by the thunder which again rolled over his head, he, with a sudden effort, forced open the door of the hut. He found himself in utter darkness: the sound, however, guided him. He was apparently unperceived; for, though he called, still the sounds continued, and no notice was taken of him. He found himself in contact with some one, whom he immediately seized; when a voice cried, "Again baffled!" to which a loud laugh succeeded; and he felt himself grappled by one whose strength seemed superhuman: determined to sell his life as dearly as he could, he struggled; but it was in vain: he was lifted from his feet and hurled with enormous force against the ground:—his enemy threw himself upon him, and kneeling upon his breast, had placed his hands upon his throat—when the glare of many torches penetrating through the hole that gave light in the day, disturbed him;— he instantly rose, and, leaving his prey, rushed through the door, and in a moment the crashing of the brandies, as he broke through the wood, was no longer heard. The storm was now still; and Aubrey, incapable of moving, was soon heard by those without. They entered; the light of their torches fell upon the mud walls, and the thatch loaded on every individual straw with heavy flakes of soot. At the desire of Aubrey they searched for her who had attracted him by her cries; he was again left in darkness; but what was his horror, when the light of the torches once more burs; upon him, to perceive the airy form of his fair conductress brought in a lifeless corse. He shut his eyes, hoping that it was but a vision arising from his disturbed imagination; but he again saw the same form, when he unclosed them, stretched by his side. There was no colour upon her cheek, not even upon her lip; yet there was a stillness about her face that seemed almost as attaching as the life that once dwelt there:—upon her neck and breast was blood, and upon her throat were the marks of teeth having opened the vein:—to this the men pointed, crying, simultaneously struck with horror, "A Vampyre! a Vampyre!" A litter was quickly formed, and Aubrey was laid by the side of her who had lately been to him the object of so many bright and fairy visions, now fallen with the flower of life that had died within her. He knew not what his thoughts were—his mind was benumbed and seemed to shun reflection, and take refuge in vacancy—he held almost unconsciously in his hand a naked dagger of a particular construction, which had been found in the hut. They were soon met by different parties who had been engaged in the search of her whom a mother had missed. Their lamentable cries, as they approached the city, forewarned the parents of some dreadful catastrophe.—To describe their grief would be impossible; but when they ascertained the cause of their child's death, they looked at Aubrey, and pointed to the corse. They were inconsolable; both died broken-hearted.

Aubrey being put to bed was seized with a most violent fever, and was often delirious; in these intervals he would call upon Lord Ruthven and upon Ianthe—by some unaccountable combination he seemed to beg of his former companion to spare the being he loved. At other times he would imprecate maledictions upon his head, and curse him as her destroyer. Lord Ruthven, chanced at this time to arrive at Athens, and, from whatever motive, upon hearing of the state of Aubrey, immediately placed himself in the same house, and became his constant attendant. When the latter recovered from his delirium, he was horrified and startled at the sight of him whose image he had now combined with that of a Vampyre; but Lord Ruthven, by his kind words, implying almost repentance for the fault that had caused their separation, and still more by the attention, anxiety, and care which he showed, soon reconciled him to his presence. His lordship seemed quite changed; he no longer appeared that apathetic being who had so astonished Aubrey; but as soon as his convalescence began to be rapid, he again gradually retired into the same state of mind, and Aubrey perceived no difference from the former man, except that at times he was surprised to meet his gaze fixed intently upon him, with a smile of malicious exultation playing upon his lips: he knew not why, but this smile haunted him. During the last stage of the invalid's recovery, Lord Ruthven was apparently engaged in watching the tideless waves raised by the cooling breeze, or in marking the progress of those orbs, circling, like our world, the moveless sun;—indeed, he appeared to wish to avoid the eyes of all.

Aubrey's mind, by this shock, was much weakened, and that elasticity of spirit which had once so distinguished him now seemed to have fled for ever. He was now as much a lover of solitude and silence as Lord Ruthven; but much as he wished for solitude, his mind could not find it in the neighbourhood of Athens; if he sought it amidst the ruins he had formerly frequented, Ianthe's form stood by his side—if he sought it in the woods, her light step would appear wandering amidst the underwood, in quest of the modest violet; then suddenly turning round, would show, to his wild imagination, her pale face and wounded throat, with a meek smile upon her lips. He determined to fly scenes, every feature of which created such bitter associations in his mind. He proposed to Lord Ruthven, to whom he held himself bound by the tender care he had taken of him during his illness, that they should visit those parts of Greece neither had yet seen. They travelled in every direction, and sought every spot to which a recollection could be attached: but though they thus hastened from place to place, yet they seemed not to heed what they gazed upon. They heard much of robbers, but they gradually began to slight these reports, which they imagined were only the invention of individuals, whose interest it was to excite the generosity of those whom they defended from pretended dangers. In consequence of thus neglecting the advice of the inhabitants, on one occasion they travelled with only a few guards, more to serve as guides than as a defence. Upon entering, however, a narrow defile, at the bottom of which was the bed of a torrent, with large masses of rock brought down from the neighbouring precipices, they had reason to repent their negligence; for scarcely were the whole of the party engaged in the narrow pass, when they were startled by the whistling of bullets close to their heads, and by the echoed report of several guns. In an instant their guards had left them, and, placing themselves behind rocks, had begun to fire in the direction whence the report came. Lord Ruthven and Aubrey, imitating their example, retired for a moment behind the sheltering turn of the defile: but ashamed of being thus detained by a foe, who with insulting shouts bade them advance, and being exposed to unresisting slaughter, if any of the robbers should climb above and take them in the rear, they determined at once to rush forward in search of the enemy. Hardly had they lost the shelter of the rock, when Lord Ruthven received a shot in the shoulder, which brought him to the ground. Aubrey hastened to his assistance; and, no longer heeding the contest or his own peril, was soon surprised by seeing the robbers' faces around him—his guards having, upon Lord Ruthven's being wounded, immediately thrown up their arms and surrendered.

By promises of great reward, Aubrey soon induced them to convey his wounded friend to a neighbouring cabin; and having agreed upon a ransom, he was no more disturbed by their presence—they being content merely to guard the entrance till their comrade should return with the promised sum, for which he had an order. Lord Ruthven's strength rapidly decreased; in two days mortification ensued, and death seemed advancing with hasty steps. His conduct and appearance had not changed; he seemed as unconscious of pain as he had been of the objects about him: but towards the close of the last evening, his mind became apparently uneasy, and his eye often fixed upon Aubrey, who was induced to offer his assistance with more than usual earnestness—"Assist me! you may save me—you may do more than that—I mean not my life, I heed the death of my existence as little as that of the passing day; but you may save my honour, your friend's honour."—"How? tell me how? I would do any thing," replied Aubrey. —"I need but little—my life ebbs apace—I cannot explain the whole—but if you would conceal all you know of me, my honour were free from stain in the world's mouth—and if my death were unknown for some time in England— I—I—but life."—"It shall not be known."—"Swear!" cried the dying man, raising himself with exultant violence, "Swear by all your soul reveres, by all your nature fears, swear that, for a year and a day you will not impart your knowledge of my crimes or death to any living being in any way, whatever may happen, or whatever you may see."—His eyes seemed bursting from their sockets: "I swear!" said Aubrey; he sunk laughing upon his pillow, and breathed no more.

Aubrey retired to rest, but did not sleep; the many circumstances attending his acquaintance with this man rose upon his mind, and he knew not why; when he remembered his oath a cold shivering came over him, as if from the presentiment of something horrible awaiting him. Rising early in the morning, he was about to enter the hovel in which he had left the corpse, when a robber met him, and informed him that it was no longer there, having been conveyed by himself and comrades, upon his retiring, to the pinnacle of a neighbouring mount, according to a promise they had given his lordship, that it should be exposed to the first cold ray of the moon that rose after his death. Aubrey astonished, and taking several of the men, determined to go and bury it upon the spot where it lay. But, when he had mounted to the summit he found no trace of either the corpse or the clothes, though the robbers swore they pointed out the identical rock: on which they had laid the body. For a time his mind was bewildered in conjectures, but he at last returned, convinced that they had buried the corpse for the sake of the clothes.

Weary of a country in which he had met with such terrible misfortunes, and in which all apparently conspired to heighten that superstitious melancholy that had seized upon his mind, he resolved to leave it, and soon arrived at Smyrna. While waiting for a vessel to convey him to Otranto, or to Naples, he occupied himself in arranging those effects he had with him belonging to Lord Ruthven. Amongst other things there was a case containing several weapons of offence, more or less adapted to ensure the death of the victim. There were several daggers and ataghans. Whilst turning them over, and examining their curious forms, what was his surprise at finding a sheath apparently ornamented in the same style as the dagger discovered in the fatal hut—he shuddered—hastening to gain further proof, he found the weapon, and his horror may be imagined when he discovered that it fitted, though peculiarly shaped, the sheath he held in his hand. His eyes seemed to need no further certainty—they seemed gazing to be bound to the dagger; yet still he wished to disbelieve; but the particular form, the same varying tints upon the haft and sheath were alike in splendour on both, and left no room for doubt; there were also drops of blood on each.

He left Smyrna, and on his way home, at Rome, his first inquiries were concerning the lady he had attempted to snatch from Lord Ruthven's seductive arts. Her parents were in distress, their fortune ruined, and she had not been heard of since the departure of his lordship. Aubrey's mind became almost broken under so many repeated horrors; he was afraid that this lady had fallen a victim to the destroyer of Ianthe. He became morose and silent; and his only occupation consisted in urging the speed of the postilions, as if he were going to save the life of some one he held dear. He arrived at Calais; a breeze, which seemed obedient to his will, soon wafted him to the English shores; and he hastened to the mansion of his fathers, and there, for a moment, appeared to lose, in the embraces and caresses of his sister, all memory of the past. If she before, by her infantine caresses, had gained his affection, now that the woman began to appear, she was still more attaching as a companion.

Miss Aubrey had not that winning grace which gains the gaze and applause of the drawing-room assemblies. There was none of that light brilliancy which only exists in the heated atmosphere of a crowded apartment. Her blue eye was never lit up by the levity of the mind beneath. There was a melancholy charm about it which did not seem to arise from misfortune, but from some feeling within, that appeared to indicate a soul conscious of a brighter realm. Her step was not that light footing, which strays where'er a butterfly or a colour may attract—it was sedate and pensive. When alone, her face was never brightened by the smile of joy; but when her brother breathed to her his affection, and would in her presence forget those griefs she knew destroyed his rest, who would have exchanged her smile for that of the voluptuary? It seemed as if those eyes,—that face were then playing in the light of their own native sphere. She was yet only eighteen, and had not been presented to the world, it having been thought by her guardians more fit that her presentation should be delayed until her brother's return from the continent, when he might be her protector. It was now, therefore, resolved that the next drawing-room, which was fast approaching, should be the epoch of her entry into the "busy scene." Aubrey would rather have remained in the mansion of his fathers, and fed upon the melancholy which overpowered him. He could not feel interest about the frivolities of fashionable strangers, when his mind had been so torn by the events he had witnessed; but he determined to sacrifice his own comfort to the protection of his sister. They soon arrived in town, and prepared for the next day, which had been announced as a drawing-room.

The crowd was excessive—a drawing-room had not been held for a long time, and all who were anxious to bask in the smile of royalty, hastened thither. Aubrey was there with his sister. While he was standing in a corner by himself, heedless of all around him, engaged in the remembrance that the first time he had seen Lord Ruthven was in that very place—he felt himself suddenly seized by the arm, and a voice he recognized too well, sounded in his ear—"Remember your oath." He had hardly courage to turn, fearful of seeing a spectre that would blast him, when he perceived, at a little distance, the same figure which had attracted his notice on this spot upon his first entry into society. He gazed till his limbs almost refusing to bear their weight, he was obliged to take the arm of a friend, and forcing a passage through the crowd, he threw himself into his carriage, and was driven home. He paced the room with hurried steps, and fixed his hands upon his head, as if he were afraid his thoughts were bursting from his brain. Lord Ruthven again before him—circumstances started up in dreadful array—the dagger—his oath.—He roused himself, he could not believe it possible—the dead rise again!—He thought his imagination had conjured up the image, his mind was resting upon. It was impossible that it could be real—he determined, therefore, to go again into society; for though he attempted to ask concerning Lord Ruthven, the name hung upon his lips, and he could not succeed in gaining information. He went a few nights after with his sister to the assembly of a near relation. Leaving her under the protection of a matron, he retired into a recess, and there gave himself up to his own devouring thoughts. Perceiving, at last, that many were leaving, he roused himself, and entering another room, found his sister surrounded by several, apparently in earnest conversation; he attempted to pass and get near her, when one, whom he requested to move, turned round, and revealed to him those features he most abhorred. He sprang forward, seized his sister's arm, and, with hurried step, forced her towards the street: at the door he found himself impeded by the crowd of servants who were waiting for their lords; and while he was engaged in passing them, he again heard that voice whisper close to him—"Remember your oath!"—He did not dare to turn, but, hurrying his sister, soon reached home.

Aubrey became almost distracted. If before his mind had been absorbed by one subject, how much more completely was it engrossed, now that the certainty of the monster's living again pressed upon his thoughts. His sister's attentions were now unheeded, and it was in vain that she intreated him to explain to her what had caused his abrupt conduct. He only uttered a few words, and those terrified her. The more he thought, the more he was bewildered. His oath startled him;—was he then to allow this monster to roam, bearing ruin upon his breath, amidst all he held dear, and not avert its progress? His very sister might have been touched by him. But even if he were to break his oath, and disclose his suspicions, who would believe him? He thought of employing his own hand to free the world from such a wretch; but death, he remembered, had been already mocked. For days he remained in this state; shut up in his room, he saw no one, and eat only when his sister came, who, with eyes streaming with tears, besought him, for her sake, to support nature. At last, no longer capable of bearing stillness and solitude, he left his house, roamed from street to street, anxious to fly that image which haunted him. His dress became neglected, and he wandered, as often exposed to the noon-day sun as to the midnight damps. He was no longer to be recognized; at first he returned with the evening to the house; but at last he laid him down to rest wherever fatigue overtook him. His sister, anxious for his safety, employed people to follow him; but they were soon distanced by him who fled from a pursuer swifter than any—from thought. His conduct, however, suddenly changed. Struck with the idea that he left by his absence the whole of his friends, with a fiend amongst them, of whose presence they were unconscious, he determined to enter again into society, and watch him closely, anxious to forewarn, in spite of his oath, all whom Lord Ruthven approached with intimacy. But when he entered into a room, his haggard and suspicious looks were so striking, his inward shudderings so visible, that his sister was at last obliged to beg of him to abstain from seeking, for her sake, a society which affected him so strongly. When, however, remonstrance proved unavailing, the guardians thought proper to interpose, and, fearing that his mind was becoming alienated, they thought it high time to resume again that trust which had been before imposed upon them by Aubrey's parents.

Desirous of saving him from the injuries and sufferings he had daily encountered in his wanderings, and of preventing him from exposing to the general eye those marks of what they considered folly, they engaged a physician to reside in the house, and take constant care of him. He hardly appeared to notice it, so completely was his mind absorbed by one terrible subject. His incoherence became at last so great, that he was confined to his chamber. There he would often lie for days, incapable of being roused. He had become emaciated, his eyes had attained a glassy lustre;—the only sign of affection and recollection remaining displayed itself upon the entry of his sister; then he would sometimes start, and, seizing her hands, with looks that severely afflicted her, he would desire her not to touch him. "Oh, do not touch him—if your love for me is aught, do not go near him!" When, however, she inquired to whom he referred, his only answer was, "True! true!" and again he sank into a state, whence not even she could rouse him. This lasted many months: gradually, however, as the year was passing, his incoherences became less frequent, and his mind threw off a portion of its gloom, whilst his guardians observed, that several times in the day he would count upon his fingers a definite number, and then smile.

The time had nearly elapsed, when, upon the last day of the year, one of his guardians entering his room, began to converse with his physician upon the melancholy circumstance of Aubrey's being in so awful a situation, when his sister was going next day to be married. Instantly Aubrey's attention was attracted; he asked anxiously to whom. Glad of this mark of returning intellect, of which they feared he had been deprived, they mentioned the name of the Earl of Marsden. Thinking this was a young Earl whom he had met with in society, Aubrey seemed pleased, and astonished them still more by his expressing his intention to be present at the nuptials, and desiring to see his sister. They answered not, but in a few minutes his sister was with him. He was apparently again capable of being affected by the influence of her lovely smile; for he pressed her to his breast, and kissed her check, wet with tears, flowing at the thought of her brother's being once more alive to the feelings of affection. He began to speak with all his wonted warmth, and to congratulate her upon her marriage with a person so distinguished for rank and every accomplishment; when he suddenly perceived a locket upon her breast; opening it, what was his surprise at beholding the features of the monster who had so long influenced his life. He seized the portrait in a paroxysm of rage, and trampled it under foot. Upon her asking him why he thus destroyed the resemblance of her future husband, he looked as if he did not understand her—then seizing her hands, and gazing on her with a frantic expression of countenance, he bade her swear that she would never wed this monster, for he—But he could not advance— it seemed as if that voice again bade him remember his oath—he turned suddenly round, thinking Lord Ruthven was near him but saw no one. In the meantime the guardians and physician, who had heard the whole, and thought this was but a return of his disorder, entered, and forcing him from Miss Aubrey, desired her to leave him. He fell upon his knees to them, he implored, he begged of them to delay but for one day. They, attributing this to the insanity they imagined had taken possession of his mind, endeavoured to pacify him, and retired.

Lord Ruthven had called the morning after the drawing-room, and had been refused with every one else. When he heard of Aubrey's ill health, he readily understood himself to be the cause of it; but when he learned that he was deemed insane, his exultation and pleasure could hardly be concealed from those among whom he had gained this information. He hastened to the house of his former companion, and, by constant attendance, and the pretence of great affection for the brother and interest in his fate, he gradually won the car of Miss Aubrey. Who could resist his power? His tongue had dangers and toils to recount—could speak of himself as of an individual having no sympathy with any being on the crowded earth, save with her to whom he addressed himself;—could tell how, since he knew her, his existence, had begun to seem worthy of preservation, if it were merely that he might listen to her soothing accents;—in fine, he knew so well how to use the serpent's art, or such was the will of fate, that he gained her affections. The title of the elder branch falling at length to him, he obtained an important embassy, which served as an excuse for hastening the marriage, (in spite of her brother's deranged state,) which was to take place the very day before his departure for the continent.

Aubrey, when he was left by the physician and his guardians, attempted to bribe the servants, but in vain. He asked for pen and paper; it was given him; he wrote a letter to his sister, conjuring her, as she valued her own happiness, her own honour, and the honour of those now in the grave, who once held her in their arms as their hope and the hope of their house, to delay but for a few hours that marriage, on which he denounced the most heavy curses. The servants promised they would deliver it; but giving it to the physician, he thought it better not to harass any more the mind of Miss Aubrey by, what he considered, the ravings of a maniac. Night passed on without rest to the busy inmates of the house; and Aubrey heard, with a horror that may more easily be conceived than described, the notes of busy preparation. Morning came, and the sound of carriages broke upon his ear. Aubrey grew almost frantic. The curiosity of the servants at last overcame their vigilance, they gradually stole away, leaving him in the custody of an helpless old woman. He seized the opportunity, with one bound was out of the room, and in a moment found himself in the apartment where all were nearly assembled. Lord Ruthven was the first to perceive him: he immediately approached, and, taking his arm by force, hurried him from the room, speechless with rage. When on the staircase, Lord Ruthven whispered in his ear— "Remember your oath, and know, if not my bride to day, your sister is dishonoured. Women are frail!" So saying, he pushed him towards his attendants, who, roused by the old woman, had come in search of him. Aubrey could no longer support himself; his rage not finding vent, had broken a blood-vessel, and he was conveyed to bed. This was not mentioned to his sister, who was not present when he entered, as the physician was afraid of agitating her. The marriage was solemnized, and the bride and bridegroom left London.

Aubrey's weakness increased; the effusion of blood produced symptoms of the near approach of death. He desired his sister's guardians might be called, and when the midnight hour had struck, he related composedly what the reader has perused—he died immediately after.

The guardians hastened to protect Miss Aubrey; but when they arrived, it was too late. Lord Ruthven had disappeared, and Aubrey's sister had glutted the thirst of a VAMPYRE!

Carwin, The Biloquist
A GOTHIC FRAGMENT

Charles Brockden Brown

---◆---

I

I was the second son of a farmer, whose place of residence was a western district of Pennsylvania. My eldest brother seemed fitted by nature for the employment to which he was destined. His wishes never led him astray from the haystack and the furrow. His ideas never ranged beyond the sphere of his vision, or suggested the possibility that to-morrow could differ from to-day. He could read and write, because he had no alternative between learning the lesson prescribed to him, and punishment. He was diligent, as long as fear urged him forward, but his exertions ceased with the cessation of this motive. The limits of his acquirements consisted in signing his name, and spelling out a chapter in the Bible.

My character was the reverse of his. My thirst of knowledge was augmented in proportion as it was supplied with gratification. The more I heard or read, the more restless and unconquerable my curiosity became. My senses were perpetually alive to novelty, my fancy teemed with visions of the future, and my attention fastened upon every thing mysterious or unknown.

My father intended that my knowledge should keep pace with that of my brother, but conceived that all beyond the mere capacity to write and read was useless or pernicious. He took as much pains to keep me within these limits, as to make the acquisitions of my brother come up to them, but his efforts were not equally successful in both cases. The most vigilant and jealous scrutiny was exerted in vain: Reproaches and blows, painful privations and ignominious penances had no power to slacken my zeal, and abate my perseverance. He might enjoin upon me the most laborious tasks, set the envy of my brother to watch me during the performance, make the most diligent search after my books, and destroy them without mercy, when they were found; but he could not out-root my darling propensity. I exerted all my powers to elude his watchfulness. Censures and stripes were sufficiently unpleasing to make me strive to avoid them. To effect this desirable end, I was incessantly employed in the invention of stratagems and the execution of expedients.

My passion was surely not deserving of blame, and I have frequently lamented the hardships to which it subjected me; yet, perhaps, the claims which were made upon my ingenuity and fortitude were not without beneficial effects upon my character.

This contention lasted from the sixth to the fourteenth year of my age. My father's opposition to my schemes was incited by a sincere though unenlightened desire for my happiness. That all his efforts were secretly eluded or obstinately repelled, was a source of the bitterest regret. He has often lamented, with tears, what he called my incorrigible depravity, and encouraged himself to perseverance by the notion of the ruin that would inevitably overtake me if I were allowed to persist in my present career. Perhaps the sufferings which arose to him from the disappointment, were equal to those which he inflicted on me.

In my fourteenth year, events happened which ascertained my future destiny. One evening I had been sent to bring cows from a meadow, some miles distant from my father's mansion. My time was limited, and I was menaced with severe chastisement if, according to my custom, I should stay beyond the period assigned.

For some time these menaces rang in my ears, and I went on my way with speed. I arrived at the meadow, but the cattle had broken the fence and escaped. It was my duty to carry home the earliest tidings of this accident, but the first suggestion was to examine the cause and manner of this escape. The field was bounded by cedar railing. Five of these rails were laid horizontally from post to post. The upper one had been broken in the middle, but the rest had merely been drawn out of the holes on one side, and rested with their ends on the ground. The means which had been used for this end, the reason why one only was broken, and that one the uppermost; how a pair of horns could be so managed as to effect that which the hands of man would have found difficult, supplied a theme of meditation.

Some accident recalled me from this reverie, and reminded me how much time had thus been consumed. I was terrified at the consequences of my delay, and sought with eagerness how they might be obviated. I asked myself if there were not a way back shorter than that by which I had come. The beaten road was rendered circuitous by a precipice that projected into a neighbouring stream, and closed up a passage by which the length of the way would have been diminished one half: at the foot of the cliff the water was of considerable depth, and agitated by an eddy. I could not estimate the danger which I should incur by plunging into it, but I was resolved to make the attempt. I have reason to think, that this experiment, if it had been tried, would have proved fatal; and my father, while he lamented my untimely fate, would have been wholly unconscious that his own unreasonable demands had occasioned it.

I turned my steps towards the spot. To reach the edge of the stream was by no means an easy undertaking, so many abrupt points and gloomy hollows were interposed. I had frequently skirted and penetrated this tract, but had never been so completely entangled in the maze as now: hence I had remained unacquainted with a narrow pass, which, at the distance of an hundred yards from the river, would conduct me, though not without danger and toil, to the opposite side of the ridge.

This glen was now discovered, and this discovery induced me to change my plan. If a passage could be here effected, it would be shorter and safer than that which led through the stream, and its practicability was to be known only by experiment. The path was narrow, steep, and overshadowed by rocks. The sun was nearly set, and the shadow of the cliff above, obscured the passage almost as much as midnight would have done: I was accustomed to despise danger when it presented itself in a sensible form, but, by a defect common in every one's education, goblins and spectres were to me the objects of the most violent apprehensions. These were unavoidably connected with solitude and darkness, and were present to my fears when I entered this gloomy recess.

These terrors are always lessened by calling the attention away to some indifferent object. I now made use of this expedient, and began to amuse myself by hallowing as loud as organs of unusual compass and vigour would enable me. I uttered the words which chanced to occur to me, and repeated in the shrill tones of a Mohock savage, "cow! cow! come home! home!" These notes were of course reverberated from the rocks which on either side towered aloft, but the echo was confused and indistinct.

I continued, for some time, thus to beguile the way, till I reached a space more than commonly abrupt, and which required all my attention. My rude ditty was suspended till I had surmounted this impediment. In a few minutes I was at leisure to renew it. After finishing the strain, I paused. In a few seconds a voice as I then imagined, uttered the same cry from the point of a rock some hundred feet behind me; the same words, with equal distinctness and deliberation, and in the same tone, appeared to be spoken. I was startled by this incident, and cast a fearful glance behind, to discover by whom it was uttered. The spot where I stood was buried in dusk, but the eminences were still invested with a luminous and vivid twilight. The speaker, however, was concealed from my view.

I had scarcely begun to wonder at this occurrence, when a new occasion for wonder, was afforded me. A few seconds, in like manner, elapsed, when my ditty was again rehearsed, with a no less perfect imitation, in a different quarter. To this quarter I eagerly turned my eyes, but no one was visible: the station, indeed, which this new speaker seemed to occupy, was inaccessible to man or beast.

If I felt astonished at this second repetition of my words, judge how much my surprise must have been augmented, when the same calls were a third time repeated, and coming still in a new direction. Five times was this ditty successively resounded, at intervals nearly equal, always from a new quarter, and with little abatement of its original distinctness and force.

A little reflection was sufficient to shew that this was no more than an echo of an extraordinary kind. My terrors were quickly supplanted by delight. The motives to dispatch were forgotten, and I amused myself for an hour, with talking to these cliffs; I placed myself in new positions, and exhausted my lungs and my invention in new clamours.

The pleasures of this new discovery were an ample compensation for the ill-treatment which I expected on my return. By some caprice in my father I escaped merely with a few reproaches. I seized the first opportunity of again visiting this recess, and repeating my amusement; time, and incessant repetition, could scarcely lessen its charms or exhaust the variety produced by new tones and new positions.

The hours in which I was most free from interruption and restraint were those of moonlight. My brother and I occupied a small room above the kitchen, disconnected, in some degree, with the rest of the house. It was the rural custom to retire early to bed, and to anticipate the rising of the sun. When the moonlight was strong enough to permit me to read, it was my custom to escape from bed, and hie with my book to some neighbouring eminence, where I would remain stretched on the mossy rock, till the sinking or o'erclouded moon forbade me to continue my employment. I was indebted for books to a friendly person in the neighbourhood, whose compliance with my solicitations was prompted partly by benevolence, and partly by enmity to my father, whom he could not more egregiously offend than by gratifying my perverse and pernicious curiosity.

In leaving my chamber I was obliged to use the utmost caution to avoid rousing my brother, whose temper disposed him to thwart me in the least of my gratifications. My purpose was surely laudable, and yet on leaving the house and returning to it, I was obliged to use the vigilance and circumspection of a thief.

One night I left my bed with this view. I posted first to my vocal glen, and thence scrambling up a neighbouring steep, which overlooked a wide extent of this romantic country, gave myself up to contemplation, and the perusal of Milton's Comus.

My reflections were naturally suggested by the singularity of this echo. To hear my own voice speak at a distance would have been formerly regarded as prodigious. To hear, too, that voice, not uttered by another, by whom it might easily be mimicked, but by myself! I cannot now recollect the transition which led me to the notion of sounds, similar to these, but produced by other means than reverberation. Could I not so dispose my organs as to make my voice appear at a distance?

From speculation I proceeded to experiment. The idea of a distant voice, like my own, was intimately present to my fancy. I exerted myself with a most ardent desire, and with something like a persuasion that I should succeed. I started with surprise, for it seemed as if success had crowned my attempts. I repeated the effort, but failed. A certain position of the organs took place on the first attempt, altogether new, unexampled and as it were, by accident, for I could not attain it on the second experiment.

You will not wonder that I exerted myself with indefatigable zeal to regain what had once, though for so short a space, been in my power. Your own ears have witnessed the success of these efforts. By perpetual exertion I gained it a second time, and now was a diligent observer of the circumstances attending it. Gradually I subjected these finer and more subtle motions to the command of my will. What was at first difficult, by exercise and habit, was rendered easy. I learned to accommodate my voice to all the varieties of distance and direction.

It cannot be denied that this faculty is wonderful and rare, but when we consider the possible modifications of muscular motion, how few of these are usually exerted, how imperfectly they are subjected to the will, and yet that the will is capable of being rendered unlimited and absolute, will not our wonder cease?

We have seen men who could hide their tongues so perfectly that even an Anatomist, after the most accurate inspection that a living subject could admit, has affirmed the organ to be wanting, but this was effected by the exertion of muscles unknown and incredible to the greater part of mankind.

The concurrence of teeth, palate, and tongue, in the formation of speech should seem to be indispensable, and yet men have spoken distinctly though wanting a tongue, and to whom, therefore, teeth and palate were superfluous. The tribe of motions requisite to this end are wholly latent and unknown to those who possess that organ.

I mean not to be more explicit. I have no reason to suppose a peculiar conformation or activity in my own organs, or that the power which I possess may not, with suitable directions and by steady efforts, be obtained by others, but I will do nothing to facilitate the acquisition. It is by far too liable to perversion for a good man to desire to possess it, or to teach it to another.

There remained but one thing to render this instrument as powerful in my hands as it was capable of being. From my childhood, I was remarkably skilful at imitation. There were few voices whether of men or birds or beasts which I could not imitate with success. To add my ancient to my newly acquired skill, to talk from a distance, and at the same time in the accents of another, was the object of my endeavours; and this object, after a certain number of trials, I finally obtained.

In my present situation every thing that denoted intellectual exertion was a crime, and exposed me to invectives if not to stripes. This circumstance induced me to be silent to all others, on the subject of my discovery. But, added to this, was a confused belief that it might be made in some way instrumental to my relief from the hardships and restraints of my present condition. For some time I was not aware of the mode in which it might be rendered subservient to this end.

II

My father's sister was an ancient lady, resident in Philadelphia, the relict of a merchant, whose decease left her the enjoyment of a frugal competence. She was without children, and had often expressed her desire that her nephew Frank, whom she always considered as a sprightly and promising lad, should be put under her care. She offered to be at the expense of my education, and to bequeath to me at her death her slender patrimony.

This arrangement was obstinately rejected by my father, because it was merely fostering and giving scope to propensities, which he considered as hurtful; and because his avarice desired that this inheritance should fall to no one but himself. To me, it was a scheme of ravishing felicity, and to be debarred from it was a source of anguish known to few. I had too much experience of my father's pertinacity ever to hope for a change in his views; yet the bliss of living with my aunt, in a new and busy scene, and in the unbounded indulgence of my literary passion, continually occupied my thoughts; for a long time these thoughts were productive only of despondency and tears.

Time only enhanced the desirableness of this scheme; my new faculty would naturally connect itself with these wishes, and the question could not fail to occur whether it might not aid me in the execution of my favourite plan.

A thousand superstitious tales were current in the family. Apparitions had been seen, and voices had been heard on a multitude of occasions. My father was a confident believer in supernatural tokens. The voice of his wife, who had been many years dead, had been twice heard at midnight whispering at his pillow. I frequently asked myself whether a scheme favourable to my views might not be built upon these foundations. Suppose (thought I) my mother should be made to enjoin upon him compliance with my wishes?

This idea bred in me a temporary consternation. To imitate the voice of the dead, to counterfeit a commission from heaven, bore the aspect of presumption and impiety. It seemed an offence which could not fail to draw after it the vengeance of the deity. My wishes for a time yielded to my fears, but this scheme, in proportion as I meditated on it, became more plausible; no other occurred to me so easy and so efficacious. I endeavoured to persuade myself that the end proposed was in the highest degree praiseworthy, and that the excellence of my purpose would justify the means employed to attain it.

My resolutions were, for a time, attended with fluctuations and misgivings. These gradually disappeared, and my purpose became firm; I was next to devise the means of effecting my views; this did not demand any tedious deliberation. It was easy to gain access to my father's chamber without notice or detection: cautious footsteps and the suppression of breath would place me, unsuspected and unthought of, by his bed side. The words I should use, and the mode of utterance were not easily settled, but having at length selected these, I made myself by much previous repetition, perfectly familiar with the use of them.

I selected a blustering and inclement night, in which the darkness was augmented by a veil of the blackest clouds. The building we inhabited was slight in its structure, and full of crevices through which the gale found easy way, and whistled in a thousand cadences. On this night the elemental music was remarkably sonorous, and was mingled not unfrequently with thunder heard remote.

I could not divest myself of secret dread. My heart faultered with a consciousness of wrong. Heaven seemed to be present and to disapprove my work; I listened to the thunder and the wind, as to the stern voice of this disapprobation. Big drops stood on my forehead, and my tremors almost incapacitated me from proceeding.

These impediments, however, I surmounted; I crept up stairs at midnight, and entered my father's chamber. The darkness was intense and I sought with outstretched hands for his bed. The darkness, added to the trepidation of my thoughts, disabled me from making a right estimate of distances. I was conscious of this, and when I advanced within the room, paused.

I endeavoured to compare the progress I had made with my knowledge of the room, and governed by the result of this comparison, proceeded cautiously and with hands still outstretched in search of the foot of the bed. At this moment lightning flashed into the room: the brightness of the gleam was dazzling, yet it afforded me an exact knowledge of my situation. I had mistaken my way, and discovered that my knees nearly touched the bedstead, and that my hands at the next step, would have touched my father's cheek. His closed eyes and every line in his countenance, were painted, as it were, for an instant on my sight.

The flash was accompanied with a burst of thunder, whose vehemence was stunning. I always entertained a dread of thunder, and now recoiled, overborne with terror. Never had I witnessed so luminous a gleam and so tremendous a shock, yet my father's slumber appeared not to be disturbed by it.

I stood irresolute and trembling: to prosecute my purpose in this state of mind was impossible. I resolved for the present to relinquish it, and turned with a view of exploring my way out of the chamber. Just then a light seen through the window, caught my eye. It was at first weak but speedily increased; no second thought was necessary to inform me that the barn, situated at a small distance from the house, and newly stored with hay, was in flames, in consequence of being struck by the lightning.

My terror at this spectacle made me careless of all consequences relative to myself. I rushed to the bed and throwing myself on my father, awakened him by loud cries. The family were speedily roused, and were compelled to remain impotent spectators of the devastation. Fortunately the wind blew in a contrary direction, so that our habitation was not injured.

The impression that was made upon me by the incidents of that night is indelible. The wind gradually rose into an hurricane; the largest branches were torn from the trees, and whirled aloft into the air; others were uprooted and laid prostrate on the ground. The barn was a spacious edifice, consisting wholly of wood, and filled with a plenteous harvest. Thus supplied with fuel, and fanned by the wind, the fire raged with incredible fury; meanwhile clouds rolled above, whose blackness was rendered more conspicuous by reflection from the flames; the vast volumes of smoke were dissipated in a moment by the storm, while glowing fragments and cinders were borne to an immense height, and tossed everywhere in wild confusion. Ever and anon the sable canopy that hung around us was streaked with lightning, and the peals by which it was accompanied were deafening, and with scarcely any intermission.

It was, doubtless, absurd to imagine any connexion between this portentous scene and the purpose that I had meditated, yet a belief of this connexion, though wavering and obscure, lurked in my mind; something more than a coincidence merely casual, appeared to have subsisted between my situation, at my father's bed side, and the flash that darted through the window, and diverted me from my design. It palsied my courage, and strengthened my conviction, that my scheme was criminal.

After some time had elapsed, and tranquillity was, in some degree, restored in the family, my father reverted to the circumstances in which I had been discovered on the first alarm of this event. The truth was impossible to be told. I felt the utmost reluctance to be guilty of a falsehood, but by falsehood only could I elude detection. That my guilt was the offspring of a fatal necessity, that the injustice of others gave it birth and made it unavoidable, afforded me slight consolation. Nothing can be more injurious than a lie, but its evil tendency chiefly respects our future conduct. Its direct consequences may be transient and few, but it facilitates a repetition, strengthens temptation, and grows into habit. I pretended some necessity had drawn me from my bed, and that discovering the condition of the barn, I hastened to inform my father.

Some time after this, my father summoned me to his presence. I had been previously guilty of disobedience to his commands, in a matter about which he was usually very scrupulous. My brother had been privy to my offence, and had threatened to be my accuser. On this occasion I expected nothing but arraignment and punishment. Weary of oppression, and hopeless of any change in my father's temper and views, I had formed the resolution of eloping from his house, and of trusting, young as I was, to the caprice of fortune. Whilst I was hesitating whether to abscond without the knowledge of the family, or to make my resolutions known to them, I received this summons.

I was employed at this time in the field; night was approaching, and I had made no preparation for departure. All the preparation in my power to make, was indeed small; a few clothes, made into a bundle, was the sum of my possessions. Time would have little influence in improving my prospects, and I resolved to execute my scheme immediately.

I left my work; intending to seek my chamber, and taking what was my own, to disappear for ever. I turned a stile that led out of the field into a bye path, when my father appeared before me, advancing in an opposite direction; to avoid him was impossible, and I summoned my fortitude to a conflict with his passion.

As soon as we met, instead of anger and upbraiding, he told me that he had been reflecting on my aunt's proposal, to take me under her protection, and had concluded that the plan was proper; if I still retained my wishes on that head, he would readily comply with them; and that if I chose, I might set off for the city next morning, as a neighbour's waggon was preparing to go.

I shall not dwell on the rapture with which this proposal was listened to: it was with difficulty that I persuaded myself that he was in earnest in making it, nor could divine the reasons, for so sudden and unexpected a change in his intentions. These I afterwards discovered. Some one had instilled into him fears, that my aunt exasperated at his opposition to her request, respecting the unfortunate Frank, would bequeath her property to strangers. To obviate this evil, which his avarice prompted him to regard as much greater than any mischief, that would accrue to me, from the change of my abode, he embraced her proposal.

I entered with exultation and triumph on this new scene; my hopes were by no means disappointed. Detested labour was exchanged for luxurious idleness. I was master of my time, and chose my own occupations. My kinswoman, on discovering that I entertained no relish for the drudgery of colleges, and was contented with the means of intellectual gratification, which I could obtain under her roof, allowed me to pursue my own choice.

III

Three tranquil years passed away, during which, each day added to my happiness, by adding to my knowledge. My biloquial faculty was not neglected. I improved it by assiduous exercise; I deeply reflected on the use to which it might be applied. I was not destitute of pure intentions; I delighted not in evil; I was incapable of knowingly contributing to another's misery: but the sole or principal end of my endeavours was not the happiness of others.

I was actuated by ambition. I was delighted to possess superior power; I was prone to manifest that superiority, and was satisfied if this were done, without much solicitude concerning consequences. I sported frequently with the apprehensions of my associates; often threw out a bait for their wonder, and supplied them with occasions for the structure of theories. It may not be amiss to enumerate one or two adventures in which I was engaged.

I had taken much pains to improve the sagacity of a favourite spaniel. It was my purpose, indeed, to ascertain to what degree of improvement the principles of reasoning and imitation could be carried in a dog. There is no doubt that the animal affixes distinct ideas to sounds. What are the possible limits of his vocabulary no one can tell. In conversing with my dog I did not use English words, but selected simple monosyllables. Habit likewise enabled him to comprehend my gestures. If I crossed my hands on my breast, he understood the signal and laid down behind me. If I joined my hands and lifted them to my breast, he returned home. If I grasped one arm above the elbow he ran before me. If I lifted my hand to my forehead, he trotted composedly behind. By one motion I could make him bark; by another I could reduce him to silence. He would howl in twenty different strains of mournfulness at my bidding. He would fetch and carry with undeviating faithfulness.

His actions being thus chiefly regulated by gestures that to a stranger would appear indifferent or casual, it was easy to produce a belief that the animal's knowledge was much greater than, in truth, it was.

One day, in a mixed company, the discourse turned upon the unrivalled abilities of Damon. Damon had, indeed, acquired in all the circles which I frequented, an extraordinary reputation. Numerous instances of his sagacity were quoted, and some of them exhibited on the spot. Much surprise was excited by the readiness with which he appeared to comprehend sentences of considerable abstraction and complexity, though, he in reality, attended to nothing but the movements of hand or fingers with which I accompanied my words. I enhanced the astonishment of some and excited the ridicule of others, by observing that my dog not only understood English when spoken by others, but actually spoke the language himself, with no small degree of precision.

This assertion could not be admitted without proof; proof, therefore, was readily produced. At a known signal, Damon began a low interrupted noise, in which the astonished hearers clearly distinguished English words. A dialogue began between the animal and his master, which was maintained, on the part of the former, with great vivacity and spirit. In this dialogue, the dog asserted the dignity of his species and capacity of intellectual improvement. The company separated lost in wonder, but perfectly convinced by the evidence that had been produced.

On a subsequent occasion a select company was assembled at a garden, at a small distance from the city. Discourse glided through a variety of topics, till it lighted at length on the subject of invisible beings. From the speculations of philosophers we proceeded to the creations of the poet. Some maintained the justness of Shakspeare's delineations of aerial beings, while others denied it. By no violent transition, Ariel and his songs were introduced, and a lady, celebrated for her musical skill, was solicited to accompany her pedal harp with the song of "Five fathom deep thy father lies"—She was known to have set, for her favourite instrument, all the songs of Shakspeare.

My youth made me little more than an auditor on this occasion. I sat apart from the rest of the company, and carefully noted every thing. The track which the conversation had taken, suggested a scheme which was not thoroughly digested when the lady began her enchanting strain.

She ended and the audience were mute with rapture. The pause continued, when a strain was wafted to our ears from another quarter. The spot where we sat was embowered by a vine. The verdant arch was lofty and the area beneath was spacious.

The sound proceeded from above. At first it was faint and scarcely audible; presently it reached a louder key, and every eye was cast up in expectation of beholding a face among the pendant clusters. The strain was easily recognized, for it was no other than that which Ariel is made to sing when finally absolved from the service of the wizard.

> Where the bee sucks, there suck I;
> In the cowslips bell I lie;
> There I couch when owl's do cry;
> On the Bat's back I do fly;
>
> After summer merrily, &c.

Their hearts palpitated as they listened: they gazed at each other for a solution of the mystery. At length the strain died away at distance, and an interval of silence was succeeded by an earnest discussion of the cause of this prodigy. One supposition only could be adopted, which was, that the strain was uttered by human organs. That the songster was stationed on the roof of the arbour, and having finished his melody had risen into the viewless fields of air.

I had been invited to spend a week at this house: this period was nearly expired when I received information that my aunt was suddenly taken sick, and that her life was in imminent danger. I immediately set out on my return to the city, but before my arrival she was dead.

This lady was entitled to my gratitude and esteem; I had received the most essential benefits at her hand. I was not destitute of sensibility, and was deeply affected by this event. I will own, however, that my grief was lessened by reflecting on the consequences of her death, with regard to my own condition. I had been ever taught to consider myself as her heir, and her death, therefore, would free me from certain restraints.

My aunt had a female servant who had lived with her for twenty years: she was married, but her husband, who was an artisan, lived apart from her. I had no reason to suspect the woman's sincerity and disinterestedness; but my aunt was no sooner consigned to the grave than a will was produced, in which Dorothy was named her sole and universal heir.

It was in vain to urge my expectations and my claims; the instrument was legibly and legally drawn up. Dorothy was exasperated by my opposition and surmises, and vigorously enforced her title. In a week after the decease of my kinswoman, I was obliged to seek a new dwelling. As all my property consisted in my cloths and my papers, this was easily done.

My condition was now calamitous and forlorn. Confiding in the acquisition of my aunt's patrimony, I had made no other provision for the future. I hated manual labour, or any task of which the object was gain. To be guided in my choice of occupations by any motive but the pleasure which the occupation was qualified to produce, was intolerable to my proud, indolent, and restive temper.

This resource was now cut off; the means of immediate subsistence were denied me. If I had determined to acquire the knowledge of some lucrative art, the acquisition would demand time, and, meanwhile, I was absolutely destitute of support. My father's house was, indeed, open to me, but I preferred to stifle myself with the filth of the kennel, rather than to return to it.

Some plan it was immediately necessary to adopt. The exigence of my affairs, and this reverse of fortune, continually occupied my thoughts; I estranged myself from society and from books, and devoted myself to lonely walks and mournful meditation.

One morning as I ranged along the bank of Schuylkill, I encountered a person, by name Ludloe, of whom I had some previous knowledge. He was from Ireland; was a man of some rank and apparently rich. I had met with him before, but in mixed companies, where little direct intercourse had taken place between us. Our last meeting was in the arbour where Ariel was so unexpectedly introduced.

Our acquaintance merely justified a transient salutation; but he did not content himself with noticing me as I passed, but joined me in my walk and entered into conversation. It was easy to advert to the occasion on which we had last met, and to the mysterious incident which then occurred. I was solicitous to dive into his thoughts upon this head and put some questions which tended to the point that I wished.

I was somewhat startled when he expressed his belief, that the performer of this mystic strain was one of the company then present, who exerted, for this end, a faculty not commonly possessed. Who this person was he did not venture to guess, and could not discover, by the tokens which he suffered to appear, that his suspicions glanced at me. He expatiated with great profoundness and fertility of ideas on the uses to which a faculty like this might be employed. No more powerful engine, he said, could be conceived, by which the ignorant and credulous might be moulded to our purposes. Managed by a man of ordinary talents, it would open for him the straightest and surest avenues to wealth and power.

His remarks excited in my mind a new strain of thoughts. I had not hitherto considered the subject in this light, though vague ideas of the importance of this art could not fail to be occasionally suggested. I ventured to inquire into his ideas of the mode, in which an art like this could be employed, so as to effect the purposes he mentioned.

He dealt chiefly in general representations. Men, he said, believed in the existence and energy of invisible powers, and in the duty of discovering and conforming to their will. This will was supposed to be sometimes made known to them through the medium of their senses. A voice coming from a quarter where no attendant form could be seen would, in most cases, be ascribed to supernal agency, and a command imposed on them, in this manner, would be obeyed with religious scrupulousness. Thus men might be imperiously directed in the disposal of their industry, their property, and even of their lives. Men, actuated by a mistaken sense of duty, might, under this influence, be led to the commission of the most flagitious, as well as the most heroic acts: If it were his desire to accumulate wealth, or institute a new sect, he should need no other instrument.

I listened to this kind of discourse with great avidity, and regretted when he thought proper to introduce new topics. He ended by requesting me to visit him, which I eagerly consented to do. When left alone, my imagination was filled with the images suggested by this conversation. The hopelessness of better fortune, which I had lately harboured, now gave place to cheering confidence. Those motives of rectitude which should deter me from this species of imposture, had never been vivid or stable, and were still more weakened by the artifices of which I had already been guilty. The utility or harmlessness of the end, justified, in my eyes, the means.

No event had been more unexpected, by me, than the bequest of my aunt to her servant. The will, under which the latter claimed, was dated prior to my coming to the city. I was not surprised, therefore, that it had once been made, but merely that it had never been cancelled or superseded by a later instrument. My wishes inclined me to suspect the existence of a later will, but I had conceived that, to ascertain its existence, was beyond my power.

Now, however, a different opinion began to be entertained. This woman like those of her sex and class was unlettered and superstitious. Her faith in spells and apparitions was of the most lively kind. Could not her conscience be awakened by a voice from the grave! Lonely and at midnight, my aunt might be introduced, upbraiding her for her injustice, and commanding her to atone for it by acknowledging the claim of the rightful proprietor.

True it was, that no subsequent will might exist, but this was the fruit of mistake, or of negligence. She probably intended to cancel the old one, but this act might, by her own weakness, or by the artifices of her servant, be delayed till death had put it out of her power. In either case a mandate from the dead could scarcely fail of being obeyed.

I considered this woman as the usurper of my property. Her husband as well as herself, were laborious and covetous; their good fortune had made no change in their mode of living; but they were as frugal and as eager to accumulate as ever. In their hands, money was inert and sterile, or it served to foster their vices. To take it from them would, therefore, be a benefit both to them and to myself; not even an imaginary injury would be inflicted. Restitution, on legal compulsion, would be reluctant and painful; but if enjoined by Heaven would be voluntary: and the performance of a seeming duty would carry with it its own reward.

These reasonings, aided by inclination, were sufficient to determine me. I have no doubt but their fallacy would have been detected in the sequel, and my scheme have been productive of nothing but confusion and remorse. From these consequences, however, my fate interposed, as in the former instance, to save me.

Having formed my resolution, many preliminaries to its execution were necessary to be settled. These demanded deliberation and delay. Meanwhile I recollected my promise to Ludloe, and paid him a visit. I met a frank and affectionate reception. It would not be easy to paint the delight which I experienced in this man's society. I was at first oppressed with the sense of my own inferiority in age, knowledge, and rank. Hence arose numberless reserves and incapacitating diffidences; but these were speedily dissipated by the fascinations of this man's address. His superiority was only rendered, by time, more conspicuous, but this superiority, by appearing never to be present to his own mind, ceased to be uneasy to me. My questions required to be frequently answered, and my mistakes to be rectified; but my keenest scrutiny, could detect in his manner, neither arrogance nor contempt. He seemed to talk merely from the overflow of his ideas, or a benevolent desire of imparting information.

My visits gradually became more frequent. Meanwhile my wants increased, and the necessity of some change in my condition became daily more urgent. This incited my reflections on the scheme which I had formed. The time and place suitable to my design, were not selected without much anxious inquiry and frequent waverings of purpose. These being at length fixed, the interval to elapse, before the carrying of my design into effect was not without perturbation and suspense. These could not be concealed from my new friend, and at length prompted him to inquire into the cause.

It was not possible to communicate the whole truth; but the warmth of his manner inspired me with some degree of ingenuousness. I did not hide from him my former hopes and my present destitute condition. He listened to my tale with no expressions of sympathy; and when I had finished, abruptly inquired, whether I had any objection to a voyage to Europe? I answered in the negative. He then said that he was preparing to depart in a fortnight and advised me to make up my mind to accompany him.

This unexpected proposal gave me pleasure and surprise, but the want of money occurred to me as an insuperable objection. On this being mentioned, "O! ho!" said he, carelessly, "that objection is easily removed, I will bear all expenses of your passage myself."

The extraordinary beneficence of this act as well as the air of incautiousness attending it, made me doubt the sincerity of his offer, and when new declarations removed this doubt, I could not forbear expressing at once my sense of his generosity and of my own unworthiness.

He replied, that generosity had been expunged from his catalogue, as having no meaning, or a vicious one. It was the scope of his exertions to be just. This was the sum of human duty, and he that ran beside, outstripped, or fell short of justice was a criminal. What he gave me was my due or not my due. If it were my due, I might reasonably demand it from him and it was wicked to withhold it. Merit on one side or gratitude on the other, were contradictory and unintelligible.

If I were fully convinced that this benefit was not my due and yet received it, he should hold me in contempt. The rectitude of my principles and conduct would be the measure of his approbation; and no benefit should he ever bestow which the receiver was not entitled to claim, and which it would not be criminal in him to refuse.

These principles were not new from the mouth of Ludloe, but they had, hitherto, been regarded as the fruits of a venturous speculation in my mind. I had never traced them into their practical consequences, and if his conduct on this occasion had not squared with his maxims, I should not have imputed to him inconsistency. I did not ponder on these reasonings at this time: objects of immediate importance engrossed my thoughts.

One obstacle to this measure was removed. When my voyage was performed how should I subsist in my new abode? I concealed not my perplexity and he commented on it in his usual manner. How did I mean to subsist, he asked, in my own country? The means of living would be, at least, as much within my reach there as here. As to the pressure of immediate and absolute want, he believed I should be exposed to little hazard. With talents such as mine, I must be hunted by a destiny peculiarly malignant, if I could not provide myself with necessaries wherever my lot were cast.

He would make allowances, however, for my diffidence and self-distrust, and would obviate my fears by expressing his own intentions with regard to me. I must be apprized, however, of his true meaning. He laboured to shun all hurtful and vicious things, and therefore carefully abstained from making or confiding in prom- ises. It was just to assist me in this voyage, and it would probably be equally just to continue to me similar assistance when it was finished. That indeed was a subject, in a great degree, within my own cognizance. His aid would be proportioned to my wants and to my merits, and I had only to take care that my claims were just, for them to be admitted.

This scheme could not but appear to me eligible. I thirsted after an acquaintance with new scenes; my present situation could not be changed for a worse; I trusted to the constancy of Ludloe's friendship; to this at least it was better to trust than to the success of my imposture on Dorothy, which was adopted merely as a desperate expedi- ent: finally I determined to embark with him.

In the course of this voyage my mind was busily employed. There were no other passengers beside ourselves, so that my own condition and the character of Ludloe, continually presented themselves to my reflections. It will be supposed that I was not a vague or indifferent observer.

There were no vicissitudes in the deportment or lapses in the discourse of my friend. His feelings appeared to preserve an unchangeable tenor, and his thoughts and words always to flow with the same rapidity. His slumber was profound and his wakeful hours serene. He was regular and temperate in all his exercises and gratifications. Hence were derived his clear perceptions and exuberant health.

This treatment of me, like all his other mental and corporal operations, was modelled by one inflexible standard. Certain scruples and delicacies were incident to my situation. Of the existence of these he seemed to be unconscious, and yet nothing escaped him inconsistent with a state of absolute equality.

I was naturally inquisitive as to his fortune and the collateral circumstances of his condition. My notions of politeness hindered me from making direct inquiries. By indirect means I could gather nothing but that his state was opulent and independent, and that he had two sisters whose situation resembled his own.

Though, in conversation, he appeared to be governed by the utmost candour; no light was let in upon the former transactions of his life. The purpose of his visit to America I could merely guess to be the gratification of curiosity.

My future pursuits must be supposed chiefly to occupy my attention. On this head I was destitute of all stedfast views. Without profession or habits of industry or sources of permanent revenue, the world appeared to me an ocean on which my bark was set afloat, without compass or sail. The world into which I was about to enter, was untried and unknown, and though I could consent to profit by the guidance I was unwilling to rely on the support of others.

This topic being nearest my heart, I frequently introduced into conversation with my friend; but on this subject he always allowed himself to be led by me, while on all others, he was zealous to point the way. To every scheme that I proposed he was sure to cause objections. All the liberal professions were censured as perverting the understanding, by giving scope to the sordid motive of gain, or imbuing the mind with erroneous principles. Skill was slowly obtained, and success, though integrity and independence must be given for it, dubious and instable. The mechanical trades were equally obnoxious; they were vicious by contributing to the spurious gratifications of the rich and multiplying the objects of luxury; they were destructive to the intellect and vigour of the artizan; they enervated his frame and brutalised his mind.

When I pointed out to him the necessity of some species of labour, he tacitly admitted that necessity, but refused to direct me in the choice of a pursuit, which though not free from defect should yet have the fewest inconveniences. He dwelt on the fewness of our actual wants, the temptations which attend the possession of wealth, the benefits of seclusion and privacy, and the duty of unfettering our minds from the prejudices which govern the world.

His discourse tended merely to unsettle my views and increase my perplexity. This effect was so uniform that I at length desisted from all allusions to this theme and endeavoured to divert my own reflections from it. When our voyage should be finished, and I should actually tread this new stage, I believed that I should be better qualified to judge of the measures to be taken by me.

IV

At length we reached Belfast. From thence we immediately repaired to Dublin. I was admitted as a member of his family. When I expressed my uncertainty as to the place to which it would be proper for me to repair, he gave me a blunt but cordial invitation to his house. My circumstances allowed me no option and I readily complied. My attention was for a time engrossed by a diversified succession of new objects. Their novelty, however, disappearing, left me at liberty to turn my eyes upon myself and my companion, and here my reflections were supplied with abundant food.

His house was spacious and commodious, and furnished with profusion and elegance. A suite of apartments was assigned to me, in which I was permitted to reign uncontrouled and access was permitted to a well furnished library. My food was furnished in my own room, prepared in the manner which I had previously directed. Occasionally Ludloe would request my company to breakfast, when an hour was usually consumed in earnest or sprightly conversation. At all other times he was invisible; and his apartments, being wholly separate from mine, I had no opportunity of discovering in what way his hours were employed.

He defended this mode of living as being most compatible with liberty. He delighted to expatiate on the evils of cohabitation. Men, subjected to the same regimen, compelled to eat and sleep and associate at certain hours, were strangers to all rational independence and liberty. Society would never be exempt from servitude and misery, till those artificial ties which held human beings together under the same roof were dissolved. He endeavoured to regulate his own conduct in pursuance of these principles, and to secure to himself as much freedom as the present regulations of society would permit. The same independence which he claimed for himself he likewise extended to me. The distribution of my own time, the selection of my own occupations and companions, should belong to myself.

But these privileges, though while listening to his arguments I could not deny them to be valuable, I would have willingly dispensed with. The solitude in which I lived became daily more painful. I ate and drank, enjoyed clothing and shelter, without the exercise of forethought or industry. I walked and sat, went out and returned for as long, and at what seasons I thought proper, yet my condition was a fertile source of discontent.

I felt myself removed to a comfortless and chilling distance from Ludloe. I wanted to share in his occupations and views. With all his ingenuousness of aspect and over-flow of thoughts, when he allowed me his company, I felt myself painfully bewildered with regard to his genuine condition and sentiments.

He had it in his power to introduce me to society; and without an introduction, it was scarcely possible to gain access to any social circle or domestic fireside. Add to this, my own obscure prospects and dubious situation. Some regular intellectual pursuit would render my state less irksome, but I had hitherto adopted no scheme of this kind.

Time tended, in no degree, to alleviate my dissatisfaction. It increased till the determination became at length formed of opening my thoughts to Ludloe. At the next breakfast interview which took place, I introduced the subject, and expatiated without reserve, on the state of my feelings. I concluded with entreating him to point out some path in which my talents might be rendered useful to himself or to mankind.

After a pause of some minutes, he said, "What would you do? You forget the immaturity of your age. If you are qualified to act a part in the theatre of life, step forth; but you are not qualified. You want knowledge, and with this you ought previously to endow yourself. Means, for this end, are within your reach. Why should you waste your time in idleness, and torment yourself with unprofitable wishes? Books are at hand; books from which most sciences and languages can be learned. Read, analyse, digest; collect facts, and investigate theories: ascertain the dictates of reason, and supply yourself with the inclination and the power to adhere to them. You will not, legally speaking, be a man in less than three years. Let this period be devoted to the acquisition of wisdom. Either stay here, or retire to a house I have on the banks of Killarney, where you will find all the conveniences of study."

I could not but reflect with wonder at this man's treatment of me. I could plead none of the rights of relationship; yet I enjoyed the privileges of a son. He had not imparted to me any scheme, by pursuit of which I might finally compensate him for the expense to which my maintenance and education would subject him. He gave me reason to hope for the continuance of his bounty. He talked and acted as if my fortune were totally disjoined from his; yet was I indebted to him for the morsel which sustained my life. Now it was proposed to withdraw myself to studious leisure, and romantic solitude. All my wants, personal and intellectual, were to be supplied gratuitously and copiously. No means were prescribed by which I might make compensation for all these benefits. In conferring them he seemed to be actuated by no view to his own ultimate advantage. He took no measures to secure my future services.

I suffered these thoughts to escape me, on this occasion, and observed that to make my application successful, or useful, it was necessary to pursue some end. I must look forward to some post which I might hereafter occupy beneficially to myself or others; and for which all the efforts of my mind should be bent to qualify myself.

These hints gave him visible pleasure; and now, for the first time, he deigned to advise me on this head. His scheme, however, was not suddenly produced. The way to it was circuitous and long. It was his business to make every new step appear to be suggested by my own reflections. His own ideas were the seeming result of the moment, and sprung out of the last idea that was uttered. Being hastily taken up, they were, of course, liable to objection. These objections, sometimes occurring to me and sometimes to him, were admitted or contested with the utmost candour. One scheme went through numerous modifications before it was proved to be ineligible, or before it yielded place to a better. It was easy to perceive, that books alone were insufficient to impart knowledge: that man must be examined with our own eyes to make us acquainted with their nature; that ideas, collected from observation and reading, must correct and illustrate each other; that the value of all principles, and their truth, lie in their practical effects. Hence, gradually arose, the usefulness of travelling, of inspecting the habits and manners of a nation, and investigating on the spot the causes of their happiness and misery. Finally, it was determined that Spain was more suitable than any other, to the views of a judicious traveller.

My language, habits, and religion were mentioned as obstacles to close and extensive views; but these difficulties successively and slowly vanished. Converse with books, and natives of Spain, a steadfast purpose and unwearied diligence would efface all differences between me and a Castilian with respect to speech. Personal habits were changeable by the same means. The bars to unbounded intercourse, rising from the religion of Spain being irreconcilably opposite to mine, cost us no little trouble to surmount, and here the skill of Ludloe was eminently displayed.

I had been accustomed to regard as unquestionable, the fallacy of the Romish faith. This persuasion was habitual and the child of prejudice, and was easily shaken by the artifices of this logician. I was first led to bestow a kind of assent on the doctrines of the Roman church; but my convictions were easily subdued by a new species of argumentation, and, in a short time, I reverted to my ancient disbelief; so that, if an exterior conformity to the rights of Spain were requisite to the attainment of my purpose, that conformity must be dissembled.

My moral principles had hitherto been vague and unsettled. My circumstances had led me to the frequent practice of insincerity; but my transgressions, as they were slight and transient, did not much excite my previous reflections or subsequent remorse. My deviations, however, though rendered easy by habit, were by no means sanctioned by my principles. Now an imposture more profound and deliberate was projected; and I could not hope to perform well my part, unless steadfastly and thoroughly persuaded of its rectitude.

My friend was the eulogist of sincerity. He delighted to trace its influence on the happiness of mankind; and proved that nothing but the universal practice of this virtue was necessary to the perfection of human society. His doctrine was splendid and beautiful. To detect its imperfections was no easy task; to lay the foundations of virtue in utility, and to limit, by that scale, the operation of general principles; to see that the value of sincerity, like that of every other mode of action, consisted in its tendency to good, and that, therefore the obligation to speak truth was not paramount or intrinsical; that my duty is modelled on a knowledge and foresight of the conduct of others; and that, since men in their actual state, are infirm and deceitful, a just estimate of consequences may sometimes make dissimulation my duty were truths that did not speedily occur. The discovery, when made, appeared to be a joint work. I saw nothing in Ludloe but proofs of candour, and a judgment incapable of bias.

The means which this man employed to fit me for his purpose, perhaps owed their success to my youth and ignorance. I may have given you exaggerated ideas of his dexterity and address. Of that I am unable to judge. Certain it is, that no time or reflection has abated my astonishment at the profoundness of his schemes, and the perseverance with which they were pursued by him. To detail their progress would expose me to the risk of being tedious, yet none but minute details would sufficiently display his patience and subtlety.

It will suffice to relate, that after a sufficient period of preparation and arrangements being made for maintaining a copious intercourse with Ludloe, I embarked for Barcelona. A restless curiosity and vigorous application have distinguished my character in every scene. Here was spacious field for the exercise of all my energies. I sought out a preceptor in my new religion. I entered into the hearts of priests and confessors,—the *hidalgo* and the peasant, the monk and the prelate, the austere and voluptuous devotee, were scrutinised in all their forms.

Man was the chief subject of my study, and the social sphere that in which I principally moved; but I was not inattentive to inanimate nature, nor unmindful of the past. If the scope of virtue were to maintain the body in health, and to furnish its highest enjoyments to every sense, to increase the number, and accuracy, and order of our intellectual stores, no virtue was ever more unblemished than mine. If to act upon our conceptions of right, and to acquit ourselves of all prejudice and selfishness in the formation of our principles, entitle us to the testimony of a good conscience, I might justly claim it.

I shall not pretend to ascertain my rank in the moral scale. If a system of deceit, pursued merely from the love of truth; if voluptuousness, never gratified at the expense of health, may incur censure, I am censurable. This, indeed, was not the limit of my deviations. Deception was often unnecessarily practised, and my biloquial faculty did not lie unemployed.

To recount these would be an endless task. They were designed as mere specimens of power, to illustrate the influence of superstition: to give sceptics the consolation of certainty: to annihilate the scruples of a tender female, or facilitate my access to the bosoms of courtiers and monks.

The first achievement of this kind took place in the convent of the Escurial. For some time the hospitality of this brotherhood allowed me a cell in that magnificent and gloomy fabric. I was drawn hither chiefly by the treasures of Arabian literature, which are preserved here in the keeping of a learned Maronite, from Lebanon. Standing one evening on the steps of the great altar, this devout friar expatiated on the miraculous evidences of his religion; and, in a moment of enthusiasm, appealed to San Lorenzo, whose martyrdom was displayed before us. No sooner was the appeal made than the saint, obsequious to the summons, whispered his responses from the shrine, and commanded the heretic to tremble and believe. This event was reported to the convent. With whatever reluctance, I could not refuse my testimony to its truth, and its influence on my faith was clearly shewn in my subsequent conduct.

A lady of rank, in Seville, who had been guilty of many unauthorized indulgences, was at last awakened to remorse by a voice from Heaven, which she imagined had commanded her to expiate her sins by an abstinence from all food for thirty days. Her friends found it impossible to outroot this persuasion, or to overcome her resolution even by force. I chanced to be one in a numerous company where she was present. This fatal illusion was mentioned, and an opportunity afforded to the lady of defending her scheme. At a pause in the discourse, a voice was heard from the ceiling, which confirmed the truth of her tale; but, at the same time, revoked the command, and, in consideration of her faith, pronounced her absolution. Satisfied with this proof, the auditors dismissed their unbelief, and the lady consented to eat.

In the course of a copious correspondence with Ludloe, the observations I had collected were given. A sentiment, which I can hardly describe, induced me to be silent on all adventures connected with my bivocal projects. On other topics, I wrote fully and without restraint. I painted, in vivid hues, the scenes with which I was daily conversant, and pursued, fearlessly every speculation on religion and government that occurred. This spirit was encouraged by Ludloe, who failed not to comment on my narrative, and multiply deductions from my principles.

He taught me to ascribe the evils that infest society to the errors of opinion. The absurd and unequal distribution of power and property gave birth to poverty and riches, and these were the sources of luxury and crimes. These positions were readily admitted; but the remedy for these ills, the means of rectifying these errors, were not easily discovered. We have been inclined to impute them to inherent defects in the moral constitution of men: that oppression and tyranny grow up by a sort of natural necessity, and that they will perish only when the human species is extinct. Ludloe laboured to prove that this was by no means the case: that man is the creature of circumstances: that he is capable of endless improvement: that his progress has been stopped by the artificial impediment of government: that by the removal of this, the fondest dreams of imagination will be realised.

From detailing and accounting for the evils which exist under our present institutions, he usually proceeded to delineate some scheme of Utopian felicity, where the empire of reason should supplant that of force; where justice should be universally understood and practised; where the interest of the whole and of the individual should be seen by all to be the same; where the public good should be the scope of all activity; where the tasks of all should be the same, and the means of subsistence equally distributed.

No one could contemplate his pictures without rapture. By their comprehensiveness and amplitude they filled the imagination. I was unwilling to believe that in no region of the world, or at no period could these ideas be realised. It was plain that the nations of Europe were tending to greater depravity, and would be the prey of perpetual vicissitude. All individual attempts at their reformation would be fruitless. He therefore who desired the diffusion of right principles, to make a just system be adopted by a whole community, must pursue some extraordinary method.

In this state of mind I recollected my native country, where a few colonists from Britain had sown the germ of populous and mighty empires. Attended, as they were, into their new abode, by all their prejudices, yet such had been the influence of new circumstances, of consulting for their own happiness, of adopting simple forms of government, and excluding nobles and kings from their system, that they enjoyed a degree of happiness far superior to their parent state.

To conquer the prejudices and change the habits of millions are impossible. The human mind, exposed to social influences, inflexibly adheres to the direction that is given to it; but for the same reason why men who begin in error, will continue, those, who commence in truth, may be expected to persist. Habit and example will operate with equal force in both instances.

Let a few, sufficiently enlightened and disinterested, take up their abode in some unvisited region. Let their social scheme be founded in equity, and how small soever their original number may be, their growth into a nation is inevitable. Among other effects of national justice, was to be ranked the swift increase of numbers. Exempt from servile obligations and perverse habits, endowed with property, wisdom, and health, hundreds will expand, with inconceivable rapidity into thousands and thousands, into millions; and a new race, tutored in truth, may, in a few centuries, overflow the habitable world.

Such were the visions of youth! I could not banish them from my mind. I knew them to be crude; but believed that deliberation would bestow upon them solidity and shape. Meanwhile I imparted them to Ludloe.

In answer to the reveries and speculations which I sent to him respecting this subject, Ludloe informed me, that they had led his mind into a new sphere of meditation. He had long and deeply considered in what way he might essentially promote my happiness. He had entertained a faint hope that I would one day be qualified for a station like that to which he himself had been advanced. This post required an elevation and stability of views which human beings seldom reach, and which could be attained by me only by a long series of heroic labours. Hitherto every new stage in my intellectual progress had added vigour to his hopes, and he cherished a stronger belief than formerly that my career would terminate auspiciously. This, however, was necessarily distant. Many preliminaries must first be settled; many arduous accomplishments be first obtained; and my virtue be subjected to severe trials. At present it was not in his power to be more explicit; but if my reflections suggested no better plan, he advised me to settle my affairs in Spain, and return to him immediately. My knowledge of this country would be of the highest use, on the supposition of my ultimately arriving at the honours to which he had alluded; and some of these preparatory measures could be taken only with his assistance, and in his company.

This intimation was eagerly obeyed, and, in a short time, I arrived at Dublin. Meanwhile my mind had copious occupation in commenting on my friend's letter. This scheme, whatever it was, seemed to be suggested by my mention of a plan of colonisation, and my preference of that mode of producing extensive and permanent effects on the condition of mankind. It was easy therefore to conjecture that this mode had been pursued under some mysterious modifications and conditions.

It had always excited my wonder that so obvious an expedient had been over-looked. The globe which we inhabit was very imperfectly known. The regions and nations unexplored, it was reasonable to believe, surpassed in extent, and perhaps in populousness, those with which we were familiar. The order of Jesuits had furnished an example of all the errors and excellences of such a scheme. Their plan was founded on erroneous notions of religion and policy, and they had absurdly chosen a scene* within reach of the injustice and ambition of an European tyrant.

It was wise and easy to profit by their example. Resting on the two props of fidelity and zeal, an association might exist for ages in the heart of Europe, whose influence might be felt, and might be boundless, in some region of the southern hemisphere; and by whom a moral and political structure might be raised, the growth of pure wisdom, and totally unlike those fragments of Roman and Gothic barbarism which cover the face of what are called the civilised nations. The belief now rose in my mind that some such scheme had actually been prosecuted, and that Ludloe was a coadjutor. On this supposition, the caution with which he approached to his point, the arduous probation which a candidate for a part on this stage must undergo, and the rigours of that test by which his fortitude and virtue must be tried, were easily explained. I was too deeply imbued with veneration for the effects of such schemes, and too sanguine in my confidence in the rectitude of Ludloe, to refuse my concurrence in any scheme by which my qualifications might at length be raised to a due point.

*Paraguay.

Our interview was frank and affectionate. I found him situated just as formerly. His aspect, manners, and deportment were the same. I entered once more on my former mode of life, but our intercourse became more frequent. We constantly breakfasted together, and our conversation was usually prolonged through half the morning.

For a time our topics were general. I thought proper to leave to him the introduction of more interesting themes; this, however, he betrayed no inclination to do. His reserve excited some surprise, and I began to suspect that whatever design he had formed with regard to me, had been laid aside. To ascertain this question, I ventured, at length, to recall his attention to the subject of his last letter, and to enquire whether subsequent reflection had made any change in his views.

He said that his views were too momentous to be hastily taken up, or hastily dismissed; the station, my attainment of which depended wholly on myself, was high above vulgar heads, and was to be gained by years of solicitude and labour. This, at least, was true with regard to minds ordinarily constituted. I, perhaps, deserved to be regarded as an exception, and might be able to accomplish in a few months that for which others were obliged to toil during half their lives.

"*Man*," continued he, "is the slave of habit. Convince him to-day that his duty leads straight forward,—he shall advance, but at every step his belief shall fade; habit will resume its empire, and tomorrow he shall turn back, or betake himself to oblique paths.

"We know not our strength till it be tried. Virtue, till confirmed by habit, is a dream. You are a man imbued by errors, and vincible by slight temptations. Deep enquiries must bestow light on your opinions, and the habit of encountering and vanquishing temptation must inspire you with fortitude. Till this be done you are unqualified for that post, in which you will be invested with divine attributes, and prescribe the condition of a large portion of mankind.

"Confide not in the firmness of your principles, or the stedfastness of your integrity. Be always vigilant and fearful. Never think you have enough of knowledge, and let not your caution slumber for a moment, for you know not when danger is near."

I acknowledged the justice of his admonitions, and professed myself willing to undergo any ordeal which reason should prescribe. What, I asked, were the conditions, on the fulfilment of which depended my advancement to the station he alluded to? Was it necessary to conceal from me the nature and obligations of this rank?

These inquiries sunk him more profoundly into meditation than I had ever before witnessed. After a pause, in which some perplexity was visible, he answered:

"I scarcely know what to say. As to promises, I claim them not from you. We are now arrived at a point, in which it is necessary to look around with caution, and that consequences should be fully known. A number of persons are leagued together for an end of some moment. To make yourself one of these is submitted to your choice. Among the conditions of their alliance are mutual fidelity and secrecy.

"Their existence depends upon this: their existence is known only to themselves. This secrecy must be obtained by all the means which are possible. When I have said thus much, I have informed you, in some degree, of their existence, but you are still ignorant of the purpose contemplated by this association, and of all the members, except myself. So far, no dangerous disclosure is yet made: but this degree of conceal-ment is not sufficient. Thus much is made known to you, because it is unavoidable. The individuals which compose this fraternity are not immortal, and the vacancies occasioned by death must be supplied from among the living. The candidate must be instructed and prepared, and they are always at liberty to recede. Their reason must approve the obligations and duties of their station, or they are unfit for it. If they recede, one duty is still incumbent upon them: they must observe an inviolable silence. To this they are not held by any promise. They must weigh consequences, and freely decide; but they must not fail to number among these consequences their own death.

"Their death will not be prompted by vengeance. The executioner will say, he that has once revealed the tale is likely to reveal it a second time; and, to prevent this, the betrayer must die. Nor is this the only consequence. To prevent the further revelation, he, to whom the secret was imparted, must likewise perish. He must not console himself with the belief that his trespass will be unknown. The knowledge cannot, by human means, be withheld from this fraternity. Rare, indeed, will it be that his purpose to disclose is not discovered before it can be effected, and the disclosure prevented by his death.

"Be well aware of your condition. What I now, or may hereafter mention, men-tion not again. Admit not even a doubt as to the propriety of hiding it from all the world. There are eyes who will discern this doubt amidst the closest folds of your heart, and your life will instantly be sacrificed.

"At present be the subject dismissed. Reflect deeply on the duty which you have already incurred. Think upon your strength of mind, and be careful not to lay your-self under impracticable obligations. It will always be in your power to recede. Even after you are solemnly enrolled a member, you may consult the dictates of your own understanding, and relinquish your post; but while you live, the obligation to be silent will perpetually attend you.

"We seek not the misery or death of any one, but we are swayed by an immutable calculation. Death is to be abhorred, but the life of the betrayer is productive of more evil than his death: his death, therefore, we choose, and our means are instantaneous and unerring.

"I love you. The first impulse of my love is to dissuade you from seeking to know more. Your mind will be full of ideas; your hands will be perpetually busy to a purpose into which no human creature, beyond the verge of your brotherhood, must pry. Believe me, who have made the experiment, that compared with this task, the task of inviolable secrecy, all others are easy. To be dumb will not suffice; never to know any remission in your zeal or your watchfulness will not suffice. If the sagacity of others detect your occupations, however strenuously you may labour for concealment, your doom is ratified, as well as that of the wretch whose evil destiny led him to pursue you.

"Yet if your fidelity fail not, great will be your recompence. For all your toils and self-devotion, ample will be the retribution. Hitherto you have been wrapt in darkness and storm; then will you be exalted to a pure and unruffled element. It is only for a time that temptation will environ you, and your path will be toilsome. In a few years you will be permitted to withdraw to a land of sages, and the remainder of your life will glide away in the enjoyments of beneficence and wisdom.

"Think deeply on what I have said. Investigate your own motives and opinions, and prepare to submit them to the test of numerous hazards and experiments."

Here my friend passed to a new topic. I was desirous of reverting to this subject, and obtaining further information concerning it, but he assiduously repelled all my attempts, and insisted on my bestowing deep and impartial attention on what had already been disclosed. I was not slow to comply with his directions. My mind refused to admit any other theme of contemplation than this.

As yet I had no glimpse of the nature of this fraternity. I was permitted to form conjectures, and previous incidents bestowed but one form upon my thoughts. In reviewing the sentiments and deportment of Ludloe, my belief continually acquired new strength. I even recollected hints and ambiguous allusions in his discourse, which were easily solved, on the supposition of the existence of a new model of society, in some unsuspected corner of the world.

I did not fully perceive the necessity of secrecy; but this necessity perhaps would be rendered apparent, when I should come to know the connection that subsisted between Europe and this imaginary colony. But what was to be done? I was willing to abide by these conditions. My understanding might not approve of all the ends proposed by this fraternity, and I had liberty to withdraw from it, or to refuse to ally myself with them. That the obligation of secrecy should still remain, was unquestionably reasonable.

IV

It appeared to be the plan of Ludloe rather to damp than to stimulate my zeal. He discouraged all attempts to renew the subject in conversation. He dwelt upon the arduousness of the office to which I aspired, the temptations to violate my duty with which I should be continually beset, the inevitable death with which the slightest breach of my engagements would be followed, and the long apprenticeship which it would be necessary for me to serve, before I should be fitted to enter into this conclave.

Sometimes my courage was depressed by these representations. My zeal, however, was sure to revive; and at length Ludloe declared himself willing to assist me in the accomplishment of my wishes. For this end, it was necessary, he said, that I should be informed of a second obligation, which every candidate must assume. Before any one could be deemed qualified, he must be thoroughly known to his associates. For this end, he must determine to disclose every fact in his history, and every secret of his heart. I must begin with making these confessions with regard to my past life, to Ludloe, and must continue to communicate, at stated seasons, every new thought, and every new occurrence, to him. This confidence was to be absolutely limitless: no exceptions were to be admitted, and no reserves to be practised; and the same penalty attended the infraction of this rule as of the former. Means would be employed, by which the slightest deviation, in either case, would be detected, and the deathful consequence would follow with instant and inevitable expedition. If secrecy were difficult to practise, sincerity, in that degree in which it was here demanded, was a task infinitely more arduous, and a period of new deliberation was necessary before I should decide. I was at liberty to pause: nay, the longer was the period of deliberation which I took, the better; but, when I had once entered this path, it was not in my power to recede. After having solemnly avowed my resolution to be thus sincere in my confession, any particle of reserve or duplicity would cost me my life.

This indeed was a subject to be deeply thought upon. Hitherto I had been guilty of concealment with regard to my friend. I had entered into no formal compact, but had been conscious to a kind of tacit obligation to hide no important transaction of my life from him. This consciousness was the source of continual anxiety. I had exerted, on numerous occasions, my bivocal faculty, but, in my intercourse with Ludloe, had suffered not the slightest intimation to escape me with regard to it. This reserve was not easily explained. It was, in a great degree, the product of habit; but I likewise considered that the efficacy of this instrument depended upon its existence being unknown. To confide the secret to one, was to put an end to my privilege: how widely the knowledge would thenceforth be diffused, I had no power to foresee.

Each day multiplied the impediments to confidence. Shame hindered me from acknowledging my past reserves. Ludloe, from the nature of our intercourse, would certainly account my reserve, in this respect, unjustifiable, and to excite his indignation or contempt was an unpleasing undertaking. Now, if I should resolve to persist in my new path, this reserve must be dismissed: I must make him master of a secret which was precious to me beyond all others; by acquainting him with past concealments, I must risk incurring his suspicion and his anger. These reflections were productive of considerable embarrassment.

There was, indeed, an avenue by which to escape these difficulties, if it did not, at the same time, plunge me into greater. My confessions might, in other respects, be unbounded, but my reserves, in this particular, might be continued. Yet should I not expose myself to formidable perils? Would my secret be for ever unsuspected and undiscovered?

When I considered the nature of this faculty, the impossibility of going farther than suspicion, since the agent could be known only by his own confession, and even this confession would not be believed by the greater part of mankind, I was tempted to conceal it.

In most cases, if I had asserted the possession of this power, I should be treated as a liar; it would be considered as an absurd and audacious expedient to free myself from the suspicion of having entered into compact with a daemon, or of being myself an emissary of the grand foe. Here, however, there was no reason to dread a similar imputation, since Ludloe had denied the preternatural pretensions of these airy sounds.

My conduct on this occasion was nowise influenced by the belief of any inherent sanctity in truth. Ludloe had taught me to model myself in this respect entirely with a view to immediate consequences. If my genuine interest, on the whole, was promoted by veracity, it was proper to adhere to it; but, if the result of my investigation were opposite, truth was to be sacrificed without scruple.

Meanwhile, in a point of so much moment, I was not hasty to determine. My delay seemed to be, by no means, unacceptable to Ludloe, who applauded my discretion, and warned me to be circumspect. My attention was chiefly absorbed by considerations connected with this subject, and little regard was paid to any foreign occupation or amusement.

One evening, after a day spent in my closet, I sought recreation by walking forth. My mind was chiefly occupied by the review of incidents which happened in Spain. I turned my face towards the fields, and recovered not from my reverie, till I had proceeded some miles on the road to Meath. The night had considerably advanced, and the darkness was rendered intense, by the setting of the moon. Being somewhat weary, as well as undetermined in what manner next to proceed, I seated myself on a grassy bank beside the road. The spot which I had chosen was aloof from passengers, and shrouded in the deepest obscurity.

Some time elapsed, when my attention was excited by the slow approach of an equipage. I presently discovered a coach and six horses, but unattended, except by coachman and postillion, and with no light to guide them on their way. Scarcely had they passed the spot where I rested, when some one leaped from beneath the hedge, and seized the head of the fore-horses. Another called upon the coachman to stop, and threatened him with instant death if he disobeyed. A third drew open the coach-door, and ordered those within to deliver their purses. A shriek of terror showed me that a lady was within, who eagerly consented to preserve her life by the loss of her money.

To walk unarmed in the neighbourhood of Dublin, especially at night, has always been accounted dangerous. I had about me the usual instruments of defence. I was desirous of rescuing this person from the danger which surrounded her, but was somewhat at a loss how to effect my purpose. My single strength was insufficient to contend with three ruffians. After a moment's debate, an expedient was suggested, which I hastened to execute.

Time had not been allowed for the ruffian who stood beside the carriage to receive the plunder, when several voices, loud, clamorous, and eager, were heard in the quarter whence the traveller had come. By trampling with quickness, it was easy to imitate the sound of many feet. The robbers were alarmed, and one called upon another to attend. The sounds increased, and, at the next moment, they betook themselves to flight, but not till a pistol was discharged. Whether it was aimed at the lady in the carriage, or at the coachman, I was not permitted to discover, for the report affrighted the horses, and they set off at full speed.

I could not hope to overtake them: I knew not whither the robbers had fled, and whether, by proceeding, I might not fall into their hands. These considerations induced me to resume my feet, and retire from the scene as expeditiously as possible. I regained my own habitation without injury.

I have said that I occupied separate apartments from those of Ludloe. To these there were means of access without disturbing the family. I hasted to my chamber, but was considerably surprised to find, on entering my apartment, Ludloe seated at a table, with a lamp before him.

My momentary confusion was greater than his. On discovering who it was, he assumed his accustomed looks, and explained appearances, by saying, that he wished to converse with me on a subject of importance, and had therefore sought me at this secret hour, in my own chamber. Contrary to his expectation, I was absent. Conceiving it possible that I might shortly return, he had waited till now. He took no further notice of my absence, nor manifested any desire to know the cause of it, but proceeded to mention the subject which had brought him hither. These were his words:

"You have nothing which the laws permit you to call your own. Justice entitles you to the supply of your physical wants, from those who are able to supply them; but there are few who will acknowledge your claim, or spare an atom of their superfluity to appease your cravings. That which they will not spontaneously give, it is not right to wrest from them by violence. What then is to be done? Property is necessary to your own subsistence. It is useful, by enabling you to supply the wants of others. To give food, and clothing, and shelter, is to give life, to annihilate temptation, to unshackle virtue, and propagate felicity. How shall property be gained?

"You may set your understanding or your hands at work. You may weave stockings or write poems, and exchange them for money; but these are tardy and meagre schemes. The means are disproportioned to the end, and I will not suffer you to pursue them. My justice will supply your wants.

"But dependence on the justice of others is a precarious condition. To be the object is a less ennobling state than to be the bestower of benefit. Doubtless you desire to be vested with competence and riches, and to hold them by virtue of the law, and not at the will of a benefactor."

He paused as if waiting for my assent to his positions. I readily expressed my concurrence, and my desire to pursue any means compatible with honesty. He resumed:

"There are various means, besides labour, violence, or fraud. It is right to select the easiest within your reach. It happens that the easiest is at hand. A revenue of some thousands a year, a stately mansion in the city, and another in Kildare, old and faithful domestics, and magnificent furniture, are good things. Will you have them?"

"A gift like that," replied I, "will be attended by momentous conditions. I cannot decide upon its value, until I know these conditions."

"The sole condition is your consent to receive them. Not even the airy obligation of gratitude will be created by acceptance. On the contrary, by accepting them, you will confer the highest benefit upon another."

"I do not comprehend you. Something surely must be given in return."

"Nothing. It may seem strange that, in accepting the absolute controul of so much property, you subject yourself to no conditions; that no claims of gratitude or service will accrue; but the wonder is greater still. The law equitably enough fetters the gift with no restraints, with respect to you that receive it; but not so with regard to the unhappy being who bestows it. That being must part, not only with property but liberty. In accepting the property, you must consent to enjoy the services of the present possessor. They cannot be disjoined.

"Of the true nature and extent of the gift, you should be fully apprised. Be aware, therefore, that, together with this property, you will receive absolute power over the liberty and person of the being who now possesses it. That being must become your domestic slave; be governed, in every particular, by your caprice.

"Happily for you, though fully invested with this power, the degree and mode in which it will be exercised will depend upon yourself. You may either totally forbear the exercise, or employ it only for the benefit of your slave. However injurious, therefore, this authority may be to the subject of it, it will, in some sense, only enhance the value of the gift to you.

"The attachment and obedience of this being will be chiefly evident in one thing. Its duty will consist in conforming, in every instance, to your will. All the powers of this being are to be devoted to your happiness; but there is one relation between you, which enables you to confer, while exacting, pleasure. This relation is sexual. Your slave is a woman; and the bond which transfers her property and person to you is—marriage."

My knowledge of Ludloe, his principles, and reasonings, ought to have precluded that surprise which I experienced at the conclusion of his discourse. I knew that he regarded the present institution of marriage as a contract of servitude, and the terms of it unequal and unjust. When my surprise had subsided, my thoughts turned upon the nature of his scheme. After a pause of reflection, I answered:

"Both law and custom have connected obligations with marriage, which, though heaviest on the female, are not light upon the male. Their weight and extent are not immutable and uniform; they are modified by various incidents, and especially by the mental and personal qualities of the lady.

"I am not sure that I should willingly accept the property and person of a woman decrepit with age, and enslaved by perverse habits and evil passions: whereas youth, beauty, and tenderness would be worth accepting, even for their own sake, and disconnected with fortune.

"As to altar vows, I believe they will not make me swerve from equity. I shall exact neither service nor affection from my spouse. The value of these, and, indeed, not only the value, but the very existence, of the latter depends upon its spontaneity. A promise to love tends rather to loosen than strengthen the tie.

"As to myself, the age of illusion is past. I shall not wed, till I find one whose moral and physical constitution will make personal fidelity easy. I shall judge without mistiness or passion, and habit will come in aid of an enlightened and deliberate choice.

"I shall not be fastidious in my choice. I do not expect, and scarcely desire, much intellectual similitude between me and my wife. Our opinions and pursuits cannot be in common. While women are formed by their education, and their education continues in its present state, tender hearts and misguided understandings are all that we can hope to meet with.

"What are the character, age, and person of the woman to whom you allude? and what prospect of success would attend my exertions to obtain her favour?"

"I have told you she is rich. She is a widow, and owes her riches to the liberality of her husband, who was a trader of great opulence, and who died while on a mercantile adventure to Spain. He was not unknown to you. Your letters from Spain often spoke of him. In short, she is the widow of Benington, whom you met at Barcelona. She is still in the prime of life; is not without many feminine attractions; has an ardent and credulous temper; and is particularly given to devotion. This temper it would be easy to regulate according to your pleasure and your interest, and I now submit to you the expediency of an alliance with her.

"I am a kinsman, and regarded by her with uncommon deference; and my commendations, therefore, will be of great service to you, and shall be given.

"I will deal ingenuously with you. It is proper you should be fully acquainted with the grounds of this proposal. The benefits of rank, and property, and independence, which I have already mentioned as likely to accrue to you from this marriage, are solid and valuable benefits; but these are not the sole advantages, and to benefit you, in these respects, is not my whole view.

"No. My treatment of you henceforth will be regulated by one principle. I regard you only as one undergoing a probation or apprenticeship; as subjected to trials of your sincerity and fortitude. The marriage I now propose to you is desirable, because it will make you independent of me. Your poverty might create an unsuitable bias in favour of proposals, one of whose effects would be to set you beyond fortune's reach. That bias will cease, when you cease to be poor and dependent.

"Love is the strongest of all human delusions. That fortitude, which is not subdued by the tenderness and blandishments of woman, may be trusted; but no fortitude, which has not undergone that test, will be trusted by us.

"This woman is a charming enthusiast. She will never marry but him whom she passionately loves. Her power over the heart that loves her will scarcely have limits. The means of prying into your transactions, of suspecting and sifting your thoughts, which her constant society with you, while sleeping and waking, her zeal and watchfulness for your welfare, and her curiosity, adroitness, and penetration will afford her, are evident. Your danger, therefore, will be imminent. Your fortitude will be obliged to have recourse, not to flight, but to vigilance. Your eye must never close.

"Alas! what human magnanimity can stand this test? How can I persuade myself that you will not fail? I waver between hope and fear. Many, it is true, have fallen, and dragged with them the author of their ruin, but some have soared above even these perils and temptations, with their fiery energies unimpaired: and great has been, as great ought to be, their recompense.

"But you are doubtless aware of your danger. I need not repeat the consequences of betraying your trust, the rigour of those who will judge your fault, the unerring and unbounded scrutiny to which your actions, the most secret and indifferent, will be subjected.

"Your conduct, however, will be voluntary. At your own option be it, to see or not to see this woman. Circumspection, deliberation forethought, are your sacred duties and highest interest."

Ludloe's remarks on the seductive and bewitching powers of women, on the difficulty of keeping a secret which they wish to know, and to gain which they employ the soft artillery of tears and prayers, and blandishments and menaces, are familiar to all men; but they had little weight with me, because they were unsupported by my own experience. I had never had any intellectual or sentimental connection with the sex. My meditations and pursuits had all led a different way; and a bias had gradually been given to my feelings, very unfavourable to the refinements of love. I acknowledge,

with shame and regret, that I was accustomed to regard the physical and sensual consequences of the sexual relation as realities; and every thing intellectual, disinterested,
and heroic, which enthusiasts connect with it, as idle dreams. Besides, said I, I am yet a
stranger to the secret, on the preservation of which so much stress is laid, and it will be
optional with me to receive it or not. If, in the progress of my acquaintance with Mrs.
Benington, I should perceive any extraordinary danger in the gift, cannot I refuse, or
at least delay to comply with any new conditions from Ludloe? Will not his candour
and his affection for me rather commend than disapprove my diffidence? In fine, I
resolved to see this lady.

     She was, it seems, the widow of Benington, whom I knew in Spain. This man was
an English merchant settled at Barcelona, to whom I had been commended by Ludloe's
letters, and through whom my pecuniary supplies were furnished. Much intercourse
and some degree of intimacy had taken place between us, and I had gained a pretty
accurate knowledge of his character. I had been informed, through different channels,
that his wife was much his superior in rank; that she possessed great wealth in her own
right; and that some disagreement of temper or views occasioned their separation. She
had married him for love, and still doated on him: the occasions for separation having
arisen, it seems, not on her side but on his. As his habits of reflection were no-wise
friendly to religion, and as hers, according to Ludloe, were of the opposite kind, it
is possible that some jarring had arisen between them from this source. Indeed, from
some casual and broken hints of Benington, especially in the latter part of his life, I had
long since gathered this conjecture. Something, thought I, may be derived from my
acquaintance with her husband favourable to my views.

     I anxiously waited for an opportunity of acquainting Ludloe with my resolution.
On the day of our last conversation, he had made a short excursion from town, intending to return the same evening, but had continued absent for several days. As soon as
he came back, I hastened to acquaint him with my wishes.

     "Have you well considered this matter?" said he. "Be assured it is of no trivial
import. The moment at which you enter the presence of this woman will decide your
future destiny. Even putting out of view the subject of our late conversations, the light
in which you shall appear to her will greatly influence your happiness, since, though
you cannot fail to love her, it is quite uncertain what return she may think proper to
make. Much, doubtless, will depend on your own perseverance and address, but you
will have many, perhaps insuperable obstacles to encounter on several accounts, and
especially in her attachment to the memory of her late husband. As to her devout tem-

per, this is nearly allied to a warm imagination in some other respects, and will operate much more in favour of an ardent and artful lover, than against him."

I still expressed my willingness to try my fortune with her.

"Well," said he, "I anticipated your consent to my proposal, and the visit I have just made was to her. I thought it best to pave the way, by informing her that I had met with one for whom she had desired me to look out. You must know that her father was one of these singular men who set a value upon things exactly in proportion to the difficulty of obtaining or comprehending them. His passion was for antiques, and his favourite pursuit during a long life was monuments in brass, marble, and parchment, of the remotest antiquity. He was wholly indifferent to the character or conduct of our present sovereign and his ministers; but was extremely solicitous about the name and exploits of a king of Ireland that lived two or three centuries before the flood. He felt no curiosity to know who was the father of his wife's child, but would travel a thousand miles, and consume months, in investigating which son of Noah it was that first landed on the coast of Munster. He would give a hundred guineas from the mint for a piece of old decayed copper no bigger than his nail, provided it had awkward characters upon it, too much defaced to be read. The whole stock of a great bookseller was, in his eyes, a cheap exchange for a shred of parchment, containing half a homily written by St. Patrick. He would have gratefully given all his patrimonial domains to one who should inform him what pendragon or druid it was who set up the first stone on Salisbury plain.

"This spirit, as you may readily suppose, being seconded by great wealth and long life, contributed to form a very large collection of venerable lumber, which, though beyond all price to the collector himself, is of no value to his heiress but so far as it is marketable. She designs to bring the whole to auction, but for this purpose a catalogue and description are necessary. Her father trusted to a faithful memory, and to vague and scarcely legible memorandums, and has left a very arduous task to any one who shall be named to the office. It occurred to me, that the best means of promoting your views was to recommend you to this office.

"You are not entirely without the antiquarian frenzy yourself. The employment, therefore, will be somewhat agreeable to you for its own sake. It will entitle you to become an inmate of the same house, and thus establish an incessant intercourse between you, and the nature of the business is such, that you may perform it in what time, and with what degree of diligence and accuracy you please."

I ventured to insinuate that, to a woman of rank and family, the character of a hireling was by no means a favourable recommendation.

He answered, that he proposed, by the account he should give of me, to obviate every scruple of that nature. Though my father was no better than a farmer, it is not absolutely certain but that my remoter ancestors had princely blood in their veins: but as long as proofs of my low extraction did not impertinently intrude themselves, my silence, or, at most, equivocal surmises, seasonably made use of, might secure me from all inconveniences on the score of birth. He should represent me, and I was such, as his friend, favourite, and equal, and my passion for antiquities should be my principal inducement to undertake this office, though my poverty would make no objection to a reasonable pecuniary recompense.

Having expressed my acquiescence in his measures, he thus proceeded: My visit was made to my kinswoman, for the purpose, as I just now told you, of paving your way into her family; but, on my arrival at her house, I found nothing but disorder and alarm. Mrs. Benington, it seems, on returning from a longer ride than customary, last Thursday evening, was attacked by robbers. Her attendants related an imperfect tale of somebody advancing at the critical moment to her rescue. It seems, however, they did more harm than good; for the horses took to flight and overturned the carriage, in consequence of which Mrs. Benington was severely bruised. She has kept her bed ever since, and a fever was likely to ensue, which has only left her out of danger to-day.

As the adventure before related, in which I had so much concern, occurred at the time mentioned by Ludloe, and as all other circumstances were alike, I could not doubt that the person whom the exertion of my mysterious powers had relieved was Mrs. Benington: but what an ill-omened interference was mine! The robbers would probably have been satisfied with the few guineas in her purse, and, on receiving these, would have left her to prosecute her journey in peace and security, but, by absurdly offering a succour, which could only operate upon the fears of her assailants, I endangered her life, first by the desperate discharge of a pistol, and next by the fright of the horses. My anxiety, which would have been less if I had not been, in some degree, myself the author of the evil, was nearly removed by Ludloe's proceeding to assure me that all danger was at an end, and that he left the lady in the road to perfect health. He had seized the earliest opportunity of acquainting her with the purpose of his visit, and had brought back with him her cheerful acceptance of my services. The next week was appointed for my introduction.

V

With such an object in view, I had little leisure to attend to any indifferent object. My thoughts were continually bent upon the expected introduction; and my impatience and curiosity drew strength, not merely from the character of Mrs. Benington, but from the nature of my new employment. Ludloe had truly observed, that I was infected with somewhat of this antiquarian mania myself, and I now remembered that Benington had frequently alluded to this collection in possession of his wife. My curiosity had then been more than once excited by his representations, and I had formed a vague resolution of making myself acquainted with this lady and her learned treasure, should I ever return to Ireland. Other incidents had driven this matter from my mind.

Meanwhile, affairs between Ludloe and myself remained stationary. Our conferences, which were regular and daily, related to general topics, and though his instructions were adapted to promote my improvement in the most useful branches of knowledge, they never afforded a glimpse towards that quarter where my curiosity was most active.

The next week now arrived, but Ludloe informed me that the state of Mrs. Benington's health required a short excursion into the country, and that he himself proposed to bear her company. The journey was to last about a fortnight, after which I might prepare myself for an introduction to her.

This was a very unexpected and disagreeable trial to my patience. The interval of solitude that now succeeded would have passed rapidly and pleasantly enough, if an event of so much moment were not in suspense. Books, of which I was passionately fond, would have afforded me delightful and incessant occupation, and Ludloe, by way of reconciling me to unavoidable delays, had given me access to a little closet, in which his rarer and more valuable books were kept.

All my amusements, both by inclination and necessity, were centred in myself and at home. Ludloe appeared to have no visitants: and though frequently abroad, or at least secluded from me, had never proposed my introduction to any of his friends except Mrs. Benington. My obligations to him were already too great to allow me to lay claim to new favours and indulgences: nor, indeed, was my disposition such as to make society needful to my happiness. My character had been, in some degree, modelled by the faculty which I possessed. This deriving all its supposed value from impenetrable secrecy, and Ludloe's admonitions tending powerfully to impress me with the necessity of wariness and circumspection in my general intercourse with mankind, I had gradually fallen into sedate, reserved, mysterious, and unsociable habits. My heart wanted not a friend.

In this temper of mind, I set myself to examine the novelties which Ludloe's private book-cases contained. It will be strange, thought I, if his favourite volume do not show some marks of my friend's character. To know a man's favourite or most constant studies cannot fail of letting in some little light upon his secret thoughts, and though he would not have given me the reading of these books, if he had thought them capable of unveiling more of his concerns than he wished, yet possibly my ingenuity may go one step farther than he dreams of. You shall judge whether I was right in my conjectures.

The books which composed this little library were chiefly the voyages and travels of the missionaries of the sixteenth and seventeenth centuries. Added to these were some works upon political economy and legislation. Those writers who have amused themselves with reducing their ideas to practice, and drawing imaginary pictures of nations or republics, whose manners or government came up to their standard of excellence, were, all of whom I had ever heard, and some I had never heard of before, to be found in this collection. A translation of Aristotle's republic, the political romances of sir Thomas Moore, Harrington, and Hume, appeared to have been much read, and Ludloe had not been sparing of his marginal comments. In these writers he appeared to find nothing but error and absurdity; and his notes were introduced for no other end than to point out groundless principles and false conclusions. The style of these remarks was already familiar to me. I saw nothing new in them, or different from the strain of those speculations with which Ludloe was accustomed to indulge himself in conversation with me.

After having turned over the leaves of the printed volumes, I at length lighted on a small book of maps, from which, of course, I could reasonably expect no information, on that point about which I was most curious. It was an Atlas, in which the maps had been drawn by the pen. None of them contained any thing remarkable, so far as I, who was indeed a smatterer in geography, was able to perceive, till I came to the end, when I noticed a map, whose prototype I was wholly unacquainted with. It was drawn on a pretty large scale, representing two islands, which bore some faint resemblance, in their relative proportions, at least, to Great Britain and Ireland. In shape they were widely different, but as to size there was no scale by which to measure them. From the great number of subdivisions, and from signs, which apparently represented towns and cities, I was allowed to infer, that the country was at least as extensive as the British isles. This map was apparently unfinished, for it had no names inscribed upon it.

I have just said, my geographical knowledge was imperfect. Though I had not enough to draw the outlines of any country by memory, I had still sufficient to recognise what I had before seen, and to discover that none of the larger islands in our globe resembled the one before me. Having such and so strong motives to curiosity, you may easily imagine my sensations on surveying this map. Suspecting, as I did, that many of Ludloe's intimations alluded to a country well known to him, though unknown to others, I was, of course, inclined to suppose that this country was now before me.

In search of some clue to this mystery, I carefully inspected the other maps in this collection. In a map of the eastern hemisphere I soon observed the outlines of islands, which, though on a scale greatly diminished, were plainly similar to that of the land above described.

It is well known that the people of Europe are strangers to very nearly one half of the surface of the globe.* From the south pole up to the equator, it is only the small space occupied by southern Africa and by South America with which we are acquainted. There is a vast extent, sufficient to receive a continent as large as North America, which our ignorance has filled only with water. In Ludloe's maps nothing was still to be seen, in these regions, but water, except in that spot where the transverse parallels of the southern tropic and the one hundred and fiftieth degree east longitude intersect each other. On this spot were Ludloe's islands placed, though without any name or inscription whatever.

I needed not to be told that this spot had never been explored by any European voyager who had published his adventures. What authority had Ludloe for fixing a habitable land in this spot? and why did he give us nothing but the courses of shores and rivers, and the scite of towns and villages, without a name?

As soon as Ludloe had set out upon his proposed journey of a fortnight, I unlocked his closet, and continued rummaging among these books and maps till night. By that time I had turned over every book and almost every leaf in this small collection, and did not open the closet again till near the end of that period. Meanwhile I had many reflections upon this remarkable circumstance. Could Ludloe have intended that I should see this Atlas? It was the only book that could be styled a manuscript on these shelves, and it was placed beneath several others, in a situation far from being obvious and forward to the eye or the hand. Was it an oversight in him to leave it in my way, or

---

* The reader must be reminded that the incidents of this narrative are supposed to have taken place before the voyages of Bougainville and Cook.

could he have intended to lead my curiosity and knowledge a little farther onward by this accidental disclosure? In either case how was I to regulate my future deportment toward him? Was I to speak and act as if this atlas had escaped my attention or not? I had already, after my first examination of it, placed the volume exactly where I found it. On every supposition I thought this was the safest way, and unlocked the closet a second time, to see that all was precisely in the original order. How was I dismayed and confounded on inspecting the shelves to perceive that the Atlas was gone. This was a theft, which, from the closet being under lock and key, and the key always in my own pocket, and also from the very nature of the thing stolen, could not be imputed to any of the domestics. After a few moments a suspicion occurred, which was soon changed into certainty by applying to the housekeeper, who told me that Ludloe had returned, apparently in much haste, the evening of the day on which he had set out upon his journey, and just after I had left the house; that he had gone into the room where this closet of books was, and, after a few minutes' stay, came out again and went away. She told me also, that he had made general inquiries after me, to which she had answered, that she had not seen me during the day, and supposed that I had spent the whole of it abroad. From this account it was plain, that Ludloe had returned for no other purpose but to remove this book out of my reach. But if he had a double key to this door, what should hinder his having access, by the same means, to every other locked up place in the house?

This suggestion made me start with terror. Of so obvious a means for possessing a knowledge of every thing under his roof, I had never been till this moment aware. Such is the infatuation which lays our most secret thoughts open to the world's scrutiny. We are frequently in most danger when we deem ourselves most safe, and our fortress is taken sometimes through a point, whose weakness nothing, it should seem, but the blindest stupidity could overlook.

My terrors, indeed, quickly subsided when I came to recollect that there was nothing in any closet or cabinet of mine which could possibly throw light upon subjects which I desired to keep in the dark. The more carefully I inspected my own drawers, and the more I reflected on the character of Ludloe, as I had known it, the less reason did there appear in my suspicions; but I drew a lesson of caution from this circumstance, which contributed to my future safety.

From this incident I could not but infer Ludloe's unwillingness to let me so far into his geographical secret, as well as the certainty of that suspicion, which had very early been suggested to my thoughts, that Ludloe's plans of civilisation had been carried into practice in some unvisited corner of the world. It was strange, however, that he should betray himself by such an inadvertency. One who talked so confidently of his own powers, to unveil any secret of mine, and, at the same time, to conceal his own transactions, had surely committed an unpardonable error in leaving this important document in my way. My reverence, indeed, for Ludloe was such, that I sometimes entertained the notion that this seeming oversight was, in truth, a regular contrivance to supply me with a knowledge, of which, when I came maturely to reflect, it was impossible for me to make any ill use. There is no use in relating what would not be believed; and should I publish to the world the existence of islands in the space allotted by Ludloe's maps to these *terræ incognitæ*, what would the world answer? That whether the space described was sea or land was of no importance. That the moral and political condition of its inhabitants was the only topic worthy of rational curiosity. Since I had gained no information upon this point; since I had nothing to disclose but vain and fantastic surmises; I might as well be ignorant of every thing. Thus, from secretly condemning Ludloe's imprudence, I gradually passed to admiration of his policy. This discovery had no other effect than to stimulate my curiosity; to keep up my zeal to prosecute the journey I had commenced under his auspices.

I had hitherto formed a resolution to stop where I was in Ludloe's confidence: to wait till the success should be ascertained of my projects with respect to Mrs. Benington, before I made any new advance in the perilous and mysterious road into which he had led my steps. But, before this tedious fortnight had elapsed, I was grown extremely impatient for an interview, and had nearly resolved to undertake whatever obligation he should lay upon me.

This obligation was indeed a heavy one, since it included the confession of my vocal powers. In itself the confession was little. To possess this faculty was neither laudable nor culpable, nor had it been exercised in a way which I should be very much ashamed to acknowledge. It had led me into many insincerities and artifices, which, though not justifiable by any creed, was entitled to some excuse, on the score of youthful ardour and temerity. The true difficulty in the way of these confessions was the not having made them already. Ludloe had long been entitled to this confidence, and, though the existence of this power was venial or wholly innocent, the obstinate concealment of it was a different matter, and would certainly expose me to suspicion and rebuke. But what was the alternative; to conceal it: to incur those dreadful punishments awarded against treason in this particular. Ludloe's menaces still rung in my ears, and appalled my heart. How should I be able to shun them? By concealing from every one what I concealed from him? How was my concealment of such a faculty to be suspected or proved? Unless I betrayed myself, who could betray me?

In this state of mind, I resolved to confess myself to Ludloe in the way that he required, reserving only the secret of this faculty. Awful, indeed, said I, is the crisis of my fate. If Ludloe's declarations are true, a horrid catastrophe awaits me. But as fast as my resolutions were shaken, they were confirmed anew by the recollection—who can betray me but myself? If I deny, who is there can prove? Suspicion can never light upon the truth; if it does, it can never be converted into certainty. Even my own lips cannot confirm it, since who will believe my testimony?

By such illusions was I fortified in my desperate resolution. Ludloe returned at the time appointed. He informed me that Mrs. Benington expected me next morning. She was ready to depart for her country residence, where she proposed to spend the ensuing summer, and would carry me along with her. In consequence of this arrangement, he said, many months would elapse before he should see me again. "You will indeed," continued he, "be pretty much shut up from all society. Your books and your new friend will be your chief, if not only companions. Her life is not a social one, because she has formed extravagant notions of the importance of lonely worship and devout solitude. Much of her time will be spent in meditation upon pious books in her closet; some of it in long solitary rides in her coach, for the sake of exercise. Little will remain for eating and sleeping; so that unless you can prevail upon her to violate her ordinary rules for your sake, you will be left pretty much to yourself. You will have the more time to reflect upon what has hitherto been the theme of our conversations. You can come to town when you want to see me. I shall generally be found in these apartments."

In the present state of my mind, though impatient to see Mrs. Benington, I was still more impatient to remove the veil between Ludloe and myself. After some pause, I ventured to enquire if there was any impediment to my advancement in the road he had already pointed out to my curiosity and ambition.

He replied, with great solemnity, that I was already acquainted with the next step to be taken in this road. If I was prepared to make him my confessor, as to the past, the present, and the future, without exception or condition, but what arose from defect of memory, he was willing to receive my confession.

I declared myself ready to do so.

"I need not," he returned, "remind you of the consequences of concealment or deceit. I have already dwelt upon these consequences. As to the past, you have already told me, perhaps, all that is of any moment to know. It is in relation to the future that caution will be chiefly necessary. Hitherto your actions have been nearly indifferent to the ends of your future existence. Confessions of the past are required, because they are an earnest of the future character and conduct. Have you then—but this is too abrupt. Take an hour to reflect and deliberate. Go by yourself; take yourself to severe task, and make up your mind with a full, entire, and unfailing resolution; for the moment in which you assume this new obligation will make you a new being. Perdition or felicity will hang upon that moment."

This conversation was late in the evening. After I had consented to postpone this subject, we parted, he telling me that he would leave his chamber door open, and as soon as my mind was made up I might come to him.

I retired accordingly to my apartment, and spent the prescribed hour in anxious and irresolute reflections. They were no other than had hitherto occurred, but they occurred with more force than ever. Some fatal obstinacy, however, got possession of me, and I persisted in the resolution of concealing one thing. We become fondly attached to objects and pursuits, frequently for no conceivable reason but the pain and trouble they cost us. In proportion to the danger in which they involve us do we cherish them. Our darling potion is the poison that scorches our vitals.

After some time, I went to Ludloe's apartment. I found him solemn, and yet benign, at my entrance. After intimating my compliance with the terms prescribed, which I did, in spite of all my labour for composure, with accents half faultering, he proceeded to put various questions to me, relative to my early history.

I knew there was no other mode of accomplishing the end in view, but by putting all that was related in the form of answers to questions; and when meditating on the character of Ludloe, I experienced excessive uneasiness as to the consummate art and penetration which his questions would manifest. Conscious of a purpose to conceal, my fancy invested my friend with the robe of a judicial inquisitor, all whose questions should aim at extracting the truth, and entrapping the liar.

In this respect, however, I was wholly disappointed. All his inquiries were general and obvious. They betokened curiosity, but not suspicion; yet there were moments when I saw, or fancied I saw, some dissatisfaction betrayed in his features; and when I arrived at that period of my story which terminated with my departure, as his companion, for Europe, his pauses were, I thought, a little longer and more museful than I liked. At this period, our first conference ended. After a talk, which had commenced at a late hour, and had continued many hours, it was time to sleep, and it was agreed that next morning the conference should be renewed.

On retiring to my pillow, and reviewing all the circumstances of this interview, my mind was filled with apprehension and disquiet. I seemed to recollect a thousand things, which showed that Ludloe was not fully satisfied with my part in this interview. A strange and nameless mixture of wrath and of pity appeared, on recollection, in the glances which, from time to time, he cast upon me. Some emotion played upon his features, in which, as my fears conceived, there was a tincture of resentment and ferocity. In vain I called my usual sophistries to my aid. In vain I pondered on the inscrutable nature of my peculiar faculty. In vain I endeavoured to persuade myself, that, by telling the truth, instead of entitling myself to Ludloe's approbation, I should only excite his anger, by what he could not but deem an attempt to impose upon his belief an incredible tale of impossible events. I had never heard or read of any instance of this faculty. I supposed the case to be absolutely singular, and I should be no more entitled to credit in proclaiming it, than if I should maintain that a certain billet of wood possessed the faculty of articulate speech. It was now, however, too late to retract. I had been guilty of a solemn and deliberate concealment. I was now in the path in which there was no turning back, and I must go forward.

The return of day's encouraging beams in some degree quieted my nocturnal terrors; and I went, at the appointed hour, to Ludloe's presence. I found him with a much more cheerful aspect than I expected, and began to chide myself in secret for the folly of my late apprehensions.

After a little pause, he reminded me, that he was only one among many, engaged in a great and arduous design. "As each of us," continued he, "is mortal, each of us must, in time, yield his post to another. Each of us is ambitious to provide himself a successor, to have his place filled by one selected and instructed by himself. All our personal feelings and affections are by no means intended to be swallowed up by a passion for the general interest; when they can be kept alive and be brought into play, in subordination and subservience to the great end, they are cherished as useful, and revered as laudable; and whatever austerity and rigour you may impute to my character, there are few more susceptible of personal regards than I am.

"You cannot know, till you are what I am, what deep, what all-absorbing interest I have in the success of my tutorship on this occasion. Most joyfully would I embrace a thousand deaths, rather than that you should prove a recreant. The consequences of any failure in your integrity will, it is true, be fatal to yourself; but there are some minds, of a generous texture, who are more impatient under ills they have inflicted upon others, than of those they have brought upon themselves; who had rather perish, themselves, in infamy, than bring infamy or death upon a benefactor.

"Perhaps of such noble materials is your mind composed. If I had not thought so, you would never have been an object of my regard, and therefore, in the motives that shall impel you to fidelity, sincerity, and perseverance, some regard to my happiness and welfare will, no doubt, have place.

"And yet I exact nothing from you on this score. If your own safety be insufficient to controul you, you are not fit for us. There is, indeed, abundant need of all possible induce-ments to make you faithful. The task of concealing nothing from me must be easy. That of concealing every thing from others must be the only arduous one. The first you can hardly fail of performing, when the exigence requires it, for what motive can you pos-sibly have to practice evasion or disguise with me? You have surely committed no crime; you have neither robbed, nor murdered, nor betrayed. If you have, there is no room for the fear of punishment or the terror of disgrace to step in, and make you hide your guilt from me. You cannot dread any farther disclosure, because I can have no interest in your ruin or your shame: and what evil could ensue the confession of the foulest murder, even before a bench of magistrates, more dreadful than that which will inevitably follow the practice of the least concealment to me, or the least undue disclosure to others?"

You cannot easily conceive the emphatical solemnity with which this was spoken. Had he fixed piercing eyes on me while he spoke; had I perceived him watching my looks, and labouring to penetrate my secret thoughts, I should doubtless have been ruined: but he fixed his eyes upon the floor, and no gesture or look indicated the small-est suspicion of my conduct. After some pause, he continued, in a more pathetic tone, while his whole frame seemed to partake of his mental agitation.

"I am greatly at a loss by what means to impress you with a full conviction of the truth of what I have just said. Endless are the sophistries by which we seduce ourselves into perilous and doubtful paths. What we do not see, we disbelieve, or we heed not. The sword may descend upon our infatuated head from above; but we who are, mean-while, busily inspecting the ground at our feet, or gazing at the scene around us, are not aware or apprehensive of its irresistible coming. In this case, it must not be seen before it is felt, or before that time comes when the danger of incurring it is over. I cannot withdraw the veil, and disclose to your view the exterminating angel. All must be vacant and blank, and the danger that stands armed with death at your elbow must continue to be totally invisible, till that moment when its vengeance is provoked or unprovokable. I will do my part to encourage you in good, or intimidate you from evil. I am anxious to set before you all the motives which are fitted to influence your conduct; but how shall I work on your convictions?"

Here another pause ensued, which I had not courage enough to interrupt. He presently resumed.

"Perhaps you recollect a visit which you paid, on Christmas day, in the year ——, to the cathedral church at Toledo. Do you remember?"

A moment's reflection recalled to my mind all the incidents of that day. I had good reason to remember them. I felt no small trepidation when Ludloe referred me to that day, for, at the moment, I was doubtful whether there had not been some bivocal agency exerted on that occasion. Luckily, however, it was almost the only similar occasion in which it had been wholly silent.

I answered in the affirmative. "I remember them perfectly."

"And yet," said Ludloe, with a smile that seemed intended to disarm this declaration of some of its terrors, "I suspect your recollection is not as exact as mine, nor, indeed, your knowledge as extensive. You met there, for the first time, a female, whose nominal uncle, but real father, a dean of that ancient church, resided in a blue stone house, the third from the west angle of the square of St. Jago."

All this was exactly true.

"This female," continued he, "fell in love with you. Her passion made her deaf to all the dictates of modesty and duty, and she gave you sufficient intimations, in subsequent interviews at the same place, of this passion; which, she being fair and enticing, you were not slow in comprehending and returning. As not only the safety of your intercourse, but even of both your lives, depended on being shielded even from suspicion, the utmost wariness and caution was observed in all your proceedings. Tell me whether you succeeded in your efforts to this end."

I replied, that, at the time, I had no doubt but I had.

"And yet," said he, drawing something from his pocket, and putting it into my hand, "there is the slip of paper, with the preconcerted emblem inscribed upon it, which the infatuated girl dropped in your sight, one evening, in the left aisle of that church. That paper you imagined you afterwards burnt in your chamber-lamp. In pursuance of this token, you deferred your intended visit, and next day the lady was accidentally drowned in passing a river. Here ended your connexion with her, and with her was buried, as you thought, all memory of this transaction.

"I leave you to draw your own inference from this disclosure. Meditate upon it when alone. Recal all the incidents of that drama, and labour to conceive the means by which my sagacity has been able to reach events that took place so far off, and under so deep a covering. If you cannot penetrate these means, learn to reverence my assertions, that I cannot be deceived; and let sincerity be henceforth the rule of your conduct towards me, not merely because it is right, but because concealment is impossible.

"We will stop here. There is no haste required of us. Yesterday's discourse will suffice for to-day, and for many days to come. Let what has already taken place be the subject of profound and mature reflection. Review, once more, the incidents of your early life, previous to your introduction to me, and, at our next conference, prepare to supply all those deficiencies occasioned by negligence, forgetfulness, or design on our first. There must be some. There must be many. The whole truth can only be disclosed after numerous and repeated conversations. These must take place at considerable intervals, and when all is told, then shall you be ready to encounter the final ordeal, and load yourself with heavy and terrific sanctions.

"I shall be the proper judge of the completeness of your confession. Knowing previously, and by unerring means, your whole history, I shall be able to detect all that is deficient, as well as all that is redundant. Your confessions have hitherto adhered to the truth; but deficient they are, and they must be; for who, at a single trial, can detail the secrets of his life? whose recollection can fully serve him at an instant's notice? who can free himself, by a single effort, from the dominion of fear and shame? We expect no miracles of fortitude and purity from our disciples. It is our discipline, our wariness, our laborious preparation that creates the excellence we have among us. We find it not ready made.

"I counsel you to join Mrs. Benington without delay. You may see me when and as often as you please. When it is proper to renew the present topic, it shall be renewed. Till then we will be silent."

Here Ludloe left me alone, but not to indifference or vacuity. Indeed I was overwhelmed with the reflections that arose from this conversation. So, said I, I am still saved, if I have wisdom enough to use the opportunity, from the consequences of past concealments. By a distinction which I had wholly overlooked, but which could not be missed by the sagacity and equity of Ludloe, I have praise for telling the truth, and an excuse for withholding some of the truth. It was, indeed, a praise to which I was entitled, for I have made no additions to the tale of my early adventures. I had no motive to exaggerate or dress out in false colours. What I sought to conceal,

I was careful to exclude entirely, that a lame or defective narrative might awaken no suspicions.

The allusion to incidents at Toledo confounded and bewildered all my thoughts. I still held the paper he had given me. So far as memory could be trusted, it was the same which, an hour after I had received it, I burnt, as I conceived, with my own hands. How Ludloe came into possession of this paper,—how he was apprised of incidents, to which only the female mentioned and myself were privy, which she had too good reason to hide from all the world, and which I had taken infinite pains to bury in oblivion, I vainly endeavoured to conjecture.

The Tapestried Chamber

OR, THE LADY IN THE SACQUE

Sir Walter Scott

———◆———

T HE FOLLOWING NARRATIVE IS GIVEN FROM THE PEN, SO FAR AS MEMORY
permits, in the same character in which it was presented to the author's
ear; nor has he claim to further praise, or to be more deeply censured,
than in proportion to the good or bad judgment which he has employed in selecting
his materials, as he has studiously avoided any attempt at ornament which might
interfere with the simplicity of the tale.

At the same time it must be admitted, that the particular class of stories which turns
on the marvellous possesses a stronger influence when told than when committed to
print. The volume taken up at noonday, though rehearsing the same incidents, conveys
a much more feeble impression than is achieved by the voice of the speaker on a circle
of fireside auditors, who hang upon the narrative as the narrator details the minute
incidents which serve to give it authenticity, and lowers his voice with an affectation of
mystery while he approaches the fearful and wonderful part. It was with such advantages that the present writer heard the following events related, more than twenty years
since, by the celebrated Miss Seward of Lichfield, who to her numerous accomplishments added, in a remarkable degree, the power of narrative in private conversation. In
its present form the tale must necessarily lose all the interest which was attached to it, by
the flexible voice and intelligent features of the gifted narrator. Yet still, read aloud, to
an undoubting audience by the doubtful light of the closing evening, or, in silence, by
a decaying taper, and amidst the solitude of a half-lighted apartment, it may redeem its
character as a good ghost-story. Miss Seward always affirmed that she had derived her
information from an authentic source, although she suppressed the names of the two
persons chiefly concerned. I will not avail myself of any particulars I may have since
received concerning the localities of the detail, but suffer them to rest under the same

general description in which they were first related to me; and, for the same reason, I will not add to, or diminish, the narrative by any circumstance, whether more or less material, but simply rehearse, as I heard it, a story of supernatural terror.

About the end of the American war, when the officers of Lord Cornwallis's army, which surrendered at Yorktown, and others, who had been made prisoners during the impolitic and ill-fated controversy, were returning to their own country, to relate their adventures, and repose themselves after their fatigues, there was amongst them a general officer, to whom Miss S. gave the name of Browne, but merely, as I understood, to save the inconvenience of introducing a nameless agent in the narrative. He was an officer of merit, as well as a gentleman of high consideration for family and attainments.

Some business had carried General Browne upon a tour through the western counties, when, in the conclusion of a morning stage, he found himself in the vicinity of a small country town, which presented a scene of uncommon beauty, and of a character peculiarly English.

The little town, with its stately old church, whose tower bore testimony to the devotion of ages long past, lay amidst pastures and corn-fields of small extent, but bounded and divided with hedgerow timber of great age and size. There were few marks of modern improvement. The environs of the place intimated neither the solitude of decay nor the bustle of novelty; the houses were old, but in good repair; and the beautiful little river murmured freely on its way to the left of the town, neither restrained by a dam nor bordered by a towing-path.

Upon a gentle eminence, nearly a mile to the southward of the town, were seen, amongst many venerable oaks and tangled thickets, the turrets of a castle, as old as the wars of York and Lancaster, but which seemed to have received important alterations during the age of Elizabeth and her successor. It had not been a place of great size; but whatever accommodation it formerly afforded was, it must be supposed, still to be obtained within its walls; at least, such was the inference which General Browne drew from observing the smoke arise merrily from several of the ancient wreathed and carved chimney-stalks. The wall of the park ran alongside of the highway for two or three hundred yards; and through the different points by which the eye found glimpses into the woodland scenery it seemed to be well stocked. Other points of view opened in succession—now a full one of the front of the old castle, and now a side glimpse at its particular towers, the former rich in all the bizarrerie of the Elizabethan school, while the simple and solid strength of other parts of the building seemed to show that they had been raised more for defense than ostentation.

Delighted with the partial glimpses which he obtained of the castle through the woods and glades by which this ancient feudal fortress was surrounded, our military traveler was determined to inquire whether it might not deserve a nearer view, and whether it contained family pictures or other objects of curiosity worthy of a stranger's visit, when, leaving the vicinity of the park, he rolled through a clean and well-paved street, and stopped at the door of a well-frequented inn.

Before ordering horses to proceed on his journey, General Browne made inquiries concerning the proprietor of the chateau which had so attracted his admiration, and was equally surprised and pleased at hearing in reply a nobleman named whom we shall call Lord Woodville. How fortunate! Much of Browne's early recollections, both at school and at college, had been connected with young Woodville whom, by a few questions, he now ascertained to be the same with the owner of this fair domain. He had been raised to the peerage by the decease of his father a few months before, and, as the General learned from the landlord, the term of mourning being ended, was now taking possession of his paternal estate in the jovial season of merry autumn, accompanied by a select party of friends, to enjoy the sports of a country famous for game.

This was delightful news to our traveller. Frank Woodville had been Richard Browne's fag at Eton, and his chosen intimate at Christ Church; their pleasures and their tasks had been the same; and the honest soldier's heart warmed to find his early friend in possession of so delightful a residence, and of an estate, as the landlord assured him with a nod and a wink, fully adequate to maintain and add to his dignity. Nothing was more natural than that the traveller should suspend a journey which there was nothing to render hurried to pay a visit to an old friend under such agreeable circumstances.

The fresh horses, therefore, had only the brief task of conveying the General's travelling carriage to Woodville Castle. A porter admitted them at a modern Gothic Lodge, built in that style to correspond with the Castle itself, and at the same time rang a bell to give warning of the approach of visitors. Apparently the sound of the bell had suspended the separation of the company, bent on the various amusements of the morning; for, on entering the court of the chateau, several young men were lounging about in their sporting dresses, looking at, and criticising the dogs which the keepers held in readiness to attend their pastime. As General Browne alighted, the young lord came to the gate of the hall, and for an instant gazed, as at a stranger, upon the countenance of his friend, on which war, with its fatigues and its wounds, had made a great alteration. But the uncertainty lasted no longer than till the visitor had spoken, and the hearty greeting which followed was such as can only be exchanged betwixt those who have passed together the merry days of careless boyhood or early youth.

"If I could have formed a wish, my dear Browne," said Lord Woodville, "it would have been to have you here, of all men, upon this occasion, which my friends are good enough to hold as a sort of holiday. Do not think you have been unwatched during the years you have been absent from us. I have traced you through your dangers, your triumphs, your misfortunes, and was delighted to see that, whether in victory or defeat, the name of my old friend was always distinguished with applause."

The General made a suitable reply, and congratulated his friend on his new dignities, and the possession of a place and domain so beautiful.

"Nay, you have seen nothing of it as yet," said Lord Woodville, "and I trust you do not mean to leave us till you are better acquainted with it. It is true, I confess, that my present party is pretty large, and the old house, like other places of the kind, does not possess so much accommodation as the extent of the outward walls appears to promise. But we can give you a comfortable old-fashioned room; and I venture to suppose that your campaigns have taught von to be glad of worse quarters."

The General shrugged his shoulders and laughed. "I presume," he said, "the worst apartment in your chateau is considerably superior to the old tobacco-cask in which I was fain to take up my night's lodging when I was in the hush, as the Virginians call it, with the light corps. There I lay, like Diogenes himself, so delighted with my covering from the elements, that I made a vain attempt to have it rolled on to my next quarters; but my commander for the time would give way to no such luxurious provision, and I took farewell of my beloved cask with tears in my eyes."

"Well, then, since you do not fear your quarters," said Lord Woodville, "you will stay with me a week at least. Of guns, dogs, fishing-rods, flies, and means of sport by sea and land, we have enough and to spare: you cannot pitch on an amusement but we will find the means of pursuing it. But if you prefer the gun and pointers, I will go with you myself, and see whether you have mended your shooting since you have been amongst the Indians of the back settlements."

The General gladly accepted his friendly host's proposal in all its points. After a morning of manly exercise, the company met at dinner, where it was the delight of Lord Woodville to conduce to the display of the high properties of his recovered friend, so as to recommend him to his guests, most of whom were persons of distinction. He led General Browne to speak of the scenes he had witnessed; and as every word marked alike the brave officer and the sensible man, who retained possession of his cool judgment under the most imminent dangers, the company looked upon the soldier with general respect, as on one who had proved himself possessed of an uncommon portion of personal courage—that attribute, of all others, of which everybody desires to be thought possessed.

The day at Woodville Castle ended as usual in such mansions. The hospitality stopped within the limits of good order; music, in which the young lord was a proficient, succeeded to the circulation of the bottle: cards and billiards, for those who preferred such amusements, were in readiness; but the exercise of the morning required early hours, and not long after eleven o'clock the guests began to retire to their several apartments.

The young lord himself conducted his friend, General Browne, to the chamber destined for him, which answered the description he had given of it being comfortable, but old-fashioned. The bed was of the massive form used in the end of the seventeenth century, and the curtains of faded silk, heavily trimmed with tarnished gold. But then the sheets, pillows, and blankets looked delightful to the campaigner, when he thought of his "mansion, the cask." There was an air of gloom in the tapestry hangings which, with their worn-out graces, curtained the walls of the little chamber and gently undulated as the autumnal breeze found its way through the ancient lattice-window, which pattered and whistled as the air gained entrance. The toilet too, with its mirror, turbaned after the manner of the beginning of the century, with a coiffure of murrey-colored silk, and its hundred strange-shaped boxes, providing for arrangements which had been obsolete for more than fifty years, had an antique, and in so far a melancholy, aspect. But nothing could blaze more brightly and cheerfully than the two large wax candles; or if aught could rival them, it was the flaming, bickering fagots in the chimney, that sent at once their gleam and their warmth through the snug apartment, which, notwithstanding the general antiquity of its appearance, was not wanting in the least convenience that modern habits rendered either necessary or desirable.

"This is an old-fashioned sleeping-apartment. General," said the young lord; "but I hope you find nothing that makes you envy your old tobacco-cask."

"I am not particular respecting my lodgings," replied the General, "yet were I to make any choice, 1 would prefer this chamber by many degrees, to the gayer and more modern rooms of your family mansion. Believe me, that when I unite its modern air of comfort with its venerable antiquity, and recollect that it is your lordship's property, I shall feel in better quarters here than if I were in the best hotel London could afford."

"I trust—I have no doubt—that you will find yourself as comfortable as I wish you, my dear General," said the young nobleman; and once more bidding his guest good-night, he shook him by the hand and withdrew.

The General once more looked round him, and internally congratulating himself on his return to peaceful life, the comforts of which were endeared by the recollection of the hardships and dangers he had lately sustained, undressed himself, and prepared for a luxurious night's rest.

Here, contrary to the custom of this species of tale, we leave the General in possession of his apartment until the next morning.

The company assembled for breakfast at an early hour, but without the appearance of General Browne, who seemed the guest that Lord Woodville was desirous of honoring above all whom his hospitality had assembled around him. He more than once expressed surprise at the General's absence, and at length sent a servant to make inquiry after him. The man brought back information that General Browne had been walking abroad since an early hour of the morning, in defiance of the weather, which was misty and ungenial.

"The custom of a soldier," said the young nobleman to his friends; "many of them acquire habitual vigilance, and cannot sleep after the early hour at which their duty usually commands them to be alert."

Yet the explanation which Lord Woodville thus offered to the company seemed hardly satisfactory to his own mind, and it was in a fit of silence and abstraction that he awaited the return of the General. It took place near an hour after the breakfast bell had rung. He looked fatigued and feverish. His hair, the powdering and arrangement of which was at this time one of the most important occupations of a man's whole day, and marked his fashion as much as, in the present time, the tying of a cravat, or the want of one, was dishevelled, uncurled, void of powder, and dank with dew. His clothes were huddled on with a careless negligence, remarkable in a military man, whose real or supposed duties are usually held to include some attention to the toilet; and his looks were haggard and ghastly in a peculiar degree.

"So you have stolen a march upon us this morning, my dear General," said Lord Woodville; "or you have not found jour bed so much to your mind as I had hoped and you seemed to expect. How did you rest last night?"

"Oh, excellently well! remarkably well! never better in my life"—said General Browne rapidly, and yet with an air of embarrassment which was obvious to his friend.

He then hastily swallowed a cup of tea, and neglecting or refusing whatever else was offered, seemed to fall into a fit of abstraction.

"You will take the gun to-day, General," said his friend and host, but had to repeat the question twice ere he received the abrupt answer, "No, my lord; I am sorry I cannot have the honor of spending another day with your lordship; my post-horses are ordered, and will be here directly."

All who were present showed surprise, and Lord Woodville immediately replied, "Post-horses, my good friend! what can you possibly want with them, when you promised to stay with me quietly for at least a week?"

"I believe," said the General, obviously much embarrassed, "that I might, in the pleasure of my first meeting with your lordship, have said something about stopping here a few days; but I have since found it altogether impossible."

"That is very extraordinary," answered the young nobleman. "You seemed quite disengaged yesterday, and you cannot have had a summons to-day; for our post has not come up from the town, and therefore you cannot have received any letters."

General Browne, without giving any further explanation, muttered something of indispensable business, and insisted on the absolute necessity of his departure in a manner which silenced all opposition on the part of his host, who saw that his resolution was taken, and forbore all further importunity.

"At least, however," he said, " permit me, my dear Browne, since go you will or must, to show you the view from the terrace, which the mist, that is now rising, will soon display."

He threw open a sash-window and stepped down upon the terrace as he spoke. The General followed him mechanically, but seemed little to attend to what his host was saying, as, looking across an extended and rich prospect, he pointed out the different objects worthy of observation. Thus they moved on till Lord Woodville had attained his purpose of drawing his guest entirely apart from the rest of the company, when, turning round upon him with an air of great solemnity, he addressed him thus:—

"Richard Browne, my old and very dear friend, we are now alone. Let me conjure you to answer me upon the word of a friend, and the honor of a soldier. How did you in reality rest during last night?"

"Most wretchedly indeed, my lord," answered the General, in the same tone of solemnity;— "so miserably, that I would not run the risk of such a second night, not only for all the lands belonging to this castle, but for all the country which I see from this elevated point of view."

"This is most extraordinary," said the young lord, as if speaking to himself; "then there must be something in the reports concerning that apartment." Again turning to the General, he said, "For God's sake, my dear friend, be candid with me, and let me know the disagreeable particulars which have befallen you under a roof, where, with consent of the owner, you should have met nothing save comfort."

The General seemed distressed by this appeal, and paused a moment before he replied. "My dear lord," he at length said, "what happened to me last night is of a nature so peculiar and so unpleasant, that I could hardly bring myself to detail it even to your lordship, were it not that, independent of my wish to gratify any request of yours, I think that sincerity on my part may lead to some explanation about a circumstance equally painful and mysterious. To others, the communication I am about to make might place me in the light of a weak-minded, superstitious fool, who suffered his own imagination to delude and bewilder him; but you have known me in childhood and youth, and will not suspect me of having adopted in manhood the feelings and frailties from which my early years were free." Here he paused, and his friend replied:—

"Do not doubt my perfect confidence in the truth of your communication, however strange it may be," replied Lord Woodville; "I know your firmness of disposition too well to suspect you could be made the object of imposition, and am aware that your honor and your friendship will equally deter you from exaggerating whatever you may have witnessed."

"Well, then," said the General, "I will proceed with my story as well as I can, relying upon your candor, and yet distinctly feeling that I would rather face a battery than recall to my mind the odious recollections of last night."

He paused a second time, and then perceiving that Lord Woodville remained silent and in an attitude of attention, he commenced, though not without obvious reluctance, the history of his night adventures in the Tapestried Chamber.

"I undressed and went to bed, so soon as your lordship left me yesterday evening; but the wood in the chimney, which nearly fronted my bed, blazed brightly and cheerfully, and, aided by a hundred exciting recollections of ray childhood and youth, which had been recalled by the unexpected pleasure of meeting your lordship, prevented me from falling immediately asleep. I ought, however, to say, that these reflections were all of a pleasant and agreeable kind, grounded on a sense of having for a time exchanged the labor, fatigues, and dangers of my profession, for the enjoyments of a peaceful life, and the reunion of those friendly and affectionate ties which I had torn asunder at the rude summons of war.

"While such pleasing reflections were stealing over my mind, and gradually lulling me to slumber, I was suddenly aroused by a sound like that of the rustling of a silken gown, and the tapping of a pair of high-heeled shoes, as if a woman were walking in the apartment. Ere I could draw the curtain to see what the matter was, the figure of a little woman passed between the bed and the fire. The back of this form was turned to me, and I could observe, from the shoulder and neck, it was that of an old woman, whose dress was an old-fashioned gown, which, I think, ladies call a sacque; that is, a sort of robe completely loose in the body, but gathered into bread plaits upon the neck and shoulders, which fall down to the ground, and terminate in a species of train.

"I thought the intrusion singular enough, but never harbored for a moment the idea that what I saw was anything more than the mortal form of some old woman about the establishment, who had a fancy to dress like her grandmother, and who having perhaps (as your lordship mentioned that you were rather straitened for room) been dislodged from her chamber for my accommodation, had forgotten the circumstance, and returned by twelve to her old haunt. Under this persuasion I moved myself in bed and coughed a little, to make the intruder sensible of my being in possession of the premises.—She turned slowly round, but, gracious heaven! my lord, what a countenance did she display to me! There was no longer any question what she was, or any thought of her being a living being. Upon a face which wore the fixed features of a corpse were imprinted the traces of the vilest and most hideous passions which had animated her while she lived. The body of some atrocious criminal seemed to have been given up from the grave, and the soul restored from the penal fire, in order to form, for a space, a union with the ancient accomplice of its guilt. I started up in bed, and sat upright, supporting myself on my palms, as I gazed on this horrible spectre. The hag made, as it seemed, a single and swift stride to the bed where I lay, and squatted herself down upon it, in precisely the same attitude which I had assumed in the extremity of horror, advancing her diabolical countenance within half a yard of mine, with a grin which seemed to intimate the malice and the derision of an incarnate fiend."

Here General Browne stopped, and wiped from his brow the cold perspiration with which the recollection of his horrible vision had covered it.

"My lord," he said, "I am no coward. I have been in all the mortal dangers incidental to my profession, and I may truly boast that no man ever knew Richard Browne dishonor the sword he wears; but in these horrible circumstances, under the eyes, and, as it seemed, almost in the grasp, of an incarnation of an evil spirit, all firmness forsook me, all manhood melted from me like wax in the furnace, and I felt my hair individually bristle. The current of my life-blood ceased to flow, and I sank back in a swoon, as very a victim to panic terror as ever was a village girl or a child of ten years old. How long I lay in this condition I cannot pretend to guess.

"But I was roused by the castle clock striking one, so loud that it seemed as if it were in the very room. It was some time before I dared open my eyes, lest they should again encounter the horrible spectacle. When, however, I summoned courage to look up, she was no longer visible. My first idea was to pull my bell, wake the servants, and remove to a garret or a hay-loft, to be ensured against a second visitation. Nay, I will confess the truth, that my resolution was altered, not by the shame of exposing myself, but by the fear that, as the bell-cord hung by the chimney, I might, in making my way to it, be again crossed by the fiendish hag, who, I figured to myself, might be still lurking about some corner of the apartment.

"I will not pretend to describe what hot and cold fever-fits tormented me for the rest of the night, through broken sleep, weary vigils, and that dubious state which forms the neutral ground between them. A hundred terrible objects appeared to haunt me; but there was the great difference betwixt the vision which I have described and those which followed, that I knew the last to be deceptions of my own fancy and over-excited nerves.

"Day at last appeared, and I rose from my bed ill in health, and humiliated in mind. I was ashamed of myself as a man and a soldier, and still more so, at feeling my own extreme desire to escape from the haunted apartment, which, however, con-quered all other considerations; so that, huddling on my clothes with the most careless haste, I made my escape from your lordship's mansion, to seek in the open air some relief to my nervous system, shaken as it was by this horrible rencounter with a visi-tant, for such I must believe her, from the other world. Your lordship has now heard the cause of my discomposure, and of my sudden desire to leave your hospitable castle. In other places I trust we may often meet; but God protect me from ever spending a second night under that roof!"

Strange as the General's tale was, he spoke with such a deep air of conviction, that it cut short all the usual commentaries which are made on such stories. Lord Woodville never once asked him if he was sure he did not dream of the apparition, or suggested any of the possibilities by which it is fashionable to explain supernatural appearances, as wild vagaries of the fancy or deceptions of the optic nerves. On the contrary, he seemed deeply impressed with the truth and reality of what he had heard; and, after a considerable pause, regretted, with much appearance of sincerity, that his early friend should in his house have suffered so severely.

"I am the more sorry for your pain, my dear Browne," he continued, "that it is the unhappy, though most unexpected, result of an experiment of my own! You must know, that for my father and grandfather's time, at least, the apartment which was assigned to you last night had been shut on account of reports that it was disturbed by supernatural sights and noises. When I came, a few weeks since, into possession of the estate, I thought the accommodation which the castle afforded for my friends was not extensive enough to permit the inhabitants of the invisible world to retain possession of a comfortable sleeping apartment. I therefore caused the Tapestried Chamber, as we call it, to be opened; and, without destroying its air of antiquity. I had such new articles of furniture placed in it as became the modern times. Yet, as the opinion that the room was haunted very strongly prevailed among the domestics, and was also known in the neighborhood and to many of my friends, I feared some prejudice might be entertained by the first occupant of the Tapestried Chamber, which might tend to revive the evil report which it had labored under, and so disappoint my purpose of rendering it an useful part of the house. I must confess, my dear Browne, that your arrival yesterday, agreeable to me for a thousand reasons besides, seemed the most favorable opportunity of removing the unpleasant rumors which attached to the room, since your courage was indubitable, and your mind free of any preoccupation on the subject. I could not, therefore, have chosen a more fitting subject for my experiment."

"Upon my life," said General Browne, somewhat hastily, "I am infinitely obliged to your lordship—very particularly indebted indeed. I am likely to remember for some time the consequences of the experiment, as your lordship is pleased to call it."

"Nay, now you are unjust, my dear friend," said Lord Woodville. "You have only to reflect for a single moment, in order to be convinced that I could not augur the possibility of the pain to which you have been so unhappily exposed. I was yesterday morning a complete sceptic on the subject of supernatural appearances. Nay, I am sure that had I told you what was said about that room, those very reports would have induced you, by your own choice, to select it for your accommodation. It was my misfortune, perhaps my error, but really cannot be termed my fault, that you have been afflicted so strangely."

"Strangely indeed!" said the General, resuming his good temper; "and I acknowledge that I have no right to be offended with your lordship for treating me like what

I used to think myself—a man of some firmness and courage.—But I see my post-horses are arrived, and I must not detain your lordship from your amusement."

"Nay, my old friend," said Lord Woodville, "since you cannot stay with us another day, which, indeed, I can no longer urge, give me at least half an hour more. You used to love pictures, and I have a gallery of portraits, some of them by Vandyke, representing ancestry to whom this property and castle formerly belonged. I think that several of them will strike you as possessing merit."

General Browne accepted the invitation, though somewhat unwillingly. It was evident he was not to breathe freely or at ease till he left Woodville Castle far behind him. He could not refuse his friend's invitation, however; and the less so, that he was a little ashamed of the peevishness which he had displayed towards his well-meaning entertainer.

The General, therefore, followed Lord Woodville through several rooms, into a long gallery hung with pictures, which the latter pointed out to his guests, telling the names, and giving some account, of the personages whose portraits presented themselves in progression. General Browne was but little interested in the details which these accounts conveyed to him. They were, indeed, of the kind which are usually found in an old family gallery. Here was a cavalier who had ruined the estate in the royal cause; there a fine lady who had reinstated it by contracting a match with a wealthy Roundhead. There hung a gallant who had been in danger for corresponding with the exiled court at St. Germain's; here one who had taken arms for William at the Revolution; and there a third that had thrown his weight alternately into the scale of Whig and Tory.

While Lord Woodville was cramming these words into his guest's ear, "against the stomach of his sense," they gained the middle of the gallery, when he beheld General Browne suddenly start, and assume an attitude of the utmost surprise, not unmixed with fear, as his eyes were caught and suddenly riveted by a portrait of an old lady in a sacque, the fashionable dress of the end of the seventeenth century.

"There she is!" he exclaimed; "there she is, in form and features, though inferior in demoniac expression to the accursed hag who visited me last night!"

"If that be the case," said the young nobleman, "there can remain no longer any doubt of the horrible reality of your apparition. That is the picture of a wretched ancestress of mine, of whose crimes a black and fearful catalogue is recorded in a family history in my charter-chest. The recital of them would be too horrible; it is enough to say, that in yon fatal apartment incest and unnatural murder were committed. I will restore it to the solitude to which the better judgment of those who preceded me had consigned it; and never shall any one, so long as I can prevent it, be exposed to a repetition of the supernatural horrors which could shake such courage as yours."

Thus the friends, who had met with such glee, parted in a very different mood: Lord Woodville to command the Tapestried Chamber to be unmantled and the door built up; and General Browne to seek in some less beautiful country, and with some less dignified friend, forgetfulness of the painful night which he had passed in Woodville Castle.

Clarimonde

Théophile Gautier

———◆———

BROTHER, YOU ASK ME IF I HAVE EVER LOVED. YES. MY STORY IS A STRANGE and terrible one; and though I am sixty-six years of age, I scarcely dare even now to disturb the ashes of that memory. To you I can refuse nothing; but I should not relate such a tale to any less experienced mind. So strange were the circumstances of my story, that I can scarcely believe myself to have ever actually been a party to them. For more than three years I remained the victim of a most singular and diabolical illusion. Poor country priest though I was, I led every night in a dream—would to God it had been all a dream!—a most worldly life, a damning life, a life of Sardanapalus. One single look too freely cast upon a woman well-nigh caused me to lose my soul; but finally by the grace of God and the assistance of my patron saint, I succeeded in casting out the evil spirit that possessed me. My daily life was long interwoven with a nocturnal life of a totally different character. By day I was a priest of the Lord, occupied with prayer and sacred things; by night, from the instant that I closed my eyes I became a young nobleman, a fine connoisseur in women, dogs, and horses; gambling, drinking, and blaspheming; and when I awoke at early daybreak, it seemed to me, on the other hand, that I had been sleeping, and had only dreamed that I was a priest. Of this somnambulistic life there now remains to me only the recollection of certain scenes and words which I cannot banish from my memory; but although I never actually left the walls of my presbytery, one would think to hear me speak that I were a man who, weary of all worldly pleasures, had become a religious, seeking to end a tempestuous life in the service of God, rather than a humble seminarist who has grown old in this obscure curacy, situated in the depths of the woods and even isolated from the life of the century.

Yes, I have loved as none in the world ever loved—with an insensate and furious passion—so violent that I am astonished it did not cause my heart to burst asunder. Ah, what nights—what nights!

From my earliest childhood I had felt a vocation to the priesthood, so that all my studies were directed with that idea in view. Up to the age of twenty-four my life had been only a prolonged novitiate. Having completed my course of theology I successively received all the minor orders, and my superiors judged me worthy, despite my youth, to pass the last awful degree. My ordination was fixed for Easter week.

I had never gone into the world. My world was confined by the walls of the college and the seminary. I knew in a vague sort of a way that there was something called Woman, but I never permitted my thoughts to dwell on such a subject, and I lived in a state of perfect innocence. Twice a year only I saw my infirm and aged mother, and in those visits were comprised my sole relations with the outer world.

I regretted nothing; I felt not the least hesitation at taking the last irrevocable step; I was filled with joy and impatience. Never did a betrothed lover count the slow hours with more feverish ardour; I slept only to dream that I was saying mass; I believed there could be nothing in the world more delightful than to be a priest; I would have refused to be a king or a poet in preference. My ambition could conceive of no loftier aim.

I tell you this in order to show you that what happened to me could not have happened in the natural order of things, and to enable you to understand that I was the victim of an inexplicable fascination.

At last the great day came. I walked to the church with a step so light that I fancied myself sustained in air, or that I had wings upon my shoulders. I believed myself an angel, and wondered at the sombre and thoughtful faces of my companions, for there were several of us. I had passed all the night in prayer, and was in a condition wellnigh bordering on ecstasy. The bishop, a venerable old man, seemed to me God the Father leaning over His Eternity, and I beheld Heaven through the vault of the temple.

You well know the details of that ceremony—the benediction, the communion under both forms, the anointing of the palms of the hands with the Oil of Catechumens, and then the holy sacrifice offered in concert with the bishop.

Ah, truly spake Job when he declared that the imprudent man is one who hath not made a covenant with his eyes! I accidentally lifted my head, which until then I had kept down, and beheld before me, so close that it seemed that I could have touched her—although she was actually a considerable distance from me and on the further side of the sanctuary railing—a young woman of extraordinary beauty, and attired with royal magnificence. It seemed as though scales had suddenly fallen from my eyes. I felt like a blind man who unexpectedly recovers his sight. The bishop, so radiantly glorious but an instant before, suddenly vanished away, the tapers paled upon their golden candlesticks like stars in the dawn, and a vast darkness seemed to fill the whole church. The charming creature appeared in bright relief against the background of that darkness, like some angelic revelation. She seemed herself radiant, and radiating light rather than receiving it.

I lowered my eyelids, firmly resolved not to again open them, that I might not be influenced by external objects, for distraction had gradually taken possession of me until I hardly knew what I was doing.

In another minute, nevertheless, I reopened my eyes, for through my eyelashes I still beheld her, all sparkling with prismatic colours, and surrounded with such a penumbra as one beholds in gazing at the sun.

Oh, how beautiful she was! The greatest painters, who followed ideal beauty into heaven itself, and thence brought back to earth the true portrait of the Madonna, never in their delineations even approached that wildly beautiful reality which I saw before me. Neither the verses of the poet nor the palette of the artist could convey any conception of her. She was rather tall, with a form and bearing of a goddess. Her hair, of a soft blonde hue, was parted in the midst and flowed back over her temples in two rivers of rippling gold; she seemed a diademed queen. Her forehead, bluish-white in its transparency, extended its calm breadth above the arches of her eyebrows, which by a strange singularity were almost black, and admirably relieved the effect of sea-green eyes of unsustainable vivacity and brilliancy. What eyes! With a single flash they could have decided a man's destiny. They had a life, a limpidity, an ardour, a humid light which I have never seen in human eyes; they shot forth rays like arrows, which I could distinctly *see* enter my heart. I know not if the fire which illumined them came from heaven or from hell, but assuredly it came from one or the other. That woman was either an angel or a demon, perhaps both. Assuredly she never sprang from the flank of Eve, our common mother. Teeth of the most lustrous pearl gleamed in her ruddy smile, and at every inflection of her lips little dimples appeared in the satiny rose of her adorable cheeks. There was a delicacy and pride in the regal outline of her nostrils bespeaking noble blood. Agate gleams played over the smooth lustrous skin of her half-bare shoulders, and strings of great blonde pearls—almost equal to her neck in beauty of colour—descended upon her bosom. From time to time she elevated her head with the undulating grace of a startled serpent or peacock, thereby imparting a quivering motion to the high lace ruff which surrounded it like a silver trellis-work.

She wore a robe of orange-red velvet, and from her wide ermine-lined sleeves there peeped forth patrician hands of infinite delicacy, and so ideally transparent that, like the fingers of Aurora, they permitted the light to shine through them.

All these details I can recollect at this moment as plainly as though they were of yesterday, for notwithstanding I was greatly troubled at the time, nothing escaped me; the faintest touch of shading, the little dark speck at the point of the chin, the imperceptible down at the corners of the lips, the velvety floss upon the brow, the quivering shadows of the eyelashes upon the cheeks—I could notice everything with astonishing lucidity of perception.

And gazing I felt opening within me gates that had until then remained closed; vents long obstructed became all clear, permitting glimpses of unfamiliar perspectives within; life suddenly made itself visible to me under a totally novel aspect. I felt as though I had just been born into a new world and a new order of things. A frightful anguish commenced to torture my heart as with red-hot pincers. Every successive minute seemed to me at once but a second and yet a century. Meanwhile the ceremony was proceeding, and I shortly found myself transported far from that world of which my newly born desires were furiously besieging the entrance. Nevertheless I answered "Yes" when I wished to say "No," though all within me protested against the violence done to my soul by my tongue. Some occult power seemed to force the words from my throat against my will. Thus it is, perhaps, that so many young girls walk to the altar firmly resolved to refuse in a startling manner the husband imposed upon them, and that yet not one ever fulfils her intention. Thus it is, doubtless, that so many poor novices take the veil, though they have resolved to tear it into shreds at the moment when called upon to utter the vows. One dares not thus cause so great a scandal to all present, nor deceive the expectation of so many people. All those eyes, all those wills seem to weigh down upon you like a cope of lead, and, moreover, measures have been so well taken, everything has been so thoroughly arranged beforehand and after a fashion so evidently irrevocable, that the will yields to the weight of circumstances and utterly breaks down.

As the ceremony proceeded the features of the fair unknown changed their expression. Her look had at first been one of caressing tenderness; it changed to an air of disdain and of mortification, as though at not having been able to make itself understood.

With an effort of will sufficient to have uprooted a mountain, I strove to cry out that I would not be a priest, but I could not speak; my tongue seemed nailed to my palate, and I found it impossible to express my will by the least syllable of negation. Though fully awake, I felt like one under the influence of a nightmare, who vainly strives to shriek out the one word upon which life depends.

She seemed conscious of the martyrdom I was undergoing, and, as though to encourage me, she gave me a look replete with divinest promise. Her eyes were a poem; their every glance was a song. She said to me:

"If thou wilt be mine, I shall make thee happier than God Himself in His paradise. The angels themselves will be jealous of thee. Tear off that funeral shroud in which thou art about to wrap thyself. I am Beauty, I am Youth, I am Life. Come to me! Together we shall be Love. Can Jehovah offer thee aught in exchange? Our lives will flow on like a dream, in one eternal kiss.

"Fling forth the wine of that chalice, and thou art free. I will conduct thee to the Unknown Isles. Thou shall sleep in my bosom upon a bed of massy gold under a silver pavilion, for I love thee and would take thee away from thy God, before whom so many noble hearts pour forth floods of love which never reach even the steps of His throne!"

These words seemed to float to my ears in a rhythm of infinite sweetness, for her look was actually sonorous, and the utterances of her eyes were reechoed in the depths of my heart as though living lips had breathed them into my life. I felt myself willing to renounce God, and yet my tongue mechanically fulfilled all the formalities of the ceremony. The fair one gave me another look, so beseeching, so despairing that keen blades seemed to pierce my heart, and I felt my bosom transfixed by more swords than those of Our Lady of Sorrows.

All was consummated; I had become a priest.

Never was deeper anguish painted on human face than upon hers. The maiden who beholds her affianced lover suddenly fall dead at her side, the mother bending over the empty cradle of her child, Eve seated at the threshold of the gate of Paradise, the miser who finds a stone substituted for his stolen treasure, the poet who accidentally permits the only manuscript of his finest work to fall into the fire, could not wear a look so despairing, so inconsolable. All the blood had abandoned her charming face, leaving it whiter than marble; her beautiful arms hung lifelessly on either side of her body as though their muscles had suddenly relaxed, and she sought the support of a pillar, for her yielding limbs almost betrayed her. As for myself, I staggered toward the door of the church, livid as death, my forehead bathed with a sweat bloodier than that of Calvary; I felt as though I were being strangled; the vault seemed to have flattened down upon my shoulders, and it seemed to me that my head alone sustained the whole weight of the dome.

As I was about to cross the threshold a hand suddenly caught mine—a woman's hand! I had never till then touched the hand of any woman. It was cold as a serpent's skin, and yet its impress remained upon my wrist, burnt there as though branded by a glowing iron. It was she. "Unhappy man! Unhappy man! What hast thou done?" she exclaimed in a low voice, and immediately disappeared in the crowd.

The aged bishop passed by. He cast a severe and scrutinising look upon me. My face presented the wildest aspect imaginable: I blushed and turned pale alternately; dazzling lights flashed before my eyes. A companion took pity on me. He seized my arm and led me out. I could not possibly have found my way back to the seminary unassisted. At the corner of a street, while the young priest's attention was momentarily turned in another direction, a negro page, fantastically garbed, approached me, and without pausing on his way slipped into my hand a little pocket-book with gold-embroidered corners, at the same time giving me a sign to hide it. I concealed it in my sleeve, and there kept it until I found myself alone in my cell. Then I opened the clasp. There were only two leaves within, bearing the words, "Clarimonde. At the Concini Palace." So little acquainted was I at that time with the things of this world that I had never heard of Clarimonde, celebrated as she was, and I had no idea as to where the Concini Palace was situated. I hazarded a thousand conjectures, each more extravagant than the last; but, in truth, I cared little whether she were a great lady or a courtesan, so that I could but see her once more.

My love, although the growth of a single hour, had taken imperishable root. I did not even dream of attempting to tear it up, so fully was I convinced such a thing would be impossible. That woman had completely taken possession of me. One look from her had sufficed to change my very nature. She had breathed her will into my life, and I no longer lived in myself, but in her and for her. I gave myself up to a thousand extravagancies. I kissed the place upon my hand which she had touched, and I repeated her name over and over again for hours in succession. I only needed to close my eyes in order to see her distinctly as though she were actually present; and I reiterated to myself the words she had uttered in my ear at the church porch: "Unhappy man! Unhappy man! What hast thou done?" I comprehended at last the full horror of my situation, and the funereal and awful restraints of the state into which I had just entered became clearly revealed to me. To be a priest!—that is, to be chaste, to never love, to observe no distinction of sex or age, to turn from the sight of all beauty, to put out one's own eyes, to hide for ever crouching in the chill shadows of some church or cloister, to visit none but the dying, to watch by unknown corpses, and ever bear about with one the black soutane as a garb of mourning for oneself, so that your very dress might serve as a pall for your coffin.

And I felt life rising within me like a subterranean lake, expanding and overflowing; my blood leaped fiercely through my arteries; my long-restrained youth suddenly burst into active being, like the aloe which blooms but once in a hundred years, and then bursts into blossom with a clap of thunder.

What could I do in order to see Clarimonde once more? I had no pretext to offer for desiring to leave the seminary, not knowing any person in the city. I would not even be able to remain there but a short time, and was only waiting my assignment to the curacy which I must thereafter occupy. I tried to remove the bars of the window; but it was at a fearful height from the ground, and I found that as I had no ladder it would be useless to think of escaping thus. And, furthermore, I could descend thence only by night in any event, and afterward how should I be able to find my way through the inextricable labyrinth of streets? All these difficulties, which to many would have appeared altogether insignificant, were gigantic to me, a poor seminarist who had fallen in love only the day before for the first time, without experience, without money, without attire.

"Ah!" cried I to myself in my blindness, "were I not a priest I could have seen her every day; I might have been her lover, her spouse. Instead of being wrapped in this dismal shroud of mine I would have had garments of silk and velvet, golden chains, a sword, and fair plumes like other handsome young cavaliers. My hair, instead of being dishonoured by the tonsure, would flow down upon my neck in waving curls; I would have a fine waxed moustache; I would be a gallant." But one hour passed before an altar, a few hastily articulated words, had for ever cut me off from the number of the living, and I had myself sealed down the stone of my own tomb; I had with my own hand bolted the gate of my prison!

I went to the window. The sky was beautifully blue; the trees had donned their spring robes; nature seemed to be making parade of an ironical joy. The *Place* was filled with people, some going, others coming; young beaux and young beauties were sauntering in couples toward the groves and gardens; merry youths passed by, cheerily trolling refrains of drinking-songs—it was all a picture of vivacity, life, animation, gaiety, which formed a bitter contrast with my mourning and my solitude. On the steps of the gate sat a young mother playing with her child. She kissed its little rosy mouth still impearled with drops of milk, and performed, in order to amuse it, a thousand divine little puerilities such as only mothers know how to invent. The father standing at a little distance smiled gently upon the charming group, and with folded arms seemed to hug his joy to his heart. I could not endure that spectacle. I closed the window with violence, and flung myself on my bed, my heart filled with frightful hate and jealousy, and gnawed my fingers and my bed-covers like a tiger that has passed ten days without food.

I know not how long I remained in this condition, but at last, while writhing on the bed in a fit of spasmodic fury, I suddenly perceived the Abbé Sérapion, who was standing erect in the centre of the room, watching me attentively. Filled with shame of myself, I let my head fall upon my breast and covered my face with my hands.

"Romuald, my friend, something very extraordinary is transpiring within you," observed Sérapion, after a few moments' silence; "your conduct is altogether inexplicable. You—always so quiet, so pious, so gentle—you to rage in your cell like a wild beast! Take heed, brother—do not listen to the suggestions of the devil. The Evil Spirit, furious that you have consecrated yourself for ever to the Lord, is prowling around you like a ravening wolf and making a last effort to obtain possession of you. Instead of allowing yourself to be conquered, my dear Romuald, make to yourself a cuirass of prayers, a buckler of mortifications, and combat the enemy like a valiant man; you will then assuredly overcome him. Virtue must be proved by temptation, and gold comes forth purer from the hands of the assayer. Fear not. Never allow yourself to become discouraged. The most watchful and steadfast souls are at moments liable to such temptation. Pray, fast, meditate, and the Evil Spirit will depart from you."

The words of the Abbé Sérapion restored me to myself, and I became a little more calm. "I came," he continued, "to tell you that you have been appointed to the curacy of C——. The priest who had charge of it has just died, and Monseigneur the Bishop has ordered me to have you installed there at once. Be ready, therefore, to start to-morrow." I responded with an inclination of the head, and the Abbé retired. I opened my missal and commenced reading some prayers, but the letters became confused and blurred under my eyes, the thread of the ideas entangled itself hopelessly in my brain, and the volume at last fell from my hands without my being aware of it.

To leave to-morrow without having been able to see her again, to add yet another barrier to the many already interposed between us, to lose for ever all hope of being able to meet her, except, indeed, through a miracle! Even to write to her, alas! would be impossible, for by whom could I dispatch my letter? With my sacred character of priest, to whom could I dare unbosom myself, in whom could I confide? I became a prey to the bitterest anxiety.

Then suddenly recurred to me the words of the Abbé Sérapion regarding the artifices of the devil; and the strange character of the adventure, the supernatural beauty of Clarimonde, the phosphoric light of her eyes, the burning imprint of her hand, the agony into which she had thrown me, the sudden change wrought within me when all my piety vanished in a single instant—these and other things clearly testified to the work of the

Evil One, and perhaps that satiny hand was but the glove which concealed his claws. Filled with terror at these fancies, I again picked up the missal which had slipped from my knees and fallen upon the floor, and once more gave myself up to prayer.

Next morning Sérapion came to take me away. Two mules freighted with our miserable valises awaited us at the gate. He mounted one, and I the other as well as I knew how.

As we passed along the streets of the city, I gazed attentively at all the windows and balconies in the hope of seeing Clarimonde, but it was yet early in the morning, and the city had hardly opened its eyes. Mine sought to penetrate the blinds and window-curtains of all the palaces before which we were passing. Sérapion doubtless attributed this curiosity to my admiration of the architecture, for he slackened the pace of his animal in order to give me time to look around me. At last we passed the city gates and commenced to mount the hill beyond. When we arrived at its summit I turned to take a last look at the place where Clarimonde dwelt. The shadow of a great cloud hung over all the city; the contrasting colours of its blue and red roofs were lost in the uniform half-tint, through which here and there floated upward, like white flakes of foam, the smoke of freshly kindled fires. By a singular optical effect one edifice, which surpassed in height all the neighbouring buildings that were still dimly veiled by the vapours, towered up, fair and lustrous with the gilding of a solitary beam of sunlight—although actually more than a league away it seemed quite near. The smallest details of its architecture were plainly distinguishable—the turrets, the platforms, the window-casements, and even the swallow-tailed weather-vanes.

"What is that palace I see over there, all lighted up by the sun?" I asked Sérapion. He shaded his eyes with his hand, and having looked in the direction indicated, replied: "It is the ancient palace which the Prince Concini has given to the courtesan Clarimonde. Awful things are done there!"

At that instant, I know not yet whether it was a reality or an illusion, I fancied I saw gliding along the terrace a shapely white figure, which gleamed for a moment in passing and as quickly vanished. It was Clarimonde.

Oh, did she know that at that very hour, all feverish and restless—from the height of the rugged road which separated me from her, and which, alas! I could never more descend—I was directing my eyes upon the palace where she dwelt, and which a mocking beam of sunlight seemed to bring nigh to me, as though inviting me to enter therein as its lord? Undoubtedly she must have known it, for her soul was too sympathetically united with mine not to have felt its least emotional thrill, and that subtle sympathy it must have been which prompted her to climb—although clad only in her nightdress—to the summit of the terrace, amid the icy dews of the morning.

The shadow gained the palace, and the scene became to the eye only a motionless ocean of roofs and gables, amid which one mountainous undulation was distinctly visible. Sérapion urged his mule forward, my own at once followed at the same gait, and a sharp angle in the road at last hid the city of S—— for ever from my eyes, as I was destined never to return thither. At the close of a weary three-days' journey through dismal country fields, we caught sight of the cock upon the steeple of the church which I was to take charge of, peeping above the trees, and after having followed some winding roads fringed with thatched cottages and little gardens, we found ourselves in front of the façade, which certainly possessed few features of magnificence. A porch ornamented with some mouldings, and two or three pillars rudely hewn from sandstone; a tiled roof with counterforts of the same sandstone as the pillars—that was all. To the left lay the cemetery, overgrown with high weeds, and having a great iron cross rising up in its centre; to the right stood the presbytery under the shadow of the church. It was a house of the most extreme simplicity and frigid cleanliness. We entered the enclosure. A few chickens were picking up some oats scattered upon the ground; accustomed, seemingly, to the black habit of ecclesiastics, they showed no fear of our presence and scarcely troubled themselves to get out of our way. A hoarse, wheezy barking fell upon our ears, and we saw an aged dog running toward us.

It was my predecessor's dog. He had dull bleared eyes, grizzled hair, and every mark of the greatest age to which a dog can possibly attain. I patted him gently, and he proceeded at once to march along beside me with an air of satisfaction unspeakable. A very old woman, who had been the housekeeper of the former curé, also came to meet us, and after having invited me into a little back parlour, asked whether I intended to retain her. I replied that I would take care of her, and the dog, and the chickens, and all the furniture her master had bequeathed her at his death. At this she became fairly transported with joy, and the Abbé Sérapion at once paid her the price which she asked for her little property.

As soon as my installation was over, the Abbé Sérapion returned to the seminary. I was, therefore, left alone, with no one but myself to look to for aid or counsel. The thought of Clarimonde again began to haunt me, and in spite of all my endeavours to banish it, I always found it present in my meditations. One evening, while promenading in my little garden along the walks bordered with box-plants, I fancied that I saw through the elm-trees the figure of a woman, who followed my every movement, and that I beheld two sea-green eyes gleaming through the foliage; but it was only an illusion, and on going round to the other side of the garden, I could find nothing except a footprint on the sanded walk—a footprint so small that it seemed to have been made by the foot of a child. The garden was enclosed by very high walls. I searched every nook and corner of it, but could discover no one there. I have never succeeded in fully accounting for this circumstance, which, after all, was nothing compared with the strange things which happened to me afterward.

For a whole year I lived thus, filling all the duties of my calling with the most scrupulous exactitude, praying and fasting, exhorting and lending ghostly aid to the sick, and bestowing alms even to the extent of frequently depriving myself of the very necessaries of life. But I felt a great aridness within me, and the sources of grace seemed closed against me. I never found that happiness which should spring from the fulfilment of a holy mission; my thoughts were far away, and the words of Clarimonde were ever upon my lips like an involuntary refrain. Oh, brother, meditate well on this! Through having but once lifted my eyes to look upon a woman, through one fault apparently so venial, I have for years remained a victim to the most miserable agonies, and the happiness of my life has been destroyed for ever.

I will not longer dwell upon those defeats, or on those inward victories invariably followed by yet more terrible falls, but will at once proceed to the facts of my story. One night my door-bell was long and violently rung. The aged housekeeper arose and opened to the stranger, and the figure of a man, whose complexion was deeply bronzed, and who was richly clad in a foreign costume, with a poniard at his girdle, appeared under the rays of Barbara's lantern. Her first impulse was one of terror, but the stranger reassured her, and stated that he desired to see me at once on matters relating to my holy calling. Barbara invited him upstairs, where I was on the point of retiring. The stranger told me that his mistress, a very noble lady, was lying at the point of death, and desired to see a priest. I replied that I was prepared to follow him, took with me the sacred articles necessary for extreme unction, and descended in all haste. Two horses black as the night itself stood without the gate, pawing the ground with impatience, and veiling their chests with long streams of smoky vapour exhaled from their nostrils. He held the stirrup and aided me to mount upon one; then, merely laying his hand upon the pommel of the saddle, he vaulted on the other, pressed the animal's sides with his knees, and loosened rein. The horse bounded forward with the velocity of an arrow. Mine, of which the stranger held the bridle, also started off at a swift gallop, keeping up with his companion. We devoured the road. The ground flowed backward beneath us in a long streaked line of pale gray, and the black silhouettes of the trees seemed fleeing by us on either side like an army in rout. We passed through a forest so profoundly gloomy that I felt my flesh creep in the chill darkness with superstitious fear. The showers of bright sparks which flew from the stony road under the ironshod feet of our horses remained glowing in our wake like a fiery trail; and had any one at that hour of the night beheld us both—my guide and myself—he must have taken us for two spectres riding upon nightmares. Witch-fires ever and anon flitted across the road before us, and the night-birds shrieked fearsomely in the depth of the woods beyond, where we beheld at intervals glow the phosphorescent eyes of wild cats. The manes of the horses became more and more dishevelled, the sweat streamed over their flanks, and their breath came through their nostrils hard and fast. But when he found them slacking pace, the guide reanimated them by uttering a strange, guttural, unearthly cry, and the gallop recommenced with fury. At last the whirlwind race ceased; a huge black mass pierced through with many bright points of light suddenly rose before us, the hoofs of our horses echoed louder upon a strong wooden draw-bridge, and we rode under a great vaulted archway which darkly yawned between two enormous towers. Some great excitement evidently reigned in the castle. Servants with torches were crossing the courtyard in every direction, and above lights were ascending and descending from landing to landing. I obtained a confused glimpse of vast masses of architecture—columns, arcades, nights of steps, stairways—a royal voluptuousness and elfin magnificence of construction worthy of fairyland. A negro page—the same who had before brought me the tablet from Clarimonde, and whom I instantly recognised—approached to aid me in dismounting, and the major-domo, attired in black velvet with a gold chain about his neck, advanced to meet me, supporting himself upon an ivory cane. Large tears were falling from his eyes and streaming over his cheeks and white beard. "Too late!" he cried, sorrowfully shaking his venerable head. "Too late, sir priest! But if you have not been able to save the soul, come at least to watch by the poor body."

He took my arm and conducted me to the death-chamber. I wept not less bitterly than he, for I had learned that the dead one was none other than that Clarimonde whom I had so deeply and so wildly loved. A *prie-dieu* stood at the foot of the bed; a bluish flame flickering in a bronze patera filled all the room with a wan, deceptive light, here and there bringing out in the darkness at intervals some projection of furniture or cornice. In a chiselled urn upon the table there was a faded white rose, whose leaves—excepting one that still held—had all fallen, like odorous tears, to the foot of the vase. A broken black mask, a fan, and disguises of every variety, which were lying on the armchairs, bore witness that death had entered suddenly and unannounced into that sumptuous dwelling. Without daring to cast my eyes upon the bed, I knelt down and commenced to repeat the Psalms for the Dead, with exceeding fervour, thanking God that He had placed the tomb between me and the memory of this woman, so that I might thereafter be able to utter her name in my prayers as a name for ever sanctified by death. But my fervour gradually weakened, and I fell insensibly into a reverie. That chamber bore no semblance to a chamber of death. In lieu of the fetid and cadaverous odours which I had been accustomed to breathe during such funereal vigils, a languorous vapour of Oriental perfume—I know not what amorous odour of woman—softly floated through the tepid air. That pale light seemed rather a twilight gloom contrived for voluptuous pleasure, than a substitute for the yellow-flickering watch-tapers which shine by the side of corpses. I thought upon the strange destiny which enabled me to meet Clarimonde again at the very moment when she was lost to me for ever, and a sigh of regretful anguish escaped from my breast. Then it seemed to me that some one behind me had also sighed, and I turned round to look. It was only an echo. But in that moment my eyes fell upon the bed of death which they had till then avoided. The red damask curtains, decorated with large flowers worked in embroidery and looped up with gold bullion, permitted me to behold the fair dead, lying at full length, with hands joined upon her bosom. She was covered with a linen wrapping of dazzling whiteness, which formed a strong contrast with the gloomy purple of the hangings, and was of so fine a texture that it concealed nothing of her body's charming form, and allowed the eye to follow those beautiful outlines—undulating like the neck of a swan—which even death had not robbed of their supple grace. She seemed an alabaster statue executed by some skilful sculptor to place upon the tomb of a queen, or rather, perhaps, like a slumbering maiden over whom the silent snow had woven a spotless veil.

I could no longer maintain my constrained attitude of prayer. The air of the alcove intoxicated me, that febrile perfume of half-faded roses penetrated my very brain, and I commenced to pace restlessly up and down the chamber, pausing at each turn before the bier to contemplate the graceful corpse lying beneath the transparency of its shroud. Wild fancies came thronging to my brain. I thought to myself that she might not, perhaps, be really dead; that she might only have feigned death for the purpose of bringing me to her castle, and then declaring her love. At one time I even thought I saw her foot move under the whiteness of the coverings, and slightly disarrange the long straight folds of the winding-sheet.

And then I asked myself: "Is this indeed Clarimonde? What proof have I that it is she? Might not that black page have passed into the service of some other lady? Surely, I must be going mad to torture and afflict myself thus!" But my heart answered with a fierce throbbing: "It is she; it is she indeed!" I approached the bed again, and fixed my eyes with redoubled attention upon the object of my incertitude. Ah, must I confess it? That exquisite perfection of bodily form, although purified and made sacred by the shadow of death, affected me more voluptuously than it should have done; and that repose so closely resembled slumber that one might well have mistaken it for such. I forgot that I had come there to perform a funeral ceremony; I fancied myself a young bridegroom entering the chamber of the bride, who all modestly hides her fair face, and through coyness seeks to keep herself wholly veiled. Heartbroken with grief, yet wild with hope, shuddering at once with fear and pleasure, I bent over her and grasped the corner of the sheet. I lifted it back, holding my breath all the while through fear of waking her. My arteries throbbed with such violence that I felt them hiss through my temples, and the sweat poured from my forehead in streams, as though I had lifted a mighty slab of marble. There, indeed, lay Clarimonde, even as I had seen her at the church on the day of my ordination. She was not less charming than then. With her, death seemed but a last coquetry. The pallor of her cheeks, the less brilliant carnation of her lips, her long eyelashes lowered and relieving their dark fringe against that white skin, lent her an unspeakably seductive aspect of melancholy chastity and mental suffering; her long loose hair, still intertwined with some little blue flowers, made a shining pillow for her head, and veiled the nudity of her shoulders with its thick ringlets; her beautiful hands, purer, more diaphanous, than the Host, were crossed on her bosom in an attitude of pious rest and silent prayer, which served to counteract all that might have proven otherwise too alluring—even after death—in the exquisite roundness and ivory polish of her bare arms from which the pearl bracelets had not yet been removed. I remained long in mute contemplation, and the more I gazed, the less could I persuade myself that life had really abandoned that beautiful body for ever. I do not know whether it was an illusion or a reflection of the lamplight, but it seemed to me that the blood was again commencing to circulate under that lifeless pallor, although she remained all motionless. I laid my hand lightly on her arm; it was cold, but not colder than her hand on the day when it touched mine at the portals of the church. I resumed my position, bending my face above her, and bathing her cheek with the warm dew of my tears. Ah, what bitter feelings of despair and helplessness, what agonies unutterable did I endure in that long watch! Vainly did I wish that I could have gathered all my life into one mass that I might give it all to her, and breathe into her chill remains the flame which devoured me. The night advanced, and feeling the moment of eternal separation approach, I could not deny myself the last sad sweet pleasure of imprinting a kiss upon the dead lips of her who had been my only love. . . . Oh, miracle! A faint breath mingled itself with my breath, and the mouth of Clarimonde responded to the passionate pressure of mine. Her eyes unclosed, and lighted up with something of their former brilliancy; she uttered a long sigh, and uncrossing her arms, passed them around my neck with a look of ineffable delight. "Ah, it is thou, Romuald!" she murmured in a voice languishingly sweet as the last vibrations of a harp. "What ailed thee, dearest? I waited so long for thee that I am dead; but we are now betrothed: I can see thee and visit thee. Adieu, Romuald, adieu! I love thee. That is all I wished to tell thee, and I give thee back the life which thy kiss for a moment recalled. We shall soon meet again."

Her head fell back, but her arms yet encircled me, as though to retain me still. A furious whirlwind suddenly burst in the window, and entered the chamber. The last remaining leaf of the white rose for a moment palpitated at the extremity of the stalk like a butterfly's wing, then it detached itself and flew forth through the open casement, bearing with it the soul of Clarimonde. The lamp was extinguished, and I fell insensible upon the bosom of the beautiful dead.

When I came to myself again I was lying on the bed in my little room at the presbytery, and the old dog of the former curé was licking my hand, which had been hanging down outside of the covers. Barbara, all trembling with age and anxiety, was busying herself about the room, opening and shutting drawers, and emptying powders into glasses. On seeing me open my eyes, the old woman uttered a cry of joy, the dog yelped and wagged his tail, but I was still so weak that I could not speak a single word or make the slightest motion. Afterward I learned that I had lain thus for three days, giving no evidence of life beyond the faintest respiration. Those three days do not reckon in my life, nor could I ever imagine whither my spirit had departed during those three days; I have no recollection of aught relating to them. Barbara told me that the same copperycomplexioned man who came to seek me on the night of my departure from the presbytery had brought me back the next morning in a close litter, and departed immediately afterward. When I became able to collect my scattered thoughts, I reviewed within my mind all the circumstances of that fateful night. At first I thought I had been the victim of some magical illusion, but ere long the recollection of other circumstances, real and palpable in themselves, came to forbid that supposition. I could not believe that I had been dreaming, since Barbara as well as myself had seen the strange man with his two black horses, and described with exactness every detail of his figure and apparel. Nevertheless it appeared that none knew of any castle in the neighbourhood answering to the description of that in which I had again found Clarimonde.

One morning I found the Abbé Sérapion in my room. Barbara had advised him that I was ill, and he had come with all speed to see me. Although this haste on his part testified to an affectionate interest in me, yet his visit did not cause me the pleasure which it should have done. The Abbé Sérapion had something penetrating and inquisitorial in his gaze which made me feel very ill at ease. His presence filled me with embarrassment and a sense of guilt. At the first glance he divined my interior trouble, and I hated him for his clairvoyance.

While he inquired after my health in hypocritically honeyed accents, he constantly kept his two great yellow lion-eyes fixed upon me, and plunged his look into my soul like a sounding-lead. Then he asked me how I directed my parish, if I was happy in it, how I passed the leisure hours allowed me in the intervals of pastoral duty, whether I had become acquainted with many of the inhabitants of the place, what was my favourite reading, and a thousand other such questions. I answered these inquiries as briefly as possible, and he, without ever waiting for my answers, passed rapidly from one subject of query to another. That conversation had evidently no connection with what he actually wished to say. At last, without any premonition, but as though repeating a piece of news which he had recalled on the instant, and feared might otherwise be forgotten subsequently, he suddenly said, in a clear vibrant voice, which rang in my ears like the trumpets of the Last Judgment:

"The great courtesan Clarimonde died a few days ago, at the close of an orgie which lasted eight days and eight nights. It was something infernally splendid. The abominations of the banquets of Belshazzar and Cleopatra were re-enacted there. Good God, what age are we living in? The guests were served by swarthy slaves who spoke an unknown tongue, and who seemed to me to be veritable demons. The livery of the very least among them would have served for the gala-dress of an emperor. There have always been very strange stories told of this Clarimonde, and all her lovers came to a violent or miserable end. They used to say that she was a ghoul, a female vampire; but I believe she was none other than Beelzebub himself."

He ceased to speak, and commenced to regard me more attentively than ever, as though to observe the effect of his words on me. I could not refrain from starting when I heard him utter the name of Clarimonde, and this news of her death, in addition to the pain it caused me by reason of its coincidence with the nocturnal scenes I had witnessed, filled me with an agony and terror which my face betrayed, despite my utmost endeavours to appear composed. Sérapion fixed an anxious and severe look upon me, and then observed: "My son, I must warn you that you are standing with foot raised upon the brink of an abyss; take heed lest you fall therein. Satan's claws are long, and tombs are not always true to their trust. The tombstone of Clarimonde should be sealed down with a triple seal, for, if report be true, it is not the first time she has died. May God watch over you, Romuald!"

And with these words the Abbé walked slowly to the door. I did not see him again at that time, for he left for S—— almost immediately.

I became completely restored to health and resumed my accustomed duties. The memory of Clarimonde and the words of the old Abbé were constantly in my mind; nevertheless no extraordinary event had occurred to verify the funereal predictions of Sérapion, and I had commenced to believe that his fears and my own terrors were over-exaggerated, when one night I had a strange dream. I had hardly fallen asleep when I heard my bed-curtains drawn apart, as their rings slided back upon the curtain rod with a sharp sound. I rose up quickly upon my elbow, and beheld the shadow of a woman standing erect before me. I recognised Clarimonde immediately. She bore in her hand a little lamp, shaped like those which are placed in tombs, and its light lent her fingers a rosy transparency, which extended itself by lessening degrees even to the opaque and milky whiteness of her bare arm. Her only garment was the linen winding-sheet which had shrouded her when lying upon the bed of death. She sought to gather its folds over her bosom as though ashamed of being so scantily clad, but her little hand was not equal to the task. She was so white that the colour of the drapery blended with that of her flesh under the pallid rays of the lamp. Enveloped with this subtle tissue which betrayed all the contour of her body, she seemed rather the marble statue of some fair antique bather than a woman endowed with life. But dead or living, statue or woman, shadow or body, her beauty was still the same, only that the green light of her eyes was less brilliant, and her mouth, once so warmly crimson, was only tinted with a faint tender rosiness, like that of her cheeks. The little blue flowers which I had noticed entwined in her hair were withered and dry, and had lost nearly all their leaves, but this did not prevent her from being charming—so charming that, notwithstanding the strange character of the adventure, and the unexplainable manner in which she had entered my room, I felt not even for a moment the least fear.

She placed the lamp on the table and seated herself at the foot of my bed; then bending toward me, she said, in that voice at once silvery clear and yet velvety in its sweet softness, such as I never heard from any lips save hers:

"I have kept thee long in waiting, dear Romuald, and it must have seemed to thee that I had forgotten thee. But I come from afar off, very far off, and from a land whence no other has ever yet returned. There is neither sun nor moon in that land whence I come: all is but space and shadow; there is neither road nor pathway: no earth for the foot, no air for the wing; and nevertheless behold me here, for Love is stronger than Death and must conquer him in the end. Oh what sad faces and fearful things I have seen on my way hither! What difficulty my soul, returned to earth through the power of will alone, has had in finding its body and reinstating itself therein! What terrible efforts I had to make ere I could lift the ponderous slab with which they had covered me! See, the palms of my poor hands are all bruised! Kiss them, sweet love, that they may be healed!" She laid the cold palms of her hands upon my mouth, one after the other. I kissed them, indeed, many times, and she the while watched me with a smile of ineffable affection.

I confess to my shame that I had entirely forgotten the advice of the Abbé Sérapion and the sacred office wherewith I had been invested. I had fallen without resistance, and at the first assault. I had not even made the least effort to repel the tempter. The fresh coolness of Clarimonde's skin penetrated my own, and I felt voluptuous tremors pass over my whole body. Poor child! in spite of all I saw afterward, I can hardly yet believe she was a demon; at least she had no appearance of being such, and never did Satan so skilfully conceal his claws and horns. She had drawn her feet up beneath her, and squatted down on the edge of the couch in an attitude full of negligent coquetry. From time to time she passed her little hand through my hair and twisted it into curls, as though trying how a new style of wearing it would become my face. I abandoned myself to her hands with the most guilty pleasure, while she accompanied her gentle play with the prettiest prattle. The most remarkable fact was that I felt no astonishment whatever at so extraordinary an adventure, and as in dreams one finds no difficulty in accepting the most fantastic events as simple facts, so all these circumstances seemed to me perfectly natural in themselves.

"I loved thee long ere I saw thee, dear Romuald, and sought thee everywhere. Thou wast my dream, and I first saw thee in the church at the fatal moment. I said at once, 'It is he!' I gave thee a look into which I threw all the love I ever had, all the love I now have, all the love I shall ever have for thee—a look that would have damned a cardinal or brought a king to his knees at my feet in view of all his court. Thou remainedst unmoved, preferring thy God to me!

"Ah, how jealous I am of that God whom thou didst love and still lovest more than me!

"Woe is me, unhappy one that I am! I can never have thy heart all to myself, I whom thou didst recall to life with a kiss—dead Clarimonde, who for thy sake bursts asunder the gates of the tomb, and comes to consecrate to thee a life which she has resumed only to make thee happy!"

All her words were accompanied with the most impassioned caresses, which bewildered my sense and my reason to such an extent, that I did not fear to utter a frightful blasphemy for the sake of consoling her, and to declare that I loved her as much as God.

Her eyes rekindled and shone like chrysoprases. "In truth?—in very truth?—as much as God!" she cried, flinging her beautiful arms around me. "Since it is so, thou wilt come with me; thou wilt follow me whithersoever I desire. Thou wilt cast away thy ugly black habit. Thou shall be the proudest and most envied of cavaliers; thou shalt be my lover! To be the acknowledged lover of Clarimonde, who has refused even a Pope! That will be something to feel proud of. Ah, the fair, unspeakably happy existence, the beautiful golden life we shall live together! And when shall we depart, my fair sir?"

"To-morrow! To-morrow!" I cried in my delirium.

"To-morrow, then, so let it be!" she answered. "In the meanwhile I shall have opportunity to change my toilet, for this is a little too light and in nowise suited for a voyage. I must also forthwith notify all my friends who believe me dead, and mourn for me as deeply as they are capable of doing. The money, the dresses, the carriages—all will be ready. I shall call for thee at this same hour. Adieu, dear heart!" And she lightly touched my forehead with her lips. The lamp went out, the curtains closed again, and all became dark; a leaden, dreamless sleep fell on me and held me unconscious until the morning following.

I awoke later than usual, and the recollection of this singular adventure troubled me during the whole day. I finally persuaded myself that it was a mere vapour of my heated imagination. Nevertheless its sensations had been so vivid that it was difficult to persuade myself that they were not real, and it was not without some presentiment of what was going to happen that I got into bed at last, after having prayed God to drive far from me all thoughts of evil, and to protect the chastity of my slumber.

I soon fell into a deep sleep, and my dream was continued. The curtains again parted, and I beheld Clarimonde, not as on the former occasion, pale in her pale winding-sheet, with the violets of death upon her cheeks, but gay, sprightly, jaunty, in a superb travelling-dress of green velvet, trimmed with gold lace, and looped up on either side to allow a glimpse of satin petticoat. Her blond hair escaped in thick ringlets from beneath a broad black felt hat, decorated with white feathers whimsically twisted into various shapes. In one hand she held a little riding-whip terminated by a golden whistle. She tapped me lightly with it, and exclaimed: "Well, my fine sleeper, is this the way you make your preparations? I thought I would find you up and dressed. Arise quickly, we have no time to lose."

I leaped out of bed at once.

"Come, dress yourself, and let us go," she continued, pointing to a little package she had brought with her. "The horses are becoming impatient of delay and champing their bits at the door. We ought to have been by this time at least ten leagues distant from here."

I dressed myself hurriedly, and she handed me the articles of apparel herself one by one, bursting into laughter from time to time at my awkwardness, as she explained to me the use of a garment when I had made a mistake. She hurriedly arranged my hair, and this done, held up before me a little pocket-mirror of Venetian crystal, rimmed with silver filigree-work, and playfully asked: "How dost find thyself now? Wilt engage me for thy valet de chambre?"

I was no longer the same person, and I could not even recognise myself. I resembled my former self no more than a finished statue resembles a block of stone. My old face seemed but a coarse daub of the one reflected in the mirror. I was handsome, and my vanity was sensibly tickled by the metamorphosis. That elegant apparel, that richly embroidered vest had made of me a totally different personage, and I marvelled at the power of transformation owned by a few yards of cloth cut after a certain pattern. The spirit of my costume penetrated my very skin and within ten minutes more I had become something of a coxcomb.

In order to feel more at ease in my new attire, I took several turns up and down the room. Clarimonde watched me with an air of maternal pleasure, and appeared well satisfied with her work. "Come, enough of this child's play! Let us start, Romuald, dear. We have far to go, and we may not get there in time." She took my hand and led me forth. All the doors opened before her at a touch, and we passed by the dog without awaking him.

At the gate we found Margheritone waiting, the same swarthy groom who had once before been my escort. He held the bridles of three horses, all black like those which bore us to the castle—one for me, one for him, one for Clarimonde. Those horses must have been Spanish genets born of mares fecundated by a zephyr, for they were fleet as the wind itself, and the moon, which had just risen at our departure to light us on the way, rolled over the sky like a wheel detached from her own chariot. We beheld her on the right leaping from tree to tree, and putting herself out of breath in the effort to keep up with us. Soon we came upon a level plain where, hard by a clump of trees, a carriage with four vigorous horses awaited us. We entered it, and the postillions urged their animals into a mad gallop. I had one arm around Clarimonde's waist, and one of her hands clasped in mine; her head leaned upon my shoulder, and I felt her bosom, half bare, lightly pressing against my arm. I had never known such intense happiness. In that hour I had forgotten everything, and I no more remembered having ever been a priest than I remembered what I had been doing in my mother's womb, so great was the fascination which the evil spirit exerted upon me. From that night my nature seemed in some sort to have become halved, and there were two men within me, neither of whom knew the other. At one moment I believed myself a priest who dreamed nightly that he was a gentleman, at another that I was a gentleman who dreamed he was a priest. I could no longer distinguish the dream from the reality, nor could I discover where the reality began or where ended the dream. The exquisite young lord and libertine railed at the priest, the priest loathed the dissolute habits of the young lord. Two spirals entangled and confounded the one with the other, yet never touching, would afford a fair representation of this bicephalic life which I lived. Despite the strange character of my condition, I do not believe that I ever inclined, even for a moment, to madness. I always retained with extreme vividness all the perceptions of my two lives. Only there was one absurd fact which I could not explain to myself—namely, that the consciousness of the same individuality existed in two men so opposite in character. It was an anomaly for which I could not account—whether I believed myself to be the cure of the little village of C——, or *Il Signor Romualdo*, the titled lover of Clarimonde.

Be that as it may, I lived, at least I believed that I lived, in Venice. I have never been able to discover rightly how much of illusion and how much of reality there was in this fantastic adventure. We dwelt in a great palace on the Canaleio, filled with frescoes and statues, and containing two Titians in the noblest style of the great master, which were hung in Clarimonde's chamber. It was a palace well worthy of a king. We had each our gondola, our *barcarolli* in family livery, our music hall, and our special poet. Clarimonde always lived upon a magnificent scale; there was something of Cleopatra in her nature. As for me, I had the retinue of a prince's son, and I was regarded with as much reverential respect as though I had been of the family of one of the twelve Apostles or the four Evangelists of the Most Serene Republic. I would not have turned aside to allow even the Doge to pass, and I do not believe that since Satan fell from heaven, any creature was ever prouder or more insolent than I. I went to the Ridotto, and played with a luck which seemed absolutely infernal. I received the best of all society—the sons of ruined families, women of the theatre, shrewd knaves, parasites, hectoring swashbucklers. But notwithstanding the dissipation of such a life, I always remained faithful to Clarimonde. I loved her wildly. She would have excited satiety itself, and chained inconstancy. To have Clarimonde was to have twenty mistresses; ay, to possess all women: so mobile, so varied of aspect, so fresh in new charms was she all in herself—a very chameleon of a woman, in sooth. She made you commit with her the infidelity you would have committed with another, by donning to perfection the character, the attraction, the style of beauty of the woman who appeared to please you. She returned my love a hundred-fold, and it was in vain that the young patricians and even the Ancients of the Council of Ten made her the most magnificent proposals. A Foscari even went so far as to offer to espouse her. She rejected all his overtures. Of gold she had enough. She wished no longer for anything but love—a love youthful, pure, evoked by herself, and which should be a first and last passion. I would have been perfectly happy but for a cursed nightmare which recurred every night, and in which I believed myself to be a poor village curé, practising mortification and penance for my excesses during the day. Reassured by my constant association with her, I never thought further of the strange manner in which I had become acquainted with Clarimonde. But the words of the Abbé Sérapion concerning her recurred often to my memory, and never ceased to cause me uneasiness.

For some time the health of Clarimonde had not been so good as usual; her complexion grew paler day by day. The physicians who were summoned could not comprehend the nature of her malady and knew not how to treat it. They all prescribed some insignificant remedies, and never called a second time. Her paleness, nevertheless, visibly increased, and she became colder and colder, until she seemed almost as white and dead as upon that memorable night in the unknown castle. I grieved with anguish unspeakable to behold her thus slowly perishing; and she, touched by my agony, smiled upon me sweetly and sadly with the fateful smile of those who feel that they must die.

One morning I was seated at her bedside, and breakfasting from a little table placed close at hand, so that I might not be obliged to leave her for a single instant. In the act of cutting some fruit I accidentally inflicted rather a deep gash on my finger. The blood immediately gushed forth in a little purple jet, and a few drops spurted upon Clarimonde. Her eyes flashed, her face suddenly assumed an expression of savage and ferocious joy such as I had never before observed in her. She leaped out of her bed with animal agility—the agility, as it were, of an ape or a cat—and sprang upon my wound, which she commenced to suck with an air of unutterable pleasure. She swallowed the blood in little mouthfuls, slowly and carefully, like a connoisseur tasting a wine from Xeres or Syracuse. Gradually her eyelids half closed, and the pupils of her green eyes became oblong instead of round. From time to time she paused in order to kiss my hand, then she would recommence to press her lips to the lips of the wound in order to coax forth a few more ruddy drops. When she found that the blood would no longer come, she arose with eyes liquid and brilliant, rosier than a May dawn; her face full and fresh, her hand warm and moist—in fine, more beautiful than ever, and in the most perfect health.

"I shall not die! I shall not die!" she cried, clinging to my neck, half mad with joy. "I can love thee yet for a long time. My life is thine, and all that is of me comes from thee. A few drops of thy rich and noble blood, more precious and more potent than all the elixirs of the earth, have given me back life."

This scene long haunted my memory, and inspired me with strange doubts in regard to Clarimonde; and the same evening, when slumber had transported me to my presbytery, I beheld the Abbé Sérapion, graver and more anxious of aspect than ever. He gazed attentively at me, and sorrowfully exclaimed: "Not content with losing your soul, you now desire also to lose your body. Wretched young man, into how terrible a plight have you fallen!" The tone in which he uttered these words powerfully affected me, but in spite of its vividness even that impression was soon dissipated, and a thousand other cares erased it from my mind. At last one evening, while looking into a mirror whose traitorous position she had not taken into account, I saw Clarimonde in the act of emptying a powder into the cup of spiced wine which she had long been in the habit of preparing after our repasts. I took the cup, feigned to carry it to my lips, and then placed it on the nearest article of furniture as though intending to finish it at my leisure. Taking advantage of a moment when the fair one's back was turned, I threw the contents under the table, after which I retired to my chamber and went to bed, fully resolved not to sleep, but to watch and discover what should come of all this mystery. I did not have to wait long, Clarimonde entered in her nightdress, and having removed her apparel, crept into bed and lay down beside me. When she felt assured that I was asleep, she bared my arm, and drawing a gold pin from her hair, commenced to murmur in a low voice:

"One drop, only one drop! One ruby at the end of my needle. . . . Since thou lovest me yet, I must not die! . . . Ah, poor love! His beautiful blood, so brightly purple, I must drink it. Sleep, my only treasure! Sleep, my god, my child! I will do thee no harm; I will only take of thy life what I must to keep my own from being for ever extinguished. But that I love thee so much, I could well resolve to have other lovers whose veins I could drain; but since I have known thee all other men have become hateful to me. . . . Ah, the beautiful arm! How round it is! How white it is! How shall I ever dare to prick this pretty blue vein!" And while thus murmuring to herself she wept, and I felt her tears raining on my arm as she clasped it with her hands. At last she took the resolve, slightly punctured me with her pin, and commenced to suck up the blood which oozed from the place. Although she swallowed only a few drops, the fear of weakening me soon seized her, and she carefully tied a little band around my arm, afterward rubbing the wound with an unguent which immediately cicatrised it.

Further doubts were impossible. The Abbé Sérapion was right. Notwithstanding this positive knowledge, however, I could not cease to love Clarimonde, and I would gladly of my own accord have given her all the blood she required to sustain her factitious life. Moreover, I felt but little fear of her. The woman seemed to plead with me for the vampire, and what I had already heard and seen sufficed to reassure me completely. In those days I had plenteous veins, which would not have been so easily exhausted as at present; and I would not have thought of bargaining for my blood, drop by drop. I would rather have opened myself the veins of my arm and said to her: "Drink, and may my love infiltrate itself throughout thy body together with my blood!" I carefully avoided ever making the least reference to the narcotic drink she had prepared for me, or to the incident of the pin, and we lived in the most perfect harmony.

Yet my priestly scruples commenced to torment me more than ever, and I was at a loss to imagine what new penance I could invent in order to mortify and subdue my flesh. Although these visions were involuntary, and though I did not actually participate in anything relating to them, I could not dare to touch the body of Christ with hands so impure and a mind defiled by such debauches whether real or imaginary. In the effort to avoid falling under the influence of these wearisome hallucinations, I strove to prevent myself from being overcome by sleep. I held my eyelids open with my fingers, and stood for hours together leaning upright against the wall, fighting sleep with all my might; but the dust of drowsiness invariably gathered upon my eyes at last, and finding all resistance useless, I would have to let my arms fall in the extremity of despairing weariness, and the current of slumber would again bear me away to the perfidious shores. Sérapion addressed me with the most vehement exhortations, severely reproaching me for my softness and want of fervour. Finally, one day when I was more wretched than usual, he said to me: "There is but one way by which you can obtain relief from this continual torment, and though it is an extreme measure it must be made use of; violent diseases require violent remedies. I know where Clarimonde is buried. It is necessary that we shall disinter her remains, and that you shall behold in how pitiable a state the object of your love is. Then you will no longer be tempted to lose your soul for the sake of an unclean corpse devoured by worms, and ready to crumble into dust. That will assuredly restore you to yourself." For my part, I was so tired of this double life that I at once consented, desiring to ascertain beyond a doubt whether a priest or a gentleman had been the victim of delusion. I had become fully resolved either to kill one of the two men within me for the benefit of the other, or else to kill both, for so terrible an existence could not last long and be endured. The Abbé Sérapion provided himself with a mattock, a lever, and a lantern, and at midnight we wended our way to the cemetery of ——, the location and place of which were perfectly familiar to him. After having directed the rays of the dark lantern upon the inscriptions of several tombs, we came at last upon a great slab, half concealed by huge weeds and devoured by mosses and parasitic plants, whereupon we deciphered the opening lines of the epitaph:

> Here lies Clarimonde
> Who was famed in her life-time
> As the fairest of women.

"It is here without a doubt," muttered Sérapion, and placing his lantern on the ground, he forced the point of the lever under the edge of the stone and commenced to raise it. The stone yielded, and he proceeded to work with the mattock. Darker and more silent than the night itself, I stood by and watched him do it, while he, bending over his dismal toil, streamed with sweat, panted, and his hard-coming breath seemed to have the harsh tone of a death rattle. It was a weird scene, and had any persons from without beheld us, they would assuredly have taken us rather for profane wretches and shroud-stealers than for priests of God. There was something grim and fierce in Sérapion's zeal which lent him the air of a demon rather than of an apostle or an angel, and his great aquiline face, with all its stern features brought out in strong relief by the lantern-light, had something fearsome in it which enhanced the unpleasant fancy. I felt an icy sweat come out upon my forehead in huge beads, and my hair stood up with a hideous fear. Within the depths of my own heart I felt that the act of the austere Sérapion was an abominable sacrilege; and I could have prayed that a triangle of fire would issue from the entrails of the dark clouds, heavily rolling above us, to reduce him to cinders. The owls which had been nestling in the cypress-trees, startled by the gleam of the lantern, flew against it from time to time, striking their dusty wings against its panes, and uttering plaintive cries of lamentation; wild foxes yelped in the far darkness, and a thousand sinister noises detached themselves from the silence. At last Sérapion's mattock struck the coffin itself, making its planks re-echo with a deep sonorous sound, with that terrible sound nothingness utters when stricken. He wrenched apart and tore up the lid, and I beheld Clarimonde, pallid as a figure of marble, with hands joined; her white winding-sheet made but one fold from her head to her feet. A little crimson drop sparkled like a speck of dew at one corner of her colourless mouth. Sérapion, at this spectacle, burst into fury: "Ah, thou art here, demon! Impure courtesan! Drinker of blood and gold!" And he flung holy water upon the corpse and the coffin, over which he traced the sign of the cross with his sprinkler. Poor Clarimonde had no sooner been touched by the blessed spray than her beautiful body crumbled into dust, and became only a shapeless and frightful mass of cinders and half-calcined bones.

"Behold your mistress, my Lord Romuald!" cried the inexorable priest, as he pointed to these sad remains. "Will you be easily tempted after this to promenade on the Lido or at Fusina with your beauty?" I covered my face with my hands, a vast ruin had taken place within me. I returned to my presbytery, and the noble Lord Romuald, the lover of Clarimonde, separated himself from the poor priest with whom he had kept such strange company so long. But once only, the following night, I saw Clarimonde. She said to me, as she had said the first time at the portals of the church: "Unhappy man! Unhappy man! What hast thou done? Wherefore have hearkened to that imbecile priest? Wert thou not happy? And what harm had I ever done thee that thou shouldst violate my poor tomb, and lay bare the miseries of my nothingness? All communication between our souls and our bodies is henceforth for ever broken. Adieu! Thou wilt yet regret me!" She vanished in air as smoke, and I never saw her more.

Alas! she spoke truly indeed. I have regretted her more than once, and I regret her still. My soul's peace has been very dearly bought. The love of God was not too much to replace such a love as hers. And this, brother, is the story of my youth. Never gaze upon a woman, and walk abroad only with eyes ever fixed upon the ground; for however chaste and watchful one may be, the error of a single moment is enough to make one lose eternity.

The Venus of Ille

Prosper Mérimée

———•———

If I am gracious, let the statue also be kind, seeing it so nobly human.

LUCIAN, PHILOPSEUDES

I DESCENDED THE LAST HILLSIDE AT CANIGOU, AND, ALTHOUGH THE SUN HAD already set, I could distinguish the houses of the little town of Ille, in the plain, toward which my steps were turned.

"You know," I said to the Catalanian who had been my guide since the previous day— "no doubt you know where M. de Peyrehorade lives?"

"Do I know it!" he exclaimed. "I know his house as well as I know my own; and if it wasn't so dark I would point it out to you. It is the prettiest in Ille. M. de Peyrehorade is a rich man; and he is marrying his son to a lady even richer than himself."

"Is the marriage to take place soon?" I asked.

"Very soon; probably the violinists are already ordered for the wedding. Perhaps it will be to-night, or to-morrow, or the day after, for all I know. It will be at Puygarrig; for the son is to marry Mademoiselle de Puygarrig. It will be a very grand affair!"

I had been introduced to M. de Peyrehorade by my friend M. de P., who told me he was a very learned antiquarian and of extreme good nature. It would give him pleasure to show me all the ruins for ten leagues round. So I was looking forward to visit with him the district surrounding Ille, which I knew to be rich in monuments belonging to ancient times and the Middle Ages. This marriage, of which I now heard for the first time, would upset all my plans. I said to myself, I should be a kill-joy; but I was expected, and as M. de P. had written to say I was coming, I should have to present myself.

"I will bet you, monsieur," said my guide to me, when we were in the plain—"I will bet you a cigar that I can guess why you are going to M. de Peyrehorade's."

"But that is not a difficult thing to guess," I replied, holding out a cigar to him. "At this hour, after traversing six leagues amongst the Canigou hills, the grand question is supper."

"Yes, but to-morrow? . . . Wait, I will bet that you have come to Ille to see the statue. I guessed that when I saw you draw pictures of the Saints at Serrabona."

"The statue! What statue?" The word had excited my curiosity.

"What! did no one tell you at Perpignan that M. de Peyrehorade had found a statue in the earth?"

"Did you mean a statue in terra-cotta, or clay?"

"Nothing of the kind. It is actually in copper, and there is enough of it to make heaps of coins. It weighs as much as a church-bell. It is deep in the ground, at the foot of an olive tree that we dug up."

"You were present, then, at the find?"

"Yes, sir. M. de Peyrehorade told Jean Coll and me, a fortnight ago, to uproot an old olive tree which had been killed by the frost last year, for there was a very severe frost, you will remember. Well, then, whilst working at it with all his might, Jean Coll gave a blow with his pickaxe, and I heard bimm! . . . as though he had struck on a bell. 'What is that?' I said. He picked and picked again, and a black hand appeared, which looked like the hand of a dead man coming out of the ground. I felt frightened; I went to the master and said to him: 'There are dead folk, master, under the olive tree; I wish you would send for the priest.' 'What dead folk?' he asked. He came, and had no sooner seen the hand than he cried out, 'An antique statue! an antique statue!' You might have thought he had discovered a treasure. And then he set to with pickaxe and hands, and worked hard; he did almost as much work as the two of us together."

"And what did you find in the end?"

"A huge black woman, more than half naked, saving your presence, sir, all in copper, and M. de Peyrehorade told us that it was an idol of pagan times . . . perhaps as old as Charlemagne!"

"I see what it is . . . some worthy Virgin in bronze which belonged to a convent that has been destroyed."

"The Blessed Virgin! Well, I never! . . . I should very soon have known if it had been the Blessed Virgin. I tell you it is an idol; you can see that plainly from its appearance. It stares at you with its great white eyes. . You might have said it was trying to put you out of countenance. It was enough to make one ashamed to look at her."

"White eyes were they? No doubt they are inlaid in the bronze; it might perhaps be a Roman statue."

"Roman! that's it. M. de Peyrehorade said that it was Roman. Ah! I can see you are as learned as he is."

"Is it whole and in good preservation?"

"Oh, it is all there, sir. It is much more beautiful and better finished than the painted plaster bust of Louis Philippe, which is at the town hall. But for all that the idol's face is not very nice to look at. She looks wicked . . . and she is so, too."

"Wicked! What mischief has she done you?"

"No mischief to me exactly; but I will tell you. We were down on all fours to raise her up on end, and M. de Peyrehorade was also tugging at the rope, although he had no more strength than a chicken, good man! With much trouble he got her straight. I picked up a tile to prop her up, when, good Lord! she fell upside down all in a heap. 'Look out there below!' I said, but I was not quick enough, for Jean Coll had not time to draw his leg out . . ."

"And was it hurt?"

"His poor leg was broken as clean as a pole. Goodness! when I saw it I was furious. I wanted to break up the idol with my pickaxe, but M. de Peyrehorade would not let me. He gave some money to Jean Coll, who, all the same, has been in bed the whole fortnight since it happened, and the doctor says that he will never walk with that leg again so well as with the other. It is a sad pity; he was our best runner, and, after M. de Peyrehorade's son, he was the cleverest tennis player. M. Alphonse de Peyrehorade was dreadfully sorry, for it was Coll against whom he played. It was fine to see them send the balls flying. Whizz! whizz! they never touched the ground."

And so we chatted till we reached Ille, and I very soon found myself in the presence of M. de Peyrehorade. He was a little old man, still hale and active; he was powdered, had a red nose, and his manner was jovial and bantering. When he had opened M. de P.'s letter he installed me in front of a well-appointed table and presented me to his wife and son as an illustrious archaeologist, whose desire it was to raise the province of Roussillon from obscurity, in which it had been left by the neglect of the learned.

Whilst I was eating with a good appetite—for nothing makes one so hungry as mountain air—I examined my hosts. I have said a word or two about M. de Peyrehorade; I should add that he was vivacity itself. He talked and ate, got up, ran to his library to bring me books, showed me engravings, and poured out drinks for me; he was never still for two minutes. His wife was rather too stout, like most Catalanian women over forty, and she seemed to me a regular provincial, solely taken up with the cares of her household. Although the supper was ample for six people at least, she ran to the kitchen, had pigeons killed and dozens of them fried, besides opening I don't know how many pots of preserves. In a trice the table was loaded with dishes and bottles, and I should assuredly have died of indigestion if I had even tasted all that was offered me. However, at each dish that I refused there were fresh excuses. They were afraid I did not get what I liked at Ille—there are so few means of getting things in the provinces, and Parisians are so hard to please!

M. Alphonse de Peyrehorade stirred no more than a statue in the midst of his parents' comings and goings. He was a tall young man of twenty-six, with beautiful and regular features, but they were wanting in expression. His figure and athletic build quite justified the reputation he had gained in the country as an indefatigable tennis player. He was that evening exquisitely dressed, exactly like the latest fashion plate. But he seemed to me to be uneasy in his garments; he was as stiff as a post in his velvet collar, and could not turn round unless with his whole body. His fat and sunburnt hands, with their short nails, contrasted strangely with his costume. They were the hands of a labouring man appearing below the sleeves of a dandy. For the rest, he only addressed me once throughout the whole evening, and that was to ask me where I had bought my watch-chain, although he studied me from head to foot very inquisitively in my capacity as a Parisian.

"Ah, now, my honoured guest," said M. de Peyrehorade to me when supper drew to its conclusion, "you belong to me. You are in my house, and I shall not give you any rest until you have seen all the curiosities among our mountains. You must learn to know our Roussillon and to do it justice. You have no idea what we can show you—Phoenician, Celtic, Roman, Arabesque and Byzantine monuments. You shall see them all—lock, stock and barrel. I will take you everywhere, and will not let you off a single stone."

A fit of coughing compelled him to stop. I took advantage of it to tell him I should be greatly distressed if I disturbed him during the interesting event about to take place in his family. If he would kindly give me the benefit of his valuable advice about the excursion I ought to take, I should be able to go without putting him to the inconvenience of accompanying me. . . .

"Ah, you are referring to this boy's marriage!" he exclaimed, interrupting me. "That is all nonsense. It takes place the day after to-morrow. You shall celebrate the wedding with us; it will take place quietly, for the bride is in mourning for an aunt, whose heiress she is. Therefore there is to be neither fête nor ball. . . . It is a pity. . . .

You would have seen our Catalanian women dance. . They are pretty, and you might perhaps have been tempted to follow Alphonse's example. One marriage, they say, leads to others. . . . On Saturday, after the young people are married, I shall be at liberty, and we will set out. I ask your forgiveness for the irksomeness of a provincial wedding. To a Parisian blasé with fêtes . . . and a wedding without a ball too! However, you will see a bride . . . such a bride . . . you must tell me what you think of her. . . . But you are not a frivolous man, and you take no notice of women. I have better things than women to show you. I am going to show you something! I have a fine surprise for you to-morrow."

"Ah," I replied, "it is not easy to have a treasure in your house without the public knowing all about it. I think I can guess the surprise you have in store for me. You are thinking of your statue. I am quite prepared to admire it, for my guide's description of it has roused my curiosity."

"Ah! he told you about the idol, for that is what they call my beautiful Venus Tur—but I will not talk of it. To-morrow, as soon as it is daylight, you shall see her, and you shall tell me if I am not right in considering her a *chef-d'oeuvre*. Upon my word, you could not have arrived at a better time! There are inscriptions which, poor ignorant, I explain after my own fashion . . . but a savant from Paris! . You will probably laugh at my interpretation, for I have written a treatise on it. . . . I—an old provincial antiquarian—I am going to venture. . . . I mean to make the press groan. If you would be so good as to read and correct it, I should be hopeful. . . . For example, I am curious to know how you would translate this inscription on the pedestal: '*CAVE*' . . .—but I do not want to ask you anything yet! To-morrow, to-morrow! Not a single word about the Venus to-day."

"You are quite right, Peyrehorade," said his wife, "to stop talking about your idol; you ought to see that you are preventing the gentle man from eating. Why, he has seen far more beautiful statues in Paris than yours. There are dozens of them in the Tuileries, and in bronze too."

"Just look at her ignorance—the blessed ignorance of the provinces!" interrupted M. de Peyrehorade. "Fancy, comparing a splendid antique statue to the flat figures of Coustou!

> How irreverently of my affairs
> The gods are pleased to talk!

"Do you know my wife wanted to have my statue melted down to make a bell for our church? She would have been its godmother—one of Myro's *chef-d'oeuvres.* "

"*Chef-d'oeuvre! chef-d'oeuvre!* a fine *chef-d'oeuvre* it is to break a man's leg!"

"Look here, wife," said M. de Peyrehorade in a determined voice, as he extended his right leg toward her, clad in a fine silk stocking, "if my Venus had broken this leg I should not have minded."

"Good gracious! Peyrehorade, how can you talk like that? Fortunately, the man is going on well. . . . And yet I can not bring myself to look at the statue which did such an evil thing as that. Poor Jean Coll!"

"Wounded by Venus, sir," said M. de Peyrehorade, laughing loudly. "The rascal complains of being wounded by Venus!

Veneris nec præmia nôris.

Who has not suffered from the wounds of Venus?"

M. Alphonse, who understood French better than Latin, winked with an understanding air, and looked at me as though to say, "Do you understand that, you Parisian?"

Supper ended at last. For an hour I had not been able to eat any more. I was tired, and could not hide my frequent yawns. Madame de Peyrehorade saw it first, and said that it was time to retire. Then began fresh apologies for the poor entertainment I should find. I should not be comfortable as in Paris; in the country things are so different! I must make allowances for the people of Roussillon. It was in vain I protested that after a journey among the mountains a bundle of straw would seem a delicious bed. They still begged me to pardon their poor rustic servants if they did not behave as well as they should. At last, accompanied by M. de Peyrehorade, I reached the room put apart for my use. The staircase, the top steps of which were of wood, led to the centre of a corridor, out of which opened several rooms.

"To the right," said my host, "is the set of rooms that I intend for the future Madame Alphonse. Your room is at the end of the passage opposite. You will understand," he added, with a look which he meant to be sly—"you will readily understand that newly married people wish to be by themselves. You are at one end of the house and they at the other."

We entered a very handsomely furnished room, where the first object that caught my eye was a bed seven feet long, six broad, and such a height that one needed a stool to get into it. My host pointed out the position of the bell, and satisfied himself that the sugar-bowl was full, and the smelling-bottles of eau de Cologne in their proper places on the toilette table; then he asked me repeatedly if I had all I wanted, wished me good-night and left me alone.

The windows were shut. Before undressing, I opened one to breathe the cool night air, which was delicious after such a lengthy supper. In front was Canigou Mountain, which is at all times beautiful, but to-night it seemed the fairest in the world, lighted up as it was by a splendid moon. I stood a few minutes to contemplate its marvellous outline, and was just going to close my window when, lowering my gaze, I saw the statue on a pedestal about forty yards from the house. It was placed in a corner of the quick-set hedge which separated a little garden from a large, perfectly level court, which, I learnt later, was the tennis ground for the town. This ground had been M. de Peyrehorade's property, but he had given it to the public at his son's urgent entreaties.

From my distance away it was difficult to make out the form of the statue; I could only judge of its height, which I guessed was about six feet. At that moment two town larrikins passed along the tennis court, close to the hedge, whistling the pretty Roussillon air, "Montagnes régalades." They stopped to look at the statue, and one of them even apostrophised her in a loud voice. He spoke the Catalanian dialect, but I had been long enough in the province of Roussillon to be able to understand almost all he said.

"Chi-ike, hussy!" (the Catalanian expression was more forcible than that). "Look here," he said, " you broke Jean Coll's leg for him! If you belonged to me I would have broken your neck."

"Bah! what with?" asked the other. "She is made of copper, and so hard that Stephen broke his file over it, trying to cut into it. It is copper from before the Flood, and harder than anything I can think."

"If I had my cold chisel" (apparently he was a locksmith's apprentice) "I would jolly soon scoop out her big white eyes; it would be like cracking a couple of nutshells for the kernels. I would do it for a *maravedi*."

They moved a few paces further off.

"I must just wish the idol good-night," said the tallest of the apprentices, stopping suddenly.

He stooped, and probably picked up a stone. I saw him stretch out his arm and throw something, and immediately after I heard a resounding blow from the bronze. At the same moment the apprentice raised his hand to his head and yelled out in pain.

"She has thrown it back at me!" he cried.

And then the two scamps took to flight as fast as they could. The stone had evidently rebounded from the metal, and had punished the rascal for the outrage done to the goddess.

I shut the window and laughed heartily.

Yet another vandal punished by Venus! Would that all destroyers of our ancient monuments could have their heads broken like that!

And with this charitable wish I fell asleep.

It was broad day when I awoke. Near my bed on one side stood M. de Peyrehorade in a dressing-gown; on the other a servant sent by his wife with a cup of chocolate in his hand.

"Come now, Parisian, get up! How lazy you people from the capital are!" said my host, while I hastily dressed myself. "It is eight o'clock, and you still in bed. I got up at six o'clock. I have been up-stairs three times; I listened at your door on tiptoe, but there was no sign of life at all. It is bad for you to sleep too much at your age. And my Venus waiting to be seen! Come, take this cup of Barcelona chocolate as fast as you can . . . it is quite contraband. You can't get such chocolate in Paris. Take in all the nourishment you can, for when you are before my Venus no one will be able to tear you away."

I was ready in five minutes; that is to say, I was only half shaved, wrongly buttoned and scalded by the chocolate which I had swallowed boiling hot. I went down-stairs into the garden and was soon in front of a wonderfully fine statue. It was indeed a Venus of extraordinary beauty. The top part of her body was bare, just as the ancients usually depicted their great deities; her right hand, raised up to her breast, was bent, with the palm inward, the thumb and two first fingers extended, whilst the other two were slightly curved. The other hand was near the hips, and held up the drapery which covered the lower part of the body. The attitude of this statue reminded me of that of the Morra player, which, for some reason or other, goes by the name of Germanicus. Perhaps they wished to depict the goddess playing at the game of Morra.

However that might be, it is impossible to conceive anything more perfect than the body of this Venus; nothing could be more harmonious or more voluptuous than its outlines, nothing more graceful or dignified than its drapery. I expected some work of the Lower Empire, and I beheld a masterpiece of the most perfect period of sculpture. I was specially struck with the exquisite truth of form, which gave the impression that it had been moulded by nature itself, if nature ever produces such perfect specimens.

The hair, which was raised off the forehead, looked as though it might have been gilded at some time. The head was small, like those of nearly all Greek statues, and bent slightly forward. As to the face, I should never be able to express its strange character; it was of quite a different type from that of any other antique statue I could recall to mind. It was not only the calm and austere beauty of the Greek sculptors, whose rule was to give a majestic immobility to every feature. Here, on the contrary, I noticed with astonishment that the artist had purposely expressed ill-nature to the point even of wickedness. Every feature was slightly contracted: the eyes were rather slanting, the mouth turned up at the corners, and the nostrils somewhat inflated. Disdain, irony, cruelty, could be traced on a face which was, notwithstanding, of incredible beauty. Indeed, the longer one looked at this wonderful statue, the more did the distressing thought obtrude itself that such marvellous beauty could be united with an utter absence of goodness.

"If the model ever existed," I said to M. de Peyrehorade, "and I doubt if Heaven ever produced such a woman, how I pity her lovers! She would delight to make them die of despair. There is something ferocious in her expression, and yet I never saw anything so beautiful."

"It is Venus herself gloating over her prey,"

cried M. de Peyrehorade, pleased with my enthusiasm.

That expression of fiendish scorn was perhaps enhanced by the contrast shown by her eyes, which were encrusted with silver, and shone brilliantly with the greenish-black colour that time had given to the whole statue. Those brilliant eyes produced a kind of illusion which recalled lifelike reality. I remembered what my guide had said, that she made those who looked at her lower their eyes. It was quite true, and I could hardly restrain an impulse of anger against myself for feeling rather ill at ease before that bronze face.

"Now that you have admired it minutely, my dear colleague in antiquarian research," said my host, "let us, by your leave, open a scientific conference. What say you to that inscription, which you have not yet noticed?"

He showed me the pedestal of the statue, and I read on it these words:

CAVE AMANTEM

"*Quid dicis, doctissime?*" he asked me, rubbing his hands together. "Let us see if we can hit on the meaning of this *CAVE AMANTEM*."

"But," I answered, "it has two meanings. It can be translated: 'Beware of him who loves thee; mistrust thy lovers.' But in that sense I do not know whether *CAVE AMANTEM* would be good Latin. Looking at the lady's diabolic expression, I would rather believe that the artist intended to put the spectator on his guard against her terrible beauty; I would therefore translate it: 'Beware if *she* loves thee.' "

"Humph!" said M. de Peyrehorade; "yes, that is an admissible interpretation; but, without wishing to displease you, I prefer the first translation, and I will tell you why. You know who Venus's lover was?"

"There were several."

"Yes, but the chief one was Vulcan. Should one not rather say, 'In spite of all thy beauty and thy scornful manner, thou shalt have for thy lover a blacksmith, a hideous cripple'? What a profound moral, monsieur, for flirts!"

I could hardly help smiling at this far-fetched explanation.

"Latin is a difficult tongue, because of its concise expression," I remarked, to avoid contradicting my antiquarian friend outright; and I stepped further away to see the statue better.

"One moment, colleague," said M. de Peyrehorade, seizing me by the aim, "you have not seen everything. There is still another inscription. Climb up on the pedestal and look at the right arm." And saying this, he helped me up.

I held on to the neck of the Venus unceremoniously, and began to make myself better acquainted with her. I only looked at her for a moment, right in the face, and I found her still more wicked, and still more beautiful. Then I discovered that there were some written characters in an ancient, running hand, it seemed to me, engraved on the arm. With the help of spectacles I spelt out the following, whilst M. de Peyrehorade repeated every word as soon as pronounced, with approving gesture and voice. It read thus:

VENERI TVRBVL . . .
EVTYCHES MYRO
IMPERIO FECIT.

After the word *TVRBVL* in the first line, I thought some letters had been effaced; but *TVRBVL* was perfectly legible.

"What do you say to that?" asked my host, radiantly smiling with malice, for he knew very well that I could not easily extricate myself from this *TVRBVL*.

"I can not explain that word yet," I said to him; "all the rest is easy. By his order Eutyches Myro made this great offering to Venus."

"Good. But what do you make of *TVRBVL*? What is *TVRBVL*?"

"*TVRBVL* puzzles me greatly; I can not think of any epithet applied to Venus which might assist me. Stay, what do you say to *TVRBVLENTA*? Venus, who troubles and disturbs. . . . You notice I am all the time thinking of her malignant expression. *TVRBVLENTA* would not be at all a bad epithet for Venus," I added modestly, for I was not myself quite satisfied with my explanation.

"Venus the turbulent! Venus the broiler! Ah! you think, then, that my Venus is a Venus of the pot-house? Nothing of the kind, monsieur. She is a Venus belonging to the great world. And now I will expound to you this *TVRBVL*. . . . You will at least promise not to divulge my discovery before my treatise is published. I shall become famous, you see, by this find. . . . You must leave us poor provincial devils a few ears to glean. You Parisian savants are rich enough."

From the top of the pedestal, where I still perched, I solemnly promised that I would never be so dishonourable as to steal his discovery.

"*TVRBVL* . . . monsieur," he said, coming nearer and lowering his voice for fear any one else but myself should hear, "read *TVRBVUSIERÆ*."

"I do not understand any better."

"Listen carefully. A league from here, at the base of the mountain, is a village called Boulternère. It is a corruption of the Latin word *TVRBVLNERA*. Nothing is commoner than such an inversion. Boulternère, monsieur, was a Roman town. I have always been doubtful about this, for I have never had any proof of it. The proof lies here. This Venus was the local goddess of the city of Boulternère; and this word Boulternère, which I have just shown to be of ancient origin, proves a still more curious thing, namely, that Boulternère, after being a Roman town, became a Phoenician one!"

He stopped a minute to take breath, and to enjoy my surprise. I had to repress a strong inclination to laugh.

"Indeed," he went on, "*TVRBVLNERA* is pure Phoenician. *TVR* pronounce *TOUR*. . . . *TOUR* and *SOUR*, are they not the same word? *SOUR* is the Phoenician name for Tyre. I need not remind you of its meaning. *BVL* is Baal, Bâl, Bel, Bul, slight differences in pronunciation. As to *NERA*, that gives me some trouble. I am tempted to think, for want of a Phoenician word, that it comes from the Greek **νηρός**— damp, marshy. That would make it a hybrid word. To justify **νηρός** I will show you at Boulternère how the mountain streams there form poisonous swamps. On the other hand, the ending *NERA* might have been added much later, in honour of Nera Pivesuvia, the wife of Tetricus, who may have done some benevolent act to the city of Turbul. But, on account of the marshes, I prefer the derivation from **νηρός** ."

He took a pinch of snuff with a satisfied air.

"But let us leave the Phoenicians and return to the inscription. I translate, then: 'To the Venus of Boulternère Myro dedicates by his command this statue, the work of his hand.'"

I took good care not to criticise his etymology, but I wanted, on my own account, to put his penetrative faculties to the proof, so I said to him: "Wait a bit, monsieur, Myro dedicated something, but I do not in the least see that it was this statue."

"What!" he exclaimed, "was not Myro a famous Greek sculptor? The talent would descend to his family; and one of his descendants made this statue. Nothing can be clearer."

"But," I replied, "I see a little hole in the arm. I fancy it has been used to hold something, perhaps a bracelet, which this Myro gave to Venus as an expiatory offering, for Myro was an unlucky lover. Venus was incensed against him, and he appeased her by consecrating a golden bracelet. You must remember that *fecit* is often used for *consecravit*. The terms are synonymous. I could show you more than one instance if I had access to Gruter or, better still, Orellius. It is natural that a lover should behold Venus in his dreams, and that he should imagine that she commanded him to give her statue a golden bracelet. Myro consecrated a bracelet to her. . . . Then the barbarians, or perhaps some sacrilegious thief—"

"Ah! it is easily seen that you are given to romancing," cried my host, lending his hand to help me down. "No, monsieur, it is a work after the School of Myro. Only look at the work, and you will agree."

Having made it a rule never to contradict pig-headed antiquarians outright, I bowed my head as though convinced, and said:

"It is a splendid piece of work."

"Ah! my God!" exclaimed M. de Peyrehorade, "here is yet another mark of vandalism! Some one has thrown a stone at my statue!"

He had just seen a white mark a little below the breast of the Venus. I noticed a similar mark on the fingers of the right hand, which at first I supposed had been scraped by the stone in passing, or perhaps a fragment of it might have broken off by the shock and rebounded upon the hand. I told my host the insult that I had witnessed and the prompt punishment which had followed. He laughed heartily, and compared the apprentice to Diomede, wishing he might see all his comrades changed into white birds, as the Greek hero did.

The breakfast bell interrupted this famous interview; and, as on the previous evening, I was forced to eat as much as four people. Then M. de Peyrehorade's tenants came to see him, and whilst he gave them audience, his son took me to see a carriage which he had bought for his *fiancée* at Toulouse, and, of course, I admired it properly. After that I went with him to the stables, where he kept me half an hour praising his horses and telling me their pedigrees and the prizes he had won at the country races. At last he spoke of his future bride, by a sudden transition from the grey mare that he intended for her.

"We shall see her to-day. I wonder if you will think her pretty. You are so difficult to please in Paris; but everybody here and at Perpignan thinks her lovely. The best of it is she is very wealthy. Her aunt, who lived at Prades, left her all her money. Oh, I am going to be ever so happy!"

I was deeply shocked to see a young man much more affected by the dowry than by the beautiful looks of his bride-to-be.

"Are you learned in jewellery?" continued M. Alphonse. "What do you think of this ring which I am going to give her to-morrow?"

So saying, he drew from the first joint of his little finger a large ring blazing with diamonds, formed by the clasping of two hands: a most poetic idea, I thought. It was of ancient workmanship, but I guessed that it had been retouched when the diamonds were set. Inside the ring was engraved in gothic letters: "*Sempr' ab ti*" ("Ever thine").

"It is a lovely ring," I said; but added, "the diamonds have taken from its original character somewhat."

"Oh, it is much prettier as it is now," he replied, smiling. "There are one thousand two hundred francs' worth of diamonds in it. My mother gave it me. It was an old family ring . . . from the days of chivalry. It was worn by my grandmother, who had it from her grandmother. Goodness knows when it was made!"

"The custom in Paris," I said, " is to give a very plain ring, usually made of two different metals, say, gold and platinum. For instance, the other ring which you have on that finger would be most suitable. This one is so large, with its diamonds and hands in relief, that no glove would go over it."

"Oh, Madame Alphonse can arrange that as she likes. I think she will be pleased enough to have it. Twelve hundred francs on one's finger is very pleasing. That little ring," he added, looking with a satisfied expression at the plain ring which he held in his hand, "was given me one Shrove Tuesday by a woman in Paris, when I was staying there two years ago. Ah! that is the place to enjoy oneself in! . . ." And he sighed regretfully.

We were to dine at Puygarrig that day, at the house of the bride's parents; we drove in carriages, and were soon at the Castle, which was about a league and a half from Ille. I was introduced and received like one of the family. I will not talk of the dinner, nor of the conversation which took place, and in which I had but little part. M. Alphonse, who sat by the side of his future bride, whispered in her ear every quarter of an hour. She hardly raised her eyes, and blushed modestly every time her intended spoke to her, though she replied without embarrassment.

Mademoiselle de Puygarrig was eighteen years of age, and her lithe, delicate figure was a great contrast to the bony limbs of her sturdy lover. She was more than beautiful: she was enchanting. I admired the perfect naturalness of all her replies. Her expression was kindly, but nevertheless was not devoid of a light touch of maliciousness which reminded me, do what I would, of my host's Venus. While making this comparison to myself I wondered if the superior beauty which undoubtedly belonged to the statue was not largely owing to her tigerish expression, for strength, even when accompanied by evil passions, always induces wonder and a sort of involuntary admiration.

What a pity, I reflected, as we left Puygarrig, that such a charming person should be so rich, and that her dowry should be the cause of her being sought by a man so unworthy of her!

Whilst on the return to Ille I found it difficult to know what to talk of to Madame de Peyrehorade, with whom I thought I ought to converse.

"You are very strong-minded people here in Roussillon," I exclaimed, "to have a wedding on a Friday. In Paris we are more superstitious; no man dare take a wife on that day."

"Oh, please don't talk of it," she said; "if it had depended only on me, I would certainly have chosen another day. But Peyrehorade wanted it, and would not give way. It troubles me, however. Suppose some misfortune should happen? There must be something in it, else why should everybody be afraid of a Friday?"

"Friday," her husband cried, "is the day dedicated to Venus. An excellent day for a wedding. You will notice, my dear colleague, that I only think of my Venus. What an honour! It was on that account I chose Friday. To-morrow, if you are willing, we will offer her a small sacrifice before the ceremony—two ring-doves and incense, if I can find any."

"For shame, Peyrehorade!" interrupted his wife, who was scandalised in the highest degree. "Offer incense to an idol! It would be an abomination! What would be said about you through the countryside?"

"At all events," said M. de Peyrehorade, "you will let me put a wreath of roses and lilies on her head?

Manibus date lilia plenis.

You see, monsieur, the charter is but a vain thing. We have no religious freedom."

The arrangements for the morrow were regulated in the following manner: Every one had to be ready and dressed for the wedding at ten o'clock prompt. After taking chocolate we were to be driven to Puygarrig. The civil marriage was to take place at the village registry, and the religious ceremony in the Castle chapel. After that there would be luncheon. Then we were to spend the time as we liked until seven o'clock, when we were all to return to M. de Peyrehorade's house, where the two families would sup together. The remainder of the time would naturally be spent in eating as much as possible, as there would be no dancing.

Ever since eight o'clock I had sat before the Venus, pencil in hand, beginning over again for the twentieth time the head of the statue, without being able to seize the expression. M. de Peyrehorade came and went, giving me advice and repeating his Phoenician derivations. Then he placed some Bengal roses on the pedestal of the statue, and addressed to it, in a tragi-comical air, vows for the couple about to live under his roof. He went in to see about his toilette toward nine o'clock, and at the same time M. Alphonse appeared, well groomed, in a new suit, white gloves, patent-leather shoes, chased buttons and a rose in his button-hole.

"You must take my wife's portrait," he said, leaning over my drawing; "she, too, is pretty."

Then began on the tennis ground, to which I have already referred, a game which at once attracted M. Alphonse's attention. I was tired, and in despair at being unable to reproduce that diabolical face, so I soon left my drawing to watch the players. There were among them several Spanish muleteers who had come the night before. They were men from Aragon and from Navarre, almost all clever players. Although the local players were encouraged by the presence and advice of M. Alphonse, they were very soon beaten by these new champions. The patriotic onlookers were filled with concern, and M. Alphonse looked at his watch. It was still only half-past nine. His mother was not ready yet. He hesitated no longer, threw off his coat, asked for a vest, and challenged the Spaniards. I looked at him with amusement and in some surprise.

"The honour of our country must be upheld," he said.

Then I saw how very handsome he was. He was roused to passion. The toilette, which had just now filled his thoughts to the exclusion of everything else, was completely forgotten. A few minutes before he hardly dared turn his head, for fear of spoiling his cravat. Now he thought nothing of his curled hair or of his beautifully got up frilled shirt. And his *fiancée*! I really believe that, if necessary, he would have adjourned the wedding. I saw him hastily put on a pair of sandals, turn up his sleeves, and with a self-satisfied manner range himself at the head of the vanquished party, like Caesar when he rallied his soldiers at Dyrrachium. I leapt the hedge and took up a position comfortably under the shade of a nettle tree in such a way as to be able to see both camps.

Contrary to general expectation, M. Alphonse missed the first ball; true, it grazed the ground, and bound with surprising force near one of the players from Aragon, who seemed the head of the Spaniards.

He was a man of about forty, strong, yet spare in appearance; he stood six feet high, and his olive skin was of almost as deep a tint as the bronze of the Venus.

M. Alphonse threw his racquet on the ground in a furious rage.

"It is this cursed ring!" he cried, "which pressed into my finger and made me miss a sure thing."

With some difficulty he took off his diamond ring, and I went nearer to take it, but he forestalled me, ran to the Venus, slipped the ring on its fourth finger, and retook his position at the head of his townsmen.

He was pale, but cool and determined. From that time he made no more fouls, and the Spaniards were completely beaten. The enthusiasm of the spectators was a fine sight: some uttered shrieks of delight and threw their caps in the air: others shook hands with him and called him the pride of their countryside. If he had repulsed an invasion, I doubt if he would have received heartier or more sincere congratulations. The disappointment of the vanquished added still more to the brilliance of his victory.

"We must have another match, my fine fellow," he said to the muleteer from Aragon in a condescending tone; "but I must give you odds."

I would have preferred M. Alphonse to be more modest, and I was almost sorry for his rival's humiliation.

The Spanish giant felt the insult keenly; I saw him go pale under his tanned skin. He looked miserably at his racquet and ground his teeth; then, in a choking voice he said: "Me lo pagaras."*

The voice of M. de Peyrehorade interrupted his son's triumph; my host was extremely astonished not to find him superintending the preparation of the new carriage, and was even more surprised to see him with racquet in hand, flushed from the game.

M. Alphonse ran to the house, bathed his face and hands, put on his new coat again and his patent-leather shoes, and five minutes after we were in full trot on the road to Puygarrig. All the tennis players of the town and a large crowd of spectators followed us with shouts of joy. The stout horses which drew us could hardly keep ahead of these dauntless Catalanians.

We were at Puygarrig, and the procession was forming into order to walk to the registry when M. Alphonse suddenly put his hand up to his head and whispered to me:

What a blunder! I have forgotten the ring! It is on Venus's finger, devil take her! Do not tell my mother, whatever happens. Perhaps she will not notice the omission."

"You could send some one for it," I said.

"No! my servant has stayed behind at Ille. I dare hardly trust these fellows here with twelve hundred francs worth of diamonds. What a temptation that will be to some one! Besides, what would the people here think of my absentmindedness? They would make fun of me. They would call me the husband of the statue. . . . If only no one steals it! Fortunately, the idol frightens the young rascals. They dare not go within arm's length of her. Well, it doesn't matter, I have another ring."

The two ceremonies, civil and religious, were accomplished with suitable state. Mademoiselle de Puygarrig received the ring which had belonged to a Paris milliner, little thinking that her *fiancé* had sacrificed another's love-token to her. Then we sat down and drank, ate and sang for long enough. I was sorry the bride had to bear the coarse jollity which went on all around her; however, she took it with a better face than I should have thought possible, and her embarrassment was neither awkward nor affected. Possibly courage springs up under occasions that need it.

The banquet broke up Lord knows when—somewhere about four o'clock. The men went for a walk in the park, which was a magnificent one, or watched the peasants of Puygarrig dance on the Castle lawn, decked in their gala dresses.

* "But you will pay for it."

In this way we passed several hours. In the meantime the women thronged round the bride, who showed them her wedding presents. Then she changed her toilette, and I noticed that she covered up her beautiful hair with a cap and a hat with feathers in it, for wives are most particular to don as quickly as possible those adornments which custom has forbidden them to wear when they are still unmarried.

It was nearly eight o'clock when we were ready to go back to Ille. But there was a pathetic scene first between Mademoiselle de Puygarrig and her aunt, who had been a mother to her, and was of advanced age and very religious: she had not been able to go to the town with us. At her departure she gave her niece a touching sermon on her wifely duties, which resulted in a flood of tears and endless embracings. M. de Peyrehorade compared this parting to the Rape of the Sabines. However, we got off at last, and during the journey every one exerted himself to cheer up the bride and make her laugh, but in vain.

At Ille supper awaited us; and *what* a supper! If the morning's coarse revel had shocked me, I was still more disgusted by the quips and jokes which circled round the bride and bridegroom. The bridegroom, who had disappeared for an instant before sitting down to supper, was pale and as chilly as an iceberg. He drank the old wine of Collioure constantly, which is almost as strong as brandy. I was on one side of him, and felt I must warn him:

"Do take care. They say this wine—"

I don't know what silly thing I said to him to show myself in harmony with the merrymakers.

"When they get up from the table I have something to say to you," he whispered, pushing my knee.

His solemn tone surprised me. I looked at him more attentively, and noticed a strange alteration in his features.

"Do you feel ill?" I asked.

"No."

And he began to drink again.

In the meantime, in the midst of cries and clapping hands, a child of eleven, who had slipped under the table, showed to the company a pretty white and rose-coloured ribbon which she had just taken from the bride's ankle. They called it her garter. It was soon cut into bits and distributed among the young people, who decorated their button-holes with it, according to a very old custom which is still preserved in a few patriarchal families. This made the bride blush to the whites of her eyes. But her confusion reached its height when M. de Peyrehorade, after calling for silence, sang some Catalanian verses to her, which he said were impromptus. I give the sense so far as I understood it.

"What is the matter with me, my friends? Has the wine I have taken made me see double? There are two Venuses here. . . ."

The bridegroom turned round suddenly and looked scared, which set everybody laughing.

"Yes," continued M. de Peyrehorade, "there are two Venuses under my roof. One I found in the earth, like a truffle; the other came down to us from the heavens to share her girdle with us."

He meant, of course, her garter.

"My son, choose between the Roman and the Catalanian Venus which you prefer. The rascal took the Catalanian, the better part, for the Roman is black and the Catalanian is white. The Roman is cold, and the Catalanian sets on fire all who come near her."

This conclusion excited such an uproar of noisy applause and loud laughter that I thought the roof would fall on our heads. There were but three grave faces at the table—those of the wedded pair and mine. I had a splitting headache; for besides, I know not why, a marriage always makes me feel melancholy. This one disgusted me rather, too.

The last couplets were sung by the deputy-mayor, and, I may say, they were very broad; then we went into the salon to witness the departure of the bride, who would soon be conducted to her chamber, as it was nearly midnight.

M. Alphonse drew me aside into the recess of a window, and said, as he turned his eyes away from me:

"You will laugh at me . . . but I do not know what is the matter with me. . . . I am bewitched, devil take it!"

My first thought was that he fancied he was threatened with some misfortune of the nature of those referred to by Montaigne and Madame de Sévigné: "The whole realm of love is filled with tragic stories."

I thought to myself that this kind of mishap only happens to men of genius.

"You have drunk too much Collioure wine, my dear M. Alphonse," I said. "I warned you."

"That may be. But this is something much more terrible."

His voice was broken, and I thought he was quite drunk.

"You know my ring?" he continued, after a pause.

"Yes. Has it been taken?"

"No."

"Therefore you have it?"

"No—I—I could not get it off the finger of that devil of a Venus."

"Nonsense! you did not pull hard enough."

"Yes, I did. . . . But the Venus . . . has clenched her finger."

He looked at me fixedly with a haggard expression, and leant against the frame-work to keep himself from falling.

"What a ridiculous tale!" I said. "You pushed the ring on too far. To-morrow you must use pincers, only take care not to injure the statue."

"No, I tell you. The finger of Venus has contracted and bent up; she closed her hand, do you hear? . . . She is my wife apparently, because I gave her my ring. . . . She will not give it back."

I shivered suddenly, and for a moment my blood ran cold. Then the deep sigh he gave sent a breath of wine into my face and all my emotion disappeared.

"The wretched man is completely drunk," I thought.

"You are an antiquarian, monsieur," the bridegroom added in dismal tones; "you know all about such statues. . . . There is perhaps some spring, some devilish catch, I do not know of. If you would go and see."

"Willingly," I said. "Come with me."

"No, I would rather you went by yourself."

So I left the salon.

The weather had changed during supper, and rain began to fall heavily. I was going to ask for an umbrella, when I stopped short and reflected. "I should be a great fool," I said to myself, "to go and verify the tale of a tipsy man! Perhaps, besides, he intended to play some stupid joke on me to amuse the country people; and at the least I should be wet through to the skin and catch a bad cold."

I cast a glance on the dripping statue from the door, and went up to my room without returning to the salon. I went to bed, but sleep was long in coming. All the scenes that had occurred during the day returned to my mind. I thought of that beautiful, innocent young girl given up to a drunken brute. "What a detestable thing," I said to myself, "is a marriage of convenience! A mayor puts on a tricoloured sash, and a priest a stole, and behold, the noblest of girls may be dedicated to the Minotaur. What can two beings who do not love each other say at such a moment, a moment that lovers would buy at the price of life itself? Can a wife ever love a man whom she has once discovered is coarse-minded? First impressions can never be obliterated, and I am certain M. Alphonse deserves to be hated."

During my monologue, which I abridge considerably, I had heard much coming and going about the house, doors open and shut, and carriages go away; then I thought I could hear the light steps of several women upon the staircase proceeding to the end of the passage opposite my room. It was probably the procession leading the bride to bed. Then they went downstairs again, and Madame de Peyrehorade's door shut. "How unhappy and strangely ill at ease that poor girl must feel!" I said to myself. I turned over on my bed in a bad temper. A bachelor cuts but a poor figure at a house where there is a wedding going on.

Silence had reigned for a long while, when it was interrupted by heavy steps coming up the stairs. The wooden stairs creaked loudly.

"What a clumsy lout!" I cried. "I bet he will fall down-stairs."

Then all became quiet again. I took up a book to change the current of my thoughts. It was a treatise on the Statistics of the Department, embellished with a preface by M. de Peyrehorade on the "Druidical Monuments of the Arrondissement of Prades." I fell into a doze at the third page.

I slept badly and waked several times. It must have been five in the morning, and I had been awake more than twenty minutes when the cock began to crow. Day had dawned. Then I distinctly heard the same heavy steps and the same creaking of the stairs that I had heard before I went to sleep. It struck me as very strange. I tried amidst my yawning to guess why M. Alphonse should rise so early; I could not think of any reason at all likely. I was going to close my eyes again when my attention was afresh excited by strange trampings, which were soon intermingled with the ringing of bells and the banging of doors, and then I could distinguish confused cries.

The drunken bridegroom must have set fire to the house! And at this reflection I leapt out of bed.

I dressed rapidly and went into the corridor. From the opposite end proceeded cries and waitings, and one piercing cry sounded above all the others—"My son! my son!" Evidently some accident had happened to M. Alphonse. I ran to the bridal chamber; it was full of people. The first sight which met my eyes was the young man, half-dressed, stretched across the bed, the wood of which was broken. He was livid and motionless, and his mother wept and cried by his side. M. de Peyrehorade was busy rubbing his son's temples with eau de Cologne and holding smelling salts under his nose. Alas! his son had been dead a long time. Upon a couch at the other end of the room was the bride in the grip of terrible convulsions. She uttered inarticulate cries, and two strapping servants had the greatest difficulty in holding her down.

"My God!" I exclaimed, "what has happened?"

I went to the bedside and raised the body of the unfortunate young man; he was already cold and stiff. His clenched teeth and black face denoted the most frightful agony. It could be easily seen that his death had been violent and his agony terrible. There was, however, no trace of blood on his clothes. I opened his shirt and found a livid mark on his breast, which extended down his sides and back. One would have thought he had been strangled by a band of iron. My foot stumbled on something hard which was under the rug; I stooped and saw the diamond ring.

I led M. de Peyrehorade and his wife away into their room; then I had the bride carried out.

"You have a daughter left," I said to them; "you must give all your care to her." I then left them to themselves.

There seemed to me no doubt that M. Alphonse had been the victim of an assassination, and the perpetrators must have found some means to get into the bride's room during the night. Those bruises, however, on the chest and the circular direction of them puzzled me much, for neither a stick nor a bar of iron could have produced them. Suddenly I recollected to have heard that in Valence the bravoes use long leather bags full of fine sand to smother people whom they want to kill. Soon, too, I remembered the muleteer from Aragon and his threat, though I could hardly think that he would take such a terrible vengeance on a light jest.

I went into the house and hunted all over for any traces of their having broken into the house, but I found none whatever. I went to the garden to see if the assassins had got in from there, but I could not find any sure indication. Last night's rain had, moreover, so soaked the ground that it would not have retained the clearest imprint. But I noticed, notwithstanding, several deep footmarks in the earth; they were in two contrary directions, but in the same line, beginning at the corner of the hedge next to the tennis ground and ending at the front door to the house. These might have been the footmarks made by M. Alphonse when he went to look for his ring on the statue's finger. On the other side the hedge at that spot was not so thick, and it must have been here that the murderers made their escape. Passing and repassing in front of the statue, I stopped short a second to look at it. I confess that this time I could not look at its expression of ironical wickedness without fear, and my head was so full of the ghastly scenes I had just witnessed that I seemed to be looking at an infernal divinity which gloated over the misfortunes that had fallen on the house.

I regained my room and remained there until noon. Then I went down and asked for news of my host and hostess. They were a little calmer. Mademoiselle de Puygarrig—or rather the widow of M. Alphonse—had regained consciousness; she had even spoken to the magistrate of Perpignan, then on a tour of inspection in Ille, and this magistrate had taken down her statement. He asked me for mine. I told him what I knew, and did not conceal my suspicions regarding the muleteer from Aragon. He gave orders for his instant arrest.

"Have you learnt anything from Madame Alphonse?" I asked the magistrate, when my deposition had been taken down and signed.

"That unhappy young lady has gone mad," he said, with a sad smile; " mad, completely mad. See what she told me:

" 'She had been in bed,' she said, 'for some moments with the curtains drawn, when the bedroom door opened and some one came in.' Now Madame Alphonse lay on the side of the bed, with her face turned to the wall. She did not stir, supposing it to be her husband. In a second the bed creaked as though it were burdened with an enormous weight. She was terribly frightened, but dared not turn round. Five minutes, or perhaps ten—she could not tell how long—passed. Then she made an involuntary movement, or else the other person who was in the bed made one, and she felt the touch of something as cold as ice—these are her very words. She sat up in the bed, trembling in every limb. Shortly after the door opened again, and some one entered, who said: 'Good-night, my little wife,' and soon after the curtains were drawn. She heard a stifled cry. The person who was in bed by her side sat up, and seemed to stretch out its arms in front. Then she turned her head round . . . and saw, so she says, her husband on his knees by the bed, with his head as high as the pillow, in the arms of a green-looking giant who was strangling him with all its might. She said—and she repeated it to me over and over twenty times, poor lady!—she said that she recognized . . . can you guess? The bronze statue of Venus belonging to M. de Peyrehorade. . . . Since it came into the country everybody dreams of it, but I will proceed with the story of the unhappy mad girl. She lost consciousness at this sight, and probably for some time her reason. She can not in any way tell how long she remained in a faint. When she came to she saw the phantom again—or the statue, as she persists in calling it—motionless, its legs and the lower half of the body in the bed, the bust and arms stretched out before it, and between its arms her lifeless husband. A cock crew, and then the statue got out of the bed, dropped the dead body, and went out. Madame Alphonse hung on to the bell, and you know the rest."

They brought in the Spaniard; he was calm, and defended himself with much coolness and presence of mind. He did not attempt to deny the remark I heard; he explained it by pretending that he meant nothing by it, but that on the following day, when he was more rested, he would have won a tennis match against his victor. I remember that he had added:

"A native of Aragon does not wait for his revenge till to-morrow when he is insulted. Had I thought M. Alphonse meant to insult me, I should have immediately stabbed him with my knife to the heart."

His shoes were compared with the footmarks in the garden; but his shoes were much larger than the marks.

Finally, the innkeeper with whom the man had lodged averred that he had spent the whole of that night in rubbing and doctoring one of his sick mules.

Moreover, this man from Aragon was quite noted and well known in the countryside, to which he came annually to trade. He was therefore released with many apologies.

I had forgotten the deposition of a servant who had been the last to see M. Alphonse alive. He saw him go up-stairs to his wife, and he had called the man and asked him in an anxious manner if he knew where I was. Then M. Alphonse heaved a sigh, and stood for a moment in silence, adding afterward:

"Well, the devil must have carried him off too!"

I asked this man if M. Alphonse had his diamond ring on when he spoke to him. The servant hesitated before he replied; then he said that he thought not, that at all events it had not attracted his attention. "If he had worn that ring," he added, correcting himself, "I should certainly have noticed it, because I believed that he had given it to Madame Alphonse."

Whilst I interrogated this man I felt a little of the superstitious horror that Madame Alphonse's deposition had spread throughout the house. The magistrate looked at me and smiled, and I refrained from pressing my questions any further.

A few hours after the funeral of M. Alphonse I prepared to leave Ille. M. de Peyrehorade's carriage was to take me to Perpignan. In spite of his state of feebleness the poor old man would accompany me to the gate of his grounds. He walked to it in silence, hardly able to drag himself along even with the help of my arm. Just as we were parting I cast a last glance at the Venus. I could see plainly that my host, although he did not share the terrors and hatred that his family felt for it, would like to get rid of the object that would ever afterward remind him of a frightful disaster. I resolved to try and persuade him to put it in a museum. I was hesitating to begin the subject when M. de Peyrehorade mechanically turned his head in the direction in which he saw me looking so attentively. He saw the statue, and immediately burst into tears. I embraced him, and, without venturing to say a single word, I stepped into the carriage.

Since my departure I have never learnt that anything was discovered to throw light on this mysterious catastrophe.

M. de Peyrehorade died some months after his son. He bequeathed me his manuscripts in his will, which some day I may publish. But I have not been able to find the treatise relating to the inscriptions on the Venus.

P. S.—My friend M. de P. has just written to me from Perpignan to tell me that the statue no longer exists. After her husband's death, the first thing Madame de Peyrehorade did was to have it melted down and made into a bell, and in this fresh form it is used in the church at Ille. But, adds M. de P., it would seem that an evil fate pursues those who possess that piece of bronze. Since that bell began to ring in Ille the vines have twice been frost-bitten.

Ligeia

Edgar Allan Poe

———◆———

And the will therein lieth, which dieth not. Who knoweth the mysteries of the will, with its vigor? For God is but a great will pervading all things by nature of its intentness. Man doth not yield himself to the angels, nor unto death utterly, save only through the weakness of his feeble will.

JOSEPH GLANVILL

I CANNOT, FOR MY SOUL, REMEMBER HOW, WHEN, OR EVEN PRECISELY WHERE, I first became acquainted with the lady Ligeia. Long years have since elapsed, and my memory is feeble through much suffering. Or, perhaps, I cannot *now* bring these points to mind, because, in truth, the character of my beloved, her rare learning, her singular yet placid cast of beauty, and the thrilling and enthralling eloquence of her low musical language, made their way into my heart by paces so steadily and stealthily progressive that they have been unnoticed and unknown. Yet I believe that I met her first and most frequently in some large, old, decaying city near the Rhine. Of her family—I have surely heard her speak. That it is of a remotely ancient date cannot be doubted. Ligeia! Ligeia! Buried in studies of a nature more than all else adapted to deaden impressions of the outward world, it is by that sweet word alone—by Ligeia— that I bring before mine eyes in fancy the image of her who is no more. And now, while I write, a recollection flashes upon me that I have *never known* the paternal name of her who was my friend and my betrothed, and who became the partner of my studies, and finally the wife of my bosom. Was it a playful charge on the part of my Ligeia? or was it a test of my strength of affection, that I should institute no inquiries upon this point? or was it rather a caprice of my own—a wildly romantic offering on the shrine of the most passionate devotion? I but indistinctly recall the fact itself—what wonder that I have utterly forgotten the circumstances which originated or attended it? And, indeed, if ever that spirit which is entitled *Romance*—if ever she, the wan and the misty-winged *Ashtophet* of idolatrous Egypt, presided, as they tell, over marriages ill-omened, then most surely she presided over mine.

There is one dear topic, however, on which my memory fails me not. It is the *person* of Ligeia. In stature she was tall, somewhat slender, and, in her latter days, even emaciated. I would in vain attempt to portray the majesty, the quiet ease, of her demeanor, or the incomprehensible lightness and elasticity of her footfall. She came and departed as a shadow. I was never made aware of her entrance into my closed study save by the dear music of her low sweet voice, as she placed her marble hand upon my shoulder. In beauty of face no maiden ever equalled her. It was the radiance of an opium dream—an airy and spirit-lifting vision more wildly divine than the phantasies which hovered about the slumbering souls of the daughters of Delos. Yet her features were not of that regular mould which we have been falsely taught to worship in the classical labors of the heathen. "There is no exquisite beauty," says Bacon, Lord Verulam, speaking truly of all the forms and *genera* of beauty, "without some *strangeness* in the proportion." Yet, although I saw that the features of Ligeia were not of a classic regularity—although I perceived that her loveliness was indeed "exquisite," and felt that there was much of "strangeness" pervading it, yet I have tried in vain to detect the irregularity and to trace home my own perception of "the strange." I examined the contour of the lofty and pale forehead—it was faultless—how cold indeed that word when applied to a majesty so divine!—the skin rivalling the purest ivory, the commanding extent and repose, the gentle prominence of the regions above the temples; and then the raven-black, the glossy, the luxuriant and naturally-curling tresses, setting forth the full force of the Homeric epithet, "hyacinthine!" I looked at the delicate outlines of the nose—and nowhere but in the graceful medallions of the Hebrews had I beheld a similar perfection. There were the same luxurious smoothness of surface, the same scarcely perceptible tendency to the aquiline, the same harmoniously curved nostrils speaking the free spirit. I regarded the sweet mouth. Here was indeed the triumph of all things heavenly—the magnificent turn of the short upper lip—the soft, voluptuous slumber of the under—the dimples which sported, and the color which spoke—the teeth glancing back, with a brilliancy almost startling, every ray of the holy light which fell upon them in her serene and placid, yet most exultingly radiant of all smiles. I scrutinized the formation of the chin—and here, too, I found the gentleness of breadth, the softness and the majesty, the fullness and the spirituality, of the Greek—the contour which the God Apollo revealed but in a dream, to Cleomenes, the son of the Athenian. And then I peered into the large eyes of Ligeia.

For eyes we have no models in the remotely antique. It might have been, too, that in these eyes of my beloved lay the secret to which Lord Verulam alludes. They were, I must believe, far larger than the ordinary eyes of our own race. They were even fuller than the fullest of the gazelle eyes of the tribe of the valley of Nourjahad. Yet it was only at intervals—in moments of intense excitement—that this peculiarity became more than slightly noticeable in Ligeia. And at such moments was her beauty—in my heated fancy thus it appeared perhaps—the beauty of beings either above or apart from the earth—the beauty of the fabulous Houri of the Turk. The hue of the orbs was the most brilliant of black, and, far over them, hung jetty lashes of great length. The brows, slightly irregular in outline, had the same tint. The "strangeness," however, which I found in the eyes, was of a nature distinct from the formation, or the color, or the brilliancy of the features, and must, after all, be referred to the *expression*. Ah, word of no meaning! behind whose vast latitude of mere sound we intrench our ignorance of so much of the spiritual. The expression of the eyes of Ligeia! How for long hours have I pondered upon it! How have I, through the whole of a midsummer night, struggled to fathom it! What was it—that something more profound than the well of Democritus—which lay far within the pupils of my beloved? What *was* it? I was possessed with a passion to discover. Those eyes! those large, those shining, those divine orbs! they became to me twin stars of Leda, and I to them devoutest of astrologers.

There is no point, among the many incomprehensible anomalies of the science of mind, more thrillingly exciting than the fact—never, I believe, noticed in the schools—that, in our endeavors to recall to memory something long forgotten, we often find ourselves *upon the very verge* of remembrance, without being able, in the end, to remember. And thus how frequently, in my intense scrutiny of Ligeia's eyes, have I felt approaching the full knowledge of their expression—felt it approaching—yet not quite be mine—and so at length entirely depart! And (strange, oh strangest mystery of all!) I found, in the commonest objects of the universe, a circle of analogies to that expression. I mean to say that, subsequently to the period when Ligeia's beauty passed into my spirit, there dwelling as in a shrine, I derived, from many existences in the material world, a sentiment such as I felt always aroused within me by her large and luminous orbs. Yet not the more could I define that sentiment, or analyze, or even steadily view it. I recognized it, let me repeat, sometimes in the survey of a rapidly-growing vine—in the contemplation of a moth, a butterfly, a chrysalis, a stream of running water. I have felt it in the ocean; in the falling of a meteor. I have felt it in the glances of unusually aged people. And there are one or two stars in heaven—(one especially, a star of the sixth magnitude, double and changeable, to be found near the large star in Lyra) in a telescopic scrutiny of which I have been made aware of the feeling. I have been filled with it by certain sounds from stringed instruments, and not unfrequently by passages from books. Among innumerable other instances, I well remember something in a volume of Joseph Glanvill, which (perhaps merely from its quaintness—who shall say?) never failed to inspire me with the sentiment;—"And the will therein lieth, which dieth not. Who knoweth the mysteries of the will, with its vigor? For God is but a great will pervading all things by nature of its intentness. Man doth not yield him to the angels, nor unto death utterly, save only through the weakness of his feeble will."

Length of years, and subsequent reflection, have enabled me to trace, indeed, some remote connection between this passage in the English moralist and a portion of the character of Ligeia. An *intensity* in thought, action, or speech, was possibly, in her, a result, or at least an index, of that gigantic volition which, during our long intercourse, failed to give other and more immediate evidence of its existence. Of all the women whom I have ever known, she, the outwardly calm, the ever-placid Ligeia, was the most violently a prey to the tumultuous vultures of stern passion. And of such passion I could form no estimate, save by the miraculous expansion of those eyes which at once so delighted and appalled me—by the almost magical melody, modulation, distinctness and placidity of her very low voice—and by the fierce energy (rendered doubly effective by contrast with her manner of utterance) of the wild words which she habitually uttered.

I have spoken of the learning of Ligeia: it was immense—such as I have never known in woman. In the classical tongues was she deeply proficient, and as far as my own acquaintance extended in regard to the modern dialects of Europe, I have never known her at fault. Indeed upon any theme of the most admired, because simply the most abstruse of the boasted erudition of the academy, have I *ever* found Ligeia at fault? How singularly—how thrillingly, this one point in the nature of my wife has forced itself, at this late period only, upon my attention! I said her knowledge was such as I have never known in woman—but where breathes the man who has traversed, and successfully, *all* the wide areas of moral, physical, and mathematical science? I saw not then what I now clearly perceive, that the acquisitions of Ligeia were gigantic, were astounding; yet I was sufficiently aware of her infinite supremacy to resign myself, with a child-like confidence, to her guidance through the chaotic world of metaphysical investigation at which I was most busily occupied during the earlier years of our marriage. With how vast a triumph—with how vivid a delight—with how much of all that is ethereal in hope—did I *feel*, as she bent over me in studies but little sought—but less known—that delicious vista by slow degrees expanding before me, down whose long, gorgeous, and all untrodden path, I might at length pass onward to the goal of a wisdom too divinely precious not to be forbidden!

How poignant, then, must have been the grief with which, after some years, I beheld my well-grounded expectations take wings to themselves and fly away! Without Ligeia I was but as a child groping benighted. Her presence, her readings alone, rendered vividly luminous the many mysteries of the transcendentalism in which we were immersed. Wanting the radiant lustre of her eyes, letters, lambent and golden, grew duller than Saturnian lead. And now those eyes shone less and less frequently upon the pages over which I pored. Ligeia grew ill. The wild eyes blazed with a too—too glorious effulgence; the pale fingers became of the transparent waxen hue of the grave, and the blue veins upon the lofty forehead swelled and sank impetuously with the tides of the most gentle emotion. I saw that she must die—and I struggled desperately in spirit with the grim Azrael. And the struggles of the passionate wife were, to my astonishment, even more energetic than my own. There had been much in her stern nature to impress me with the belief that, to her, death would have come without its terrors;—but not so. Words are impotent to convey any just idea of the fierceness of resistance with which she wrestled with the Shadow. I groaned in anguish at the pitiable spectacle. I would have soothed—I would have reasoned; but, in the intensity of her wild desire for life—for life—*but* for life—solace and reason were alike the uttermost of folly. Yet not until the last instance, amid the most convulsive writhings of her fierce spirit, was shaken the external placidity of her demeanor. Her voice grew more gentle—grew more low—yet I would not wish to dwell upon the wild meaning of the quietly uttered words. My brain reeled as I hearkened entranced, to a melody more than mortal—to assumptions and aspirations which mortality had never before known.

That she loved me I should not have doubted; and I might have been easily aware that, in a bosom such as hers, love would have reigned no ordinary passion. But in death only, was I fully impressed with the strength of her affection. For long hours, detaining my hand, would she pour out before me the overflowing of a heart whose more than passionate devotion amounted to idolatry. How had I deserved to be so blessed by such confessions?—how had I deserved to be so cursed with the removal of my beloved in the hour of her making them? But upon this subject I cannot bear to dilate. Let me say only, that in Ligeia's more than womanly abandonment to a love, alas! all unmerited, all unworthily bestowed, I at length recognized the principle of her longing with so wildly earnest a desire for the life which was now fleeing so rapidly away. It is this wild longing—it is this eager vehemence of desire for life—*but* for life—that I have no power to portray—no utterance capable of expressing.

At high noon of the night in which she departed, beckoning me, peremptorily, to her side, she bade me repeat certain verses composed by herself not many days before. I obeyed her.—They were these:

> Lo! 'tis a gala night
>   Within the lonesome latter years!
> An angel throng, bewinged, bedight
>   In veils, and drowned in tears,
> Sit in a theatre, to see
>   A play of hopes and fears,
> While the orchestra breathes fitfully
>   The music of the spheres.
>
> Mimes, in the form of God on high,
>   Mutter and mumble low,
> And hither and thither fly;—
>   Mere puppets they, who come and go
> At bidding of vast formless things
>   That shift the scenery to and fro,
> Flapping from out their Condor wings
>   Invisible Wo!
>
> That motley drama!—oh, be sure
>   It shall not be forgot!
> With its Phantom chased forevermore,
>   By a crowd that seize it not,
> Through a circle that ever returneth in
>   To the self-same spot,
> And much of Madness and more of Sin,
>   And Horror, the soul of the plot.

But see, amid the mimic rout,
    A crawling shape intrude!
A blood-red thing that writhes from out
    The scenic solitude!
It writhes!—it writhes!—with mortal pangs
    The mimes become its food,
And the seraphs sob at vermin fangs
    In human gore imbued.

Out—out are the lights—out all!
    And over each quivering form,
The curtain, a funeral pall,
    Comes down with the rush of a storm,
And the angels, all pallid and wan,
    Uprising, unveiling, affirm
That the play is the tragedy, "Man,"
    And its hero, the Conqueror Worm.

"O God!" half shrieked Ligeia, leaping to her feet and extending her arms aloft with a spasmodic movement, as I made an end of these lines—"O God! O Divine Father!—shall these things be undeviatingly so?—shall this Conqueror be not once conquered? Are we not part and parcel in Thee? Who—who knoweth the mysteries of the will with its vigor? Man doth not yield him to the angels, *nor unto death utterly*, save only through the weakness of his feeble will."

And now, as if exhausted with emotion, she suffered her white arms to fall, and returned solemnly to her bed of Death. And as she breathed her last sighs, there came mingled with them a low murmur from her lips. I bent to them my ear and distinguished, again, the concluding words of the passage in Glanvill:— *"Man doth not yield him to the angels, nor unto death utterly, save only through the weakness of his feeble will."*

She died;—and I, crushed into the very dust with sorrow, could no longer endure the lonely desolation of my dwelling in the dim and decaying city by the Rhine. I had no lack of what the world calls wealth. Ligeia had brought me far more, very far more, than ordinarily falls to the lot of mortals. After a few months, therefore, of weary and aimless wandering, I purchased, and put in some repair, an abbey, which I shall not name, in one of the wildest and least frequented portions of fair England. The gloomy and dreary grandeur of the building, the almost savage aspect of the domain, the many melancholy and time-honored memories connected with both, had much in unison with the feelings of utter abandonment which had driven me into that remote and unsocial region of the country. Yet although the external abbey, with its verdant decay hanging about it, suffered but little alteration, I gave way, with a child-like perversity, and perchance with a faint hope of alleviating my sorrows, to a display of more than regal magnificence within.—For such follies, even in childhood, I had imbibed a taste and now they came back to me as if in the dotage of grief. Alas, I feel how much even of incipient madness might have been discovered in the gorgeous and fantastic draperies, in the solemn carvings of Egypt, in the wild cornices and furniture, in the Bedlam patterns of the carpets of tufted gold! I had become a bounden slave in the trammels of opium, and my labors and my orders had taken a coloring from my dreams. But these absurdities I must not pause to detail. Let me speak only of that one chamber, ever accursed, whither in a moment of mental alienation, I led from the altar as my bride—as the successor of the unforgotten Ligeia—the fair-haired and blue-eyed Lady Rowena Trevanion, of Tremaine.

There is no individual portion of the architecture and decoration of that bridal chamber which is not now visibly before me. Where were the souls of the haughty family of the bride, when, through thirst of gold, they permitted to pass the threshold of an apartment *so* bedecked, a maiden and a daughter so beloved? I have said that I minutely remember the details of the chamber—yet I am sadly forgetful on topics of deep moment;—and here there was no system, no keeping, in the fantastic display, to take hold upon the memory. The room lay in a high turret of the castellated abbey, was pentagonal in shape, and of capacious size. Occupying the whole southern face of the pentagon was the sole window—an immense sheet of unbroken glass from Venice—a single pane, and tinted of a leaden hue, so that the rays of either the sun or moon, passing through it, fell with a ghastly lustre on the objects within. Over the upper portion of this huge window, extended the trellice-work of an aged vine, which clambered up the massy walls of the turret. The ceiling, of gloomy-looking oak, was excessively lofty, vaulted, and elaborately fretted with the wildest and most grotesque specimens of a semi-Gothic, semi-Druidical device. From out the most central recess of this melancholy vaulting, depended, by a single chain of gold with long links, a huge censer of the same metal, Saracenic in pattern, and with many perforations so contrived that there writhed in and out of them, as if endued with a serpent vitality, a continual succession of parti-colored fires.

Some few ottomans and golden candelabra, of Eastern figure, were in various stations about—and there was the couch, too—the bridal couch—of an Indian model, and low, and sculptured of solid ebony, with a pall-like canopy above. In each of the angles of the chamber stood on end a gigantic sarcophagus of black granite, from the tombs of the kings over against Luxor, with their aged lids full of immemorial sculpture. But in the draping of the apartment lay, alas! the chief phantasy of all. The lofty walls, gigantic in height—even unproportionably so—were hung from summit to foot, in vast folds, with a heavy and massive-looking tapestry—tapestry of a material which was found alike as a carpet on the floor, as a covering for the ottomans and the ebony bed, as a canopy for the bed, and as the gorgeous volutes of the curtains which partially shaded the window. The material was the richest cloth of gold. It was spotted all over, at irregular intervals, with arabesque figures, about a foot in diameter, and wrought upon the cloth in patterns of the most jetty black. But these figures partook of the true character of the arabesque only when regarded from a single point of view. By a contrivance now common, and indeed traceable to a very remote period of antiquity, they were made changeable in aspect. To one entering the room, they bore the appearance of simple monstrosities; but upon a farther advance, this appearance gradually departed; and step by step, as the visiter moved his station in the chamber, he saw himself surrounded by an endless succession of the ghastly forms which belong to the superstition of the Norman, or arise in the guilty slumbers of the monk. The phantasmagoric effect was vastly heightened by the artificial introduction of a strong continual current of wind behind the draperies—giving a hideous and uneasy animation to the whole.

In halls such as these—in a bridal chamber such as this—I passed, with the Lady of Tremaine, the unhallowed hours of the first month of our marriage—passed them with but little disquietude. That my wife dreaded the fierce moodiness of my temper—that she shunned me and loved me but little—I could not help perceiving; but it gave me rather pleasure than otherwise. I loathed her with a hatred belonging more to demon than to man. My memory flew back, (oh, with what intensity of regret!) to Ligeia, the beloved, the august, the beautiful, the entombed. I revelled in recollections of her purity, of her wisdom, of her lofty, her ethereal nature, of her passionate, her idolatrous love. Now, then, did my spirit fully and freely burn with more than all the fires of her own. In the excitement of my opium dreams (for I was habitually fettered in the shackles of the drug) I would call aloud upon her name, during the silence of the night, or among the sheltered recesses of the glens by day, as if, through the wild eagerness, the solemn passion, the consuming ardor of my longing for the departed, I could restore her to the pathway she had abandoned—ah, *could* it be forever?—upon the earth.

About the commencement of the second month of the marriage, the Lady Rowena was attacked with sudden illness, from which her recovery was slow. The fever which consumed her rendered her nights uneasy; and in her perturbed state of half-slumber, she spoke of sounds, and of motions, in and about the chamber of the turret, which I concluded had no origin save in the distemper of her fancy, or perhaps in the phantas-magoric influences of the chamber itself. She became at length convalescent—finally, well. Yet but a brief period elapsed, ere a second more violent disorder again threw her upon a bed of suffering; and from this attack her frame, at all times feeble, never altogether recovered. Her illnesses were, after this epoch, of alarming character, and of more alarming recurrence, defying alike the knowledge and the great exertions of her physicians. With the increase of the chronic disease which had thus, apparently, taken too sure hold upon her constitution to be eradicated by human means, I could not fail to observe a similar increase in the nervous irritation of her temperament, and in her excitability by trivial causes of fear. She spoke again, and now more frequently and pertinaciously, of the sounds—of the slight sounds—and of the unusual motions among the tapestries, to which she had formerly alluded.

One night, near the closing in of September, she pressed this distressing subject with more than usual emphasis upon my attention. She had just awakened from an unquiet slumber, and I had been watching, with feelings half of anxiety, half of vague terror, the workings of her emaciated countenance. I sat by the side of her ebony bed, upon one of the ottomans of India. She partly arose, and spoke, in an earnest low whisper, of sounds which she *then* heard, but which I could not hear—of motions which she *then* saw, but which I could not perceive. The wind was rushing hurriedly behind the tapestries, and I wished to show her (what, let me confess it, I could not *all* believe) that those almost inarticulate breathings, and those very gentle variations of the figures upon the wall, were but the natural effects of that customary rushing of the wind. But a deadly pallor, overspreading her face, had proved to me that my exertions to reassure her would be fruitless. She appeared to be fainting, and no atten-dants were within call. I remembered where was deposited a decanter of light wine which had been ordered by her physicians, and hastened across the chamber to procure it. But, as I stepped beneath the light of the censer, two circumstances of a startling nature attracted my attention. I had felt that some palpable although invisible object had passed lightly by my person; and I saw that there lay upon the golden carpet, in the very middle of the rich lustre thrown from the censer, a shadow—a faint, indefinite shadow of angelic aspect—such as might be fancied for the shadow of a shade. But I was wild with the excitement of an immoderate dose of opium, and heeded these things but little, nor spoke of them to Rowena. Having found the wine, I recrossed the chamber, and poured out a goblet-ful, which I held to the lips of the fainting lady. She had now partially recovered, however, and took the vessel herself, while I sank upon an ottoman near me, with my eyes fastened upon her person. It was then that I became distinctly aware of a gentle foot-fall upon the carpet, and near the couch; and in a second thereafter, as Rowena was in the act of raising the wine to her lips, I saw, or may have dreamed that I saw, fall within the goblet, as if from some invisible spring in the atmosphere of the room, three or four large drops of a brilliant and ruby colored fluid. If this I saw—not so Rowena. She swallowed the wine unhesitatingly, and I forbore to speak to her of a circumstance which must, after all, I considered, have been but the suggestion of a vivid imagination, rendered morbidly active by the terror of the lady, by the opium, and by the hour.

Yet I cannot conceal it from my own perception that, immediately subsequent to the fall of the ruby-drops, a rapid change for the worse took place in the disorder of my wife; so that, on the third subsequent night, the hands of her menials prepared her for the tomb, and on the fourth, I sat alone, with her shrouded body, in that fantastic chamber which had received her as my bride.—Wild visions, opium-engendered, flitted, shadow-like, before me. I gazed with unquiet eye upon the sarcophagi in the angles of the room, upon the varying figures of the drapery, and upon the writhing of the parti-colored fires in the censer overhead. My eyes then fell, as I called to mind the circumstances of a former night, to the spot beneath the glare of the censer where I had seen the faint traces of the shadow. It was there, however, no longer; and breathing with greater freedom, I turned my glances to the pallid and rigid figure upon the bed. Then rushed upon me a thousand memories of Ligeia—and then came back upon my heart, with the turbulent violence of a flood, the whole of that unutterable wo with which I had regarded *her* thus enshrouded. The night waned; and still, with a bosom full of bitter thoughts of the one only and supremely beloved, I remained gazing upon the body of Rowena.

It might have been midnight, or perhaps earlier, or later, for I had taken no note of time, when a sob, low, gentle, but very distinct, startled me from my revery.—I *felt* that it came from the bed of ebony—the bed of death. I listened in an agony of superstitious terror—but there was no repetition of the sound. I strained my vision to detect any motion in the corpse—but there was not the slightest perceptible. Yet I could not have been deceived. I had heard the noise, however faint, and my soul was awakened within me. I resolutely and perseveringly kept my attention riveted upon the body. Many minutes elapsed before any circumstance occurred tending to throw light upon the mystery. At length it became evident that a slight, a very feeble, and barely noticeable tinge of color had flushed up within the cheeks, and along the sunken small veins of the eyelids. Through a species of unutterable horror and awe, for which the language of mortality has no sufficiently energetic expression, I felt my heart cease to beat, my limbs grow rigid where I sat. Yet a sense of duty finally operated to restore my self-possession. I could no longer doubt that we had been precipitate in our preparations—that Rowena still lived. It was necessary that some immediate exertion be made; yet the turret was altogether apart from the portion of the abbey tenanted by the servants—there were none within call—I had no means of summoning them to my aid without leaving the room for many minutes—and this I could not venture to do. I therefore struggled alone in my endeavors to call back the spirit still hovering. In a short period it was certain, however, that a relapse had taken place; the color disappeared from both eyelid and cheek, leaving a wanness even more than that of marble; the lips became doubly shrivelled and pinched up in the ghastly expression of death; a repulsive clamminess and coldness overspread rapidly the surface of the body; and all the usual rigorous stiffness immediately supervened. I fell back with a shudder upon the couch from which I had been so startlingly aroused, and again gave myself up to passionate waking visions of Ligeia.

An hour thus elapsed when (could it be possible?) I was a second time aware of some vague sound issuing from the region of the bed. I listened—in extremity of horror. The sound came again—it was a sigh. Rushing to the corpse, I saw—distinctly saw—a tremor upon the lips. In a minute afterward they relaxed, disclosing a bright line of the pearly teeth. Amazement now struggled in my bosom with the profound awe which had hitherto reigned there alone. I felt that my vision grew dim, that my reason wandered; and it was only by a violent effort that I at length succeeded in nerving myself to the task which duty thus once more had pointed out. There was now a partial glow upon the forehead and upon the cheek and throat; a perceptible warmth pervaded the whole frame; there was even a slight pulsation at the heart. The lady *lived*; and with redoubled ardor I betook myself to the task of restoration. I chafed and bathed the temples and the hands, and used every exertion which experience, and no little medical reading, could suggest. But in vain. Suddenly, the color fled, the pulsation ceased, the lips resumed the expression of the dead, and, in an instant afterward, the whole body took upon itself the icy chilliness, the livid hue, the intense rigidity, the sunken outline, and all the loathsome peculiarities of that which has been, for many days, a tenant of the tomb.

And again I sunk into visions of Ligeia—and again, (what marvel that I shudder while I write?) *again* there reached my ears a low sob from the region of the ebony bed. But why shall I minutely detail the unspeakable horrors of that night? Why shall I pause to relate how, time after time, until near the period of the gray dawn, this hideous drama of revivification was repeated; how each terrific relapse was only into a sterner and apparently more irredeemable death; how each agony wore the aspect of a struggle with some invisible foe; and how each struggle was succeeded by I know not what of wild change in the personal appearance of the corpse? Let me hurry to a conclusion.

The greater part of the fearful night had worn away, and she who had been dead, once again stirred—and now more vigorously than hitherto, although arousing from a dissolution more appalling in its utter hopelessness than any. I had long ceased to struggle or to move, and remained sitting rigidly upon the ottoman, a helpless prey to a whirl of violent emotions, of which extreme awe was perhaps the least terrible, the least consuming. The corpse, I repeat, stirred, and now more vigorously than before. The hues of life flushed up with unwonted energy into the countenance—the limbs relaxed—and, save that the eyelids were yet pressed heavily together, and that the bandages and draperies of the grave still imparted their charnel character to the figure, I might have dreamed that Rowena had indeed shaken off, utterly, the fetters of Death. But if this idea was not, even then, altogether adopted, I could at least doubt no longer, when, arising from the bed, tottering, with feeble steps, with closed eyes, and with the manner of one bewildered in a dream, the thing that was enshrouded advanced bodily and palpably into the middle of the apartment.

I trembled not—I stirred not—for a crowd of unutterable fancies connected with the air, the stature, the demeanor of the figure, rushing hurriedly through my brain, had paralyzed—had chilled me into stone. I stirred not—but gazed upon the apparition. There was a mad disorder in my thoughts—a tumult unappeasable. Could it, indeed, be the *living* Rowena who confronted me? Could it indeed be Rowena *at all*—the fair-haired, the blue-eyed Lady Rowena Trevanion of Tremaine? Why, *why* should I doubt it? The bandage lay heavily about the mouth—but then might it not be the mouth of the breathing Lady of Tremaine? And the cheeks—there were the roses as in her noon of life—yes, these might indeed be the fair cheeks of the living Lady of Tremaine. And the chin, with its dimples, as in health, might it not be hers?—but *had she then grown taller since her malady?* What inexpressible madness seized me with that thought? One bound, and I had reached her feet! Shrinking from my touch, she let fall from her head the ghastly cerements which had confined it, and there streamed forth, into the rushing atmosphere of the chamber, huge masses of long and dishevelled hair; *it was blacker than the wings of the midnight!* And now slowly opened *the eyes* of the figure which stood before me. "Here then, at least," I shrieked aloud, "can I never—can I never be mistaken—these are the full, and the black, and the wild eyes—of my lost love—of the lady—of the LADY LIGEIA."

The Were-Wolf

H. B. Marryatt

———◆———

MY FATHER WAS NOT BORN, OR ORIGINALLY A RESIDENT, IN THE HARTZ Mountains; he was the serf of an Hungarian nobleman, of great posses- sions, in Transylvania; but, although a serf, he was not by any means a poor or illiterate man. In fact, he was rich, and his intelligence and respectability were such, that he had been raised by his lord to the stewardship; but, whoever may happen to be born a serf, a serf must he remain, even though he become a wealthy man; such was the condition of my father. My father had been married for about five years; and, by his marriage, had three children—my eldest brother Cæsar, myself (Hermann), and a sister named Marcella. Latin is still the language spoken in that country; and that will account for our high-sounding names. My mother was a very beautiful woman, unfortunately more beautiful than virtuous: she was seen and admired by the lord of the soil; my father was sent away upon some mission; and, during his absence, my mother, flattered by the attentions, and won by the assiduities, of this nobleman, yielded to his wishes. It so happened that my father returned very unexpectedly, and discovered the intrigue. The evidence of my mother's shame was positive: he surprised her in the company of her seducer! Carried away by the impetuosity of his feelings, he watched the opportunity of a meeting taking place between them, and murdered both his wife and her seducer. Conscious that, as a serf, not even the provocation which he had received would be allowed as a justification of his conduct, he hastily collected together what money he could lay his hands upon, and, as we were then in the depth of winter, he put his horses to the sleigh, and taking his children with him, he set off in the middle of the night, and was far away before the tragical circumstance had transpired. Aware that he would be pursued, and that he had no chance of escape if he remained in any portion of his native country (in which the authorities could lay hold of him), he continued his flight without intermission until he had buried himself in the intricacies and seclusion of the Hartz Mountains. Of course, all that I have now told you I learned afterwards. My oldest recollections are knit to a rude, yet comfortable cottage, in which I lived with my father, brother, and sister. It was on the confines of one of those vast forests which cover the northern part of Germany; around it were a few acres of ground, which, during the summer months, my father cultivated, and which, though they yielded a doubtful harvest, were sufficient for our support. In the winter we remained much in doors, for, as my father followed the chase, we were left alone, and the wolves, during that season, incessantly prowled about. My father had purchased the cottage, and land about it, of one of the rude foresters, who gain their livelihood partly by hunting, and partly by burning charcoal, for the purpose of smelting the ore from the neighbouring mines; it was distant about two miles from any other habitation. I can call to mind the whole landscape now: the tall pines which rose up on the mountain above us, and the wide expanse of forest beneath, on the topmost boughs and heads of whose trees we looked down from our cottage, as the mountain below us rapidly descended into the distant valley. In summer time the prospect was beautiful; but during the severe winter, a more desolate scene could not well be imagined.

I said that, in the winter, my father occupied himself with the chase; every day he left us, and often would he lock the door, that we might not leave the cottage. He had no one to assist him, or to take care of us—indeed, it was not easy to find a female servant who would live in such a solitude; but, could he have found one, my father would not have received her, for he had imbibed a horror of the sex, as a difference of his conduct toward us, his two boys, and my poor little sister, Marcella, evidently proved. You may suppose we were sadly neglected; indeed, we suffered much, for my father, fearful that we might come to some harm, would not allow us fuel, when he left the cottage; and we were obliged, therefore, to creep under the heaps of bears'-skins, and there to keep ourselves as warm as we could until he returned in the evening, when a blazing fire was our delight. That my father chose this restless sort of life may appear strange, but the fact was that he could not remain quiet; whether from remorse for having committed murder, or from the misery consequent on his change of situation, or from both combined, he was never happy unless he was in a state of activity. Children, however, when left much to themselves, acquire a thoughtfulness not common to their age. So it was with us; and during the short cold days of winter we would sit silent, longing for the happy hours when the snow would melt, and the leaves burst out, and the birds begin their songs, and when we should again be set at liberty.

Such was our peculiar and savage sort of life until my brother Cæsar was nine, myself seven, and my sister five, years old, when the circumstances occurred on which is based the extraordinary narrative which I am about to relate.

One evening my father returned home rather later than usual; he had been unsuccessful, and, as the weather was very severe, and many feet of snow were upon the ground, he was not only very cold, but in a very bad humour. He had brought in wood, and we were all three of us gladly assisting each other in blowing on the embers to create the blaze, when he caught poor little Marcella by the arm and threw her aside; the child fell, struck her mouth, and bled very much. My brother ran to raise her up. Accustomed to ill usage, and afraid of my father, she did not dare to cry, but looked up in his face very piteously. My father drew his stool nearer to the hearth, muttered something in abuse of women, and busied himself with the fire, which both my brother and I had deserted when our sister was so unkindly treated. A cheerful blaze was soon the result of his exertions; but we did not, as usual, crowd round it. Marcella, still bleeding, retired to a corner, and my brother and I took our seats beside her, while my father hung over the fire gloomily and alone. Such had been our position for about half-an-hour, when the howl of a wolf, close under the window of the cottage, fell on our ears. My father started up, and seized his gun; the howl was repeated, he examined the priming, and then hastily left the cottage, shutting the door after him. We all waited (anxiously listening), for we thought that if he succeeded in shooting the wolf, he would return in a better humour; and although he was harsh to all of us, and particularly so to our little sister, still we loved our father, and loved to see him cheerful and happy, for what else had we to look up to? And I may here observe, that perhaps there never were three children who were fonder of each other; we did not, like other children, fight and dispute together; and if, by chance, any disagreement did arise between my elder brother and me, little Marcella would run to us, and kissing us both, seal, through her entreaties, the peace between us. Marcella was a lovely, amiable child; I can recall her beautiful features even now—Alas! poor little Marcella.

We waited for some time, but the report of the gun did not reach us, and my elder brother then said, "Our father has followed the wolf, and will not be back for some time. Marcella, let us wash the blood from your mouth, and then we will leave this corner, and go to the fire and warm ourselves."

We did so, and remained there until near midnight, every minute wondering, as it grew later, why our father did not return. We had no idea that he was in any danger, but we thought that he must have chased the wolf for a very long time. "I will look out and see if father is coming," said my brother Cæsar, going to the door. "Take care," said Marcella, "the wolves must be about now, and we cannot kill them, brother." My brother opened the door very cautiously, and but a few inches; he peeped out.— "I see nothing," said he, after a time, and once more he joined us at the fire. "We have had no supper," said I, for my father usually cooked the meat as soon as he came home; and during his absence we had nothing but the fragments of the preceding day.

"And if our father comes home after his hunt, Cæsar," said Marcella, "he will be pleased to have some supper; let us cook it for him and for ourselves." Cæsar climbed upon the stool, and reached down some meat—I forget now whether it was venison or bear's meat; but we cut off the usual quantity, and proceeded to dress it, as we used to do under our father's superintendence. We were all busied putting it into the platters before the fire, to await his coming, when we heard the sound of a horn. We listened— there was a noise outside, and a minute afterwards my father entered, ushering in a young female, and a large dark man in a hunter's dress.

Perhaps I had better now relate, what was only known to me many years after- wards. When my father had left the cottage, he perceived a large white wolf about thirty yards from him; as soon as the animal saw my father, it retreated slowly, growl- ing and snarling. My father followed; the animal did not run, but always kept at some distance; and my father did not like to fire until he was pretty certain that his ball would take effect: thus they went on for some time, the wolf now leaving my father far behind, and then stopping and snarling defiance at him, and then again, on his approach, setting off at speed.

Anxious to shoot the animal (for the white wolf is very rare), my father continued the pursuit for several hours, during which he continually ascended the mountain.

You must know that there are peculiar spots on those mountains which are supposed, and, as my story will prove, truly supposed, to be inhabited by the evil influences; they are well known to the huntsmen, who invariably avoid them. Now, one of these spots, an open space in the pine forests above us, had been pointed out to my father as dangerous on that account. But, whether he disbelieved these wild stories, or whether, in his eager pursuit of the chase, he disregarded them, I know not; certain, however, it is that he was decoyed by the white wolf to this open space, when the ani- mal appeared to slacken her speed. My father approached, came close up to her, raised his gun to his shoulder, and was about to fire, when the wolf suddenly disappeared. He thought that the snow on the ground must have dazzled his sight, and he let down his gun to look for the beast—but she was gone; how she could have escaped over the clearance, without his seeing her, was beyond his comprehension. Mortified at the ill success of his chase, he was about to retrace his steps, when he heard the distant sound of a horn. Astonishment at such a sound—at such an hour—in such a wilderness, made him forget for the moment his disappointment, and he remained riveted to the spot. In a minute the horn was blown a second time, and at no great distance; my father stood still, and listened: a third time it was blown. I forget the term used to express it, but it was the signal which, my father well knew, implied that the party was lost in the woods. In a few minutes more my father beheld a man on horseback, with a female seated on the crupper, enter the cleared space, and ride up to him. At first, my father called to mind the strange stories which he had heard of the supernatural beings who were said to frequent these mountains; but the nearer approach of the parties satisfied him that they were mortals like himself. As soon as they came up to him, the man who guided the horse accosted him. "Friend Hunter, you are out late, the better fortune for us: we have ridden far, and are in fear of our lives, which are eagerly sought after. These mountains have enabled us to elude our pursuers; but if we find not shelter and refreshment, that will avail us little, as we must perish from hunger and the inclemency of the night. My daughter, who rides behind me, is now more dead than alive—say, can you assist us in our difficulty?"

"My cottage is some few miles distant," replied my father, " but I have little to offer you besides a shelter from the weather; to the little I have you are welcome. May I ask whence you come?"

"Yes, friend, it is no secret now; we have escaped from Transylvania, where my daughter's honour and my life were equally in jeopardy!"

This information was quite enough to raise an interest in my father's heart. He remembered his own escape: he remembered the loss of his wife's honour, and the tragedy by which it was wound up. He immediately, and warmly, offered all the assistance which he could afford them.

"There is no time to be lost, then, good sir," observed the horseman; "my daughter is chilled with the frost, and cannot hold out much longer against the severity of the weather."

"Follow me," replied my father, leading the way towards his home.

"I was lured away in pursuit of a large white wolf," observed my father; " it came to the very window of my hut, or I should not have been out at this time of night."

"The creature passed by us just as we came out of the wood," said the female in a silvery tone.

"I was nearly discharging my piece at it," observed the hunter; "but since it did us such good service, I am glad that I allowed it to escape."

In about an hour and a half, during which my father walked at a rapid pace, the party arrived at the cottage, and, as I said before, came in.

"We are in good time, apparently," observed the dark hunter, catching the smell of the roasted meat, as he walked to the fire and surveyed my brother and sister, and myself. "You have young cooks here, Mynheer." "I am glad that we shall not have to wait," replied my father. "Come, mistress, seat yourself by the fire; you require warmth after your cold ride." "And where can I put up my horse, Mynheer?" observed the huntsman. "I will take care of him," replied my father, going out of the cottage door.

The female must, however, be particularly described. She was young, and apparently twenty years of age. She was dressed in a travelling dress, deeply bordered with white fur, and wore a cap of white ermine on her head. Her features were very beautiful, at least I thought so, and so my father has since declared. Her hair was flaxen, glossy and shining, and bright as a mirror; and her mouth, although somewhat large when it was open, showed the most brilliant teeth I have ever beheld. But there was something about her eyes, bright as they were, which made us children afraid; they were so restless, so furtive; I could not at that time tell why, but I felt as if there was cruelty in her eye; and when she beckoned us to come to her, we approached her with fear and trembling. Still she was beautiful, very beautiful. She spoke kindly to my brother and myself, patted our heads, and caressed us; but Marcella would not come near her; on the contrary, she slunk away, and hid herself in the bed, and would not wait for the supper, which half an hour before she had been so anxious for.

My father, having put the horse into a close shed, soon returned, and supper was placed upon the table. When it was over, my father requested that the young lady would take possession of his bed, and he would remain at the fire, and sit up with her father. After some hesitation on her part, this arrangement was agreed to, and I and my brother crept into the other bed with Marcella, for we had as yet always slept together.

But we could not sleep; there was something so unusual, not only in seeing strange people, but in having those people sleep at the cottage, that we were bewildered. As for poor little Marcella, she was quiet, but I perceived that she trembled during the whole night, and sometimes I thought that she was checking a sob. My father had brought out some spirits, which he rarely used, and he and the strange hunter remained drinking and talking before the fire. Our ears were ready to catch the slightest whisper—so much was our curiosity excited.

"You said you came from Transylvania?" observed my father.

"Even so, Mynheer," replied the hunter. "I was a serf to the noble house of ———; my master would insist upon my surrendering up my fair girl to his wishes; it ended in my giving him a few inches of my hunting-knife."

"We are countrymen, and brothers in misfortune," replied my father, taking the huntsman's hand, and pressing it warmly.

"Indeed! Are you, then, from that country?"

"Yes; and I too have fled for my life. But mine is a melancholy tale."

"Your name?" inquired the hunter.

"Krantz."

"What! Krantz of—I have heard your tale; you need not renew your grief by repeating it now. Welcome, most welcome, Mynheer, and, I may say, my worthy kinsman. I am your second cousin, Wilfred of Barnsdorf," cried the hunter, rising up and embracing my father.

They filled their horn mugs to the brim, and drank to one another, after the German fashion. The conversation was then carried on in a low tone; all that we could collect from it was, that our new relative and his daughter were to take up their abode in our cottage, at least for the present. In about an hour they both fell back in their chairs, and appeared to sleep.

"Marcella, dear, did you hear?" said my brother in a low tone.

"Yes," replied Marcella, in a whisper; "I heard all. Oh! brother, I cannot bear to look upon that woman— I feel so frightened."

My brother made no reply, and shortly afterwards we were all three fast asleep.

When we awoke the next morning, we found that the hunter's daughter had risen before us. I thought she looked more beautiful than ever. She came up to little Marcella and caressed her; the child burst into tears, and sobbed as if her heart would break.

But, not to detain you with too long a story, the huntsman and his daughter were accommodated in the cottage. My father and he went out hunting daily, leaving Christina with us. She performed all the household duties; was very kind to us children; and, gradually, the dislike even of little Marcella wore away. But a great change took place in my father; he appeared to have conquered his aversion to the sex, and was most attentive to Christina. Often, after her father and we were in bed, would he sit up with her, conversing in a low tone by the fire. I ought to have mentioned, that my father and the huntsman Wilfred, slept in another portion of the cottage, and that the bed which he formerly occupied, and which was in the same room as ours, had been given up to the use of Christina. These visitors had been about three weeks at the cottage, when, one night, after we children had been sent to bed, a consultation was held. My father had asked Christina in marriage, and had obtained both her own consent and that of Wilfred; after this a conversation took place, which was, as nearly as I can recollect, as follows:

"You may take my child, Mynheer Krantz, and my blessing with her, and I shall then leave you and seek some other habitation—it matters little where."

"Why not remain here, Wilfred?"

"No, no, I am called elsewhere; let that suffice, and ask no more questions. You have my child."

"I thank you for her, and will duly value her; but there is one difficulty."

"I know what you would say; there is no priest here in this wild country: true, neither is there any law to bind; still must some ceremony pass between you, to satisfy a father. Will you consent to marry her after my fashion? if so, I will marry you directly."

"I will," replied my father.

"Then take her by the hand. Now, Mynheer, swear."

"I swear," repeated my father.

"By all the spirits of the Hartz Mountains—"

"Nay, why not by Heaven? " interrupted my father.

"Because it is not my humour," rejoined Wilfred; "if I prefer that oath, less binding perhaps, than another, surely you will not thwart me."

"Well, be it so then; have your humour. Will you make me swear by that in which I do not believe?"

"Yet many do so, who in outward appearance are Christians," rejoined Wilfred; "say, will you be married, or shall I take my daughter away with me?"

"Proceed," replied my father, impatiently.

"I swear by all the spirits of the Hartz Mountains, by all their power for good or for evil, that I take Christina for my wedded wife; that I will ever protect her, cherish her, and love her; that my hand shall never be raised against her to harm her."

My father repeated the words after Wilfred.

"And if I fail in this, my vow, may all the vengeance of the spirits fall upon me and upon my children; may they perish by the vulture, by the wolf, or other beasts of the forest; may their flesh be torn from their limbs, and their bones blanch in the wilderness; all this I swear."

My father hesitated, as he repeated the last words; little Marcella could not restrain herself, and as my father repeated the last sentence, she burst into tears. This sudden interruption appeared to discompose the party, particularly my father; he spoke harshly to the child, who controlled her sobs, burying her face under the bed-clothes.

Such was the second marriage of my father. The next morning, the hunter Wilfred mounted his horse and rode away.

My father resumed his bed, which was in the same room as ours; and things went on much as before the marriage, except that our new mother-in-law did not show any kindness towards us; indeed, during my father's absence, she would often beat us, particularly little Marcella, and her eyes would flash fire, as she looked eagerly upon the fair and lovely child.

One night, my sister awoke me and my brother.

"What is the matter?" said Cæsar.

"She has gone out," whispered Marcella.

"Gone out!"

"Yes, gone out at the door, in her night-clothes," replied the child; "I saw her get out of bed, look at my father to see if he slept, and then she went out at the door."

What could induce her to leave her bed, and all undressed to go out, in such bitter wintry weather, with the snow deep on the ground, was to us incomprehensible; we lay awake, and in about an hour we heard the growl of a wolf, close under the window.

"There is a wolf," said Cæsar, "she will be torn to pieces."

"Oh, no!" cried Marcella.

In a few minutes afterwards our mother-in-law appeared; she was in her night-dress, as Marcella had stated. She let down the latch of the door, so as to make no noise, went to a pail of water, and washed her face and hands, and then slipped into the bed where my father lay.

We all three trembled, we hardly knew why, but we resolved to watch the next night: we did so—and not only on the ensuing night, but on many others, and always at about the same hour, would our mother-in-law rise from her bed, and leave the cottage—and after she was gone, we invariably heard the growl of a wolf under our window, and always saw her, on her return, wash herself before she retired to bed. We observed, also, that she seldom sat down to meals, and that when she did, she appeared to eat with dislike; but when the meat was taken down, to be prepared for dinner, she would often furtively put a raw piece into her mouth.

My brother Cæsar was a courageous boy; he did not like to speak to my father until he knew more. He resolved that he would follow her out, and ascertain what she did. Marcella and I endeavoured to dissuade him from this project; but he would not be controlled, and, the very next night he lay down in his clothes, and as soon as our mother-in-law had left the cottage, he jumped up, took down my father's gun, and followed her.

You may imagine in what a state of suspense Marcella and I remained, during his absence. After a few minutes, we heard the report of a gun. It did not awaken my father, and we lay trembling with anxiety. In a minute afterwards we saw our mother-in-law enter the cottage—her dress was bloody. I put my hand to Marcella's mouth to prevent her crying out, although I was myself in great alarm. Our mother-in-law approached my father's bed, looked to see if he was asleep, and then went to the chimney, and blew up the embers into a blaze.

"Who is there?" said my father, waking up.

"Lie still, dearest," replied my mother-in-law, "it is only me; I have lighted the fire to warm some water; I am not quite well."

My father turned round and was soon asleep; but we watched our mother-in-law. She changed her linen, and threw the garments she had worn into the fire; and we then perceived that her right leg was bleeding profusely, as if from a gun-shot wound. She bandaged it up, and then dressing herself, remained before the fire until the break of day.

Poor little Marcella, her heart beat quick as she pressed me to her side—so indeed did mine. Where was our brother, Cæsar? How did my mother-in-law receive the wound unless from his gun? At last my father rose, and then, for the first time I spoke, saying, "Father, where is my brother, Cæsar?"

"Your brother!" exclaimed he, "why, where can he be?"

"Merciful Heaven! I thought as I lay very restless last night," observed our mother-in-law, "that I heard somebody open the latch of the door; and, dear me, husband, what has become of your gun?"

My father cast his eyes up above the chimney, and perceived that his gun was missing. For a moment he looked perplexed, then seizing a broad axe, he went out of the cottage without saying another word.

He did not remain away from us long: in a few minutes he returned, bearing in his arms the mangled body of my poor brother; he laid it down, and covered up his face.

My mother-in-law rose up, and looked at the body, while Marcella and I threw ourselves by its side wailing and sobbing bitterly.

"Go to bed again, children," said she sharply. "Husband," continued she, "your boy must have taken the gun down to shoot a wolf, and the animal has been too powerful for him. Poor boy! He has paid dearly for his rashness."

My father made no reply; I wished to speak—to tell all—but Marcella, who perceived my intention, held me by the arm, and looked at me so imploringly, that I desisted.

My father, therefore, was left in his error; but Marcella and I, although we could not comprehend it, were conscious that our mother-in-law was in some way connected with my brother's death.

That day my father went out and dug a grave, and when he laid the body in the earth, he piled up stones over it, so that the wolves should not be able to dig it up. The shock of this catastrophe was to my poor father very severe; for several days he never went to the chase, although at times he would utter bitter anathemas and vengeance against the wolves.

But during this time of mourning on his part, my mother-in-law's nocturnal wanderings continued with the same regularity as before.

At last, my father took down his gun, to repair to the forest; but he soon returned, and appeared much annoyed.

"Would you believe it, Christina, that the wolves—perdition to the whole race—have actually contrived to dig up the body of my poor boy, and now there is nothing left of him but his bones?"

"Indeed!" replied my mother-in-law. Marcella looked at me, and I saw in her intelligent eye all she would have uttered.

"A wolf growls under our window every night, father," said I.

"Aye, indeed?—why did you not tell me, boy?—wake me the next time you hear it."

I saw my mother-in-law turn away; her eyes flashed fire, and she gnashed her teeth.

My father went out again, and covered up with a larger pile of stones the little remnants of my poor brother which the wolves had spared. Such was the first act of the tragedy.

The spring now came on: the snow disappeared, and we were permitted to leave the cottage; but never would I quit, for one moment, my dear little sister, to whom, since the death of my brother, I was more ardently attached than ever; indeed I was afraid to leave her alone with my mother-in-law, who appeared to have a particular pleasure in ill-treating the child. My father was now employed upon his little farm, and I was able to render him some assistance.

Marcella used to sit by us while we were at work, leaving my mother-in-law alone in the cottage. I ought to observe that, as the spring advanced, so did my mother decrease her nocturnal rambles, and that we never heard the growl of the wolf under the window after I had spoken of it to my father.

One day, when my father and I were in the field, Marcella being with us, my mother-in-law came out, saying that she was going into the forest, to collect some herbs my father wanted, and that Marcella must go to the cottage and watch the dinner. Marcella went, and my mother-in-law soon disappeared in the forest, taking a direction quite contrary to that in which the cottage stood, and leaving my father and I, as it were, between her and Marcella.

About an hour afterwards we were startled by shrieks from the cottage, evidently the shrieks of little Marcella. "Marcella has burnt herself, father," said I, throwing down my spade. My father threw down his, and we both hastened to the cottage. Before we could gain the door, out darted a large white wolf, which fled with the utmost celerity. My father had no weapon; he rushed into the cottage, and there saw poor little Marcella expiring; her body was dreadfully mangled, and the blood pouring from it had formed a large pool on the cottage floor. My father's first intention had been to seize his gun and pursue, but he was checked by this horrid spectacle; he knelt down by his dying child, and burst into tears: Marcella could just look kindly on us for a few seconds, and then her eyes were closed in death.

My father and I were still hanging over my poor sister's body, when my mother-in-law came in. At the dreadful sight she expressed much concern, but she did not appear to recoil from the sight of blood, as most women do.

"Poor child!" said she, "it must have been that great white wolf which passed me just now, and frightened me so—she's quite dead, Krantz."

"I know it—I know it!" cried my father in agony.

I thought my father would never recover from the effects of this second tragedy: he mourned bitterly over the body of his sweet child, and for several days would not consign it to its grave, although frequently requested by my mother-in-law to do so. At last he yielded, and dug a grave for her close by that of my poor brother, and took every precaution that the wolves should not violate her remains.

I was now really miserable, as I lay alone in the bed which I had formerly shared with my brother and sister. I could not help thinking that my mother-in-law was implicated in both their deaths, although I could not account for the manner; but I no longer felt afraid of her: my little heart was full of hatred and revenge.

The night after my sister had been buried, as I lay awake, I perceived my mother-in-law get up and go out of the cottage. I waited for some time, then dressed myself, and looked out through the door, which I half-opened. The moon shone bright, and I could see the spot where my brother and my sister had been buried; and what was my horror, when I perceived my mother-in-law busily removing the stones from Marcella's grave.

She was in her white night-dress, and the moon shone full upon her. She was digging with her hands, and throwing away the stones behind her with all the ferocity of a wild beast. It was some time before I could collect my senses and decide what I should do. At last, I perceived that she had arrived at the body, and raised it up to the side of the grave. I could bear it no longer; I ran to my father and awoke him.

"Father! father!" cried I, "dress yourself, and get your gun."

"What!" cried my father, "the wolves are there, are they?"

He jumped out of bed, threw on his clothes, and in his anxiety did not appear to perceive the absence of his wife. As soon as he was ready, I opened the door, he went out, and I followed him.

Imagine his horror, when (unprepared as he was for such a sight) he beheld, as he advanced towards the grave, not a wolf, but his wife, in her night-dress, on her hands and knees, crouching by the body of my sister, and tearing off large pieces of the flesh, and devouring them with all the avidity of a wolf. She was too busy to be aware of our approach. My father dropped his gun, his hair stood on end; so did mine; he breathed heavily, and then his breath for a time stopped. I picked up the gun and put it into his hand. Suddenly he appeared as if concentrated rage had restored him to double vigour; he levelled his piece, fired, and with a loud shriek, down fell the wretch whom he had fostered in his bosom.

"God of Heaven!" cried my father, sinking down upon the earth in a swoon, as soon as he had discharged his gun.

I remained some time by his side before he recovered. "Where am I?" said he, "what has happened?—Oh!—yes, yes! I recollect now. Heaven forgive me!"

He rose and we walked up to the grave; what again was our astonishment and horror to find that instead of the dead body of my mother-in-law, as we expected, there was lying over the remains of my poor sister, a large, white she wolf.

"The white wolf!" exclaimed my father, "the white wolf which decoyed me into the forest—I see it all now—I have dealt with the spirits of the Hartz Mountains."

For some time my father remained in silence and deep thought. He then carefully lifted up the body of my sister, replaced it in the grave, and covered it over as before, having struck the head of the dead animal with the heel of his boot, and raving like a madman. He walked back to the cottage, shut the door, and threw himself on the bed; I did the same, for I was in a stupor of amazement.

Early in the morning we were both roused by a loud knocking at the door, and in rushed the hunter Wilfred.

"My daughter!—man—my daughter!—where is my daughter!" cried he in a rage.

"Where the wretch, the fiend, should be, I trust," replied my father, starting up and displaying equal choler; "where she should be—in hell!—Leave this cottage or you may fare worse."

"Ha-ha!" replied the hunter, "would you harm a potent spirit of the Hartz Mountains? Poor mortal, who must needs wed a were wolf."

"Out, demon! I defy thee and thy power."

"Yet shall you feel it; remember your oath—your solemn oath—never to raise your hand against her to harm her."

"I made no compact with evil spirits."

"You did; and if you failed in your vow, you were to meet the vengeance of the spirits. Your children were to perish by the vulture, the wolf——"

"Out, out, demon!"

"And their bones blanch in the wilderness. Ha!-ha!"

My father, frantic with rage, seized his axe, and raised it over Wilfred's head to strike.

"All this I swear," continued the huntsman, mockingly.

The axe descended; but it passed through the form of the hunter, and my father lost his balance, and fell heavily on the floor.

"Mortal!" said the hunter, striding over my father's body, "we have power over those only who have committed murder. You have been guilty of a double murder—you shall pay the penalty attached to your marriage vow. Two of your children are gone; the third is yet to follow—and follow them he will, for your oath is registered. Go—it were kindness to kill thee—your punishment is—that you live!"

Ethan Brand

A CHAPTER FROM AN ABORTIVE ROMANCE

Nathaniel Hawthorne

———◆———

BARTRAM THE LIME-BURNER, A ROUGH, HEAVY-LOOKING MAN, BEGRIMED with charcoal, sat watching his kiln, at nightfall, while his little son played at building houses with the scattered fragments of marble, when, on the hillside below them, they heard a roar of laughter, not mirthful, but slow, and even solemn, like a wind shaking the boughs of the forest.

"Father, what is that?" asked the little boy, leaving his play, and pressing betwixt his father's knees.

"O, some drunken man, I suppose," answered the lime-burner; "some merry fellow from the bar-room in the village, who dared not laugh loud enough within doors lest he should blow the roof of the house off. So here he is, shaking his jolly sides at the foot of Graylock."

"But, father," said the child, more sensitive than the obtuse, middle-aged clown, "he does not laugh like a man that is glad. So the noise frightens me!"

"Don't be a fool, child! " cried his father, gruffly. "You will never make a man, I do believe; there is too much of your mother in you. I have known the rustling of a leaf startle you. Hark! Here comes the merry fellow now. You shall see that there is no harm in him."

Bartram and his little son, while they were talking thus, sat watching the same lime-kiln that had been the scene of Ethan Brand's solitary and meditative life, before he began his search for the Unpardonable Sin. Many years, as we have seen, had now elapsed, since that portentous night when the Idea was first developed. The kiln, however, on the mountain-side, stood unimpaired, and was in nothing changed since he had thrown his dark thoughts into the intense glow of its furnace, and melted them, as it were, into the one thought that took possession of his life. It was a rude, round, tower-like structure, about twenty feet high, heavily built of rough stones, and with a hillock of earth heaped about the larger part of its circumference; so that the blocks and fragments of marble might be drawn by cart-loads, and thrown in at the top. There was an opening at the bottom of the tower, like an oven-mouth, but large enough to admit a man in a stooping posture, and provided with a massive iron door. With the smoke and jets of flame issuing from the chinks and crevices of this door, which seemed to give admittance into the hillside, it resembled nothing so much as the private entrance to the infernal regions, which the shepherds of the Delectable Mountains were accustomed to show to pilgrims.

There are many such lime-kilns in that tract of country, for the purpose of burning the white marble which composes a large part of the substance of the hills. Some of them, built years ago, and long deserted, with weeds growing in the vacant round of the interior, which is open to the sky, and grass and wild-flowers rooting themselves into the chinks of the stones, look already like relics of antiquity, and may yet be overspread with the lichens of centuries to come. Others, where the lime-burner still feeds his daily and night-long fire, afford points of interest to the wanderer among the hills, who seats himself on a log of wood or a fragment of marble, to hold a chat with the solitary man. It is a lonesome, and, when the character is inclined to thought, may be an intensely thoughtful occupation; as it proved in the case of Ethan Brand, who had mused to such strange purpose, in days gone by, while the fire in this very kiln was burning.

The man who now watched the fire was of a different order, and troubled himself with no thoughts save the very few that were requisite to his business. At frequent intervals, he flung back the clashing weight of the iron door, and, turning his face from the insufferable glare, thrust in huge logs of oak, or stirred the immense brands with a long pole. Within the furnace were seen the curling and riotous flames, and the burning marble, almost molten with the intensity of heat; while without, the reflection of the fire quivered on the dark intricacy of the surrounding forest, and showed in the foreground a bright and ruddy little picture of the hut, the spring beside its door, the athletic and coal-begrimed figure of the lime-burner, and the half-frightened child, shrinking into the protection of his father's shadow. And when again the iron door was closed, then reappeared the tender light of the half-full moon, which vainly strove to trace out the indistinct shapes of the neighboring mountains; and, in the upper sky, there was a flitting congregation of clouds, still faintly tinged with the rosy sunset, though thus far down into the valley the sunshine had vanished long and long ago.

The little boy now crept still closer to his father, as footsteps were heard ascending the hillside, and a human form thrust aside the bushes that clustered beneath the trees.

"Halloo! who is it?" cried the lime-burner, vexed at his son's timidity, yet half infected by it. "Come forward, and show yourself, like a man, or I'll fling this chunk of marble at your head!"

"You offer me a rough welcome," said a gloomy voice, as the unknown man drew nigh. "Yet I neither claim nor desire a kinder one, even at my own fireside."

To obtain a distincter view, Bartram threw open the iron door of the kiln, whence immediately issued a gush of fierce light, that smote full upon the stranger's face and figure. To a careless eye there appeared nothing very remarkable in his aspect, which was that of a man in a coarse, brown, country-made suit of clothes, tall and thin, with the staff and heavy shoes of a wayfarer. As he advanced, he fixed his eyes—which were very bright—intently upon the brightness of the furnace, as if he beheld, or expected to behold, some object worthy of note within it.

"Good evening, stranger," said the lime-burner; "whence come you, so late in the day?"

"I come from my search," answered the wayfarer; "for, at last, it is finished."

"Drunk!—or crazy!" muttered Bartram to himself. "I shall have trouble with the fellow. The sooner I drive him away, the better."

The little boy, all in a tremble, whispered to his father, and begged him to shut the door of the kiln, so that there might not be so much light; for that there was something in the man's face which he was afraid to look at, yet could not look away from. And, indeed, even the lime-burner's dull and torpid sense began to be impressed by an indescribable something in that thin, rugged, thoughtful visage, with the grizzled hair hanging wildly about it, and those deeply sunken eyes, which gleamed like fires within the entrance of a mysterious cavern. But, as he closed the door, the stranger turned towards him, and spoke in a quiet, familiar way, that made Bartram feel as if he were a sane and sensible man, after all.

"Your task draws to an end, I see," said he. "This marble has already been burning three days. A few hours more will convert the stone to lime."

"Why, who are you?" exclaimed the lime-burner. "You seem as well acquainted with my business as I am myself."

"And well I may be," said the stranger; "for I followed the same craft many a long year, and here, too, on this very spot. But you are a new-comer in these parts. Did you never hear of Ethan Brand?"

"The man that went in search of the Unpardonable Sin?" asked Bartram, with a laugh.

"The same," answered the stranger. "He has found what he sought, and therefore he comes back again."

"What! then you are Ethan Brand himself?" cried the lime-burner, in amazement. "I am a new-comer here, as you say, and they call it eighteen years since you left the foot of Graylock. But, I can tell you, the good folks still talk about Ethan Brand, in the village yonder, and what a strange errand took him away from his lime-kiln. Well, and so you have found the Unpardonable Sin?"

"Even so!" said the stranger, calmly.

"If the question is a fair one," proceeded Bartram, "where might it be?"

Ethan Brand laid his finger on his own heart.

"Here!" replied he.

And then, without mirth in his countenance, but as if moved by an involuntary recognition of the infinite absurdity of seeking throughout the world for what was the closest of all things to himself, and looking into every heart, save his own, for what was hidden in no other breast, he broke into a laugh of scorn. It was the same slow, heavy laugh, that had almost appalled the lime-burner when it heralded the wayfarer's approach.

The solitary mountain-side was made dismal by it. Laughter, when out of place, mistimed, or bursting forth from a disordered state of feeling, may be the most terrible modulation of the human voice. The laughter of one asleep, even if it be a little child,—the madman's laugh,—the wild, screaming laugh of a born idiot,—are sounds that we sometimes tremble to hear, and would always willingly forget. Poets have imagined no utterance of fiends or hobgoblins so fearfully appropriate as a laugh. And even the obtuse lime-burner felt his nerves shaken, as this strange man looked inward at his own heart, and burst into laughter that rolled away into the night, and was indistinctly reverberated among the hills.

"Joe," said he to his little son, "scamper down to the tavern in the village, and tell the jolly fellows there that Ethan Brand has come back, and that he has found the Unpardonable Sin!"

The boy darted away on his errand, to which Ethan Brand made no objection, nor seemed hardly to notice it. He sat on a log of wood, looking steadfastly at the iron door of the kiln. When the child was out of sight, and his swift and light footsteps ceased to be heard treading first on the fallen leaves and then on the rocky mountain-path, the lime-burner began to regret his departure. He felt that the little fellow's presence had been a barrier between his guest and himself, and that he must now deal, heart to heart, with a man who, on his own confession, had committed the one only crime for which Heaven could afford no mercy. That crime, in its indistinct blackness, seemed to over-shadow him. The lime-burner's own sins rose up within him, and made his memory riotous with a throng of evil shapes that asserted their kindred with the Master Sin, whatever it might be, which it was within the scope of man's corrupted nature to con-ceive and cherish. They were all of one family; they went to and fro between his breast and Ethan Brand's, and carried dark greetings from one to the other.

Then Bartram remembered the stories which had grown traditionary in reference to this strange man, who had come upon him like a shadow of the night, and was mak-ing himself at home in his old place, after so long absence that the dead people, dead and buried for years, would have had more right to be at home, in any familiar spot, than he. Ethan Brand, it was said, had conversed with Satan himself in the lurid blaze of this very kiln. The legend had been matter of mirth heretofore, but looked grisly now. According to this tale, before Ethan Brand departed on his search, he had been accustomed to evoke a fiend from the hot furnace of the lime-kiln, night after night, in order to confer with him about the Unpardonable Sin; the man and the fiend each laboring to frame the image of some mode of guilt which could neither be atoned for nor forgiven. And, with the first gleam of light upon the mountain-top, the fiend crept in at the iron door, there to abide the intensest element of fire, until again summoned forth to share in the dreadful task of extending man's possible guilt beyond the scope of Heaven's else infinite mercy.

While the lime-burner was struggling with the horror of these thoughts, Ethan Brand rose from the log, and flung open the door of the kiln. The action was in such accordance with the idea in Bartram's mind, that he almost expected to see the Evil One issue forth, red-hot from the raging furnace.

"Hold! hold!" cried he, with a tremulous attempt to laugh; for he was ashamed of his fears, although they overmastered him. "Don't, for mercy's sake, bring out your Devil now!"

"Man!" sternly replied Ethan Brand, "what need have I of the Devil? I have left him behind me, on my track. It is with such half-way sinners as you that he busies himself. Fear not, because I open the door. I do but act by old custom, and am going to trim your fire, like a lime-burner, as I was once."

He stirred the vast coals, thrust in more wood, and bent forward to gaze into the hollow prison-house of the fire, regardless of the fierce glow that reddened upon his face. The lime-burner sat watching him, and half suspected his strange guest of a purpose, if not to evoke a fiend, at least to plunge bodily into the flames, and thus vanish from the eight of man. Ethan Brand, however, drew quietly back, and closed the door of the kiln.

"I have looked," said he, "into many a human heart that was seven times hotter with sinful passions than yonder furnace is with fire. But I found not there what I sought. No, not the Unpardonable Sin!"

"What is the Unpardonable Sin?" asked the lime-burner; and then he shrank farther from his companion, trembling lest his question should be answered.

"It is a sin that grew within my own breast," replied Ethan Brand, standing erect, with a pride that distinguishes all enthusiasts of his stamp. "A sin that grew nowhere else! The sin of an intellect that triumphed over the sense of brotherhood with man and reverence for God, and sacrificed everything to its own mighty claims! The only sin that deserves a recompense of immortal agony! Freely, were it to do again, would I incur the guilt. Unshrinkingly I accept the retribution!"

"The man's head is turned," muttered the lime-burner to himself. "He may be a sinner, like the rest of us,—nothing more likely,—but, I'll be sworn, he is a madman too."

Nevertheless, he felt uncomfortable at his situation, alone with Ethan Brand on the wild mountain-side, and was right glad to hear the rough murmur of tongues, and the footsteps of what seemed a pretty numerous party, stumbling over the stones and rustling through the underbrush. Soon appeared the whole lazy regiment that was wont to infest the village tavern, comprehending three or four individuals who had drunk flip beside the bar-room fire through all the winters, and smoked their pipes beneath the stoop through all the summers, since Ethan Brand's departure. Laughing boisterously, and mingling all their voices together in unceremonious talk, they now burst into the moonshine and narrow streaks of firelight that illuminated the open space before the lime-kiln. Bartram set the door ajar again, flooding the spot with light, that the whole company might get a fair view of Ethan Brand, and he of them.

There, among other old acquaintances, was a once ubiquitous man, now almost extinct, but whom we were formerly sure to encounter at the hotel of every thriving village throughout the country. It was the stage-agent. The present specimen of the genus was a wilted and smoke-dried man, wrinkled and red-nosed, in a smartly cut, brown, bobtailed coat, with brass buttons, who, for a length of time unknown, had kept his desk and corner in the bar-room, and was still puffing what seemed to be the same cigar that he had lighted twenty years before. He had great fame as a dry joker, though, perhaps, less on account of any intrinsic humor than from a certain flavor of brandy-toddy and tobacco-smoke, which impregnated all his ideas and expressions, as well as his person.

Another well-remembered though strangely altered face was that of Lawyer Giles, as people still called him in courtesy; an elderly ragamuffin, in his soiled shirt-sleeves and tow-cloth trousers. This poor fellow had been an attorney, in what ha called his better days, a sharp practitioner, and in great vogue among the village litigants; but flip, and sling, and toddy, and cocktails, imbibed at all hours, morning, noon, and night, had caused him to slide from intellectual to various kinds and degrees of bodily labor, till, at last, to adopt his own phrase, he slid into a soap-vat. In other words, Giles was now a soap-boiler, in a small way. He had come to be but the fragment of a human being, a part of one foot having been chopped off by an axe, and an entire hand torn away by the devilish grip of a steam-engine. Yet, though the corporeal hand was gone, a spiritual member remained; for, stretching forth the stump, Giles steadfastly averred that he felt an invisible thumb and fingers with as vivid a sensation as before the real ones were amputated. A maimed and miserable wretch he was; but one, nevertheless, whom the world could not trample on, and had no right to scorn, either in this or any previous stage of his misfortunes, since he had still kept up the courage and spirit of a man, asked nothing in charity, and with his one hand—and that the left one—fought a stern battle against want and hostile circumstances.

Among the throng, too, came another personage, who, with certain points of similarity to Lawyer Giles, had many more of difference. It was the village doctor; a man of some fifty years, whom, at an earlier period of his life, we introduced as paying a professional visit to Ethan Brand during the latter's supposed insanity. He was now a purple-visaged, rude, and brutal, yet half-gentlemanly figure, with something wild, ruined, and desperate in his talk, and in all the details of his gesture and manners. Brandy possessed this man like an evil spirit, and made him as surly and savage as a wild beast, and as miserable as a lost soul; but there was supposed to be in him such wonderful skill, such native gifts of healing, beyond any which medical science could impart, that society caught hold of him, and would not let him sink out of its reach. So, swaying to and fro upon his horse, and grumbling thick accents at the bedside, he visited all the sick-chambers for miles about among the mountain towns, and sometimes raised a dying man, as it were, by miracle, or quite as often, no doubt, sent his patient to a grave that was dug many a year too soon. The doctor had an everlasting pipe in his mouth, and, as somebody said, in allusion to his habit of swearing, it was always alight with hell-fire.

These three worthies pressed forward, and greeted Ethan Brand each after his own fashion, earnestly inviting him to partake of the contents of a certain black bottle, in which, as they averred, he would find something far better worth seeking for than the Unpardonable Sin. No mind, which has wrought itself by intense and solitary meditation into a high state of enthusiasm, can endure the kind of contact with low and vulgar modes of thought and feeling to which Ethan Brand was now subjected. It made him doubt—and, strange to say, it was a painful doubt—whether he had indeed found the Unpardonable Sin and found it within himself. The whole question on which he had exhausted life, and more than life, looked like a delusion.

"Leave me," he said bitterly, "ye brute beasts, that have made yourselves so, shrivelling up your souls with fiery liquors! I have done with you. Years and years ago, I groped into your hearts, and found nothing there for my purpose. Get ye gone!"

"Why, you uncivil scoundrel," cried the fierce doctor, "is that the way you respond to the kindness of your best friends? Then let me tell you the truth. You have no more found the Unpardonable Sin than yonder boy Joe has. You are but a crazy fellow,—I told you so twenty years ago,—neither better nor worse than a crazy fellow, and the fit companion of old Humphrey, here!"

He pointed to an old man, shabbily dressed, with long white hair, thin visage, and unsteady eyes. For some years past this aged person had been wandering about among the hills, inquiring of all travellers whom he met for his daughter. The girl, it seemed, had gone off with a company of circus-performers; and occasionally tidings of her came to the village, and fine stories were told of her glittering appearance as she rode on horseback in the ring, or performed marvellous feats on the tight-rope.

The white-haired father now approached Ethan Brand, and gazed unsteadily into his face.

"They tell me you have been all over the earth," said he, wringing his hands with earnestness. "You must have seen my daughter, for she makes a grand figure in the world, and everybody goes to see her. Did she send any word to her old father, or say when she was coming back?"

Ethan Brand's eye quailed beneath the old man's. That daughter, from whom he so earnestly desired a word of greeting, was the Esther of our tale, the very girl whom, with such cold and remorseless purpose, Ethan Brand had made the subject of a psychological experiment, and wasted, absorbed, and perhaps annihilated her soul, in the process.

"Yes," murmured he, turning away from the hoary wanderer; "it is no delusion. There is an Unpardonable Sin!"

While these things were passing, a merry scene was going forward in the area of cheerful light, beside the spring and before the door of the hut. A number of the youth of the village, young men and girls, had hurried up the hillside, impelled by curiosity to see Ethan Brand, the hero of so many a legend familiar to their childhood. Finding nothing, however, very remarkable in his aspect,—nothing but a sunburnt wayfarer, in plain garb and dusty shoes, who sat looking into the fire, as if he fancied pictures among the coals,—these young people speedily grew tired of observing him. As it happened, there was other amusement at hand. An old German Jew, travelling with a diorama on his back, was passing down the mountain-road towards the village just as the party turned aside from it, and, in hopes of eking out the profits of the day, the showman had kept them company to the lime-kiln.

"Come, old Dutchman," cried one of the young men, "let us see your pictures, if you can swear they are worth looking at!"

"O yes, Captain," answered the Jew,—whether as a matter of courtesy or craft, he styled everybody Captain,— "I shall show you, indeed, some very superb pictures!"

So, placing his box in a proper position, he invited the young men and girls to look through the glass orifices of the machine, and proceeded to exhibit a series of the most outrageous scratchings and daubings, as specimens of the fine arts, that ever an itinerant showman had the face to impose upon his circle of spectators. The pictures were worn out, moreover, tattered, full of cracks and wrinkles, dingy with tobacco-smoke, and otherwise in a most pitiable condition. Some purported to be cities, public edifices, and ruined castles in Europe; others represented Napoleon's battles and Nelson's sea-fights; and in the midst of these would be seen a gigantic, brown, hairy hand,— which might have been mistaken for the Hand of Destiny, though, in truth, it was only the showman's,—pointing its forefinger to various scenes of the conflict, while its owner gave historical illustrations. When, with much merriment at its abominable deficiency of merit, the exhibition was concluded, the German bade little Joe put his head into the box. Viewed through the magnifying-glasses, the boy's round, rosy visage assumed the strangest imaginable aspect of an immense Titanic child, the mouth grinning broadly, and the eyes and every other feature overflowing with fun at the joke. Suddenly, however, that merry face turned pale, and its expression changed to horror, for this easily impressed and excitable child had become sensible that the eye of Ethan Brand was fixed upon him through the glass.

"You make the little man to be afraid, Captain," said the German Jew, turning up the dark and strong outline of his visage, from his stooping posture. "But look again, and, by chance, I shall cause you to see somewhat that is very fine, upon my word!"

Ethan Brand gazed into the box for an instant, and then starting back, looked fixedly at the German. What had he seen? Nothing, apparently; for a curious youth, who had peeped in almost at the same moment, beheld only a vacant space of canvas.

"I remember you now," muttered Ethan Brand to the showman.

"Ah, Captain," whispered the Jew of Nuremburg, with a dark smile, "I find it to be a heavy matter in my show-box,—this Unpardonable Sin! By my faith, Captain, it has wearied my shoulders, this long day, to carry it over the mountain."

"Peace," answered Ethan Brand, sternly, "or get thee into the furnace yonder!"

The Jew's exhibition had scarcely concluded, when a great, elderly dog—who seemed to be his own master, as no person in the company laid claim to him—saw fit to render himself the object of public notice. Hitherto, he had shown himself a very quiet, well disposed old dog, going round from one to another, and, by way of being sociable, offering his rough head to be patted by any kindly hand that would take so much trouble. But now, all of a sudden, this grave and venerable quadruped, of his own mere motion, and without the slightest suggestion from anybody else, began to run round after his tall, which, to heighten the absurdity of the proceeding, was a great deal shorter than it should have been. Never was seen such headlong eagerness in pursuit of an object that could not possibly be attained; never was heard such a tremendous outbreak of growling, snarling, barking, and snapping—as if one end of the ridiculous brute's body were at deadly and most unforgivable enmity with the other. Faster and faster, roundabout went the cur; and faster and still faster fled the unapproachable brevity of his tail; and louder and fiercer grew his yells of rage and animosity; until, utterly exhausted, and as far from the goal as ever, the foolish old dog ceased his performance as suddenly as he had begun it. The next moment he was as mild, quiet, sensible, and respectable in his deportment, as when he first scraped acquaintance with the company.

As may be supposed, the exhibition was greeted with universal laughter, clapping of hands, and shouts of encore, to which the canine performer responded by wagging all that there was to wag of his tail, but appeared totally unable to repeat his very successful effort to amuse the spectators.

Meanwhile, Ethan Brand had resumed his seat upon the log, and moved, it might be, by a perception of some remote analogy between his own case and that of this self-pursuing cur, he broke into the awful laugh, which, more than any other token, expressed the condition of his inward being. From that moment, the merriment of the party was at an end; they stood aghast, dreading lest the inauspicious sound should be reverberated around the horizon, and that mountain would thunder it to mountain, and so the horror be prolonged upon their ears. Then, whispering one to another that it was late,—that the moon was almost down,—that the August night was growing chill,—they hurried homewards, leaving the lime-burner and little Joe to deal as they might with their unwelcome guest. Save for these three human beings, the open space on the hillside was a solitude, set in a vast gloom of forest. Beyond that darksome verge, the firelight glimmered on the stately trunks and almost black foliage of pines, intermixed with the lighter verdure of sapling oaks, maples, and poplars, while here and there lay the gigantic corpses of dead trees, decaying on the leaf-strewn soil. And it seemed to little Joe—a timorous and imaginative child—that the silent forest was holding its breath, until some fearful thing should happen.

Ethan Brand thrust more wood into the fire, and closed the door of the kiln; then looking over his shoulder at the lime-burner and his son, he bade, rather than advised, them to retire to rest.

"For myself, I cannot sleep," said he. "I have matters that it concerns me to meditate upon. I will watch the fire, as I used to do in the old time."

"And call the Devil out of the furnace to keep you company, I suppose," muttered Bartram, who had been making intimate acquaintance with the black bottle above mentioned. "But watch, if you like, and call as many devils as you like! For my part, I shall be all the better for a snooze. Come, Joe!"

As the boy followed his father into the hut, he looked back at the wayfarer, and the tears came into his eyes, for his tender spirit had an intuition of the bleak and terrible loneliness in which this man had enveloped himself.

When they had gone, Ethan Brand sat listening to the crackling of the kindled wood, and looking at the little spirts of fire that issued through the chinks of the door. These trifles, however, once so familiar, had but the slightest hold of his attention, while deep within his mind he was reviewing the gradual but marvellous change that had been wrought upon him by the search to which he had devoted himself. He remembered how the night dew had fallen upon him,—how the dark forest had whispered to him,—how the stars had gleamed upon him,—a simple and loving man, watching his fire in the years gone by, and ever musing as it burned. He remembered with what tenderness, with what love and sympathy for mankind, and what pity for human guilt and woe, he had first begun to contemplate those ideas which afterwards became the inspiration of his life; with what reverence he had then looked into the heart of man, viewing it as a temple originally divine, and, however desecrated, still to be held sacred by a brother; with what awful fear he had deprecated the success of his pursuit, and prayed that the Unpardonable Sin might never be revealed to him. Then ensued that vast intellectual development, which, in its progress, disturbed the counterpoise between his mind and heart. The Idea that possessed his life had operated as a means of education; it had gone on cultivating his powers to the highest point of which they were susceptible; it had raised him from the level of an unlettered laborer to stand on a star-lit eminence, whither the philosophers of the earth, laden with the lore of universities, might vainly strive to clamber after him. So much for the intellect! But where was the heart? That, indeed, had withered,—had contracted,—had hardened,—had perished! It had ceased to partake of the universal throb. He had lost his hold of the magnetic chain of humanity. He was no longer a brother-man, opening the chambers of the dungeons of our common nature by the key of holy sympathy, which gave him a right to share in all its secrets; he was now a cold observer, looking on mankind as the subject of his experiment, and, at length, converting man and woman to be his puppets, and pulling the wires that moved them to such degrees of crime as were demanded for his study.

Thus Ethan Brand became a fiend. He began to be so from the moment that his moral nature had ceased to keep the pace of improvement with his intellect. And now, as his highest effort and inevitable development,—as the bright and gorgeous flower, and rich, delicious fruit of his life's labor,— he had produced the Unpardonable Sin!

"What more have I to seek? what more to achieve?" said Ethan Brand to himself. "My task is done, and well done!"

Starting from the log with a certain alacrity in his gait and ascending the hillock of earth that was raised against the stone circumference of the lime-kiln, he thus reached the top of the structure. It was a space of perhaps ten feet across, from edge to edge, presenting a view of the upper surface of the immense mass of broken marble with which the kiln was heaped. All these innumerable blocks and fragments of marble were red-hot and vividly on fire, sending up great spouts of blue flame, which quivered aloft and danced madly, as within a magic circle, and sank and rose again, with continual and multitudinous activity. As the lonely man bent forward over this terrible body of fire, the blasting heat smote up against his person with a breath that, it might be supposed, would have scorched and shrivelled him up in a moment.

Ethan Brand stood erect, and raised his arms on high. The blue flames played upon his face, and imparted the wild and ghastly light which alone could have suited its expression; it was that of a fiend on the verge of plunging into his gulf of intensest torment.

"O Mother Earth," cried he, "who art no more my Mother, and into whose bosom this frame shall never be resolved! O mankind, whose brotherhood I have cast off, and trampled thy great heart beneath my feet! O stars of heaven, that shone on me of old, as if to light me onward and upward!—farewell all, and forever. Come, deadly element of Fire,—henceforth my familiar frame! Embrace me, as I do thee!"

That night the sound of a fearful peal of laughter rolled heavily through the sleep of the lime-burner and his little son; dim shapes of horror and anguish haunted their dreams, and seemed still present in the rude hovel, when they opened their eyes to the daylight.

"Up, boy, up!" cried the lime-burner, staring about him. "Thank Heaven, the night is gone, at last; and rather than pass such another, I would watch my lime-kiln, wide awake, for a twelvemonth. This Ethan Brand, with his humbug of an Unpardonable Sin, has done me no such mighty favor, in taking my place!"

He issued from the hut, followed by little Joe, who kept fast hold of his father's hand. The early sunshine was already pouring its gold upon the mountain-tops; and though the valleys were still in shadow, they smiled cheerfully in the promise of the bright day that was hastening onward. The village, completely shut in by hills, which swelled away gently about it, looked as if it had rested peacefully in the hollow of the great hand of Providence. Every dwelling was distinctly visible; the little spires of the two churches pointed upwards, and caught a fore-glimmering of brightness from the sun-gilt skies upon their gilded weathercocks. The tavern was astir, and the figure of the old, smoke-dried stage-agent, cigar in mouth, was seen beneath the stoop. Old Graylock was glorified with a golden cloud upon his head. Scattered likewise over the breasts of the surrounding mountains, there were heaps of hoary mist, in fantastic shapes, some of them far down into the valley, others high up towards the summits, and still others, of the same family of mist or cloud, hovering in the gold radiance of the upper atmosphere. Stepping from one to another of the clouds that rested on the hills, and thence to the loftier brotherhood that sailed in air, it seemed almost as if a mortal man might thus ascend into the heavenly regions. Earth was so mingled with sky that it was a day-dream to look at it.

To supply that charm of the familiar and homely, which Nature so readily adopts into a scene like this, the stage-coach was rattling down the mountain-road, and the driver sounded his horn, while echo caught up the notes, and intertwined them into a rich and varied and elaborate harmony, of which the original performer could lay claim to little share. The great hills played a concert among themselves, each contributing a strain of airy sweetness.

Little Joe's face brightened at once.

"Dear father," cried he, skipping cheerily to and fro, "that strange man is gone, and the sky and the mountains all seem glad of it!"

"Yes," growled the lime-burner, with an oath, "but he has let the fire go down, and no thanks to him if five hundred bushels of lime are not spoiled. If I catch the fellow hereabouts again, I shall feel like tossing him into the furnace!"

With his long pole in his hand, he ascended to the top of the kiln. After a moment's pause, he called to his son.

"Come up here, Joe!" said he.

So little Joe ran up the hillock, and stood by his father's side. The marble was all burnt into perfect, snow-white lime. But on its surface, in the midst of the circle,—snow-white too, and thoroughly converted into lime,—lay a human skeleton, in the attitude of a person who, after long toil, lies down to long repose. Within the ribs—strange to say —was the shape of a human heart.

"Was the fellow's heart made of marble?" cried Bartram, in some perplexity at this phenomenon. "At any rate, it is burnt into what looks like special good lime; and, taking all the bones together, my kiln is half a bushel the richer for him."

So saying, the rude lime-burner lifted his pole, and, letting it fall upon the skeleton, the relics of Ethan Brand were crumbled into fragments.

What Was It?

Fitz-James O'Brien

———◆———

I T IS, I CONFESS, WITH CONSIDERABLE DIFFIDENCE, THAT I APPROACH THE strange narrative which I am about to relate. The events which I purpose detailing are of so extraordinary a character that I am quite prepared to meet with an unusual amount of incredulity and scorn. I accept all such beforehand. I have, I trust, the literary courage to face unbelief. I have, after mature consideration resolved to narrate, in as simple and straightforward a manner as I can compass, some facts that passed under my observation, in the month of July last, and which, in the annals of the mysteries of physical science, are wholly unparalleled.

I live at No. ——— Twenty-sixth Street, in New York. The house is in some respects a curious one. It has enjoyed for the last two years the reputation of being haunted. It is a large and stately residence, surrounded by what was once a garden, but which is now only a green enclosure used for bleaching clothes. The dry basin of what has been a fountain, and a few fruit trees ragged and unpruned, indicate that this spot in past days was a pleasant, shady retreat, filled with fruits and flowers and the sweet murmur of waters.

The house is very spacious. A hall of noble size leads to a large spiral staircase winding through its center, while the various apartments are of imposing dimensions. It was built some fifteen or twenty years since by Mr. A———, the well-known New York merchant, who five years ago threw the commercial world into convulsions by a stupendous bank fraud. Mr. A———, as everyone knows, escaped to Europe, and died not long after, of a broken heart. Almost immediately after the news of his decease reached this country and was verified, the report spread in Twenty-sixth Street that No. ——— was haunted. Legal measures had dispossessed the widow of its former owner, and it was inhabited merely by a caretaker and his wife, placed there by the house agent into whose hands it had passed for the purposes of renting or sale. These people declared that they were troubled with unnatural noises. Doors were opened without any visible agency. The remnants of furniture scattered through the various rooms were, during the night, piled one upon the other by unknown hands. Invisible feet passed up and down the stairs in broad daylight, accompanied by the rustle of unseen silk dresses, and the gliding of viewless hands along the massive balusters. The caretaker and his wife declared they would live there no longer. The house agent laughed, dismissed them, and put others in their place. The noises and supernatural manifestations continued. The neighborhood caught up the story, and the house remained untenanted for three years. Several persons negotiated for it; but, somehow, always before the bargain was closed they heard the unpleasant rumors and declined to treat any further.

It was in this state of things that my landlady, who at that time kept a boarding-house in Bleecker Street, and who wished to move further up town, conceived the bold idea of renting No. —— Twenty-sixth Street. Happening to have in her house rather a plucky and philosophical set of boarders, she laid her scheme before us, stating candidly everything she had heard respecting the ghostly qualities of the establishment to which she wished to remove us. With the exception of two timid persons,—a sea-captain and a returned Californian, who immediately gave notice that they would leave,—all of Mrs. Moffat's guests declared that they would accompany her in her chivalric incursion into the abode of spirits.

Our removal was effected in the month of May, and we were charmed with our new residence. The portion of Twenty-sixth Street where our house is situated, between Seventh and Eighth Avenues, is one of the pleasantest localities in New York. The gardens back of the houses, running down nearly to the Hudson, form, in the summer time, a perfect avenue of verdure. The air is pure and invigorating, sweeping, as it does, straight across the river from the Weehawken heights, and even the ragged garden which surrounded the house, although displaying on washing days rather too much clothes-line, still gave us a piece of greensward to look at, and a cool retreat in the summer evenings, where we smoked our cigars in the dusk, and watched the fire-flies flashing their dark lanterns in the long grass.

Of course we had no sooner established ourselves at No. —— than we began to expect ghosts. We absolutely awaited their advent with eagerness. Our dinner conversation was supernatural. One of the boarders, who had purchased Mrs. Crowe's *Night Side of Nature* for his own private delectation, was regarded as a public enemy by the entire household for not having bought twenty copies. The man led a life of supreme wretchedness while he was reading this volume. A system of espionage was established, of which he was the victim. If he incautiously laid the book down for an instant and left the room, it was immediately seized and read aloud in secret places to a select few. I found myself a person of immense importance, it having leaked out that I was tolerably well versed in the history of supernaturalism, and had once written a story the foundation of which was a ghost. If a table or a wainscot panel happened to warp when we were assembled in the large drawing-room, there was an instant silence, and everyone was prepared for an immediate clanking of chains and a spectral form.

After a month of psychological excitement, it was with the utmost dissatisfaction that we were forced to acknowledge that nothing in the remotest degree approaching the supernatural had manifested itself. Once the black butler asseverated that his candle had been blown out by some invisible agency while he was undressing himself for the night; but as I had more than once discovered this colored gentleman in a condition when one candle must have appeared to him like two, thought it possible that, by going a step further in his potations, he might have reversed this phenomenon, and seen no candle at all where he ought to have beheld one.

Things were in this state when an accident took place so awful and inexplicable in its character that my reason fairly reels at the bare memory of the occurrence. It was the tenth of July. After dinner was over I repaired, with my friend Dr. Hammond, to the garden to smoke my evening pipe. Independent of certain mental sympathies which existed between the Doctor and myself, we were linked together by a vice. We both smoked opium. We knew each other's secret, and respected it. We enjoyed together that wonderful expansion of thought, that marvelous intensifying of the perceptive faculties, that boundless feeling of existence when we seem to have points of contact with the whole universe,—in short, that unimaginable spiritual bliss, which I would not surrender for a throne, and which I hope you, reader, will never—never taste.

Those hours of opium happiness which the Doctor and I spent together in secret were regulated with a scientific accuracy. We did not blindly smoke the drug of paradise, and leave our dreams to chance. While smoking, we carefully steered our conversation through the brightest and calmest channels of thought. We talked of the East, and endeavored to recall the magical panorama of its glowing scenery. We criticized the most sensuous poets,—those who painted life ruddy with health, brimming with passion, happy in the possession of youth and strength and beauty. If we talked of Shakespeare's Tempest, we lingered over Ariel, and avoided Caliban. Like the Guebers, we turned our faces to the East, and saw only the sunny side of the world.

This skillful coloring of our train of thought produced in our subsequent visions a corresponding tone. The splendors of Arabian fairyland dyed our dreams. We paced the narrow strip of grass with the tread and port of kings. The song of the *rana arborea*, while he clung to the bark of the ragged plum-tree, sounded like the strains of divine musicians. Houses, walls, and streets melted like rain clouds, and vistas of unimaginable glory stretched away before us. It was a rapturous companionship. We enjoyed the vast delight more perfectly because, even in our most ecstatic moments, we were conscious of each other's presence. Our pleasures, while individual, were still twin, vibrating and moving in musical accord.

On the evening in question, the tenth of July, the Doctor and myself drifted into an unusually metaphysical mood. We lit our large meerschaums, filled with fine Turkish tobacco, in the core of which burned a little black nut of opium, that, like the nut in the fairy tale, held within its narrow limits wonders beyond the reach of kings; we paced to and fro, conversing. A strange perversity dominated the currents of our thought. They would *not* flow through the sun-lit channels into which we strove to divert them. For some unaccountable reason, they constantly diverged into dark and lonesome beds, where a continual gloom brooded. It was in vain that, after our old fashion, we flung ourselves on the shores of the East, and talked of its gay bazaars, of the splendors of the time of Haroun, of harems and golden palaces. Black afreets continually arose from the depths of our talk, and expanded, like the one the fisherman released from the copper vessel, until they blotted everything bright from our vision. Insensibly, we yielded to the occult force that swayed us, and indulged in gloomy speculation. We had talked some time upon the proneness of the human mind to mysticism, and the almost universal love of the terrible, when Hammond suddenly said to me. "What do you consider to be the greatest element of terror?"

The question puzzled me. That many things were terrible, I knew. Stumbling over a corpse in the dark; beholding, as I once did, a woman floating down a deep and rapid river, with wildly lifted arms, and awful, upturned face, uttering, as she drifted, shrieks that rent one's heart while we, spectators, stood frozen at a window which overhung the river at a height of sixty feet, unable to make the slightest effort to save her, but dumbly watching her last supreme agony and her disappearance. A shattered wreck, with no life visible, encountered floating listlessly on the ocean, is a terrible object, for it suggests a huge terror, the proportions of which are veiled. But it now struck me, for the first time, that there must be one great and ruling embodiment of fear,—a King of

Terrors, to which all others must succumb. What might it be? To what train of circum-stances would it owe its existence?

"I confess, Hammond," I replied to my friend, "I never considered the subject before. That there must be one Something more terrible than any other thing, I feel. I cannot attempt, however, even the most vague definition."

"I am somewhat like you, Harry," he answered. "I feel my capacity to experi-ence a terror greater than anything yet conceived by the human mind;—something combining in fearful and unnatural amalgamation hitherto supposed incompatible ele-ments. The calling of the voices in Brockden Brown's novel of *Wieland* is awful; so is the picture of the Dweller of the Threshold, in Bulwer's *Zanoni*; but," he added, shak-ing his head gloomily, "there is something more horrible still than those."

"Look here, Hammond," I rejoined, "let us drop this kind of talk, for Heaven's sake! We shall suffer for it, depend on it."

"I don't know what's the matter with me to-night," he replied, "but my brain is running upon all sorts of weird and awful thoughts. I feel as if I could write a story like Hoffman, to-night, if I were only master of a literary style."

"Well, if we are going to be Hoffmanesque in our talk, I'm off to bed. Opium and nightmares should never be brought together. How sultry it is! Good-night, Hammond."

"Good-night, Harry. Pleasant dreams to you."

"To you, gloomy wretch, afreets, ghouls, and enchanters."

We parted, and each sought his respective chamber. I undressed quickly and got into bed, taking with me, according to my usual custom, a book, over which I gener-ally read myself to sleep. I opened the volume as soon as I had laid my head upon the pillow, and instantly flung it to the other side of the room. It was Goudon's *History of Monsters*,—a curious French work, which I had lately imported from Paris, but which, in the state of mind I had then reached, was anything but an agreeable companion. I resolved to go to sleep at once; so, turning down my gas until nothing but a little blue point of light glimmered on the top of the tube, I composed myself to rest.

The room was in total darkness. The atom of gas that still remained alight did not illuminate a distance of three inches round the burner. I desperately drew my arm across my eyes, as if to shut out even the darkness, and tried to think of nothing. It was in vain. The confounded themes touched on by Hammond in the garden kept obtrud-ing themselves on my brain. I battled against them. I erected ramparts of would-be blackness of intellect to keep them out. They still crowded upon me. While I was lying still as a corpse, hoping that by a perfect physical inaction I should hasten mental repose, an awful incident occurred. A Something dropped, as it seemed, from the ceiling, plumb upon my chest, and the next instant I felt two bony hands encircling my throat, endeavoring to choke me.

I am no coward, and am possessed of considerable physical strength. The suddenness of the attack, instead of stunning me, strung every nerve to its highest tension. My body acted from instinct, before my brain had time to realize the terrors of my position. In an instant I wound two muscular arms around the creature, and squeezed it, with all the strength of despair, against my chest. In a few seconds the bony hands that had fastened on my throat loosened their hold, and I was free to breathe once more. Then commenced a struggle of awful intensity. Immersed in the most profound darkness, totally ignorant of the nature of the Thing by which I was so suddenly attacked, finding my grasp slipping every moment, by reason, it seemed to me, of the entire nakedness of my assailant, bitten with sharp teeth in the shoulder, neck, and chest, having every moment to protect my throat against a pair of sinewy, agile hands, which my utmost efforts could not confine,—these were a combination of circumstances to combat which required all the strength, skill, and courage that I possessed.

At last, after a silent, deadly, exhausting struggle, I got my assailant under by a series of incredible efforts of strength. Once pinned, with my knee on what I made out to be its chest, I knew that I was victor. I rested for a moment to breathe. I heard the creature beneath me panting in the darkness, and felt the violent throbbing of a heart. It was apparently as exhausted as I was; that was one comfort. At this moment I remembered that I usually placed under my pillow, before going to bed, a large yellow silk pocket handkerchief. I felt for it instantly; it was there. In a few seconds more I had, after a fashion, pinioned the creature's arms.

I now felt tolerably secure. There was nothing more to be done but to turn on the gas, and, having first seen what my midnight assailant was like, arouse the household. I will confess to being actuated by a certain pride in not giving the alarm before; I wished to make the capture alone and unaided.

Never losing my hold for an instant, I slipped from the bed to the floor, dragging my captive with me. I had but a few steps to make to reach the gas-burner; these I made with the greatest caution, holding the creature in a grip like a vice. At last I got within arm's length of the tiny speck of blue light which told me where the gas-burner lay. Quick as lightning I released my grasp with one hand and let on the full flood of light. Then I turned to look at my captive.

I cannot even attempt to give any definition of my sensations the instant after I turned on the gas. I suppose I must have shrieked with terror, for in less than a minute afterward my room was crowded with the inmates of the house. I shudder now as I think of that awful moment. *I saw nothing!* Yes; I had one arm firmly clasped round a breathing, panting, corporeal shape, my other hand gripped with all its strength a throat as warm, as apparently fleshy, as my own; and yet, with this living substance in my grasp, with its body pressed against my own, and all in the bright glare of a large jet of gas, I absolutely beheld nothing! Not even an outline,—a vapor!

I do not, even at this hour, realize the situation in which I found myself. I cannot recall the astounding incident thoroughly. Imagination in vain tries to compass the awful paradox.

It breathed. I felt its warm breath upon my cheek. It struggled fiercely. It had hands. They clutched me. Its skin was smooth, like my own. There it lay, pressed close up against me, solid as stone,—and yet utterly invisible!

I wonder that I did not faint or go mad on the instant. Some wonderful instinct must have sustained me; for, absolutely, in place of loosening my hold on the terrible Enigma, I seemed to gain an additional strength in my moment of horror, and tightened my grasp with such wonderful force that I felt the creature shivering with agony.

Just then Hammond entered my room at the head of the household. As soon as he beheld my face—which, I suppose, must have been an awful sight to look at—he hastened forward, crying, "Great heaven, Harry! what has happened?"

"Hammond! Hammond!" I cried, "come here. O, this is awful! I have been attacked in bed by something or other, which I have hold of; but I can't see it,—I can't see it!"

Hammond, doubtless struck by the unfeigned horror expressed in my countenance, made one or two steps forward with an anxious yet puzzled expression. A very audible titter burst from the remainder of my visitors. This suppressed laughter made me furious. To laugh at a human being in my position! It was the worst species of cruelty. *Now*, I can understand why the appearance of a man struggling violently, as it would seem, with an airy nothing, and calling for assistance against a vision, should have appeared ludicrous. *Then*, so great was my rage against the mocking crowd that had I the power I would have stricken them dead where they stood.

"Hammond! Hammond!" I cried again, despairingly, "for God's sake come to me. I can hold the—the thing but a short while longer. It is overpowering me. Help me! Help me!"

"Harry," whispered Hammond, approaching me, "you have been smoking too much opium."

"I swear to you, Hammond, that this is no vision," I answered, in the same low tone. "Don't you see how it shakes my whole frame with its struggles? If you don't believe me, convince yourself. Feel it,—touch it."

Hammond advanced and laid his hand in the spot I indicated. A wild cry of horror burst from him. He had felt it!

In a moment he had discovered somewhere in my room a long piece of cord and was the next instant winding it and knotting it about the body of the unseen being that I clasped in my arms.

"Harry," he said, in a hoarse, agitated voice, for, though he preserved his presence of mind, he was deeply moved, "Harry, it's all safe now. You may let go, old fellow, if you're tired. The Thing can't move."

I was utterly exhausted, and I gladly loosed my hold.

Hammond stood holding the ends of the cord that bound the Invisible, twisted round his hand, while before him, self-supporting as it were, he beheld a rope laced and interlaced, and stretching tightly around a vacant space. I never saw a man look so thoroughly stricken with awe. Nevertheless his face expressed all the courage and determination which I knew him to possess. His lips, although white, were set firmly, and one could perceive at a glance that, although stricken with fear, he was not daunted.

The confusion that ensued among the guests of the house who were witnesses of this extraordinary scene between Hammond and myself,—who beheld the pantomime of binding this struggling Something,—who beheld me almost sinking from physical exhaustion when my task of jailer was over,—the confusion and terror that took possession of the bystanders, when they saw all this, was beyond description. The weaker ones fled from the apartment. The few who remained clustered near the door and could not be induced to approach Hammond and his Charge. Still incredulity broke out through their terror. They had not the courage to satisfy themselves, and yet they doubted. It was in vain that I begged of some of the men to come near and convince themselves by touch of the existence in that room of a living being which was invisible. They were incredulous, but did not dare to undeceive themselves. How could a solid, living, breathing body be invisible, they asked. My reply was this. I gave a sign to Hammond, and both of us—conquering our fearful repugnance to touch the invisible creature—lifted it from the ground, manacled as it was, and took it to my bed. Its weight was about that of a boy of fourteen.

"Now, my friends," I said, as Hammond and myself held the creature suspended over the bed, "I can give you self-evident proof that here is a solid, ponderable body, which, nevertheless, you cannot see. Be good enough to watch the surface of the bed attentively."

I was astonished at my own courage in treating this strange event so calmly; but I had recovered from my first terror, and felt a sort of scientific pride in the affair, which dominated every other feeling.

The eyes of the bystanders were immediately fixed on my bed. At a given signal Hammond and I let the creature fall. There was a dull sound of a heavy body alighting on a soft mass. The timbers of the bed creaked. A deep impression marked itself distinctly on the pillow, and on the bed itself. The crowd who witnessed this gave a low cry, and rushed from the room. Hammond and I were left alone with our Mystery.

We remained silent for some time, listening to the low, irregular breathing of the creature on the bed, and watching the rustle of the bedclothes as it impotently struggled to free itself from confinement. Then Hammond spoke.

"Harry, this is awful."

"Ay, awful."

"But not unaccountable."

"Not unaccountable! What do you mean? Such a thing has never occurred since the birth of the world. I know not what to think, Hammond. God grant that I am not mad, and that this is not an insane fantasy!"

"Let us reason a little, Harry. Here is a solid body which we touch, but which we cannot see. The fact is so unusual that it strikes us with terror. Is there no parallel, though, for such a phenomenon? Take a piece of pure glass. It is tangible and transparent. A certain chemical coarseness is all that prevents its being so entirely transparent as to be totally invisible. It is not theoretically impossible, mind you, to make a glass which shall not reflect a single ray of light,—a glass so pure and homogeneous in its atoms that the rays from the sun will pass through it as they do through the air, refracted but not reflected. We do not see the air, and yet we feel it."

"That's all very well, Hammond, but these are inanimate substances. Glass does not breathe, air does not breathe. *This* thing has a heart that palpitates,—a will that moves it,—lungs that play, and inspire and respire."

"You forget the phenomena of which we have so often heard of late," answered the Doctor, gravely. "At the meetings called 'spirit circles,' invisible hands have been thrust into the hands of those persons round the table,—warm, fleshly hands that seemed to pulsate with mortal life."

"What? Do you think, then, that this thing is—"

"I don't know what it is," was the solemn reply; "but please the gods I will, with your assistance, thoroughly investigate it."

We watched together, smoking many pipes, all night long, by the bedside of the unearthly being that tossed and panted until it was apparently wearied out. Then we learned by the low, regular breathing that it slept.

The next morning the house was all astir. The boarders congregated on the landing outside my room, and Hammond and myself were lions. We had to answer a thousand questions as to the state of our extraordinary prisoner, for as yet not one person in the house except ourselves could be induced to set foot in the apartment.

The creature was awake. This was evidenced by the convulsive manner in which the bed-clothes were moved in its efforts to escape. There was something truly terrible in beholding, as it were, those second-hand indications of the terrible writhings and agonized struggles for liberty which themselves were invisible.

Hammond and myself had racked our brains during the long night to discover some means by which we might realize the shape and general appearance of the Enigma. As well as we could make out by passing our hands over the creature's form, its outlines and lineaments were human. There was a mouth; a round, smooth head without hair; a nose, which, however, was little elevated above the cheeks; and its hands and feet felt like those of a boy. At first we thought of placing the being on a smooth surface and tracing its outlines with chalk, as shoemakers trace the outline of the foot. This plan was given up as being of no value. Such an outline would give not the slightest idea of its conformation.

A happy thought struck me. We would take a cast of it in plaster of Paris. This would give us the solid figure, and satisfy all our wishes. But how to do it? The movements of the creature would disturb the setting of the plastic covering, and distort the mold. Another thought. Why not give it chloroform? It had respiratory organs,— that was evident by its breathing. Once reduced to a state of insensibility, we could do with it what we would. Doctor X—— was sent for; and after the worthy physician had recovered from the first shock of amazement, he proceeded to administer the chloroform. In three minutes afterward we were enabled to remove the fetters from the creature's body, and a modeler was busily engaged in covering the invisible form with the moist clay. In five minutes more we had a mold, and before evening a rough fac-simile of the Mystery. It was shaped like a man—distorted, uncouth, and horrible, but still a man. It was small, not over four feet and some inches in height, and its limbs revealed a muscular development that was unparalleled. Its face surpassed in hideousness anything I had ever seen. Gustav Doré, or Callot, or Tony Johannot, never conceived anything so horrible. There is a face in one of the latter's illustrations to *Un Voyage où il vous plaira*, which somewhat approaches the countenance of this creature, but does not equal it. It was the physiognomy of what I should fancy a ghoul might be. It looked as if it was capable of feeding on human flesh.

Having satisfied our curiosity, and bound every one in the house to secrecy, it became a question what was to be done with our Enigma? It was impossible that we should keep such a horror in our house; it was equally impossible that such an awful being should be let loose upon the world. I confess that I would have gladly voted for the creature's destruction. But who would shoulder the responsibility? Who would undertake the execution of this horrible semblance of a human being? Day after day this question was deliberated gravely. The boarders all left the house. Mrs. Moffat was in despair, and threatened Hammond and myself with all sorts of legal penalties if we did not remove the Horror. Our answer was, "We will go if you like, but we decline taking this creature with us. Remove it yourself if you please. It appeared in your house. On you the responsibility rests." To this there was, of course, no answer. Mrs. Moffat could not obtain for love or money a person who would even approach the Mystery.

The most singular part of the affair was that we were entirely ignorant of what the creature habitually fed on. Everything in the way of nutriment that we could think of was placed before it, but was never touched. It was awful to stand by, day after day, and see the clothes toss, and hear the hard breathing, and know that it was starving.

Ten, twelve days, a fortnight passed, and it still lived. The pulsations of the heart, however, were daily growing fainter, and had now nearly ceased. It was evident that the creature was dying for want of sustenance. While this terrible life-struggle was going on, I felt miserable. I could not sleep. Horrible as the creature was, it was pitiful to think of the pangs it was suffering.

At last it died. Hammond and I found it cold and stiff one morning in the bed. The heart had ceased to beat, the lungs to inspire. We hastened to bury it in the garden. It was a strange funeral, the dropping of that viewless corpse into the damp hole. The cast of its form I gave to Doctor X——, who keeps it in his museum in Tenth Street.

As I am on the eve of a long journey from which I may not return, I have drawn up this narrative of an event the most singular that has ever come to my knowledge.

The Waters of Death

Erckmann-Chatrian

———◆———

THE WARM MINERAL WATERS OF SPINBRONN, SITUATED IN THE Hundsrück, several leagues from Pirmesens, formerly enjoyed a magnificent reputation. All who were afflicted with gout or gravel in Germany repaired thither; the savage aspect of the country did not deter them. They lodged in pretty cottages at the head of the defile; they bathed in the cascade, which fell in large sheets of foam from the summit of the rocks; they drank one or two decanters of mineral water daily, and the doctor of the place, Daniel Hâselnoss, who distributed his prescriptions clad in a great wig and chestnut coat, had an excellent practice.

To-day the waters of Spinbronn figure no longer in the "Codex"; in this poor village one no longer sees anyone but a few miserable woodcutters, and, sad to say, Dr. Hâselnoss has left!

All this resulted from a series of very strange catastrophes which lawyer Brêmer of Pirmesens told me about the other day.

You should know, Master Frantz (said he), that the spring of Spinbronn issues from a sort of cavern, about five feet high and twelve or fifteen feet wide; the water has a warmth of sixty-seven degrees Centigrade; it is salt. As for the cavern, entirely covered without with moss, ivy, and brushwood, its depth is unknown because the hot exhalations prevent all entrance.

Nevertheless, strangely enough, it was noticed early in the last century that birds of the neighborhood—thrushes, doves, hawks—were engulfed in it in full flight, and it was never known to what mysterious influence to attribute this particular.

In 1801, at the height of the season, owing to some circumstance which is still unexplained, the spring became more abundant, and the bathers, walking below on the greensward, saw a human skeleton as white as snow fall from the cascade.

You may judge, Master Frantz, of the general fright; it was thought naturally that a murder had been committed at Spinbronn in a recent year, and that the body of the victim had been thrown in the spring. But the skeleton weighed no more than a dozen francs, and Hâselnoss concluded that it must have sojourned more than three centuries in the sand to have become reduced to such a state of desiccation.

This very plausible reasoning did not prevent a crowd of patrons, wild at the idea of having drunk the saline water, from leaving before the end of the day; those worst afflicted with gout and gravel consoled themselves. But the overflow continuing, all the rubbish, slime, and detritus which the cavern contained was disgorged on the following days; a veritable bone-yard came down from the mountain: skeletons of animals of every kind—of quadrupeds, birds, and reptiles—in short, all that one could conceive as most horrible.

Hâselnoss issued a pamphlet demonstrating that all these bones were derived from an antediluvian world: that they were fossil bones, accumulated there in a sort of funnel during the universal flood—that is to say, four thousand years before Christ, and that, consequently, one might consider them as nothing but stones, and that it was needless to be disgusted. But his work had scarcely reassured the gouty when, one fine morning, the corpse of a fox, then that of a hawk with all its feathers, fell from the cascade.

It was impossible to establish that these remains antedated the Flood. Anyway, the disgust was so great that everybody tied up his bundle and went to take the waters elsewhere.

"How infamous!" cried the beautiful ladies—"how horrible! So that's what the virtue of these mineral waters came from! Oh, 'twere better to die of gravel than continue such a remedy!"

At the end of a week there remained at Spinbronn only a big Englishman who had gout in his hands as well as in his feet, who had himself addressed as Sir Thomas Hawerburch, Commodore; and he brought a large retinue, according to the usage of a British subject in a foreign land.

This personage, big and fat, with a florid complexion, but with hands simply knotted with gout, would have drunk skeleton soup if it would have cured his infirmity. He laughed heartily over the desertion of the other sufferers, and installed himself in the prettiest *châlet* at half price, announcing his design to pass the winter at Spinbronn.

(Here lawyer Brêmer slowly absorbed an ample pinch of snuff as if to quicken his reminiscences; he shook his laced ruff with his finger tips and continued:)

* * *

Five or six years before the Revolution of 1789, a young doctor of Pirmesens, named
Christian Weber, had gone out to San Domingo in the hope of making his fortune. He
had actually amassed some hundred thousand francs in the exercise of his profession
when the negro revolt broke out.

I need not recall to you the barbarous treatment to which our unfortunate fellow countrymen were subjected at Haiti. Dr. Weber had the good luck to escape the
massacre and to save part of his fortune. Then he traveled in South America, and especially in French Guiana. In 1801 he returned to Pirmesens, and established himself at
Spinbronn, where Dr. Hâselnoss made over his house and defunct practice.

Christian Weber brought with him an old negress called Agatha: a frightful
creature, with a flat nose and lips as large as your fist, and her head tied up in three
bandanas of razor-edged colors. This poor old woman adored red; she had earrings
which hung down to her shoulders, and the mountaineers of Hundsrück came from six
leagues around to stare at her.

As for Dr. Weber, he was a tall, lean man, invariably dressed in a sky-blue coat
with codfish tails and deerskin breeches. He wore a hat of flexible straw and boots with
bright yellow tops, on the front of which hung two silver tassels. He talked little; his
laugh was like a nervous attack, and his gray eyes, usually calm and meditative, shone
with singular brilliance at the least sign of contradiction. Every morning he fetched a
turn round about the mountain, letting his horse ramble at a venture, whistling forever
the same tune, some negro melody or other. Lastly, this rum chap had brought from
Haiti a lot of bandboxes filled with queer insects—some black and reddish brown, big
as eggs; others little and shimmering like sparks. He seemed to set greater store by
them than by his patients, and, from time to time, on coming back from his rides, he
brought a quantity of butterflies pinned to his hat brim.

Scarcely was he settled in Hâselnoss's vast house when he peopled the back yard
with outlandish birds—Barbary geese with scarlet cheeks, Guinea hens, and a white
peacock, which perched habitually on the garden wall, and which divided with the
negress the admiration of the mountaineers.

If I enter into these details, Master Frantz, it's because they recall my early youth;
Dr. Christian found himself to be at the same time my cousin and my tutor, and as
early as on his return to Germany he had come to take me and install me in his house
at Spinbronn. The black Agatha at first sight inspired me with some fright, and I only
got seasoned to that fantastic visage with considerable difficulty; but she was such a

good woman—she knew so well how to make spiced patties, she hummed such strange songs in a guttural voice, snapping her fingers and keeping time with a heavy shuffle, that I ended by taking her in fast friendship.

Dr. Weber was naturally thick with Sir Thomas Hawerburch, as representing the only one of his clientele then in evidence, and I was not slow in perceiving that these two eccentrics held long conventicles together. They conversed on mysterious matters, on the transmission of fluids, and indulged in certain odd signs which one or the other had picked up in his voyages—Sir Thomas in the Orient, and my tutor in America. This puzzled me greatly. As children will, I was always lying in wait for what they seemed to want to conceal from me; but despairing in the end of discovering anything, I took the course of questioning Agatha, and the poor old woman, after making me promise to say nothing about it, admitted that my tutor was a sorcerer.

For the rest, Dr. Weber exercised a singular influence over the mind of this negress, and this woman, habitually so gay and forever ready to be amused by nothing, trembled like a leaf when her master's gray eyes chanced to alight on her.

All this, Master Frantz, seems to have no bearing on the springs of Spinbronn. But wait, wait—you shall see by what a singular concourse of circumstances my story is connected with it. I told you that birds darted into the cavern, and even other and larger creatures. After the final departure of the patrons, some of the old inhabitants of the village recalled that a young girl named Louise Müller, who lived with her infirm old grandmother in a cottage on the pitch of the slope, had suddenly disappeared half a hundred years before. She had gone out to look for herbs in the forest, and there had never been any more news of her afterwards, except that, three or four days later, some woodcutters who were descending the mountain had found her sickle and her apron a few steps from the cavern.

From that moment it was evident to everyone that the skeleton which had fallen from the cascade, on the subject of which Hâselnoss had turned such fine phrases, was no other than that of Louise Müller. The poor girl had doubtless been drawn into the gulf by the mysterious influence which almost daily overcame weaker beings!

What could this influence be? None knew. But the inhabitants of Spinbronn, superstitious like all mountaineers, maintained that the devil lived in the cavern, and terror spread in the whole region.

Now one afternoon in the middle of the month of July, 1802, my cousin undertook a new classification of the insects in his bandboxes. He had secured several rather curious ones the preceding afternoon. I was with him, holding the lighted candle with one hand and with the other a needle which I heated red-hot.

Sir Thomas, seated, his chair tipped back against the sill of a window, his feet on a stool, watched us work, and smoked his cigar with a dreamy air.

I stood in with Sir Thomas Hawerburch, and I accompanied him every day to the woods in his carriage. He enjoyed hearing me chatter in English, and wished to make of me, as he said, a thorough gentleman. The butterflies labeled, Dr. Weber at last opened the box of the largest insects, and said:

"Yesterday I secured a magnificent horn beetle, the great *Lucanus cervus* of the oaks of the Hartz. It has this peculiarity—the right claw divides in five branches. It's a rare specimen."

At the same time I offered him the needle, and as he pierced the insect before fixing it on the cork, Sir Thomas, until then impassive, got up, and, drawing near a bandbox, he began to examine the spider crab of Guiana with a feeling of horror which was strikingly portrayed on his fat vermilion face.

"That is certainly," he cried, "the most frightful work of the creation. The mere sight of it—it makes me shudder!"

In truth, a sudden pallor overspread his face.

"Bah!" said my tutor, "all that is only a prejudice from childhood—one hears his nurse cry out—one is afraid—and the impression sticks. But if you should consider the spider with a strong microscope, you would be astonished at the finish of his members, at their admirable arrangement, and even at their elegance."

"It disgusts me," interrupted the commodore brusquely. "Pouah!"

It had turned over in his fingers.

"Oh! I don't know why," he declared, "spiders have always frozen my blood!"

Dr. Weber began to laugh, and I, who shared the feelings of Sir Thomas, exclaimed:

"Yes, cousin, you ought to take this villainous beast out of the box—it is disgusting—it spoils all the rest."

"Little chump," he said, his eyes sparkling, "what makes you look at it? If you don't like it, go take yourself off somewhere."

Evidently he had taken offense; and Sir Thomas, who was then before the window contemplating the mountain, turned suddenly, took me by the hand, and said to me in a manner full of good will:

"Your tutor, Frantz, sets great store by his spider; we like the trees better—the verdure. Come, let's go for a walk."

"Yes, go," cried the doctor, "and come back for supper at six o'clock."

Then raising his voice:

"No hard feelings, Sir Hawerburch."

The commodore replied laughingly, and we got into the carriage, which was always waiting in front of the door of the house.

Sir Thomas wanted to drive himself and dismissed his servant. He made me sit beside him on the same seat and we started off for Rothalps.

While the carriage was slowly ascending the sandy path, an invincible sadness possessed itself of my spirit. Sir Thomas, on his part, was grave. He perceived my sadness and said:

"You don't like spiders, Frantz, nor do I either. But thank Heaven, there aren't any dangerous ones in this country. The spider crab which your tutor has in his box comes from French Guiana. It inhabits the great, swampy forests filled with warm vapors, with scalding exhalations; this temperature is necessary to its life. Its web, or rather its vast snare, envelops an entire thicket. In it it takes birds as our spiders take flies. But drive these disgusting images from your mind, and drink a swallow of my old Burgundy."

Then turning, he raised the cover of the rear seat, and drew from the straw a sort of gourd from which he poured me a full bumper in a leather goblet.

When I had drunk all my good humor returned and I began to laugh at my fright.

The carriage was drawn by a little Ardennes horse, thin and nervous as a goat, which clambered up the nearly perpendicular path. Thousands of insects hummed in the bushes. At our right, at a hundred paces or more, the somber outskirts of the Rothalp forests extended below us, the profound shades of which, choked with briers and foul brush, showed here and there an opening filled with light. On our left tumbled the stream of Spinbronn, and the more we climbed the more did its silvered sheets, floating in the abyss, grow tinged with azure and redouble their sound of cymbals.

I was captivated by this spectacle. Sir Thomas, leaning back in the seat, his knees as high as his chin, abandoned himself to his habitual reveries, while the horse, laboring with his feet and hanging his head on his chest as a counter-weight to the carriage, held on as if suspended on the flank of the rock. Soon, however, we reached a pitch less steep: the haunt of the roebuck, surrounded by tremulous shadows. I always lost my head, and my eyes too, in an immense perspective. At the apparition of the shadows I turned my head and saw the cavern of Spinbronn close at hand. The encompassing mists were a magnificent green, and the stream which, before falling, extends over a bed of black sand and pebbles, was so clear that one would have thought it frozen if pale vapors did not follow its surface.

The horse had just stopped of his own accord to breathe; Sir Thomas, rising, cast his eye over the countryside.

"How calm everything is!" said he.

Then, after an instant of silence: "If you weren't here, Frantz, I should certainly bathe in the basin."

"But, Commodore," said I, "why not bathe? I would do well to stroll around in the neighborhood. On the next hill is a great glade filled with wild strawberries. I'll go and pick some. I'll be back in an hour."

"Ha! I should like to, Frantz; it's a good idea. Dr. Weber contends that I drink too much Burgundy. It's necessary to offset wine with mineral water. This little bed of sand pleases me."

Then, having set both feet on the ground, he hitched the horse to the trunk of a little birch and waved his hand as if to say:

"You may go." I saw him sit down on the moss and draw off his boots. As I moved away he turned and called out:

"In an hour, Frantz."

They were his last words.

An hour later I returned to the spring. The horse, the carriage, and the clothes of Sir Thomas alone met my eyes. The sun was setting. The shadows were getting long. Not a bird's song under the foliage, not the hum of an insect in the tall grass. A silence like death looked down on this solitude! The silence frightened me. I climbed up on the rock which overlooks the cavern; I looked to the right and to the left. Nobody! I called. No answer! The sound of my voice, repeated by the echoes, filled me with fear. Night settled down slowly. A vague sense of horror oppressed me. Suddenly the story of the young girl who had disappeared occurred to me; and I began to descend on the run; but, arriving before the cavern, I stopped, seized with unaccountable terror: in casting a glance in the deep shadows of the spring I had caught sight of two motion-less red points. Then I saw long lines wavering in a strange manner in the midst of the darkness, and that at a depth where no human eye had ever penetrated. Fear lent my sight, and all my senses, an unheard-of subtlety of perception. For several seconds I heard very distinctly the evening plaint of a cricket down at the edge of the wood, a dog barking far away, very far in the valley. Then my heart, compressed for an instant by emotion, began to beat furiously and I no longer heard anything!

Then uttering a horrible cry, I fled, abandoning the horse, the carriage. In less than twenty minutes, bounding over the rocks and brush, I reached the threshold of our house, and cried in a stifled voice:

"Run! Run! Sir Hawerburch is dead! Sir Hawerburch is in the cavern—!"

After these words, spoken in the presence of my tutor, of the old woman Agatha, and of two or three people invited in that evening by the doctor, I fainted. I have learned since that during a whole hour I raved deliriously.

The whole village had gone in search of the commodore. Christian Weber hurried them off. At ten o'clock in the evening all the crowd came back, bringing the carriage, and in the carriage the clothes of Sir Hawerburch. They had discovered nothing. It was impossible to take ten steps in the cavern without being suffocated.

During their absence Agatha and I waited, sitting in the chimney corner. I, howling incoherent words of terror; she, with hands crossed on her knees, eyes wide open, going from time to time to the window to see what was taking place, for from the foot of the mountain one could see torches flitting in the woods. One could hear hoarse voices, in the distance, calling to each other in the night.

At the approach of her master, Agatha began to tremble. The doctor entered brusquely, pale, his lips compressed, despair written on his face. A score of woodcutters followed him tumultuously, in great felt hats with wide brims—swarthy visaged—shaking the ash from their torches. Scarcely was he in the hall when my tutor's glittering eyes seemed to look for something. He caught sight of the negress, and without a word having passed between them, the poor woman began to cry:

"No! no! I don't want to!"

"And I wish it," replied the doctor in a hard tone.

One would have said that the negress had been seized by an invincible power. She shuddered from head to foot, and Christian Weber showing her a bench, she sat down with a corpse-like stiffness.

All the bystanders, witnesses of this shocking spectacle, good folk with primitive and crude manners, but full of pious sentiments, made the sign of the cross, and I who knew not then, even by name, of the terrible magnetic power of the will, began to tremble, believing that Agatha was dead.

Christian Weber approached the negress, and making a rapid pass over her forehead:

"Are you there?" said he.

"Yes, master."

"Sir Thomas Hawerburch?"

At these words she shuddered again.

"Do you see him?"

"Yes—yes," she gasped in a strangling voice, "I see him."

"Where is he?"

"Up there—in the back of the cavern—dead!"

"Dead!" said the doctor, "how?"

"The spider—Oh! the spider crab—Oh!—"

"Control your agitation," said the doctor, who was quite pale, "tell us plainly—"

"The spider crab holds him by the throat—he is there—at the back—under the rock—wound round by webs—Ah!"

Christian Weber cast a cold glance toward his assistants, who, crowding around, with their eyes sticking out of their heads, were listening intently, and I heard him murmur:

"It's horrible! horrible!"

Then he resumed:

"You see him?"

"I see him—"

"And the spider—is it big?"

"Oh, master, never—never have I seen such a large one—not even on the banks of the Mocaris—nor in the lowlands of Konanama. It is as large as my head—!"

There was a long silence. All the assistants looked at each other, their faces livid, their hair standing up. Christian Weber alone seemed calm; having passed his hand several times over the negress's forehead, he continued:

"Agatha, tell us how death befell Sir Hawerburch."

"He was bathing in the basin of the spring—the spider saw him from behind, with his bare back. It was hungry, it had fasted for a long time; it saw him with his arms on the water. Suddenly it came out like a flash and placed its fangs around the commodore's neck, and he cried out: "Oh! oh! my God!" It stung and fled. Sir Hawerburch sank down in the water and died. Then the spider returned and surrounded him with its web, and he floated gently, gently, to the back of the cavern. It drew in on the web. Now he is all black."

The doctor, turning to me, who no longer felt the shock, asked:

"Is it true, Frantz, that the commodore went in bathing?"

"Yes, Cousin Christian."

"At what time?"

"At four o'clock."

"At four o'clock—it was very warm, wasn't it?"

"Oh, yes!"

"It's certainly so," said he, striking his forehead. "The monster could come out without fear——"

He pronounced a few unintelligible words, and then, looking toward the mountaineers:

"My friends," he cried, "that is where this mass of débris came from—of skeletons—which spread terror among the bathers. That is what has ruined you all—it is the spider crab! It is there—hidden in its web—awaiting its prey in the back of the cavern! Who can tell the number of its victims?"

And full of fury, he led the way, shouting:

"Fagots! Fagots!"

The woodcutters followed him, vociferating.

Ten minutes later two large wagons laden with fagots were slowly mounting the slope. A long file of woodcutters, their backs bent double, followed, enveloped in the somber night. My tutor and I walked ahead, leading the horses by their bridles, and the melancholy moon vaguely lighted this funereal march. From time to time the wheels grated. Then the carts, raised by the irregularities of the rocky road, fell again in the track with a heavy jolt.

As we drew near the cavern, on the playground of the roebucks, our cortége halted. The torches were lit, and the crowd advanced toward the gulf. The limpid water, running over the sand, reflected the bluish flame of the resinous torches, the rays of which revealed the tops of the black firs leaning over the rock.

"This is the place to unload," the doctor then said. "It's necessary to block up the mouth of the cavern."

And it was not without a feeling of terror that each undertook the duty of executing his orders. The fagots fell from the top of the loads. A few stakes driven down before the opening of the spring prevented the water from carrying them away.

Toward midnight the mouth of the cavern was completely closed. The water running over spread to both sides on the moss. The top fagots were perfectly dry; then Dr. Weber, supplying himself with a torch, himself lit the fire. The flames ran from twig to twig with an angry crackling, and soon leaped toward the sky, chasing clouds of smoke before them.

It was a strange and savage spectacle, the great pile with trembling shadows lit up in this way.

This cavern poured forth black smoke, unceasingly renewed and disgorged. All around stood the woodcutters, somber, motionless, expectant, their eyes fixed on the opening; and I, although trembling from head to foot in fear, could not tear away my gaze.

It was a good quarter of an hour that we waited, and Dr. Weber was beginning to grow impatient, when a black object, with long hooked claws, appeared suddenly in the shadow and precipitated itself toward the opening.

A cry resounded about the pyre.

The spider, driven back by the live coals, reentered its cave. Then, smothered doubtless by the smoke, it returned to the charge and leaped out into the midst of the flames. Its long legs curled up. It was as large as my head, and of a violet red.

One of the woodcutters, fearing lest it leap clear of the fire, threw his hatchet at it, and with such good aim that on the instant the fire around it was covered with blood. But soon the flames burst out more vigorously over it and consumed the horrible destroyer.

Such, Master Frantz, was the strange event which destroyed the fine reputation which the waters of Spinbronn formerly enjoyed. I can certify the scrupulous precision of my account. But as for giving you an explanation, that would be impossible for me to do. At the same time, allow me to tell you that it does not seem to me absurd to admit that a spider, under the influence of a temperature raised by thermal waters, which affords the same conditions of life and development as the scorching climates of Africa and South America, should attain a fabulous size. It was this same extreme heat which explains the prodigious exuberance of the antediluvian creation!

However that may be, my tutor, judging that it would be impossible after this event to reestablish the waters of Spinbronn, sold the house back to Hâselnoss, in order to return to America with his negress and collections. I was sent to board in Strasbourg, where I remained until 1809.

The great political events of the epoch then absorbing the attention of Germany and France explain why the affair I have just told you about passed completely unobserved.

On the River

Guy de Maupassant

————— ◆ —————

L AST SUMMER I RENTED A COUNTRY COTTAGE ON THE BANKS OF THE Seine, several miles from Paris, and I used to go out to sleep there every night. After a while, I formed the acquaintance of one of my neighbors, a man between thirty and forty years of age, who really was one of the queerest characters I have ever met. He was an old boating-man, crazy on the subject of boats, and was always either in, or on, or by the water. He must have been born in a boat, and probably he will die in one, some day, while taking a last outing.

One evening, as we were walking along the banks of the Seine, I asked him to tell me about some of his nautical experiences. Immediately his face lighted up, and he became eloquent, almost poetical, for his heart was full of an all-absorbing, irresistible, devouring passion—a love for the river.

"Ah!" said he, "how many recollections I have of the river that flows at our feet! You street-dwellers have no idea what the river really is. But let a fisherman pronounce the word. To him it means mystery, the unknown, a land of mirage and phantasmagoria, where odd things that have no real existence are seen at night and strange noises are heard; where one trembles without knowing the reason why, as when passing through a cemetery,—and indeed the river is a sinister cemetery without graves.

"Land, for a fisherman, has boundaries, but the river, on moonless nights, appears to him unlimited A sailor doesn't feel the same way about the sea. The sea is often cruel, but it roars and foams, it gives us fair warning; the river is silent and treacherous. It flows stealthily, without a murmur, and the eternal gentle motion of the water is more awful to me than the big ocean waves.

"Dreamers believe that the deep hides immense lands of blue, where the drowned roll around among the big fish, in strange forests or in crystal caves. The river has only black depths, where the dead decay in the slime. But it's beautiful when the sun shines on it, and the waters splash softly on the banks covered with whispering reeds.

"In speaking of the ocean the poet says:

> "Oh! what tragic tales of the vast, blue deep,—
> The vast blue deep prayerful mothers fear,—
> The sad waves tell when at night, we hear,
> Their ceaseless moanings in our sleep!

Well, I believe that the stories the slender reeds tell one another in their wee, silvery voices are even more appalling than the ghastly tragedies related by the roaring waves.

"But as you have asked me to relate some of my recollections, I will tell you a strange adventure that happened to me here, about ten years ago.

"Then, as now, I lived in old mother Lafon's house and one of my best friends, Louis Bernet, who since has given up boating, as well as his happy-go-lucky ways, to become a State Councillor, was camping out in the village of C———, two miles away. We used to take dinner together every day, either at his place or at mine.

"One evening, as I was returning home alone, feeling rather tired, and with difficulty rowing the twelve-foot boat that I always took out at night, I stopped to rest a little while near that point over there, formed by reeds, about two hundred yards in front of the railway bridge. The weather was magnificent; the moon was shining very brightly, and the air was soft and still. The calmness of the surroundings tempted me, and I thought how pleasant it would be to fill my pipe here and smoke. No sooner said than done, and, laying hold of the anchor, I dropped it overboard. The boat, which was following the stream, slid to the end of the chain and came to a stop; I settled myself aft on a rug, as comfortably as I could. There was not a sound to be heard nor a movement to be seen, though sometimes I noticed the almost imperceptible rippling of the water on the banks, and watched the highest clumps of reeds, which at times assumed strange shapes that appeared to move.

"The river was perfectly calm, but I was affected by the extraordinary stillness that enveloped me. The frogs and toads, the nocturnal musicians of the swamps, were voiceless. Suddenly, at my right, a frog croaked. I started; it stopped, and all was silent. I resolved to light my pipe for distraction. But, strange to say, though I was an inveterate smoker I failed to enjoy it, and after a few puffs I grew sick and stopped smoking. Then I began to hum an air, but the sound of my voice depressed me.

"At last I lay down in the boat and watched the sky. For a while I remained quiet, but presently the slight pitching of the boat disturbed me. I felt as if it were swaying to and fro from one side of the river to the other, and that an invisible force or being was drawing it slowly to the bottom and then raising it to let it drop again. I was knocked about as if in a storm; I heard strange noises; I jumped up; the water was shining and all was still. Then I knew that my nerves were slightly shaken, and decided to leave the river. I pulled on the chain. The boat moved along, but presently I felt some resistance and pulled harder. The anchor refused to come up; it had caught in something at the bottom and remained stuck. I pulled and tugged but to no avail. With the oars I turned the boat around and forced her up-stream, in order to alter the position of the anchor. This was all in vain, however, for the anchor did not yield; so in a rage, I began to shake at the chain, which wouldn't budge.

"I sat down discouraged, to ponder over my mishap. It was impossible to break the chain or to separate it from the boat, as it was enormous and was riveted to a piece of wood as big as my arm; but as the weather continued fine, I did not doubt but that some fisherman would come along and rescue me. The accident calmed me so much that I managed to remain quiet and smoke my pipe. I had a bottle of rum with me so I drank two or three glasses of it and began to laugh at my situation. It was so warm that it would not have mattered much had I been obliged to spend all night out of doors.

"Suddenly something jarred slightly against the side of the boat. I started, and a cold sweat broke over me from head to foot. The noise was due to a piece of wood drifting along with the current, but it proved sufficient to disturb my mind, and once more I seized the chain and tugged in desperation. I felt the same strange nervousness creep over me. The anchor remained firm. I seated myself again, exhausted.

"Meantime the river was covering itself with a white mist that lay close to the water, so that when I stood up neither the stream, nor my feet, nor the boat, were visible to me; I could distinguish only the ends of the reeds and, a little farther away, the meadow, ashen in the moonlight, with large black patches formed by groups of Italian poplars reaching toward the sky. I was buried up to my waist in something that looked like a blanket of down of a peculiar whiteness; and all kinds of fantastic visions arose before me. I imagined that some one was trying to crawl into the boat, which I could no longer see, and that the river hidden under the thick fog was full of strange creatures that were swimming all around me. I felt a horrible depression steal over me, my temples throbbed, my heart beat wildly, and, losing all control over myself, I was ready to plunge overboard and swim to safety. But this idea suddenly filled me with horror. I imagined myself lost in the dense mist, floundering about aimlessly among the reeds and water-plants, unable to find the banks of the river or the boat; and I felt as if I should certainly be drawn by my feet to the bottom of the dark waters. As I really should have had to swim against the current for at least five hundred yards before reaching a spot where I could safely land, it was nine chances to ten that, being unable to see in the fog, I should drown, although I was a fine swimmer.

"I tried to overcome my dread. I determined not to be afraid, but there was something in me besides my will and that something was faint-hearted. I asked myself what there was to fear; my courageous self railed at the other, the timid one; never before had I so fully realised the opposition that exists between the two beings we have in us; the one willing, the other resisting, and each one triumphing in turn. But this foolish and unaccountable fear was growing worse and worse, and was becoming positive terror. I remained motionless, with open eyes and straining ears, waiting. For what? I scarcely knew, but it must have been for something terrible. I believe that had a fish suddenly taken it into its head to jump out of the water, as frequently happens, I should have fallen in a dead faint. However, I managed to keep my senses after a violent effort to control myself. I took my bottle of rum and again raised it to my lips.

"Suddenly I began to shout at the top of my voice, turning successively toward the four points of the horizon. After my throat had become completely paralyzed with shouting, I listened. A dog was barking in the distance.

"I drank some more rum and lay down in the bottom of the boat. I remained thus at least one hour, perhaps two, without sleeping, my eyes open, visited by nightmares. I did not dare to sit up, though I had an insane desire to do so; I put it off from second to second, saying: 'Now then, I'll get up,' but I was afraid to move. At last I raised myself with infinite care, as if my life depended on the slightest sound I might make, and peered over the edge of the boat. I was greeted by the most marvellous, stupendous sight that it is possible to imagine. It was a vision of fairyland, one of those phenomena that travellers in distant countries tell us about, but that we are unable to believe.

The mist, which two hours ago hung over the water, had lifted and settled on the banks of the stream. It formed on each side an unbroken hill, six or seven yards in height, that shone in the moonlight with the dazzling whiteness of snow. Nothing could be seen but the flashing river, moving between the two white mountains, and overhead a full moon that illuminated the milky-blue sky.

"All the hosts of the water had awakened; the frogs were croaking dismally, while from time to time a toad sent its short, monotonous, and gloomy note to the stars. Strange to say, I was no longer frightened; I was surrounded by a landscape so utterly unreal that the strangest freaks of nature would not have surprised me at all.

"How long this situation lasted I am unable to tell, for I finally dozed off to sleep. When I awoke, the moon was gone and the sky was covered with clouds. The water splashed dismally, the wind was blowing, it was cold and completely dark. I finished the rum and lay listening to the rustling of the reeds and the murmur of the river. I tried to see, but failed to distinguish the boat or even my hands, although I held them close to my eyes. The darkness, however, was slowly decreasing. Suddenly I thought I saw a shadow glide past me. I shouted to it and a voice responded: it was a fisherman. I called to him and told him of my plight. He brought his boat alongside mine and both began tugging at the chain. The anchor still would not yield. A cold, rainy day was setting in, one of those days that bring disaster and sadness. I perceived another boat, which we hailed. The owner added his strength to ours, and little by little the anchor gave way. It came up very slowly, laden with considerable weight. Finally a black heap appeared and we dragged it into my boat. It was the body of an old woman, with a big stone tied around her neck!"

The Ghostly Kiss

Lafcadio Hearn

———◆———

THE THEATRE WAS FULL. I CANNOT REMEMBER WHAT THEY WERE PLAYING. I did not have time to observe the actors. I only remember how vast the building seemed. Looking back, I saw an ocean of faces stretching away almost beyond the eye's power of definition to the far circles where the seats rose tier above tier in lines of illumination. The ceiling was blue, and in the midst a great mellow lamp hung suspended like a moon, at a height so lofty that I could not see the suspending chain. All the seats were black. I fancied that the theatre was hung with hangings of black velvet, bordered with a silver fringe that glimmered like tears. The audience were all in white.

All in white!—I asked myself whether I was not in some theatre of some tropical city—why all in white? I could not guess. I fancied at moments that I could perceive a moonlit landscape through far distant oriel windows, and the crests of palms casting moving shadows like gigantic spiders. The air was sweet with a strange and a new perfume; it was a drowsy air—a poppied air, in which the waving of innumerable white fans made no rustle, no sound.

There was a strange stillness and a strange silence. All eyes were turned toward the stage, except my own. I gazed in every direction but that of the stage! I cannot imagine why it was that I rarely looked toward the stage. No one noticed me; no one appeared to perceive that I was the only person in all that vast assembly clad in black— a tiny dark speck in a sea of white light.

Gradually the voices of the actors seemed to me to become fainter and fainter— thin sounds like whispers from another world—a world of ghosts!—and the music seemed not music, but only an echo in the mind of the hearer, like a memory of songs heard and forgotten in forgotten years.

There were faces that I thought strangely familiar—faces I fancied I had seen somewhere else in some other time. But none recognized me.

* * *

A woman sat before me—a fair woman with hair as brightly golden as the locks of Aphrodite. I asked my heart why it beat so strangely when I turned my eyes upon her. I felt as if it sought to leap from my breast and fling itself all palpitating under her feet. I watched the delicate movements of her neck, where a few loose bright curls were straying, like strands of gold clinging to a column of ivory;—the soft curve of the cheek flushed by a faint ruddiness like the velvet surface of a half-ripe peach;—the grace of the curving lips—lips sweet as those of the Cnidian Venus, which even after two thousand years still seem humid, as with the kisses of the last lover. But the eyes I could not see.

And a strange desire rose within me—an intense wish to kiss those lips. My heart said, Yes;—my reason whispered, No. I thought of the ten thousand thousand eyes that might suddenly be turned upon me. I looked back; and it seemed to me as if the whole theatre had grown vaster! The circles of seats had receded;—the great centre lamp seemed to have mounted higher;—the audience seemed vast as that we dream of in visions of the Last Judgment. And my heart beat so violently that I heard its passionate pulsation, louder than the voices of the actors and I feared lest it should betray me to all the host of white-clad men and women above me. But none seemed to hear or to see me. I trembled as I thought of the consequences of obeying the mad impulse that became every moment more overpowering and uncontrollable.

And my heart answered, "One kiss of those lips were worth the pain of ten thousand deaths."

I do not remember that I arose. I only remember finding myself beside her, close to her, breathing her perfumed breath, and gazing into eyes deep as the amethystine heaven of a tropical night. I pressed my lips passionately to hers;—I felt a thrill of inexpressible delight and triumph;—I felt the warm soft lips curl back to meet mine, and give me back my kiss!

And a great fear suddenly came upon me. And all the multitude of white-clad men and women arose in silence; and ten thousand thousand eyes looked upon me.

I heard a voice, faint, sweet,—such a voice as we hear when dead loves visit us in dreams.

"Thou hast kissed me: the compact is sealed forever."

And raising my eyes once more I saw that all the seats were graves and all the white dresses shrouds. Above me a light still shone in the blue roof, but only the light of a white moon in the eternal azure of heaven. White tombs stretched away in weird file to the verge of the horizon;—where it had seemed to me that I beheld a play, I saw only a lofty mausoleum;—and I knew that the perfume of the night was but the breath of flowers dying upon the tombs!

The Phantom 'Rickshaw

Rudyard Kipling

———— ◆ ————

May no ill dreams disturb my rest,
Nor Powers of Darkness me molest.
EVENING HYMN

ONE OF THE FEW ADVANTAGES THAT INDIA HAS OVER ENGLAND IS A great Knowability. After five years' service a man is directly or indirectly acquainted with the two or three hundred Civilians in his Province, all the Messes of ten or twelve Regiments and Batteries, and some fifteen hundred other people of the non-official caste. In ten years his knowledge should be doubled, and at the end of twenty he knows, or knows something about, every Englishman in the Empire, and may travel anywhere and everywhere without paying hotel-bills.

Globe-trotters who expect entertainment as a right, have, even within my memory, blunted this open-heartedness, but none the less to-day, if you belong to the Inner Circle and are neither a Bear nor a Black Sheep, all houses are open to you, and our small world is very, very kind and helpful.

Rickett of Kamartha stayed with Polder of Kumaon some fifteen years ago. He meant to stay two nights, but was knocked down by rheumatic fever, and for six weeks disorganized Polder's establishment, stopped Polder's work, and nearly died in Polder's bedroom. Polder behaves as though he had been placed under eternal obligation by Rickett, and yearly sends the little Ricketts a box of presents and toys. It is the same everywhere. The men who do not take the trouble to conceal from you their opinion that you are an incompetent ass, and the women who blacken your character and misunderstand your wife's amusements, will work themselves to the bone in your behalf if you fall sick or into serious trouble.

Heatherlegh, the Doctor, kept, in addition to his regular practice, a hospital on his private account—an arrangement of loose boxes for Incurables, his friend called it— but it was really a sort of fitting-up shed for craft that had been damaged by stress of weather. The weather in India is often sultry, and since the tale of bricks is always a fixed quantity, and the only liberty allowed is permission to work overtime and get no thanks, men occasionally break down and become as mixed as the metaphors in this sentence.

Heatherlegh is the dearest doctor that ever was, and his invariable prescription to all his patients is, "lie low, go slow, and keep cool." He says that more men are killed by overwork than the importance of this world justifies. He maintains that overwork slew Pansay, who died under his hands about three years ago. He has, of course, the right to speak authoritatively, and he laughs at my theory that there was a crack in Pansay's head and a little bit of the Dark World came through and pressed him to death. "Pansay went off the handle," says Heatherlegh, "after the stimulus of long leave at Home. He may or he may not have behaved like a blackguard to Mrs. Keith-Wessington. My notion is that the work of the Katabundi Settlement ran him off his legs, and that he took to brooding and making much of an ordinary P. & O. flirtation. He certainly was engaged to Miss Mannering, and she certainly broke off the engagement. Then he took a feverish chill and all that nonsense about ghosts developed. Overwork started his illness, kept it alight, and killed him poor devil. Write him off to the System—one man to take the work of two and a half men."

I do not believe this. I used to sit up with Pansay sometimes when Heatherlegh was called out to patients, and I happened to be within claim. The man would make me most unhappy by describing in a low, even voice, the procession that was always passing at the bottom of his bed. He had a sick man's command of language. When he recovered I suggested that he should write out the whole affair from beginning to end, knowing that ink might assist him to ease his mind. When little boys have learned a new bad word they are never happy till they have chalked it up on a door. And this also is Literature.

He was in a high fever while he was writing, and the blood-and-thunder Magazine diction he adopted did not calm him. Two months afterward he was reported fit for duty, but, in spite of the fact that he was urgently needed to help an undermanned Commission stagger through a deficit, he preferred to die; vowing at the last that he was hag-ridden. I got his manuscript before he died, and this is his version of the affair, dated 1885:—

My doctor tells me that I need rest and change of air. It is not improbable that I shall get both ere long—rest that neither the red-coated messenger nor the mid-day gun can break, and change of air far beyond that which any homeward-bound steamer can give me. In the meantime I am resolved to stay where I am; and, in flat defiance of my doctor's orders, to take all the world into my confidence. You shall learn for yourselves the precise nature of my malady; and shall, too, judge for yourselves whether any man born of woman on this weary earth was ever so tormented as I.

Speaking now as a condemned criminal might speak ere the drop-bolts are drawn, my story, wild and hideously improbable as it may appear, demands at least attention. That it will ever receive credence I utterly disbelieve. Two months ago I should have scouted as mad or drunk the man who had dared tell me the like. Two months ago I was the happiest man in India. To-day, from Peshawar to the sea, there is no one more wretched. My doctor and I are the only two who know this. His explanation is, that my brain, digestion, and eyesight are all slightly affected; giving rise to my frequent and persistent "delusions." Delusions, indeed! I call him a fool; but he attends me still with the same unwearied smile, the same bland professional manner, the same neatly trimmed red whiskers, till I begin to suspect that I am an ungrateful, evil-tempered invalid. But you shall judge for yourselves.

Three years ago it was my fortune—my great misfortune—to sail from Gravesend to Bombay, on return from long leave, with one Agnes Keith-Wessington, wife of an officer on the Bombay side. It does not in the least concern you to know what manner of woman she was. Be content with the knowledge that, ere the voyage had ended, both she and I were desperately and unreasoningly in love with one another. Heaven knows that I can make the admission now without one particle of vanity. In matters of this sort there is always one who gives and another who accepts. From the first day of our ill-omened attachment, I was conscious that Agnes's passion was a stronger, a more dominant, and—if I may use the expression—a purer sentiment than mine. Whether she recognized the fact then, I do not know. Afterward it was bitterly plain to both of us.

Arrived at Bombay in the spring of the year, we went our respective ways, to meet no more for the next three or four months, when my leave and her love took us both to Simla. There we spent the season together; and there my fire of straw burned itself out to a pitiful end with the closing year. I attempt no excuse. I make no apology. Mrs. Wessington had given up much for my sake, and was prepared to give up all. From my own lips, in August, 1882, she learned that I was sick of her presence, tired of her company, and weary of the sound of her voice. Ninety-nine women out of a hundred would have wearied of me as I wearied of them; seventy-five of that number would have promptly avenged themselves by active and obtrusive flirtation with other men. Mrs. Wessington was the hundredth. On her neither my openly expressed aversion nor the cutting brutalities with which I garnished our interviews had the least effect.

"Jack, darling!" was her one eternal cuckoo cry: "I'm sure it's all a mistake—a hideous mistake; and we'll be good friends again some day. *Please* forgive me, Jack, dear."

I was the offender, and I knew it. That knowledge transformed my pity into passive endurance, and, eventually, into blind hate—the same instinct, I suppose, which prompts a man to savagely stamp on the spider he has but half killed. And with this hate in my bosom the season of 1882 came to an end.

Next year we met again at Simla—she with her monotonous face and timid attempts at reconciliation, and I with loathing of her in every fibre of my frame. Several times I could not avoid meeting her alone; and on each occasion her words were identically the same. Still the unreasoning wail that it was all a "mistake"; and still the hope of eventually "making friends." I might have seen had I cared to look, that that hope only was keeping her alive. She grew more wan and thin month by month. You will agree with me, at least, that such conduct would have driven any one to despair. It was uncalled for; childish; unwomanly. I maintain that she was much to blame. And again, sometimes, in the black, fever-stricken night-watches, I have begun to think that I might have been a little kinder to her. But that really is a "delusion." I could not have continued pretending to love her when I didn't; could I? It would have been unfair to us both.

Last year we met again—on the same terms as before. The same weary appeal, and the same curt answers from my lips. At least I would make her see how wholly wrong and hopeless were her attempts at resuming the old relationship. As the season wore on, we fell apart—that is to say, she found it difficult to meet me, for I had other and more absorbing interests to attend to. When I think it over quietly in my sick-room, the season of 1884 seems a confused nightmare wherein light and shade were fantastically intermingled—my courtship of little Kitty Mannering; my hopes, doubts, and fears; our long rides together; my trembling avowal of attachment; her reply; and now and again a vision of a white face flitting by in the 'rickshaw with the black and white liveries I once watched for so earnestly; the wave of Mrs. Wessington's gloved hand; and, when she met me alone, which was but seldom, the irksome monotony of her appeal. I loved Kitty Mannering; honestly, heartily loved her, and with my love for her grew my hatred for Agnes. In August Kitty and I were engaged. The next day I met those accursed "magpie" *jhampanies* at the back of Jakko, and, moved by some passing sentiment of pity, stopped to tell Mrs. Wessington everything. She knew it already.

"So I hear you're engaged, Jack dear." Then, without a moment's pause:—"I'm sure it's all a mistake—a hideous mistake. We shall be as good friends some day, Jack, as we ever were."

My answer might have made even a man wince. It cut the dying woman before me like the blow of a whip. "Please forgive me, Jack; I didn't mean to make you angry; but it's true, it's true!"

And Mrs. Wessington broke down completely. I turned away and left her to finish her journey in peace, feeling, but only for a moment or two, that I had been an unutterably mean hound. I looked back, and saw that she had turned her 'rickshaw with the idea, I suppose, of overtaking me.

The scene and its surroundings were photographed on my memory. The rain-swept sky (we were at the end of the wet weather), the sodden, dingy pines, the muddy road, and the black powder-riven cliffs formed a gloomy background against which the black and white liveries of the *jhampanies*, the yellow-paneled 'rickshaw and Mrs. Wessington's down-bowed golden head stood out clearly. She was holding her handkerchief in her left hand and was leaning back exhausted against the 'rickshaw cushions. I turned my horse up a bypath near the Sanjowlie Reservoir and literally ran away. Once I fancied I heard a faint call of "Jack!" This may have been imagination. I never stopped to verify it. Ten minutes later I came across Kitty on horseback; and, in the delight of a long ride with her, forgot all about the interview.

A week later Mrs. Wessington died, and the inexpressible burden of her existence was removed from my life. I went Plainsward perfectly happy. Before three months were over I had forgotten all about her, except that at times the discovery of some of her old letters reminded me unpleasantly of our bygone relationship. By January I had disinterred what was left of our correspondence from among my scattered belongings and had burned it. At the beginning of April of this year, 1885, I was at Simla—semi-deserted Simla—once more, and was deep in lover's talks and walks with Kitty. It was decided that we should be married at the end of June. You will understand, therefore, that, loving Kitty as I did, I am not saying too much when I pronounce myself to have been, at that time, the happiest man in India.

Fourteen delightful days passed almost before I noticed their flight. Then, aroused to the sense of what was proper among mortals circumstanced as we were, I pointed out to Kitty that an engagement ring was the outward and visible sign of her dignity as an engaged girl; and that she must forthwith come to Hamilton's to be measured for one. Up to that moment, I give you my word, we had completely forgotten so trivial a matter. To Hamilton's we accordingly went on the 15th of April, 1885. Remember that—whatever my doctor may say to the contrary—I was then in perfect health, enjoying a well-balanced mind and an *absolutely* tranquil spirit. Kitty and I entered Hamilton's shop together, and there, regardless of the order of affairs, I measured Kitty for the ring in the presence of the amused assistant. The ring was a sapphire with two diamonds. We then rode out down the slope that leads to the Combermere Bridge and Peliti's shop.

While my Waler was cautiously feeling his way over the loose shale, and Kitty was laughing and chattering at my side—while all Simla, that is to say as much of it as had then come from the Plains, was grouped round the Reading-room and Peliti's veranda,—I was aware that some one, apparently at a vast distance, was calling me by my Christian name. It struck me that I had heard the voice before, but when and where I could not at once determine. In the short space it took to cover the road between the path from Hamilton's shop and the first plank of the Combermere Bridge I had thought over half a dozen people who might have committed such a solecism, and had eventually decided that it must have been singing in my ears. Immediately opposite Peliti's shop my eye was arrested by the sight of four *jhampanies* in "magpie" livery, pulling a yellow-paneled, cheap, bazar 'rickshaw. In a moment my mind flew back to the previous season and Mrs. Wessington with a sense of irritation and disgust. Was it not enough that the woman was dead and done with, without her black and white servitors reappearing to spoil the day's happiness? Whoever employed them now I thought I would call upon, and ask as a personal favor to change her *jhampanies'* livery. I would hire the men myself, and, if necessary, buy their coats from off their backs. It is impossible to say here what a flood of undesirable memories their presence evoked.

"Kitty," I cried, "there are poor Mrs. Wessington's *jhampanies* turned up again! I wonder who has them now?"

Kitty had known Mrs. Wessington slightly last season, and had always been interested in the sickly woman.

"What? Where?" she asked. "I can't see them anywhere."

Even as she spoke her horse, swerving from a laden mule, threw himself directly in front of the advancing 'rickshaw. I had scarcely time to utter a word of warning when, to my unutterable horror, horse and rider passed *through* men and carriage as if they had been thin air.

"What's the matter?" cried Kitty; "what made you call out so foolishly, Jack? If I *am* engaged I don't want all creation to know about it. There was lots of space between the mule and the veranda; and, if you think I can't ride—There!"

Whereupon wilful Kitty set off, her dainty little head in the air, at a hand-gallop in the direction of the Band-stand; fully expecting, as she herself afterward told me, that I should follow her. What was the matter? Nothing indeed. Either that I was mad or drunk, or that Simla was haunted with devils. I reined in my impatient cob, and turned round. The 'rickshaw had turned too, and now stood immediately facing me, near the left railing of the Combermere Bridge.

"Jack! Jack, darling!" (There was no mistake about the words this time: they rang through my brain as if they had been shouted in my ear.) "It's some hideous mistake, I'm sure. *Please* forgive me, Jack, and let's be friends again."

The 'rickshaw-hood had fallen back, and inside, as I hope and pray daily for the death I dread by night, sat Mrs. Keith-Wessington, handkerchief in hand, and golden head bowed on her breast.

How long I stared motionless I do not know. Finally, I was aroused by my syce taking the Waler's bridle and asking whether I was ill. From the horrible to the commonplace is but a step. I tumbled off my horse and dashed, half fainting, into Peliti's for a glass of cherry-brandy. There two or three couples were gathered round the coffee-tables discussing the gossip of the day. Their trivialities were more comforting to me just then than the consolations of religion could have been. I plunged into the midst of the conversation at once; chatted, laughed, and jested with a face (when I caught a glimpse of it in a mirror) as white and drawn as that of a corpse. Three or four men noticed my condition; and, evidently setting it down to the results of over-many pegs, charitably endeavoured to draw me apart from the rest of the loungers. But I refused to be led away. I wanted the company of my kind—as a child rushes into the midst of the dinner-party after a fright in the dark. I must have talked for about ten minutes or so, though it seemed an eternity to me, when I heard Kitty's clear voice outside inquiring for me. In another minute she had entered the shop, prepared to roundly upbraid me for failing so signally in my duties. Something in my face stopped her.

"Why, Jack," she cried, "what *have* you been doing? What *has* happened? Are you ill?" Thus driven into a direct lie, I said that the sun had been a little too much for me. It was close upon five o'clock of a cloudy April afternoon, and the sun had been hidden all day. I saw my mistake as soon as the words were out of my mouth: attempted to recover it; blundered hopelessly and followed Kitty in a regal rage, out of doors, amid the smiles of my acquaintances. I made some excuse (I have forgotten what) on the score of my feeling faint; and cantered away to my hotel, leaving Kitty to finish the ride by herself.

In my room I sat down and tried calmly to reason out the matter. Here was I, Theobald Jack Pansay, a well-educated Bengal Civilian in the year of grace, 1885, presumably sane, certainly healthy, driven in terror from my sweetheart's side by the apparition of a woman who had been dead and buried eight months ago. These were facts that I could not blink. Nothing was further from my thought than any memory of Mrs. Wessington when Kitty and I left Hamilton's shop. Nothing was more utterly commonplace than the stretch of wall opposite Peliti's. It was broad daylight. The road was full of people; and yet here, look you, in defiance of every law of probability, in direct outrage of Nature's ordinance, there had appeared to me a face from the grave.

Kitty's Arab had gone *through* the 'rickshaw: so that my first hope that some woman marvelously like Mrs. Wessington had hired the carriage and the coolies with their old livery was lost. Again and again I went round this treadmill of thought; and again and again gave up baffled and in despair. The voice was as inexplicable as the apparition. I had originally some wild notion of confiding it all to Kitty; of begging her to marry me at once; and in her arms defying the ghostly occupant of the 'rickshaw. "After all," I argued, "the presence of the 'rickshaw is in itself enough to prove the existence of a spectral illusion. One may see ghosts of men and women, but surely never of coolies and carriages. The whole thing is absurd. Fancy the ghost of a hillman!"

Next morning I sent a penitent note to Kitty, imploring her to overlook my strange conduct of the previous afternoon. My Divinity was still very wroth, and a personal apology was necessary. I explained, with a fluency born of night-long pondering over a falsehood, that I had been attacked with sudden palpitation of the heart—the result of indigestion. This eminently practical solution had its effect; and Kitty and I rode out that afternoon with the shadow of my first lie dividing us.

Nothing would please her save a canter round Jakko. With my nerves still unstrung from the previous night I feebly protested against the notion, suggesting Observatory Hill, Jutogh, the Boileaugunge road—anything rather than the Jakko round. Kitty was angry and a little hurt: so I yielded from fear of provoking further misunderstanding, and we set out together toward Chota Simla. We walked a greater part of the way, and, according to our custom, cantered from a mile or so below the Convent to the stretch of level road by the Sanjowlie Reservoir. The wretched horses appeared to fly, and my heart beat quicker and quicker as we neared the crest of the ascent. My mind had been full of Mrs. Wessington all the afternoon; and every inch of the Jakko road bore witness to our old-time walks and talks. The bowlders were full of it; the pines sang it aloud overhead; the rain-fed torrents giggled and chuckled unseen over the shameful story; and the wind in my ears chanted the iniquity aloud.

As a fitting climax, in the middle of the level men call the Ladies' Mile the Horror was awaiting me. No other 'rickshaw was in sight—only the four black and white *jhampanies*, the yellow-paneled carriage, and the golden head of the woman within—all apparently just as I had left them eight months and one fortnight ago! For an instant I fancied that Kitty *must* see what I saw—we were so marvelously sympathetic in all things. Her next words undeceived me—"Not a soul in sight! Come along, Jack, and I'll race you to the Reservoir buildings!" Her wiry little Arab was off like a bird, my Waler following close behind, and in this order we dashed under the cliffs. Half a minute brought us within fifty yards of the 'rickshaw. I pulled my Waler and fell back a little. The 'rickshaw was directly in the middle of the road; and once more the Arab passed through it, my horse following. "Jack! Jack dear! *Please* forgive me," rang with a wail in my ears, and, after an interval:—"It's all a mistake, a hideous mistake!"

I spurred my horse like a man possessed. When I turned my head at the Reservoir works, the black and white liveries were still waiting—patiently waiting—under the gray hillside, and the wind brought me a mocking echo of the words I had just heard. Kitty bantered me a good deal on my silence throughout the remainder of the ride. I had been talking up till then wildly and at random. To save my life I could not speak afterward naturally, and from Sanjowlie to the Church wisely held my tongue.

I was to dine with the Mannerings that night, and had barely time to canter home to dress. On the road to Elysium Hill I overheard two men talking together in the dusk.—"It's a curious thing," said one, "how completely all trace of it disappeared. You know my wife was insanely fond of the woman ('never could see anything in her myself), and wanted me to pick up her old 'rickshaw and coolies if they were to be got for love or money. Morbid sort of fancy I call it; but I've got to do what the *Memsahib* tells me. Would you believe that the man she hired it from tells me that all four of the men—they were brothers—died of cholera on the way to Hardwar, poor devils; and the ' rickshaw has been broken up by the man himself. 'Told me he never used a dead *Memsahib's* 'rickshaw. 'Spoilt his luck. Queer notion, wasn't it? Fancy poor little Mrs. Wessington spoiling any one's luck except her own!" I laughed aloud at this point; and my laugh jarred on me as I uttered it. So there *were* ghosts of 'rickshaws after all, and ghostly employments in the other world! How much did Mrs. Wessington give her men? What were their hours? Where did they go?

And for visible answer to my last question I saw the infernal Thing blocking my path in the twilight. The dead travel fast, and by short cuts unknown to ordinary coolies. I laughed aloud a second time and checked my laughter suddenly, for I was afraid I was going mad. Mad to a certain extent I must have been, for I recollect that I reined in my horse at the head of the 'rickshaw, and politely wished Mrs. Wessington "Good-evening." Her answer was one I knew only too well. I listened to the end; and replied that I had heard it all before, but should be delighted if she had anything further to say. Some malignant devil stronger than I must have entered into me that evening, for I have a dim recollection of talking the commonplaces of the day for five minutes to the Thing in front of me.

"Mad as a hatter, poor devil—or drunk. Max, try and get him to come home."

Surely *that* was not Mrs. Wessington's voice! The two men had overheard me speaking to the empty air, and had returned to look after me. They were very kind and considerate, and from their words evidently gathered that I was extremely drunk. I thanked them confusedly and cantered away to my hotel, there changed, and arrived at the Mannerings' ten minutes late. I pleaded the darkness of the night as an excuse; was rebuked by Kitty for my unlover-like tardiness; and sat down.

The conversation had already become general; and under cover of it, I was addressing some tender small talk to my sweetheart when I was aware that at the further end of the table a short red-whiskered man was describing, with much broidery, his encounter with a mad unknown that evening.

A few sentences convinced me that he was repeating the incident of half an hour ago. In the middle of the story he looked round for applause, as professional story-tellers do, caught my eye, and straightway collapsed. There was a moment's awkward silence, and the red-whiskered man muttered something to the effect that he had "forgotten the rest," thereby sacrificing a reputation as a good story-teller which he had built up for six seasons past. I blessed him from the bottom of my heart, and—went on with my fish.

In the fulness of time that dinner came to an end; and with genuine regret I tore myself away from Kitty—as certain as I was of my own existence that It would be waiting for me outside the door. The red-whiskered man, who had been introduced to me as Doctor Heatherlegh, of Simla, volunteered to bear me company as far as our roads lay together. I accepted his offer with gratitude.

My instinct had not deceived me. It lay in readiness in the Mall, and, in what seemed devilish mockery of our ways, with a lighted head-lamp. The red-whiskered man went to the point at once, in a manner that showed he had been thinking over it all dinner time.

"I say, Pansay, what the deuce was the matter with you this evening on the Elysium road?" The suddenness of the question wrenched an answer from me before I was aware.

"That!" said I, pointing to It.

"*That* may be either D. T. or Eyes for aught I know. Now you don't liquor. I saw as much at dinner, so it can't be *D. T.* There's nothing whatever where you're pointing, though you're sweating and trembling with fright like a scared pony. Therefore, I conclude that it's Eyes. And I ought to understand all about them. Come along home with me. I'm on the Blessington lower road."

To my intense delight the 'rickshaw instead of waiting for us kept about twenty yards ahead—and this, too whether we walked, trotted, or cantered. In the course of that long night ride I had told my companion almost as much as I have told you here.

"Well, you've spoiled one of the best tales I've ever laid tongue to," said he, "but I'll forgive you for the sake of what you've gone through. Now come home and do what I tell you; and when I've cured you, young man, let this be a lesson to you to steer clear of women and indigestible food till the day of your death."

The 'rickshaw kept steady in front; and my red-whiskered friend seemed to derive great pleasure from my account of its exact whereabouts.

"Eyes, Pansay—all Eyes, Brain, and Stomach. And the greatest of these three is Stomach. You've too much conceited Brain, too little Stomach, and thoroughly unhealthy Eyes. Get your Stomach straight and the rest follows. And all that's French for a liver pill. I'll take sole medical charge of you from this hour! for you're too interesting a phenomenon to be passed over."

By this time we were deep in the shadow of the Blessington lower road and the 'rickshaw came to a dead stop under a pine-clad, over-hanging shale cliff. Instinctively I halted too, giving my reason. Heatherlegh rapped out an oath.

"Now, if you think I'm going to spend a cold night on the hillside for the sake of a stomach-*cum*-Brain-*cum*-Eye illusion . . . Lord, ha' mercy! What's that?"

There was a muffled report, a blinding smother of dust just in front of us, a crack, the noise of rent boughs, and about ten yards of the cliff-side—pines, undergrowth, and all—slid down into the road below, completely blocking it up. The uprooted trees swayed and tottered for a moment like drunken giants in the gloom, and then fell prone among their fellows with a thunderous crash. Our two horses stood motionless and sweating with fear. As soon as the rattle of falling earth and stone had subsided, my companion muttered:—"Man, if we'd gone forward we should have been ten feet deep in our graves by now. 'There are more things in heaven and earth' . . . Come home, Pansay, and thank God. I want a peg badly."

We retraced our way over the Church Ridge, and I arrived at Dr. Heatherlegh's house shortly after midnight.

His attempts toward my cure commenced almost immediately, and for a week I never left his sight. Many a time in the course of that week did I bless the good-fortune which had thrown me in contact with Simla's best and kindest doctor. Day by day my spirits grew lighter and more equable. Day by day, too, I became more and more inclined to fall in with Heatherlegh's "spectral illusion" theory, implicating eyes, brain, and stomach. I wrote to Kitty, telling her that a slight sprain caused by a fall from my horse kept me indoors for a few days; and that I should be recovered before she had time to regret my absence.

Heatherlegh's treatment was simple to a degree. It consisted of liver pills, cold-water baths, and strong exercise, taken in the dusk or at early dawn—for, as he sagely observed:—"A man with a sprained ankle doesn't walk a dozen miles a day, and your young woman might be wondering if she saw you."

At the end of the week, after much examination of pupil and pulse, and strict injunctions as to diet and pedestrianism, Heatherlegh dismissed me as brusquely as he had taken charge of me. Here is his parting benediction: "Man, I can certify to your mental cure, and that's as much as to say I've cured most of your bodily ailments. Now, get your traps out of this as soon as you can; and be off to make love to Miss Kitty."

I was endeavoring to express my thanks for his kindness. He cut me short.

"Don't think I did this because I like you. I gather that you've behaved like a blackguard all through. But, all the same, you're a phenomenon, and as queer a phe-nomenon as you are a blackguard. No!"—checking me a second time—"not a rupee, please. Go out and see if you can find the eyes-brain-and-stomach business again. I'll give you a lakh for each time you see it."

Half an hour later I was in the Mannerings' drawing-room with Kitty—drunk with the intoxication of present happiness and the foreknowledge that I should never more be troubled with Its hideous presence. Strong in the sense of my new-found security, I proposed a ride at once; and, by preference, a canter round Jakko.

Never had I felt so well, so overladen with vitality and mere animal spirits, as I did on the afternoon of the 30th of April. Kitty was delighted at the change in my appear-ance, and complimented me on it in her delightfully frank and outspoken manner.

We left the Mannerings' house together, laughing and talking, and cantered along the Chota Simla road as of old.

I was in haste to reach the Sanjowlie Reservoir and there make my assurance doubly sure. The horses did their best, but seemed all too slow to my impatient mind. Kitty was astonished at my boisterousness. "Why, Jack!" she cried at last, "you are behaving like a child. What are you doing?"

We were just below the Convent, and from sheer wantonness I was making my Waler plunge and curvet across the road as I tickled it with the loop of my riding-whip.

"Doing?" I answered; "nothing, dear. That's just it. If you'd been doing nothing for a week except lie up, you'd be as riotous as I.

> "Singing and murmuring in your feastful mirth,
>   Joying to feel yourself alive;
> Lord over Nature, Lord of the visible Earth,
>   Lord of the senses five."

My quotation was hardly out of my lips before we had rounded the corner above the Convent; and a few yards further on could see across to Sanjowlie. In the centre of the level road stood the black and white liveries, the yellow-paneled 'rickshaw, and Mrs. Keith-Wessington. I pulled up, looked, rubbed my eyes, and, I believe must have said something. The next thing I knew was that I was lying face downward on the road with Kitty kneeling above me in tears.

"Has it gone, child!" I gasped. Kitty only wept more bitterly.

"Has what gone, Jack dear? what does it all mean? There must be a mistake somewhere, Jack. A hideous mistake." Her last words brought me to my feet—mad—raving for the time being.

"Yes, there *is* a mistake somewhere," I repeated, "a hideous mistake. Come and look at It."

I have an indistinct idea that I dragged Kitty by the wrist along the road up to where It stood, and implored her for pity's sake to speak to It; to tell It that we were betrothed; that neither Death nor Hell could break the tie between us; and Kitty only knows how much more to the same effect. Now and again I appealed passionately to the Terror in the 'rickshaw to bear witness to all I had said, and to release me from a torture that was killing me. As I talked I suppose I must have told Kitty of my old relations with Mrs. Wessington, for I saw her listen intently with white face and blazing eyes.

"Thank you, Mr. Pansay," she said, "that's *quite* enough. *Syce ghora láo.*"

The syces, impassive as Orientals always are, had come up with the recaptured horses; and as Kitty sprang into her saddle I caught hold of the bridle, entreating her to hear me out and forgive. My answer was the cut of her riding-whip across my face from mouth to eye, and a word or two of farewell that even now I cannot write down. So I judged, and judged rightly, that Kitty knew all; and I staggered back to the side of the 'rickshaw. My face was cut and bleeding, and the blow of the riding-whip had raised a livid blue wheal on it. I had no self-respect. Just then, Heatherlegh, who must have been following Kitty and me at a distance, cantered up.

"Doctor," I said, pointing to my face, "here's Miss Mannering's signature to my order of dismissal and . . . I'll thank you for that lakh as soon as convenient."

Heatherlegh's face, even in my abject misery, moved me to laughter.

"I'll stake my professional reputation"—he began. "Don't be a fool," I whispered. "I've lost my life's happiness and you'd better take me home."

As I spoke the 'rickshaw was gone. Then I lost all knowledge of what was passing. The crest of Jakko seemed to heave and roll like the crest of a cloud and fall in upon me.

Seven days later (on the 7th of May, that is to say) I was aware that I was lying in Heatherlegh's room as weak as a little child. Heatherlegh was watching me intently from behind the papers on his writing-table. His first words were not encouraging; but I was too far spent to be much moved by them.

"Here's Miss Kitty has sent back your letters. You corresponded a good deal, you young people. Here's a packet that looks like a ring, and a cheerful sort of a note from Mannering Papa, which I've taken the liberty of reading and burning. The old gentleman's not pleased with you."

"And Kitty?" I asked, dully.

"Rather more drawn than her father from what she says. By the same token you must have been letting out any number of queer reminiscences just before I met you. 'Says that a man who would have behaved to a woman as you did to Mrs. Wessington ought to kill himself out of sheer pity for his kind. She's a hot-headed little virago, your mash. 'Will have it too that you were suffering from *D. T.* when that row on the Jakko road turned up. 'Says she'll die before she ever speaks to you again."

I groaned and turned over to the other side.

"Now you've got your choice, my friend. This engagement has to be broken off; and the Mannerings don't want to be too hard on you. Was it broken through *D. T.* or epileptic fits? Sorry I can't offer you a better exchange unless you'd prefer hereditary insanity. Say the word and I'll tell 'em it's fits. All Simla knows about that scene on the Ladies' Mile. Come! I'll give you five minutes to think over it."

During those five minutes I believe that I explored thoroughly the lowest circles of the Inferno which it is permitted man to tread on earth. And at the same time I myself was watching myself faltering through the dark labyrinths of doubt, misery, and utter despair. I wondered, as Heatherlegh in his chair might have wondered, which dreadful alternative I should adopt. Presently I heard myself answering in a voice that I hardly recognized—

"They're confoundedly particular about morality in these parts. Give 'em fits, Heatherlegh, and my love. Now let me sleep a bit longer."

Then my two selves joined, and it was only I (half crazed, devil-driven I) that tossed in my bed, tracing step by step the history of the past month.

"But I am in Simla," I kept repeating to myself. "I, Jack Pansay, am in Simla and there are no ghosts here. It's unreasonable of that woman to pretend there are. Why couldn't Agnes have left me alone? I never did her any harm. It might just as well have been me as Agnes. Only I'd never have come hack on purpose to kill *her*. Why can't I be left alone—left alone and happy?"

It was high noon when I first awoke: and the sun was low in the sky before I slept—slept as the tortured criminal sleeps on his rack, too worn to feel further pain.

Next day I could not leave my bed. Heatherlegh told me in the morning that he had received an answer from Mr. Mannering, and that, thanks to his (Heatherlegh's) friendly offices, the story of my affliction had traveled through the length and breadth of Simla, where I was on all sides much pitied.

"And that's rather more than you deserve," he concluded, pleasantly, "though the Lord knows you've been going through a pretty severe mill. Never mind; we'll cure you yet, you perverse phenomenon."

I declined firmly to be cured. "You've been much too good to me already, old man," said I; "but I don't think I need trouble you further."

In my heart I knew that nothing Heatherlegh could do would lighten the burden that had been laid upon me.

With that knowledge came also a sense of hopeless, impotent rebellion against the unreasonableness of it all. There were scores of men no better than I whose punishments had at least been reserved for another world; and I felt that it was bitterly, cruelly unfair that I alone should have been singled out for so hideous a fate. This mood would in time give place to another where it seemed that the 'rickshaw and I were the only realities in a world of shadows; that Kitty was a ghost; that Mannering, Heatherlegh, and all the other men and women I knew were all ghosts; and the great, gray hills themselves but vain shadows devised to torture me. From mood to mood I tossed backward and forward for seven weary days; my body growing daily stronger and stronger, until the bedroom looking-glass told me that I had returned to every-day life, and was as other men once more. Curiously enough my face showed no signs of the struggle I had gone through. It was pale indeed, but as expressionless and commonplace as ever. I had expected some permanent alteration—visible evidence of the disease that was eating me away. I found nothing.

On the 15th of May, I left Heatherlegh's house at eleven o'clock in the morning; and the instinct of the bachelor drove me to the Club. There I found that every man knew my story as told by Heatherlegh, and was, in clumsy fashion, abnormally kind and attentive. Nevertheless I recognized that for the rest of my natural life I should be among but not of my fellows; and I envied very bitterly indeed the laughing coolies on the Mall below. I lunched at the Club, and at four o'clock wandered aimlessly down the Mall in the vague hope of meeting Kitty. Close to the Band-stand the black and white liveries joined me; and I heard Mrs. Wessington's old appeal at my side. I had been expecting this ever since I came out; and was only surprised at her delay. The phantom 'rickshaw and I went side by side along the Chota Simla road in silence. Close to the bazar, Kitty and a man on horseback overtook and passed us. For any sign she gave I might have been a dog in the road. She did not even pay me the compliment of quickening her pace; though the rainy afternoon had served for an excuse.

So Kitty and her companion, and I and my ghostly Light-o'-Love, crept round Jakko in couples. The road was streaming with water; the pines dripped like roof-pipes on the rocks below, and the air was full of fine, driving rain. Two or three times I found myself saying to myself almost aloud: "I'm Jack Pansay on leave at Simla—*at Simla!* Everyday, ordinary Simla. I mustn't forget that—I mustn't forget that." Then I would try to recollect some of the gossip I had heard at the Club: the prices of So-and-So's horses—anything, in fact, that related to the workaday Anglo-Indian world I knew so well. I even repeated the multiplication-table rapidly to myself, to make quite sure that I was not taking leave of my senses. It gave me much comfort; and must have prevented my hearing Mrs. Wessington for a time.

Once more I wearily climbed the Convent slope and entered the level road. Here Kitty and the man started off at a canter, and I was left alone with Mrs. Wessington.

"Agnes," said I, "will you put back your hood and tell me what it all means?" The hood dropped noiselessly, and I was face to face with my dead and buried mistress. She was wearing the dress in which I had last seen her alive; carried the same tiny handkerchief in her right hand; and the same card-case in her left. (A woman eight months dead with a card-case!) I had to pin myself down to the multiplication-table, and to set both hands on the stone parapet of the road, to assure myself that that at least was real.

"Agnes," I repeated, "for pity's sake tell me what it all means." Mrs. Wessington leaned forward, with that odd, quick turn of the head I used to know so well, and spoke.

If my story had not already so madly overleaped the bounds of all human belief I should apologize to you now. As I know that no one—no, not even Kitty, for whom it is written as some sort of justification of my conduct—will believe me, I will go on. Mrs. Wessington spoke and I walked with her from the Sanjowlie road to the turning below the Commander-in-Chief's house as I might walk by the side of any living woman's 'rickshaw, deep in conversation. The second and most tormenting of my moods of sickness had suddenly laid hold upon me, and like the Prince in Tennyson's poem, "I seemed to move amid a world of ghosts." There had been a garden-party at the Commander-in-Chief's, and we two joined the crowd of homeward-bound folk. As I saw them then it seemed that *they* were the shadows—impalpable, fantastic shadows—that divided for Mrs. Wessington's 'rickshaw to pass through. What we said during the course of that weird interview I cannot—indeed, I dare not—tell. Heatherlegh's comment would have been a short laugh and a remark that I had been "mashing a brain-eye-and-stomach chimera." It was a ghastly and yet in some indefinable way a marvelously dear experience. Could it be possible, I wondered, that I was in this life to woo a second time the woman I had killed by my own neglect and cruelty?

I met Kitty on the homeward road—a shadow among shadows.

If I were to describe all the incidents of the next fortnight in their order, my story would never come to an end; and your patience would be exhausted. Morning after morning and evening after evening the ghostly 'rickshaw and I used to wander through Simla together. Wherever I went there the four black and white liveries followed me and bore me company to and from my hotel. At the Theatre I found them amid the crowd or yelling *jhampanies*; outside the Club veranda, after a long evening of whist; at the Birthday Ball, waiting patiently for my reappearance; and in broad daylight when I went calling. Save that it cast no shadow, the 'rickshaw was in every respect as real to look upon as one of wood and iron. More than once, indeed, I have had to check myself from warning some hard-riding friend against cantering over it. More than once I have walked down the Mall deep in conversation with Mrs. Wessington to the unspeakable amazement of the passers-by.

Before I had been out and about a week I learned that the "fit" theory had been discarded in favor of insanity. However, I made no change in my mode of life. I called, rode, and dined out as freely as ever. I had a passion for the society of my kind which I had never felt before; I hungered to be among the realities of life; and at the same time I felt vaguely unhappy when I had been separated too long from my ghostly companion. It would be almost impossible to describe my varying moods from the 15th of May up to to-day.

The presence of the 'rickshaw filled me by turns with horror, blind fear, a dim sort of pleasure, and utter despair. I dared not leave Simla; and I knew that my stay there was killing me. I knew, moreover, that it was my destiny to die slowly and a little every day. My only anxiety was to get the penance over as quietly as might be. Alternately I hungered for a sight of Kitty and watched her outrageous flirtations with my successor—to speak more accurately, my successors—with amused interest. She was as much out of my life as I was out of hers. By day I wandered with Mrs. Wessington almost content. By night I implored Heaven to let me return to the world as I used to know it. Above all these varying moods lay the sensation of dull, numbing wonder that the Seen and the Unseen should mingle so strangely on this earth to hound one poor soul to its grave.

* * *

August 27. Heatherlegh has been indefatigable in his attendance on me; and only yesterday told me that I ought to send in an application for sick leave. An application to escape the company of a phantom! A request that the Government would graciously permit me to get rid of five ghosts and an airy 'rickshaw by going to England. Heatherlegh's proposition moved me to almost hysterical laughter. I told him that I should await the end quietly at Simla; and I am sure that the end is not far off. Believe me that I dread its advent more than any word can say; and I torture myself nightly with a thousand speculations as to the manner of my death.

Shall I die in my bed decently and as an English gentleman should die; or, in one last walk on the Mall, will my soul be wrenched from me to take its place forever and ever by the side of that ghastly phantasm? Shall I return to my old lost allegiance in the next world, or shall I meet Agnes loathing her and bound to her side through all eternity? Shall we two hover over the scene of our lives till the end of Time? As the day of my death draws nearer, the intense horror that all living flesh feels toward escaped spirits from beyond the grave grows more and more powerful. It is an awful thing to go down quick among the dead with scarcely one-half of your life completed. It is a thousand times more awful to wait as I do in your midst, for I know not what unimaginable terror. Pity me, at least on the score of my "delusion," for I know you will never believe what I have written here. Yet as surely as ever a man was done to death by the Powers of Darkness I am that man.

In justice, too, pity her. For as surely as ever woman was killed by man, I killed Mrs. Wessington. And the last portion of my punishment is ever now upon me.

The Were-Wolf

Clemence Housman

———◆———

THE GREAT FARM HALL WAS ABLAZE WITH THE FIRE-LIGHT, AND NOISY with laughter and talk and many-sounding work. None could be idle but the very young and the very old: little Rol, who was hugging a puppy, and old Trella, whose palsied hand fumbled over her knitting. The early evening had closed in, and the farm-servants, come from their outdoor work, had assembled in the ample hall, which gave space for a score or more of workers. Several of the men were engaged in carving, and to these were yielded the best place and light; others made or repaired fishing-tackle and harness, and a great seine net occupied three pairs of hands. Of the women most were sorting and mixing eider feather and chopping straw to add to it. Looms were there, though not in present use, but three wheels whirred emulously, and the finest and swiftest thread of the three ran between the fingers of the house-mistress. Near her were some children, busy too, plaiting wicks for candles and lamps. Each group of workers had a lamp in its centre, and those farthest from the fire had live heat from two braziers filled with glowing wood embers, replenished now and again from the generous hearth. But the flicker of the great fire was manifest to remotest corners, and prevailed beyond the limits of the weaker lights.

Little Rol grew tired of his puppy, dropped it incontinently, and made an onslaught on Tyr, the old wolf-hound, who basked dozing, whimpering and twitching in his hunting dreams. Prone went Rol beside Tyr, his young arms round the shaggy neck, his curls against the black jowl. Tyr gave a perfunctory lick, and stretched with a sleepy sigh. Rol growled and rolled and shoved invitingly, but could only gain from the old dog placid toleration and a half-observant blink. "Take that then!" said Rol, indignant at this ignoring of his advances, and sent the puppy sprawling against the dignity that disdained him as playmate. The dog took no notice, and the child wandered off to find amusement elsewhere.

The baskets of white eider feathers caught his eye far off in a distant corner. He slipped under the table, and crept along on all-fours, the ordinary common-place custom of walking down a room upright not being to his fancy. When close to the women he lay still for a moment watching, with his elbows on the floor and his chin in his palms. One of the women seeing him nodded and smiled, and presently he crept out behind her skirts and passed, hardly noticed, from one to another, till he found opportunity to possess himself of a large handful of feathers. With these he traversed the length of the room, under the table again, and emerged near the spinners. At the feet of the youngest he curled himself round, sheltered by her knees from the observation of the others, and disarmed her of interference by secretly displaying his handful with a confiding smile. A dubious nod satisfied him, and presently he started on the play he had devised. He took a tuft of the white down, and gently shook it free of his fingers close to the whirl of the wheel. The wind of the swift motion took it, spun it round and round in widening circles, till it floated above like a slow white moth. Little Rol's eyes danced, and the row of his small teeth shone in a silent laugh of delight. Another and another of the white tufts was sent whirling round like a winged thing in a spider's web, and floating clear at last. Presently the handful failed.

Rol sprawled forward to survey the room, and contemplate another journey under the table. His shoulder, thrusting forward, checked the wheel for an instant; he shifted hastily. The wheel flew on with a jerk, and the thread snapped. "Naughty Rol!" said the girl. The swiftest wheel stopped also, and the house-mistress, Rol's aunt, leaned forward, and sighting the low curly head, gave a warning against mischief, and sent him off to old Trella's corner.

Rol obeyed, and after a discreet period of obedience, sidled out again down the length of the room farthest from his aunt's eye. As he slipped in among the men, they looked up to see that their tools might be, as far as possible, out of reach of Rol's hands, and close to their own. Nevertheless, before long he managed to secure a fine chisel and take off its point on the leg of the table. The carver's strong objections to this disconcerted Rol, who for five minutes thereafter effaced himself under the table.

During this seclusion he contemplated the many pairs of legs that surrounded him, and almost shut out the light of the fire. How very odd some of the legs were: some were curved where they should be straight, some were straight where they should be curved, and, as Rol said to himself, "they all seemed screwed on differently." Some were tucked away modestly under the benches, others were thrust far out under the table, encroaching on Rol's own particular domain. He stretched out his own short legs and regarded them critically, and, after comparison, favourably. Why were not all legs made like his, or like *his*?

These legs approved by Rol were a little apart from the rest. He crawled opposite and again made comparison. His face grew quite solemn as he thought of the innumerable days to come before his legs could be as long and strong. He hoped they would be just like those, his models, as straight as to bone, as curved as to muscle.

A few moments later Sweyn of the long legs felt a small hand caressing his foot, and looking down, met the upturned eyes of his little cousin Rol. Lying on his back, still softly patting and stroking the young man's foot, the child was quiet and happy for a good while. He watched the movement of the strong deft hands, and the shifting of the bright tools. Now and then, minute chips of wood, puffed off by Sweyn, fell down upon his face. At last he raised himself, very gently, lest a jog should wake impatience in the carver, and crossing his own legs round Sweyn's ankle, clasping with his arms too, laid his head against the knee. Such act is evidence of a child's most wonderful hero-worship. Quite content was Rol, and more than content when Sweyn paused a minute to joke, and pat his head and pull his curls. Quiet he remained, as long as quiescence is possible to limbs young as his. Sweyn forgot he was near, hardly noticed when his leg was gently released, and never saw the stealthy abstraction of one of his tools.

Ten minutes thereafter was a lamentable wail from low on the floor, rising to the full pitch of Rol's healthy lungs; for his hand was gashed across, and the copious bleeding terrified him. Then was there soothing and comforting, washing and binding, and a modicum of scolding, till the loud outcry sank into occasional sobs, and the child, tear-stained and subdued, was returned to the chimney-corner settle, where Trella nodded.

In the reaction after pain and fright, Rol found that the quiet of that fire-lit corner was to his mind. Tyr, too, disdained him no longer, but, roused by his sobs, showed all the concern and sympathy that a dog can by licking and wistful watching. A little shame weighed also upon his spirits. He wished he had not cried quite so much. He remembered how once Sweyn had come home with his arm torn down from the shoulder, and a dead bear; and how he had never winced nor said a word, though his lips turned white with pain. Poor little Rol gave another sighing sob over his own faint-hearted shortcomings.

The light and motion of the great fire began to tell strange stories to the child, and the wind in the chimney roared a corroborative note now and then. The great black mouth of the chimney, impending high over the hearth, received as into a mysterious gulf murky coils of smoke and brightness of aspiring sparks; and beyond, in the high darkness, were muttering and wailing and strange doings, so that sometimes the smoke rushed back in panic, and curled out and up to the roof, and condensed itself to invisibility among the rafters. And then the wind would rage after its lost prey, and rush round the house, rattling and shrieking at window and door.

In a lull, after one such loud gust, Rol lifted his head in surprise and listened. A lull had also come on the babel of talk, and thus could be heard with strange distinctness a sound outside the door—the sound of a child's voice, a child's hands. "Open, open; let me in!" piped the little voice from low down, lower than the handle, and the latch rattled as though a tiptoe child reached up to it, and soft small knocks were struck. One near the door sprang up and opened it. "No one is here," he said. Tyr lifted his head and gave utterance to a howl, loud, prolonged, most dismal.

Sweyn, not able to believe that his ears had deceived him, got up and went to the door. It was a dark night; the clouds were heavy with snow, that had fallen fitfully when the wind lulled. Untrodden snow lay up to the porch; there was no sight nor sound of any human being. Sweyn strained his eyes far and near, only to see dark sky, pure snow, and a line of black fir trees on a hill brow, bowing down before the wind. "It must have been the wind," he said, and closed the door.

Many faces looked scared. The sound of a child's voice had been so distinct—and the words "Open, open; let me in!" The wind might creak the wood, or rattle the latch, but could not speak with a child's voice, nor knock with the soft plain blows that a plump fist gives. And the strange unusual howl of the wolf-hound was an omen to be feared, be the rest what it might. Strange things were said by one and another, till the rebuke of the house-mistress quelled them into far-off whispers. For a time after there was uneasiness, constraint, and silence; then the chill fear thawed by degrees, and the babble of talk flowed on again.

Yet half-an-hour later a very slight noise outside the door sufficed to arrest every hand, every tongue. Every head was raised, every eye fixed in one direction. "It is Christian; he is late," said Sweyn.

No, no; this is a feeble shuffle, not a young man's tread. With the sound of uncertain feet came the hard tap-tap of a stick against the door, and the high-pitched voice of eld, "Open, open; let me in!" Again Tyr flung up his head in a long doleful howl.

Before the echo of the tapping stick and the high voice had fairly died away, Sweyn had sprung across to the door and flung it wide. "No one again," he said in a steady voice, though his eyes looked startled as he stared out. He saw the lonely expanse of snow, the clouds swagging low, and between the two the line of dark fir-trees bowing in the wind. He closed the door without a word of comment, and re-crossed the room.

A score of blanched faces were turned to him as though he must be solver of the enigma. He could not be unconscious of this mute eye-questioning, and it disturbed his resolute air of composure. He hesitated, glanced towards his mother, the house-mistress, then back at the frightened folk, and gravely, before them all, made the sign of the cross. There was a flutter of hands as the sign was repeated by all, and the dead silence was stirred as by a huge sigh, for the held breath of many was freed as though the sign gave magic relief.

Even the house-mistress was perturbed. She left her wheel and crossed the room to her son, and spoke with him for a moment in a low tone that none could overhear. But a moment later her voice was high-pitched and loud, so that all might benefit by her rebuke of the "heathen chatter" of one of the girls. Perhaps she essayed to silence thus her own misgivings and forebodings.

No other voice dared speak now with its natural fulness. Low tones made inter-mittent murmurs, and now and then silence drifted over the whole room. The handling of tools was as noiseless as might be, and suspended on the instant if the door rattled in a gust of wind. After a time Sweyn left his work, joined the group nearest the door, and loitered there on the pretence of giving advice and help to the unskilful.

A man's tread was heard outside in the porch. "Christian!" said Sweyn and his mother simultaneously, he confidently, she authoritatively, to set the checked wheels going again. But Tyr flung up his head with an appalling howl.

"Open, open; let me in!"

It was a man's voice, and the door shook and rattled as a man's strength beat against it. Sweyn could feel the planks quivering, as on the instant his hand was upon the door, flinging it open, to face the blank porch, and beyond only snow and sky, and firs aslant in the wind.

He stood for a long minute with the open door in his hand. The bitter wind swept in with its icy chill, but a deadlier chill of fear came swifter, and seemed to freeze the beating of hearts. Sweyn stepped back to snatch up a great bearskin cloak.

"Sweyn, where are you going?"

"No farther than the porch, mother," and he stepped out and closed the door.

He wrapped himself in the heavy fur, and leaning against the most sheltered wall of the porch, steeled his nerves to face the devil and all his works. No sound of voices came from within; the most distinct sound was the crackle and roar of the fire.

It was bitterly cold. His feet grew numb, but he forbore stamping them into warmth lest the sound should strike panic within; nor would he leave the porch, nor print a foot-mark on the untrodden white that declared so absolutely how no human voices and hands could have approached the door since snow fell two hours or more ago. "When the wind drops there will be more snow," thought Sweyn.

For the best part of an hour he kept his watch, and saw no living thing—heard no unwonted sound. "I will freeze here no longer," he muttered, and re-entered.

One woman gave a half-suppressed scream as his hand was laid on the latch, and then a gasp of relief as he came in. No one questioned him, only his mother said, in a tone of forced unconcern, "Could you not see Christian coming?" as though she were made anxious only by the absence of her younger son. Hardly had Sweyn stamped near to the fire than clear knocking was heard at the door. Tyr leapt from the hearth, his eyes red as the fire, his fangs showing white in the black jowl, his neck ridged and bristling; and overleaping Rol, ramped at the door, barking furiously.

Outside the door a clear mellow voice was calling. Tyr's bark made the words undistinguishable. No one offered to stir towards the door before Sweyn.

He stalked down the room resolutely, lifted the latch, and swung back the door.

A white-robed woman glided in.

No wraith! Living—beautiful—young.

Tyr leapt upon her.

Lithely she baulked the sharp fangs with folds of her long fur robe, and snatching from her girdle a small two-edged axe, whirled it up for a blow of defence.

Sweyn caught the dog by the collar, and dragged him off yelling and struggling.

The stranger stood in the doorway motionless, one foot set forward, one arm flung up, till the house-mistress hurried down the room; and Sweyn, relinquishing to others the furious Tyr, turned again to close the door, and offer excuse for so fierce a greeting. Then she lowered her arm, slung the axe in its place at her waist, loosened the furs about her face, and shook over her shoulders the long white robe—all as it were with the sway of one movement.

She was a maiden, tall and very fair. The fashion of her dress was strange, half masculine, yet not unwomanly. A fine fur tunic, reaching but little below the knee, was all the skirt she wore; below were the cross-bound shoes and leggings that a hunter wears. A white fur cap was set low upon the brows, and from its edge strips of fur fell lappet-wise about her shoulders; two of these at her entrance had been drawn forward and crossed about her throat, but now, loosened and thrust back, left unhidden long plaits of fair hair that lay forward on shoulder and breast, down to the ivory-studded girdle where the axe gleamed.

Sweyn and his mother led the stranger to the hearth without question or sign of curiosity, till she voluntarily told her tale of a long journey to distant kindred, a promised guide unmet, and signals and landmarks mistaken.

"Alone!" exclaimed Sweyn in astonishment. "Have you journeyed thus far, a hundred leagues, alone?"

She answered "Yes" with a little smile.

"Over the hills and the wastes! Why, the folk there are savage and wild as beasts."

She dropped her hand upon her axe with a laugh of some scorn.

"I fear neither man nor beast; some few fear me." And then she told strange tales of fierce attack and defence, and of the bold free huntress life she had led.

Her words came a little slowly and deliberately, as though she spoke in a scarce familiar tongue; now and then she hesitated, and stopped in a phrase, as though for lack of some word.

She became the centre of a group of listeners. The interest she excited dissipated, in some degree, the dread inspired by the mysterious voices. There was nothing ominous about this young, bright, fair reality, though her aspect was strange.

Little Rol crept near, staring at the stranger with all his might. Unnoticed, he softly stroked and patted a corner of her soft white robe that reached to the floor in ample folds. He laid his cheek against it caressingly, and then edged up close to her knees.

"What is your name?" he asked.

The stranger's smile and ready answer, as she looked down, saved Rol from the rebuke merited by his unmannerly question.

"My real name," she said, "would be uncouth to your ears and tongue. The folk of this country have given me another name, and from this" (she laid her hand on the fur robe) "they call me 'White Fell.' "

Little Rol repeated it to himself, stroking and patting as before. "White Fell, White Fell."

The fair face, and soft, beautiful dress pleased Rol. He knelt up, with his eyes on her face and an air of uncertain determination, like a robin's on a doorstep, and plumped his elbows into her lap with a little gasp at his own audacity.

"Rol!" exclaimed his aunt; but, "Oh, let him!" said White Fell, smiling and stroking his head; and Rol stayed.

He advanced farther, and panting at his own adventurousness in the face of his aunt's authority, climbed up on to her knees. Her welcoming arms hindered any protest. He nestled happily, fingering the axe head, the ivory studs in her girdle, the ivory clasp at her throat, the plaits of fair hair; rubbing his head against the softness of her fur-clad shoulder, with a child's full confidence in the kindness of beauty.

White Fell had not uncovered her head, only knotted the pendant fur loosely behind her neck. Rol reached up his hand towards it, whispering her name to himself, "White Fell, White Fell," then slid his arms round her neck, and kissed her—once—twice. She laughed delightedly, and kissed him again.

"The child plagues you?" said Sweyn.

"No, indeed," she answered, with an earnestness so intense as to seem disproportionate to the occasion.

Rol settled himself again on her lap, and began to unwind the bandage bound round his hand. He paused a little when he saw where the blood had soaked through; then went on till his hand was bare and the cut displayed, gaping and long, though only skin deep. He held it up towards White Fell, desirous of her pity and sympathy.

At sight of it, and the blood-stained linen, she drew in her breath suddenly, clasped Rol to her—hard, hard—till he began to struggle. Her face was hidden behind the boy, so that none could see its expression. It had lighted up with a most awful glee.

Afar, beyond the fir-grove, beyond the low hill behind, the absent Christian was hastening his return. From daybreak he had been afoot, carrying notice of a bear hunt to all the best hunters of the farms and hamlets that lay within a radius of twelve miles. Nevertheless, having been detained till a late hour, he now broke into a run, going with a long smooth stride of apparent ease that fast made the miles diminish.

He entered the midnight blackness of the fir-grove with scarcely slackened pace, though the path was invisible; and passing through into the open again, sighted the farm lying a furlong off down the slope. Then he sprang out freely, and almost on the instant gave one great sideways leap, and stood still. There in the snow was the track of a great wolf.

His hand went to his knife, his only weapon. He stooped, knelt down, to bring his eyes to the level of a beast, and peered about; his teeth set, his heart beat a little harder than the pace of his running insisted on. A solitary wolf, nearly always savage and of large size, is a formidable beast that will not hesitate to attack a single man. This wolf-track was the largest Christian had ever seen, and, so far as he could judge, recently made. It led from under the fir-trees down the slope. Well for him, he thought, was the delay that had so vexed him before: well for him that he had not passed through the dark fir-grove when that danger of jaws lurked there. Going warily, he followed the track.

It led down the slope, across a broad ice-bound stream, along the level beyond, making towards the farm. A less precise knowledge had doubted, and guessed that here might have come straying big Tyr or his like; but Christian was sure, knowing better than to mistake between footmark of dog and wolf.

Straight on—straight on towards the farm.

Surprised and anxious grew Christian, that a prowling wolf should dare so near. He drew his knife and pressed on, more hastily, more keen-eyed. Oh that Tyr were with him!

Straight on, straight on, even to the very door, where the snow failed. His heart seemed to give a great leap and then stop. There the track *ended*.

Nothing lurked in the porch, and there was no sign of return. The firs stood straight against the sky, the clouds lay low; for the wind had fallen and a few snow-flakes came drifting down. In a horror of surprise, Christian stood dazed a moment: then he lifted the latch and went in. His glance took in all the old familiar forms and faces, and with them that of the stranger, fur-clad and beautiful. The awful truth flashed upon him: he knew what she was.

Only a few were startled by the rattle of the latch as he entered. The room was filled with bustle and movement, for it was the supper hour, when all tools were laid aside, and trestles and tables shifted. Christian had no knowledge of what he said and did; he moved and spoke mechanically, half thinking that soon he must wake from this horrible dream. Sweyn and his mother supposed him to be cold and dead-tired, and spared all unnecessary questions. And he found himself seated beside the hearth, opposite that dreadful Thing that looked like a beautiful girl; watching her every movement, curdling with horror to see her fondle the child Rol.

Sweyn stood near them both, intent upon White Fell also; but how differently! She seemed unconscious of the gaze of both—neither aware of the chill dread in the eyes of Christian, nor of Sweyn's warm admiration.

These two brothers, who were twins, contrasted greatly, despite their striking likeness. They were alike in regular profile, fair brown hair, and deep blue eyes; but Sweyn's features were perfect as a young god's, while Christian's showed faulty details. Thus, the line of his mouth was set too straight, the eyes shelved too deeply back, and the contour of the face flowed in less generous curves than Sweyn's. Their height was the same, but Christian was too slender for perfect proportion, while Sweyn's well-knit frame, broad shoulders, and muscular arms, made him pre-eminent for manly beauty as well as for strength. As a hunter Sweyn was without rival; as a fisher without rival. All the countryside acknowledged him to be the best wrestler, rider, dancer, singer. Only in speed could he be surpassed, and in that only by his younger brother. All others Sweyn could distance fairly; but Christian could outrun him easily. Ay, he could keep pace with Sweyn's most breathless burst, and laugh and talk the while. Christian took little pride in his fleetness of foot, counting a man's legs to be the least worthy of his members. He had no envy of his brother's athletic superiority, though to several feats he had made a moderate second. He loved as only a twin can love—proud of all that Sweyn did, content with all that Sweyn was; humbly content also that his own great love should not be so exceedingly returned, since he knew himself to be so far less love-worthy.

Christian dared not, in the midst of women and children, launch the horror that he knew into words. He waited to consult his brother; but Sweyn did not, or would not, notice the signal he made, and kept his face always turned towards White Fell. Christian drew away from the hearth, unable to remain passive with that dread upon him.

"Where is Tyr?" he said suddenly. Then, catching sight of the dog in a distant corner, "Why is he chained there?"

"He flew at the stranger," one answered.

Christian's eyes glowed. "Yes?" he said, interrogatively.

"He was within an ace of having his brain knocked out."

"Tyr?"

"Yes; she was nimbly up with that little axe she has at her waist. It was well for old Tyr that his master throttled him off."

Christian went without a word to the corner where Tyr was chained. The dog rose up to meet him, as piteous and indignant as a dumb beast can be. He stroked the black head. "Good Tyr! brave dog!"

They knew, they only; and the man and the dumb dog had comfort of each other.

Christian's eyes turned again towards White Fell: Tyr's also, and he strained against the length of the chain. Christian's hand lay on the dog's neck, and he felt it ridge and bristle with the quivering of impotent fury. Then he began to quiver in like manner, with a fury born of reason, not instinct; as impotent morally as was Tyr physically. Oh! the woman's form that he dare not touch! Anything but that, and he with Tyr would be free to kill or be killed.

Then he returned to ask fresh questions.

"How long has the stranger been here?"

"She came about half-an-hour before you."

"Who opened the door to her?"

"Sweyn: no one else dared."

The tone of the answer was mysterious.

"Why?" queried Christian. "Has anything strange happened? Tell me."

For answer he was told in a low undertone of the summons at the door thrice repeated without human agency; and of Tyr's ominous howls; and of Sweyn's fruitless watch outside.

Christian turned towards his brother in a torment of impatience for a word apart. The board was spread, and Sweyn was leading White Fell to the guest's place. This was more awful: she would break bread with them under the roof-tree!

He started forward, and touching Sweyn's arm, whispered an urgent entreaty. Sweyn stared, and shook his head in angry impatience.

Thereupon Christian would take no morsel of food.

His opportunity came at last. White Fell questioned of the landmarks of the country, and of one Cairn Hill, which was an appointed meeting-place at which she was due that night. The house-mistress and Sweyn both exclaimed.

"It is three long miles away," said Sweyn; "with no place for shelter but a wretched hut. Stay with us this night, and I will show you the way to-morrow."

White Fell seemed to hesitate. "Three miles," she said; "then I should be able to see or hear a signal."

"I will look out," said Sweyn; "then, if there be no signal, you must not leave us."

He went to the door. Christian rose silently, and followed him out.

"Sweyn, do you know what she is?"

Sweyn, surprised at the vehement grasp, and low hoarse voice, made answer: "She? Who? White Fell?"

"Yes."

"She is the most beautiful girl I have ever seen."

"She is a Were-Wolf."

Sweyn burst out laughing. "Are you mad?" he asked.

"No; here, see for yourself."

Christian drew him out of the porch, pointing to the snow where the footmarks had been. Had been, for now they were not. Snow was falling fast, and every dint was blotted out.

"Well?" asked Sweyn.

"Had you come when I signed to you, you would have seen for yourself."

"Seen what?"

"The footprints of a wolf leading up to the door; none leading away."

It was impossible not to be startled by the tone alone, though it was hardly above a whisper. Sweyn eyed his brother anxiously, but in the darkness could make nothing of his face. Then he laid his hands kindly and re-assuringly on Christian's shoulders and felt how he was quivering with excitement and horror.

"One sees strange things," he said, "when the cold has got into the brain behind the eyes; you came in cold and worn out."

"No," interrupted Christian. "I saw the track first on the brow of the slope, and followed it down right here to the door. This is no delusion."

Sweyn in his heart felt positive that it was. Christian was given to day-dreams and strange fancies, though never had he been possessed with so mad a notion before.

"Don't you believe me?" said Christian desperately. "You must. I swear it is sane truth. Are you blind? Why, even Tyr knows."

"You will be clearer headed to-morrow after a night's rest. Then come too, if you will, with White Fell, to the Hill Cairn; and if you have doubts still, watch and follow, and see what footprints she leaves."

Galled by Sweyn's evident contempt Christian turned abruptly to the door. Sweyn caught him back.

"What now, Christian? What are you going to do?"

"You do not believe me; my mother shall."

Sweyn's grasp tightened. "You shall not tell her," he said authoritatively.

Customarily Christian was so docile to his brother's mastery that it was now a surprising thing when he wrenched himself free vigorously, and said as determinedly as Sweyn, "She shall know!" but Sweyn was nearer the door and would not let him pass.

"There has been scare enough for one night already. If this notion of yours will keep, broach it to-morrow." Christian would not yield.

"Women are so easily scared," pursued Sweyn, "and are ready to believe any folly without shadow of proof. Be a man, Christian, and fight this notion of a Were-Wolf by yourself."

"If you would believe me," began Christian.

"I believe you to be a fool," said Sweyn, losing patience. "Another, who was not your brother, might believe you to be a knave, and guess that you had transformed White Fell into a Were-Wolf because she smiled more readily on me than on you."

The jest was not without foundation, for the grace of White Fell's bright looks had been bestowed on him, on Christian never a whit. Sweyn's coxcombery was always frank, and most forgiveable, and not without fair colour.

"If you want an ally," continued Sweyn, "confide in old Trella. Out of her stores of wisdom, if her memory holds good, she can instruct you in the orthodox manner of tackling a Were-Wolf. If I remember aright, you should watch the suspected person till midnight, when the beast's form must be resumed, and retained ever after if a human eye sees the change; or, better still, sprinkle hands and feet with holy water, which is certain death. Oh! never fear, but old Trella will be equal to the occasion."

Sweyn's contempt was no longer good-humoured; some touch of irritation or resentment rose at this monstrous doubt of White Fell. But Christian was too deeply distressed to take offence.

"You speak of them as old wives' tales; but if you had seen the proof I have seen, you would be ready at least to wish them true, if not also to put them to the test."

"Well," said Sweyn, with a laugh that had a little sneer in it, "put them to the test! I will not object to that, if you will only keep your notions to yourself. Now, Christian, give me your word for silence, and we will freeze here no longer."

Christian remained silent.

Sweyn put his hands on his shoulders again and vainly tried to see his face in the darkness.

"We have never quarrelled yet, Christian?"

"*I* have never quarrelled," returned the other, aware for the first time that his dictatorial brother had sometimes offered occasion for quarrel, had he been ready to take it.

"Well," said Sweyn emphatically, "if you speak against White Fell to any other, as to-night you have spoken to me—*we shall*."

He delivered the words like an ultimatum, turned sharp round, and re-entered the house. Christian, more fearful and wretched than before, followed.

"Snow is falling fast: not a single light is to be seen."

White Fell's eyes passed over Christian without apparent notice, and turned bright and shining upon Sweyn.

"Nor any signal to be heard?" she queried. "Did you not hear the sound of a sea-horn?"

"I saw nothing, and heard nothing; and signal or no signal, the heavy snow would keep you here perforce."

She smiled her thanks beautifully. And Christian's heart sank like lead with a deadly foreboding, as he noted what a light was kindled in Sweyn's eyes by her smile.

That night, when all others slept, Christian, the weariest of all, watched outside the guest-chamber till midnight was past. No sound, not the faintest, could be heard. Could the old tale be true of the midnight change? What was on the other side of the door, a woman or a beast? he would have given his right hand to know. Instinctively he laid his hand on the latch, and drew it softly, though believing that bolts fastened the inner side. The door yielded to his hand; he stood on the threshold; a keen gust of air cut at him; the window stood open; the room was empty.

So Christian could sleep with a somewhat lightened heart.

In the morning there was surprise and conjecture when White Fell's absence was discovered. Christian held his peace. Not even to his brother did he say how he knew that she had fled before midnight; and Sweyn, though evidently greatly chagrined, seemed to disdain reference to the subject of Christian's fears.

The elder brother alone joined the bear hunt; Christian found pretext to stay behind. Sweyn, being out of humour, manifested his contempt by uttering not a single expostulation.

All that day, and for many a day after, Christian would never go out of sight of his home. Sweyn alone noticed how he manœuvred for this, and was clearly annoyed by it. White Fell's name was never mentioned between them, though not seldom was it heard in general talk. Hardly a day passed but little Rol asked when White Fell would come again: pretty White Fell, who kissed like a snowflake. And if Sweyn answered, Christian would be quite sure that the light in his eyes, kindled by White Fell's smile, had not yet died out.

Little Rol! Naughty, merry, fair-haired little Rol. A day came when his feet raced over the threshold never to return; when his chatter and laugh were heard no more; when tears of anguish were wept by eyes that never would see his bright head again: never again, living or dead.

He was seen at dusk for the last time, escaping from the house with his puppy, in freakish rebellion against old Trella. Later, when his absence had begun to cause anxiety, his puppy crept back to the farm, cowed, whimpering and yelping, a pitiful, dumb lump of terror, without intelligence or courage to guide the frightened search.

Rol was never found, nor any trace of him. Where he had perished was never known; how he had perished was known only by an awful guess—a wild beast had devoured him.

Christian heard the conjecture "a wolf"; and a horrible certainty flashed upon him that he knew what wolf it was. He tried to declare what he knew, but Sweyn saw him start at the words with white face and struggling lips; and, guessing his purpose, pulled him back, and kept him silent, hardly, by his imperious grip and wrathful eyes, and one low whisper.

That Christian should retain his most irrational suspicion against beautiful White Fell was, to Sweyn, evidence of a weak obstinacy of mind that would but thrive upon expostulation and argument. But this evident intention to direct the passions of grief and anguish to a hatred and fear of the fair stranger, such as his own, was intolerable, and Sweyn set his will against it. Again Christian yielded to his brother's stronger words and will, and against his own judgment consented to silence.

Repentance came before the new moon, the first of the year, was old. White Fell came again, smiling as she entered, as though assured of a glad and kindly welcome; and, in truth, there was only one who saw again her fair face and strange white garb without pleasure. Sweyn's face glowed with delight, while Christian's grew pale and rigid as death. He had given his word to keep silence; but he had not thought that she would dare to come again. Silence was impossible, face to face with that Thing, impossible. Irrepressibly he cried out:

"Where is Rol?"

Not a quiver disturbed White Fell's face. She heard, yet remained bright and tranquil. Sweyn's eyes flashed round at his brother dangerously. Among the women some tears fell at the poor child's name; but none caught alarm from its sudden utterance, for the thought of Rol rose naturally. Where was little Rol, who had nestled in the stranger's arms, kissing her; and watched for her since; and prattled of her daily?

Christian went out silently. One only thing there was that he could do, and he must not delay. His horror overmastered any curiosity to hear White Fell's smooth excuses and smiling apologies for her strange and uncourteous departure; or her easy tale of the circumstances of her return; or to watch her bearing as she heard the sad tale of little Rol.

The swiftest runner of the country-side had started on his hardest race: little less than three leagues and back, which he reckoned to accomplish in two hours, though the night was moonless and the way rugged. He rushed against the still cold air till it felt like a wind upon his face. The dim homestead sank below the ridges at his back, and fresh ridges of snowlands rose out of the obscure horizon-level to drive past him as the stirless air drove, and sink away behind into obscure level again. He took no conscious heed of landmarks, not even when all sign of a path was gone under depths of snow. His will was set to reach his goal with unexampled speed; and thither by instinct his physical forces bore him, without one definite thought to guide.

And the idle brain lay passive, inert, receiving into its vacancy restless siftings of past sights and sounds: Rol, weeping, laughing, playing, coiled in the arms of that dreadful Thing: Tyr—O Tyr!—white fangs in the black jowl: the women who wept on the foolish puppy, precious for the child's last touch: footprints from pine wood to door: the smiling face among furs, of such womanly beauty—smiling—smiling: and Sweyn's face.

"Sweyn, Sweyn, O Sweyn, my brother!"

Sweyn's angry laugh possessed his ear within the sound of the wind of his speed; Sweyn's scorn assailed more quick and keen than the biting cold at his throat. And yet he was unimpressed by any thought of how Sweyn's anger and scorn would rise, if this errand were known.

Sweyn was a sceptic. His utter disbelief in Christian's testimony regarding the footprints was based upon positive scepticism. His reason refused to bend in accepting the possibility of the supernatural materialised. That a living beast could ever be other than palpably bestial—pawed, toothed, shagged, and eared as such, was to him incredible; far more that a human presence could be transformed from its god-like aspect, upright, free-handed, with brows, and speech, and laughter. The wild and fearful legends that he had known from childhood and then believed, he regarded now as built upon facts distorted, overlaid by imagination, and quickened by superstition. Even the strange summons at the threshold, that he himself had vainly answered, was, after the first shock of surprise, rationally explained by him as malicious foolery on the part of some clever trickster, who withheld the key to the enigma.

To the younger brother all life was a spiritual mystery, veiled from his clear knowledge by the density of flesh. Since he knew his own body to be linked to the complex and antagonistic forces that constitute one soul, it seemed to him not impossibly strange that one spiritual force should possess divers forms for widely various manifestation. Nor, to him, was it great effort to believe that as pure water washes away all natural foulness, so water, holy by consecration, must needs cleanse God's world from that supernatural evil Thing. Therefore, faster than ever man's foot had covered those leagues, he sped under the dark, still night, over the waste, trackless snow-ridges to the far-away church, where salvation lay in the holy-water stoup at the door. His faith was as firm as any that wrought miracles in days past, simple as a child's wish, strong as a man's will.

He was hardly missed during these hours, every second of which was by him fulfilled to its utmost extent by extremest effort that sinews and nerves could attain. Within the homestead the while, the easy moments went bright with words and looks of unwonted animation, for the kindly, hospitable instincts of the inmates were roused into cordial expression of welcome and interest by the grace and beauty of the returned stranger.

But Sweyn was eager and earnest, with more than a host's courteous warmth. The impression that at her first coming had charmed him, that had lived since through memory, deepened now in her actual presence. Sweyn, the matchless among men, acknowledged in this fair White Fell a spirit high and bold as his own, and a frame so firm and capable that only bulk was lacking for equal strength. Yet the white skin was moulded most smoothly, without such muscular swelling as made his might evident. Such love as his frank self-love could concede was called forth by an ardent admiration for this supreme stranger. More admiration than love was in his passion, and therefore he was free from a lover's hesitancy and delicate reserve and doubts. Frankly and boldly he courted her favour by looks and tones, and an address that came of natural ease, needless of skill by practice.

Nor was she a woman to be wooed otherwise. Tender whispers and sighs would never gain her ear; but her eyes would brighten and shine if she heard of a brave feat, and her prompt hand in sympathy fall swiftly on the axe-haft and clasp it hard. That movement ever fired Sweyn's admiration anew; he watched for it, strove to elicit it, and glowed when it came. Wonderful and beautiful was that wrist, slender and steel-strong; also the smooth shapely hand, that curved so fast and firm, ready to deal instant death.

Desiring to feel the pressure of these hands, this bold lover schemed with palpable directness, proposing that she should hear how their hunting songs were sung, with a chorus that signalled hands to be clasped. So his splendid voice gave the verses, and, as the chorus was taken up, he claimed her hands, and, even through the easy grip, felt, as he desired, the strength that was latent, and the vigour that quickened the very fingertips, as the song fired her, and her voice was caught out of her by the rhythmic swell, and rang clear on the top of the closing surge.

Afterwards she sang alone. For contrast, or in the pride of swaying moods by her voice, she chose a mournful song that drifted along in a minor chant, sad as a wind that dirges:

"Oh, let me go!
Around spin wreaths of snow;
The dark earth sleeps below.

"Far up the plain
Moans on a voice of pain:
'Where shall my babe be lain?'

"In my white breast
Lay the sweet life to rest!
Lay, where it can lie best!

"'Hush! hush its cries!
Dense night is on the skies:
Two stars are in thine eyes.'

"Come, babe, away!
But lie thou till dawn be grey,
Who must be dead by day.

"This cannot last;
But, ere the sickening blast,
All sorrow shall be past;

"And kings shall be
Low bending at thy knee,
Worshipping life from thee.

"For men long sore
To hope of what's before,—
To leave the things of yore.

"Mine, and not thine,
How deep their jewels shine!
Peace laps thy head, not mine."

Old Trella came tottering from her corner, shaken to additional palsy by an aroused memory. She strained her dim eyes towards the singer, and then bent her head, that the one ear yet sensible to sound might avail of every note. At the close, groping forward, she murmured with the high-pitched quaver of old age:

"So she sang, my Thora; my last and brightest. What is she like, she whose voice is like my dead Thora's? Are her eyes blue?"

"Blue as the sky."

"So were my Thora's! Is her hair fair, and in plaits to the waist?"

"Even so," answered White Fell herself, and met the advancing hands with her own, and guided them to corroborate her words by touch.

"Like my dead Thora's," repeated the old woman; and then her trembling hands rested on the fur-clad shoulders, and she bent forward and kissed the smooth fair face that White Fell upturned, nothing loth, to receive and return the caress.

So Christian saw them as he entered.

He stood a moment. After the starless darkness and the icy night air, and the fierce silent two hours' race, his senses reeled on sudden entrance into warmth, and light, and the cheery hum of voices. A sudden unforeseen anguish assailed him, as now first he entertained the possibility of being overmatched by her wiles and her daring, if at the approach of pure death she should start up at bay transformed to a terrible beast, and achieve a savage glut at the last. He looked with horror and pity on the harmless, helpless folk, so unwitting of outrage to their comfort and security. The dreadful Thing in their midst, that was veiled from their knowledge by womanly beauty, was a centre of pleasant interest. There, before him, signally impressive, was poor old Trella, weakest and feeblest of all, in fond nearness. And a moment might bring about the revelation of a monstrous horror—a ghastly, deadly danger, set loose and at bay, in a circle of girls and women and careless defenceless men: so hideous and terrible a thing as might crack the brain, or curdle the heart stone dead.

And he alone of the throng prepared!

For one breathing space he faltered, no longer than that, while over him swept the agony of compunction that yet could not make him surrender his purpose.

He alone? Nay, but Tyr also; and he crossed to the dumb sole sharer of his knowledge.

So timeless is thought that a few seconds only lay between his lifting of the latch and his loosening of Tyr's collar; but in those few seconds succeeding his first glance, as lightning-swift had been the impulses of others, their motion as quick and sure. Sweyn's vigilant eye had darted upon him, and instantly his every fibre was alert with hostile instinct; and, half divining, half incredulous, of Christian's object in stooping to Tyr, he came hastily, wary, wrathful, resolute to oppose the malice of his wild-eyed brother.

But beyond Sweyn rose White Fell, blanching white as her furs, and with eyes grown fierce and wild. She leapt down the room to the door, whirling her long robe closely to her. "Hark!" she panted. "The signal horn! Hark, I must go!" as she snatched at the latch to be out and away.

For one precious moment Christian had hesitated on the half-loosened collar; for, except the womanly form were exchanged for the bestial, Tyr's jaws would gnash to rags his honour of manhood. Then he heard her voice, and turned—too late.

As she tugged at the door, he sprang across grasping his flask, but Sweyn dashed between, and caught him back irresistibly, so that a most frantic effort only availed to wrench one arm free. With that, on the impulse of sheer despair, he cast at her with all his force. The door swung behind her, and the flask flew into fragments against it. Then, as Sweyn's grasp slackened, and he met the questioning astonishment of surrounding faces, with a hoarse inarticulate cry: "God help us all!" he said. "She is a Were-Wolf."

Sweyn turned upon him, "Liar, coward!" and his hands gripped his brother's throat with deadly force, as though the spoken word could be killed so; and as Christian struggled, lifted him clear off his feet and flung him crashing backward. So furious was he, that, as his brother lay motionless, he stirred him roughly with his foot, till their mother came between, crying shame; and yet then he stood by, his teeth set, his brows knit, his hands clenched, ready to enforce silence again violently, as Christian rose staggering and bewildered.

But utter silence and submission were more than he expected, and turned his anger into contempt for one so easily cowed and held in subjection by mere force. "He is mad!" he said, turning on his heel as he spoke, so that he lost his mother's look of pained reproach at this sudden free utterance of what was a lurking dread within her.

Christian was too spent for the effort of speech. His hard-drawn breath laboured in great sobs; his limbs were powerless and unstrung in utter relax after hard service. Failure in his endeavour induced a stupor of misery and despair. In addition was the wretched humiliation of open violence and strife with his brother, and the distress of hearing misjudging contempt expressed without reserve; for he was aware that Sweyn had turned to allay the scared excitement half by imperious mastery, half by explanation and argument, that showed painful disregard of brotherly consideration. All this unkindness of his twin he charged upon the fell Thing who had wrought this their first dissension, and, ah! most terrible thought, interposed between them so effectually, that Sweyn was wilfully blind and deaf on her account, resentful of interference, arbitrary beyond reason.

Dread and perplexity unfathomable darkened upon him; unshared, the burden was overwhelming: a foreboding of unspeakable calamity, based upon his ghastly discovery, bore down upon him, crushing out hope of power to withstand impending fate.

Sweyn the while was observant of his brother, despite the continual check of finding, turn and glance when he would, Christian's eyes always upon him, with a strange look of helpless distress, discomposing enough to the angry aggressor. "Like a beaten dog!" he said to himself, rallying contempt to withstand compunction. Observation set him wondering on Christian's exhausted condition. The heavy labouring breath and the slack inert fall of the limbs told surely of unusual and prolonged exertion. And then why had close upon two hours' absence been followed by open hostility against White Fell?

Suddenly, the fragments of the flask giving a clue, he guessed all, and faced about to stare at his brother in amaze. He forgot that the motive scheme was against White Fell, demanding derision and resentment from him; that was swept out of remembrance by astonishment and admiration for the feat of speed and endurance. In eagerness to question he inclined to attempt a generous part and frankly offer to heal the breach; but Christian's depression and sad following gaze provoked him to self-justification by recalling the offence of that outrageous utterance against White Fell; and the impulse passed. Then other considerations counselled silence; and afterwards a humour possessed him to wait and see how Christian would find opportunity to proclaim his performance and establish the fact, without exciting ridicule on account of the absurdity of the errand.

This expectation remained unfulfilled. Christian never attempted the proud avowal that would have placed his feat on record to be told to the next generation.

That night Sweyn and his mother talked long and late together, shaping into certainty the suspicion that Christian's mind had lost its balance, and discussing the evident cause. For Sweyn, declaring his own love for White Fell, suggested that his unfortunate brother, with a like passion, they being twins in loves as in birth, had through jealousy and despair turned from love to hate, until reason failed at the strain, and a craze developed, which the malice and treachery of madness made a serious and dangerous force.

So Sweyn theorised, convincing himself as he spoke; convincing afterwards others who advanced doubts against White Fell; fettering his judgment by his advocacy, and by his staunch defence of her hurried flight silencing his own inner consciousness of the unaccountability of her action.

But a little time and Sweyn lost his vantage in the shock of a fresh horror at the homestead. Trella was no more, and her end a mystery. The poor old woman crawled out in a bright gleam to visit a bed-ridden gossip living beyond the fir-grove. Under the trees she was last seen, halting for her companion, sent back for a forgotten present. Quick alarm sprang, calling every man to the search. Her stick was found among the brushwood only a few paces from the path, but no track or stain, for a gusty wind was sifting the snow from the branches, and hid all sign of how she came by her death.

So panic-stricken were the farm folk that none dared go singly on the search. Known danger could be braced, but not this stealthy Death that walked by day invisible, that cut off alike the child in his play and the aged woman so near to her quiet grave.

"Rol she kissed; Trella she kissed!" So rang Christian's frantic cry again and again, till Sweyn dragged him away and strove to keep him apart, albeit in his agony of grief and remorse he accused himself wildly as answerable for the tragedy, and gave clear proof that the charge of madness was well founded, if strange looks and desperate, incoherent words were evidence enough.

But thenceforward all Sweyn's reasoning and mastery could not uphold White Fell above suspicion. He was not called upon to defend her from accusation when Christian had been brought to silence again; but he well knew the significance of this fact, that her name, formerly uttered freely and often, he never heard now: it was huddled away into whispers that he could not catch.

The passing of time did not sweep away the superstitious fears that Sweyn despised. He was angry and anxious; eager that White Fell should return, and, merely by her bright gracious presence, reinstate herself in favour; but doubtful if all his authority and example could keep from her notice an altered aspect of welcome; and he foresaw clearly that Christian would prove unmanageable, and might be capable of some dangerous outbreak.

For a time the twins' variance was marked, on Sweyn's part by an air of rigid indifference, on Christian's by heavy downcast silence, and a nervous apprehensive observation of his brother. Superadded to his remorse and foreboding, Sweyn's displeasure weighed upon him intolerably, and the remembrance of their violent rupture was a ceaseless misery. The elder brother, self-sufficient and insensitive, could little know how deeply his unkindness stabbed. A depth and force of affection such as Christian's was unknown to him. The loyal subservience that he could not appreciate had encouraged him to domineer; this strenuous opposition to his reason and will was accounted as furious malice, if not sheer insanity.

Christian's surveillance galled him incessantly, and embarrassment and danger he foresaw as the outcome. Therefore, that suspicion might be lulled, he judged it wise to make overtures for peace. Most easily done. A little kindliness, a few evidences of consideration, a slight return of the old brotherly imperiousness, and Christian replied by a gratefulness and relief that might have touched him had he understood all, but instead, increased his secret contempt.

So successful was this finesse, that when, late on a day, a message summoning Christian to a distance was transmitted by Sweyn, no doubt of its genuineness occurred. When, his errand proved useless, he set out to return, mistake or misapprehension was all that he surmised. Not till he sighted the homestead, lying low between the night-grey snow ridges, did vivid recollection of the time when he had tracked that horror to the door rouse an intense dread, and with it a hardly-defined suspicion.

His grasp tightened on the bear-spear that he carried as a staff; every sense was alert, every muscle strung; excitement urged him on, caution checked him, and the two governed his long stride, swiftly, noiselessly, to the climax he felt was at hand.

As he drew near to the outer gates, a light shadow stirred and went, as though the grey of the snow had taken detached motion. A darker shadow stayed and faced Christian, striking his life-blood chill with utmost despair.

Sweyn stood before him, and surely, the shadow that went was White Fell.

They had been together—close. Had she not been in his arms, near enough for lips to meet?

There was no moon, but the stars gave light enough to show that Sweyn's face was flushed and elate. The flush remained, though the expression changed quickly at sight of his brother. How, if Christian had seen all, should one of his frenzied outbursts be met and managed: by resolution? by indifference? He halted between the two, and as a result, he swaggered.

"White Fell?" questioned Christian, hoarse and breathless.

"Yes?"

Sweyn's answer was a query, with an intonation that implied he was clearing the ground for action.

From Christian came: "Have you kissed her?" like a bolt direct, staggering Sweyn by its sheer prompt temerity.

He flushed yet darker, and yet half-smiled over this earnest of success he had won. Had there been really between himself and Christian the rivalry that he imagined, his face had enough of the insolence of triumph to exasperate jealous rage.

"You dare ask this!"

"Sweyn, O Sweyn, I must know! You have!"

The ring of despair and anguish in his tone angered Sweyn, misconstruing it. Jealousy urging to such presumption was intolerable.

"Mad fool!" he said, constraining himself no longer. "Win for yourself a woman to kiss. Leave mine without question. Such an one as I should desire to kiss is such an one as shall never allow a kiss to you."

Then Christian fully understood his supposition.

"I—I!" he cried. "White Fell—that deadly Thing! Sweyn, are you blind, mad? I would save you from her: a Were-Wolf!"

Sweyn maddened again at the accusation—a dastardly way of revenge, as he conceived; and instantly, for the second time, the brothers were at strife violently.

But Christian was now too desperate to be scrupulous; for a dim glimpse had shot a possibility into his mind, and to be free to follow it the striking of his brother was a necessity. Thank God! he was armed, and so Sweyn's equal.

Facing his assailant with the bear-spear, he struck up his arms, and with the butt end hit hard so that he fell. The matchless runner leapt away on the instant, to follow a forlorn hope.

Sweyn, on regaining his feet, was as amazed as angry at this unaccountable flight. He knew in his heart that his brother was no coward, and that it was unlike him to shrink from an encounter because defeat was certain, and cruel humiliation from a vindictive victor probable. Of the uselessness of pursuit he was well aware: he must abide his chagrin, content to know that his time for advantage would come. Since White Fell had parted to the right, Christian to the left, the event of a sequent encounter did not occur to him.

And now Christian, acting on the dim glimpse he had had, just as Sweyn turned upon him, of something that moved against the sky along the ridge behind the homestead, was staking his only hope on a chance, and his own superlative speed. If what he saw was really White Fell, he guessed she was bending her steps towards the open wastes; and there was just a possibility that, by a straight dash, and a desperate perilous leap over a sheer bluff, he might yet meet her or head her. And then: he had no further thought.

It was past, the quick, fierce race, and the chance of death at the leap; and he halted in a hollow to fetch his breath and to look: did she come? had she gone?

She came.

She came with a smooth, gliding, noiseless speed, that was neither walking nor running; her arms were folded in her furs that were drawn tight about her body; the white lappets from her head were wrapped and knotted closely beneath her face; her eyes were set on a far distance. So she went till the even sway of her going was startled to a pause by Christian.

"Fell!"

She drew a quick, sharp breath at the sound of her name thus mutilated, and faced Sweyn's brother. Her eyes glittered; her upper lip was lifted, and shewed the teeth. The half of her name, impressed with an ominous sense as uttered by him, warned her of the aspect of a deadly foe. Yet she cast loose her robes till they trailed ample, and spoke as a mild woman.

"What would you?"

Then Christian answered with his solemn dreadful accusation:

"You kissed Rol—and Rol is dead! You kissed Trella: she is dead! You have kissed Sweyn, my brother; but he shall not die!"

He added: "You may live till midnight."

The edge of the teeth and the glitter of the eyes stayed a moment, and her right hand also slid down to the axe haft. Then, without a word, she swerved from him, and sprang out and away swiftly over the snow.

And Christian sprang out and away, and followed her swiftly over the snow, keeping behind, but half-a-stride's length from her side.

So they went running together, silent, towards the vast wastes of snow, where no living thing but they two moved under the stars of night.

Never before had Christian so rejoiced in his powers. The gift of speed, and the training of use and endurance were priceless to him now. Though midnight was hours away, he was confident that, go where that Fell Thing would, hasten as she would, she could not outstrip him nor escape from him. Then, when came the time for transformation, when the woman's form made no longer a shield against a man's hand, he could slay or be slain to save Sweyn. He had struck his dear brother in dire extremity, but he could not, though reason urged, strike a woman.

For one mile, for two miles they ran: White Fell ever foremost, Christian ever at equal distance from her side, so near that, now and again, her out-flying furs touched him. She spoke no word; nor he. She never turned her head to look at him, nor swerved to evade him; but, with set face looking forward, sped straight on, over rough, over smooth, aware of his nearness by the regular beat of his feet, and the sound of his breath behind.

In a while she quickened her pace. From the first, Christian had judged of her speed as admirable, yet with exulting security in his own excelling and enduring whatever her efforts. But, when the pace increased, he found himself put to the test as never had he been before in any race. Her feet, indeed, flew faster than his; it was only by his length of stride that he kept his place at her side. But his heart was high and resolute, and he did not fear failure yet.

So the desperate race flew on. Their feet struck up the powdery snow, their breath smoked into the sharp clear air, and they were gone before the air was cleared of snow and vapour. Now and then Christian glanced up to judge, by the rising of the stars, of the coming of midnight. So long—so long!

White Fell held on without slack. She, it was evident, with confidence in her speed proving matchless, as resolute to outrun her pursuer as he to endure till midnight and fulfil his purpose. And Christian held on, still self-assured. He could not fail; he would not fail. To avenge Rol and Trella was motive enough for him to do what man could do; but for Sweyn more. She had kissed Sweyn, but he should not die too: with Sweyn to save he could not fail.

Never before was such a race as this; no, not when in old Greece man and maid raced together with two fates at stake; for the hard running was sustained unabated, while star after star rose and went wheeling up towards midnight, for one hour, for two hours.

Then Christian saw and heard what shot him through with fear. Where a fringe of trees hung round a slope he saw something dark moving, and heard a yelp, followed by a full horrid cry, and the dark spread out upon the snow, a pack of wolves in pursuit.

Of the beasts alone he had little cause for fear; at the pace he held he could distance them, four-footed though they were. But of White Fell's wiles he had infinite apprehension, for how might she not avail herself of the savage jaws of these wolves, akin as they were to half her nature. She vouchsafed to them nor look nor sign; but Christian, on an impulse to assure himself that she should not escape him, caught and held the back-flung edge of her furs, running still.

She turned like a flash with a beastly snarl, teeth and eyes gleaming again. Her axe shone, on the upstroke, on the downstroke, as she hacked at his hand. She had lopped it off at the wrist, but that he parried with the bear-spear. Even then, she shore through the shaft and shattered the bones of the hand at the same blow, so that he loosed perforce.

Then again they raced on as before, Christian not losing a pace, though his left hand swung useless, bleeding and broken.

The snarl, indubitable, though modified from a woman's organs, the vicious fury revealed in teeth and eyes, the sharp arrogant pain of her maiming blow, caught away Christian's heed of the beasts behind, by striking into him close vivid realisation of the infinitely greater danger that ran before him in that deadly Thing.

When he bethought him to look behind, lo! the pack had but reached their tracks, and instantly slunk aside, cowed; the yell of pursuit changing to yelps and whines. So abhorrent was that fell creature to beast as to man.

She had drawn her furs more closely to her, disposing them so that, instead of flying loose to her heels, no drapery hung lower than her knees, and this without a check to her wonderful speed, nor embarrassment by the cumbering of the folds. She held her head as before; her lips were firmly set, only the tense nostrils gave her breath; not a sign of distress witnessed to the long sustaining of that terrible speed.

But on Christian by now the strain was telling palpably. His head weighed heavy, and his breath came labouring in great sobs; the bear spear would have been a burden now. His heart was beating like a hammer, but such a dulness oppressed his brain, that it was only by degrees he could realise his helpless state; wounded and weaponless, chasing that terrible Thing, that was a fierce, desperate, axe-armed woman, except she should assume the beast with fangs yet more formidable.

And still the far slow stars went lingering nearly an hour from midnight.

So far was his brain astray that an impression took him that she was fleeing from the midnight stars, whose gain was by such slow degrees that a time equalling days and days had gone in the race round the northern circle of the world, and days and days as long might last before the end—except she slackened, or except he failed.

But he would not fail yet.

How long had he been praying so? He had started with a self-confidence and reliance that had felt no need for that aid; and now it seemed the only means by which to restrain his heart from swelling beyond the compass of his body, by which to cherish his brain from dwindling and shrivelling quite away. Some sharp-toothed creature kept tearing and dragging on his maimed left hand; he never could see it, he could not shake it off; but he prayed it off at times.

The clear stars before him took to shuddering, and he knew why: they shuddered at sight of what was behind him. He had never divined before that strange things hid themselves from men under pretence of being snow-clad mounds or swaying trees; but now they came slipping out from their harmless covers to follow him, and mock at his impotence to make a kindred Thing resolve to truer form. He knew the air behind him was thronged; he heard the hum of innumerable murmurings together; but his eyes could never catch them, they were too swift and nimble. Yet he knew they were there, because, on a backward glance, he saw the snow mounds surge as they grovelled flatlings out of sight; he saw the trees reel as they screwed themselves rigid past recognition among the boughs.

And after such glance the stars for awhile returned to steadfastness, and an infinite stretch of silence froze upon the chill grey world, only deranged by the swift even beat of the flying feet, and his own—slower from the longer stride, and the sound of his breath. And for some clear moments he knew that his only concern was, to sustain his speed regardless of pain and distress, to deny with every nerve he had her power to outstrip him or to widen the space between them, till the stars crept up to midnight. Then out again would come that crowd invisible, humming and hustling behind, dense and dark enough, he knew, to blot out the stars at his back, yet ever skipping and jerking from his sight.

A hideous check came to the race. White Fell swirled about and leapt to the right, and Christian, unprepared for so prompt a lurch, found close at his feet a deep pit yawning, and his own impetus past control. But he snatched at her as he bore past, clasping her right arm with his one whole hand, and the two swung together upon the brink.

And her straining away in self preservation was vigorous enough to counterbalance his headlong impulse, and brought them reeling together to safety.

Then, before he was verily sure that they were not to perish so, crashing down, he saw her gnashing in wild pale fury as she wrenched to be free; and since her right hand was in his grasp, used her axe left-handed, striking back at him.

The blow was effectual enough even so; his right arm dropped powerless, gashed, and with the lesser bone broken, that jarred with horrid pain when he let it swing as he leaped out again, and ran to recover the few feet she had gained from his pause at the shock.

The near escape and this new quick pain made again every faculty alive and intense. He knew that what he followed was most surely Death animate: wounded and helpless, he was utterly at her mercy if so she should realise and take action. Hopeless to avenge, hopeless to save, his very despair for Sweyn swept him on to follow, and follow, and precede the kiss-doomed to death. Could he yet fail to hunt that Thing past midnight, out of the womanly form alluring and treacherous, into lasting restraint of the bestial, which was the last shred of hope left from the confident purpose of the outset?

"Sweyn, Sweyn, O Sweyn!" He thought he was praying, though his heart wrung out nothing but this: "Sweyn, Sweyn, O Sweyn!"

The last hour from midnight had lost half its quarters, and the stars went lifting up the great minutes; and again his greatening heart, and his shrinking brain, and the sickening agony that swung at either side, conspired to appal the will that had only seeming empire over his feet.

Now White Fell's body was so closely enveloped that not a lap nor an edge flew free. She stretched forward strangely aslant, leaning from the upright poise of a runner. She cleared the ground at times by long bounds, gaining an increase of speed that Christian agonised to equal.

Because the stars pointed that the end was nearing, the black brood came behind again, and followed, noising. Ah! if they could but be kept quiet and still, nor slip their usual harmless masks to encourage with their interest the last speed of their most deadly congener. What shape had they? Should he ever know? If it were not that he was bound to compel the fell Thing that ran before him into her truer form, he might face about and follow them. No—no—not so; if he might do anything but what he did—race, race, and racing bear this agony, he would just stand still and die, to be quit of the pain of breathing.

He grew bewildered, uncertain of his own identity, doubting of his own true form. He could not be really a man, no more than that running Thing was really a woman; his real form was only hidden under embodiment of a man, but what it was he did not know. And Sweyn's real form he did not know. Sweyn lay fallen at his feet, where he had struck him down—his own brother—he: he stumbled over him, and had to overleap him and race harder because she who had kissed Sweyn leapt so fast. "Sweyn, Sweyn, O Sweyn!"

Why did the stars stop to shudder? Midnight else had surely come!

The leaning, leaping Thing looked back at him with a wild, fierce look, and laughed in savage scorn and triumph. He saw in a flash why, for within a time measurable by seconds she would have escaped him utterly. As the land lay, a slope of ice sunk on the one hand; on the other hand a steep rose, shouldering forwards; between the two was space for a foot to be planted, but none for a body to stand; yet a juniper bough, thrusting out, gave a handhold secure enough for one with a resolute grasp to swing past the perilous place, and pass on safe.

Though the first seconds of the last moment were going, she dared to flash back a wicked look, and laugh at the pursuer who was impotent to grasp.

The crisis struck convulsive life into his last supreme effort; his will surged up indomitable, his speed proved matchless yet. He leapt with a rush, passed her before her laugh had time to go out, and turned short, barring the way, and braced to withstand her.

She came hurling desperate, with a feint to the right hand, and then launched herself upon him with a spring like a wild beast when it leaps to kill. And he, with one strong arm and a hand that could not hold, with one strong hand and an arm that could not guide and sustain, he caught and held her even so. And they fell together. And because he felt his whole arm slipping, and his whole hand loosing, to slack the dreadful agony of the wrenched bone above, he caught and held with his teeth the tunic at her knee, as she struggled up and wrung off his hands to overleap him victorious.

Like lightning she snatched her axe, and struck him on the neck, deep—once, twice—his life-blood gushed out, staining her feet.

The stars touched midnight.

The death scream he heard was not his, for his set teeth had hardly yet relaxed when it rang out; and the dreadful cry began with a woman's shriek, and changed and ended as the yell of a beast. And before the final blank overtook his dying eyes, he saw that She gave place to It; he saw more, that Life gave place to Death—causelessly, incomprehensibly.

For he did not presume that no holy water could be more holy, more potent to destroy an evil thing than the life-blood of a pure heart poured out for another in free willing devotion.

His own true hidden reality that he had desired to know grew palpable, recognisable. It seemed to him just this: a great glad abounding hope that he had saved his brother; too expansive to be contained by the limited form of a sole man, it yearned for a new embodiment infinite as the stars.

What did it matter to that true reality that the man's brain shrank, shrank, till it was nothing; that the man's body could not retain the huge pain of his heart, and heaved it out through the red exit riven at the neck; that the black noise came again hurtling from behind, reinforced by that dissolved shape, and blotted out for ever the man's sight, hearing, sense.

* * *

In the early grey of day Sweyn chanced upon the footprints of a man—of a runner, as he saw by the shifted snow; and the direction they had taken aroused curiosity, since a little farther their line must be crossed by the edge of a sheer height. He turned to trace them. And so doing, the length of the stride struck his attention—a stride long as his own if he ran. He knew he was following Christian.

In his anger he had hardened himself to be indifferent to the night-long absence of his brother; but now, seeing where the footsteps went, he was seized with compunction and dread. He had failed to give thought and care to his poor frantic twin, who might—was it possible?—have rushed to a frantic death.

His heart stood still when he came to the place where the leap had been taken. A piled edge of snow had fallen too, and nothing but snow lay below when he peered. Along the upper edge he ran for a furlong, till he came to a dip where he could slip and climb down, and then back again on the lower level to the pile of fallen snow. There he saw that the vigorous running had started afresh.

He stood pondering; vexed that any man should have taken that leap where he had not ventured to follow; vexed that he had been beguiled to such painful emotions; guessing vainly at Christian's object in this mad freak. He began sauntering along, half unconsciously following his brother's track; and so in a while he came to the place where the footprints were doubled.

Small prints were these others, small as a woman's, though the pace from one to another was longer than that which the skirts of women allow.

Did not White Fell tread so?

A dreadful guess appalled him, so dreadful that he recoiled from belief. Yet his face grew ashy white, and he gasped to fetch back motion to his checked heart. Unbelievable? Closer attention showed how the smaller footfall had altered for greater speed, striking into the snow with a deeper onset and a lighter pressure on the heels. Unbelievable? Could any woman but White Fell run so? Could any man but Christian run so? The guess became a certainty. He was following where alone in the dark night White Fell had fled from Christian pursuing.

Such villainy set heart and brain on fire with rage and indignation: such villainy in his own brother, till lately love-worthy, praiseworthy, though a fool for meekness. He would kill Christian; had he lives many as the footprints he had trodden, vengeance should demand them all. In a tempest of murderous hate he followed on in haste, for the track was plain enough, starting with such a burst of speed as could not be maintained, but brought him back soon to a plod for the spent, sobbing breath to be regulated. He cursed Christian aloud and called White Fell's name on high in a frenzied expense of passion. His grief itself was a rage, being such an intolerable anguish of pity and shame at the thought of his love, White Fell, who had parted from his kiss free and radiant, to be hounded straightway by his brother mad with jealousy, fleeing for more than life while her lover was housed at his ease. If he had but known, he raved, in impotent rebellion at the cruelty of events, if he had but known that his strength and love might have availed in her defence; now the only service to her that he could render was to kill Christian.

As a woman he knew she was matchless in speed, matchless in strength; but Christian was matchless in speed among men, nor easily to be matched in strength. Brave and swift and strong though she were, what chance had she against a man of his strength and inches, frantic, too, and intent on horrid revenge against his brother, his successful rival?

Mile after mile he followed with a bursting heart; more piteous, more tragic, seemed the case at this evidence of White Fell's splendid supremacy, holding her own so long against Christian's famous speed. So long, so long that his love and admiration grew more and more boundless, and his grief and indignation therewith also. Whenever the track lay clear he ran, with such reckless prodigality of strength, that it soon was spent, and he dragged on heavily, till, sometimes on the ice of a mere, sometimes on a wind-swept place, all signs were lost; but, so undeviating had been their line that a course straight on, and then short questing to either hand, recovered them again.

Hour after hour had gone by through more than half that winter day, before ever he came to the place where the trampled snow showed that a scurry of feet had come—and gone! Wolves' feet—and gone most amazingly! Only a little beyond he came to the lopped point of Christian's bear-spear; farther on he would see where the remnant of the useless shaft had been dropped. The snow here was dashed with blood, and the footsteps of the two had fallen closer together. Some hoarse sound of exultation came from him that might have been a laugh had breath sufficed. "O White Fell, my poor, brave love! Well struck!" he groaned, torn by his pity and great admiration, as he guessed surely how she had turned and dealt a blow.

The sight of the blood inflamed him as it might a beast that ravens. He grew mad with a desire to have Christian by the throat once again, not to loose this time till he had crushed out his life, or beat out his life, or stabbed out his life; or all these, and torn him piecemeal likewise: and ah! then, not till then, bleed his heart with weeping, like a child, like a girl, over the piteous fate of his poor lost love.

On—on—on—through the aching time, toiling and straining in the track of those two superb runners, aware of the marvel of their endurance, but unaware of the marvel of their speed, that, in the three hours before midnight had overpassed all that vast distance that he could only traverse from twilight to twilight. For clear daylight was passing when he came to the edge of an old marl-pit, and saw how the two who had gone before had stamped and trampled together in desperate peril on the verge. And here fresh blood stains spoke to him of a valiant defence against his infamous brother; and he followed where the blood had dripped till the cold had staunched its flow, taking a savage gratification from this evidence that Christian had been gashed deeply, maddening afresh with desire to do likewise more excellently, and so slake his murderous hate. And he began to know that through all his despair he had entertained a germ of hope, that grew apace, rained upon by his brother's blood.

He strove on as best he might, wrung now by an access of hope, now of despair, in agony to reach the end, however terrible, sick with the aching of the toiled miles that deferred it.

And the light went lingering out of the sky, giving place to uncertain stars.

He came to the finish.

Two bodies lay in a narrow place. Christian's was one, but the other beyond not White Fell's. There where the footsteps ended lay a great white wolf.

At the sight Sweyn's strength was blasted; body and soul he was struck down grovelling.

The stars had grown sure and intense before he stirred from where he had dropped prone. Very feebly he crawled to his dead brother, and laid his hands upon him, and crouched so, afraid to look or stir farther.

Cold, stiff, hours dead. Yet the dead body was his only shelter and stay in that most dreadful hour. His soul, stripped bare of all sceptic comfort, cowered, shivering, naked, abject; and the living clung to the dead out of piteous need for grace from the soul that had passed away.

He rose to his knees, lifting the body. Christian had fallen face forward in the snow, with his arms flung up and wide, and so had the frost made him rigid: strange, ghastly, unyielding to Sweyn's lifting, so that he laid him down again and crouched above, with his arms fast round him, and a low heart-wrung groan.

When at last he found force to raise his brother's body and gather it in his arms, tight clasped to his breast, he tried to face the Thing that lay beyond. The sight set his limbs in a palsy with horror and dread. His senses had failed and fainted in utter cowardice, but for the strength that came from holding dead Christian in his arms, enabling him to compel his eyes to endure the sight, and take into the brain the complete aspect of the Thing. No wound, only blood stains on the feet. The great grim jaws had a savage grin, though dead-stiff. And his kiss: he could bear it no longer, and turned away, nor ever looked again.

And the dead man in his arms, knowing the full horror, had followed and faced it for his sake; had suffered agony and death for his sake; in the neck was the deep death gash, one arm and both hands were dark with frozen blood, for his sake! Dead he knew him, as in life he had not known him, to give the right meed of love and worship. Because the outward man lacked perfection and strength equal to his, he had taken the love and worship of that great pure heart as his due; he, so unworthy in the inner reality, so mean, so despicable, callous, and contemptuous towards the brother who had laid down his life to save him. He longed for utter annihilation, that so he might lose the agony of knowing himself so unworthy such perfect love. The frozen calm of death on the face appalled him. He dared not touch it with lips that had cursed so lately, with lips fouled by kiss of the horror that had been death.

He struggled to his feet, still clasping Christian. The dead man stood upright within his arm, frozen rigid. The eyes were not quite closed; the head had stiffened, bowed slightly to one side; the arms stayed straight and wide. It was the figure of one crucified, the blood-stained hands also conforming.

So living and dead went back along the track that one had passed in the deepest passion of love, and one in the deepest passion of hate. All that night Sweyn toiled through the snow, bearing the weight of dead Christian, treading back along the steps he before had trodden, when he was wronging with vilest thoughts, and cursing with murderous hatred, the brother who all the while lay dead for his sake.

Cold, silence, darkness encompassed the strong man bowed with the dolorous burden; and yet he knew surely that that night he entered hell, and trod hell-fire along the homeward road, and endured through it only because Christian was with him. And he knew surely that to him Christian had been as Christ, and had suffered and died to save him from his sins.

The Death of Halpin Frayser

Ambrose Bierce

———◆———

For by death is wrought greater change than hath been shown. Whereas in general the spirit that removed cometh back upon occasion, and is sometimes seen of those in flesh (appearing in the form of the body it bore) yet it hath happened that the veritable body without the spirit hath walked. And it is attested of those encountering who have lived to speak thereon that a lich so raised up hath no natural affection, nor remembrance thereof, but only hate. Also, it is known that some spirits which in life were benign become by death evil altogether.

—HALI

I

One dark night in midsummer a man waking from a dreamless sleep in a forest lifted his head from the earth, and staring a few moments into the blackness, said: "Catherine Larue." He said nothing more; no reason was known to him why he should have said so much.

The man was Halpin Frayser. He lived in St. Helena, but where he lives now is uncertain, for he is dead. One who practices sleeping in the woods with nothing under him but the dry leaves and the damp earth, and nothing over him but the branches from which the leaves have fallen and the sky from which the earth has fallen, cannot hope for great longevity, and Frayser had already attained the age of thirty-two. There are persons in this world, millions of persons, and far and away the best persons, who regard that as a very advanced age. They are the children. To those who view the voyage of life from the port of departure the bark that has accomplished any considerable distance appears already in close approach to the farther shore. However, it is not certain that Halpin Frayser came to his death by exposure.

He had been all day in the hills west of the Napa Valley, looking for doves and such small game as was in season. Late in the afternoon it had come on to be cloudy, and he had lost his bearings; and although he had only to go always downhill—everywhere the way to safety when one is lost—the absence of trails had so impeded him that he was overtaken by night while still in the forest. Unable in the darkness to penetrate the thickets of manzanita and other undergrowth, utterly bewildered and overcome with fatigue, he had lain down near the root of a large madrono and fallen into a dreamless sleep. It was hours later, in the very middle of the night, that one of God's mysterious messengers, gliding ahead of the incalculable host of his companions sweeping westward with the dawn line, pronounced the awakening word in the ear of the sleeper, who sat upright and spoke, he knew not why, a name, he knew not whose.

Halpin Frayser was not much of a philosopher, nor a scientist. The circumstance that, waking from a deep sleep at night in the midst of a forest, he had spoken aloud a name that he had not in memory and hardly had in mind did not arouse an enlightened curiosity to investigate the phenomenon. He thought it odd, and with a little perfunctory shiver, as if in deference to a seasonal presumption that the night was chill, he lay down again and went to sleep. But his sleep was no longer dreamless.

He thought he was walking along a dusty road that showed white in the gathering darkness of a summer night. Whence and whither it led, and why he traveled it, he did not know, though all seemed simple and natural, as is the way in dreams; for in the Land Beyond the Bed surprises cease from troubling and the judgment is at rest. Soon he came to a parting of the ways; leading from the highway was a road less traveled, having the appearance, indeed, of having been long abandoned, because, he thought, it led to something evil; yet he turned into it without hesitation, impelled by some imperious necessity.

As he pressed forward he became conscious that his way was haunted by invisible existences whom he could not definitely figure to his mind. From among the trees on either side he caught broken and incoherent whispers in a strange tongue which yet he partly understood. They seemed to him fragmentary utterances of a monstrous conspiracy against his body and soul.

It was now long after nightfall, yet the interminable forest through which he journeyed was lit with a wan glimmer having no point of diffusion, for in its mysterious lumination nothing cast a shadow. A shallow pool in the guttered depression of an old wheel rut, as from a recent rain, met his eye with a crimson gleam. He stooped and plunged his hand into it. It stained his fingers; it was blood! Blood, he then observed, was about him everywhere. The weeds growing rankly by the roadside showed it in blots and splashes on their big, broad leaves. Patches of dry dust between the wheelways were pitted and spattered as with a red rain. Defiling the trunks of the trees were broad maculations of crimson, and blood dripped like dew from their foliage.

All this he observed with a terror which seemed not incompatible with the fulfill-
ment of a natural expectation. It seemed to him that it was all in expiation of some crime
which, though conscious of his guilt, he could not rightly remember. To the menaces
and mysteries of his surroundings the consciousness was an added horror. Vainly he
sought by tracing life backward in memory, to reproduce the moment of his sin; scenes
and incidents came crowding tumultuously into his mind, one picture effacing another,
or commingling with it in confusion and obscurity, but nowhere could he catch a glimpse
of what he sought. The failure augmented his terror; he felt as one who has murdered
in the dark, not knowing whom nor why. So frightful was the situation—the mysterious
light burned with so silent and awful a menace; the noxious plants, the trees that by common consent are invested with a melancholy or baleful character, so openly in his sight
conspired against his peace; from overhead and all about came so audible and startling
whispers and the sighs of creatures so obviously not of earth—that he could endure it
no longer, and with a great effort to break some malign spell that bound his faculties to
silence and inaction, he shouted with the full strength of his lungs! His voice broken, it
seemed, into an infinite multitude of unfamiliar sounds, went babbling and stammering
away into the distant reaches of the forest, died into silence, and all was as before. But he
had made a beginning at resistance and was encouraged. He said:

"I will not submit unheard. There may be powers that are not malignant traveling
this accursed road. I shall leave them a record and an appeal. I shall relate my wrongs,
the persecutions that I endure—I, a helpless mortal, a penitent, an unoffending poet!"
Halpin Frayser was a poet only as he was a penitent: in his dream.

Taking from his clothing a small red-leather pocketbook, one-half of which was
leaved for memoranda, he discovered that he was without a pencil. He broke a twig
from a bush, dipped it into a pool of blood and wrote rapidly. He had hardly touched
the paper with the point of his twig when a low, wild peal of laughter broke out at a
measureless distance away, and growing ever louder, seemed approaching ever nearer;
a soulless, heartless, and unjoyous laugh, like that of the loon, solitary by the lakeside
at midnight; a laugh which culminated in an unearthly shout close at hand, then died
away by slow gradations, as if the accursed being that uttered it had withdrawn over
the verge of the world whence it had come. But the man felt that this was not so—that
it was near by and had not moved.

A strange sensation began slowly to take possession of his body and his mind.
He could not have said which, if any, of his senses was affected; he felt it rather as
a consciousness—a mysterious mental assurance of some overpowering presence—

some supernatural malevolence different in kind from the invisible existences that swarmed about him, and superior to them in power. He knew that it had uttered that hideous laugh. And now it seemed to be approaching him; from what direction he did not know—dared not conjecture. All his former fears were forgotten or merged in the gigantic terror that now held him in thrall. Apart from that, he had but one thought: to complete his written appeal to the benign powers who, traversing the haunted wood, might some time rescue him if he should be denied the blessing of annihilation. He wrote with terrible rapidity, the twig in his fingers rilling blood without renewal; but in the middle of a sentence his hands denied their service to his will, his arms fell to his sides, the book to the earth; and powerless to move or cry out, he found himself staring into the sharply drawn face and blank, dead eyes of his own mother, standing white and silent in the garments of the grave!

II

In his youth Halpin Frayser had lived with his parents in Nashville, Tennessee. The Fraysers were well-to-do, having a good position in such society as had survived the wreck wrought by civil war. Their children had the social and educational opportunities of their time and place, and had responded to good associations and instruction with agreeable manners and cultivated minds. Halpin being the youngest and not over robust was perhaps a trifle "spoiled." He had the double disadvantage of a mother's assiduity and a father's neglect. Frayser *père* was what no Southern man of means is not—a politician. His country, or rather his section and State, made demands upon his time and attention so exacting that to those of his family he was compelled to turn an ear partly deafened by the thunder of the political captains and the shouting, his own included.

Young Halpin was of a dreamy, indolent and rather romantic turn, somewhat more addicted to literature than law, the profession to which he was bred. Among those of his relations who professed the modern faith of heredity it was well understood that in him the character of the late Myron Bayne, a maternal great-grandfather, had revisited the glimpses of the moon—by which orb Bayne had in his lifetime been sufficiently affected to be a poet of no small Colonial distinction. If not specially observed, it was observable that while a Frayser who was not the proud possessor of a sumptuous copy of the ancestral "poetical works" (printed at the family expense, and long ago withdrawn from an inhospitable market) was a rare Frayser indeed, there was an illogical indisposition to honor the great deceased in the person of his spiritual successor. Halpin was pretty generally deprecated as an intellectual black sheep who was likely at any moment to disgrace the flock by bleating in meter. The Tennessee Fraysers were a practical folk—not practical in the popular sense of devotion to sordid pursuits, but having a robust contempt for any qualities unfitting a man for the wholesome vocation of politics.

In justice to young Halpin it should be said that while in him were pretty faithfully reproduced most of the mental and moral characteristics ascribed by history and family tradition to the famous Colonial bard, his succession to the gift and faculty divine was purely inferential. Not only had he never been known to court the muse, but in truth he could not have written correctly a line of verse to save himself from the Killer of the Wise. Still, there was no knowing when the dormant faculty might wake and smite the lyre.

In the meantime the young man was rather a loose fish, anyhow. Between him and his mother was the most perfect sympathy, for secretly the lady was herself a devout disciple of the late and great Myron Bayne, though with the tact so generally and justly admired in her sex (despite the hardy calumniators who insist that it is essentially the same thing as cunning) she had always taken care to conceal her weakness from all eyes but those of him who shared it. Their common guilt in respect of that was an added tie between them. If in Halpin's youth his mother had "spoiled" him, he had assuredly done his part toward being spoiled. As he grew to such manhood as is attainable by a Southerner who does not care which way elections go the attachment between him and his beautiful mother—whom from early childhood he had called Katy—became yearly stronger and more tender. In these two romantic natures was manifest in a signal way that neglected phenomenon, the dominance of the sexual element in all the relations of life, strengthening, softening, and beautifying even those of consanguinity. The two were nearly inseparable, and by strangers observing their manner were not infrequently mistaken for lovers.

Entering his mother's boudoir one day Halpin Frayser kissed her upon the forehead, toyed for a moment with a lock of her dark hair which had escaped from its confining pins, and said, with an obvious effort at calmness:

"Would you greatly mind, Katy, if I were called away to California for a few weeks?"

It was hardly needful for Katy to answer with her lips a question to which her telltale cheeks had made instant reply. Evidently she would greatly mind; and the tears, too, sprang into her large brown eyes as corroborative testimony.

"Ah, my son," she said, looking up into his face with infinite tenderness, "I should have known that this was coming. Did I not lie awake a half of the night weeping because, during the other half, Grandfather Bayne had come to me in a dream, and standing by his portrait—young, too, and handsome as that—pointed to yours on the same wall? And when I looked it seemed that I could not see the features; you had been painted with a face cloth, such as we put upon the dead. Your father has laughed at me, but you and I, dear, know that such things are not for nothing. And I saw below the edge of the cloth the marks of hands on your throat—forgive me, but we have not been used to keep such things from each other. Perhaps you have another interpretation. Perhaps it does not mean that you will go to California. Or maybe you will take me with you?"

It must be confessed that this ingenious interpretation of the dream in the light of newly discovered evidence did not wholly commend itself to the son's more logical mind; he had, for the moment at least, a conviction that it foreshadowed a more simple and immediate, if less tragic, disaster than a visit to the Pacific Coast. It was Halpin Frayser's impression that he was to be garroted on his native heath.

"Are there not medicinal springs in California?" Mrs. Frayser resumed before he had time to give her the true reading of the dream—"places where one recovers from rheumatism and neuralgia? Look—my fingers feel so stiff; and I am almost sure they have been giving me great pain while I slept."

She held out her hands for his inspection. What diagnosis of her case the young man may have thought it best to conceal with a smile the historian is unable to state, but for himself he feels bound to say that fingers looking less stiff, and showing fewer evidences of even insensible pain, have seldom been submitted for medical inspection by even the fairest patient desiring a prescription of unfamiliar scenes.

The outcome of it was that of these two odd persons having equally odd notions of duty, the one went to California, as the interest of his client required, and the other remained at home in compliance with a wish that her husband was scarcely conscious of entertaining.

While in San Francisco Halpin Frayser was walking one dark night along the water front of the city, when, with a suddenness that surprised and disconcerted him, he became a sailor. He was in fact "shanghaied" aboard a gallant, gallant ship, and sailed for a far countree. Nor did his misfortunes end with the voyage; for the ship was cast ashore on an island of the South Pacific, and it was six years afterward when the survivors were taken off by a venturesome trading schooner and brought back to San Francisco.

Though poor in purse, Frayser was no less proud in spirit than he had been in the years that seemed ages and ages ago. He would accept no assistance from strangers, and it was while living with a fellow survivor near the town of St. Helena, awaiting news and remittances from home, that he had gone gunning and dreaming.

III

The apparition confronting the dreamer in the haunted wood—the thing so like, yet so unlike his mother—was horrible! It stirred no love nor longing in his heart; it came unattended with pleasant memories of a golden past—inspired no sentiment of any kind; all the finer emotions were swallowed up in fear. He tried to turn and run from before it, but his legs were as lead; he was unable to lift his feet from the ground. His arms hung helpless at his sides; of his eyes only he retained control, and these he dared not remove from the lusterless orbs of the apparition, which he knew was not a soul without a body, but that most dreadful of all existences infesting that haunted wood—a body without a soul! In its blank stare was neither love, nor pity, nor intelligence—nothing to which to address an appeal for mercy. "An appeal will not lie," he thought, with an absurd reversion to professional slang, making the situation more horrible, as the fire of a cigar might light up a tomb.

For a time, which seemed so long that the world grew gray with age and sin, and the haunted forest, having fulfilled its purpose in this monstrous culmination of its terrors, vanished out of his consciousness with all its sights and sounds, the apparition stood within a pace, regarding him with the mindless malevolence of a wild brute; then thrust its hands forward and sprang upon him with appalling ferocity! The act released his physical energies without unfettering his will; his mind was still spellbound, but his powerful body and agile limbs, endowed with a blind, insensate life of their own, resisted stoutly and well. For an instant he seemed to see this unnatural contest between a dead intelligence and a breathing mechanism only as a spectator—such fancies are in dreams; then he regained his identity almost as if by a leap forward into his body, and the straining automaton had a directing will as alert and fierce as that of its hideous antagonist.

But what mortal can cope with a creature of his dream? The imagination creating the enemy is already vanquished; the combat's result is the combat's cause. Despite his struggles—despite his strength and activity, which seemed wasted in a void, he felt the cold fingers close upon his throat. Borne backward to the earth, he saw above him the dead and drawn face within a hand's breadth of his own, and then all was black. A sound as of the beating of distant drums—a murmur of swarming voices, a sharp, far cry signing all to silence, and Halpin Frayser dreamed that he was dead.

IV

A warm, clear night had been followed by a morning of drenching fog. At about the middle of the afternoon of the preceding day a little whiff of light vapor—a mere thickening of the atmosphere, the ghost of a cloud—had been observed clinging to the western side of Mount St. Helena, away up along the barren altitudes near the summit. It was so thin, so diaphanous, so like a fancy made visible, that one would have said: "Look quickly! in a moment it will be gone."

In a moment it was visibly larger and denser. While with one edge it clung to the mountain, with the other it reached farther and farther out into the air above the lower slopes. At the same time it extended itself to north and south, joining small patches of mist that appeared to come out of the mountainside on exactly the same level, with an intelligent design to be absorbed. And so it grew and grew until the summit was shut out of view from the valley, and over the valley itself was an ever-extending canopy, opaque and gray. At Calistoga, which lies near the head of the valley and the foot of the mountain, there were a starless night and a sunless morning. The fog, sinking into the valley, had reached southward, swallowing up ranch after ranch, until it had blotted out the town of St. Helena, nine miles away. The dust in the road was laid; trees were adrip with moisture; birds sat silent in their coverts; the morning light was wan and ghastly, with neither color nor fire.

Two men left the town of St. Helena at the first glimmer of dawn, and walked along the road northward up the valley toward Calistoga. They carried guns on their shoulders, yet no one having knowledge of such matters could have mistaken them for hunters of bird or beast. They were a deputy sheriff from Napa and a detective from San Francisco— Holker and Jaralson, respectively. Their business was man-hunting.

"How far is it?" inquired Holker, as they strode along, their feet stirring white the dust beneath the damp surface of the road.

"The White Church? Only a half mile farther," the other answered. "By the way," he added, "it is neither white nor a church; it is an abandoned schoolhouse, gray with age and neglect. Religious services were once held in it—when it was white, and there is a graveyard that would delight a poet. Can you guess why I sent for you, and told you to come heeled?"

"Oh, I never have bothered you about things of that kind. I've always found you communicative when the time came. But if I may hazard a guess, you want me to help you arrest one of the corpses in the graveyard."

"You remember Branscom?" said Jaralson, treating his companion's wit with the inattention that it deserved.

"The chap who cut his wife's throat? I ought; I wasted a week's work on him and had my expenses for my trouble. There is a reward of five hundred dollars, but none of us ever got a sight of him. You don't mean to say——"

"Yes, I do. He has been under the noses of you fellows all the time. He comes by night to the old graveyard at the White Church."

"The devil! That's where they buried his wife."

"Well, you fellows might have had sense enough to suspect that he would return to her grave some time."

"The very last place that anyone would have expected him to return to."

"But you had exhausted all the other places. Learning your failure at them, I 'laid for him' there."

"And you found him?"

"Damn it! he found *me*. The rascal got the drop on me—regularly held me up and made me travel. It's God's mercy that he didn't go through me. Oh, he's a good one, and I fancy the half of that reward is enough for me if you're needy."

Holker laughed good humoredly, and explained that his creditors were never more importunate.

"I wanted merely to show you the ground, and arrange a plan with you," the detective explained. "I thought it as well for us to be heeled, even in daylight."

"The man must be insane," said the deputy sheriff. "The reward is for his capture and conviction. If he's mad he won't be convicted."

Mr. Holker was so profoundly affected by that possible failure of justice that he involuntarily stopped in the middle of the road, then resumed his walk with abated zeal.

"Well, he looks it," assented Jaralson. "I'm bound to admit that a more unshaven, unshorn, unkempt, and uneverything wretch I never saw outside the ancient and honorable order of tramps. But I've gone in for him, and can't make up my mind to let go. There's glory in it for us, anyhow. Not another soul knows that he is this side of the Mountains of the Moon."

"All right," Holker said; "we will go and view the ground," and he added, in the words of a once favorite inscription for tombstones: " 'where you must shortly lie'—I mean, if old Branscom ever gets tired of you and your impertinent intrusion. By the way, I heard the other day that 'Branscom' was not his real name."

"What is?"

"I can't recall it. I had lost all interest in the wretch, and it did not fix itself in my memory—something like Pardee. The woman whose throat he had the bad taste to cut was a widow when he met her. She had come to California to look up some relatives—there are persons who will do that sometimes. But you know all that."

"Naturally."

"But not knowing the right name, by what happy inspiration did you find the right grave? The man who told me what the name was said it had been cut on the headboard."

"I don't know the right grave." Jaralson was apparently a trifle reluctant to admit his ignorance of so important a point of his plan. "I have been watching about the place generally. A part of our work this morning will be to identify that grave. Here is the White Church."

For a long distance the road had been bordered by fields on both sides, but now on the left there was a forest of oaks, madronos, and gigantic spruces whose lower parts only could be seen, dim and ghostly in the fog. The undergrowth was, in places, thick, but nowhere impenetrable. For some moments Holker saw nothing of the building, but as they turned into the woods it revealed itself in faint gray outline through the fog, looking huge and far away. A few steps more, and it was within an arm's length, distinct, dark with moisture, and insignificant in size. It had the usual country-schoolhouse form—belonged to the packing-box order of architecture; had an underpinning of stones, a moss-grown roof, and blank window spaces, whence both glass and sash had long departed. It was ruined, but not a ruin—a typical Californian substitute for what are known to guide-bookers abroad as "monuments of the past." With scarcely a glance at this uninteresting structure Jaralson moved on into the dripping undergrowth beyond.

"I will show you where he held me up," he said. "This is the graveyard."

Here and there among the bushes were small inclosures containing graves, sometimes no more than one. They were recognized as graves by the discolored stones or rotting boards at head and foot, leaning at all angles, some prostrate; by the ruined picket fences surrounding them; or, infrequently, by the mound itself showing its gravel through the fallen leaves. In many instances nothing marked the spot where lay the vestiges of some poor mortal—who, leaving "a large circle of sorrowing friends," had been left by them in turn—except a depression in the earth, more lasting than that in the spirits of the mourners. The paths, if any paths had been, were long obliterated; trees of a considerable size had been permitted to grow up from the graves and thrust aside with root or branch the inclosing fences. Over all was that air of abandonment and decay which seems nowhere so fit and significant as in a village of the forgotten dead.

As the two men, Jaralson leading, pushed their way through the growth of young trees, that enterprising man suddenly stopped and brought up his shotgun to the height of his breast, uttered a low note of warning, and stood motionless, his eyes fixed upon something ahead. As well as he could, obstructed by brush, his companion, though seeing nothing, imitated the posture and so stood, prepared for what might ensue. A moment later Jaralson moved cautiously forward, the other following.

Under the branches of an enormous spruce lay the dead body of a man. Standing silent above it they noted such particulars as first strike the attention—the face, the attitude, the clothing; whatever most promptly and plainly answers the unspoken question of a sympathetic curiosity.

The body lay upon its back, the legs wide apart. One arm was thrust upward, the other outward; but the latter was bent acutely, and the hand was near the throat. Both hands were tightly clenched. The whole attitude was that of desperate but ineffectual resistance to—what?

Near by lay a shotgun and a game bag through the meshes of which was seen the plumage of shot birds. All about were evidences of a furious struggle; small sprouts of poison-oak were bent and denuded of leaf and bark; dead and rotting leaves had been pushed into heaps and ridges on both sides of the legs by the action of other feet than theirs; alongside the hips were unmistakable impressions of human knees.

The nature of the struggle was made clear by a glance at the dead man's throat and face. While breast and hands were white, those were purple—almost black. The shoulders lay upon a low mound, and the head was turned back at an angle otherwise impossible, the expanded eyes staring blankly backward in a direction opposite to that of the feet. From the froth filling the open mouth the tongue protruded, black and swollen. The throat showed horrible contusions; not mere finger-marks, but bruises and lacerations wrought by two strong hands that must have buried themselves in the yielding flesh, maintaining their terrible grasp until long after death. Breast, throat, face, were wet; the clothing was saturated; drops of water, condensed from the fog, studded the hair and mustache.

All this the two men observed without speaking—almost at a glance. Then Holker said:

"Poor devil! he had a rough deal."

Jaralson was making a vigilant circumspection of the forest, his shotgun held in both hands and at full cock, his finger upon the trigger.

"The work of a maniac," he said, without withdrawing his eyes from the inclosing wood. "It was done by Branscom—Pardee."

Something half hidden by the disturbed leaves on the earth caught Holker's attention. It was a red-leather pocketbook. He picked it up and opened it. It contained leaves of white paper for memoranda, and upon the first leaf was the name "Halpin Frayser." Written in red on several succeeding leaves—scrawled as if in haste and barely legible—were the following lines, which Holker read aloud, while his companion continued scanning the dim gray confines of their narrow world and hearing matter of apprehension in the drip of water from every burdened branch:

"Enthralled by some mysterious spell, I stood
In the lit gloom of an enchanted wood.
　　The cypress there and myrtle twined their boughs,
Significant, in baleful brotherhood.

"The brooding willow whispered to the yew;
Beneath, the deadly nightshade and the rue,
　　With immortelles self-woven into strange
Funereal shapes, and horrid nettles grew.

"No song of bird nor any drone of bees,
Nor light leaf lifted by the wholesome breeze:
　　The air was stagnant all, and Silence was
A living thing that breathed among the trees.

"Conspiring spirits whispered in the gloom,
Half-heard, the stilly secrets of the tomb.
　　With blood the trees were all adrip; the leaves
Shone in the witch-light with a ruddy bloom.

"I cried aloud!—the spell, unbroken still,
Rested upon my spirit and my will.
　　Unsouled, unhearted, hopeless and forlorn,
I strove with monstrous presages of ill!

"At last the viewless—"

Holker ceased reading; there was no more to read. The manuscript broke off in the middle of a line.

"That sounds like Bayne," said Jaralson, who was something of a scholar in his way. He had abated his vigilance and stood looking down at the body.

"Who's Bayne?" Holker asked rather incuriously.

"Myron Bayne, a chap who flourished in the early years of the nation—more than a century ago. Wrote mighty dismal stuff; I have his collected works. That poem is not among them, but it must have been omitted by mistake."

"It is cold," said Holker; "let us leave here; we must have up the coroner from Napa."

Jaralson said nothing, but made a movement in compliance. Passing the end of the slight elevation of earth upon which the dead man's head and shoulders lay, his foot struck some hard substance under the rotting forest leaves, and he took the trouble to kick it into view. It was a fallen headboard, and painted on it were the hardly decipherable words, "Catharine Larue."

"Larue, Larue!" exclaimed Holker, with sudden animation. "Why, that is the real name of Branscom—not Pardee. And—bless my soul! how it all comes to me—the murdered woman's name had been Frayser!"

"There is some rascally mystery here," said Detective Jaralson. "I hate anything of that kind."

There came to them out of the fog—seemingly from a great distance—the sound of a laugh, a low, deliberate, soulless laugh, which had no more of joy than that of a hyena night-prowling in the desert; a laugh that rose by slow gradation, louder and louder, clearer, more distinct and terrible, until it seemed barely outside the narrow circle of their vision; a laugh so unnatural, so unhuman, so devilish, that it filled those hardy man-hunters with a sense of dread unspeakable! They did not move their weapons nor think of them; the menace of that horrible sound was not of the kind to be met with arms. As it had grown out of silence, so now it died away; from a culminating shout which had seemed almost in their ears, it drew itself away into the distance, until its failing notes, joyless and mechanical to the last, sank to silence at a measureless remove.

Lot No. 249

Arthur Conan Doyle

——— • ———

OF THE DEALINGS OF EDWARD BELLINGHAM WITH WILLIAM Monkhouse Lee, and of the cause of the great terror of Abercrombie Smith, it may be that no absolute and final judgment will ever be delivered. It is true that we have the full and clear narrative of Smith himself, and such corroboration as he could look for from Thomas Styles the servant, from the Reverend Plumptree Peterson, Fellow of Old's, and from such other people as chanced to gain some passing glance at this or that incident in a singular chain of events. Yet, in the main, the story must rest upon Smith alone, and the most will think that it is more likely that one brain, however outwardly sane, has some subtle warp in its texture, some strange flaw in its workings, than that the path of Nature has been overstepped in open day in so famed a centre of learning and light as the University of Oxford. Yet when we think how narrow and how devious this path of Nature is, how dimly we can trace it, for all our lamps of science, and how from the darkness which girds it round great and terrible possibilities loom ever shadowly upwards, it is a bold and confident man who will put a limit to the strange by-paths into which the human spirit may wander.

In a certain wing of what we will call Old College in Oxford there is a corner turret of an exceeding great age. The heavy arch which spans the open door has bent downwards in the centre under the weight of its years, and the grey lichen-blotched blocks of stone are bound and knitted together with withes and strand of ivy, as though the old mother had set herself to brace them up against wind and weather. From a door a stone stair curves upwards spirally, passing two landings, and terrninating in a third one, its steps all shapeless and hollowed by the tread of so many generations of the seekers aft knowledge. Life has flowed like water down this winding stair, and, water-like, has left these smooth-worn grooves behind it. From the long-gowned pedantic scholars of Plantagenet days down to the young bloods of a later age, how full and strong had been that tide of young English life. And what was left now of all those hopes, those strivings, those fiery energies, save here and there in some old-world churchyard a few scratches upon a stone and perchance a handful of dust in a mouldering coffin? Yet here were the silent stair and the grey old wall, with bend and saltire and many another heraldic device still to be read upon its surface, like grotesque shadows thrown back from the days that had passed.

In the month of May, in the year 1884, three young men occupied the sets of rooms which opened on to the separate landings of the old stair. Each set consisted simply of a sitting-room and a bedroom, while the two corresponding rooms upon the ground-floor were used, the one as a coal-cellar, and the other as the living-room of the servant, or scout, Thomas Styles, whose duty it was to wait upon the three men above him. To right and to left was a line of lecture-rooms and of offices, so that the dwellers in the old turret enjoyed a certain seclusion, which made the chambers popular among the more studious undergraduates. Such were the three who occupied them now—Abercrombie Smith above, Edward Bellingham beneath him, and William Monkhouse Lee upon the lowest story.

It was ten o'clock on a bright spring night, and Abercrombie Smith lay back in his armchair, his feet upon the fender, and his briar-root pipe between his lips. In a similar chair, and equally at his ease, there lounged on the other side of the fireplace his old school friend Jephro Hastie. Both men were in flannels, for they had spent their evening upon the river, but apart from their dress no one could look at their hard-cut, alert faces without seeing that they were open-air men—men whose minds and tastes turned naturally to all that was manly and robust. Hastie, indeed, was stroke of his college boat, and Smith was an even better oar, but a coming examination had already cast its shadow over him and held him to his work, save for the few hours a week which health demanded. A litter of medical books upon the table, with scattered bones, models, and anatomical plates, pointed to the extent as well as the nature of his studies, while a couple of single-sticks and a set of boxing-gloves above the mantel-piece hinted at the means by which, with Hastie's help, he might take his exercise in its most compressed and least distant form. They knew each other very well—so well that they could sit now in that soothing silence which is the very highest development of companionship.

"Have some whisky," said Abercrombie Smith at last between two cloudbursts. "Scotch in the jug and Irish in the bottle."

"No, thanks. I'm in for the sculls. I don't liquor when I'm training. How about you?"

"I'm reading hard. I think it best to leave it alone."

Hastie nodded, and they relapsed into a contented silence.

"By the way, Smith," asked Hastie, presently, "have you made the acquaintance of either of the fellows on your stair yet?"

"Just a nod when we pass. Nothing more."

"Hum! I should be inclined to let it stand at that. I know something of them both. Not much, but as much as I want. I don't think I should take them to my bosom if I were you. Not that there's much amiss with Monkhouse Lee."

"Meaning the thin one?"

"Precisely. He is a gentlemanly little fellow. I don't think there is any vice in him. But then you can't know him without knowing Bellingham."

"Meaning the fat one?"

"Yes, the fat one. And he's a man whom I, for one, would rather not know."

Abercrombie Smith raised his eyebrows and glanced across at his companion.

"What's up, then?" he asked. "Drink? Cards? Cad? You used not to be censorious."

"Ah! you evidently don't know the man, or you wouldn't ask. There's something damnable about him—something reptilian. My gorge always rises at him. I should put him down as a man with secret vices—an evil liver. He's no fool, though. They say that he is one of the best men in his line that they have ever had in the college."

"Medicine or classics?"

"Eastern languages. He's a demon at them. Chillingworth met him somewhere above the second cataract last long, and he told me that he just prattled to the Arabs as if he had been born and nursed and weaned among them. He talked Coptic to the Copts, and Hebrew to the Jews, and Arabic to the Bedouins, and they were all ready to kiss the hem of his frock-coat. There are some old hermit Johnnies up in those parts who sit on rocks and scowl and spit at the casual stranger. Well, when they saw this chap Bellingham, before he had said five words they just lay down on their bellies and wriggled. Chillingworth said that he never saw anything like it. Bellingham seemed to take it as his right, too, and strutted about among them and talked down to them like a Dutch uncle. Pretty good for an undergrad. of Old's, wasn't it?"

"Why do you say you can't know Lee without knowing Bellingham?"

"Because Bellingham is engaged to his sister Eveline. Such a bright little girl, Smith! I know the whole family well. It's disgusting to see that brute with her. A toad and a dove, that's what they always remind me of."

Abercrombie Smith grinned and knocked his ashes out against the side of the grate.

"You show every card in your hand, old chap," said he. "What a prejudiced, green-eyed, evil-thinking old man it is! You have really nothing against the fellow except that."

"Well, I've known her ever since she was as long as that cherry-wood pipe, and I don't like to see her taking risks. And it is a risk. He looks beastly. And he has a beastly temper, a venomous temper. You remember his row with Long Norton?"

"No; you always forget that I am a freshman."

"Ah, it was last winter. Of course. Well, you know the towpath along by the river. There were several fellows going along it, Bellingham in front, when they came on an old market-woman coming the other way. It had been raining—you know what those fields are like when it has rained—and the path ran between the river and a great puddle that was nearly as broad. Well, what does this swine do but keep the path, and push the old girl into the mud, where she and her marketings came to terrible grief. It was a blackguard thing to do, and Long Norton, who is as gentle a fellow as ever stepped, told him what he thought of it. One word led to another, and it ended in Norton laying his stick across the fellow's shoulders. There was the deuce of a fuss about it, and it's a treat to see the way in which Bellingham looks at Norton when they meet now. By Jove, Smith, it's nearly eleven o'clock!"

"No hurry. Light your pipe again."

"Not I. I'm supposed to be in training. Here I've been sitting gossiping when I ought to have been safely tucked up. I'll borrow your skull, if you can share it. Williams has had mine for a month. I'll take the little bones of your ear, too, if you are sure you won't need them. Thanks very much. Never mind a bag, I can carry them very well under my arm. Good-night, my son, and take my tip as to your neighbour."

When Hastie, bearing his anatomical plunder, had clattered off down the winding stair, Abercrombie Smith hurled his pipe into the wastepaper basket, and drawing his chair nearer to the lamp, plunged into a formidable green-covered volume, adorned with great coloured maps of that strange internal kingdom of which we are the hapless and helpless monarchs. Though a freshman at Oxford, the student was not so in medicine, for he had worked for four years at Glasgow and at Berlin, and this coming examination would place him finally as a member of his profession. With his firm mouth, broad forehead, and clear-cut, somewhat hard-featured face, he was a man who, if he had no brilliant talent, was yet so dogged, so patient, and so strong that he might in the end overtop a more showy genius. A man who can hold his own among Scotchmen and North Germans is not a man to be easily set back. Smith had left a name at Glasgow and at Berlin, and he was bent now upon doing as much at Oxford, if hard work and devotion could accomplish it.

He had sat reading for about an hour, and the hands of the noisy carriage clock upon the side table were rapidly closing together upon the twelve, when a sudden sound fell upon the student's ear—a sharp, rather shrill sound, like the hissing intake of a man's breath who gasps under some strong emotion. Smith laid down his book and slanted his ear to listen. There was no one on either side or above him, so that the interruption came certainly from the neighbour beneath—the same neighbour of whom Hastie had given so unsavory an account. Smith knew him only as a flabby, pale-faced man of silent and studious habits, a man whose lamp threw a golden bar from the old turret even after he had extinguished his own. This community in lateness had formed a certain silent bond between them. It was soothing to Smith when the hours stole on towards dawning to feel that there was another so close who set as small a value upon his sleep as he did. Even now, as his thoughts turned towards him, Smith's feelings were kindly. Hastie was a good fellow, but he was rough, strong-fibred, with no imagination or sympathy. He could not tolerate departures from what he looked upon as the model type of manliness. If a man could not be measured by a public-school standard, then he was beyond the pale with Hastie. Like so many who are themselves robust, he was apt to confuse the constitution with the character, to ascribe to want of principle what was really a want of circulation. Smith, with his stronger mind, knew his friend's habit, and made allowance for it now as his thoughts turned towards the man beneath him.

There was no return of the singular sound, and Smith was about to turn to his work once more, when suddenly there broke out in the silence of the night a hoarse cry, a positive scream—the call of a man who is moved and shaken beyond all control. Smith sprang out of his chair and dropped his book. He was a man of fairly firm fibre, but there was something in this sudden, uncontrollable shriek of horror which chilled his blood and pringled in his skin. Coming in such a place and at such an hour, it brought a thousand fantastic possibilities into his head. Should he rush down, or was it better to wait? He had all the national hatred of making a scene, and he knew so little of his neighbour that he would not lightly intrude upon his affairs. For a moment he stood in doubt and even as he balanced the matter there was a quick rattle of footsteps upon the stairs, and young Monkhouse Lee, half dressed and as white as ashes, burst into his room.

"Come down!" he gasped. "Bellingham's ill."

Abercrombie Smith followed him closely downstairs into the sitting-room which was beneath his own, and intent as he was upon the matter in hand, he could not but take an amazed glance around him as he crossed the threshold. It was such a chamber as he had never seen before—a museum rather than a study. Walls and ceiling were thickly covered with a thousand strange relics from Egypt and the East. Tall, angular figures bearing burdens or weapons stalked in an uncouth frieze round the apartments. Above were bull-headed, stork-headed, cat-headed, owl-headed statues, with viper-crowned, almond-eyed monarchs, and strange, beetle-like deities cut out of the blue Egyptian lapis lazuli. Horus and Isis and Osiris peeped down from every niche and shelf, while across the ceiling a true son of Old Nile, a great, hanging-jawed crocodile, was slung in a double noose.

In the centre of this singular chamber was a large, square table, littered with papers, bottles, and the dried leaves of some graceful, palm-like plant. These varied objects had all been heaped together in order to make room for a mummy case, which had been conveyed from the wall, as was evident from the gap there, and laid across the front of the table. The mummy itself, a horrid, black, withered thing, like a charred head on a gnarled bush, was lying half out of the case, with its clawlike hand and bony forearm resting upon the table. Propped up against the sarcophagus was an old yellow scroll of papyrus, and in front of it, in a wooden armchair, sat the owner of the room, his head thrown back, his widely-opened eyes directed in a horrified stare to the crocodile above him, and his blue, thick lips puffing loudly with every expiration.

"My God! he's dying!" cried Monkhouse Lee distractedly.

He was a slim, handsome young fellow, olive-skinned and dark-eyed, of a Spanish rather than of an English type, with a Celtic intensity of manner which contrasted with the Saxon phlegm of Abercrombie Smith.

"Only a faint, I think," said the medical student. "Just give me a hand with him. You take his feet. Now on to the sofa. Can you kick all those little wooden devils off? What a litter it is! Now he will be all right if we undo his collar and give him some water. What has he been up to at all?"

"I don't know. I heard him cry out. I ran up. I know him pretty well, you know. It is very good of you to come down."

"His heart is going like a pair of castanets," said Smith, laying his hand on the breast of the unconscious man. "He seems to me to be frightened all to pieces. Chuck the water over him! What a face he has got on him!"

It was indeed a strange and most repellent face, for colour and outline were equally unnatural. It was white, not with the ordinary pallor of fear, but with an absolutely bloodless white, like the under side of a sole. He was very fat, but gave the impression of having at some time been considerably fatter, for his skin hung loosely in creases and folds, and was shot with a meshwork of wrinkles. Short, stubbly brown hair bristled up from his scalp, with a pair of thick, wrinkled ears protruding at the sides. His light grey eyes were still open, the pupils dilated and the balls projecting in a fixed and horrid stare. It seemed to Smith as he looked down upon him that he had never seen Nature's danger signals flying so plainly upon a man's countenance, and his thoughts turned more seriously to the warning which Hastie had given him an hour before.

"What the deuce can have frightened him so?" he asked.

"It's the mummy."

"The mummy? How, then?"

"I don't know. It's beastly and morbid. I wish he would drop it. It's the second fright he has given me. It was the same last winter. I found him just like this, with that horrid thing in front of him."

"What does he want with the mummy, then?"

"Oh, he's a crank, you know. It's his hobby. He knows more about these things than any man in England. But I wish he wouldn't! Ah, he's beginning to come to."

A faint tinge of colour had begun to steal back into Bellingham's ghastly cheeks, and his eyelids shivered like a sail after a calm. He clasped and unclasped his hands, drew a long, thin breath between his teeth, and suddenly jerking up his head, threw a glance of recognition around him. As his eyes fell upon the mummy, he sprang off the sofa, seized the roll of papyrus, thrust it into a drawer, turned the key, and then staggered back on to the sofa.

"What's up?" he asked. "What do you chaps want?"

"You've been shrieking out and making no end of a fuss," said Monkhouse Lee. "If our neighbour here from above hadn't come down, I'm sure I don't know what I should have done with you."

"Ah, it's Abercrombie Smith," said Bellingham, glancing up at him. "How very good of you to come in! What a fool I am! Oh, my God, what a fool I am!"

He sunk his head on to his hands, and burst into peal after peal of hysterical laughter.

"Look here! Drop it!" cried Smith, shaking him roughly by the shoulder.

"Your nerves are all in a jangle. You must drop these little midnight games with mummies, or you'll be going off your chump. You're all on wires now."

"I wonder," said Bellingham, "whether you would be as cool as I am if you had seen—"

"What then?"

"Oh, nothing. I meant that I wonder if you could sit up at night with a mummy without trying your nerves. I have no doubt that you are quite right. I dare say that I have been taking it out of myself too much lately. But I am all right now. Please don't go, though. Just wait for a few minutes until I am quite myself."

"The room is very close," remarked Lee, throwing open the window and letting in the cool night air.

"It's balsamic resin," said Bellingham. He lifted up one of the dried palmate leaves from the table and frizzled it over the chimney of the lamp. It broke away into heavy smoke wreaths, and a pungent, biting odour filled the chamber. "It's the sacred plant—the plant of the priests," he remarked. "Do you know anything of Eastern languages, Smith?"

"Nothing at all. Not a word."

The answer seemed to lift a weight from the Egyptologist's mind.

"By the way," he continued, "how long was it from the time that you ran down, until I came to my senses?"

"Not long. Some four or five minutes."

"I thought it could not be very long," said he, drawing a long breath. "But what a strange thing unconsciousness is! There is no measurement to it. I could not tell from my own sensations if it were seconds or weeks. Now that gentleman on the table was packed up in the days of the eleventh dynasty, some forty centuries ago, and yet if he could find his tongue, he would tell us that this lapse of time has been but a closing of the eyes and a reopening of them. He is a singularly fine mummy, Smith."

Smith stepped over to the table and looked down with a professional eye at the black and twisted form in front of him. The features, though horribly discoloured, were perfect, and two little nut-like eyes still lurked in the depths of the black, hollow sockets. The blotched skin was drawn tightly from bone to bone, and a tangled wrap of black coarse hair fell over the ears. Two thin teeth, like those of a rat, overlay the shrivelled lower lip. In its crouching position, with bent joints and craned head, there was a suggestion of energy about the horrid thing which made Smith's gorge rise. The gaunt ribs, with their parchment-like covering, were exposed, and the sunken, leaden-hued abdomen, with the long slit where the embalmer had left his mark; but the lower limbs were wrapped round with coarse yellow bandages. A number of little clove-like pieces of myrrh and of cassia were sprinkled over the body, and lay scattered on the inside of the case.

"I don't know his name," said Bellingham, passing his hand over the shrivelled head. "You see the outer sarcophagus with the inscriptions is missing. Lot 249 is all the title he has now. You see it printed on his case. That was his number in the auction at which I picked him up."

"He has been a very pretty sort of fellow in his day," remarked Abercrombie Smith. "He has been a giant. His mummy is six feet seven in length, and that would be a giant over there, for they were never a very robust race. Feel these great knotted bones, too. He would be a nasty fellow to tackle."

"Perhaps these very hands helped to build the stones into the pyramids," suggested Monkhouse Lee, looking down with disgust in his eyes at the crooked, unclean talons.

"No fear. This fellow has been pickled in natron, and looked after in the most approved style. They did not serve hodsmen in that fashion. Salt or bitumen was enough for them. It has been calculated that this sort of thing cost about seven hundred and thirty pounds in our money. Our friend was a noble at the least. What do you make of that small inscription near his feet, Smith?"

"I told you that I know no Eastern tongue."

"Ah, so you did. It is the name of the embalmer, I take it. A very conscientious worker he must have been. I wonder how many modern works will survive four thousand years?"

He kept on speaking lightly and rapidly, but it was evident to Abercrombie Smith that he was still palpitating with fear. His hands shook, his lower lip trembled, and look where he would, his eye always came sliding round to his gruesome companion. Through all his fear, however, there was a suspicion of triumph in his tone and manner. His eyes shone, and his footstep, as he paced the room, was brisk and jaunty. He gave the impression of a man who has gone through an ordeal, the marks of which he still bears upon him, but which has helped him to his end.

"You're not going yet?" he cried, as Smith rose from the sofa.

At the prospect of solitude, his fears seemed to crowd back upon him, and he stretched out a hand to detain him.

"Yes, I must go. I have my work to do. You are all right now. I think that with your nervous system you should take up some less morbid study."

"Oh, I am not nervous as a rule; and I have unwrapped mummies before."

"You fainted last time," observed Monkhouse Lee.

"Ah, yes, so I did. Well, I must have a nerve tonic or a course of electricity. You are not going, Lee?"

"I'll do whatever you wish, Ned."

"Then I'll come down with you and have a shakedown on your sofa. Good-night, Smith. I am so sorry to have disturbed you with my foolishness."

They shook hands, and as the medical student stumbled up the spiral and irregular stair he heard a key turn in a door, and the steps of his two new acquaintances as they descended to the lower floor.

In this strange way began the acquaintance between Edward Bellingham and Abercrombie Smith, an acquaintance which the latter, at least, had no desire to push forward. Bellingham, however, appeared to have taken a fancy to his rough-spoken neighbour, and made his advances in such a way that he could hardly be repulsed without absolute brutality. Twice be called to thank Smith for his assistance, and mam times afterwards he looked in with books, papers and such other civilities as two bachelor neighbours can offer each other. He was, as Smith soon found, a man of wide reading, with catholic tastes and an extraordinary memory. His manner, too, was so pleasing and suave that one came, after a time, to overlook his repellent appearance. For a jaded and wearied man he was no unpleasant companion, and Smith found himself, after a time, looking forward to his visits, and even returning them.

Clever as he undoubtedly was, however, the medical student seemed to detect a dash of insanity in the man. He broke out at times into a high, inflated style of talk which was in contrast with the simplicity of his life.

"It is a wonderful thing," he cried, "to feel that one can command powers of good and of evil—a ministering angel or a demon of vengeance." And again, of Monkhouse Lee, he said,—"Lee is a good fellow, an honest fellow, but he is without strength or ambition. He would not make a fit partner for a man with a great enterprise. He would not make a fit partner for me."

At such hints and innuendoes stolid Smith, puffing solemnly at his pipe, would simply raise his eyebrows and shake his head, with little interjections of medical wisdom as to earlier hours and fresher air.

One habit Bellingham had developed of late which Smith knew to be a frequent herald of a weakening mind. He appeared to be for ever talking to himself. At late hours of the night, when there could be no visitor with him, Smith could still hear his voice beneath him in a low, muffled monologue, sunk almost to a whisper, and yet very audible in the silence. This solitary babbling annoyed and distracted the student, so that he spoke more than once to his neighbour about it. Bellingham, however, flushed up at the charge, and denied curtly that he had uttered a sound; indeed, he showed more annoyance over the matter than the occasion seemed to demand.

Had Abercrombie Smith had any doubt as to his own ears he had not to go far to find corroboration. Tom Styles, the little wrinkled man-servant who had attended to the wants of the lodgers in the turret for a longer time than any man's memory could carry him, was sorely put to it over the same matter.

"If you please, sir," said he, as he tidied down the top chamber one morning, "do you think Mr. Bellingham is all right, sir?"

"All right, Styles?"

"Yes, sir. Right in his head, sir."

"Why should he not be, then?"

"Well, I don't know, sir. His habits has changed of late. He's not the same man he used to be, though I make free to say that he was never quite one of my gentlemen, like Mr. Hastie or yourself, sir. He's took to talkin' to himself something awful. I wonder it don't disturb you. I don't know what to make of him, sir."

"I don't know what business it is of yours, Styles."

"Well, I takes an interest, Mr. Smith. It may be forward of me, but I can't help it. I feel sometimes as if I was mother and father to my young gentlemen. It all falls on me when things go wrong and the relations come. But Mr. Bellingham, sir. I want to know what it is that walks about his room sometimes when he's out and when the door's locked on the outside."

"Eh? you're talking nonsense, Styles."

"Maybe so, sir; but I heard it more'n once with my own ears."

"Rubbish, Styles."

"Very good, sir. You'll ring the bell if you want me."

Abercrombie Smith gave little heed to the gossip of the old man-servant, but a small incident occurred a few days later which left an unpleasant effect upon his mind, and brought the words of Styles forcibly to his memory.

Bellingham had come up to see him late one night, and was entertaining him with an interesting account of the rock tombs of Beni Hassan in Upper Egypt, when Smith, whose hearing was remarkably acute, distinctly heard the sound of a door opening on the landing below.

"There's some fellow gone in or out of your room," he remarked.

Bellingham sprang up and stood helpless for a moment, with the expression of a man who is half incredulous and half afraid.

"I surely locked it. I am almost positive that I locked it," he stammered. "No one could have opened it."

"Why, I hear some one coming up the steps now," said Smith.

Bellingham rushed out through the door, slammed it loudly behind him, and hurried down the stairs. About half-way down Smith heard him stop, and thought he caught the sound of whispering. A moment later the door beneath him shut, a key creaked in a lock, and Bellingham, with beads of moisture upon his pale face, ascended the stairs once more, and reentered the room.

"It's all right," he said, throwing himself down in a chair. "It was that fool of a dog. He had pushed the door open. I don't know how I came to forget to lock it."

"I didn't know you kept a dog," said Smith, looking very thoughtfully at the disturbed face of his companion.

"Yes, I haven't had him long. I must get rid of him. He's a great nuisance."

"He must be, if you find it so hard to shut him up. I should have thought that shutting the door would have been enough, without locking it."

"I want to prevent old Styles from letting him out. He's of some value, you know, and it would be awkward to lose him."

"I am a bit of a dog-fancier myself," said Smith, still gazing hard at his companion from the corner of his eyes. "Perhaps you'll let me have a look at it."

"Certainly. But I am afraid it cannot be to-night; I have an appointment. Is that clock right? Then I am a quarter of an hour late already. You'll excuse me, I am sure."

He picked up his cap and hurried from the room. In spite of his appointment, Smith heard him reenter his own chamber and lock his door upon the inside.

This interview left a disagreeable impression upon the medical student's mind. Bellingham had lied to him, and lied so clumsily that it looked as if he had desperate reasons for concealing the truth. Smith knew that his neighbour had no dog. He knew, also, that the step which he had heard upon the stairs was not the step of an animal. But if it were not, then what could it be? There was old Styles's statement about the something which used to pace the room at times when the owner was absent. Could it be a woman? Smith rather inclined to the view. If so, it would mean disgrace and expulsion to Bellingham if it were discovered by the authorities, so that his anxiety and falsehoods might be accounted for. And yet it was inconceivable that an undergraduate could keep a woman in his rooms without being instantly detected. Be the explanation what it might, there was something ugly about it, and Smith determined, as he turned to his books, to discourage all further attempts at intimacy on the part of his soft-spoken and ill-favoured neighbour.

But his work was destined to interruption that night. He had hardly caught up the broken threads when a firm, heavy footfall came three steps at a time from below, and Hastie, in blazer and flannels, burst into the room.

"Still at it!" said he, plumping down into his wonted arm-chair. "What a chap you are to stew! I believe an earthquake might come and knock Oxford into a cocked hat, and you would sit perfectly placid with four books among the ruins. However, I won't bore you long. Three whiffs of baccy, and I am off."

"What's the news, then?" asked Smith, cramming a plug of bird's-eye into his briar with his forefinger.

"Nothing very much. Wilson made 70 for the freshmen against the eleven. They say that they will play him instead of Buddicomb, for Buddicomb is clean off colour. He used to be able to bowl a little, but it's nothing but half-volleys and long hops now."

"Medium right," suggested Smith, with the intense gravity which comes upon a 'varsity man when he speaks of athletics.

"Inclining to fast, with a work from leg. Comes with the arm about three inches or so. He used to be nasty on a wet wicket. Oh, by-the-way, have you heard about Long Norton?"

"What's that?"

"He's been attacked."

"Attacked?"

"Yes, just as he was turning out of the High Street, and within a hundred yards of the gate of Old's."

"But who—"

"Ah, that's the rub! If you said 'what,' you would be more grammatical. Norton swears that it was not human, and, indeed, from the scratches on his throat, I should be inclined to agree with him."

"What, then? Have we come down to spooks?"

Abercrombie Smith puffed his scientific contempt.

"Well, no; I don't think that is quite the idea, either. I am inclined to think that if any showman has lost a great ape lately, and the brute is in these parts, a jury would find a true bill against it. Norton passes that way every night, you know, about the same hour. There's a tree that hangs low over the path—the big elm from Rainy's garden. Norton thinks the thing dropped on him out of the tree. Anyhow, he was nearly strangled by two arms, which, he says, were as strong and as thin as steel bands. He saw nothing; only those beastly arms that tightened and tightened on him. He yelled his head nearly off, and a couple of chaps came running, and the thing went over the wall like a cat. He never got a fair sight of it the whole time. It gave Norton a shake up, I can tell you. I tell him it has been as good as a change at the seaside for him."

"A garrotter, most likely," said Smith.

"Very possible. Norton says not; but we don't mind what he says. The garrotter had long nails, and was pretty smart at swinging himself over walls. By-the-way, your beautiful neighbour would be pleased if he heard about it. He had a grudge against Norton, and he's not a man, from what I know of him, to forget his little debts. But hallo, old chap, what have you got in your noddle?"

"Nothing," Smith answered curtly.

He had started in his chair, and the look had flashed over his face which comes upon a man who is struck suddenly by some unpleasant idea.

"You looked as if something I had said had taken you on the raw. By-the-way, you have made the acquaintance of Master B. since I looked in last, have you not? Young Monkhouse Lee told me something to that effect."

"Yes; I know him slightly. He has been up here once or twice."

"Well, you're big enough and ugly enough to take care of yourself. He's not what I should call exactly a healthy sort of Johnny, though, no doubt, he's very clever, and all that. But you'll soon find out for yourself. Lee is all right; he's a very decent little fellow. Well, so long, old chap! I row Mullins for the Vice-Chancellor's pot on Wednesday week, so mind you come down, in case I don't see you before."

Bovine Smith laid down his pipe and turned stolidly to his books once more. But with all the will in the world, he found it very hard to keep his mind upon his work. It would slip away to brood upon the man beneath him, and upon the little mystery which hung round his chambers. Then his thoughts turned to this singular attack of which Hastie had spoken, and to the grudge which Bellingham was said to owe the object of it. The two ideas would persist in rising together in his mind, as though there were some close and intimate connection between them. And yet the suspicion was so dim and vague that it could not be put down in words.

"Confound the chap!" cried Smith, as he shied his book on pathology across the room. "He has spoiled my night's reading, and that's reason enough, if there were no other, why I should steer clear of him in the future."

For ten days the medical student confined himself so closely to his studies that he neither saw nor heard anything of either of the men beneath him. At the hours when Bellingham had been accustomed to visit him, he took care to sport his oak, and though he more than once heard a knocking at his outer door, he resolutely refused to answer it. One afternoon, however, he was descending the stairs when, just as he was passing it, Bellingham's door flew open, and young Monkhouse Lee came out with his eyes sparkling and a dark flush of anger upon his olive cheeks. Close at his heels followed Bellingham, his fat, unhealthy face all quivering with malignant passion.

"You fool!" he hissed. "You'll be sorry."

"Very likely," cried the other. "Mind what I say, It's off! I won't hear of it!"

"You've promised, anyhow."

"Oh, I'll keep that! I won't speak. But I'd rather little Eva was in her grave. Once for all, it's off. She'll do what I say. We don't want to see you again."

So much Smith could not avoid hearing, but he hurried on, for he had no wish to be involved in their dispute. There had been a serious breach between them, that was clear enough, and Lee was going to cause the engagement with his sister to be broken off. Smith thought of Hastie's comparison of the toad and the dove, and was glad to think that the matter was at an end. Bellingham's face when he was in a passion was not pleasant to look upon. He was not a man to whom an innocent girl could be trusted for life. As he walked, Smith wondered languidly what could have caused the quarrel, and what the promise might be which Bellingham had been so anxious that Monkhouse Lee should keep.

It was the day of the sculling match between Hastie and Mullins, and a stream of men were making their way down to the banks of the Isis. A May sun was shining brightly, and the yellow path was barred with the black shadows of the tall elm-trees. On either side the grey colleges lay back from the road, the hoary old mothers of minds looking out from their high, mullioned windows at the tide of young life which swept so merrily past them. Black-clad tutors, prim officials, pale reading men, brown-faced, straw-hatted young athletes in white sweaters or many-coloured blazers, all were hurrying towards the blue winding river which curves through the Oxford meadows.

Abercrombie Smith, with the intuition of an old oarsman, chose his position at the point where he knew that the struggle, if there were a struggle, would come. Far off he heard the hum which announced the start, the gathering roar of the approach, the thunder of running feet, and the shouts of the men in the boats beneath him. A spray of half-clad, deep-breathing runners shot past him, and craning over their shoulders, he saw Hastie pulling a steady thirty-six, while his opponent, with a jerky forty, was a good boat's length behind him. Smith gave a cheer for his friend, and pulling out his watch, was starting off again for his chambers, when he felt a touch upon his shoulder, and found that young Monkhouse Lee was beside him.

"I saw you there," he said, in a timid, deprecating way. "I wanted to speak to you, if you could spare me a half-hour. This cottage is mine. I share it with Harrington of King's. Come in and have a cup of tea."

"I must be back presently," said Smith. "I am hard on the grind at present. But I'll come in for a few minutes with pleasure. I wouldn't have come out only Hastie is a friend of mine."

"So he is of mine. Hasn't he a beautiful style? Mullins wasn't in it. But come into the cottage. It's a little den of a place, but it is pleasant to work in during the summer months."

It was a small, square, white building, with green doors and shutters, and a rustic trellis-work porch, standing back some fifty yards from the river's bank. Inside, the main room was roughly fitted up as a study—deal table, unpainted shelves with books, and a few cheap oleographs upon the wall. A kettle sang upon a spirit-stove, and there were tea things upon a tray on the table.

"Try that chair and have a cigarette," said Lee. "Let me pour you out a cup of tea. It's so good of you to come in, for I know that your time is a good deal taken up. I wanted to say to you that, if I were you, I should change my rooms at once."

"Eh?"

Smith sat staring with a lighted match in one hand and his unlit cigarette in the other.

"Yes; it must seem very extraordinary, and the worst of it is that I cannot give my reasons, for I am under a solemn promise—a very solemn promise. But I may go so far as to say that I don't think Bellingham is a very safe man to live near. I intend to camp out here as much as I can for a time."

"Not safe! What do you mean?"

"Ah, that's what I mustn't say. But do take my advice, and move your rooms. We had a grand row to-day. You must have heard us, for you came down the stairs."

"I saw that you had fallen out."

"He's a horrible chap, Smith. That is the only word for it. I have had doubts about him ever since that night when he fainted—you remember, when you came down. I taxed him to-day, and he told me things that made my hair rise, and wanted me to stand in with him. I'm not strait-laced, but I am a clergyman's son, you know, and I think there are some things which are quite beyond the pale. I only thank God that I found him out before it was too late, for he was to have married into my family.

"This is all very fine, Lee," said Abercrombie Smith curtly. "But either you are saying a great deal too much or a great deal too little."

"I give you a warning."

"If there is real reason for warning, no promise can bind you. If I see a rascal about to blow a place up with dynamite no pledge will stand in my way of preventing him."

"Ah, but I cannot prevent him, and I can do nothing but warn you."

"Without saying what you warn me against."

"Against Bellingham."

"But that is childish. Why should I fear him, or any man?"

"I can't tell you. I can only entreat you to change your rooms. You are in danger where you are. I don't even say that Bellingham would wish to injure you. But it might happen, for he is a dangerous neighbour just now."

"Perhaps I know more than you think," said Smith, looking keenly at the young man's boyish, earnest face. "Suppose I tell you that some one else shares Bellingham's rooms."

Monkhouse Lee sprang from his chair in uncontrollable excitement.

"You know, then?" he gasped.

"A woman."

Lee dropped back again with a groan.

"My lips are sealed," he said. "I must not speak."

"Well, anyhow," said Smith, rising, "it is not likely that I should allow myself to be frightened out of rooms which suit me very nicely. It would be a little too feeble for me to move out all my goods and chattels because you say that Bellingham might in some unexplained way do me an injury. I think that I'll just take my chance, and stay where I am, and as I see that it's nearly five o'clock, I must ask you to excuse me."

He bade the young student adieu in a few curt words, and made his way homeward through the sweet spring evening, feeling half-ruffled, half-amused, as any other strong, unimaginative man might who has been menaced by a vague and shadowy danger.

There was one little indulgence which Abercrombie Smith always allowed himself, however closely his work might press upon him. Twice a week, on the Tuesday and the Friday, it was his invariable custom to walk over to Farlingford, the residence of Doctor Plumptree Peterson, situated about a mile and a half out of Oxford. Peterson had been a close friend of Smith's elder brother Francis, and as he was a bachelor, fairly well-to-do, with a good cellar and a better library, his house was a pleasant goal for a man who was in need of a brisk walk. Twice a week, then, the medical student would swing out there along the dark country roads, and spend a pleasant hour in Peterson's comfortable study, discussing, over a glass of old port, the gossip of the 'varsity or the latest developments of medicine or of surgery.

On the day which followed his interview with Monkhouse Lee, Smith shut up his books at a quarter past eight, the hour when he usually started for his friend's house. As he was leaving his room, however, his eyes chanced to fall upon one of the books which Bellingham had lent him, and his conscience pricked him for not having returned it. However repellent the man might be, he should not be treated with discourtesy. Taking the book, he walked downstairs and knocked at his neighbour's door. There was no answer; but on turning the handle he found that it was unlocked. Pleased at the thought of avoiding an interview, he stepped inside, and placed the book with his card upon the table.

The lamp was turned half down, but Smith could see the details of the room plainly enough. It was all much as he had seen it before—the frieze, the animal-headed gods, the hanging crocodile, and the table littered over with papers and dried leaves. The mummy case stood upright against the wall, but the mummy itself was missing. There was no sign of any second occupant of the room, and he felt as he withdrew that he had probably done Bellingham an injustice. Had he a guilty secret to preserve, he would hardly leave his door open so that all the world might enter.

The spiral stair was as black as pitch, and Smith was slowly making his way down its irregular steps, when he was suddenly conscious that something had passed him in the darkness. There was a faint sound, a whiff of air, a light brushing past his elbow, but so slight that he could scarcely be certain of it. He stopped and listened, but the wind was rustling among the ivy outside, and he could hear nothing else.

"Is that you, Styles?" he shouted.

There was no answer, and all was still behind him. It must have been a sudden gust of air, for there were crannies and cracks in the old turret. And yet he could almost have sworn that he heard a footfall by his very side. He had emerged into the quadrangle, still turning the matter over in his head, when a man came running swiftly across the smooth-cropped lawn.

"Is that you, Smith?"

"Hullo, Hastie!"

"For God's sake come at once! Young Lee is drowned! Here's Harrington of King's with the news. The doctor is out. You'll do, but come along at once. There may be life in him."

"Have you brandy?"

"No."

"I'll bring some. There's a flask on my table."

Smith bounded up the stairs, taking three at a time, seized the flask, and was rushing down with it, when, as he passed Bellingham's room, his eyes fell upon something which left him gasping and staring upon the landing.

The door, which he had closed behind him, was now open, and right in front of him, with the lamp-light shining upon it, was the mummy case. Three minutes ago it had been empty. He could swear to that. Now it framed the lank body of its horrible occupant, who stood, grim and stark, with his black shrivelled face towards the door. The form was lifeless and inert, but it seemed to Smith as he gazed that there still lingered a lurid spark of vitality, some faint sign of consciousness in the little eyes which lurked in the depths of the hollow sockets. So astounded and shaken was he that he had forgotten his errand, and was still staring at the lean, sunken figure when the voice of his friend below recalled him to himself.

"Come on, Smith!" he shouted. "It's life and death, you know. Hurry up! Now, then," he added, as the medical student reappeared, "let us do a sprint. It is well under a mile, and we should do it in five minutes. A human life is better worth running for than a pot."

Neck and neck they dashed through the darkness, and did not pull up until panting and spent, they had reached the little cottage by the river. Young Lee, limp and dripping like a broken water-plant, was stretched upon the sofa, the green scum of the river upon his black hair, and a fringe of white foam upon his leaden-hued lips. Beside him knelt his fellow student, Harrington, endeavouring to chafe some warmth back into his rigid limbs.

"I think there's life in him," said Smith, with his hand to the lad's side. "Put your watch glass to his lips. Yes, there's dimming on it. You take one arm, Hastie. Now work it as I do, and we'll soon pull him round."

For ten minutes they worked in silence, inflating and depressing the chest of the unconscious man. At the end of that time a shiver ran through his body, his lips trembled, and he opened his eyes. The three students burst out into an irrepressible cheer.

"Wake up, old chap. You've frightened us quite enough."

"Have some brandy. Take a sip from the flask."

"He's all right now," said his companion Harrington. "Heavens, what a fright I got! I was reading here, and had gone out for a stroll as far as the river, when I heard a scream and a splash. Out I ran, and by the time I could find him and fish him out, all life seemed to have gone. Then Simpson couldn't get a doctor, for he has a game-leg, and I had to run, and I don't know what I'd have done without you fellows. That's right, old chap. Sit up."

Monkhouse Lee had raised himself on his hands, and looked wildly about him.

"What's up?" he asked. "I've been in the water. Ah, yes; I remember."

A look of fear came into his eyes, and he sank his face into his hands.

"How did you fall in?"

"I didn't fall in."

"How then?"

"I was thrown in. I was standing by the bank, and something from behind picked me up like a feather and hurled me in. I heard nothing, and I saw nothing. But I know what it was, for all that."

"And so do I," whispered Smith.

Lee looked up with a quick glance of surprise.

"You've learned, then?" he said. "You remember the advice I gave you?"

"Yes, and I begin to think that I shall take it."

"I don't know what the deuce you fellows are talking about," said Hastie, "but I think, if I were you, Harrington, I should get Lee to bed at once. It will be time enough to discuss the why and the wherefore when he is a little stronger. I think, Smith, you and I can leave him alone now. I am walking back to college; if you are coming in that direction, we can have a chat."

But it was little chat that they had upon their homeward path. Smith's mind was too full of the incidents of the evening, the absence of the mummy from his neighbour's rooms, the step that passed him on the stair, the reappearance—the extraordinary, inexplicable reappearance of the grisly thing—and then this attack upon Lee, corresponding so closely to the previous outrage upon another man against whom Bellingham bore a grudge. All this settled in his thoughts, together with the many little incidents which had previously turned him against his neighbour, and the singular circumstances under which he was first called in to him. What had been a dim suspicion, a vague, fantastic conjecture, had suddenly taken form, and stood out in his mind as a grim fact, a thing not to be denied. And yet, how monstrous it was! how unheard of!

how entirely beyond all bounds of human experience. An impartial judge, or even the friend who walked by his side, would simply tell him that his eyes had deceived him, that the mummy had been there all the time, that young Lee had tumbled into the river as any other man tumbles into a river, and that blue pill was the best thing for a disordered liver. He felt that he would have said as much if the positions had been reversed. And yet he could swear that Bellingham was a murderer at heart, and that he wielded a weapon such as no man had ever used in all the grim history of crime.

Hastie had branched off to his rooms with a few crisp and emphatic comments upon his friend's unsociability, and Abercrombie Smith crossed the quadrangle to his corner turret with a strong feeling of repulsion for his chambers and their associations. He would take Lee's advice, and move his quarters as soon as possible, for how could a man study when his ear was ever straining for every murmur or footstep in the room below? He observed, as he crossed over the lawn, that the light was still shining in Bellingham's window, and as he passed up the staircase the door opened, and the man himself looked out at him. With his fat, evil face he was like some bloated spider fresh from the weaving of his poisonous web.

"Good-evening," said he. "Won't you come in?"

"No," cried Smith fiercely.

"No? You are busy as ever? I wanted to ask you about Lee. I was sorry to hear that there was a rumour that something was amiss with him."

His features were grave, but there was the gleam of a hidden laugh in his eyes as he spoke. Smith saw it, and he could have knocked him down for it.

"You'll be sorrier still to hear that Monkhouse Lee is doing very well, and is out of all danger," he answered. "Your hellish tricks have not come off this time. Oh, you needn't try to brazen it out. I know all about it."

Bellingham took a step back from the angry student, and half-closed the door as if to protect himself.

"You are mad," he said. "What do you mean? Do you assert that I had anything to do with Lee's accident?"

"Yes," thundered Smith. "You and that bag of bones behind you; you worked it between you. I tell you what it is, Master B., they have given up burning folk like you, but we still keep a hangman, and, by George! if any man in this college meets his death while you are here, I'll have you up, and if you don't swing for it, it won't be my fault. You'll find that your filthy Egyptian tricks won't answer in England."

"You're a raving lunatic," said Bellingham.

"All right. You just remember what I say, for you'll find that I'll be better than my word."

The door slammed, and Smith went fuming up to his chamber, where he locked the door upon the inside, and spent half the night in smoking his old briar and brooding over the strange events of the evening.

Next morning Abercrombie Smith heard nothing of his neighbour, but Harrington called upon him in the afternoon to say that Lee was almost himself again. All day Smith stuck fast to his work, but in the evening he determined to pay the visit to his friend Doctor Peterson upon which he had started the night before. A good walk and a friendly chat would be welcome to his jangled nerves.

Bellingham's door was shut as he passed, but glancing back when he was some distance from the turret, he saw his neighbour's head at the window outlined against the lamp-light, his face pressed apparently against the glass as he gazed out into the darkness. It was a blessing to be away from all contact with him, if but for a few hours, and Smith stepped out briskly, and breathed the soft spring air into his lungs. The half-moon lay in the west between two Gothic pinnacles, and threw upon the silvered street a dark tracery from the stone-work above. There was a brisk breeze, and light, fleecy clouds drifted swiftly across the sky. Old's was on the very border of the town, and in five minutes Smith found himself beyond the houses and between the hedges of a May-scented Oxfordshire lane.

It was a lonely and little frequented road which led to his friend's house. Early as it was, Smith did not meet a single soul upon his way. He walked briskly along until he came to the avenue gate, which opened into the long gravel drive leading up to Farlingford. In front of him he could see the cosy red light of the windows glimmering through the foliage. He stood with his hand upon the iron latch of the swinging gate, and he glanced back at the road along which he had come. Something was coming swiftly down it.

It moved in the shadow of the hedge, silently and furtively, a dark, crouching figure, dimly visible against the black background. Even as he gazed back at it, it had lessened its distance by twenty paces, and was fast closing upon him. Out of the darkness he had a glimpse of a scraggy neck, and of two eyes that will ever haunt him in his dreams. He turned, and with a cry of terror he ran for his life up the avenue. There were the red lights, the signals of safety, almost within a stone's-throw of him. He was a famous runner, but never had he run as he ran that night.

The heavy gate had swung into place behind him, but he heard it dash open again before his pursuer. As he rushed madly and wildly through the night, he could hear a swift, dry patter behind him, and could see, as he threw back a glance, that this horror was bounding like a tiger at his heels, with blazing eyes and one stringy arm out-thrown. Thank God, the door was ajar. He could see the thin bar of light which shot from the lamp in the hall. Nearer yet sounded the clatter from behind. He heard a hoarse gurgling at his very shoulder. With a shriek he flung himself against the door, slammed and bolted it behind him, and sank half-fainting on to the hall chair.

"My goodness, Smith, what's the matter?" asked Peterson, appearing at the door of his study.

"Give me some brandy."

Peterson disappeared, and came rushing out again with a glass and a decanter.

"You need it," he said, as his visitor drank off what he poured out for him. "Why, man, you are as white as a cheese."

Smith laid down his glass, rose up, and took a deep breath.

"I am my own man again now," said he. "I was never so unmanned before. But, with your leave, Peterson, I will sleep here to-night, for I don't think I could face that road again except by daylight. It's weak, I know, but I can't help it."

Peterson looked at his visitor with a very questioning eye.

"Of course you shall sleep here if you wish. I'll tell Mrs. Burney to make up the spare bed. Where are you off to now?"

"Come up with me to the window that overlooks the door. I want you to see what I have seen."

They went up to the window of the upper hall whence they could look down upon the approach to the house. The drive and the fields on either side lay quiet and still, bathed in the peaceful moonlight.

"Well, really, Smith," remarked Peterson, "it is well that I know you to be an abstemious man. What in the world can have frightened you?"

"I'll tell you presently. But where can it have gone? Ah, now, look, look! See the curve of the road just beyond your gate."

"Yes, I see; you needn't pinch my arm off. I saw some one pass. I should say a man, rather thin, apparently, and tall, very tall. But what of him? And what of yourself? You are still shaking like an aspen leaf."

"I have been within hand-grip of the devil, that's all. But come down to your study, and I shall tell you the whole story."

He did so. Under the cheery lamp-light, with a glass of wine on the table beside him, and the portly form and florid face of his friend in front, he narrated, in their order, all the events, great and small, which had formed so singular a chain, from the night on which he had found Bellingham fainting in front of the mummy case until this horrid experience of an hour ago.

"There now," he said as he concluded, "that's the whole black business. It is monstrous and incredible, but it is true."

Doctor Plumptree Peterson sat for some time in silence with a very puzzled expression upon his face.

"I never heard of such a thing in my life, never!" he said at last. "You have told me the facts. Now tell me your inferences."

"You can draw your own."

"But I should like to hear yours. You have thought over the matter, and I have not."

"Well, it must be a little vague in detail, but the main points seem to me to be clear enough. This fellow Bellingham, in his Eastern studies, has got hold of some infernal secret by which a mummy—or possibly only this particular mummy—can be temporarily brought to life. He was trying this disgusting business on the night when he fainted. No doubt the sight of the creature moving had shaken his nerve, even though he had expected it. You remember that almost the first words he said were to call out upon himself as a fool. Well, he got more hardened afterwards, and carried the matter through without fainting. The vitality which he could put into it was evidently only a passing thing, for I have seen it continually in its case as dead as this table. He has some elaborate process, I fancy, by which he brings the thing to pass. Having done it, he naturally bethought him that he might use the creature as an agent. It has intelligence and it has strength. For some purpose he took Lee into his confidence; but Lee, like a decent Christian, would have nothing to do with such a business. Then they had a row, and Lee vowed that he would tell his sister of Bellingham's true character. Bellingham's game was to prevent him, and he nearly managed it, by setting this creature of his on his track. He had already tried its powers upon another man— Norton—towards whom, he had a grudge. It is the merest chance that he has not two murders upon his soul. Then, when I taxed him with the matter, he had the strongest reasons for wishing me out of the way, before I could convey my knowledge to any one else. He got his chance when I went out, for he knew my habits and where I was bound for. I have had a narrow shave, Peterson, and it is mere luck you didn't find me on your doorstep in the morning. I'm not a nervous man as a rule, and I never thought to have the fear of death put upon me as it was to-night."

"My dear boy, you take the matter too seriously," said his companion. "Your nerves are out of order with your work, and you make too much of it. How could such a thing as this stride about the streets of Oxford, even at night, without being seen?"

"It has been seen. There is quite a scare in the town about an escaped ape, as they imagine the creature to be. It is the talk of the place."

"Well, it's a striking chain of events. And yet, my dear fellow, you must allow that each incident in itself is capable of a more natural explanation."

"What! even my adventure of to-night?"

"Certainly. You come out with your nerves all unstrung, and your head full of this theory of yours. Some gaunt, half-famished tramp steals after you, and seeing you run, is emboldened to pursue you. Your fears and imagination do the rest."

"It won't do, Peterson; it won't do."

"And again, in the instance of your finding the mummy case empty, and then a few moments later with an occupant, you know that it was lamp-light, that the lamp was half turned down, and that you had no special reason to look hard at the case. It is quite possible that you may have overlooked the creature in the first instance."

"No, no; it is out of the question."

"And then Lee may have fallen into the river, and Norton been garrotted. It is certainly a formidable indictment that you have against Bellingham; but if you were to place it before a police magistrate, he would simply laugh in your face."

"I know he would. That is why I mean to take the matter into my own hands."

"Eh?"

"Yes; I feel that a public duty rests upon me, and, besides, I must do it for my own safety, unless I choose to allow myself to be hunted by this beast out of the college, and that would be a little too feeble. I have quite made up my mind what I shall do. And first of all, may I use your paper and pens for an hour?"

"Most certainly. You will find all that you want upon that side-table."

Abercrombie Smith sat down before a sheet of foolscap, and for an hour, and then for a second hour his pen travelled swiftly over it. Page after page was finished and tossed aside while his friend leaned back in his arm-chair, looking across at him with patient curiosity. At last, with an exclamation of satisfaction, Smith sprang to his feet, gathered his papers up into order, and laid the last one upon Peterson's desk.

"Kindly sign this as a witness," he said.

"A witness? Of what?"

"Of my signature, and of the date. The date is the most important. Why, Peterson, my life might hang upon it."

"My dear Smith, you are talking wildly. Let me beg you to go to bed."

"On the contrary, I never spoke so deliberately in my life. And I will promise to go to bed the moment you have signed it."

"But what is it?"

"It is a statement of all that I have been telling you to-night. I wish you to witness it."

"Certainly," said Peterson, signing his name under that of his companion. "There you are! But what is the idea?"

"You will kindly retain it, and produce it in case I am arrested."

"Arrested? For what?"

"For murder. It is quite on the cards. I wish to be ready for every event. There is only one course open to me, and I am determined to take it"

"For Heaven's sake, don't do anything rash!"

"Believe me, it would be far more rash to adopt any other course. I hope that we won't need to bother you, but it will ease my mind to know that you have this statement of my motives. And now I am ready to take your advice and to go to roost, for I want to be at my best in the morning."

Abercrombie Smith was not an entirely pleasant man to have as an enemy. Slow and easy-tempered, he was formidable when driven to action. He brought to every purpose in life the same deliberate resoluteness which had distinguished him as a scientific student. He had laid his studies aside for a day, but he intended that the day should not be wasted. Not a word did he say to his host as to his plans, but by nine o'clock he was well on his way to Oxford.

In the High Street he stopped at Clifford's the gunmaker's, and bought a heavy revolver, with a box of central-fire cartridges. Six of them he slipped into the chambers, and half-cocking the weapon, placed it in the pocket of his coat. He then made his way to Hastie's rooms, where the big oarsman was lounging over his breakfast, with the *Sporting Times* propped up against the coffee-pot.

"Hullo! What's up?" he asked. "Have some coffee?"

"No, thank you. I want you to come with me, Hastie, and do what I ask you."

"Certainly, my boy."

"And bring a heavy stick with you."

"Hullo!" Hastie stared. "Here's a hunting crop that would fell an ox."

"One other thing. You have a box of amputating knives. Give me the longest of them."

"There you are. You seem to be fairly on the war trail. Anything else?"

"No; that will do." Smith placed the knife inside his coat, and led the way to the quadrangle. "We are neither of us chickens, Hastie," said he. "I think I can do this job alone, but I take you as a precaution. I am going to have a little talk with Bellingham. If I have only him to deal with, I won't, of course, need you. If I shout, however, up you come, and lam out with your whip as hard as you can lick. Do you understand?"

"All right. I'll come if I hear you bellow."

"Stay here, then. I may be a little time, but don't budge until I come down."

"I'm a fixture."

Smith ascended the stairs, opened Bellingham's door and stepped in. Bellingham was seated behind his table, writing. Beside him, among his litter of strange possessions, towered the mummy case, with its sale number 249 still stuck upon its front, and its hideous occupant stiff and stark within it. Smith looked very deliberately round him, closed the door, and then stepping across to the fire-place, struck a match and set the fire alight. Bellingham sat staring, with amazement and rage upon his bloated face.

"Well, really now, you make yourself at home," he gasped.

Smith sat himself deliberately down, placing his watch upon the table, drew out his pistol, cocked it, and laid it in his lap. Then he took the long amputating knife from his bosom, and threw it down in front of Bellingham.

"Now, then," said he, "just get to work and cut up that mummy."

"Oh, is that it?" said Bellingham with a sneer.

"Yes, that is it. They tell me that the law can't touch you. But I have a law that will set matters straight. If in five minutes you have not set to work, I swear by the God who made me that I will put a bullet through your brain!"

"You would murder me?"

Bellingham had half risen, and his face was the colour of putty.

"Yes."

"And for what?"

"To stop your mischief. One minute has gone."

"But what have I done?"

"I know and you know."

"This is mere bullying."

"Two minutes are gone."

"But you must give reasons. You are a madman—a dangerous madman. Why should I destroy my own property? It is a valuable mummy."

"You must cut it up, and you must burn it."

"I will do no such thing."

"Four minutes are gone."

Smith took up the pistol and he looked towards Bellingham with an inexorable face. As the second-hand stole round, he raised his hand, and the finger twitched upon the trigger.

"There! there! I'll do it!" screamed Bellingham.

In frantic haste he caught up the knife and hacked at the figure of the mummy, ever glancing round to see the eye and the weapon of his terrible visitor bent upon him. The creature crackled and snapped under every stab of the keen blade. A thick yellow dust rose up from it. Spices and dried essences rained down upon the floor. Suddenly, with a rending crack, its backbone snapped asunder, and it fell, a brown heap of sprawling limbs, upon the floor.

"Now into the fire!" said Smith.

The flames leaped and roared as the dried and tinder-like debris was piled upon it. The little room was like the stoke-hole of a steamer and the sweat ran down the faces of the two men; but still the one stooped and worked, while the other sat watching him with a set face. A thick, fat smoke oozed out from the fire, and a heavy smell of burned rosin and singed hair filled the air. In a quarter of an hour a few charred and brittle sticks were all that was left of Lot No. 249.

"Perhaps that will satisfy you," snarled Bellingham, with hate and fear in his little grey eyes as he glanced back at his tormentor.

"No; I must make a clean sweep of all your materials. We must have no more devil's tricks. In with all these leaves! They may have something to do with it."

"And what now?" asked Bellingham, when the leaves also had been added to the blaze.

"Now the roll of papyrus which you had on the table that night. It is in that drawer, I think."

"No, no," shouted Bellingham. "Don't burn that! Why, man, you don't know what you do. It is unique: it contains wisdom which is nowhere else to be found."

"Out with it!"

"But look here, Smith, you can't really mean it. I'll share the knowledge with you. I'll teach you all that is in it. Or, stay, let me only copy it before you burn it!"

Smith stepped forward and turned the key in the drawer. Taking out the yellow, curled roll of paper, he threw it into the fire, and pressed it down with his heel. Bellingham screamed, and grabbed at it; but Smith pushed him back and stood over it until it was reduced to a formless grey ash.

"Now, Master B.," said he, "I think I have pretty well drawn your teeth. You'll hear from me again, if you return to your old tricks. And now good-morning, for I must go back to my studies."

And such is the narrative of Abercrombie Smith as to the singular events which occurred in Old College, Oxford, in the spring of '84. As Bellingham left the university immediately afterwards, and was last heard of in the Soudan, there is no one who can contradict his statement. But the wisdom of men is small, and the ways of Nature are strange, and who shall put a bound to the dark things which may be found by those who seek for them?

The Dead Valley

Ralph Adams Cram

———————◆———————

I HAVE A FRIEND, OLOF EHRENSVÄRD, A SWEDE BY BIRTH, WHO YET, BY REASON of a strange and melancholy mischance of his early boyhood, has thrown his lot with that of the New World. It is a curious story of a headstrong boy and a proud and relentless family: the details do not matter here, but they are sufficient to weave a web of romance around the tall yellow-bearded man with the sad eyes and the voice that gives itself perfectly to plaintive little Swedish songs remembered out of childhood. In the winter evenings we play chess together, he and I, and after some close, fierce battle has been fought to a finish—usually with my own defeat—we fill our pipes again, and Ehrensvärd tells me stories of the far, half-remembered days in the fatherland, before he went to sea: stories that grow very strange and incredible as the night deepens and the fire falls together, but stories that, nevertheless, I fully believe.

One of them made a strong impression on me, so I set it down here, only regretting that I cannot reproduce the curiously perfect English and the delicate accent which to me increased the fascination of the tale. Yet, as best I can remember it, here it is.

"I never told you how Nils and I went over the hills to Hallsberg, and how we found the Dead Valley, did I? Well, this is the way it happened. I must have been about twelve years old, and Nils Sjöberg, whose father's estate joined ours, was a few months younger. We were inseparable just at that time, and whatever we did, we did together.

"Once a week it was market day in Engelholm, and Nils and I went always there to see the strange sights that the market gathered from all the surrounding country. One day we quite lost our hearts, for an old man from across the Elfborg had brought a little dog to sell, that seemed to us the most beautiful dog in all the world. He was a round, woolly puppy, so funny that Nils and I sat down on the ground and laughed at him, until he came and played with us in so jolly a way that we felt that there was only one really desirable thing in life, and that was the little dog of the old man from across the hills. But alas! we had not half money enough wherewith to buy him, so we were forced to beg the old man not to sell him before the next market day, promising that we would bring the money for him then. He gave us his word, and we ran home very fast and implored our mothers to give us money for the little dog.

"We got the money, but we could not wait for the next market day. Suppose the puppy should be sold! The thought frightened us so that we begged and implored that we might be allowed to go over the hills to Hallsberg where the old man lived, and get the little dog ourselves, and at last they told us we might go. By starting early in the morning we should reach Hallsberg by three o'clock, and it was arranged that we should stay there that night with Nils's aunt, and, leaving by noon the next day, be home again by sunset.

"Soon after sunrise we were on our way, after having received minute instructions as to just what we should do in all possible and impossible circumstances, and finally a repeated injunction that we should start for home at the same hour the next day, so that we might get safely back before nightfall.

"For us, it was magnificent sport, and we started off with our rifles, full of the sense of our very great importance: yet the journey was simple enough, along a good road, across the big hills we knew so well, for Nils and I had shot over half the territory this side of the dividing ridge of the Elfborg. Back of Engelholm lay a long valley, from which rose the low mountains, and we had to cross this, and then follow the road along the side of the hills for three or four miles, before a narrow path branched off to the left, leading up through the pass.

"Nothing occurred of interest on the way over, and we reached Hallsberg in due season, found to our inexpressible joy that the little dog was not sold, secured him, and so went to the house of Nils's aunt to spend the night.

"Why we did not leave early on the following day, I can't quite remember; at all events, I know we stopped at a shooting range just outside of the town, where most attractive pasteboard pigs were sliding slowly through painted foliage, serving so as beautiful marks. The result was that we did not get fairly started for home until afternoon, and as we found ourselves at last pushing up the side of the mountain with the sun dangerously near their summits, I think we were a little scared at the prospect of the examination and possible punishment that awaited us when we got home at midnight.

"Therefore we hurried as fast as possible up the mountain side, while the blue dusk closed in about us, and the light died in the purple sky. At first we had talked hilariously, and the little dog had leaped ahead of us with the utmost joy. Latterly, however, a curious oppression came on us; we did not speak or even whistle, while the dog fell behind, following us with hesitation in every muscle.

"We had passed through the foothills and the low spurs of the mountains, and were almost at the top of the main range, when life seemed to go out of everything, leaving the world dead, so suddenly silent the forest became, so stagnant the air. Instinctively we halted to listen.

"Perfect silence,—the crushing silence of deep forests at night; and more, for always, even in the most impenetrable fastnesses of the wooded mountains, is the multitudinous murmur of little lives, awakened by the darkness, exaggerated and intensified by the stillness of the air and the great dark: but here and now the silence seemed unbroken even by the turn of a leaf, the movement of a twig, the note of night bird or insect. I could hear the blood beat through my veins; and the crushing of the grass under our feet as we advanced with hesitating steps sounded like the falling of trees.

"And the air was stagnant,—dead. The atmosphere seemed to lie upon the body like the weight of sea on a diver who has ventured too far into its awful depths. What we usually call silence seems so only in relation to the din of ordinary experience. This was silence in the absolute, and it crushed the mind while it intensified the senses, bringing down the awful weight of inextinguishable fear.

"I know that Nils and I stared towards each other in abject terror, listening to our quick, heavy breathing, that sounded to our acute senses like the fitful rush of waters. And the poor little dog we were leading justified our terror. The black oppression seemed to crush him even as it did us. He lay close on the ground, moaning feebly, and dragging himself painfully and slowly closer to Nils's feet. I think this exhibition of utter animal fear was the last touch, and must inevitably have blasted our reason— mine anyway; but just then, as we stood quaking on the bounds of madness, came a sound, so awful, so ghastly, so horrible, that it seemed to rouse us from the dead spell that was on us.

"In the depth of the silence came a cry, beginning as a low, sorrowful moan, rising to a tremulous shriek, culminating in a yell that seemed to tear the night in sunder and rend the world as by a cataclysm. So fearful was it that I could not believe it had actual existence: it passed previous experience, the powers of belief, and for a moment I thought it the result of my own animal terror, an hallucination born of tottering reason.

"A glance at Nils dispelled this thought in a flash. In the pale light of the high stars he was the embodiment of all possible human fear, quaking with an ague, his jaw fallen, his tongue out, his eyes protruding like those of a hanged man. Without a word we fled, the panic of fear giving us strength, and together, the little dog caught close in Nils's arms, we sped down the side of the cursed mountains,—anywhere, goal was of no account: we had but one impulse—to get away from that place.

"So under the black trees and the far white stars that flashed through the still leaves overhead, we leaped down the mountain side, regardless of path or landmark, straight through the tangled underbrush, across mountain streams, through fens and copses, anywhere, so only that our course was downward.

"How long we ran thus, I have no idea, but by and by the forest fell behind, and we found ourselves among the foothills, and fell exhausted on the dry short grass, panting like tired dogs.

"It was lighter here in the open, and presently we looked around to see where we were, and how we were to strike out in order to find the path that would lead us home. We looked in vain for a familiar sign. Behind us rose the great wall of black forest on the flank of the mountain: before us lay the undulating mounds of low foothills, unbroken by trees or rocks, and beyond, only the fall of black sky bright with multitudinous stars that turned its velvet depth to a luminous gray.

"As I remember, we did not speak to each other once: the terror was too heavy on us for that, but by and by we rose simultaneously and started out across the hills.

"Still the same silence, the same dead, motionless air—air that was at once sultry and chilling: a heavy heat struck through with an icy chill that felt almost like the burning of frozen steel. Still carrying the helpless dog, Nils pressed on through the hills, and I followed close behind. At last, in front of us, rose a slope of moor touching the white stars. We climbed it wearily, reached the top, and found ourselves gazing down into a great, smooth valley, filled half way to the brim with—what?

"As far as the eye could see stretched a level plain of ashy white, faintly phosphorescent, a sea of velvet fog that lay like motionless water, or rather like a floor of alabaster, so dense did it appear, so seemingly capable of sustaining weight. If it were possible, I think that sea of dead white mist struck even greater terror into my soul than the heavy silence or the deadly cry—so ominous was it, so utterly unreal, so phantasmal, so impossible, as it lay there like a dead ocean under the steady stars. Yet through that mist *we must go*! there seemed no other way home, and, shattered with abject fear, mad with the one desire to get back, we started down the slope to where the sea of milky mist ceased, sharp and distinct around the stems of the rough grass.

"I put one foot into the ghostly fog. A chill as of death struck through me, stopping my heart, and I threw myself backward on the slope. At that instant came again the shriek, close, close, right in our ears, in ourselves, and far out across that damnable sea I saw the cold fog lift like a water-spout and toss itself high in writhing convolutions towards the sky. The stars began to grow dim as thick vapor swept across them, and in the growing dark I saw a great, watery moon lift itself slowly above the palpitating sea, vast and vague in the gathering mist.

"This was enough: we turned and fled along the margin of the white sea that throbbed now with fitful motion below us, rising, rising, slowly and steadily, driving us higher and higher up the side of the foothills.

"It was a race for life; that we knew. How we kept it up I cannot understand, but we did, and at last we saw the white sea fall behind us as we staggered up the end of the valley, and then down into a region that we knew, and so into the old path. The last thing I remember was hearing a strange voice, that of Nils, but horribly changed, stammer brokenly, 'The dog is dead!' and then the whole world turned around twice, slowly and resistlessly, and consciousness went out with a crash.

"It was some three weeks later, as I remember, that I awoke in my own room, and found my mother sitting beside the bed. I could not think very well at first, but as I slowly grew strong again, vague flashes of recollection began to come to me, and little by little the whole sequence of events of that awful night in the Dead Valley came back. All that I could gain from what was told me was that three weeks before I had been found in my own bed, raging sick, and that my illness grew fast into brain fever. I tried to speak of the dread things that had happened to me, but I saw at once that no one looked on them save as the hauntings of a dying frenzy, and so I closed my mouth and kept my own counsel.

"I must see Nils, however, and so I asked for him. My mother told me that he also had been ill with a strange fever, but that he was now quite well again. Presently they brought him in, and when we were alone I began to speak to him of the night on the mountain. I shall never forget the shock that struck me down on my pillow when the boy denied everything: denied having gone with me, ever having heard the cry, having seen the valley, or feeling the deadly chill of the ghostly fog. Nothing would shake his determined ignorance, and in spite of myself I was forced to admit that his denials came from no policy of concealment, but from blank oblivion.

"My weakened brain was in a turmoil. Was it all but the floating phantasm of delirium? Or had the horror of the real thing blotted Nils's mind into blankness so far as the events of the night in the Dead Valley were concerned? The latter explanation seemed the only one, else how explain the sudden illness which in a night had struck us both down? I said nothing more, either to Nils or to my own people, but waited, with a growing determination that, once well again, I would find that valley if it really existed.

"It was some weeks before I was really well enough to go, but finally, late in September, I chose a bright, warm, still day, the last smile of the dying summer, and started early in the morning along the path that led to Hallsberg. I was sure I knew where the trail struck off to the right, down which we had come from the valley of dead water, for a great tree grew by the Hallsberg path at the point where, with a sense of salvation, we had found the home road. Presently I saw it to the right, a little distance ahead.

"I think the bright sunlight and the clear air had worked as a tonic to me, for by the time I came to the foot of the great pine, I had quite lost faith in the verity of the vision that haunted me, believing at last that it was indeed but the nightmare of madness. Nevertheless, I turned sharply to the right, at the base of the tree, into a narrow path that led through a dense thicket. As I did so I tripped over something. A swarm of flies sung into the air around me, and looking down I saw the matted fleece, with the poor little bones thrusting through, of the dog we had bought in Hallsberg.

"Then my courage went out with a puff, and I knew that it all was true, and that now I was frightened. Pride and the desire for adventure urged me on, however, and I pressed into the close thicket that barred my way. The path was hardly visible: merely the worn road of some small beasts, for, though it showed in the crisp grass, the bushes above grew thick and hardly penetrable. The land rose slowly, and rising grew clearer, until at last I came out on a great slope of hill, unbroken by trees or shrubs, very like my memory of that rise of land we had topped in order that we might find the dead valley and the icy fog. I looked at the sun; it was bright and clear, and all around insects were humming in the autumn air, and birds were darting to and fro. Surely there was no danger, not until nightfall at least; so I began to whistle, and with a rush mounted the last crest of brown hill.

"There lay the Dead Valley! A great oval basin, almost as smooth and regular as though made by man. On all sides the grass crept over the brink of the encircling hills, dusty green on the crests, then fading into ashy brown, and so to a deadly white, this last color forming a thin ring, running in a long line around the slope. And then? Nothing. Bare, brown, hard earth, glittering with grains of alkali, but otherwise dead and barren. Not a tuft of grass, not a stick of brushwood, not even a stone, but only the vast expanse of beaten clay.

"In the midst of the basin, perhaps a mile and a half away, the level expanse was broken by a great dead tree, rising leafless and gaunt into the air. Without a moment's hesitation I started down into the valley and made for this goal. Every particle of fear seemed to have left me, and even the valley itself did not look so very terrifying. At all events, I was driven by an overwhelming curiosity, and there seemed to be but one thing in the world to do,—to get to that Tree! As I trudged along over the hard earth, I noticed that the multitudinous voices of birds and insects had died away. No bee or butterfly hovered through the air, no insects leaped or crept over the dull earth. The very air itself was stagnant.

"As I drew near the skeleton tree, I noticed the glint of sunlight on a kind of white mound around its roots, and I wondered curiously. It was not until I had come close that I saw its nature.

"All around the roots and barkless trunk was heaped a wilderness of little bones. Tiny skulls of rodents and of birds, thousands of them, rising about the dead tree and streaming off for several yards in all directions, until the dreadful pile ended in isolated skulls and scattered skeletons. Here and there a larger bone appeared,—the thigh of a sheep, the hoofs of a horse, and to one side, grinning slowly, a human skull.

"I stood quite still, staring with all my eyes, when suddenly the dense silence was broken by a faint, forlorn cry high over my head. I looked up and saw a great falcon turning and sailing downward just over the tree. In a moment more she fell motionless on the bleaching bones.

"Horror struck me, and I rushed for home, my brain whirling, a strange numbness growing in me. I ran steadily, on and on. At last I glanced up. Where was the rise of hill? I looked around wildly. Close before me was the dead tree with its pile of bones. I had circled it round and round, and the valley wall was still a mile and a half away.

"I stood dazed and frozen. The sun was sinking, red and dull, towards the line of hills. In the east the dark was growing fast. Was there still time? *Time!* It was not *that* I wanted, it was *will*! My feet seemed clogged as in a nightmare. I could hardly drag them over the barren earth. And then I felt the slow chill creeping through me. I looked down. Out of the earth a thin mist was rising, collecting in little pools that grew ever larger until they joined here and there, their currents swirling slowly like thin blue smoke. The western hills halved the copper sun. When it was dark I should hear that shriek again, and then I should die. I knew that, and with every remaining atom of will I staggered towards the red west through the writhing mist that crept clammily around my ankles, retarding my steps.

"And as I fought my way off from the Tree, the horror grew, until at last I thought I was going to die. The silence pursued me like dumb ghosts, the still air held my breath, the hellish fog caught at my feet like cold hands.

"But I won! though not a moment too soon. As I crawled on my hands and knees up the brown slope, I heard, far away and high in the air, the cry that already had almost bereft me of reason. It was faint and vague, but unmistakable in its horrible intensity. I glanced behind. The fog was dense and pallid, heaving undulously up the brown slope. The sky was gold under the setting sun, but below was the ashy gray of death. I stood for a moment on the brink of this sea of hell, and then leaped down the slope. The sunset opened before me, the night closed behind, and as I crawled home weak and tired, darkness shut down on the Dead Valley."

The Red Room

H. G. Wells

———◆———

I CAN ASSURE YOU," SAID I, "THAT IT WILL TAKE A VERY TANGIBLE GHOST TO frighten me." And I stood up before the fire with my glass in my hand.

"It is your own choosing," said the man with the withered arm, and glanced at me askance.

"Eight-and-twenty years," said I, "I have lived, and never a ghost have I seen as yet."

The old woman sat staring hard into the fire, her pale eyes wide open. "Ay," she broke in; "and eight-and-twenty years you have lived and never seen the likes of this house, I reckon. There's a many things to see, when one's still but eight-and-twenty." She swayed her head slowly from side to side. "A many things to see and sorrow for."

I half-suspected the old people were trying to enhance the spiritual terrors of their house by their droning insistence. I put down my empty glass on the table and looked about the room, and caught a glimpse of myself, abbreviated and broadened to an impossible sturdiness, in the queer old mirror at the end of the room. "Well," I said, "if I see anything to-night, I shall be so much the wiser. For I come to the business with an open mind."

"It's your own choosing," said the man with the withered arm once more.

I heard the sound of a stick and a shambling step on the flags in the passage outside, and the door creaked on its hinges as a second old man entered, more bent, more wrinkled, more aged even than the first. He supported himself by a single crutch, his eyes were covered by a shade, and his lower lip, half-averted, hung pale and pink from his decaying yellow teeth. He made straight for an arm-chair on the opposite side of the table, sat down clumsily, and began to cough. The man with the withered arm gave this new-comer a short glance of positive dislike; the old woman took no notice of his arrival, but remained with her eyes fixed steadily on the fire.

"I said—it's your own choosing," said the man with the withered arm, when the coughing had ceased for awhile.

"It's my own choosing," I answered.

The man with the shade became aware of my presence for the first time, and threw his head back for a moment and sideways, to see me. I caught a momentary glimpse of his eyes, small and bright and inflamed. Then he began to cough and splutter again.

"Why don't you drink?" said the man with the withered arm, pushing the beer towards him. The man with the shade poured out a glassful with a shaky arm that splashed half as much again on the deal table. A monstrous shadow of him crouched upon the wall and mocked his action as he poured and drank. I must confess I had scarce expected these grotesque custodians. There is to my mind something inhuman in senility, something crouching and atavistic; the human qualities seem to drop from old people insensibly day by day. The three of them made me feel uncomfortable, with their gaunt silences, their bent carriage, their evident unfriendliness to me and to one another.

"If," said I, "you will show me to this haunted room of yours, I will make myself comfortable there."

The old man with the cough jerked his head back so suddenly that it startled me, and shot another glance of his red eyes at me from under the shade; but no one answered me. I waited a minute, glancing from one to the other.

"If," I said a little louder, "if you will show me to this haunted room of yours, I will relieve you from the task of entertaining me."

"There's a candle on the slab outside the door," said the man with the withered arm, looking at my feet as he addressed me. "But if you go to the red room to-night—"

("This night of all nights!" said the old woman.)

"You go alone."

"Very well," I answered. "And which way do I go?"

"You go along the passage for a bit," said he, "until you come to a door, and through that is a spiral staircase, and half-way up that is a landing and another door covered with baize. Go through that and down the long corridor to the end, and the red room is on your left up the steps."

"Have I got that right?" I said, and repeated his directions. He corrected me in one particular.

"And are you really going?" said the man with the shade, looking at me again for the third time, with that queer, unnatural tilting of the face.

("This night of all nights!" said the old woman.)

"It is what I came for," I said, and moved towards the door. As I did so, the old man with the shade rose and staggered round the table, so as to be closer to the others and to the fire. At the door I turned and looked at them, and saw they were all close together, dark against the firelight, staring at me over their shoulders, with an intent expression on their ancient faces.

"Good-night," I said, setting the door open.

"It's your own choosing," said the man with the withered arm.

I left the door wide open until the candle was well alight, and then I shut them in and walked down the chilly, echoing passage.

I must confess that the oddness of these three old pensioners in whose charge her ladyship had left the castle, and the deep-toned, old-fashioned furniture of the house-keeper's room in which they foregathered, affected me in spite of my efforts to keep myself at a matter-of-fact phase. They seemed to belong to another age, an older age, an age when things spiritual were different from this of ours, less certain; an age when omens and witches were credible, and ghosts beyond denying. Their very existence was spectral; the cut of their clothing, fashions born in dead brains. The ornaments and con-veniences of the room about them were ghostly—the thoughts of vanished men, which still haunted rather than participated in the world of to-day. But with an effort I sent such thoughts to the right-about. The long, draughty subterranean passage was chilly and dusty, and my candle flared and made the shadows cower and quiver. The echoes rang up and down the spiral staircase, and a shadow came sweeping up after me, and one fled before me into the darkness overhead. I came to the landing and stopped there for a moment, listening to a rustling that I fancied I heard; then, satisfied of the absolute silence, I pushed open the baize-covered door and stood in the corridor.

The effect was scarcely what I expected, for the moonlight, coming in by the great window on the grand staircase, picked out everything in vivid black shadow or silvery illumination. Everything was in its place: the house might have been deserted on the yesterday instead of eighteen months ago. There were candles in the sockets of the sconces, and whatever dust had gathered on the carpets or upon the polished flooring was distributed so evenly as to be invisible in the moonlight. I was about to advance, and stopped abruptly. A bronze group stood upon the landing, hidden from me by the corner of the wall, but its shadow fell with marvellous distinctness upon the white panelling, and gave me the impression of some one crouching to waylay me. I stood rigid for half a minute perhaps. Then, with my hand in the pocket that held my revolver, I advanced, only to discover a Ganymede and Eagle glistening in the moon-light. That incident for a time restored my nerve, and a porcelain Chinaman on a buhl table, whose head rocked silently as I passed him, scarcely startled me.

The door to the red room and the steps up to it were in a shadowy corner. I moved my candle from side to side, in order to see clearly the nature of the recess in which I stood before opening the door. Here it was, thought I, that my predecessor was found, and the memory of that story gave me a sudden twinge of apprehension. I glanced over my shoulder at the Ganymede in the moonlight, and opened the door of the red room rather hastily, with my face half turned to the pallid silence of the landing.

I entered, closed the door behind me at once, turned the key I found in the lock within, and stood with the candle held aloft, surveying the scene of my vigil, the great red room of Lorraine Castle, in which the young duke had died. Or, rather, in which he had begun his dying, for he had opened the door and fallen headlong down the steps I had just ascended. That had been the end of his vigil, of his gallant attempt to conquer the ghostly tradition of the place, and never, I thought, had apoplexy better served the ends of superstition. And there were other and older stories that clung to the room, back to the half-credible beginning of it all, the tale of a timid wife and the tragic end that came to her husband's jest of frightening her. And looking around that large shadowy room, with its shadowy window bays, its recesses and alcoves, one could well understand the legends that had sprouted in its black corners, its germinating darkness. My candle was a little tongue of light in its vastness, that failed to pierce the opposite end of the room, and left an ocean of mystery and suggestion beyond its island of light.

I resolved to make a systematic examination of the place at once, and dispel the fanciful suggestions of its obscurity before they obtained a hold upon me. After satisfying myself of the fastening of the door, I began to walk about the room, peering round each article of furniture, tucking up the valances of the bed, and opening its curtains wide. I pulled up the blinds and examined the fastenings of the several windows before closing the shutters, leant forward and looked up the blackness of the wide chimney, and tapped the dark oak panelling for any secret opening. There were two big mirrors in the room, each with a pair of sconces bearing candles, and on the mantel-shelf, too, were more candles in china candlesticks. All these I lit one after the other. The fire was laid,—an unexpected consideration from the old housekeeper,—and I lit it, to keep down any disposition to shiver, and when it was burning well, I stood round with my back to it and regarded the room again. I had pulled up a chintz-covered armchair and a table, to form a kind of barricade before me, and on this lay my revolver ready to hand. My precise examination had done me good, but I still found the remoter darkness of the place, and its perfect stillness, too stimulating for the imagination. The echoing of the stir and crackling of the fire was no sort of comfort to me. The shadow in the alcove, at the end in particular, had that undefinable quality of a presence, that odd suggestion of a lurking living thing, that comes so easily in silence and solitude. At last, to reassure myself, I walked with a candle into it, and satisfied myself that there was nothing tangible there. I stood that candle upon the floor of the alcove, and left it in that position.

By this time I was in a state of considerable nervous tension, although to my reason there was no adequate cause for the condition. My mind, however, was perfectly clear. I postulated quite unreservedly that nothing supernatural could happen, and to pass the time I began to string some rhymes together, Ingoldsby fashion, of the original legend of the place. A few I spoke aloud, but the echoes were not pleasant. For the same reason I also abandoned, after a time, a conversation with myself upon the impossibility of ghosts and haunting. My mind reverted to the three old and distorted people downstairs, and I tried to keep it upon that topic. The sombre reds and blacks of the room troubled me; even with seven candles the place was merely dim. The one in the alcove flared in a draught, and the fire-flickering kept the shadows and penumbra perpetually shifting and stirring. Casting about for a remedy, I recalled the candles I had seen in the passage, and, with a slight effort, walked out into the moonlight, carrying a candle and leaving the door open, and presently returned with as many as ten. These I put in various knick-knacks of china with which the room was sparsely adorned, lit and placed where the shadows had lain deepest, some on the floor, some in the window recesses, until at last my seventeen candles were so arranged that not an inch of the room but had the direct light of at least one of them. It occurred to me that when the ghost came, I could warn him not to trip over them. The room was now quite brightly illuminated. There was something very cheery and reassuring in these little streaming flames, and snuffing them gave me an occupation, and afforded a reassuring sense of the passage of time.

Even with that, however, the brooding expectation of the vigil weighed heavily upon me. It was after midnight that the candle in the alcove suddenly went out, and the black shadow sprang back to its place there. I did not see the candle go out; I simply turned and saw that the darkness was there, as one might start and see the unexpected presence of a stranger. "By Jove!" said I aloud; "that draught's a strong one!" and, taking the matches from the table, I walked across the room in a leisurely manner to relight the corner again. My first match would not strike, and as I succeeded with the second, something seemed to blink on the wall before me. I turned my head involuntarily, and saw that the two candles on the little table by the fireplace were extinguished. I rose at once to my feet.

"Odd!" I said. "Did I do that myself in a flash of absent-mindedness?"

I walked back, relit one, and as I did so, I saw the candle in the right sconce of one of the mirrors wink and go right out, and almost immediately its companion followed it. There was no mistake about it. The flame vanished, as if the wicks had been suddenly nipped between a finger and a thumb, leaving the wick neither glowing nor smoking, but black. While I stood gaping, the candle at the foot of the bed went out, and the shadows seemed to take another step towards me.

"This won't do!" said I, and first one and then another candle on the mantel-shelf followed.

"What's up?" I cried, with a queer high note getting into my voice somehow. At that the candle on the wardrobe went out, and the one I had relit in the alcove followed.

"Steady on!" I said. "These candles are wanted," speaking with a half-hysterical facetiousness, and scratching away at a match the while for the mantel candlesticks. My hands trembled so much that twice I missed the rough paper of the matchbox. As the mantel emerged from darkness again, two candles in the remoter end of the window were eclipsed. But with the same match I also relit the larger mirror candles, and those on the floor near the doorway, so that for the moment I seemed to gain on the extinctions. But then in a volley there vanished four lights at once in different corners of the room, and I struck another match in quivering haste, and stood hesitating whither to take it.

As I stood undecided, an invisible hand seemed to sweep out the two candles on the table. With a cry of terror, I dashed at the alcove, then into the corner, and then into the window, relighting three, as two more vanished by the fireplace; then, perceiving a better way, I dropped the matches on the iron-bound deed-box in the corner, and caught up the bedroom candlestick. With this I avoided the delay of striking matches; but for all that the steady process of extinction went on, and the shadows I feared and fought against returned, and crept in upon me, first a step gained on this side of me and then on that. It was like a ragged storm-cloud sweeping out the stars. Now and then one returned for a minute, and was lost again. I was now almost frantic with the horror of the coming darkness, and my self-possession deserted me. I leaped, panting and dishevelled, from candle to candle, in a vain struggle against that remorseless advance.

I bruised myself on the thigh against the table, I sent a chair headlong, I stumbled and fell and whisked the cloth from the table in my fall. My candle rolled away from me, and I snatched another as I rose. Abruptly this was blown out, as I swung it off the table, by the wind of my sudden movement, and immediately the two remaining candles followed. But there was light still in the room, a red light that staved off the shadows from me. The fire! Of course, I could still thrust my candle between the bars and relight it!

I turned to where the flames were still dancing between the glowing coals, and splashing red reflections upon the furniture, made two steps towards the grate, and incontinently the flames dwindled and vanished, the glow vanished, the reflections rushed together and vanished, and as I thrust the candle between the bars, darkness closed upon me like the shutting of an eye, wrapped about me in a stifling embrace, sealed my vision, and crushed the last vestiges of reason from my brain. The candle fell from my hand. I flung out my arms in a vain effort to thrust that ponderous blackness away from me, and, lifting up my voice, screamed with all my might—once, twice, thrice. Then I think I must have staggered to my feet. I know I thought suddenly of the moonlit corridor, and, with my head bowed and my arms over my face, made a run for the door.

But I had forgotten the exact position of the door, and struck myself heavily against the corner of the bed. I staggered back, turned, and was either struck or struck myself against some other bulky furniture. I have a vague memory of battering myself thus, to and fro in the darkness, of a cramped struggle, and of my own wild crying as I darted to and fro, of a heavy blow at last upon my forehead, a horrible sensation of falling that lasted an age, of my last frantic effort to keep my footing, and then I remember no more.

I opened my eyes in daylight. My head was roughly bandaged, and the man with the withered arm was watching my face. I looked about me, trying to remember what had happened, and for a space I could not recollect. I rolled my eyes into the corner, and saw the old woman, no longer abstracted, pouring out some drops of medicine from a little blue phial into a glass. "Where am I?" I asked. "I seem to remember you, and yet I cannot remember who you are."

They told me then, and I heard of the haunted red room as one who hears a tale. "We found you at dawn," said he, " and there was blood on your forehead and lips."

It was very slowly I recovered my memory of my experience. "You believe now," said the old man, "that the room is haunted?" He spoke no longer as one who greets an intruder, but as one who grieves for a broken friend.

"Yes," said I; "the room is haunted."

"And you have seen it. And we, who have lived here all our lives, have never set eyes upon it. Because we have never dared.—Tell us, is it truly the old earl who—"

"No," said I; "it is not."

"I told you so," said the old lady, with the glass in her hand. "It is his poor young countess who was frightened—"

"It is not," I said. "There is neither ghost of earl nor ghost of countess in that room, there is no ghost there at all; but worse, far worse—"

"Well?" they said.

"The worst of all the things that haunt poor mortal man," said I; "and that is, in all its nakedness—*Fear!* Fear that will not have light nor sound, that will not bear with reason, that deafens and darkens and overwhelms. It followed me through the corridor, it fought against me in the room—"

I stopped abruptly. There was an interval of silence. My hand went up to my bandages.

Then the man with the shade sighed and spoke. "That is it," said he. "I knew that was it. A Power of Darkness. To put such a curse upon a woman! It lurks there always. You can feel it even in the daytime, even of a bright summer's day, in the hangings, in the curtains, keeping behind you however you face about. In the dusk it creeps along the corridor and follows you, so that you dare not turn. There is Fear in that room of hers—black Fear, and there will be—so long as this house of sin endures."

The Monkey's Paw

W. W. Jacobs

I

Without, the night was cold and wet, but in the small parlour of Laburnam Villa the blinds were drawn and the fire burned brightly. Father and son were at chess, the former, who possessed ideas about the game involving radical changes, putting his king into such sharp and unnecessary perils that it even provoked comment from the white-haired old lady knitting placidly by the fire.

"Hark at the wind," said Mr. White, who, having seen a fatal mistake after it was too late, was amiably desirous of preventing his son from seeing it.

"I'm listening," said the latter, grimly surveying the board as he stretched out his hand. "Check."

"I should hardly think that he'd come tonight," said his father, with his hand poised over the board.

"Mate," replied the son.

"That's the worst of living so far out," bawled Mr. White, with sudden and unlooked-for violence; "of all the beastly, slushy, out-of-the-way places to live in, this is the worst. Pathway's a bog, and the road's a torrent. I don't know what people are thinking about. I suppose because only two houses in the road are let, they think it doesn't matter."

"Never mind, dear," said his wife, soothingly; "perhaps you'll win the next one."

Mr. White looked up sharply, just in time to intercept a knowing glance between mother and son. The words died away on his lips, and he hid a guilty grin in his thin grey beard.

"There he is," said Herbert White, as the gate banged to loudly and heavy footsteps came toward the door.

The old man rose with hospitable haste, and opening the door, was heard condoling with the new arrival. The new arrival also condoled with himself, so that Mrs. White said, "Tut, tut!" and coughed gently as her husband entered the room, followed by a tall, burly man, beady of eye and rubicund of visage.

"Sergeant-Major Morris," he said, introducing him.

The sergeant-major shook hands, and taking the proffered seat by the fire, watched contentedly while his host got out whiskey and tumblers and stood a small copper kettle on the fire.

At the third glass his eyes got brighter, and he began to talk, the little family circle regarding with eager interest this visitor from distant parts, as he squared his broad shoulders in the chair and spoke of wild scenes and doughty deeds; of wars and plagues and strange peoples.

"Twenty-one years of it," said Mr. White, nodding at his wife and son. "When he went away he was a slip of a youth in the warehouse. Now look at him."

"He don't look to have taken much harm," said Mrs. White, politely.

"I'd like to go to India myself," said the old man, "just to look round a bit, you know."

"Better where you are," said the sergeant-major, shaking his head. He put down the empty glass, and sighing softly, shook it again.

"I should like to see those old temples and fakirs and jugglers," said the old man. "What was that you started telling me the other day about a monkey's paw or something, Morris?"

"Nothing," said the soldier, hastily. "Least-ways nothing worth hearing."

"Monkey's paw?" said Mrs. White, curiously.

"Well, it's just a bit of what you might call magic, perhaps," said the sergeant-major, off-handedly.

His three listeners leaned forward eagerly. The visitor absent-mindedly put his empty glass to his lips and then set it down again. His host filled it for him.

"To look at," said the sergeant-major, fumbling in his pocket, "it's just an ordinary little paw, dried to a mummy."

He took something out of his pocket and proffered it. Mrs. White drew back with a grimace, but her son, taking it, examined it curiously.

"And what is there special about it?" inquired Mr. White as he took it from his son, and having examined it, placed it upon the table.

"It had a spell put on it by an old fakir," said the sergeant-major, "a very holy man. He wanted to show that fate ruled people's lives, and that those who interfered with it did so to their sorrow. He put a spell on it so that three separate men could each have three wishes from it."

His manner was so impressive that his hearers were conscious that their light laughter jarred somewhat.

"Well, why don't you have three, sir?" said Herbert White, cleverly.

The soldier regarded him in the way that middle age is wont to regard presumptuous youth. "I have," he said, quietly, and his blotchy face whitened.

"And did you really have the three wishes granted?" asked Mrs. White.

"I did," said the sergeant-major, and his glass tapped against his strong teeth.

"And has anybody else wished?" persisted the old lady.

"The first man had his three wishes. Yes," was the reply; "I don't know what the first two were, but the third was for death. That's how I got the paw."

His tones were so grave that a hush fell upon the group.

"If you've had your three wishes, it's no good to you now, then, Morris," said the old man at last. "What do you keep it for?"

The soldier shook his head. "Fancy, I suppose," he said, slowly. "I did have some idea of selling it, but I don't think I will. It has caused enough mischief already. Besides, people won't buy. They think it's a fairy tale; some of them, and those who do think anything of it want to try it first and pay me afterward."

"If you could have another three wishes," said the old man, eyeing him keenly, "would you have them?"

"I don't know," said the other. "I don't know."

He took the paw, and dangling it between his forefinger and thumb, suddenly threw it upon the fire. White, with a slight cry, stooped down and snatched it off.

"Better let it burn," said the soldier, solemnly.

"If you don't want it, Morris," said the other, "give it to me."

"I won't," said his friend, doggedly. "I threw it on the fire. If you keep it, don't blame me for what happens. Pitch it on the fire again like a sensible man."

The other shook his head and examined his new possession closely. "How do you do it?" he inquired.

"Hold it up in your right hand and wish aloud," said the sergeant-major, "but I warn you of the consequences."

"Sounds like the *Arabian Nights*," said Mrs. White, as she rose and began to set the supper. "Don't you think you might wish for four pairs of hands for me?"

Her husband drew the talisman from pocket, and then all three burst into laughter as the sergeant-major, with a look of alarm on his face, caught him by the arm.

"If you must wish," he said, gruffly, "wish for something sensible."

Mr. White dropped it back in his pocket, and placing chairs, motioned his friend to the table. In the business of supper the talisman was partly forgotten, and afterward the three sat listening in an enthralled fashion to a second instalment of the soldier's adventures in India.

"If the tale about the monkey's paw is not more truthful than those he has been telling us," said Herbert, as the door closed behind their guest, just in time for him to catch the last train, "we sha'nt make much out of it."

"Did you give him anything for it, father?" inquired Mrs. White, regarding her husband closely.

"A trifle," said he, colouring slightly. "He didn't want it, but I made him take it. And he pressed me again to throw it away."

"Likely," said Herbert, with pretended horror. "Why, we're going to be rich, and famous and happy. Wish to be an emperor, father, to begin with; then you can't be henpecked."

He darted round the table, pursued by the maligned Mrs. White armed with an antimacassar.

Mr. White took the paw from his pocket and eyed it dubiously. "I don't know what to wish for, and that's a fact," he said, slowly. "It seems to me I've got all I want."

"If you only cleared the house, you'd be quite happy, wouldn't you?" said Herbert, with his hand on his shoulder. "Well, wish for two hundred pounds, then; that'll just do it."

His father, smiling shamefacedly at his own credulity, held up the talisman, as his son, with a solemn face, somewhat marred by a wink at his mother, sat down at the piano and struck a few impressive chords.

"I wish for two hundred pounds," said the old man distinctly.

A fine crash from the piano greeted the words, interrupted by a shuddering cry from the old man. His wife and son ran toward him.

"It moved," he cried, with a glance of disgust at the object as it lay on the floor. "As I wished, it twisted in my hand like a snake."

"Well, I don't see the money," said his son as he picked it up and placed it on the table, "and I bet I never shall."

"It must have been your fancy, father," said his wife, regarding him anxiously.

He shook his head. "Never mind, though; there's no harm done, but it gave me a shock all the same."

They sat down by the fire again while the two men finished their pipes. Outside, the wind was higher than ever, and the old man started nervously at the sound of a door banging upstairs. A silence unusual and depressing settled upon all three, which lasted until the old couple rose to retire for the night.

"I expect you'll find the cash tied up in a big bag in the middle of your bed," said Herbert, as he bade them good-night, "and something horrible squatting up on top of the wardrobe watching you as you pocket your ill-gotten gains."

He sat alone in the darkness, gazing at the dying fire, and seeing faces in it. The last face was so horrible and so simian that he gazed at it in amazement. It got so vivid that, with a little uneasy laugh, he felt on the table for a glass containing a little water to throw over it. His hand grasped the monkey's paw, and with a little shiver he wiped his hand on his coat and went up to bed.

II

In the brightness of the wintry sun next morning as it streamed over the breakfast table he laughed at his fears. There was an air of prosaic wholesomeness about the room which it had lacked on the previous night, and the dirty, shrivelled little paw was pitched on the sideboard with a carelessness which betokened no great belief in its virtues.

"I suppose all old soldiers are the same," said Mrs. White. "The idea of our listening to such nonsense! How could wishes be granted in these days? And if they could, how could two hundred pounds hurt you, father?"

"Might drop on his head from the sky," said the frivolous Herbert.

"Morris said the things happened so naturally," said his father, "that you might if you so wished attribute it to coincidence."

"Well, don't break into the money before I come back," said Herbert as he rose from the table. "I'm afraid it'll turn you into a mean, avaricious man, and we shall have to disown you."

His mother laughed, and following him to the door, watched him down the road; and returning to the breakfast table, was very happy at the expense of her husband's credulity. All of which did not prevent her from scurrying to the door at the postman's knock, nor prevent her from referring somewhat shortly to retired sergeant-majors of bibulous habits when she found that the post brought a tailor's bill.

"Herbert will have some more of his funny remarks, I expect, when he comes home," she said, as they sat at dinner.

"I dare say," said Mr. White, pouring himself out some beer; "but for all that, the thing moved in my hand; that I'll swear to."

"You thought it did," said the old lady soothingly.

"I say it did," replied the other. "There was no thought about it; I had just— What's the matter?"

His wife made no reply. She was watching the mysterious movements of a man outside, who, peering in an undecided fashion at the house, appeared to be trying to make up his mind to enter. In mental connection with the two hundred pounds, she noticed that the stranger was well dressed, and wore a silk hat of glossy newness. Three times he paused at the gate, and then walked on again. The fourth time he stood with his hand upon it, and then with sudden resolution flung it open and walked up the path. Mrs. White at the same moment placed her hands behind her, and hurriedly unfastening the strings of her apron, put that useful article of apparel beneath the cushion of her chair.

She brought the stranger, who seemed ill at ease, into the room. He gazed at her furtively, and listened in a preoccupied fashion as the old lady apologized for the appearance of the room, and her husband's coat, a garment which he usually reserved for the garden. She then waited as patiently as her sex would permit, for him to broach his business, but he was at first strangely silent.

"I—was asked to call," he said at last, and stooped and picked a piece of cotton from his trousers. "I come from 'Maw and Meggins.' "

The old lady started. "Is anything the matter?" she asked, breathlessly. "Has anything happened to Herbert? What is it? What is it?"

Her husband interposed. "There, there, mother," he said, hastily. "Sit down, and don't jump to conclusions. You've not brought bad news, I'm sure, sir"; and he eyed the other wistfully.

"I'm sorry—" began the visitor.

"Is he hurt?" demanded the mother, wildly.

The visitor bowed in assent. "Badly hurt," he said, quietly, "but he is not in any pain."

"Oh, thank God!" said the old woman, clasping her hands. "Thank God for that! Thank——"

She broke off suddenly as the sinister meaning of the assurance dawned upon her and she saw the awful confirmation of her fears in the other's perverted face. She caught her breath, and turning to her slower-witted husband, laid her trembling old hand upon his. There was a long silence.

"He was caught in the machinery," said the visitor at length in a low voice.

"Caught in the machinery," repeated Mr. White, in a dazed fashion, "yes."

He sat staring blankly out at the window, and taking his wife's hand between his own, pressed it as he had been wont to do in their old courting-days nearly forty years before.

"He was the only one left to us," he said, turning gently to the visitor. "It is hard."

The other coughed, and rising, walked slowly to the window. "The firm wished me to convey their sincere sympathy with you in your great loss," he said, without looking round. "I beg that you will understand I am only their servant and merely obeying orders."

There was no reply; the old woman's face was white, her eyes staring, and her breath inaudible; on the husband's face was a look such as his friend the sergeant might have carried into his first action.

"I was to say that Maw and Meggins disclaim all responsibility," continued the other. "They admit no liability at all, but in consideration of your son's services, they wish to present you with a certain sum as compensation."

Mr. White dropped his wife's hand, and rising to his feet, gazed with a look of horror at his visitor. His dry lips shaped the words, "How much?"

"Two hundred pounds," was the answer.

Unconscious of his wife's shriek, the old man smiled faintly, put out his hands like a sightless man, and dropped, a senseless heap, to the floor.

III

In the huge new cemetery, some two miles distant, the old people buried their dead, and came back to a house steeped in shadow and silence. It was all over so quickly that at first they could hardly realize it, and remained in a state of expectation as though of something else to happen—something else which was to lighten this load, too heavy for old hearts to bear.

But the days passed, and expectation gave place to resignation—the hopeless resignation of the old, sometimes miscalled, apathy. Sometimes they hardly exchanged a word, for now they had nothing to talk about, and their days were long to weariness.

It was about a week after that the old man, waking suddenly in the night, stretched out his hand and found himself alone. The room was in darkness, and the sound of subdued weeping came from the window. He raised himself in bed and listened.

"Come back," he said, tenderly. "You will be cold."

"It is colder for my son," said the old woman, and wept afresh.

The sound of her sobs died away on his ears. The bed was warm, and his eyes heavy with sleep. He dozed fitfully, and then slept until a sudden wild cry from his wife awoke him with a start.

"*The paw!*" she cried wildly. "The monkey's paw!"

He started up in alarm. "Where? Where is it? What's the matter?"

She came stumbling across the room toward him. "I want it," she said, quietly. "You've not destroyed it?"

"It's in the parlour, on the bracket," he replied, marvelling. "Why?"

She cried and laughed together, and bending over, kissed his cheek.

"I only just thought of it," she said, hysterically. "Why didn't I think of it before? Why didn't *you* think of it?"

"Think of what?" he questioned.

"The other two wishes," she replied, rapidly. "We've only had one."

"Was not that enough?" he demanded, fiercely.

"No," she cried, triumphantly; "we'll have one more. Go down and get it quickly, and wish our boy alive again."

The man sat up in bed and flung the bedclothes from his quaking limbs. "Good God, you are mad!" he cried, aghast.

"Get it," she panted; "get it quickly, and wish—Oh, my boy, my boy!"

Her husband struck a match and lit the candle. "Get back to bed," he said, unsteadily. "You don't know what you are saying."

"We had the first wish granted," said the old woman, feverishly; "why not the second?"

"A coincidence," stammered the old man.

"Go and get it and wish," cried his wife, quivering with excitement.

The old man turned and regarded her, and his voice shook. "He has been dead ten days, and besides he—I would not tell you else, but—I could only recognize him by his clothing. If he was too terrible for you to see then, how now?"

"Bring him back," cried the old woman, and dragged him toward the door. "Do you think I fear the child I have nursed?"

He went down in the darkness, and felt his way to the parlour, and then to the mantelpiece. The talisman was in its place, and a horrible fear that the unspoken wish might bring his mutilated son before him ere he could escape from the room seized upon him, and he caught his breath as he found that he had lost the direction of the door. His brow cold with sweat, he felt his way round the table, and groped along the wall until he found himself in the small passage with the unwholesome thing in his hand.

Even his wife's face seemed changed as he entered the room. It was white and expectant, and to his fears seemed to have an unnatural look upon it. He was afraid of her.

"*Wish!*" she cried, in a strong voice.

"It is foolish and wicked," he faltered.

"*Wish!*" repeated his wife.

He raised his hand. "I wish my son alive again."

The talisman fell to the floor, and he regarded it fearfully. Then he sank trembling into a chair as the old woman, with burning eyes, walked to the window and raised the blind.

He sat until he was chilled with the cold, glancing occasionally at the figure of the old woman peering through the window. The candle-end, which had burned below the rim of the china candlestick, was throwing pulsating shadows on the ceiling and walls, until, with a flicker larger than the rest, it expired. The old man, with an unspeakable sense of relief at the failure of the talisman, crept back to his bed, and a minute or two afterward the old woman came silently and apathetically beside him.

Neither spoke, but lay silently listening to the ticking of the clock. A stair creaked, and a squeaky mouse scurried noisily through the wall. The darkness was oppressive, and after lying for some time screwing up his courage, he took the box of matches, and striking one, went downstairs for a candle.

At the foot of the stairs the match went out, and he paused to strike another; and at the same moment a knock, so quiet and stealthy as to be scarcely audible, sounded on the front door.

The matches fell from his hand and spilled in the passage. He stood motionless, his breath suspended until the knock was repeated. Then he turned and fled swiftly back to his room, and closed the door behind him. A third knock sounded through the house.

"*What's that?*" cried the old woman, starting up.

"A rat," said the old man in shaking tones—"a rat. It passed me on the stairs."

His wife sat up in bed listening. A loud knock resounded through the house.

"It's Herbert!" she screamed. "It's Herbert!"

She ran to the door, but her husband was before her, and catching her by the arm, held her tightly.

"What are you going to do?" he whispered hoarsely.

"It's my boy; it's Herbert!" she cried, struggling mechanically. "I forgot it was two miles away. What are you holding me for? Let go. I must open the door."

"For God's sake don't let it in," cried the old man, trembling.

"You're afraid of your own son," she cried, struggling. "Let me go. I'm coming, Herbert; I'm coming."

There was another knock, and another. The old woman with a sudden wrench broke free and ran from the room. Her husband followed to the landing, and called after her appealingly as she hurried downstairs. He hard the chain rattle back and the bottom bolt drawn slowly and stiffly from the socket. Then the old woman's voice, strained and panting.

"The bolt," she cried loudly. "Come down. I can't reach it."

But her husband was on his hands and knees groping wildly on the floor in search of the paw. If he could only find it before the thing outside got in. A perfect fusillade of knocks reverberated through the house, and he heard the scraping of a chair as his wife put it down in the passage against the door. He heard the creaking of the bolt as it came slowly back, and at the same moment he found the monkey's paw, and frantically breathed his third and last wish.

The knocking ceased suddenly, although the echoes of it were still in the house. He heard the chair drawn back, and the door opened. A cold wind rushed up the staircase, and a long loud wail of disappointment and misery from his wife gave him courage to run down to her side, and then to the gate beyond. The street lamp flickering opposite shone on a quiet and deserted road.

The Southwest Chamber

Mary E. Wilkins Freeman

———◆———

THAT SCHOOL-TEACHER FROM ACTON IS COMING TO-DAY," SAID THE elder Miss Gill, Sophia.

"So she is," assented the younger Miss Gill, Amanda.

"I have decided to put her in the southwest chamber," said Sophia.

Amanda looked at her sister with an expression of mingled doubt and terror. "You don't suppose she would—" she began hesitatingly.

"Would what?" demanded Sophia, sharply. She was more incisive than her sister. Both were below the medium height, and stout, but Sophia was firm where Amanda was flabby. Amanda wore a baggy old muslin (it was a hot day), and Sophia was uncompromisingly hooked up in a starched and boned cambric over her high shelving figure.

"I didn't know but she would object to sleeping in that room, as long as Aunt Harriet died there such a little time ago," faltered Amanda.

"Well!" said Sophia, "of all the silly notions! If you are going to pick out rooms in this house where nobody has died, for the boarders, you'll have your hands full. Grandfather Ackley had seven children; four of them died here to my certain knowledge, besides grandfather and grandmother. I think Great-grandmother Ackley, grandfather's mother, died here, too; she must have; and Great-grandfather Ackley, and grandfather's unmarried sister, Great-aunt Fanny Ackley. I don't believe there's a room nor a bed in this house that somebody hasn't passed away in."

"Well, I suppose I am silly to think of it, and she had better go in there," said Amanda.

"I know she had. The northeast room is small and hot, and she's stout and likely to feel the heat, and she's saved money and is able to board out summers, and maybe she'll come here another year if she's well accommodated," said Sophia. "Now I guess you'd better go in there and see if any dust has settled on anything since it was cleaned, and open the west windows and let the sun in, while I see to that cake."

Amanda went to her task in the southwest chamber while her sister stepped heavily down the back stairs on her way to the kitchen.

"It seems to me you had better open the bed while you air and dust, then make it up again," she called back.

"Yes, sister," Amanda answered, shudderingly.

Nobody knew how this elderly woman with the untrammeled imagination of a child dreaded to enter the southwest chamber, and yet she could not have told why she had the dread. She had entered and occupied rooms which had been once tenanted by persons now dead. The room which had been hers in the little house in which she and her sister had lived before coming here had been her dead mother's. She had never reflected upon the fact with anything but loving awe and reverence. There had never been any fear. But this was different. She entered and her heart beat thickly in her ears. Her hands were cold. The room was a very large one. The four windows, two facing south, two west, were closed, the blinds also. The room was in a film of green gloom. The furniture loomed out vaguely. The gilt frame of a blurred old engraving on the wall caught a little light. The white counterpane on the bed showed like a blank page.

Amanda crossed the room, opened with a straining motion of her thin back and shoulders one of the west windows, and threw back the blind. Then the room revealed itself an apartment full of an aged and worn but no less valid state. Pieces of old mahogany swelled forth; a peacock-patterned chintz draped the bedstead. This chintz also covered a great easy chair which had been the favourite seat of the former occupant of the room. The closet door stood ajar. Amanda noticed that with wonder. There was a glimpse of purple drapery floating from a peg inside the closet. Amanda went across and took down the garment hanging there. She wondered how her sister had happened to leave it when she cleaned the room. It was an old loose gown which had belonged to her aunt. She took it down, shuddering, and closed the closet door after a fearful glance into its dark depths. It was a long closet with a strong odour of lovage. The Aunt Harriet had had a habit of eating lovage and had carried it constantly in her pocket. There was very likely some of the pleasant root in the pocket of the musty purple gown which Amanda threw over the easy chair.

Amanda perceived the odour with a start as if before an actual presence. Odour seems in a sense a vital part of a personality. It can survive the flesh to which it has clung like a persistent shadow, seeming to have in itself something of the substance of that to which it pertained. Amanda was always conscious of this fragrance of lovage as she tidied the room. She dusted the heavy mahogany pieces punctiliously after she had opened the bed as her sister had directed. She spread fresh towels over the wash-stand and the bureau; she made the bed. Then she thought to take the purple gown from the easy chair and carry it to the garret and put it in the trunk with the other articles of the dead woman's wardrobe which had been packed away there; *but the purple gown was not on the chair!*

Amanda Gill was not a woman of strong convictions even as to her own actions. She directly thought that possibly she had been mistaken and had not removed it from the closet. She glanced at the closet door and saw with surprise that it was open, and she had thought she had closed it, but she instantly was not sure of that. So she entered the closet and looked for the purple gown. *It was not there!*

Amanda Gill went feebly out of the closet and looked at the easy chair again. The purple gown was not there! She looked wildly around the room. She went down on her trembling knees and peered under the bed, she opened the bureau drawers, she looked again in the closet. Then she stood in the middle of the floor and fairly wrung her hands.

"What does it mean?" she said in a shocked whisper.

She had certainly seen that loose purple gown of her dead Aunt Harriet's.

There is a limit at which self-refutation must stop in any sane person. Amanda Gill had reached it. She knew that she had seen that purple gown in that closet; she knew that she had removed it and put it on the easy chair. She also knew that she had not taken it out of the room. She felt a curious sense of being inverted mentally. It was as if all her traditions and laws of life were on their heads. Never in her simple record had any garment not remained where she had placed it unless removed by some palpable human agency.

Then the thought occurred to her that possibly her sister Sophia might have entered the room unobserved while her back was turned and removed the dress. A sensation of relief came over her. Her blood seemed to flow back into its usual channels; the tension of her nerves relaxed.

"How silly I am," she said aloud.

She hurried out and downstairs into the kitchen where Sophia was making cake, stirring with splendid circular sweeps of a wooden spoon a creamy yellow mass. She looked up as her sister entered.

"Have you got it done?" said she.

"Yes," replied Amanda. Then she hesitated. A sudden terror overcame her. It did not seem as if it were at all probable that Sophia had left that foamy cake mixture a second to go to Aunt Harriet's chamber and remove that purple gown.

"Well," said Sophia, "if you have got that done I wish you would take hold and string those beans. The first thing we know there won't be time to boil them for dinner."

Amanda moved toward the pan of beans on the table, then she looked at her sister.

"Did you come up in Aunt Harriet's room while I was there?" she asked weakly.

She knew while she asked what the answer would be.

"Up in Aunt Harriet's room? Of course I didn't. I couldn't leave this cake without having it fall. You know that well enough. Why?"

"Nothing," replied Amanda.

Suddenly she realized that she could not tell her sister what had happened, for before the utter absurdity of the whole thing her belief in her own reason quailed. She knew what Sophia would say if she told her. She could hear her.

"Amanda Gill, have you gone stark staring mad?"

She resolved that she would never tell Sophia. She dropped into a chair and begun shelling the beans with nerveless fingers. Sophia looked at her curiously.

"Amanda Gill, what on earth ails you?" she asked.

"Nothing," replied Amanda. She bent her head very low over the green pods.

"Yes, there is, too! You are as white as a sheet, and your hands are shaking so you can hardly string those beans. I did think you had more sense, Amanda Gill."

"I don't know what you mean, Sophia."

"Yes, you do know what I mean, too; you needn't pretend you don't. Why did you ask me if I had been in that room, and why do you act so queer?"

Amanda hesitated. She had been trained to truth. Then she lied.

"I wondered if you'd noticed how it had leaked in on the paper over by the bureau, that last rain," said she.

"What makes you look so pale then?"

"I don't know. I guess the heat sort of overcame me."

"I shouldn't think it could have been very hot in that room when it had been shut up so long," said Sophia.

She was evidently not satisfied, but then the grocer came to the door and the matter dropped.

For the next hour the two women were very busy. They kept no servant. When they had come into possession of this fine old place by the death of their aunt it had seemed a doubtful blessing. There was not a cent with which to pay for repairs and taxes and insurance, except the twelve hundred dollars which they had obtained from the sale of the little house in which they had been born and lived all their lives. There had been a division in the old Ackley family years before. One of the daughters had married against her mother's wish and had been disinherited. She had married a poor man by the name of Gill, and shared his humble lot in sight of her former home and her sister and mother living in prosperity, until she had borne three daughters; then she died, worn out with overwork and worry.

The mother and the elder sister had been pitiless to the last. Neither had ever spoken to her since she left her home the night of her marriage. They were hard women.

The three daughters of the disinherited sister had lived quiet and poor, but not actually needy lives. Jane, the middle daughter, had married, and died in less than a year. Amanda and Sophia had taken the girl baby she left when the father married again. Sophia had taught a primary school for many years; she had saved enough to buy the little house in which they lived. Amanda had crocheted lace, and embroidered flannel, and made tidies and pincushions, and had earned enough for her clothes and the child's, little Flora Scott.

Their father, William Gill, had died before they were thirty, and now in their late middle life had come the death of the aunt to whom they had never spoken, although they had often seen her, who had lived in solitary state in the old Ackley mansion until she was more than eighty. There had been no will, and they were the only heirs with the exception of young Flora Scott, the daughter of the dead sister.

Sophia and Amanda thought directly of Flora when they knew of the inheritance.

"It will be a splendid thing for her; she will have enough to live on when we are gone," Sophia said.

She had promptly decided what was to be done. The small house was to be sold, and they were to move into the old Ackley house and take boarders to pay for its keeping. She scouted the idea of selling it. She had an enormous family pride. She had always held her head high when she had walked past that fine old mansion, the cradle of her race, which she was forbidden to enter. She was unmoved when the lawyer who was advising her disclosed to her the fact that Harriet Ackley had used every cent of the Ackley money.

"I realize that we have to work," said she, "but my sister and I have determined to keep the place."

That was the end of the discussion. Sophia and Amanda Gill had been living in the old Ackley house a fortnight, and they had three boarders: an elderly widow with a comfortable income, a young Congregationalist clergyman, and the middle-aged single woman who had charge of the village library. Now the school-teacher from Acton, Miss Louisa Stark, was expected for the summer, and would make four.

Sophia considered that they were comfortably provided for. Her wants and her sister's were very few, and even the niece, although a young girl, had small expenses, since her wardrobe was supplied for years to come from that of the deceased aunt. There were stored away in the garret of the Ackley house enough voluminous black silks and satins and bombazines to keep her clad in somber richness for years to come.

Flora was a very gentle girl, with large, serious blue eyes, a seldom-smiling, pretty mouth, and smooth flaxen hair. She was delicate and very young—sixteen on her next birthday.

She came home soon now with her parcels of sugar and tea from the grocer's. She entered the kitchen gravely and deposited them on the table by which her Aunt Amanda was seated stringing beans. Flora wore an obsolete turban-shaped hat of black straw which had belonged to the dead aunt; it set high like a crown, revealing her forehead. Her dress was an ancient purple-and-white print, too long and too large except over the chest, where it held her like a straight waistcoat.

"You had better take off your hat, Flora," said Sophia. She turned suddenly to Amanda. "Did you fill the water-pitcher in that chamber for the schoolteacher?" she asked severely. She was quite sure that Amanda had not filled the water-pitcher.

Amanda blushed and started guiltily. "I declare, I don't believe I did," said she.

"I didn't think you had," said her sister with sarcastic emphasis.

"Flora, you go up to the room that was your Great-aunt Harriet's, and take the water-pitcher off the wash-stand and fill it with water. Be real careful, and don't break the pitcher, and don't spill the water."

"In *that* chamber?" asked Flora. She spoke very quietly, but her face changed a little.

"Yes, in that chamber," returned her Aunt Sophia sharply. "Go right along."

Flora went, and her light footstep was heard on the stairs. Very soon she returned with the blue-and-white water-pitcher and filled it carefully at the kitchen sink.

"Now be careful and not spill it," said Sophia as she went out of the room carrying it gingerly.

Amanda gave a timidly curious glance at her; she wondered if she had seen the purple gown.

Then she started, for the village stagecoach was seen driving around to the front of the house. The house stood on a corner.

"Here, Amanda, you look better than I do; you go and meet her," said Sophia. "I'll just put the cake in the pan and get it in the oven and I'll come. Show her right up to her room."

Amanda removed her apron hastily and obeyed. Sophia hurried with her cake, pouring it into the baking-tins. She had just put it in the oven, when the door opened and Flora entered carrying the blue water-pitcher.

"What are you bringing down that pitcher again for?" asked Sophia.

"She wants some water, and Aunt Amanda sent me," replied Flora.

Her pretty pale face had a bewildered expression.

"For the land sake, she hasn't used all that great pitcherful of water so quick?"

"There wasn't any water in it," replied Flora.

Her high, childish forehead was contracted slightly with a puzzled frown as she looked at her aunt.

"Wasn't any water in it?"

"No, ma'am."

"Didn't I see you filling the pitcher with water not ten minutes ago, I want to know?"

"Yes, ma'am."

"What did you do with that water?"

"Nothing."

"Did you carry that pitcherful of water up to that room and set it on the wash-stand?"

"Yes, ma'am."

"Didn't you spill it?"

"No, ma'am."

"Now, Flora Scott, I want the truth! Did you fill that pitcher with water and carry it up there, and wasn't there any there when she came to use it?"

"Yes, ma'am."

"Let me see that pitcher." Sophia examined the pitcher. It was not only perfectly dry from top to bottom, but even a little dusty. She turned severely on the young girl. "That shows," said she, "you did not fill the pitcher at all. You let the water run at the side because you didn't want to carry it upstairs. I am ashamed of you. It's bad enough to be so lazy, but when it comes to not telling the truth—"

The young girl's face broke up suddenly into piteous confusion, and her blue eyes became filmy with tears.

"I did fill the pitcher, honest," she faltered, "I did, Aunt Sophia. You ask Aunt Amanda."

"I'll ask nobody. This pitcher is proof enough. Water don't go off and leave the pitcher dusty on the inside if it was put in ten minutes ago. Now you fill that pitcher full quick, and you carry it upstairs, and if you spill a drop there'll be something besides talk."

Flora filled the pitcher, with the tears falling over her cheeks. She sniveled softly as she went out, balancing it carefully against her slender hip. Sophia followed her.

"Stop crying," said she sharply; "you ought to be ashamed of yourself. What do you suppose Miss Louisa Stark will think. No water in her pitcher in the first place, and then you come back crying as if you didn't want to get it."

In spite of herself, Sophia's voice was soothing. She was very fond of the girl. She followed her up the stairs to the chamber where Miss Louisa Stark was waiting for the water to remove the soil of travel. She had removed her bonnet, and its tuft of red geraniums lightened the obscurity of the mahogany dresser. She had placed her little beaded cape carefully on the bed. She was replying to a tremulous remark of Amanda's, who was nearly fainting from the new mystery of the water-pitcher, that it was warm and she suffered a good deal in warm weather.

Louisa Stark was stout and solidly built. She was much larger than either of the Gill sisters. She was a masterly woman inured to command from years of school-teaching. She carried her swelling bulk with majesty; even her face, moist and red with the heat, lost nothing of its dignity of expression.

She was standing in the middle of the floor with an air which gave the effect of her standing upon an elevation. She turned when Sophia and Flora, carrying the water-pitcher, entered.

"This is my sister Sophia," said Amanda tremulously.

Sophia advanced, shook hands with Miss Louisa Stark and bade her welcome and hoped she would like her room. Then she moved toward the closet. "There is a nice large closet in this room—the best closet in the house. You might have your trunk—" she said, then she stopped short.

The closet door was ajar, and a purple garment seemed suddenly to swing into view as if impelled by some wind.

"Why, here is something left in this closet," Sophia said in a mortified tone. "I thought all those things had been taken away."

She pulled down the garment with a jerk, and as she did so Amanda passed her in a weak rush for the door.

"I am afraid your sister is not well," said the school-teacher from Acton. "She looked very pale when you took that dress down. I noticed it at once. Hadn't you better go and see what the matter is? She may be going to faint."

"She is not subject to fainting spells," replied Sophia, but she followed Amanda.

She found her in the room which they occupied together, lying on the bed, very pale and gasping. She leaned over her.

"Amanda, what is the matter; don't you feel well?" she asked.

"I feel a little faint."

Sophia got a camphor bottle and began rubbing her sister's forehead.

"Do you feel better?" she said.

Amanda nodded.

"I guess it was that green apple pie you ate this noon," said Sophia. "I declare, what did I do with that dress of Aunt Harriet's? I guess if you feel better I'll just run and get it and take it up garret. I'll stop in here again when I come down. You'd better lay still. Flora can bring you up a cup of tea. I wouldn't try to eat any supper."

Sophia's tone as she left the room was full of loving concern. Presently she returned; she looked disturbed, but angrily so. There was not the slightest hint of any fear in her expression.

"I want to know," said she, looking sharply and quickly around, "if I brought that purple dress in here, after all?"

"I didn't see you," replied Amanda.

"I must have. It isn't in that chamber, nor the closet. You aren't lying on it, are you?"

"I lay down before you came in," replied Amanda.

"So you did. Well, I'll go and look again."

Presently Amanda heard her sister's heavy step on the garret stairs. Then she returned with a queer defiant expression on her face.

"I carried it up garret, after all, and put it in the trunk," said, she. "I declare, I forgot it. I suppose your being faint sort of put it out of my head. There it was, folded up just as nice, right where I put it."

Sophia's mouth was set; her eyes upon her sister's scared, agitated face were full of hard challenge.

"Yes," murmured Amanda.

"I must go right down and see to that cake," said Sophia, going out of the room. "If you don't feel well, you pound on the floor with the umbrella."

Amanda looked after her. She knew that Sophia had not put that purple dress of her dead Aunt Harriet in the trunk in the garret.

Meantime Miss Louisa Stark was settling herself in the southwest chamber. She unpacked her trunk and hung her dresses carefully in the closet. She filled the bureau drawers with nicely folded linen and small articles of dress. She was a very punctilious woman. She put on a black India silk dress with purple flowers. She combed her grayish-blond hair in smooth ridges back from her broad forehead. She pinned her lace at her throat with a brooch, very handsome, although somewhat obsolete—a bunch of pearl grapes on black onyx, set in gold filagree. She had purchased it several years ago with a considerable portion of the stipend from her spring term of school-teaching.

As she surveyed herself in the little swing mirror surmounting the old-fashioned mahogany bureau she suddenly bent forward and looked closely at the brooch. It seemed to her that something was wrong with it. As she looked she became sure. Instead of the familiar bunch of pearl grapes on the black onyx, she saw a knot of blonde and black hair under glass surrounded by a border of twisted gold. She felt a thrill of horror, though she could not tell why. She unpinned the brooch, and it was her own familiar one, the pearl grapes and the onyx. "How very foolish I am," she thought. She thrust the pin in the laces at her throat and again looked at herself in the glass, and there it was again—the knot of blond and black hair and the twisted gold.

Louisa Stark looked at her own large, firm face above the brooch and it was full of terror and dismay which were new to it. She straightway began to wonder if there could be anything wrong with her mind. She remembered that an aunt of her mother's had been insane. A sort of fury with herself possessed her. She stared at the brooch in the glass with eyes at once angry and terrified. Then she removed it again and there was her own old brooch. Finally she thrust the gold pin through the lace again, fastened it and turning a defiant back on the glass, went down to supper.

At the supper table she met the other boarders—the elderly widow, the young clergyman and the middle-aged librarian. She viewed the elderly widow with reserve, the clergyman with respect, the middle-aged librarian with suspicion. The latter wore a very youthful shirt-waist, and her hair in a girlish fashion which the school-teacher, who twisted hers severely from the straining roots at the nape of her neck to the small, smooth coil at the top, condemned as straining after effects no longer hers by right.

The librarian, who had a quick acridness of manner, addressed her, asking what room she had, and asked the second time in spite of the school-teacher's evident reluctance to hear her. She even, since she sat next to her, nudged her familiarly in her rigid black silk side.

"What room are you in, Miss Stark?" said she.

"I am at a loss how to designate the room," replied Miss Stark stiffly.

"Is it the big southwest room?"

"It evidently faces in that direction," said Miss Stark.

The librarian, whose name was Eliza Lippincott, turned abruptly to Miss Amanda Gill, over whose delicate face a curious colour compounded of flush and pallour was stealing.

"What room did your aunt die in, Miss Amanda?" asked she abruptly.

Amanda cast a terrified glance at her sister, who was serving a second plate of pudding for the minister.

"That room," she replied feebly.

"That's what I thought," said the librarian with a certain triumph. "I calculated that must be the room she died in, for it's the best room in the house, and you haven't put anybody in it before. Somehow the room that anybody has died in lately is generally the last room that anybody is put in. I suppose *you* are so strong-minded you don't object to sleeping in a room where anybody died a few weeks ago?" she inquired of Louisa Stark with sharp eyes on her face.

"No, I do not," replied Miss stark with emphasis.

"Nor in the same bed?" persisted Eliza Lippincott with a kittenish reflection.

The young minister looked up from his pudding. He was very spiritual, but he had had poor pickings in his previous boarding place, and he could not help a certain abstract enjoyment over Miss Gill's cooking.

"You would certainly not be afraid, Miss Lippincott?" he remarked, with his gentle, almost caressing inflection of tone. "You do not for a minute believe that a higher power would allow any manifestation on the part of a disembodied spirit—who we trust is in her heavenly home—to harm one of His servants?"

"Oh, Mr. Dunn, of course not," replied Eliza Lippincott with a blush. "Of course not. I never meant to imply—"

"I could not believe you did," said the minister gently. He was very young, but he already had a wrinkle of permanent anxiety between his eyes and a smile of permanent ingratiation on his lips. The lines of the smile were as deeply marked as the wrinkle.

"Of course dear Miss Harriet Gill was a professing Christian," remarked the widow, "and I don't suppose a professing Christian would come back and scare folks if she could. I wouldn't be a mite afraid to sleep in that room; I'd rather have it than the one I've got. If I was afraid to sleep in a room where a good woman died, I wouldn't tell of it. If I saw things or heard things I'd think the fault must be with my own guilty conscience." Then she turned to Miss Stark. "Any time you feel timid in that room I'm ready and willing to change with you," said she.

"Thank you; I have no desire to change. I am perfectly satisfied with my room," replied Miss Stark with freezing dignity, which was thrown away upon the widow.

"Well," said she, "any time, if you should feel timid, you know what to do. I've got a real nice room; it faces east and gets the morning sun, but it isn't so nice as yours, according to my way of thinking. I'd rather take my chances any day in a room anybody had died in than in one that was hot in summer. I'm more afraid of a sunstroke than of spooks, for my part."

Miss Sophia Gill, who had not spoken one word, but whose mouth had become more and more rigidly compressed, suddenly rose from the table, forcing the minister to leave a little pudding, at which he glanced regretfully.

Miss Louisa Stark did not sit down in the parlour with the other boarders. She went straight to her room. She felt tired after her journey, and meditated a loose wrapper and writing a few letters quietly before she went to bed. Then, too, she was conscious of a feeling that if she delayed, the going there at all might assume more terrifying proportions. She was full of defiance against herself and her own lurking weakness.

So she went resolutely and entered the southwest chamber. There was through the room a soft twilight. She could dimly discern everything, the white satin scroll-work on the wall paper and the white counterpane on the bed being most evident. Consequently both arrested her attention first. She saw against the wall-paper directly facing the door the waist of her best black satin dress hung over a picture.

"That is very strange," she said to herself, and again a thrill of vague horror came over her.

She knew, or thought she knew, that she had put that black satin dress waist away nicely folded between towels in her trunk. She was very choice of her black satin dress.

She took down the black waist and laid it on the bed preparatory to folding it, but when she attempted to do so she discovered that the two sleeves were firmly sewed together. Louisa Stark stared at the sewed sleeves. "What does this mean?" she asked herself. She examined the sewing carefully; the stitches were small, and even, and firm, of black silk.

She looked around the room. On the stand beside the bed was something which she had not noticed before: a little old-fashioned work-box with a picture of a little boy in a pinafore on the top. Beside this work-box lay, as if just laid down by the user, a spool of black silk, a pair of scissors, and a large steel thimble with a hole in the top, after an old style. Louisa stared at these, then at the sleeves of her dress. She moved toward the door. For a moment she thought that this was something legitimate about which she might demand information; then she became doubtful. Suppose that work-box had been there all the time; suppose she had forgotten; suppose she herself had done this absurd thing, or suppose that she had not, what was to hinder the others from thinking so; what was to hinder a doubt being cast upon her own memory and reasoning powers?

Louisa Stark had been on the verge of a nervous breakdown in spite of her iron constitution and her great will power. No woman can teach school for forty years with absolute impunity. She was more credulous as to her own possible failings than she had ever been in her whole life. She was cold with horror and terror, and yet not so much horror and terror of the supernatural as of her own self. The weakness of belief in the supernatural was nearly impossible for this strong nature. She could more easily believe in her own failing powers.

"I don't know but I'm going to be like Aunt Marcia," she said to herself, and her fat face took on a long rigidity of fear.

She started toward the mirror to unfasten her dress, then she remembered the strange circumstance of the brooch and stopped short. Then she straightened herself defiantly and marched up to the bureau and looked in the glass. She saw reflected therein, fastening the lace at her throat, the old-fashioned thing of a large oval, a knot of fair and black hair under glass, set in a rim of twisted gold. She unfastened it with trembling fingers and looked at it. It was her own brooch, the cluster of pearl grapes on black onyx. Louisa Stark placed the trinket in its little box on the nest of pink cotton and put it away in the bureau drawer. Only death could disturb her habit of order.

Her fingers were so cold they felt fairly numb as she unfastened her dress; she staggered when she slipped it over her head. She went to the closet to hang it up and recoiled. A strong smell of lovage came in her nostrils; a purple gown near the door swung softly against her face as if impelled by some wind from within. All the pegs were filled with garments not her own, mostly of somber black, but there were some strange-patterned silk things and satins.

Suddenly Louisa Stark recovered her nerve. This, she told herself, was something distinctly tangible. Somebody had been taking liberties with her wardrobe. Somebody had been hanging some one else's clothes in her closet. She hastily slipped on her dress again and marched straight down to the parlour. The people were seated there; the widow and the minister were playing backgammon. The librarian was watching them. Miss Amanda Gill was mending beside the large lamp on the centre table. They all looked up with amazement as Louisa Stark entered. There was something strange in her expression. She noticed none of them except Amanda.

"Where is your sister?" she asked peremptorily of her.

"She's in the kitchen mixing up bread," Amanda quavered; "is there anything—" But the school-teacher was gone.

She found Sophia Gill standing by the kitchen table kneading dough with dignity. The young girl Flora was bringing some flour from the pantry. She stopped and stared at Miss Stark, and her pretty, delicate young face took on an expression of alarm.

Miss Stark opened at once upon the subject in her mind.

"Miss Gill," said she, with her utmost school-teacher manner, "I wish to inquire why you have had my own clothes removed from the closet in my room and others substituted?"

Sophia Gill stood with her hands fast in the dough, regarding her. Her own face paled slowly and reluctantly, her mouth stiffened.

"What? I don't quite understand what you mean, Miss Stark," said she.

"My clothes are not in the closet in my room and it is full of things which do not belong to me," said Louisa Stark.

"Bring me that flour," said Sophia sharply to the young girl, who obeyed, casting timid, startled glances at Miss Stark as she passed her. Sophia Gill began rubbing her hands clear of the dough. "I am sure I know nothing about it," she said with a certain tempered asperity. "Do you know anything about it, Flora?"

"Oh, no, I don't know anything about it, Aunt Sophia," answered the young girl, fluttering.

Then Sophia turned to Miss Stark. "I'll go upstairs with you, Miss Stark," said she, "and see what the trouble is. There must be some mistake." She spoke stiffly with constrained civility.

"Very well," said Miss Stark with dignity. Then she and Miss Sophia went upstairs. Flora stood staring after them.

Sophia and Louisa Stark went up to the southwest chamber. The closet door was shut. Sophia threw it open, then she looked at Miss Stark. On the pegs hung the school-teacher's own garments in ordinary array.

"I can't see that there is anything wrong," remarked Sophia grimly.

Miss Stark strove to speak but she could not. She sank down on the nearest chair. She did not even attempt to defend herself. She saw her own clothes in the closet. She knew there had been no time for any human being to remove those which she thought she had seen and put hers in their places. She knew it was impossible. Again the awful horror of herself overwhelmed her.

"You must have been mistaken," she heard Sophia say.

She muttered something, she scarcely knew what. Sophia then went out of the room. Presently she undressed and went to bed. In the morning she did not go down to breakfast, and when Sophia came to inquire, requested that the stage be ordered for the noon train. She said that she was sorry, but was ill, and feared lest she might be worse, and she felt that she must return home at once. She looked ill, and could not take even the toast and tea which Sophia had prepared for her. Sophia felt a certain pity for her, but it was largely mixed with indignation. She felt that she knew the true reason for the school-teacher's illness and sudden departure, and it incensed her.

"If folks are going to act like fools we shall never be able to keep this house," she said to Amanda after Miss Stark had gone; and Amanda knew what she meant.

Directly the widow, Mrs. Elvira Simmons, knew that the school-teacher had gone and the southwest room was vacant, she begged to have it in exchange for her own. Sophia hesitated a moment; she eyed the widow sharply. There was something about the large, roseate face worn in firm lines of humour and decision which reassured her.

"I have no objection, Mrs. Simmons," said she, "if—"

"If what?" asked the widow.

"If you have common sense enough not to keep fussing because the room happens to be the one my aunt died in," said Sophia bluntly.

"Fiddlesticks!" said the widow, Mrs. Elvira Simmons.

That very afternoon she moved into the southwest chamber. The young girl Flora assisted her, though much against her will.

"Now I want you to carry Mrs. Simmons' dresses into the closet in that room and hang them up nicely, and see that she has everything she wants," said Sophia Gill. "And you can change the bed and put on fresh sheets. What are you looking at me that way for?"

"Oh, Aunt Sophia, can't I do something else?"

"What do you want to do something else for?"

"I am afraid."

"Afraid of what? I should think you'd hang your head. No; you go right in there and do what I tell you."

Pretty soon Flora came running into the sitting-room where Sophia was, as pale as death, and in her hand she held a queer, old-fashioned frilled nightcap.

"What's that?" demanded Sophia.

"I found it under the pillow."

"What pillow?"

"In the southwest room."

Sophia took it and looked at it sternly.

"It's Great-aunt Harriet's," said Flora faintly.

"You run down street and do that errand at the grocer's for me and I'll see that room," said Sophia with dignity. She carried the nightcap away and put it in the trunk in the garret where she had supposed it stored with the rest of the dead woman's belongings. Then she went into the southwest chamber and made the bed and assisted Mrs. Simmons to move, and there was no further incident.

The widow was openly triumphant over her new room. She talked a deal about it at the dinner-table.

"It is the best room in the house, and I expect you all to be envious of me," said she.

"And you are sure you don't feel afraid of ghosts?" said the librarian.

"Ghosts!" repeated the widow with scorn. "If a ghost comes I'll send her over to you. You are just across the hall from the southwest room."

"You needn't," returned Eliza Lippincott with a shudder. "I wouldn't sleep in that room, after—" she checked herself with an eye on the minister.

"After what?" asked the widow.

"Nothing," replied Eliza Lippincott in an embarrassed fashion.

"I trust Miss Lippincott has too good sense and too great faith to believe in anything of that sort," said the minister.

"I trust so, too," replied Eliza hurriedly.

"You did see or hear something—now what was it, I want to know?" said the widow that evening when they were alone in the parlour. The minister had gone to make a call.

Eliza hesitated.

"What was it?" insisted the widow.

"Well," said Eliza hesitatingly, "if you'll promise not to tell."

"Yes, I promise; what was it?"

"Well, one day last week, just before the school-teacher came, I went in that room to see if there were any clouds. I wanted to wear my gray dress, and I was afraid it was going to rain, so I wanted to look at the sky at all points, so I went in there, and—"

"And what?"

"Well, you know that chintz over the bed, and the valance, and the easy chair; what pattern should you say it was?"

"Why, peacocks on a blue ground. Good land, I shouldn't think any one who had ever seen that would forget it."

"Peacocks on a blue ground, you are sure?"

"Of course I am. Why?"

"Only when I went in there that afternoon it was not peacocks on a blue ground; it was great red roses on a yellow ground."

"Why, what do you mean?"

"What I say."

"Did Miss Sophia have it changed?"

"No. I went in there again an hour later and the peacocks were there."

"You didn't see straight the first time."

"I expected you would say that."

"The peacocks are there now; I saw them just now."

"Yes, I suppose so; I suppose they flew back."

"But they couldn't."

"Looks as if they did."

"Why, how could such a thing be? It couldn't be."

"Well, all I know is those peacocks were gone for an hour that afternoon and the red roses on the yellow ground were there instead."

The widow stared at her a moment, then she began to laugh rather hysterically.

"Well," said she, "I guess I sha'n't give up my nice room for any such tomfoolery as that. I guess I would just as soon have red roses on a yellow ground as peacocks on a blue; but there's no use talking, you couldn't have seen straight. How could such a thing have happened?"

"I don't know," said Eliza Lippincott; "but I know I wouldn't sleep in that room if you'd give me a thousand dollars."

"Well, I would," said the widow, "and I'm going to."

When Mrs. Simmons went to the southwest chamber that night she cast a glance at the bed-hanging and the easy chair. There were the peacocks on the blue ground. She gave a contemptuous thought to Eliza Lippincott.

"I don't believe but she's getting nervous," she thought. "I wonder if any of her family have been out at all."

But just before Mrs. Simmons was ready to get into bed she looked again at the hangings and the easy chair, and there were the red roses on the yellow ground instead of the peacocks on the blue. She looked long and sharply. Then she shut her eyes, and then opened them and looked. She still saw the red roses. Then she crossed the room, turned her back to the bed, and looked out at the night from the south window. It was clear and the full moon was shining. She watched it a moment sailing over the dark blue in its nimbus of gold. Then she looked around at the bed hangings. She still saw the red roses on the yellow ground.

Mrs. Simmons was struck in her most vulnerable point. This apparent contradiction of the reasonable as manifested in such a commonplace thing as chintz of a bed-hanging affected this ordinarily unimaginative woman as no ghostly appearance could have done. Those red roses on the yellow ground were to her much more ghostly than any strange figure clad in the white robes of the grave entering the room.

She took a step toward the door, then she turned with a resolute air. "As for going downstairs and owning up I'm scared and having that Lippincott girl crowing over me, I won't for any red roses instead of peacocks. I guess they can't hurt me, and as long as we've both of us seen 'em I guess we can't both be getting loony," she said.

Mrs. Elvira Simmons blew out her light and got into bed and lay staring out between the chintz hangings at the moonlit room. She said her prayers in bed always as being more comfortable, and presumably just as acceptable in the case of a faithful servant with a stout habit of body. Then after a little she fell asleep; she was of too practical a nature to be kept long awake by anything which had no power of actual bodily effect upon her. No stress of the spirit had ever disturbed her slumbers. So she slumbered between the red roses, or the peacocks, she did not know which.

But she was awakened about midnight by a strange sensation in her throat. She had dreamed that some one with long white fingers was strangling her, and she saw bending over her the face of an old woman in a white cap. When she waked there was no old woman, the room was almost as light as day in the full moonlight, and looked very peaceful; but the strangling sensation at her throat continued, and besides that, her face and ears felt muffled. She put up her hand and felt that her head was covered with a ruffled nightcap tied under her chin so tightly that it was exceedingly uncomfortable. A great qualm of horror shot over her. She tore the thing off frantically and flung it from her with a convulsive effort as if it had been a spider. She gave, as she did so, a quick, short scream of terror. She sprang out of bed and was going toward the door, when she stopped.

It had suddenly occurred to her that Eliza Lippincott might have entered the room and tied on the cap while she was asleep. She had not locked her door. She looked in the closet, under the bed; there was no one there. Then she tried to open the door, but to her astonishment found that it was locked—bolted on the inside. "I must have locked it, after all," she reflected with wonder, for she never locked her door. Then she could scarcely conceal from herself that there was something out of the usual about it all. Certainly no one could have entered the room and departed locking the door on the inside. She could not control the long shiver of horror that crept over her, but she was still resolute. She resolved that she would throw the cap out of the window. "I'll see if I have tricks like that played on me, I don't care who does it," said she quite aloud. She was still unable to believe wholly in the supernatural. The idea of some human agency was still in her mind, filling her with anger.

She went toward the spot where she had thrown the cap—she had stepped over it on her way to the door—but it was not there. She searched the whole room, lighting her lamp, but she could not find the cap. Finally she gave it up. She extinguished her lamp and went back to bed. She fell asleep again, to be again awakened in the same fashion. That time she tore off the cap as before, but she did not fling it on the floor as before. Instead she held to it with a fierce grip. Her blood was up.

Holding fast to the white flimsy thing, she sprang out of bed, ran to the window which was open, slipped the screen, and flung it out; but a sudden gust of wind, though the night was calm, arose and it floated back in her face. She brushed it aside like a cobweb and she clutched at it. She was actually furious. It eluded her clutching fingers. Then she did not see it at all. She examined the floor, she lighted her lamp again and searched, but there was no sign of it.

Mrs. Simmons was then in such a rage that all terror had disappeared for the time. She did not know with what she was angry, but she had a sense of some mocking presence which was silently proving too strong against her weakness, and she was aroused to the utmost power of resistance. To be baffled like this and resisted by something which was as nothing to her straining senses filled her with intensest resentment.

Finally she got back into bed again; she did not go to sleep. She felt strangely drowsy, but she fought against it. She was wide awake, staring at the moonlight, when she suddenly felt the soft white strings of the thing tighten around her throat and realized that her enemy was again upon her. She seized the strings, untied them, twitched off the cap, ran with it to the table where her scissors lay and furiously cut it into small bits. She cut and tore, feeling an insane fury of gratification.

"There!" said she quite aloud. "I guess I sha'n't have any more trouble with this old cap."

She tossed the bits of muslin into a basket and went back to bed. Almost immediately she felt the soft strings tighten around her throat. Then at last she yielded, vanquished. This new refutal of all laws of reason by which she had learned, as it were, to spell her theory of life, was too much for her equilibrium. She pulled off the clinging strings feebly, drew the thing from her head, slid weakly out of bed, caught up her wrapper and hastened out of the room. She went noiselessly along the hall to her own old room: she entered, got into her familiar bed, and lay there the rest of the night shuddering and listening, and if she dozed, waking with a start at the feeling of the pressure upon her throat to find that it was not there, yet still to be unable to shake off entirely the horror.

When daylight came she crept back to the southwest chamber and hurriedly got some clothes in which to dress herself. It took all her resolution to enter the room, but nothing unusual happened while she was there. She hastened back to her old chamber, dressed herself and went down to breakfast with an imperturbable face. Her colour had not faded. When asked by Eliza Lippincott how she had slept, she replied with an appearance of calmness which was bewildering that she had not slept very well. She never did sleep very well in a new bed, and she thought she would go back to her old room.

Eliza Lippincott was not deceived, however, neither were the Gill sisters, nor the young girl, Flora. Eliza Lippincott spoke out bluntly.

"You needn't talk to me about sleeping well," said she. "I know something queer happened in that room last night by the way you act."

They all looked at Mrs. Simmons, inquiringly—the librarian with malicious curiosity and triumph, the minister with sad incredulity, Sophia Gill with fear and indignation, Amanda and the young girl with unmixed terror. The widow bore herself with dignity.

"I saw nothing nor heard nothing which I trust could not have been accounted for in some rational manner," said she.

"What was it?" persisted Eliza Lippincott.

"I do not wish to discuss the matter any further," replied Mrs. Simmons shortly. Then she passed her plate for more creamed potato. She felt that she would die before she confessed to the ghastly absurdity of that nightcap, or to having been disturbed by the flight of peacocks off a blue field of chintz after she had scoffed at the possibility of such a thing. She left the whole matter so vague that in a fashion she came off the mistress of the situation. She at all events impressed everybody by her coolness in the face of no one knew what nightly terror.

After breakfast, with the assistance of Amanda and Flora, she moved back into her old room. Scarcely a word was spoken during the process of moving, but they all worked with trembling haste and looked guilty when they met one another's eyes, as if conscious of betraying a common fear.

That afternoon the young minister, John Dunn, went to Sophia Gill and requested permission to occupy the southwest chamber that night.

"I don't ask to have my effects moved there," said he, "for I could scarcely afford a room so much superior to the one I now occupy, but I would like, if you please, to sleep there to-night for the purpose of refuting in my own person any unfortunate superstition which may have obtained root here."

Sophia Gill thanked the minister gratefully and eagerly accepted his offer.

"How anybody with common sense can believe for a minute in any such nonsense passes my comprehension," said she.

"It certainly passes mine how anybody with Christian faith can believe in ghosts," said the minister gently, and Sophia Gill felt a certain feminine contentment in hearing him. The minister was a child to her; she regarded him with no tincture of sentiment, and yet she loved to hear two other women covertly condemned by him and she herself thereby exalted.

That night about twelve o'clock the Reverend John Dunn essayed to go to his nightly slumber in the southwest chamber. He had been sitting up until that hour preparing his sermon.

He traversed the hall with a little night-lamp in his hand, opened the door of the southwest chamber, and essayed to enter. He might as well have essayed to enter the solid side of a house. He could not believe his senses. The door was certainly open; he could look into the room full of soft lights and shadows under the moonlight which streamed into the windows. He could see the bed in which he had expected to pass the night, but he could not enter. Whenever he strove to do so he had a curious sensation as if he were trying to press against an invisible person who met him with a force of opposition impossible to overcome. The minister was not an athletic man, yet he had considerable strength. He squared his elbows, set his mouth hard, and strove to push his way through into the room. The opposition which he met was as sternly and mutely terrible as the rocky fastness of a mountain in his way.

For a half hour John Dunn, doubting, raging, overwhelmed with spiritual agony as to the state of his own soul rather than fear, strove to enter that southwest chamber. He was simply powerless against this uncanny obstacle. Finally a great horror as of evil itself came over him. He was a nervous man and very young. He fairly fled to his own chamber and locked himself in like a terror-stricken girl.

The next morning he went to Miss Gill and told her frankly what had happened, and begged her to say nothing about it lest he should have injured the cause by the betrayal of such weakness, for he actually had come to believe that there was something wrong with the room.

"What it is I know not, Miss Sophia," said he, "but I firmly believe, against my will, that there is in that room some accursed evil power at work, of which modern faith and modern science know nothing."

Miss Sophia Gill listened with grimly lowering face. She had an inborn respect for the clergy, but she was bound to hold that southwest chamber in the dearly beloved old house of her fathers free of blame.

"I think I will sleep in that room myself to-night," she said, when the minister had finished.

He looked at her in doubt and dismay.

"I have great admiration for your faith and courage, Miss Sophia," he said, "but are you wise?"

"I am fully resolved to sleep in that room to-night," said she conclusively. There were occasions when Miss Sophia Gill could put on a manner of majesty, and she did now.

It was ten o'clock that night when Sophia Gill entered the southwest chamber. She had told her sister what she intended doing and had been proof against her tearful entreaties. Amanda was charged not to tell the young girl, Flora.

"There is no use in frightening that child over nothing," said Sophia.

Sophia, when she entered the southwest chamber, set the lamp which she carried on the bureau, and began moving about the rooms pulling down the curtains, taking off the nice white counterpane of the bed, and preparing generally for the night.

As she did so, moving with great coolness and deliberation, she became conscious that she was thinking some thoughts that were foreign to her. She began remembering what she could not have remembered, since she was not then born: the trouble over her mother's marriage, the bitter opposition, the shutting the door upon her, the ostracizing her from heart and home. She became aware of a most singular sensation as of bitter resentment herself, and not against the mother and sister who had so treated her own mother, but against her own mother, and then she became aware of a like bitterness extended to her own self. She felt malignant toward her mother as a young girl whom she remembered, though she could not have remembered, and she felt malignant toward her own self, and her sister Amanda, and Flora. Evil suggestions surged in her brain—suggestions which turned her heart to stone and which still fascinated her. And all the time by a sort of double consciousness she knew that what she thought was strange and not due to her own volition. She knew that she was thinking the thoughts of some other person, and she knew who. She felt herself possessed.

But there was tremendous strength in the woman's nature. She had inherited strength for good and righteous self-assertion, from the evil strength of her ancestors. They had turned their own weapons against themselves. She made an effort which seemed almost mortal, but was conscious that the hideous thing was gone from her. She thought her own thoughts. Then she scouted to herself the idea of anything supernatural about the terrific experience. "I am imagining everything," she told herself. She went on with her preparations; she went to the bureau to take down her hair. She looked in the glass and saw, instead of her softly parted waves of hair, harsh lines of iron-gray under the black borders of an old-fashioned head-dress. She saw instead of her smooth, broad forehead, a high one wrinkled with the intensest concentration of selfish reflections of a long life; she saw instead of her steady blue eyes, black ones with depths of malignant reserve, behind a broad meaning of ill will; she saw instead of her firm, benevolent mouth one with a hard, thin line, a network of melancholic wrinkles. She saw instead of her own face, middle-aged and good to see, the expression of a life of honesty and good will to others and patience under trials, the face of a very old woman scowling forever with unceasing hatred and misery at herself and all others, at life, and death, at that which had been and that which was to come. She saw instead of her own face in the glass, the face of her dead Aunt Harriet, topping her own shoulders in her own well-known dress!

Sophia Gill left the room. She went into the one which she shared with her sister Amanda. Amanda looked up and saw her standing there. She had set the lamp on a table, and she stood holding a handkerchief over her face. Amanda looked at her with terror.

"What is it? What is it, Sophia?" she gasped.

Sophia still stood with the handkerchief pressed to her face.

"Oh, Sophia, let me call somebody. Is your face hurt? Sophia, what is the matter with your face?" fairly shrieked Amanda.

Suddenly Sophia took the handkerchief from her face.

"Look at me, Amanda Gill," she said in an awful voice.

Amanda looked, shrinking.

"What is it? Oh, what is it? You don't look hurt. What is it, Sophia?"

"What do you see?"

"Why, I see you."

"Me?"

"Yes, you. What did you think I would see?"

Sophia Gill looked at her sister. "Never as long as I live will I tell you what I thought you would see, and you must never ask me," said she.

"Well, I never will, Sophia," replied Amanda, half weeping with terror.

"You won't try to sleep in that room again, Sophia?"

"No," said Sophia; "and I am going to sell this house."

The Man Who Went Too Far

E. F. Benson

———◆———

THE LITTLE VILLAGE OF ST. FAITH'S NESTLES IN A HOLLOW OF WOODED hill up on the north bank of the river Fawn in the county of Hampshire, huddling close round its gray Norman church as if for spiritual protection against the fays and fairies, the trolls and "little people," who might be supposed still to linger in the vast empty spaces of the New Forest, and to come after dusk and do their doubtful businesses. Once outside the hamlet you may walk in any direction (so long as you avoid the high road which leads to Brockenhurst) for the length of a summer afternoon without seeing sign of human habitation, or possibly even catching sight of another human being. Shaggy wild ponies may stop their feeding for a moment as you pass, the white scuts of rabbits will vanish into their burrows, a brown viper perhaps will glide from your path into a clump of heather, and unseen birds will chuckle in the bushes, but it may easily happen that for a long day you will see nothing human. But you will not feel in the least lonely; in summer, at any rate, the sunlight will be gay with butterflies, and the air thick with all those woodland sounds which like instruments in an orchestra combine to play the great symphony of the yearly festival of June. Winds whisper in the birches, and sigh among the firs; bees are busy with their redolent labor among the heather, a myriad birds chirp in the green temples of the forest trees, and the voice of the river prattling over stony places, bubbling into pools, chuckling and gulping round corners, gives you the sense that many presences and companions are near at hand.

Yet, oddly enough, though one would have thought that these benign and cheerful influences of wholesome air and spaciousness of forest were very healthful comrades for a man, in so far as nature can really influence this wonderful human genus which has in these centuries learned to defy her most violent storms in its well-established houses, to bridle her torrents and make them light its streets, to tunnel her mountains and plow her seas, the inhabitants of St. Faith's will not willingly venture into the forest after dark. For in spite of the silence and loneliness of the hooded night it seems that a man is not sure in what company he may suddenly find himself, and though it is difficult to get from these villagers any very clear story of occult appearances, the feeling is widespread. One story indeed I have heard with some definiteness, the tale of a monstrous goat that has been seen to skip with hellish glee about the woods and shady places, and this perhaps is connected with the story which I have here attempted to piece together. It too is well-known to them; for all remember the young artist who died here not long ago, a young man, or so he struck the beholder, of great personal beauty, with something about him that made men's faces to smile and brighten when they looked on him. His ghost they will tell you "walks" constantly by the stream and through the woods which he loved so, and in especial it haunts a certain house, the last of the village, where he lived, and its garden in which he was done to death. For my part I am inclined to think that the terror of the Forest dates chiefly from that day. So, such as the story is, I have set it forth in connected form. It is based partly on the accounts of the villagers, but mainly on that of Darcy, a friend of mine and a friend of the man with whom these events were chiefly concerned.

The day had been one of untarnished midsummer splendor, and as the sun drew near to its setting, the glory of the evening grew every moment more crystalline, more miraculous. Westward from St. Faith's the beechwood which stretched for some miles toward the heathery upland beyond already cast its veil of clear shadow over the red roofs of the village, but the spire of the gray church, over-topping all, still pointed a flaming orange finger into the sky. The river Fawn, which runs below, lay in sheets of sky-reflected blue, and wound its dreamy devious course round the edge of this wood, where a rough two-planked bridge crossed from the bottom of the garden of the last house in the village, and communicated by means of a little wicker gate with the wood itself. Then once out of the shadow of the wood the stream lay in flaming pools of the molten crimson of the sunset, and lost itself in the haze of woodland distances.

This house at the end of the village stood outside the shadow, and the lawn which sloped down to the river was still flecked with sunlight. Garden-beds of dazzling color lined its gravel walks, and down the middle of it ran a brick pergola, half-hidden in clusters of rambler-rose and purple with starry clematis. At the bottom end of it, between two of its pillars, was slung a hammock containing a shirt-sleeved figure.

The house itself lay somewhat remote from the rest of the village, and a footpath leading across two fields, now tall and fragrant with hay, was its only communication with the high road. It was low-built, only two stories in height, and like the garden, its walls were a mass of flowering roses. A narrow stone terrace ran along the garden front, over which was stretched an awning, and on the terrace a young silent-footed man-servant was busied with the laying of the table for dinner. He was neat-handed and quick with his job, and having finished it he went back into the house, and reappeared again with a large rough bath-towel on his arm. With this he went to the hammock in the pergola.

"Nearly eight, sir," he said.

"Has Mr. Darcy come yet?" asked a voice from the hammock.

"No, sir."

"If I'm not back when he comes, tell him that I'm just having a bathe before dinner."

The servant went back to the house, and after a moment or two Frank Halton struggled to a sitting posture, and slipped out on to the grass. He was of medium height and rather slender in build, but the supple ease and grace of his movements gave the impression of great physical strength: even his descent from the hammock was not an awkward performance. His face and hands were of very dark complexion, either from constant exposure to wind and sun, or, as his black hair and dark eyes tended to show, from some strain of southern blood. His head was small, his face of an exquisite beauty of modeling, while the smoothness of its contour would have led you to believe that he was a beardless lad still in his teens. But something, some look which living and experience alone can give, seemed to contradict that, and finding yourself completely puzzled as to his age, you would next moment probably cease to think about that, and only look at this glorious specimen of young manhood with wondering satisfaction.

He was dressed as became the season and the heat, and wore only a shirt open at the neck, and a pair of flannel trousers. His head, covered very thickly with a somewhat rebellious crop of short curly hair, was bare as he strolled across the lawn to the bathing-place that lay below. Then for a moment there was silence, then the sound of splashed and divided waters, and presently after, a great shout of ecstatic joy, as he swam up-stream with the foamed water standing in a frill round his neck. Then after some five minutes of limb-stretching struggle with the flood, he turned over on his back, and with arms thrown wide, floated down-stream, ripple-cradled and inert. His eyes were shut, and between half-parted lips he talked gently to himself.

"I am one with it," he said to himself, "the river and I, I and the river. The coolness and splash of it is I, and the water-herbs that wave in it are I also. And my strength and my limbs are not mine but the river's. It is all one, all one, dear Fawn."

A quarter of an hour later he appeared again at the bottom of the lawn, dressed as before, his wet hair already drying into its crisp short curls again. There he paused a moment, looking back at the stream with the smile with which men look on the face of a friend, then turned towards the house. Simultaneously his servant came to the door leading on to the terrace, followed by a man who appeared to be some half-way through the fourth decade of his years. Frank and he saw each other across the bushes and garden-beds, and each quickening his step, they met suddenly face to face round an angle of the garden walk, in the fragrance of syringa.

"My dear Darcy," cried Frank, "I am charmed to see you."

But the other stared at him in amazement.

"Frank!" he exclaimed.

"Yes, that is my name," he said laughing, "what is the matter?"

Darcy took his hand.

"What have you done to yourself?" he asked. "You are a boy again."

"Ah, I have a lot to tell you," said Frank. "Lots that you will hardly believe, but I shall convince you——"

He broke off suddenly, and held up his hand.

"Hush, there is my nightingale," he said.

The smile of recognition and welcome with which he had greeted his friend faded from his face, and a look of rapt wonder took its place, as of a lover listening to the voice of his beloved. His mouth parted slightly, showing the white line of teeth, and his eyes looked out and out till they seemed to Darcy to be focused on things beyond the vision of man. Then something perhaps startled the bird, for the song ceased.

"Yes, lots to tell you," he said. "Really I am delighted to see you. But you look rather white and pulled down; no wonder after that fever. And there is to be no nonsense about this visit. It is June now, you stop here till you are fit to begin work again. Two months at least."

"Ah, I can't trespass quite to that extent."

Frank took his arm and walked him down the grass.

"Trespass? Who talks of trespass? I shall tell you quite openly when I am tired of you, but you know when we had the studio together, we used not to bore each other. However, it is ill talking of going away on the moment of your arrival. Just a stroll to the river, and then it will be dinner-time."

Darcy took out his cigarette case, and offered it to the other.

Frank laughed.

"No, not for me. Dear me, I suppose I used to smoke once. How very odd!"

"Given it up?"

"I don't know. I suppose I must have. Anyhow I don't do it now. I would as soon think of eating meat."

"Another victim on the smoking altar of vegetarianism?"

"Victim?" asked Frank. "Do I strike you as such?"

He paused on the margin of the stream and whistled softly. Next moment a moorhen made its splashing flight across the river, and ran up the bank. Frank took it very gently in his hands and stroked its head, as the creature lay against his shirt.

"And is the house among the reeds still secure?" he half-crooned to it. "And is the missus quite well, and are the neighbors flourishing? There, dear, home with you," and he flung it into the air.

"That bird's very tame," said Darcy, slightly bewildered.

"It is rather," said Frank, following its flight.

During dinner Frank chiefly occupied himself in bringing himself up-to-date in the movements and achievements of this old friend whom he had not seen for six years. Those six years, it now appeared, had been full of incident and success for Darcy; he had made a name for himself as a portrait painter which bade fair to outlast the vogue of a couple of seasons, and his leisure time had been brief. Then some four months previously he had been through a severe attack of typhoid, the result of which as concerns this story was that he had come down to this sequestered place to recruit.

"Yes, you've got on," said Frank at the end. "I always knew you would. A.R.A. with more in prospect. Money? You roll in it, I suppose, and, O Darcy, how much happiness have you had all these years? That is the only imperishable possession. And how much have you learned? Oh, I don't mean in Art. Even I could have done well in that."

Darcy laughed.

"Done well? My dear fellow, all I have learned in these six years you knew, so to speak, in your cradle. Your old pictures fetch huge prices. Do you never paint now?"

Frank shook his head.

"No, I'm too busy," he said.

"Doing what? Please tell me. That is what every one is for ever asking me."

"Doing? I suppose you would say I do nothing."

Darcy glanced up at the brilliant young face opposite him.

"It seems to suit you, that way of being busy," he said. "Now, it's your turn. Do you read? Do you study? I remember you saying that it would do us all—all us artists, I mean—a great deal of good if we would study any one human face carefully for a year, without recording a line. Have you been doing that?"

Frank shook his head again.

"I mean exactly what I say," he said, "I have been *doing* nothing. And I have never been so occupied. Look at me; have I not done something to myself to begin with?"

"You are two years younger than I," said Darcy, "at least you used to be. You therefore are thirty-five. But had I never seen you before I should say you were just twenty. But was it worth while to spend six years of greatly-occupied life in order to look twenty? Seems rather like a woman of fashion."

Frank laughed boisterously.

"First time I've ever been compared to that particular bird of prey," he said. "No, that has not been my occupation—in fact I am only very rarely conscious that one effect of my occupation has been that. Of course, it must have been if one comes to think of it. It is not very important. Quite true my body has become young. But that is very little; I have become young."

Darcy pushed back his chair and sat sideways to the table looking at the other.

"Has that been your occupation then?" he asked.

"Yes, that anyhow is one aspect of it. Think what youth means! It is the capacity for growth, mind, body, spirit, all grow, all get stronger, all have a fuller, firmer life every day. That is something, considering that every day that passes after the ordinary man reaches the full-blown flower of his strength, weakens his hold on life. A man reaches his prime, and remains, we say, in his prime, for ten years, or perhaps twenty. But after his primest prime is reached, he slowly, insensibly weakens. These are the signs of age in you, in your body, in your art probably, in your mind. You are less electric than you were. But I, when I reach my prime—I am nearing it—ah, you shall see."

The stars had begun to appear in the blue velvet of the sky, and to the east the horizon seen above the black silhouette of the village was growing dove-colored with the approach of moon-rise. White moths hovered dimly over the garden-beds, and the footsteps of night tip-toed through the bushes. Suddenly Frank rose.

"Ah, it is the supreme moment," he said softly. "Now more than at any other time the current of life, the eternal imperishable current runs so close to me that I am almost enveloped in it. Be silent a minute."

He advanced to the edge of the terrace and looked out standing stretched with arms outspread. Darcy heard him draw a long breath into his lungs, and after many seconds expel it again. Six or eight times he did this, then turned back into the lamplight.

"It will sound to you quite mad, I expect," he said, "but if you want to hear the soberest truth I have ever spoken and shall ever speak, I will tell you about myself. But come into the garden if it is not too damp for you. I have never told any one yet, but I shall like to tell you. It is long, in fact, since I have even tried to classify what I have learned."

They wandered into the fragrant dimness of the pergola, and sat down. Then Frank began:

"Years ago, do you remember," he said, "we used often to talk about the decay of joy in the world. Many impulses, we settled, had contributed to this decay, some of which were good in themselves, others that were quite completely bad. Among the good things, I put what we may call certain Christian virtues, renunciation, resignation, sympathy with suffering, and the desire to relieve sufferers. But out of those things spring very bad ones, useless renunciations, asceticism for its own sake, mortification of the flesh with nothing to follow, no corresponding gain that is, and that awful and terrible disease which devastated England some centuries ago, and from which by heredity of spirit we suffer now, Puritanism. That was a dreadful plague, the brutes held and taught that joy and laughter and merriment were evil: it was a doctrine the most profane and wicked. Why, what is the commonest crime one sees? A sullen face. That is the truth of the matter.

"Now all my life I have believed that we are intended to be happy, that joy is of all gifts the most divine. And when I left London, abandoned my career, such as it was, I did so because I intended to devote my life to the cultivation of joy, and, by continuous and unsparing effort, to be happy. Among people, and in constant intercourse with others, I did not find it possible; there were too many distractions in towns and workrooms, and also too much suffering. So I took one step backwards or forwards, as you may choose to put it, and went straight to Nature, to trees, birds, animals, to all those things which quite clearly pursue one aim only, which blindly follow the great native instinct to be happy without any care at all for morality, or human law or divine law. I wanted, you understand, to get all joy first-hand and unadulterated, and I think it scarcely exists among men; it is obsolete."

Darcy turned in his chair.

"Ah, but what makes birds and animals happy?" he asked. "Food, food and mating."

Frank laughed gently in the stillness.

"Do not think I became a sensualist," he said. "I did not make that mistake. For the sensualist carries his miseries pick-a-back, and round his feet is wound the shroud that shall soon enwrap him. I may be mad, it is true, but I am not so stupid anyhow as to have tried that. No, what is it that makes puppies play with their own tails, that sends cats on their prowling ecstatic errands at night?"

He paused a moment.

"So I went to Nature," he said. "I sat down here in this New Forest, sat down fair and square, and looked. That was my first difficulty, to sit here quiet without being bored, to wait without being impatient, to be receptive and very alert, though for a long time nothing particular happened. The change in fact was slow in those early stages."

"Nothing happened?" asked Darcy rather impatiently, with the sturdy revolt against any new idea which to the English mind is synonymous with nonsense. "Why, what in the world *should* happen?"

Now Frank as he had known him was the most generous but most quick-tempered of mortal men; in other words his anger would flare to a prodigious beacon, under almost no provocation, only to be quenched again under a gust of no less impulsive kindliness. Thus the moment Darcy had spoken, an apology for his hasty question was half-way up his tongue. But there was no need for it to have traveled even so far, for Frank laughed again with kindly, genuine mirth.

"Oh, how I should have resented that a few years ago," he said. "Thank goodness that resentment is one of the things I have got rid of. I certainly wish that you should believe my story—in fact, you are going to—but that you at this moment should imply that you do not, does not concern me."

"Ah, your solitary sojournings have made you inhuman," said Darcy, still very English.

"No, human," said Frank. "Rather more human, at least rather less of an ape."

"Well, that was my first quest," he continued, after a moment, "the deliberate and unswerving pursuit of joy, and my method, the eager contemplation of Nature. As far as motive went, I daresay it was purely selfish, but as far as effect goes, it seems to me about the best thing one can do for one's fellow-creatures, for happiness is more infectious than small-pox. So, as I said, I sat down and waited; I looked at happy things, zealously avoided the sight of anything unhappy, and by degrees a little trickle of the happiness of this blissful world began to filter into me. The trickle grew more abundant, and now, my dear fellow, if I could for a moment divert from me into you one half of the torrent of joy that pours through me day and night, you would throw the world, art, everything aside, and just live, exist. When a man's body dies, it passes into trees and flowers. Well, that is what I have been trying to do with my soul before death."

The servant had brought into the pergola a table with syphons and spirits, and had set a lamp upon it. As Frank spoke he leaned forward towards the other, and Darcy for all his matter-of-fact commonsense could have sworn that his companion's face shone, was luminous in itself. His dark brown eyes glowed from within, the unconscious smile of a child irradiated and transformed his face. Darcy felt suddenly excited, exhilarated.

"Go on," he said. "Go on. I can feel you are somehow telling me sober truth. I daresay you are mad; but I don't see that matters."

Frank laughed again.

"Mad?" he said. "Yes, certainly, if you wish. But I prefer to call it sane. However, nothing matters less than what anybody chooses to call things. God never labels his gifts; He just puts them into our hands; just as he put animals in the garden of Eden, for Adam to name if he felt disposed."

"So by the continual observance and study of things that were happy," continued he, "I got happiness, I got joy. But seeking it, as I did, from Nature, I got much more which I did not seek, but stumbled upon originally by accident. It is difficult to explain, but I will try.

"About three years ago I was sitting one morning in a place I will show you tomorrow. It is down by the river brink, very green, dappled with shade and sun, and the river passes there through some little clumps of reeds. Well, as I sat there, doing nothing, but just looking and listening, I heard the sound quite distinctly of some flute-like instrument playing a strange unending melody. I thought at first it was some musical yokel on the highway and did not pay much attention. But before long the strangeness and indescribable beauty of the tune struck me. It never repeated itself, but it never came to an end, phrase after phrase ran its sweet course, it worked gradually and inevitably up to a climax, and having attained it, it went on; another climax was reached and another and another. Then with a sudden gasp of wonder I localized where it came from. It came from the reeds and from the sky and from the trees. It was everywhere, it was the sound of life. It was, my dear Darcy, as the Greeks would have said, it was Pan playing on his pipes, the voice of Nature. It was the life-melody, the world-melody."

Darcy was far too interested to interrupt, though there was a question he would have liked to ask, and Frank went on:

"Well, for the moment I was terrified, terrified with the impotent horror of nightmare, and I stopped my ears and just ran from the place and got back to the house panting, trembling, literally in a panic. Unknowingly, for at that time I only pursued joy, I had begun, since I drew my joy from Nature, to get in touch with Nature. Nature, force, God, call it what you will, had drawn across my face a little gossamer web of essential life. I saw that when I emerged from my terror, and I went very humbly back to where I had heard the Pan-pipes. But it was nearly six months before I heard them again."

"Why was that?" asked Darcy.

"Surely because I had revolted, rebelled, and worst of all been frightened. For I believe that just as there is nothing in the world which so injures one's body as fear, so there is nothing that so much shuts up the soul. I was afraid, you see, of the one thing in the world which has real existence. No wonder its manifestation was withdrawn."

"And after six months?"

"After six months one blessed morning I heard the piping again. I wasn't afraid that time. And since then it has grown louder, it has become more constant. I now hear it often, and I can put myself into such an attitude towards Nature that the pipes will almost certainly sound. And never yet have they played the same tune, it is always something new, something fuller, richer, more complete than before."

"What do you mean by 'such an attitude towards Nature'?" asked Darcy.

"I can't explain that; but by translating it into a bodily attitude it is this."

Frank sat up for a moment quite straight in his chair, then slowly sunk back with arms outspread and head drooped.

"That," he said, "an effortless attitude, but open, resting, receptive. It is just that which you must do with your soul."

Then he sat up again.

"One word more," he said, "and I will bore you no further. Nor unless you ask me questions shall I talk about it again. You will find me, in fact, quite sane in my mode of life. Birds and beasts you will see behaving somewhat intimately to me, like that moor-hen, but that is all. I will walk with you, ride with you, play golf with you, and talk with you on any subject you like. But I wanted you on the threshold to know what has happened to me. And one thing more will happen."

He paused again, and a slight look of fear crossed his eyes.

"There will be a final revelation," he said, "a complete and blinding stroke which will throw open to me, once and for all, the full knowledge, the full realization and comprehension that I am one, just as you are, with life. In reality there is no 'me,' no 'you,' no 'it.' Everything is part of the one and only thing which is life. I know that that is so, but the realization of it is not yet mine. But it will be, and on that day, so I take it, I shall see Pan. It may mean death, the death of my body, that is, but I don't care. It may mean immortal, eternal life lived here and now and for ever. Then having gained that, ah, my dear Darcy, I shall preach such a gospel of joy, showing myself as the living proof of the truth, that Puritanism, the dismal religion of sour faces, shall vanish like a breath of smoke, and be dispersed and disappear in the sunlit air. But first the full knowledge must be mine."

Darcy watched his face narrowly.

"You are afraid of that moment," he said.

Frank smiled at him.

"Quite true; you are quick to have seen that. But when it comes I hope I shall not be afraid."

For some little time there was silence; then Darcy rose.

"You have bewitched me, you extraordinary boy," he said. "You have been telling me a fairy-story, and I find myself saying, 'Promise me it is true.' "

"I promise you that," said the other.

"And I know I shan't sleep," added Darcy.

Frank looked at him with a sort of mild wonder as if he scarcely understood.

"Well, what does that matter?" he said.

"I assure you it does. I am wretched unless I sleep."

"Of course I can make you sleep if I want," said Frank in a rather bored voice.

"Well, do."

"Very good: go to bed. I'll come upstairs in ten minutes."

Frank busied himself for a little after the other had gone, moving the table back under the awning of the veranda and quenching the lamp. Then he went with his quick silent tread upstairs and into Darcy's room. The latter was already in bed, but very wide-eyed and wakeful, and Frank with an amused smile of indulgence, as for a fretful child, sat down on the edge of the bed.

"Look at me," he said, and Darcy looked.

"The birds are sleeping in the brake," said Frank softly, "and the winds are asleep. The sea sleeps, and the tides are but the heaving of its breast. The stars swing slow, rocked in the great cradle of the Heavens, and—"

He stopped suddenly, gently blew out Darcy's candle, and left him sleeping.

Morning brought to Darcy a flood of hard commonsense, as clear and crisp as the sunshine that filled his room. Slowly as he woke he gathered together the broken threads of the memories of the evening which had ended, so he told himself, in a trick of common hypnotism. That accounted for it all; the whole strange talk he had had was under a spell of suggestion from the extraordinary vivid boy who had once been a man; all his own excitement, his acceptance of the incredible had been merely the effect of a stronger, more potent will imposed on his own. How strong that will was, he guessed from his own instantaneous obedience to Frank's suggestion of sleep. And armed with impenetrable commonsense he came down to breakfast. Frank had already begun, and was consuming a large plateful of porridge and milk with the most prosaic and healthy appetite.

"Slept well?" he asked.

"Yes, of course. Where did you learn hypnotism?"

"By the side of the river."

"You talked an amazing quantity of nonsense last night," remarked Darcy, in a voice prickly with reason.

"Rather. I felt quite giddy. Look, I remembered to order a dreadful daily paper for you. You can read about money markets or politics or cricket matches."

Darcy looked at him closely. In the morning light Frank looked even fresher, younger, more vital than he had done the night before, and the sight of him somehow dinted Darcy's armor of commonsense.

"You are the most extraordinary fellow I ever saw," he said. "I want to ask you some more questions."

"Ask away," said Frank.

For the next day or two Darcy plied his friend with many questions, objections and criticisms on the theory of life and gradually got out of him a coherent and complete account of his experience. In brief then, Frank believed that "by lying naked," as he put it, to the force which controls the passage of the stars, the breaking of a wave, the budding of a tree, the love of a youth and maiden, he had succeeded in a way hitherto undreamed of in possessing himself of the essential principle of life. Day by day, so he thought, he was getting nearer to, and in closer union with the great power itself which caused all life to be, the spirit of nature, of force, or the spirit of God. For himself, he confessed to what others would call paganism; it was sufficient for him that there existed a principle of life. He did not worship it, he did not pray to it, he did not praise it. Some of it existed in all human beings, just as it existed in trees and animals; to realize and make living to himself the fact that it was all one, was his sole aim and object.

Here perhaps Darcy would put in a word of warning. "Take care," he said. "To see Pan meant death, did it not?"

Frank's eyebrows would rise at this.

"What does that matter?" he said. "True, the Greeks were always right, and they said so, but there is another possibility. For the nearer I get to it, the more living, the more vital and young I become."

"What then do you expect the final revelation will do for you?"

"I have told you," said he. "It will make me immortal."

But it was not so much from speech and argument that Darcy grew to grasp his friend's conception, as from the ordinary conduct of his life. They were passing, for instance, one morning down the village street, when an old woman, very bent and decrepit, but with an extraordinary cheerfulness of face, hobbled out from her cottage. Frank instantly stopped when he saw her.

"You old darling! How goes it all?" he said.

But she did not answer, her dim old eyes were riveted on his face; she seemed to drink in like a thirsty creature the beautiful radiance which shone there. Suddenly she put her two withered old hands on his shoulders.

"You're just the sunshine itself," she said, and he kissed her and passed on.

But scarcely a hundred yards further a strange contradiction of such tenderness occurred. A child running along the path towards them fell on its face, and set up a dismal cry of fright and pain. A look of horror came into Frank's eyes, and, putting his fingers in his ears, he fled at full speed down the street, and did not pause till he was out of hearing. Darcy, having ascertained that the child was not really hurt, followed him in bewilderment.

"Are you without pity then?" he asked.

Frank shook his head impatiently.

"Can't you see?" he asked. "Can't you understand that that sort of thing, pain, anger, anything unlovely throws me back, retards the coming of the great hour! Perhaps when it comes I shall be able to piece that side of life on to the other, on to the true religion of joy. At present I can't."

"But the old woman. Was she not ugly?"

Frank's radiance gradually returned.

"Ah, no. She was like me. She longed for joy, and knew it when she saw it, the old darling."

Another question suggested itself.

"Then what about Christianity?" asked Darcy.

"I can't accept it. I can't believe in any creed of which the central doctrine is that God who is Joy should have had to suffer. Perhaps it was so; in some inscrutable way I believe it may have been so, but I don't understand how it was possible. So I leave it alone; my affair is joy."

They had come to the weir above the village, and the thunder of riotous cool water was heavy in the air. Trees dipped into the translucent stream with slender trailing branches, and the meadow where they stood was starred with midsummer blossomings. Larks shot up caroling into the crystal dome of blue, and a thousand voices of June sang round them. Frank, bare-headed as was his wont, with his coat slung over his arm and his shirt sleeves rolled up above the elbow, stood there like some beautiful wild animal with eyes half-shut and mouth half-open, drinking in the scented warmth of the air. Then suddenly he flung himself face downwards on the grass at the edge of the stream, burying his face in the daisies and cowslips, and lay stretched there in wide-armed ecstasy, with his long fingers pressing and stroking the dewy herbs of the field. Never before had Darcy seen him thus fully possessed by his idea; his caressing fingers, his half-buried face pressed close to the grass, even the clothed lines of his figure were instinct with a vitality that somehow was different from that of other men. And some faint glow from it reached Darcy, some thrill, some vibration from that charged recumbent body passed to him, and for a moment he understood as he had not understood before, despite his persistent questions and the candid answers they received, how real, and how realized by Frank, his idea was.

Then suddenly the muscles in Frank's neck became stiff and alert, and he half-raised his head, whispering, "The Pan-pipes, the Pan-pipes. Close, oh, so close."

Very slowly, as if a sudden movement might interrupt the melody, he raised himself and leaned on the elbow of his bent arm. His eyes opened wider, the lower lids drooped as if he focused his eyes on something very far away, and the smile on his face broadened and quivered like sunlight on still water, till the exultance of its happiness was scarcely human. So he remained motionless and rapt for some minutes, then the look of listening died from his face, and he bowed his head satisfied.

"Ah, that was good," he said. "How is it possible you did not hear? Oh, you poor fellow! Did you really hear nothing?"

A week of this outdoor and stimulating life did wonders in restoring to Darcy the vigor and health which his weeks of fever had filched from him, and as his normal activity and higher pressure of vitality returned, he seemed to himself to fall even more under the spell which the miracle of Frank's youth cast over him. Twenty times a day he found himself saying to himself suddenly at the end of some ten minutes' silent resistance to the absurdity of Frank's idea: "But it isn't possible; it can't be possible," and from the fact of his having to assure himself so frequently of this, he knew that he was struggling and arguing with a conclusion which already had taken root in his mind. For in any case a visible living miracle confronted him, since it was equally impossible that this youth, this boy, trembling on the verge of manhood, was thirty-five. Yet such was the fact.

July was ushered in by a couple of days of blustering and fretful rain, and Darcy, unwilling to risk a chill, kept to the house. But to Frank this weeping change of weather seemed to have no bearing on the behavior of man, and he spent his days exactly as he did under the suns of June, lying in his hammock, stretched on the dripping grass, or making huge rambling excursions into the forest, the birds hopping from tree to tree after him, to return in the evening, drenched and soaked, but with the same unquench-able flame of joy burning within him.

"Catch cold?" he would ask, "I've forgotten how to do it, I think. I suppose it makes one's body more sensible always to sleep out-of-doors. People who live indoors always remind me of something peeled and skinless."

"Do you mean to say you slept out-of-doors last night in that deluge?" asked Darcy. "And where, may I ask?"

Frank thought a moment.

"I slept in the hammock till nearly dawn," he said. "For I remember the light blinked in the east when I awoke. Then I went—where did I go?—oh, yes, to the meadow where the Pan-pipes sounded so close a week ago. You were with me, do you remember? But I always have a rug if it is wet."

And he went whistling upstairs.

Somehow that little touch, his obvious effort to recall where he had slept, brought strangely home to Darcy the wonderful romance of which he was the still half-incred-ulous beholder. Sleep till close on dawn in a hammock, then the tramp—or probably scamper—underneath the windy and weeping heavens to the remote and lonely meadow by the weir! The picture of other such nights rose before him; Frank sleep-ing perhaps by the bathing-place under the filtered twilight of the stars, or the white blaze of moon-shine, a stir and awakening at some dead hour, perhaps a space of silent wide-eyed thought, and then a wandering through the hushed woods to some other dormitory, alone with his happiness, alone with the joy and the life that suffused and enveloped him, without other thought or desire or aim except the hourly and never-ceasing communion with the joy of nature.

They were in the middle of dinner that night, talking on indifferent subjects, when Darcy suddenly broke off in the middle of a sentence.

"I've got it," he said. "At last I've got it."

"Congratulate you," said Frank. "But what?"

"The radical unsoundness of your idea. It is this: All nature from highest to lowest is full, crammed full of suffering; every living organism in nature preys on another, yet in your aim to get close to, to be one with nature, you leave suffering altogether out; you run away from it, you refuse to recognize it. And you are waiting, you say, for the final revelation."

Frank's brow clouded slightly.

"Well?" he asked, rather wearily.

"Cannot you guess then when the final revelation will be? In joy you are supreme, I grant you that; I did not know a man could be so master of it. You have learned perhaps practically all that nature can teach. And if, as you think, the final revelation is coming to you, it will be the revelation of horror, suffering, death, pain in all its hideous forms. Suffering does exist: you hate it and fear it."

Frank held up his hand.

"Stop; let me think," he said.

There was silence for a long minute.

"That never struck me," he said at length. "It is possible that what you suggest is true. Does the sight of Pan mean that, do you think? Is it that nature, take it alto-gether, suffers horribly, suffers to a hideous inconceivable extent? Shall I be shown all the suffering?"

He got up and came round to where Darcy sat.

"If it is so, so be it," he said. "Because, my dear fellow, I am near, so splendidly near to the final revelation. To-day the pipes have sounded almost without pause. I have even heard the rustle in the bushes, I believe, of Pan's coming. I have seen, yes, I saw to-day, the bushes pushed aside as if by a hand, and piece of a face, not human, peered through. But I was not frightened, at least I did not run away this time."

He took a turn up to the window and back again.

"Yes, there is suffering all through," he said, "and I have left it all out of my search. Perhaps, as you say, the revelation will be that. And in that case, it will be good-bye. I have gone on one line. I shall have gone too far along one road, without having explored the other. But I can't go back now. I wouldn't if I could; not a step would I retrace! In any case, whatever the revelation is, it will be God. I'm sure of that."

The rainy weather soon passed, and with the return of the sun Darcy again joined Frank in long rambling days. It grew extraordinarily hotter, and with the fresh bursting of life, after the rain, Frank's vitality seemed to blaze higher and higher. Then, as is the habit of the English weather, one evening clouds began to bank themselves up in the west, the sun went down in a glare of coppery thunder-rack, and the whole earth broiling under an unspeakable oppression and sultriness paused and panted for the storm. After sunset the remote fires of lightning began to wink and flicker on the horizon, but when bed-time came the storm seemed to have moved no nearer, though a very low unceasing noise of thunder was audible. Weary and oppressed by the stress of the day, Darcy fell at once into a heavy uncomforting sleep.

He woke suddenly into full consciousness, with the din of some appalling explosion of thunder in his ears, and sat up in bed with racing heart. Then for a moment, as he recovered himself from the panic-land which lies between sleeping and waking, there was silence, except for the steady hissing of rain on the shrubs outside his window. But suddenly that silence was shattered and shredded into fragments by a scream from somewhere close at hand outside in the black garden, a scream of supreme and despairing terror. Again, and once again it shrilled up, and then a babble of awful words was interjected. A quivering sobbing voice that he knew, said:

"My God, oh, my God; oh, Christ!"

And then followed a little mocking, bleating laugh. Then was silence again; only the rain hissed on the shrubs.

All this was but the affair of a moment, and without pause either to put on clothes or light a candle, Darcy was already fumbling at his door-handle. Even as he opened it he met a terror-stricken face outside, that of the man-servant who carried a light.

"Did you hear?" he asked.

The man's face was bleached to a dull shining whiteness.

"Yes, sir," he said. "It was the master's voice."

* * *

Together they hurried down the stairs, and through the dining-room where an orderly table for breakfast had already been laid, and out on to the terrace. The rain for the moment had been utterly stayed, as if the tap of the heavens had been turned off, and under the lowering black sky, not quite dark, since the moon rode somewhere serene behind the conglomerated thunder-clouds, Darcy stumbled into the garden, followed by the servant with the candle. The monstrous leaping shadow of himself was cast before him on the lawn; lost and wandering odors of rose and lily and damp earth were thick about him, but more pungent was some sharp and acrid smell that suddenly reminded him of a certain châlet in which he had once taken refuge in the Alps. In the blackness of the hazy light from the sky, and the vague tossing of the candle behind him, he saw that the hammock in which Frank so often lay was tenanted. A gleam of white shirt was there, as if a man sitting up in it, but across that there was an obscure dark shadow, and as he approached the acrid odor grew more intense.

He was now only some few yards away, when suddenly the black shadow seemed to jump into the air, then came down with tappings of hard hoofs on the brick path that ran down the pergola, and with frolicsome skippings galloped off into the bushes. When that was gone Darcy could see quite clearly that a shirted figure sat up in the hammock. For one moment, from sheer terror of the unseen, he hung on his step, and the servant joining him they walked together to the hammock.

It was Frank. He was in shirt and trousers only, and he sat up with braced arms. For one half-second he stared at them, his face a mask of horrible contorted terror. His upper lip was drawn back so that the gums of the teeth appeared, and his eyes were focused not on the two who approached him but on something quite close to him; his nostrils were widely expanded, as if he panted for breath, and terror incarnate and repulsion and deathly anguish ruled dreadful lines on his smooth cheeks and forehead. Then even as they looked the body sank backwards, and the ropes of the hammock wheezed and strained.

Darcy lifted him out and carried him indoors. Once he thought there was a faint convulsive stir of the limbs that lay with so dead a weight in his arms, but when they got inside, there was no trace of life. But the look of supreme terror and agony of fear had gone from his face, a boy tired with play but still smiling in his sleep was the burden he laid on the floor. His eyes had closed, and the beautiful mouth lay in smiling curves, even as when a few mornings ago, in the meadow by the weir, it had quivered to the music of the unheard melody of Pan's pipes. Then they looked further.

Frank had come back from his bath before dinner that night in his usual costume of shirt and trousers only. He had not dressed, and during dinner, so Darcy remembered, he had rolled up the sleeves of his shirt to above the elbow. Later, as they sat and talked after dinner on the close sultriness of the evening, he had unbuttoned the front of his shirt to let what little breath of wind there was play on his skin. The sleeves were rolled up now, the front of the shirt was unbuttoned, and on his arms and on the brown skin of his chest were strange discolorations which grew momently more clear and defined, till they saw that the marks were pointed prints, as if caused by the hoofs of some monstrous goat that had leaped and stamped upon him.

The Treasure of Abbot Thomas

M. R. James

────◆────

I

Verum usque in præsentem diem multa garriunt inter se Canonici de abscondito quodam istius Abbatis Thomæ thesauro, quem sæpe, quanquam ahduc incassum, quaesiverunt Steinfeldenses. Ipsum enim Thomam adhuc florida in ætate existentem ingentem auri massam circa monasterium defodisse perhibent; de quo multoties interrogatus ubi esset, cum risu respondere solitus erat: "Job, Johannes, et Zacharias vel vobis vel posteris indicabunt"; idemque aliquando adiicere se inventuris minime invisurum. Inter alia huius Abbatis opera, hoc memoria praecipue dignum indico quod fenestram magnam in orientali parte alæe australis in ecclesia sua imaginibus optime in vitro depictis impleverit: id quod et ipsius effigies et insignia ibidem posita demonstrant. Domum quoque Abbatialem fere totam restauravit: puteo in atrio ipsius effosso et lapidibus marmoreis pulchre cælatis exornato. Decessit autem, morte aliquantulum subitanea perculsus, ætatis suæ anno lxxiido, incarnationis vero Dominicae mdxxixo.

I suppose I shall have to translate this," said the antiquary to himself, as he finished copying the above lines from that rather rare and exceedingly diffuse book, the Sertum Steinfeldense Norbertinum.* "Well, it may as well be done first as last," and accordingly the following rendering was very quickly produced:

Up to the present day there is much gossip among the Canons about a certain hidden treasure of this Abbot Thomas, for which those of Steinfeld have often made search, though hitherto in vain. The story is that Thomas, while

---

* An account of the Premonstratensian abbey of Steinfeld, in the Eiffel, with lives of the Abbots, published at Cologne in 1712 by Christian Albert Erhard, a resident in the district. The epithet *Norbertinum* is due to the fact that St Norbert was founder of the Premonstratensian Order.

yet in the vigour of life, concealed a very large quantity of gold somewhere in the monastery. He was often asked where it was, and always answered, with a laugh: "Job, John, and Zechariah will tell either you or your successors." He sometimes added that he should feel no grudge against those who might find it. Among other works carried out by this Abbot I may specially mention his filling the great window at the east end of the south aisle of the church with figures admirably painted on glass, as his effigy and arms in the window attest. He also restored almost the whole of the Abbot's lodging, and dug a well in the court of it, which he adorned with beautiful carvings in marble. He died rather suddenly in the seventy-second year of his age, a.d. 1529.

The object which the antiquary had before him at the moment was that of tracing the whereabouts of the painted windows of the Abbey Church at Steinfeld. Shortly after the Revolution, a very large quantity of painted glass made its way from the dissolved abbeys of Germany and Belgium to this country, and may now be seen adorning various of our parish churches, cathedrals, and private chapels. Steinfeld Abbey was among the most considerable of these involuntary contributors to our artistic possession (I am quoting the somewhat ponderous preamble of the book which the antiquary wrote), and the greater part of the glass from that institution can be identified without much difficulty by the help, either of the numerous inscriptions in which the place is mentioned, or of the subjects of the windows, in which several well-defined cycles or narratives were represented.

The passage with which I began my story had set the antiquary on the track of another identification. In a private chapel—no matter where—he had seen three large figures, each occupying a whole light in a window, and evidently the work of one artist. Their style made it plain that that artist had been a German of the sixteenth century; but hitherto the more exact localizing of them had been a puzzle. They represented—will you be surprised to hear it?—Job Patriarcha, Johannes Evangelista, Zacharias Propheta, and each of them held a book or scroll, inscribed with a sentence from his writings. These, as a matter of course, the antiquary had noted, and had been struck by the curious way in which they differed from any text of the Vulgate that he had been able to examine. Thus the scroll in Job's hand was inscribed: "Auro est locus in quo absconditur" (for "conflatur")*; on the book

---

* There is a place for gold where it is hidden.

of John was: "Habent in vestimentis suis scripturam quam nemo novit"* (for in "vestimento scriptum," the following words being taken from another verse); and Zacharias had: "Super lapidem unum septem oculi sunt"** (which alone of the three presents an unaltered text).

A sad perplexity it had been to our investigator to think why these three personages should have been placed together in one window. There was no bond of connexion between them, either historic, symbolic, or doctrinal, and he could only suppose that they must have formed part of a very large series of Prophets and Apostles, which might have filled, say, all the clerestory windows of some capacious church. But the passage from the *Sertum* had altered the situation by showing that the names of the actual personages represented in the glass now in Lord D——'s chapel had been constantly on the lips of Abbot Thomas von Eschenhausen of Steinfeld, and that this Abbot had put up a painted window, probably about the year 1520, in the south aisle of his abbey church. It was no very wild conjecture that the three figures might have formed part of Abbot Thomas's offering; it was one which, moreover, could probably be confirmed or set aside by another careful examination of the glass. And, as Mr. Somerton was a man of leisure, he set out on pilgrimage to the private chapel with very little delay. His conjecture was confirmed to the full. Not only did the style and technique of the glass suit perfectly with the date and place required, but in another window of the chapel he found some glass, known to have been bought along with the figures, which contained the arms of Abbot Thomas von Eschenhausen.

At intervals during his researches Mr. Somerton had been haunted by the recollection of the gossip about the hidden treasure, and, as he thought the matter over, it became more and more obvious to him that if the Abbot meant anything by the enigmatical answer which he gave to his questioners, he must have meant that the secret was to be found somewhere in the window he had placed in the abbey church. It was undeniable, furthermore, that the first of the curiously-selected texts on the scrolls in the window might be taken to have a reference to hidden treasure.

Every feature, therefore, or mark which could possibly assist in elucidating the riddle which, he felt sure, the Abbot had set to posterity he noted with scrupulous care, and, returning to his Berkshire manor-house, consumed many a pint of the midnight oil over his tracings and sketches. After two or three weeks, a day came when

---

* They have on their raiment a writing which no man knoweth.
** Upon one stone are seven eyes.

Mr. Somerton announced to his man that he must pack his own and his master's things for a short journey abroad, whither for the moment we will not follow him.

II

Mr. Gregory, the Rector of Parsbury, had strolled out before breakfast, it being a fine autumn morning, as far as the gate of his carriage-drive, with intent to meet the postman and sniff the cool air. Nor was he disappointed of either purpose. Before he had had time to answer more than ten or eleven of the miscellaneous questions propounded to him in the lightness of their hearts by his young offspring, who had accompanied him, the postman was seen approaching; and among the morning's budget was one letter bearing a foreign postmark and stamp (which became at once the objects of an eager competition among the youthful Gregorys), and addressed in an uneducated, but plainly an English hand.

When the Rector opened it, and turned to the signature, he realized that it came from the confidential valet of his friend and squire, Mr. Somerton. Thus it ran:

HONOURED SIR,

Has I am in a great anxeity about Master I write at is Wish to beg you Sir if you could be so good as Step over. Master Has add a Nastey Shock and keeps His Bedd. I never Have known Him like this but No wonder and Nothing will serve but you Sir. Master says would I mintion the Short Way Here is Drive to Cobblince and take a Trap. Hopeing I Have maid all Plain, but am much Confused in Myself what with Anxiatey and Weakfulness at Night. If I might be so Bold Sir it will be a Pleasure to see a Honnest Brish Face among all These Forig ones.

I am Sir
Your obedt Servt
WILLIAM BROWN

P.S.—The Village for Town I will not Turm. It is name Steenfeld.

The reader must be left to picture to himself in detail the surprise, confusion, and hurry of preparation into which the receipt of such a letter would be likely to plunge a quiet Berkshire parsonage in the year of grace 1859. It is enough for me to say that a train to town was caught in the course of the day, and that Mr. Gregory was able to secure a cabin in the Antwerp boat and a place in the Coblenz train. Nor was it difficult to manage the transit from that centre to Steinfeld.

I labour under a grave disadvantage as narrator of this story in that I have never visited Steinfeld myself, and that neither of the principal actors in the episode (from whom I derive my information) was able to give me anything but a vague and rather dismal idea of its appearance. I gather that it is a small place, with a large church despoiled of its ancient fittings; a number of rather ruinous great buildings, mostly of the seventeenth century, surround this church; for the abbey, in common with most of those on the Continent, was rebuilt in a luxurious fashion by its inhabitants at that period. It has not seemed to me worth while to lavish money on a visit to the place, for though it is probably far more attractive than either Mr. Somerton or Mr. Gregory thought it, there is evidently little, if anything, of first-rate interest to be seen—except, perhaps, one thing, which I should not care to see.

The inn where the English gentleman and his servant were lodged is, or was, the only "possible" one in the village. Mr. Gregory was taken to it at once by his driver, and found Mr. Brown waiting at the door. Mr. Brown, a model when in his Berkshire home of the impassive whiskered race who are known as confidential valets, was now egregiously out of his element, in a light tweed suit, anxious, almost irritable, and plainly anything but master of the situation. His relief at the sight of the "honest British face" of his Rector was unmeasured, but words to describe it were denied him. He could only say:

"Well, I ham pleased, I'm sure, sir, to see you. And so I'm sure, sir, will master."

"How *is* your master, Brown?" Mr. Gregory eagerly put in.

"I think he's better, sir, thank you; but he's had a dreadful time of it. I 'ope he's gettin' some sleep now, but——"

"What has been the matter—I couldn't make out from your letter? Was it an accident of any kind?"

"Well, sir, I 'ardly know whether I'd better speak about it. Master was very particker he should be the one to tell you. But there's no bones broke—that's one thing I'm sure we ought to be thankful——"

"What does the doctor say?" asked Mr. Gregory.

They were by this time outside Mr. Somerton's bedroom door, and speaking in low tones. Mr. Gregory, who happened to be in front, was feeling for the handle, and chanced to run his fingers over the panels. Before Brown could answer, there was a terrible cry from within the room.

"In God's name, who is that?" were the first words they heard. "Brown, is it?"

"Yes, sir—me, sir, and Mr. Gregory," Brown hastened to answer, and there was an audible groan of relief in reply.

They entered the room, which was darkened against the afternoon sun, and Mr. Gregory saw, with a shock of pity, how drawn, how damp with drops of fear, was the usually calm face of his friend, who, sitting up in the curtained bed, stretched out a shaking hand to welcome him.

"Better for seeing you, my dear Gregory," was the reply to the Rector's first question, and it was palpably true.

After five minutes of conversation Mr.. Somerton was more his own man, Brown afterwards reported, than he had been for days. He was able to eat a more than respectable dinner, and talked confidently of being fit to stand a journey to Coblenz within twenty-four hours.

"But there's one thing," he said, with a return of agitation which Mr. Gregory did not like to see, "which I must beg you to do for me, my dear Gregory. Don't," he went on, laying his hand on Gregory's to forestall any interruption—"don't ask me what it is, or why I want it done. I'm not up to explaining it yet; it would throw me back—undo all the good you have done me by coming. The only word I will say about it is that you run no risk whatever by doing it, and that Brown can and will show you tomorrow what it is. It's merely to put back—to keep—something——No; I can't speak of it yet. Do you mind calling Brown?"

"Well, Somerton," said Mr. Gregory, as he crossed the room to the door. "I won't ask for any explanations till you see fit to give them. And if this bit of business is as easy as you represent it to be, I will very gladly undertake it for you the first thing in the morning."

"Ah, I was sure you would, my dear Gregory; I was certain I could rely on you. I shall owe you more thanks than I can tell. Now, here is Brown. Brown, one word with you."

"Shall I go?" interjected Mr. Gregory.

"Not at all. Dear me, no. Brown, the first thing to-morrow morning—(you don't mind early hours, I know, Gregory)—you must take the Rector to—*there*, you know' (a nod from Brown, who looked grave and anxious), "and he and you will put that back. You needn't be in the least alarmed; it's *perfectly* safe in the daytime. You know what I mean. It lies on the step, you know, where—where we put it." (Brown swallowed dryly once or twice, and, failing to speak, bowed.) "And—yes, that's all. Only this one other word, my dear Gregory. If you *can* manage to keep from questioning Brown about this matter, I shall be still more bound to you. To-morrow evening, at latest, if all goes well, I shall be able, I believe, to tell you the whole story from start to finish. And now I'll wish you good-night. Brown will be with me—he sleeps here— and if I were you, I should lock my door. Yes, be particular to do that. They—they like it, the people here, and it's better. Good-night, good-night."

They parted upon this, and if Mr. Gregory woke once or twice in the small hours and fancied he heard a fumbling about the lower part of his locked door, it was, perhaps, no more than what a quiet man, suddenly plunged into a strange bed and the heart of a mystery, might reasonably expect. Certainly he thought, to the end of his days, that he had heard such a sound twice or three times between midnight and dawn.

He was up with the sun, and out in company with Brown soon after. Perplexing as was the service he had been asked to perform for Mr. Somerton, it was not a difficult or an alarming one, and within half an hour from his leaving the inn it was over. What it was I shall not as yet divulge.

Later in the morning Mr. Somerton, now almost himself again, was able to make a start from Steinfeld; and that same evening, whether at Coblenz or at some intermediate stage on the journey I am not certain, he settled down to the promised explanation. Brown was present, but how much of the matter was ever really made plain to his comprehension he would never say, and I am unable to conjecture.

III

This was Mr. Somerton's story:

"You know roughly, both of you, that this expedition of mine was undertaken with the object of tracing something in connexion with some old painted glass in Lord D——'s private chapel. Well, the starting-point of the whole matter lies in this passage from an old printed book, to which I will ask your attention."

And at this point Mr. Somerton went carefully over some ground with which we are already familiar.

"On my second visit to the chapel," he went on, "my purpose was to take every note I could of figures, lettering, diamond-scratchings on the glass, and even apparently accidental markings. The first point which I tackled was that of the inscribed scrolls. I could not doubt that the first of these, that of Job—'There is a place for the gold where it is hidden'—with its intentional alteration, must refer to the treasure; so I applied myself with some confidence to the next, that of St John—'They have on their vestures a writing which no man knoweth.' The natural question will have occurred to you: Was there an inscription on the robes of the figures? I could see none; each of the three had a broad black border to his mantle, which made a conspicuous and rather ugly feature in the window. I was nonplussed, I will own, and, but for a curious bit of luck, I think I should have left the search where the Canons of Steinfeld had left it before me. But it so happened that there was a good deal of dust on the surface of the glass, and Lord D——, happening to come in, noticed my blackened hands, and kindly insisted on sending for a Turk's head broom to clean down the window. There must, I suppose, have been a rough piece in the broom; anyhow, as it passed over the border of one of the mantles, I noticed that it left a long scratch, and that some yellow stain instantly showed up. I asked the man to stop his work for a moment, and ran up the ladder to examine the place. The yellow stain was there, sure enough, and what had come away was a thick black pigment, which had evidently been laid on with the brush after the glass had been burnt, and could therefore be easily scraped off without doing any harm. I scraped, accordingly, and you will hardly believe—no, I do you an injustice; you will have guessed already—that I found under this black pigment two or three clearly-formed capital letters in yellow stain on a clear ground. Of course, I could hardly contain my delight.

"I told Lord D—— that I had detected an inscription which I thought might be very interesting, and begged to be allowed to uncover the whole of it. He made no difficulty about it whatever, told me to do exactly as I pleased, and then, having an engagement, was obliged—rather to my relief, I must say—to leave me. I set to work at once, and found the task a fairly easy one. The pigment, disintegrated, of course, by time, came off almost at a touch, and I don't think that it took me a couple of hours, all told, to clean the whole of the black borders in all three lights. Each of the figures had, as the inscription said, 'a writing on their vestures which nobody knew.'

"This discovery, of course, made it absolutely certain to my mind that I was on the right track. And, now, what was the inscription? While I was cleaning the glass I almost took pains not to read the lettering, saving up the treat until I had got the whole thing clear. And when that was done, my dear Gregory, I assure you I could almost have cried from sheer disappointment. What I read was only the most hopeless jumble of letters that was ever shaken up in a hat. Here it is:

Job.   DREVICIOPEDMOOMSMVIVLISLC
AVIBASBATAOVT

St John.   RDIIEAMRLESIPVSPODSEEIRSET
               TAAESGIAVNNR

Zechariah.   FTEEAILNQDPVAIVMTLEEATTOH
               IOONVMCAAT.H.Q.E.

"Blank as I felt and must have looked for the first few minutes, my disappointment didn't last long. I realized almost at once that I was dealing with a cipher or
cryptogram; and I reflected that it was likely to be of a pretty simple kind, considering
its early date. So I copied the letters with the most anxious care. Another little point, I
may tell you, turned up in the process which confirmed my belief in the cipher. After
copying the letters on Job's robe I counted them, to make sure that I had them right.
There were thirty-eight; and, just as I finished going through them, my eye fell on
a scratching made with a sharp point on the edge of the border. It was simply the
number xxxviii in Roman numerals. To cut the matter short, there was a similar note,
as I may call it, in each of the other lights; and that made it plain to me that the glass-
painter had had very strict orders from Abbot Thomas about the inscription and had
taken pains to get it correct.

"Well, after that discovery you may imagine how minutely I went over the whole
surface of the glass in search of further light. Of course, I did not neglect the inscription on the scroll of Zechariah—'Upon one stone are seven eyes,' but I very quickly
concluded that this must refer to some mark on a stone which could only be found
in situ, where the treasure was concealed. To be short, I made all possible notes and
sketches and tracings, and then came back to Parsbury to work out the cipher at leisure. Oh, the agonies I went through! I thought myself very clever at first, for I made
sure that the key would be found in some of the old books on secret writing. The
Steganographia of Joachim Trithemius, who was an earlier contemporary of Abbot
Thomas, seemed particularly promising; so I got that and Selenius's *Cryptographia* and
Bacon's *de Augmentis Scientiarum* and some more. But I could hit upon nothing. Then
I tried the principle of the 'most frequent letter,' taking first Latin and then German
as a basis. That didn't help, either; whether it ought to have done so, I am not clear.
And then I came back to the window itself, and read over my notes, hoping almost
against hope that the Abbot might himself have somewhere supplied the key I wanted.
I could make nothing out of the colour or pattern of the robes. There were no landscape backgrounds with subsidiary objects; there was nothing in the canopies. The
only resource possible seemed to be in the attitudes of the figures. 'Job,' I read: 'scroll

in left hand, forefinger of right hand extended upwards. John: holds inscribed book in left hand; with right hand blesses, with two fingers. Zechariah: scroll in left hand; right hand extended upwards, as Job, but with three fingers pointing up.' In other words, I reflected, Job has *one* finger extended, John has *two*, Zechariah has *three*. May not there be a numerical key concealed in that? My dear Gregory," said Mr. Somerton, laying his hand on his friend's knee, "that *was* the key. I didn't get it to fit at first, but after two or three trials I saw what was meant. After the first letter of the inscription you skip *one* letter, after the next you skip *two*, and after that skip *three*. Now look at the result I got. I've underlined the letters which form words:

DREVICIOPEDMOOMSMVIVLISLCAVIBASBATAOVT

RDIIEAMRLESIPVSPODSEEIRSETTA AESGIAVNNR

FTEEAILNQDPVAIVMTLEEATTOHIOO NVMCAAT.H.Q.E.

"Do you see it? 'Decem millia auri reposita sunt in puteo in at ...' (Ten thousand [pieces] of gold are laid up in a well in . . . , followed by an incomplete word beginning *at*. So far so good. I tried the same plan with the remaining letters; but it wouldn't work, and I fancied that perhaps the placing of dots after the three last letters might indicate some difference of procedure. Then I thought to myself, 'Wasn't there some allusion to a well in the account of Abbot Thomas in that book the *Sertum*?' Yes, there was; he built a *puteus in atrio* (a well in the court). There, of course, was my word atrio. The next step was to copy out the remaining letters of the inscription, omitting those I had already used. That gave what you will see on this slip:

RVIIOPDOOSMVVISCAVBSBTAOTDIEAMLSIVSPDEERSETAEGIANR
FEEALQD VAIMLEATTHOOVMCA.H.Q.E.

"Now, I knew what the three first letters I wanted were—namely, *rio*—to complete the word *atrio*; and, as you will see, these are all to be found in the first five letters. I was a little confused at first by the occurrence of two *i*'s, but very soon I saw that every alternate letter must be taken in the remainder of the inscription. You can work it out for yourself; the result, continuing where the first "round" left off, is this:

'rio domus abbatialis de Steinfeld a me, Thoma, qui posui custodem super ea. Gare à qui la touche.'

"So the whole secret was out:

'Ten thousand pieces of gold are laid up in the well in the court of the Abbot's house of Steinfeld by me, Thomas, who have set a guardian over them. Gare à qui la louche.'

"The last words, I ought to say, are a device which Abbot Thomas had adopted. I found it with his arms in another piece of glass at Lord D——'s, and he drafted it bodily into his cipher, though it doesn't quite fit in point of grammar.

"Well, what would any human being have been tempted to do, my dear Gregory, in my place? Could he have helped setting off, as I did, to Steinfeld, and tracing the secret literally to the fountain-head? I don't believe he could. Anyhow, I couldn't, and, as I needn't tell you, I found myself at Steinfeld as soon as the resources of civilization could put me there, and installed myself in the inn you saw. I must tell you that I was not altogether free from forebodings—on one hand of disappointment, on the other of danger. There was always the possibility that Abbot Thomas's well might have been wholly obliterated, or else that someone, ignorant of cryptograms, and guided only by luck, might have stumbled on the treasure before me. And then"—there was a very perceptible shaking of the voice here—"I was not entirely easy, I need not mind confessing, as to the meaning of the words about the guardian of the treasure. But, if you don't mind, I'll say no more about that until—until it becomes necessary.

"At the first possible opportunity Brown and I began exploring the place. I had naturally represented myself as being interested in the remains of the abbey, and we could not avoid paying a visit to the church, impatient as I was to be elsewhere. Still, it did interest me to see the windows where the glass had been, and especially that at the east end of the south aisle. In the tracery lights of that I was startled to see some fragments and coats-of-arms remaining—Abbot Thomas's shield was there, and a small figure with a scroll inscribed "Oculos habent, et non videbunt" (They have eyes, and shall not see), which, I take it, was a hit of the Abbot at his Canons.

"But, of course, the principal object was to find the Abbot's house. There is no prescribed place for this, so far as I know, in the plan of a monastery; you can't predict of it, as you can of the chapter-house, that it will be on the eastern side of the cloister, or, as of the dormitory, that it will communicate with a transept of the church. I felt that if I asked many questions I might awaken lingering memories of the treasure, and I thought it best to try first to discover it for myself. It was not a very long or difficult search. That three-sided court south-east of the church, with deserted piles of building round it, and grass-grown pavement, which you saw this morning, was the place. And glad enough I was to see that it was put to no use, and was neither very far from our inn nor overlooked by any inhabited building; there were only orchards and paddocks on the slopes east of the church. I can tell you that fine stone glowed wonderfully in the rather watery yellow sunset that we had on the Tuesday afternoon.

"Next, what about the well? There was not much doubt about that, as you can testify. It is really a very remarkable thing. That curb is, I think, of Italian marble, and the carving I thought must be Italian also. There were reliefs, you will perhaps remember, of Eliezer and Rebekah, and of Jacob opening the well for Rachel, and similar subjects; but, by way of disarming suspicion, I suppose, the Abbot had carefully abstained from any of his cynical and allusive inscriptions.

"I examined the whole structure with the keenest interest, of course—a square well-head with an opening in one side; an arch over it, with a wheel for the rope to pass over, evidently in very good condition still, for it had been used within sixty years, or perhaps even later though not quite recently. Then there was the question of depth and access to the interior. I suppose the depth was about sixty to seventy feet; and as to the other point, it really seemed as if the Abbot had wished to lead searchers up to the very door of his treasure-house, for, as you tested for yourself, there were big blocks of stone bonded into the masonry, and leading down in a regular staircase round and round the inside of the well.

"It seemed almost too good to be true. I wondered if there was a trap—if the stones were so contrived as to tip over when a weight was placed on them; but I tried a good many with my own weight and with my stick, and all seemed, and actually were, perfectly firm. Of course, I resolved that Brown and I would make an experiment that very night.

"I was well prepared. Knowing the sort of place I should have to explore, I had brought a sufficiency of good rope and bands of webbing to surround my body, and crossbars to hold to, as well as lanterns and candles and crowbars, all of which would go into a single carpet-bag and excite no suspicion. I satisfied myself that my rope would be long enough, and that the wheel for the bucket was in good working order, and then we went home to dinner.

"I had a little cautious conversation with the landlord, and made out that he would not be overmuch surprised if I went out for a stroll with my man about nine o'clock, to make (Heaven forgive me!) a sketch of the abbey by moonlight. I asked no questions about the well, and am not likely to do so now. I fancy I know as much about it as anyone in Steinfeld: at least"—with a strong shudder—"I don't want to know any more.

"Now we come to the crisis, and, though I hate to think of it, I feel sure, Gregory, that it will be better for me in all ways to recall it just as it happened. We started, Brown and I, at about nine with our bag, and attracted no attention; for we managed to slip out at the hinder end of the inn-yard into an alley which brought us quite to the edge of the village. In five minutes we were at the well, and for some little time we sat on the edge of the well-head to make sure that no one was stirring or spying on us. All we heard was some horses cropping grass out of sight farther down the eastern slope. We were perfectly unobserved, and had plenty of light from the gorgeous full moon to allow us to get the rope properly fitted over the wheel. Then I secured the band round my body beneath the arms. We attached the end of the rope very securely to a ring in the stonework. Brown took the lighted lantern and followed me; I had a crowbar. And so we began to descend cautiously, feeling every step before we set foot on it, and scanning the walls in search of any marked stone.

"Half aloud I counted the steps as we went down, and we got as far as the thirty-eighth before I noted anything at all irregular in the surface of the masonry. Even here there was no mark, and I began to feel very blank, and to wonder if the Abbot's cryptogram could possibly be an elaborate hoax. At the forty-ninth step the staircase ceased. It was with a very sinking heart that I began retracing my steps, and when I was back on the thirty-eighth—Brown, with the lantern, being a step or two above me—I scrutinized the little bit of irregularity in the stonework with all my might; but there was no vestige of a mark.

"Then it struck me that the texture of the surface looked just a little smoother than the rest, or, at least, in some way different. It might possibly be cement and not stone. I gave it a good blow with my iron bar. There was a decidedly hollow sound, though that might be the result of our being in a well. But there was more. A great flake of cement dropped on to my feet, and I saw marks on the stone underneath. I had tracked the Abbot down, my dear Gregory; even now I think of it with a certain pride. It took but a very few more taps to clear the whole of the cement away, and I saw a slab of stone about two feet square, upon which was engraven a cross. Disappointment again, but only for a moment. It was you, Brown, who reassured me by a casual remark. You said, if I remember right:

" 'It's a funny cross: looks like a lot of eyes.'

"I snatched the lantern out of your hand, and saw with inexpressible pleasure that the cross *was* composed of seven eyes, four in a vertical line, three horizontal. The last of the scrolls in the window was explained in the way I had anticipated. Here was my 'stone with the seven eyes.' So far the Abbot's data had been exact, and as I thought of this, the anxiety about the 'guardian' returned upon me with increased force. Still I wasn't going to retreat now.

"Without giving myself time to think, I knocked away the cement all round the marked stone, and then gave it a prise on the right side with my crowbar. It moved at once, and I saw that it was but a thin light slab, such as I could easily lift out myself, and that it stopped the entrance to a cavity. I did lift it out unbroken, and set it on the step, for it might be very important to us to be able to replace it. Then I waited for several minutes on the step just above. I don't know why, but I think to see if any dreadful thing would rush out. Nothing happened. Next I lit a candle, and very cautiously I placed it inside the cavity, with some idea of seeing whether there were foul air, and of getting a glimpse of what was inside. There *was* some foulness of air which nearly extinguished the flame, but in no long time it burned quite steadily. The hole went some little way back, and also on the right and left of the entrance, and I could see some rounded light-coloured objects within which might be bags. There was no use in waiting. I faced the cavity, and looked in. There was nothing immediately in the front of the hole. I put my arm in and felt to the right, very gingerly. . . .

"Just give me a glass of cognac, Brown. I'll go on in a moment, Gregory. . . .

"Well, I felt to the right, and my fingers touched something curved, that felt—yes—more or less like leather; dampish it was, and evidently part of a heavy, full thing. There was nothing, I must say, to alarm one. I grew bolder, and putting both hands in as well as I could, I pulled it to me, and it came. It was heavy, but moved more easily than I had expected. As I pulled it towards the entrance, my left elbow knocked over and extinguished the candle. I got the thing fairly in front of the mouth and began drawing it out. Just then Brown gave a sharp ejaculation and ran quickly up the steps with the lantern. He will tell you why in a moment. Startled as I was, I looked round after him, and saw him stand for a minute at the top and then walk away a few yards. Then I heard him call softly, 'All right, sir,' and went on pulling out the great bag, in complete darkness. It hung for an instant on the edge of the hole, then slipped forward on to my chest, and *put its arms round my neck*.

"My dear Gregory, I am telling you the exact truth. I believe I am now acquainted with the extremity of terror and repulsion which a man can endure without losing his mind. I can only just manage to tell you now the bare outline of the experience. I was conscious of a most horrible smell of mould, and of a cold kind of face pressed against my own, and moving slowly over it, and of several—I don't know how many—legs or arms or tentacles or something clinging to my body. I screamed out, Brown says, like a beast, and fell away backward from the step on which I stood, and the creature slipped downwards, I suppose, on to that same step. Providentially the band round me held firm. Brown did not lose his head, and was strong enough to pull me up to the top and get me over the edge quite promptly. How he managed it exactly I don't know, and I think he would find it hard to tell you. I believe he contrived to hide our implements in the deserted building near by, and with very great difficulty he got me back to the inn. I was in no state to make explanations, and Brown knows no German; but next morning I told the people some tale of having had a bad fall in the abbey ruins, which I suppose they believed. And now, before I go further, I should just like you to hear what Brown's experiences during those few minutes were. Tell the Rector, Brown, what you told me."

"Well, sir," said Brown, speaking low and nervously, "it was just this way. Master was busy down in front of the 'ole, and I was 'olding the lantern and looking on, when I 'eard somethink drop in the water from the top, as I thought. So I looked up, and I see someone's 'ead lookin' over at us. I s'pose I must ha' said somethink, and I 'eld the light up and run up the steps, and my light shone right on the face. That was a bad un, sir, if ever I see one! A holdish man, and the face very much fell in, and larfin, as I thought. And I got up the steps as quick pretty nigh as I'm tellin' you, and when I was out on the ground there warn't a sign of any person. There 'adn't been the time for anyone to get away, let alone a hold chap, and I made sure he warn't crouching down by the well, nor nothink. Next thing I hear master cry out somethink 'orrible, and hall I see was him hanging out by the rope, and, as master says, 'owever I got him up I couldn't tell you."

"You hear that, Gregory?" said Mr. Somerton. "Now, does any explanation of that incident strike you?"

"The whole thing is so ghastly and abnormal that I must own it puts me quite off my balance; but the thought did occur to me that possibly the—well, the person who set the trap might have come to see the success of his plan."

"Just so, Gregory, just so. I can think of nothing else so—*likely*, I should say, if such a word had a place anywhere in my story. I think it must have been the Abbot . . . . Well, I haven't much more to tell you. I spent a miserable night, Brown sitting up with me. Next day I was no better; unable to get up; no doctor to be had; and if one had been available, I doubt if he could have done much for me. I made Brown write off to you, and spent a second terrible night. And, Gregory, of this I am sure, and I think it affected me more than the first shock, for it lasted longer: there was someone or something on the watch outside my door the whole night. I almost fancy there were two. It wasn't only the faint noises I heard from time to time all through the dark hours, but there was the smell—the hideous smell of mould. Every rag I had had on me on that first evening I had stripped off and made Brown take it away. I believe he stuffed the things into the stove in his room; and yet the smell was there, as intense as it had been in the well; and, what is more, it came from outside the door. But with the first glimmer of dawn it faded out, and the sounds ceased, too; and that convinced me that the thing or things were creatures of darkness, and could not stand the daylight; and so I was sure that if anyone could put back the stone, it or they would be powerless until someone else took it away again. I had to wait until you came to get that done. Of course, I couldn't send Brown to do it by himself, and still less could I tell anyone who belonged to the place.

"Well, there is my story; and, if you don't believe it, I can't help it. But I think you do."

"Indeed," said Mr. Gregory, "I can find no alternative. I *must* believe it! I saw the well and the stone myself, and had a glimpse, I thought, of the bags or something else in the hole. And, to be plain with you, Somerton, I believe my door was watched last night, too."

"I dare say it was, Gregory; but, thank goodness, that is over. Have you, by the way, anything to tell about your visit to that dreadful place?"

"Very little," was the answer. "Brown and I managed easily enough to get the slab into its place, and he fixed it very firmly with the irons and wedges you had desired him to get, and we contrived to smear the surface with mud so that it looks just like the rest of the wall. One thing I did notice in the carving on the well-head, which I think must have escaped you. It was a horrid, grotesque shape—perhaps more like a toad than anything else, and there was a label by it inscribed with the two words, 'Depositum custodi.' "*

* "Keep that which is committed to thee."

The Story of a Panic

E. M. Forster

———◆———

I

Eustace's career—if career it can be called—certainly dates from that afternoon in the chestnut woods above Ravello. I confess at once that I am a plain, simple man, with no pretensions to literary style. Still, I do flatter myself that I can tell a story without exaggerating, and I have therefore decided to give an unbiassed account of the extraordinary events of eight years ago.

Ravello is a delightful place with a delightful little hotel in which we met some charming people. There were the two Miss Robinsons, who had been there for six weeks with Eustace, their nephew, then a boy of about fourteen. Mr. Sandbach had also been there some time. He had held a curacy in the north of England, which he had been compelled to resign on account of ill-health, and while he was recruiting at Ravello he had taken in hand Eustace's education—which was then sadly deficient—and was endeavouring to fit him for one of our great public schools. Then there was Mr. Leyland, a would-be artist, and, finally, there was the nice landlady, Signora Scafetti, and the nice English-speaking waiter, Emmanuele—though at the time of which I am speaking Emmanuele was away, visiting a sick father.

To this little circle, I, my wife, and my two daughters made, I venture to think, a not unwelcome addition. But though I liked most of the company well enough, there were two of them to whom I did not take at all. They were the artist, Leyland, and the Miss Robinsons' nephew, Eustace.

Leyland was simply conceited and odious, and, as those qualities will be amply illustrated in my narrative, I need not enlarge upon them here. But Eustace was something besides: he was indescribably repellent.

I am fond of boys as a rule, and was quite disposed to be friendly. I and my daughters offered to take him out—"No, walking was such a fag." Then I asked him to come and bathe—"No, he could not swim."

"Every English boy should be able to swim," I said, "I will teach you myself."

"There, Eustace dear," said Miss Robinson; "here is a chance for you."

But he said he was afraid of the water!—a boy afraid!—and of course I said no more.

I would not have minded so much if he had been a really studious boy, but he neither played hard nor worked hard. His favourite occupations were lounging on the terrace in an easy chair and loafing along the high road, with his feet shuffling up the dust and his shoulders stooping forward. Naturally enough, his features were pale, his chest contracted, and his muscles undeveloped. His aunts thought him delicate; what he really needed was discipline.

That memorable day we all arranged to go for a picnic up in the chestnut woods—all, that is, except Janet, who stopped behind to finish her water-colour of the Cathedral—not a very successful attempt, I am afraid.

I wander off into these irrelevant details, because in my mind I cannot separate them from an account of the day; and it is the same with the conversation during the picnic: all is imprinted on my brain together. After a couple of hours' ascent, we left the donkeys that had carried the Miss Robinsons and my wife, and all proceeded on foot to the head of the valley—Vallone Fontana Caroso is its proper name, I find.

I have visited a good deal of fine scenery before and since, but have found little that has pleased me more. The valley ended in a vast hollow, shaped like a cup, into which radiated ravines from the precipitous hills around. Both the valley and the ravines and the ribs of hill that divided the ravines were covered with leafy, chestnut, so that the general appearance was that of a many fingered green hand, palm upwards, which was clutching, convulsively to keep us in its grasp. Far down the valley we could see Ravello and the sea, but that was the only sign of another world.

"Oh, what a perfectly lovely place," said my daughter Rose. "What a picture it would make!"

"Yes," said Mr. Sandbach. "Many a famous European gallery would be proud to have a landscape a tithe as beautiful as this upon its walls."

"On the contrary," said Leyland, "it would make a very poor picture. Indeed, it is not paintable at all."

"And why is that?" said Rose, with far more deference than he deserved.

"Look, in the first place," he replied, "how intolerably straight against the sky is the line of the hill. It would need breaking up and diversifying. And where we are standing the whole thing is out of perspective. Besides, all the colouring is monotonous and crude."

"I do not know anything about pictures," I put in, "and I do not pretend to know: but I know what is beautiful when I see it, and I am thoroughly content with this."

"Indeed, who could help being contented!" said the elder Miss Robinson and Mr. Sandbach said the same.

"Ah!" said Leyland, "you all confuse the artistic view of nature with the photographic."

Poor Rose had brought her camera with her, so I thought this positively rude. I did not wish any unpleasantness; so I merely turned away and assisted my wife and Miss Mary Robinson to put out the lunch—not a very nice lunch.

"Eustace, dear," said his aunt, "come and help us here."

He was in a particularly bad temper that morning. He had, as usual, not wanted to come, and his aunts had nearly allowed him to stop at the hotel to vex Janet. But I, with their permission, spoke to him rather sharply on the subject of exercise; and the result was that he had come, but was even more taciturn and moody than usual.

Obedience was not his strong point. He invariably questioned every command, and only executed it grumbling. I should always insist on prompt and cheerful obedience, if I had a son.

"I'm—coming—Aunt—Mary," he at last replied, and dawdled to cut a piece of wood to make a whistle, taking care not to arrive till we had finished.

"Well, well, sir!" said I, "you stroll in at the end and profit by our labours." He sighed, for he could not endure being chaffed. Miss Mary, very unwisely, insisted on giving him the wing of the chicken, in spite of all my attempts to prevent her. I remember that I had a moment's vexation when I thought that, instead of enjoying the sun, and the air, and the woods, we were all engaged in wrangling over the diet of a spoilt boy.

But, after lunch, he was a little less in evidence. He withdrew to a tree trunk, and began to loosen the bark from his whistle. I was thankful to see him employed, for once in a way. We reclined, and took a *dolce far niente*.

Those sweet chestnuts of the South are puny striplings compared with our robust Northerners. But they clothed the contours of the hills and valleys in a most pleasing way, their veil being only broken by two clearings, in one of which we were sitting.

And because these few trees were cut down, Leyland burst into a petty indictment of the proprietor.

"All the poetry is going from Nature," he cried, "her lakes and marshes are drained, her seas banked up, her forests cut down. Everywhere we see the vulgarity of desolation spreading."

I have had some experience of estates, and answered that cutting was very necessary for the health of the larger trees. Besides, it was unreasonable to expect the proprietor to derive no income from his lands.

"If you take the commercial side of landscape, you may feel pleasure in the owner's activity. But to me the mere thought that a tree is convertible into cash is disgusting."

"I see no reason," I observed politely, "to despise the gifts of Nature, because they are of value."

It did not stop him. "It is no matter," he went on, "we are all hopelessly steeped in vulgarity. I do not except myself. It is through us, and to our shame, that the Nereids have left the waters and the Oreads the mountains, that the woods no longer give shelter to Pan."

"Pan!" cried Mr. Sandbach, his mellow voice filling the valley as if it had been a great green church, "Pan is dead. That is why the woods do not shelter him." And he began to tell the striking story of the mariners who were sailing near the coast at the time of the birth of Christ, and three times heard a loud voice saying: "The great God Pan is dead."

"Yes. The great God Pan is dead," said Leyland. And he abandoned himself to that mock misery in which artistic people are so fond of indulging. His cigar went out, and he had to ask me for a match.

"How very interesting," said Rose. "I do wish I knew some ancient history."

"It is not worth your notice," said Mr. Sandbach. "Eh, Eustace?"

Eustace was finishing his whistle. He looked up, with the irritable frown in which his aunts allowed him to indulge, and made no reply.

The conversation turned to various topics and then died out. It was a cloudless afternoon in May, and the pale green of the young chestnut leaves made a pretty contrast with the dark blue of the sky. We were all sitting at the edge of the small clearing for the sake of the view, and the shade of the chestnut saplings behind us was manifestly insufficient. All sounds died away—at least that is my account: Miss Robinson says that the clamour of the birds was the first sign of uneasiness that she discerned. All sounds died away, except that, far in the distance, I could hear two boughs of a great chestnut grinding together as the tree swayed. The grinds grew shorter and shorter, and finally that sound stopped also. As I looked over the green fingers of the valley, everything was absolutely motionless and still; and that feeling of suspense which one so often experiences when Nature is in repose, began to steal over me.

Suddenly, we were all electrified by the excruciating noise of Eustace's whistle. I never heard any instrument give forth so ear-splitting and discordant a sound.

"Eustace, dear," said Miss Mary Robinson, "you might have thought of your poor Aunt Julia's head."

Leyland who had apparently been asleep, sat up.

"It is astonishing how blind a boy is to anything that is elevating or beautiful," he observed. "I should not have thought he could have found the wherewithal out here to spoil our pleasure like this."

Then the terrible silence fell upon us again. I was now standing up and watching a catspaw of wind that was running down one of the ridges opposite, turning the light green to dark as it travelled. A fanciful feeling of foreboding came over me; so I turned away, to find to my amazement, that all the others were also on their feet, watching it too.

It is not possible to describe coherently what happened next: but I, for one, am not ashamed to confess that, though the fair blue sky was above me, and the green spring woods beneath me, and the kindest of friends around me, yet I became terribly frightened, more frightened than I ever wish to become again, frightened in a way I never have known either before or after. And in the eyes of the others, too, I saw blank, expressionless fear, while their mouths strove in vain to speak and their hands to gesticulate. Yet, all around us were prosperity, beauty, and peace, and all was motionless, save the catspaw of wind, now travelling up the ridge on which we stood.

Who moved first has never been settled. It is enough to say that in one second we were tearing away along the hillside. Leyland was in front, then Mr. Sandbach, then my wife. But I only saw for a brief moment; for I ran across the little clearing and through the woods and over the undergrowth and the rocks and down the dry torrent beds into the valley below. The sky might have been black as I ran, and the trees short grass, and the hillside a level road; for I saw nothing and heard nothing and felt nothing, since all the channels of sense and reason were blocked. It was not the spiritual fear that one has known at other times, but brutal overmastering physical fear, stopping up the ears, and dropping clouds before the eyes, and filling the mouth with foul tastes. And it was no ordinary humiliation that survived; for I had been afraid, not as a man, but as a beast.

II

I cannot describe our finish any better than our start; for our fear passed away as it had come, without cause. Suddenly I was able to see, and hear, and cough, and clear my mouth. Looking back, I saw that the others were stopping too; and, in a short time, we were all together, though it was long before we could speak, and longer before we dared to.

No one was seriously injured. My poor wife had sprained her ankle, Leyland had torn one of his nails on a tree trunk, and I myself had scraped and damaged my ear. I never noticed it till I had stopped.

We were all silent, searching one another's faces. Suddenly Miss Mary Robinson gave a terrible shriek. "Oh, merciful heavens! where is Eustace?" And then she would have fallen, if Mr. Sandbach had not caught her.

"We must go back, we must go back at once," said my Rose, who was quite the most collected of the party. "But I hope—I feel he is safe."

Such was the cowardice of Leyland, that he objected. But, finding himself in a minority, and being afraid of being left alone, he gave in. Rose and I supported my poor wife, Mr. Sandbach and Miss Robinson helped Miss Mary, and we returned slowly and silently, taking forty minutes to ascend the path that we had descended in ten.

Our conversation was naturally disjointed, as no one wished to offer an opinion on what had happened. Rose was the most talkative: she startled us all by saying that she had very nearly stopped where she was.

"Do you mean to say that you weren't—that you didn't feel compelled to go?" said Mr. Sandbach.

"Oh, of course, I did feel frightened"—she was the first to use the word—"but I somehow felt that if I could stop on it would be quite different, that I shouldn't be frightened at all, so to speak." Rose never did express herself clearly: still, it is greatly to her credit that she, the youngest of us, should have held on so long at that terrible time.

"I should have stopped, I do believe," she continued, "if I had not seen mamma go."

Rose's experience comforted us a little about Eustace. But a feeling of terrible foreboding was on us all, as we painfully climbed the chestnut-covered slopes and neared the little clearing. When we reached it our tongues broke loose. There, at the further side, were the remains of our lunch, and close to them, lying motionless on his back, was Eustace.

With some presence of mind I at once cried out: "Hey, you young monkey! jump up!" But he made no reply, nor did he answer when his poor aunts spoke to him. And, to my unspeakable horror, I saw one of those green lizards dart out from under his shirt-cuff as we approached.

We stood watching him as he lay there so silently, and my ears began to tingle in expectation of the outbursts of lamentations and tears.

Miss Mary fell on her knees beside him and touched his hand, which was convulsively entwined in the long grass.

As she did so, he opened his eyes and smiled.

I have often seen that peculiar smile since, both on the possessor's face and on the photographs of him that are beginning to get into the illustrated papers. But, till then, Eustace had always worn a peevish, discontented frown; and we were all unused to this disquieting smile, which always seemed to be without adequate reason.

His aunts showered kisses on him, which he did not reciprocate, and then there was an awkward pause, Eustace seemed so natural and undisturbed, yet, if he had not had astonishing experiences himself, he ought to have been all the more astonished at our extraordinary behaviour. My wife, with ready tact, endeavoured to behave as if nothing had happened.

"Well, Mr. Eustace," she said, sitting down as she spoke, to ease her foot, "how have you been amusing yourself since we have been away?"

"Thank you, Mrs. Tytler, I have been very happy."

"And where have you been?"

"Here."

"And lying down all the time, you idle boy?"

"No, not all the time."

"What were you doing before?"

"Oh; standing or sitting."

"Stood and sat doing nothing! Don't you know the poem 'Satan finds some mischief still for——' "

"Oh, my dear madam, hush! hush!" Mr. Sandbach's voice broke in; and my wife, naturally mortified by the interruption, said no more and moved away. I was surprised to see Rose immediately take her place, and, with more freedom than she generally displayed, run her fingers through the boy's tousled hair.

"Eustace! Eustace!" she said, hurriedly, "tell me everything—every single thing."

Slowly he sat up—till then he had lain on his back.

"Oh, Rose—," he whispered, and, my curiosity being aroused, I moved nearer to hear what he was going to say. As I did so, I caught sight of some goats' footmarks in the moist earth beneath the trees.

"Apparently you have had a visit from some goats," I observed. "I had no idea they fed up here."

Eustace laboriously got on to his feet and came to see; and when he saw the footmarks he lay down and rolled on them, as a dog rolls in dirt.

After that there was a grave silence, broken at length by the solemn speech of Mr. Sandbach.

"My dear friends," he said, "it is best to confess the truth bravely. I know that what I am going to say now is what you are all now feeling. The Evil One has been very near us in bodily form. Time may yet discover some injury that he has wrought among us. But, at present, for myself at all events, I wish to offer up thanks for a merciful deliverance."

With that he knelt down, and, as the others knelt, I knelt too, though I do not believe in the Devil being allowed to assail us in visible form, as I told Mr. Sandbach afterwards. Eustace came too, and knelt quietly enough between his aunts after they had beckoned to him. But when it was over he at once got up, and began hunting for something.

"Why! Someone has cut my whistle in two," he said. (I had seen Leyland with an open knife in his hand—a superstitious act which I could hardly approve.)

"Well, it doesn't matter," he continued.

"And why doesn't it matter?" said Mr. Sandbach, who has ever since tried to entrap Eustace into an account of that mysterious hour.

"Because I don't want it any more."

"Why?"

At that he smiled; and, as no one seemed to have anything more to say, I set off as fast as I could through the wood, and hauled up a donkey to carry my poor wife home. Nothing occurred in my absence, except that Rose had again asked Eustace to tell her what had happened; and he, this time, had turned away his head, and had not answered her a single word.

As soon as I returned, we all set off. Eustace walked with difficulty, almost with pain, so that, when we reached the other donkeys, his aunts wished him to mount one of them and ride all the way home. I make it a rule never to interfere between relatives, but I put my foot down at this. As it turned out, I was perfectly right, for the healthy exercise, I suppose, began to thaw Eustace's sluggish blood and loosen his stiffened muscles. He stepped out manfully, for the first time in his life, holding his head up and taking deep draughts of air into his chest. I observed with satisfaction to Miss Mary Robinson, that Eustace was at last taking some pride in his personal appearance.

Mr. Sandbach sighed, and said that Eustace must be carefully watched, for we none of us understood him yet. Miss Mary Robinson being very much—over much, I think—guided by him, sighed too.

"Come, come. Miss Robinson," I said, "there's nothing wrong with Eustace. Our experiences are mysterious, not his. He was astonished at our sudden departure, that's why he was so strange when we returned. He's right enough—improved, if anything."

"And is the worship of athletics, the cult of insensate activity, to be counted as an improvement?" put in Leyland, fixing a large, sorrowful eye on Eustace, who had stopped to scramble on to a rock to pick some cyclamen. "The passionate desire to rend from Nature the few beauties that have been still left her—that is to be counted as an improvement too?"

It is mere waste of time to reply to such remarks, especially when they come from an unsuccessful artist, suffering from a damaged finger. I changed the conversation by asking what we should say at the hotel. After some discussion, it was agreed that we should say nothing, either there or in our letters home. Importunate truth-telling, which brings only bewilderment and discomfort to the hearers, is, in my opinion, a mistake; and, after a long discussion, I managed to make Mr. Sandbach acquiesce in my view.

Eustace did not share in our conversation. He was racing about, like a real boy, in the wood to the right. A strange feeling of shame; prevented us from openly mentioning our fright to him. Indeed, it seemed almost reasonable to conclude that it had made but little impression on him. So it disconcerted us when he bounded back with an armful of flowering acanthus, calling out:

"Do you suppose Gennaro'll be there when we get back?"

Gennaro was the stop-gap waiter, a clumsy, impertinent fisher-lad, who had been had up from Minori in the absence of the nice English-speaking Emmanuele. It was to him that we owed our scrappy lunch; and I could not conceive why Eustace desired to see him, unless it was to make mock with him of our behaviour.

"Yes, of course he will be there," said Miss Robinson. "Why do you ask, dear?"

"Oh, I thought I'd like to see him."

"And why?" snapped Mr. Sandbach.

"Because, because I do, I do; because, because I do." He danced away into the darkening wood to the rhythm of his words.

"This is very extraordinary," said Mr. Sandbach. "Did he like Gennaro before?"

"Gennaro has only been here two days," said Rose, "and I know that they haven't spoken to each other a dozen times."

Each time Eustace returned from the wood his spirits were higher. Once he came whooping down on us as a wild Indian, and another time he made believe to be a dog. The last time he came back with a poor dazed hare, too frightened to move, sitting on his arm. He was getting too uproarious, I thought; and we were all glad to leave the wood, and start upon the steep staircase path that leads down into Ravello. It was late and turning dark; and we made all the speed we could, Eustace scurrying in front of us like a goat.

Just where the staircase path debouches on the white high road, the next extraordinary incident of this extraordinary day occurred. Three old women were standing by the wayside. They, like ourselves, had come down from the woods, and they were resting their heavy bundles of fuel on the low parapet of the road. Eustace stopped in front of them, and, after a moment's deliberation, stepped forward and—kissed the left-hand one on the cheek!

"My good fellow!" exclaimed Mr. Sandbach, "are you quite crazy?"

Eustace said nothing, but offered the old woman some of his flowers, and then hurried on. I looked back; and the old woman's companions seemed as much astonished at the proceeding as we were. But she herself had put the flowers in her bosom, and was murmuring blessings.

This salutation of the old lady was the first example of Eustace's strange behaviour, and we were both surprised and alarmed. It was useless talking to him, for he either made silly replies, or else bounded away without replying at all.

He made no reference on the way home to Gennaro, and I hoped that that was forgotten. But, when we came to the Piazza, in front of the Cathedral, he screamed out: "Gennaro! Gennaro!" at the top of his voice, and began running up the little alley that led to the hotel. Sure enough, there was Gennaro at the end of it, with his arms and legs sticking out of the nice little English-speaking waiter's dress suit, and a dirty fisherman's cap on his head—for, as the poor landlady truly said, however much she superintended his toilette, he always managed to introduce something incongruous into it before he had done.

Eustace sprang to meet him, and leapt right up into his arms, and put his own arms round his neck. And this in the presence, not only of us, but also of the landlady, the chambermaid, the facchino, and of two American ladies who were coming for a few days' visit to the little hotel.

I always make a point of behaving pleasantly to Italians, however little they may deserve it; but this habit of promiscuous intimacy was perfectly intolerable and could only lead to familiarity and mortification for all. Taking Miss Robinson aside, I asked her permission to speak seriously to Eustace on the subject of intercourse with social inferiors. She granted it; but I determined to wait till the absurd boy had calmed down a little from the excitement of the day. Meanwhile, Gennaro, instead of attending to the wants of the two new ladies, carried Eustace into the house, as if it was the most natural thing in the world.

"Ho capito," I heard him say as he passed me. "Ho capito" is the Italian for "I have understood"; but, as Eustace had not spoken to him, I could not see the force of the remark. It served to increase our bewilderment, and, by the time we sat down at the dinner-table, our imaginations and our tongues were alike exhausted.

I omit from this account the various comments that were made, as few of them seem worthy of being recorded. But, for three or four hours, seven of us were pouring forth our bewilderment in a stream of appropriate and inappropriate exclamations. Some traced a connection between our behaviour in the afternoon and the behaviour of Eustace now. Others saw no connexion at all. Mr. Sandbach still held to the possibility of infernal influences, and also said that he ought to have a doctor. Leyland only saw the development of "that unspeakable Philistine, the boy." Rose maintained, to my surprise, that everything was excusable; while I began to see that the young gentleman wanted a sound thrashing. The poor Miss Robinsons swayed helplessly about between these diverse opinions; inclining now to careful supervision, now to acquiescence, now to corporal chastisement, now to Eno's Fruit Salt.

Dinner passed off fairly well, though Eustace was terribly fidgety, Gennaro as usual dropping the knives and spoons, and hawking and clearing his throat. He only knew a few words of English, and we were all reduced to Italian for making known our wants. Eustace, who had picked up a little somehow, asked for some oranges. To my annoyance, Gennaro, in his answer made use of the second person singular—a form only used when addressing those who are both intimates and equals. Eustace had brought it on himself; but an impertinence of this kind was an affront to us all, and I was determined to speak, and to speak at once.

When I heard him clearing the table I went in, and, summoning up my Italian, or rather Neapolitan—the Southern dialects are execrable—I said, "Gennaro! I heard you address Signor Eustace with 'Tu.'"

"It is true."

"You are not right. You must use 'Lei' or 'Voi'—more polite forms. And remember that, though Signor Eustace is sometimes silly and foolish—this afternoon for example—yet you must always behave respectfully to him; for he is a young English gentleman, and you are a poor Italian fisher-boy."

I know that speech sounds terribly snobbish, but in Italian one can say things that one would never dream of saying in English. Besides, it is no good speaking delicately to persons of that class. Unless you put things plainly, they take a vicious pleasure in misunderstanding you.

An honest English fisherman would have landed me one in the eye in a minute for such a remark, but the wretched down-trodden Italians have no pride. Gennaro only sighed, and said: "It is true."

"Quite so," I said, and turned to go. To my indignation I heard him add: "But sometimes it is not important."

"What do you mean?" I shouted.

He came close up to me with horrid gesticulating fingers.

"Signor Tytler, I wish to say this. If Eustazio asks me to call him 'Voi,' I will call him 'Voi.' Otherwise, no."

With that he seized up a tray of dinner things, and fled from the room with them; and I heard two more wine-glasses go on the court-yard floor.

I was now fairly angry, and strode out to interview Eustace. But he had gone to bed, and the landlady, to whom I also wished to speak, was engaged. After more vague wonderings, obscurely expressed owing to the presence of Janet and the two American ladies, we all went to bed, too, after a harassing and most extraordinary day.

III

But the day was nothing to the night.

I suppose I had slept for about four hours, when I woke suddenly thinking I heard a noise in the garden. And, immediately, before my eyes were open, cold terrible fear seized me—not fear of something that was happening, like the fear in the wood, but fear of something that might happen.

Our room was on the first floor, looking out on to the garden—or terrace, it was rather: a wedge-shaped block of ground covered with roses and vines, and intersected with little asphalt paths. It was bounded on the small side by the house; round the two long sides ran a wall, only three feet above the terrace level, but with a good twenty feet drop over it into the olive yards, for the ground fell very precipitously away.

Trembling all over I stole to the window. There, pattering up and down the asphalt paths, was something white. I was too much alarmed to see clearly; and in the uncertain light of the stars the thing took all manner of curious shapes. Now it was a great dog, now an enormous white bat, now a mass of quickly travelling cloud. It would bounce like a ball, or take short flights like a bird, or glide slowly; like a wraith. It gave no sound—save the pattering sound of what, after all, must be human feet. And at last the obvious explanation forced itself upon my disordered mind; and I realized that Eustace had got out of bed, and that we were in for something more.

I hastily dressed myself, and went down into the dining-room which opened upon the terrace. The door was already unfastened. My terror had almost entirely passed away, but for quite five minutes I struggled with a curious cowardly feeling, which bade me not interfere with the poor strange boy, but leave him to his ghostly patterings, and merely watch him from the window, to see he took no harm.

But better impulses prevailed and, opening the door, I called out:

"Eustace! what on earth are you doing? Come in at once."

He stopped his antics, and said: "I hate my bedroom. I could not stop in it, it is too small."

"Come! come! I'm tired of affectation. You've never complained of it before."

"Besides I can't see anything—no flowers, no leaves, no sky: only a stone wall." The outlook of Eustace's room certainly was limited; but, as I told him, he had never complained of it before.

"Eustace, you talk like a child. Come in! Prompt obedience, if you please."

He did not move.

"Very well: I shall carry you in by force." I added, and made a few steps towards him. But I was soon convinced of the futility of pursuing a boy through a tangle of asphalt paths, and went in instead, to call Mr. Sandbach and Leyland to my aid.

When I returned with them he was worse than ever. He would not even answer us when we spoke, but began singing and chattering to himself in a most alarming way.

"It's a case for the doctor now," said Mr. Sandbach, gravely tapping his forehead.

He had stopped his running and was singing, first low, then loud—singing five-finger exercises, scales, hymn tunes, scraps of Wagner—anything that came into his head. His voice—a very untuneful voice—grew stronger and stronger, and he ended with a tremendous shout which boomed like a gun among the mountains, and awoke everyone who was still sleeping in the hotel. My poor wife and the two girls appeared at their respective windows, and the American ladies were heard violently ringing their bell.

"Eustace," we all cried, "stop! stop, dear boy, and come into the house."

He shook his head, and started off again—talking this time. Never have I listened to such an extraordinary speech. At any other time it would have been ludicrous, for here was a boy, with no sense of beauty and a puerile command of words, attempting to tackle themes which the greatest poets have found almost beyond their power. Eustace Robinson, aged fourteen, was standing in his nightshirt saluting, praising, and blessing, the great forces and manifestations of Nature.

He spoke first of night and the stars and planets above his head, of the swarms of fire-flies below him, of the invisible sea below the fire-flies, of the great rocks covered with anemones and shells that were slumbering in the invisible sea. He spoke of the rivers and water-falls, of the ripening bunches of grapes, of the smoking cone of Vesuvius and the hidden fire-channels that made the smoke, of the myriads of lizards who were lying curled up in the crannies of the sultry earth, of the showers of white rose-leaves that were tangled in his hair. And then he spoke of the rain and the wind by which all things are changed, of the air through which all things live, and of the woods in which all things can be hidden.

Of course, it was all absurdly high faluting: yet I could have kicked Leyland for audibly observing that it was "a diabolical caricature of all that was most holy and beautiful in life."

"And then,"—Eustace was going on in the pitiable conversational doggerel which was his only mode of expression—"and then there are men, but I can't make them out so well." He knelt down by the parapet, and rested his head on his arms.

"Now's the time," whispered Leyland. I hate stealth, but we darted forward and endeavoured to catch hold of him from behind. He was away in a twinkling, but turned round at once to look at us. As far as I could see in the starlight, he was crying. Leyland rushed at him again, and we tried to corner him among the asphalt paths, but without the slightest approach to success.

We returned, breathless and discomfited, leaving him to his madness in the further corner of the terrace. But my Rose had an inspiration.

"Papa," she called from the window, "if you get Gennaro, he might be able to catch him for you."

I had no wish to ask a favour of Gennaro, but, as the landlady had by now appeared on the scene, I begged her to summon him from the charcoal-bin in which he slept, and make him try what he could do.

She soon returned, and was shortly followed by Gennaro, attired in a dress coat, without either waistcoat, shirt, or vest, and a ragged pair of what had been trousers, cut short above the knees for purposes of wading. The landlady, who had quite picked up English ways, rebuked him for the incongruous and even indecent appearance which he presented.

"I have a coat and I have trousers. What more do you desire?"

"Never mind, Signora Scafetti," I put in, "As there are no ladies here, it is not of the slightest consequence." Then, turning to Gennaro, I said: "The aunts of Signor Eustace wish you to fetch him into the house."

He did not answer.

"Do you hear me? He is not well. I order you to fetch him into the house."

"Fetch! fetch!" said Signora Scafetti, and shook him roughly by the arm.

"Eustazio is well where he is."

"Fetch! fetch!" Signora Scafetti screamed, and let loose a flood of Italian, most of which, I am glad to say, I could not follow. I glanced up nervously at the girls' window, but they hardly know as much as I do, and I am thankful to say that none of us caught one word of Gennaro's answer.

The two yelled and shouted at each other for quite ten minutes, at the end of which Gennaro rushed back to his charcoal-bin and Signora Scafetti burst into tears, as well she might, for she greatly valued her English guests.

"He says," she sobbed, "that Signer Eustace is well where he is, and that he will not fetch him. I can do no more."

But I could, for, in my stupid British way, I have got some insight into the Italian character. I followed Mr. Gennaro to his place of repose, and found him wriggling down on to a dirty sack.

"I wish you to fetch Signor Eustace to me," I began.

He hurled at me an unintelligible reply.

"If you fetch him, I will give you this." And out of my pocket I took a new ten lira note.

This time he did not answer.

"This note is equal to ten lire in silver," I continued, for I knew that the poor-class Italian is unable to conceive of a single large sum.

"I know it."

"That is, two hundred soldi."

"I do not desire them. Eustazio is my friend."

I put the note into my pocket.

"Besides, you would not give it me."

"I am an Englishman. The English always do what they promise."

"That is true." It is astonishing how the most dishonest of nations trust us. Indeed they often trust us more than we trust one another. Gennaro knelt up on his sack. It was too dark to see his face, but I could feel his warm garlicky breath coming out in gasps, and I knew that the eternal avarice of the South had laid hold upon him.

"I could not fetch Eustazio to the house. He might die there."

"You need not do that," I replied patiently. "You need only bring him to me; and I will stand outside in the garden." And to this, as if it were something quite different, the pitiable youth consented.

"But give me first the ten lire."

"No"—for I knew the kind of person with whom I had to deal. Once faithless, always faithless.

We returned to the terrace, and Gennaro, without a single word, pattered off towards the pattering that could be heard at the remoter end. Mr. Sandbach, Leyland, and myself moved away a little from the house, and stood in the shadow of the white climbing roses, practically invisible.

We heard "Eustazio" called, followed by absurd cries of pleasure from the poor boy. The pattering ceased, and we heard them talking. Their voices got nearer, and presently I could discern them through the creepers, the grotesque figure of the young man, and the slim little white-robed boy. Gennaro had his arm round Eustace's neck, and Eustace was talking away in his fluent, slip-shod Italian.

"I understand almost everything," I heard him say. "The trees, hills, stars, water, I can see all. But isn't it odd! I can't make out men a bit. Do you know what I mean?"

"Ho capito," said Gennaro gravely, and took his arm off Eustace's shoulder. But I made the new note crackle in my pocket; and he heard it. He stuck his hand out with a jerk; and the unsuspecting Eustace gripped it in his own.

"It is odd!" Eustace went on—they were quite close now—"It almost seems as if—as if—"

I darted out and caught hold of his arm, and Leyland got hold of the other arm, and Mr. Sandbach hung on to his feet. He gave shrill heart-piercing screams; and the white roses, which were falling early that year, descended in showers on him as we dragged him into the house.

As soon as we entered the house he stopped shrieking; but floods of tears silently burst forth, and spread over his upturned face.

"Not to my room," he pleaded. "It is so small."

His infinitely dolorous look filled me with strange pity, but what could I do? Besides, his window was the only one that had bars to it.

"Never mind, dear boy," said kind Mr. Sandbach. "I will bear you company till the morning."

At this his convulsive struggles began again. "Oh, please, not that. Anything but that. I will promise to lie still and not to cry more than I can help, if I am left alone."

So we laid him on the bed, and drew the sheets over him, and left him sobbing bitterly, and saying: "I nearly saw everything, and now I can see nothing at all."

We informed the Miss Robinsons of all that had happened, and returned to the dining-room, where we found Signora Scafetti and Gennaro whispering together. Mr. Sandbach got pen and paper, and began writing to the English doctor at Naples. I at once drew out the note, and flung it down on the table to Gennaro.

"Here is your pay," I said sternly, for I was thinking of the Thirty Pieces of Silver.

"Thank you very much, sir," said Gennaro, and grabbed it.

He was going off, when Leyland, whose interest and indifference were always equally misplaced, asked him what Eustace had meant by saying "he could not make out men a bit."

"I cannot say. Signor Eustazio" (I was glad to observe a little deference at last) "has a subtle brain. He understands many things."

"But I heard you say you understood," Leyland persisted.

"I understand, but I cannot explain. I am a poor Italian fisher-lad. Yet, listen: I will try." I saw to my alarm that his manner was changing, and tried to stop him.

But he sat down on the edge of the table and started off, with some absolutely incoherent remarks.

"It is sad," he observed at last. "What has happened is very sad. But what can I do? I am poor. It is not I."

I turned away in contempt. Leyland went on asking questions. He wanted to know who it was that Eustace had in his mind when he spoke.

"That is easy to say," Gennaro gravely answered. "It is you, it is I. It is all in this house, and many outside it. If he wishes for mirth, we discomfort him. If he asks to be alone, we disturb him. He longed for a friend, and found none for fifteen years. Then he found me, and the first night I—I who have been in the woods and understood things too—betray him to you, and send him in to die. But what could I do?"

"Gently, gently," said I.

"Oh, assuredly he will die. He will lie in the small room all night, and in the morning he will be dead. That I know for certain."

"There, that will do," said Mr. Sandbach. "I shall be sitting with him."

"Filomena Giusti sat all night with Caterina, but Caterina was dead in the morning. They would not let her out, though I begged, and prayed, and cursed, and beat the door, and climbed the wall. They were ignorant fools, and thought I wished to carry her away. And in the morning she was dead."

"What is all this?" I asked Signora Scafetti.

"All kinds of stories will get about," she replied, "and he, least of anyone, has reason to repeat them."

"And I am alive now," he went on, "because I had neither parents nor relatives nor friends, so that, when the first night came, I could run through the woods, and climb the rocks, and plunge into the water, until I had accomplished my desire!"

We heard a cry from Eustace's room—a faint but steady sound, like the sound of wind in a distant wood, heard by one standing in tranquillity.

"That," said Gennaro, "was the last noise of Caterina. I was hanging on to her window then, and it blew out past me."

And, lifting up his hand, in which my ten lira note was safely packed, he solemnly cursed Mr. Sandbach, and Leyland, and myself, and Fate, because Eustace was dying in the upstairs room. Such is the working of the Southern mind; and I verily believe that he would not have moved even then, had not Leyland, that unspeakable idiot, upset the lamp with his elbow. It was a patent self-extinguishing lamp, bought by Signora Scafetti, at my special request, to replace the dangerous thing that she was using. The result was, that it went out; and the mere physical change from light to darkness had more power over the ignorant animal nature of Gennaro than the most obvious dictates of logic and reason.

I felt, rather than saw, that he had left the room, and shouted out to Mr. Sandbach: "Have you got the key of Eustace's room in your pocket?" But Mr. Sandbach and Leyland were both on the floor, having mistaken each other for Gennaro, and some more precious time was wasted in finding a match. Mr. Sandbach had only just time to say that he had left the key in the door, in case the Miss Robinsons wished to pay Eustace a visit, when we heard a noise on the stairs, and there was Gennaro, carrying Eustace down.

We rushed out and blocked up the passage, and they lost heart and retreated to the upper landing.

"Now they are caught," cried Signora Scafetti. "There is no other way out."

We were cautiously ascending the staircase, when there was a terrific scream from my wife's room, followed by a heavy thud on the asphalt path. They had leapt out of her window.

I reached the terrace just in time to see Eustace jumping over the parapet of the garden wall. This time I knew for certain he would be killed. But he alighted in an olive tree, looking like a great white moth; and from the tree he slid on to the earth. And as soon as his bare feet touched the clods of earth he uttered a strange loud cry, such as I should not have thought the human voice could have produced, and disappeared among the trees below.

"He has understood and he is saved," cried Gennaro, who was still sitting on the asphalt path. "Now, instead of dying he will live!"

"And you, instead of keeping the ten lire, will give them up," I retorted, for at this theatrical remark I could contain myself no longer.

"The ten lire are mine," he hissed back, in a scarcely audible voice. He clasped his hand over his breast to protect his ill-gotten gains, and, as he did so, he swayed forward and fell upon his face on the path. He had not broken any limbs, and a leap like that would never have killed an Englishman, for the drop was not great. But those miserable Italians have no stamina. Something had gone wrong inside him, and he was dead.

The morning was still far off, but the morning breeze had begun, and more rose leaves fell on us as we carried him in. Signora Scafetti burst into screams at the sight of the dead body, and, far down the valley towards the sea, there still resounded the shouts and the laughter of the escaping boy.

The White People

Arthur Machen

———◆———

PROLOGUE

Sorcery and sanctity," said Ambrose, "these are the only realities. Each is an ecstasy, a withdrawal from the common life."

Cotgrave listened, interested. He had been brought by a friend to this mouldering house in a northern suburb, through an old garden to the room where Ambrose the recluse dozed and dreamed over his books.

"Yes," he went on, "magic is justified of her children. There are many, I think, who eat dry crusts and drink water, with a joy infinitely sharper than anything within the experience of the 'practical' epicure."

"You are speaking of the saints?"

"Yes, and of the sinners, too. I think you are falling into the very general error of confining the spiritual world to the supremely good; but the supremely wicked, necessarily, have their portion in it. The merely carnal, sensual man can no more be a great sinner than he can be a great saint. Most of us are just indifferent, mixed-up creatures; we muddle through the world without realizing the meaning and the inner sense of things, and, consequently, our wickedness and our goodness are alike second-rate, unimportant."

"And you think the great sinner, then, will be an ascetic, as well as the great saint?"

"Great people of all kinds forsake the imperfect copies and go to the perfect originals. I have no doubt but that many of the very highest among the saints have never done a 'good action' (using the words in their ordinary sense). And, on the other hand, there have been those who have sounded the very depths of sin, who all their lives have never done an 'ill deed.' "

He went out of the room for a moment, and Cotgrave, in high delight, turned to his friend and thanked him for the introduction.

"He's grand," he said. "I never saw that kind of lunatic before."

Ambrose returned with more whisky and helped the two men in a liberal manner. He abused the teetotal sect with ferocity, as he handed the seltzer, and pouring out a glass of water for himself, was about to resume his monologue, when Cotgrave broke in—

"I can't stand it, you know," he said, "your paradoxes are too monstrous. A man may be a great sinner and yet never do anything sinful! Come!"

"You're quite wrong," said Ambrose. "I never make paradoxes; I wish I could. I merely said that a man may have an exquisite taste in Romanee Conti, and yet never have even smelt four ale. That's all, and it's more like a truism than a paradox, isn't it? Your surprise at my remark is due to the fact that you haven't realized what sin is. Oh, yes, there is a sort of connexion between Sin with the capital letter, and actions which are commonly called sinful: with murder, theft, adultery, and so forth. Much the same connexion that there is between the A, B, C and fine literature. But I believe that the misconception—it is all but universal—arises in great measure from our looking at the matter through social spectacles. We think that a man who does evil to *us* and to his neighbours must be very evil. So he is, from a social standpoint; but can't you realize that Evil in its essence is a lonely thing, a passion of the solitary, individual soul? Really, the average murderer, *quâ* murderer, is not by any means a sinner in the true sense of the word. He is simply a wild beast that we have to get rid of to save our own necks from his knife. I should class him rather with tigers than with sinners."

"It seems a little strange."

"I think not. The murderer murders not from positive qualities, but from negative ones; he lacks something which non-murderers possess. Evil, of course, is wholly positive—only it is on the wrong side. You may believe me that sin in its proper sense is very rare; it is probable that there have been far fewer sinners than saints. Yes, your standpoint is all very well for practical, social purposes; we are naturally inclined to think that a person who is very disagreeable to us must be a very great sinner! It is very disagreeable to have one's pocket picked, and we pronounce the thief to be a very great sinner. In truth, he is merely an undeveloped man. He cannot be a saint, of course; but he may be, and often is, an infinitely better creature than thousands who have never broken a single commandment. He is a great nuisance to *us*, I admit, and we very properly lock him up if we catch him; but between his troublesome and unsocial action and evil—Oh, the connexion is of the weakest."

It was getting very late. The man who had brought Cotgrave had probably heard all this before, since he assisted with a bland and judicious smile, but Cotgrave began to think that his "lunatic" was turning into a sage.

"Do you know," he said, "you interest me immensely? You think, then, that we do not understand the real nature of evil?"

"No, I don't think we do. We over-estimate it and we under-estimate it. We take the very numerous infractions of our social 'bye-laws'—the very necessary and very proper regulations which keep the human company together—and we get frightened at the prevalence of 'sin' and 'evil.' But this is really nonsense. Take theft, for example. Have you any *horror* at the thought of Robin Hood, of the Highland caterans of the seventeenth century, of the moss-troopers, of the company promoters of our day?

"Then, on the other hand, we underrate evil. We attach such an enormous importance to the 'sin' of meddling with our pockets (and our wives) that we have quite forgotten the awfulness of real sin."

"And what is sin?" said Cotgrave.

"I think I must reply to your question by another. What would your feelings be, seriously, if your cat or your dog began to talk to you, and to dispute with you in human accents? You would be overwhelmed with horror. I am sure of it. And if the roses in your garden sang a weird song, you would go mad. And suppose the stones in the road began to swell and grow before your eyes, and if the pebble that you noticed at night had shot out stony blossoms in the morning?

"Well, these examples may give you some notion of what sin really is."

"Look here," said the third man, hitherto placid, "you two seem pretty well wound up. But I'm going home. I've missed my tram, and I shall have to walk."

Ambrose and Cotgrave seemed to settle down more profoundly when the other had gone out into the early misty morning and the pale light of the lamps.

"You astonish me," said Cotgrave. "I had never thought of that. If that is really so, one must turn everything upside down. Then the essence of sin really is—"

"In the taking of heaven by storm, it seems to me," said Ambrose. "It appears to me that it is simply an attempt to penetrate into another and higher sphere in a forbidden manner. You can understand why it is so rare. There are few, indeed, who wish to penetrate into other spheres, higher or lower, in ways allowed or forbidden. Men, in the mass, are amply content with life as they find it. Therefore there are few saints, and sinners (in the proper sense) are fewer still, and men of genius, who partake sometimes of each character, are rare also. Yes; on the whole, it is, perhaps, harder to be a great sinner than a great saint."

"There is something profoundly unnatural about sin? Is that what you mean?"

"Exactly. Holiness requires as great, or almost as great, an effort; but holiness works on lines that *were* natural once; it is an effort to recover the ecstasy that was before the Fall. But sin is an effort to gain the ecstasy and the knowledge that pertain alone to angels, and in making this effort man becomes a demon. I told you that the mere murderer is not *therefore* a sinner; that is true, but the sinner is sometimes a murderer. Gilles de Raiz is an instance. So you see that while the good and the evil are unnatural to man as he now is—to man the social, civilized being—evil is unnatural in a much deeper sense than good. The saint endeavours to recover a gift which he has lost; the sinner tries to obtain something which was never his. In brief, he repeats the Fall."

"But are you a Catholic?" said Cotgrave.

"Yes; I am a member of the persecuted Anglican Church."

"Then, how about those texts which seem to reckon as sin that which you would set down as a mere trivial dereliction?"

"Yes; but in one place the word 'sorcerers' comes in the same sentence, doesn't it? That seems to me to give the key-note. Consider: can you imagine for a moment that a false statement which saves an innocent man's life is a sin? No; very good, then, it is not the mere liar who is excluded by those words; it is, above all, the 'sorcerers' who use the material life, who use the failings incidental to material life as instruments to obtain their infinitely wicked ends. And let me tell you this: our higher senses are so blunted, we are so drenched with materialism, that we should probably fail to recognize real wickedness if we encountered it."

"But shouldn't we experience a certain horror—a terror such as you hinted we would experience if a rose tree sang—in the mere presence of an evil man?"

"We should if we were natural: children and women feel this horror you speak of, even animals experience it. But with most of us convention and civilization and education have blinded and deafened and obscured the natural reason. No, sometimes we may recognize evil by its hatred of the good—one doesn't need much penetration to guess at the influence which dictated, quite unconsciously, the 'Blackwood' review of Keats—but this is purely incidental; and, as a rule, I suspect that the Hierarchs of Tophet pass quite unnoticed, or, perhaps, in certain cases, as good but mistaken men."

"But you used the word 'unconscious' just now, of Keats' reviewers. Is wickedness ever unconscious?"

"Always. It must be so. It is like holiness and genius in this as in other points; it is a certain rapture or ecstasy of the soul; a transcendent effort to surpass the ordinary bounds. So, surpassing these, it surpasses also the understanding, the faculty that takes note of that which comes before it. No, a man may be infinitely and horribly wicked and never suspect it. But I tell you, evil in this, its certain and true sense, is rare, and I think it is growing rarer."

"I am trying to get hold of it all," said Cotgrave. "From what you say, I gather that the true evil differs generically from that which we call evil?"

"Quite so. There is, no doubt, an analogy between the two; a resemblance such as enables us to use, quite legitimately, such terms as the 'foot of the mountain' and the 'leg of the table.' And, sometimes, of course, the two speak, as it were, in the same language. The rough miner, or 'puddler,' the untrained, undeveloped 'tiger-man,' heated by a quart or two above his usual measure, comes home and kicks his irritating and injudicious wife to death. He is a murderer. And Gilles de Raiz was a murderer. But you see the gulf that separates the two? The 'word,' if I may so speak, is accidentally the same in each case, but the 'meaning' is utterly different. It is flagrant 'Hobson Jobson' to confuse the two, or rather, it is as if one supposed that Juggernaut and the Argonauts had something to do etymologically with one another. And no doubt the same weak likeness, or analogy, runs between all the 'social' sins and the real spiritual sins, and in some cases, perhaps, the lesser may be 'schoolmasters' to lead one on to the greater—from the shadow to the reality. If you are anything of a Theologian, you will see the importance of all this."

"I am sorry to say," remarked Cotgrave, "that I have devoted very little of my time to theology. Indeed, I have often wondered on what grounds theologians have claimed the title of Science of Sciences for their favourite study; since the 'theological' books I have looked into have always seemed to me to be concerned with feeble and obvious pieties, or with the kings of Israel and Judah. I do not care to hear about those kings."

Ambrose grinned.

"We must try to avoid theological discussion," he said. "I perceive that you would be a bitter disputant. But perhaps the 'dates of the kings' have as much to do with theology as the hobnails of the murderous puddler with evil."

"Then, to return to our main subject, you think that sin is an esoteric, occult thing?"

"Yes. It is the infernal miracle as holiness is the supernal. Now and then it is raised to such a pitch that we entirely fail to suspect its existence; it is like the note of the great pedal pipes of the organ, which is so deep that we cannot hear it. In other cases it may lead to the lunatic asylum, or to still stranger issues. But you must never confuse it with mere social misdoing. Remember how the Apostle, speaking of the 'other side,' distinguishes between 'charitable' actions and charity. And as one may give all one's goods to the poor, and yet lack charity; so, remember, one may avoid every crime and yet be a sinner."

"Your psychology is very strange to me," said Cotgrave, "but I confess I like it, and I suppose that one might fairly deduce from your premises the conclusion that the real sinner might very possibly strike the observer as a harmless personage enough?"

"Certainly; because the true evil has nothing to do with social life or social laws, or if it has, only incidentally and accidentally. It is a lonely passion of the soul—or a passion of the lonely soul—whichever you like. If, by chance, we understand it, and grasp its full significance, then, indeed, it will fill us with horror and with awe. But this emotion is widely distinguished from the fear and the disgust with which we regard the ordinary criminal, since this latter is largely or entirely founded on the regard which we have for our own skins or purses. We hate a murderer, because we know that we should hate to be murdered, or to have any one that we like murdered. So, on the 'other side,' we venerate the saints, but we don't 'like' them as we like our friends. Can you persuade yourself that you would have 'enjoyed' St. Paul's company? Do you think that you and I would have 'got on' with Sir Galahad?"

"So with the sinners, as with the saints. If you met a very evil man, and recognized his evil; he would, no doubt, fill you with horror and awe; but there is no reason why you should 'dislike' him. On the contrary, it is quite possible that if you could succeed in putting the sin out of your mind you might find the sinner capital company, and in a little while you might have to reason yourself back into horror. Still, how awful it is. If the roses and the lilies suddenly sang on this coming morning; if the furniture began to move in procession, as in De Maupassant's tale!"

"I am glad you have come back to that comparison," said Cotgrave, "because I wanted to ask you what it is that corresponds in humanity to these imaginary feats of inanimate things. In a word—what is sin? You have given me, I know, an abstract definition, but I should like a concrete example."

"I told you it was very rare," said Ambrose, who appeared willing to avoid the giving of a direct answer. "The materialism of the age, which has done a good deal to suppress sanctity, has done perhaps more to suppress evil. We find the earth so very comfortable that we have no inclination either for ascents or descents. It would seem as if the scholar who decided to 'specialize' in Tophet, would be reduced to purely antiquarian researches. No palaeontologist could show you a *live* pterodactyl."

"And yet you, I think, have 'specialized,' and I believe that your researches have descended to our modern times."

"You are really interested, I see. Well, I confess, that I have dabbled a little, and if you like I can show you something that bears on the very curious subject we have been discussing."

Ambrose took a candle and went away to a far, dim corner of the room. Cotgrave saw him open a venerable bureau that stood there, and from some secret recess he drew out a parcel, and came back to the window where they had been sitting.

Ambrose undid a wrapping of paper, and produced a green pocket-book.

"You will take care of it?" he said. "Don't leave it lying about. It is one of the choicer pieces in my collection, and I should be very sorry if it were lost."

He fondled the faded binding.

"I knew the girl who wrote this," he said. "When you read it, you will see how it illustrates the talk we have had to-night. There is a sequel, too, but I won't talk of that."

"There was an odd article in one of the reviews some months ago," he began again, with the air of a man who changes the subject. "It was written by a doctor— Dr. Coryn, I think, was the name. He says that a lady, watching her little girl play- ing at the drawing-room window, suddenly saw the heavy sash give way and fall on the child's fingers. The lady fainted, I think, but at any rate the doctor was summoned, and when he had dressed the child's wounded and maimed fingers he was summoned to the mother. She was groaning with pain, and it was found that three fingers of her hand, corresponding with those that had been injured on the child's hand, were swol- len and inflamed, and later, in the doctor's language, purulent sloughing set in."

Ambrose still handled delicately the green volume.

"Well, here it is," he said at last, parting with difficulty, it seemed, from his treasure.

"You will bring it back as soon as you have read it," he said, as they went out into the hall, into the old garden, faint with the odour of white lilies.

There was a broad red band in the east as Cotgrave turned to go, and from the high ground where he stood he saw that awful spectacle of London in a dream.

THE GREEN BOOK

The morocco binding of the book was faded, and the colour had grown faint, but there were no stains nor bruises nor marks of usage. The book looked as if it had been bought "on a visit to London" some seventy or eighty years ago, and had somehow been forgotten and suffered to lie away out of sight. There was an old, delicate, lingering odour about it, such an odour as sometimes haunts an ancient piece of furniture for a century or more. The end-papers, inside the binding, were oddly decorated with coloured patterns and faded gold. It looked small, but the paper was fine, and there were many leaves, closely covered with minute, painfully formed characters.

I found this book (the manuscript began) in a drawer in the old bureau that stands on the landing. It was a very rainy day and I could not go out, so in the afternoon I got a candle and rummaged in the bureau. Nearly all the drawers were full of old dresses, but one of the small ones looked empty, and I found this book hidden right at the back. I wanted a book like this, so I took it to write in. It is full of secrets. I have a great many other books of secrets I have written, hidden in a safe place, and I am going to write here many of the old secrets and some new ones; but there are some I shall not put down at all. I must not write down the real names of the days and months which I found out a year ago, nor the way to make the Aklo letters, or the Chian language, or the great beautiful Circles, nor the Mao Games, nor the chief songs. I may write something about all these things but not the way to do them, for peculiar reasons. And I must not say who the Nymphs are, or the Dols, or Jeelo, or what voolas mean. All these are most secret secrets, and I am glad when I remember what they are, and how many wonderful languages I know, but there are some things that I call the secrets of the secrets of the secrets that I dare not think of unless I am quite alone, and then I shut my eyes, and put my hands over them and whisper the word, and the Alala comes. I only do this at night in my room or in certain woods that I know, but I must not describe them, as they are secret woods. Then there are the Ceremonies, which are all of them important, but some are more delightful than others—there are the White Ceremonies, and the Green Ceremonies, and the Scarlet Ceremonies. The Scarlet Ceremonies are the best, but there is only one place where they can be performed properly, though there is a very nice imitation which I have done in other places. Besides these, I have the dances, and the Comedy, and I have done the Comedy sometimes when the others were looking, and they didn't understand anything about it. I was very little when I first knew about these things.

When I was very small, and mother was alive, I can remember remembering things before that, only it has all got confused. But I remember when I was five or six I heard them talking about me when they thought I was not noticing. They were saying how queer I was a year or two before, and how nurse had called my mother to come and listen to me talking all to myself, and I was saying words that nobody could understand.

I was speaking the Xu language, but I only remember a very few of the words, as it was about the little white faces that used to look at me when I was lying in my cradle. They used to talk to me, and I learnt their language and talked to them in it about some great white place where they lived, where the trees and the grass were all white, and there were white hills as high up as the moon, and a cold wind. I have often dreamed of it afterwards, but the faces went away when I was very little. But a wonderful thing happened when I was about five. My nurse was carrying me on her shoulder; there was a field of yellow corn, and we went through it, it was very hot. Then we came to a path through a wood, and a tall man came after us, and went with us till we came to a place where there was a deep pool, and it was very dark and shady. Nurse put me down on the soft moss under a tree, and she said: "She can't get to the pond now." So they left me there, and I sat quite still and watched, and out of the water and out of the wood came two wonderful white people, and they began to play and dance and sing. They were a kind of creamy white like the old ivory figure in the drawing-room; one was a beautiful lady with kind dark eyes, and a grave face, and long black hair, and she smiled such a strange sad smile at the other, who laughed and came to her. They played together, and danced round and round the pool, and they sang a song till I fell asleep. Nurse woke me up when she came back, and she was looking something like the lady had looked, so I told her all about it, and asked her why she looked like that. At first she cried, and then she looked very frightened, and turned quite pale. She put me down on the grass and stared at me, and I could see she was shaking all over. Then she said I had been dreaming, but I knew I hadn't. Then she made me promise not to say a word about it to anybody, and if I did I should be thrown into the black pit. I was not frightened at all, though nurse was, and I never forgot about it, because when I shut my eyes and it was quite quiet, and I was all alone, I could see them again, very faint and far away, but very splendid; and little bits of the song they sang came into my head, but I couldn't sing it.

I was thirteen, nearly fourteen, when I had a very singular adventure, so strange that the day on which it happened is always called the White Day. My mother had been dead for more than a year, and in the morning I had lessons, but they let me go out for walks in the afternoon. And this afternoon I walked a new way, and a little brook led me into a new country, but I tore my frock getting through some of the difficult places, as the way was through many bushes, and beneath the low branches of trees, and up thorny thickets on the hills, and by dark woods full of creeping thorns. And it was a long, long way. It seemed as if I was going on for ever and ever, and I had to creep by a place like a tunnel where a brook must have been, but all the water had dried up, and the floor was rocky, and the bushes had grown overhead till they met, so that it was quite dark. And I went on and on through that dark place; it was a long, long way. And I came to a hill that I never saw before. I was in a dismal thicket full of black twisted boughs that tore me as I went through them, and I cried out because I was smarting all over, and then I found that I was climbing, and I went up and up a long way, till at last the thicket stopped and I came out crying just under the top of a big bare place, where there were ugly grey stones lying all about on the grass, and here and there a little twisted, stunted tree came out from under a stone, like a snake. And I went up, right to the top, a long way. I never saw such big ugly stones before; they came out of the earth some of them, and some looked as if they had been rolled to where they were, and they went on and on as far as I could see, a long, long way. I looked out from them and saw the country, but it was strange. It was winter time, and there were black terrible woods hanging from the hills all round; it was like seeing a large room hung with black curtains, and the shape of the trees seemed quite different from any I had ever seen before. I was afraid. Then beyond the woods there were other hills round in a great ring, but I had never seen any of them; it all looked black, and everything had a voor over it. It was all so still and silent, and the sky was heavy and grey and sad, like a wicked voorish dome in Deep Dendo. I went on into the dreadful rocks. There were hundreds and hundreds of them. Some were like horrid-grinning men; I could see their faces as if they would jump at me out of the stone, and catch hold of me, and drag me with them back into the rock, so that I should always be there. And there were other rocks that were like animals, creeping, horrible animals, putting out their tongues, and others were like words that I could not say, and others like dead people lying on the grass. I went on among them, though they frightened me, and my heart was full of wicked songs that they put into it; and I wanted to make faces and twist myself about in the way they did, and I went on and on a long way till at last I liked the rocks, and they didn't frighten me any more. I sang the songs I thought of; songs full of words that must not be spoken or written down. Then I made faces like the faces on the rocks, and I twisted myself about like the twisted ones, and I lay down flat on the ground like the dead ones, and I went up to one that was grinning, and put my arms round him and hugged him. And so I went on and on through the rocks till I came to a round mound in the middle of them. It was higher than a mound, it was nearly as high as our house, and it was like a great basin turned upside down, all smooth and round and green, with one stone, like a post, sticking up at the top. I climbed up the sides, but they were so steep I had to stop or I should have rolled all the way down again, and I should have knocked against the stones at the bottom, and perhaps been killed. But I wanted to get up to the very top of the big round mound, so I lay down flat on my face, and took hold of the grass with my hands and drew myself up, bit by bit, till I was at the top. Then I sat down on the stone in the middle, and looked all round about. I felt I had come such a long, long way, just as if I were a hundred miles from home, or in some other country, or in one of the strange places I had read about in the "Tales of the Genie" and the "Arabian Nights," or as if I had gone across the sea, far away, for years and I had found another world that nobody had ever seen or heard of before, or as if I had somehow flown through the sky and fallen on one of the stars I had read about where everything is dead and cold and grey, and there is no air, and the wind doesn't blow. I sat on the stone and looked all round and down and round about me. It was just as if I was sitting on a tower in the middle of a great empty town, because I could see nothing all around but the grey rocks on the ground. I couldn't make out their shapes any more, but I could see them on and on for a long way, and I looked at them, and they seemed as if they had been arranged into patterns, and shapes, and figures. I knew they couldn't be, because I had seen a lot of them coming right out of the earth, joined to the deep rocks below, so I looked again, but still I saw nothing but circles, and small circles inside big ones, and pyramids, and domes, and spires, and they seemed all to go round and round the place where I was sitting, and the more I looked, the more I saw great big rings of rocks, getting bigger and bigger, and I stared so long that it felt as if they were all moving and turning, like a great wheel, and I was turning, too, in the middle. I got quite dizzy and queer in the head, and everything began to be hazy and not clear, and I saw little sparks of blue light, and the stones looked as if they were springing and dancing and twisting as they went round and round and round. I was frightened again, and I cried out loud, and jumped up from the stone I was sitting on, and fell down. When I got up I was so glad they all looked still, and I sat down on the top and slid down the mound, and went on again. I danced as I went in the peculiar way the rocks had danced when I got giddy, and I was so glad I could do it quite well, and I danced and danced along, and sang extraordinary songs that came into my head. At last I came to the edge of that great flat hill, and there were no more rocks, and the way went again through a dark thicket in a hollow. It was just as bad as the other one I went through climbing up, but I didn't mind this one, because I was so glad I had seen those singular dances and could imitate them. I went down, creeping through the bushes, and a tall nettle stung me on my leg, and made me burn, but I didn't mind it, and I tingled with the boughs and the thorns, but I only laughed and sang. Then I got out of the thicket into a close

valley, a little secret place like a dark passage that nobody ever knows of, because it
was so narrow and deep and the woods were so thick round it. There is a steep bank
with trees hanging over it, and there the ferns keep green all through the winter, when
they are dead and brown upon the hill, and the ferns there have a sweet, rich smell like
what oozes out of fir trees. There was a little stream of water running down this valley,
so small that I could easily step across it. I drank the water with my hand, and it tasted
like bright, yellow wine, and it sparkled and bubbled as it ran down over beautiful red
and yellow and green stones, so that it seemed alive and all colours at once. I drank it,
and I drank more with my hand, but I couldn't drink enough, so I lay down and bent
my head and sucked the water up with my lips. It tasted much better, drinking it that
way, and a ripple would come up to my mouth and give me a kiss, and I laughed, and
drank again, and pretended there was a nymph, like the one in the old picture at home,
who lived in the water and was kissing me. So I bent low down to the water, and put
my lips softly to it, and whispered to the nymph that I would come again. I felt sure it
could not be common water, I was so glad when I got up and went on; and I danced
again and went up and up the valley, under hanging hills. And when I came to the top,
the ground rose up in front of me, tall and steep as a wall, and there was nothing but
the green wall and the sky. I thought of "for ever and for ever, world without end,
Amen"; and I thought I must have really found the end of the world, because it was
like the end of everything, as if there could be nothing at all beyond, except the kingdom of Voor, where the light goes when it is put out, and the water goes when the sun
takes it away. I began to think of all the long, long way I had journeyed, how I had
found a brook and followed it, and followed it on, and gone through bushes and thorny
thickets, and dark woods full of creeping thorns. Then I had crept up a tunnel under
trees, and climbed a thicket, and seen all the grey rocks, and sat in the middle of them
when they turned round, and then I had gone on through the grey rocks and come
down the hill through the stinging thicket and up the dark valley, all a long, long way.
I wondered how I should get home again, if I could ever find the way, and if my home
was there any more, or if it were turned and everybody in it into grey rocks, as in the
"Arabian Nights." So I sat down on the grass and thought what I should do next. I was
tired, and my feet were hot with walking, and as I looked about I saw there was a wonderful well just under the high, steep wall of grass. All the ground round it was covered
with bright, green, dripping moss; there was every kind of moss there, moss like beautiful little ferns, and like palms and fir trees, and it was all green as jewellery, and drops
of water hung on it like diamonds. And in the middle was the great well, deep and

shining and beautiful, so clear that it looked as if I could touch the red sand at the bottom, but it was far below. I stood by it and looked in, as if I were looking in a glass. At the bottom of the well, in the middle of it, the red grains of sand were moving and stirring all the time, and I saw how the water bubbled up, but at the top it was quite smooth, and full and brimming. It was a great well, large like a bath, and with the shining, glittering green moss about it, it looked like a great white jewel, with green jewels all round. My feet were so hot and tired that I took off my boots and stockings, and let my feet down into the water, and the water was soft and cold, and when I got up I wasn't tired any more, and I felt I must go on, farther and farther, and see what was on the other side of the wall. I climbed up it very slowly, going sideways all the time, and when I got to the top and looked over, I was in the queerest country I had seen, stranger even than the hill of the grey rocks. It looked as if earth-children had been playing there with their spades, as it was all hills and hollows, and castles and walls made of earth and covered with grass. There were two mounds like big beehives, round and great and solemn, and then hollow basins, and then a steep mounting wall like the ones I saw once by the seaside where the big guns and the soldiers were. I nearly fell into one of the round hollows, it went away from under my feet so suddenly, and I ran fast down the side and stood at the bottom and looked up. It was strange and solemn to look up. There was nothing but the grey, heavy sky and the sides of the hollow; everything else had gone away, and the hollow was the whole world, and I thought that at night it must be full of ghosts and moving shadows and pale things when the moon shone down to the bottom at the dead of the night, and the wind wailed up above. It was so strange and solemn and lonely, like a hollow temple of dead heathen gods. It reminded me of a tale my nurse had told me when I was quite little; it was the same nurse that took me into the wood where I saw the beautiful white people. And I remembered how nurse had told me the story one winter night, when the wind was beating the trees against the wall, and crying and moaning in the nursery chimney. She said there was, somewhere or other, a hollow pit, just like the one I was standing in, everybody was afraid to go into it or near it, it was such a bad place. But once upon a time there was a poor girl who said she would go into the hollow pit, and everybody tried to stop her, but she would go. And she went down into the pit and came back laughing, and said there was nothing there at all, except green grass and red stones, and white stones and yellow flowers. And soon after people saw she had most beautiful emerald earrings, and they asked how she got them, as she and her mother were quite poor. But she laughed, and said her earrings were not made of emeralds at all, but only of green grass. Then, one day, she wore on her breast the reddest ruby that any one had ever seen, and it was as big as a hen's egg, and glowed and sparkled like a hot burning coal of fire. And they asked how she got it, as she and her mother were quite poor. But she laughed, and said it was not a ruby at all, but only a red stone. Then one day she wore round her neck the loveliest necklace that any one had ever seen, much finer than the queen's finest, and it was made of great bright diamonds, hundreds of them, and they shone like all the stars on a night in June. So they asked her how she got it, as she and her mother were quite poor. But she laughed, and said they were not diamonds at all, but only white stones. And one day she went to the Court, and she wore on her head a crown of pure angel-gold, so nurse said, and it shone like the sun, and it was much more splendid than the crown the king was wearing himself, and in her ears she wore the emeralds, and the big ruby was the brooch on her breast, and the great diamond necklace was sparkling on her neck. And the king and queen thought she was some great princess from a long way off, and got down from their thrones and went to meet her, but somebody told the king and queen who she was, and that she was quite poor. So the king asked why she wore a gold crown, and how she got it, as she and her mother were so poor. And she laughed, and said it wasn't a gold crown at all, but only some yellow flowers she had put in her hair. And the king thought it was very strange, and said she should stay at the Court, and they would see what would happen next. And she was so lovely that everybody said that her eyes were greener than the emeralds, that her lips were redder than the ruby, that her skin was whiter than the diamonds, and that her hair was brighter than the golden crown. So the king's son said he would marry her, and the king said he might. And the bishop married them, and there was a great supper, and afterwards the king's son went to his wife's room. But just when he had his hand on the door, he saw a tall, black man, with a dreadful face, standing in front of the door, and a voice said—

"Venture not upon your life,
This is mine own wedded wife."

Then the king's son fell down on the ground in a fit. And they came and tried to get into the room, but they couldn't, and they hacked at the door with hatchets, but the wood had turned hard as iron, and at last everybody ran away, they were so frightened at the screaming and laughing and shrieking and crying that came out of the room. But next day they went in, and found there was nothing in the room but thick black smoke, because the black man had come and taken her away. And on the bed there were two knots of faded grass and a red stone, and some white stones, and some faded yellow flowers. I remembered this tale of nurse's while I was standing at the bottom of the deep hollow; it was so strange and solitary there, and I felt afraid. I could not see any stones or flowers, but I was afraid of bringing them away without knowing, and I thought I would do a charm that came into my head to keep the black man away. So I stood right in the very middle of the hollow, and I made sure that I had none of those things on me, and then I walked round the place, and touched my eyes, and my lips, and my hair in a peculiar manner, and whispered some queer words that nurse taught me to keep bad things away. Then I felt safe and climbed up out of the hollow, and went on through all those mounds and hollows and walls, till I came to the end, which was high above all the rest, and I could see that all the different shapes of the earth were arranged in patterns, something like the grey rocks, only the pattern was different. It was getting late, and the air was indistinct, but it looked from where I was standing something like two great figures of people lying on the grass. And I went on, and at last I found a certain wood, which is too secret to be described, and nobody knows of the passage into it, which I found out in a very curious manner, by seeing some little animal run into the wood through it. So I went after the animal by a very narrow dark way, under thorns and bushes, and it was almost dark when I came to a kind of open place in the middle. And there I saw the most wonderful sight I have ever seen, but it was only for a minute, as I ran away directly, and crept out of the wood by the passage I had come by, and ran and ran as fast as ever I could, because I was afraid, what I had seen was so wonderful and so strange and beautiful. But I wanted to get home and think of it, and I did not know what might not happen if I stayed by the wood. I was hot all over and trembling, and my heart was beating, and strange cries that I could not help came from me as I ran from the wood. I was glad that a great white moon came up from over a round hill and showed me the way, so I went back through the mounds and hollows and down the close valley, and up through the thicket over the place of the grey rocks, and so at last I got home again. My father was busy in his study, and the servants had not told about my not coming home, though they were frightened, and wondered what they ought to do, so I told them I had lost my way, but I did not let them find out the real way I had been. I went to bed and lay awake all through the night, thinking of what I had seen. When I came out of the narrow way, and it looked all shining, though the air was dark, it seemed so certain, and all the way home I was quite sure that I had seen it, and I wanted to be alone in my room, and be glad over it all to myself, and shut my eyes and pretend it was there, and do all the things I would have done if I had not been so afraid. But when I shut my eyes the sight would not come, and I began to think about my adventures all over again, and I remembered how dusky and queer it was at the end, and I was afraid it must be all a mistake, because it seemed impossible it could happen. It seemed like one of nurse's tales, which I didn't really believe in, though I was frightened at the bottom of the hollow; and the stories she told me when I was little came back into my head, and I wondered whether it was really there what I thought I had seen, or whether any of her tales could have happened a long time ago. It was so queer; I lay awake there in my room at the back of the house, and the moon was shining on the other side towards the river, so the bright light did not fall upon the wall. And the house was quite still. I had heard my father come upstairs, and just after the clock struck twelve, and after the house was still and empty, as if there was nobody alive in it. And though it was all dark and indistinct in my room, a pale glimmering kind of light shone in through the white blind, and once I got up and looked out, and there was a great black shadow of the house covering the garden, looking like a prison where men are hanged; and then beyond it was all white; and the wood shone white with black gulfs between the trees. It was still and clear, and there were no clouds on the sky. I wanted to think of what I had seen but I couldn't, and I began to think of all the tales that nurse had told me so long ago that I thought I had forgotten, but they all came back, and mixed up with the thickets and the grey rocks and the hollows in the earth and the secret wood, till I hardly knew what was new and what was old, or whether it was not all dreaming. And then I remembered that hot summer afternoon, so long ago, when nurse left me by myself in the shade, and the white people came out of the water and out of the wood, and played, and danced, and sang, and I began to fancy that nurse told me about something like it before I saw them, only I couldn't recollect exactly what she told me. Then I wondered whether she had been the white lady, as I remembered she was just as white and beautiful, and had the same dark eyes and black hair; and sometimes she smiled and looked like the lady had looked, when she was telling me some of her stories, beginning with "Once on a time," or "In the time of the fairies." But I thought she couldn't be the lady, as she seemed to have gone a different way into the wood, and I didn't think the man who came after us could be the other, or I couldn't have seen that wonderful secret in the secret wood. I thought of the moon: but it was afterwards when I was in the middle of the wild land, where the earth was made into the shape of great figures, and it was all walls, and mysterious hollows, and smooth round mounds, that I saw the great white moon come up over a round hill. I was wondering about all these things, till at last I got quite frightened, because I was afraid something had happened to me, and I remembered nurse's tale of the poor girl who went into the hollow pit, and was carried away at last by the black man. I knew I had gone into a hollow pit too, and perhaps it was the same, and I had done something dreadful. So I did the charm over again, and touched my eyes and my lips and my hair in a peculiar manner, and said the old words from the fairy language, so that I might be sure I had not been carried away. I tried again to see the secret wood, and to creep up the passage and see what I had seen there, but somehow I couldn't, and I kept on thinking of nurse's stories. There was one I remembered about a young man who once upon a time went hunting, and all the day he and his hounds hunted everywhere, and they crossed the rivers and went into all the woods, and went round the marshes, but they couldn't find anything at all, and they hunted all day till the sun sank down and began to set behind the mountain. And the young man was angry because he couldn't find anything, and he was going to turn back, when just as the sun touched the mountain, he saw come out of a brake in front of him a beautiful white stag. And he cheered to his hounds, but they whined and would not follow, and he cheered to his horse, but it shivered and stood stock still, and the young man jumped off the horse and left the hounds and began to follow the white stag all alone. And soon it was quite dark, and the sky was black, without a single star shining in it, and the stag went away into the darkness. And though the man had brought his gun with him he never shot at the stag, because he wanted to catch it, and he was afraid he would lose it in the night. But he never lost it once, though the sky was so black and the air was so dark, and the stag went on and on till the young man didn't know a bit where he was. And they went through enormous woods where the air was full of whispers and a pale, dead light came out from the rotten trunks that were lying on the ground, and just as the man thought he had lost the stag, he would see it all white and shining in front of him, and he would run fast to catch it, but the stag always ran faster, so he did not catch it. And they went through the enormous woods, and they swam across rivers, and they waded through black marshes where the ground bubbled, and the air was full of will-o'-the-wisps, and the stag fled away down into rocky narrow valleys, where the air was like the smell of a vault, and the man went after it. And they went over the great mountains and the man heard the wind come down from the sky, and the stag went on and the man went after. At last the sun rose and the young man found he was in a country that he had never seen before; it was a beautiful valley with a bright stream running through it, and a great, big round hill in the middle. And the stag went down the valley, towards the hill, and it seemed to be getting tired and went slower and slower, and though the man was tired, too, he began to run faster, and he was sure he would catch the stag at last. But just as they got to the bottom of the hill, and the man stretched out his hand to catch the stag, it vanished into the earth, and the man began to cry; he was so sorry that he had lost it after all his long hunting. But as he was crying he saw there was a door in the hill, just in front of him, and he went in, and it was quite dark, but he went on, as he thought he would find the white stag. And all of a sudden it got light, and there was the sky, and the sun shining, and birds singing in the trees, and there was a beautiful fountain. And by the fountain a lovely lady was sitting, who was the queen of the fairies, and she told the man that she had changed herself into a stag to bring him there because she loved him so much. Then she brought out a great gold cup, covered with jewels, from her fairy palace, and she offered him wine in the cup to drink. And he drank, and the more he drank the more he longed to drink, because the wine was enchanted. So he kissed the lovely lady, and she became his wife, and he stayed all that day and all that night in the hill where she lived, and when he woke he found he was lying on the ground, close to where he had seen the stag first, and his horse was there and his hounds were there waiting, and he looked up, and the sun sank behind the mountain. And he went home and lived a long time, but he would never kiss any other lady because he had kissed the queen of the fairies, and he would never drink common wine any more, because he had drunk enchanted wine. And sometimes nurse told me tales that she had heard from her great-grandmother, who was very old, and lived in a cottage on the mountain all alone, and most of these tales were about a hill where people used to meet at night long ago, and they used to play all sorts of strange games and do queer things that nurse told me of, but I couldn't understand, and now, she said, everybody but her great-grandmother had forgotten all about it, and nobody knew where the hill was, not even her great-grandmother. But she told me one very strange story about the hill, and I trembled when I remembered it. She said that people always went there in summer, when it was very hot, and they had to dance a good deal. It would be all dark at first, and there were trees there, which made it much darker, and people would come, one by one, from all directions, by a secret path which nobody else knew, and two persons would keep the gate, and every one as they came up had to give a very curious sign, which nurse showed me as well as she could, but she said she couldn't show me properly. And all kinds of people would come; there would be gentle folks and village folks, and some old people and boys and girls, and quite small children, who sat and watched. And it would all be dark as they came in, except in one corner where some one was burning something that smelt strong and sweet, and made them laugh, and there one would see a glaring of coals, and the smoke mounting up red. So they would all come in, and when the last had come there was no door any more, so that no one else could get in, even if they knew there was anything beyond. And once a gentleman who was a stranger and had ridden a long way, lost his path at night, and his horse took him into the very middle of the wild country, where everything was upside down, and there were dreadful marshes and great stones everywhere, and holes underfoot, and the trees looked like gibbet-posts, because they had great black arms that stretched out across the way. And this strange gentleman was very frightened, and his horse began to shiver all over, and at last it stopped and wouldn't go any farther, and the gentleman got down and tried to lead the horse, but it wouldn't move, and it was all covered with a sweat, like death. So the gentleman went on all alone, going farther and farther into the wild country, till at last he came to a dark place, where he heard shouting and singing and crying, like nothing he had ever heard before. It all sounded quite close to him, but he couldn't get in, and so he began to call, and while he was calling, something came behind him, and in a minute his mouth and arms and legs were all bound up, and he fell into a swoon. And when he came to himself, he was lying by the roadside, just where he had first lost his way, under a blasted oak with a black trunk, and his horse was tied beside him. So he rode on to the town and told the people there what had happened, and some of them were amazed; but others knew. So when once everybody had come, there was no door at all for anybody else to pass in by. And when they were all inside, round in a ring, touching each other, some one began to sing in the darkness, and some one else would make a noise like thunder with a thing they had on purpose, and on still nights people would hear the thundering noise far, far away beyond the wild land, and some of them, who thought they knew what it was, used to make a sign on their breasts when they woke up in their beds at dead of night and heard that terrible deep noise, like thunder on the mountains. And the noise and the singing would go on and on for a long time, and the people who were in a ring swayed a little to and fro; and the song was in an old, old language that nobody knows now, and the tune was queer. Nurse said her great-grandmother had known some one who remembered a little of it, when she was quite a little girl, and nurse tried to sing some of it to me, and it was so strange a tune that I turned all cold and my flesh crept as if I had put my hand on something dead. Sometimes it was a man that sang and sometimes it was a woman, and sometimes the one who sang it did it so well that two or three of the people who were there fell to the ground shrieking and tearing with their hands. The singing went on, and the people in the ring kept swaying to and fro for a long time, and at last the moon would rise over a place they called the Tole Deol, and came up and showed them swinging and swaying from side to side, with the sweet thick smoke curling up from the burning coals, and floating in circles all around them. Then they had their supper. A boy and a girl brought it to them; the boy carried a great cup of wine, and the girl carried a cake of bread, and they passed the bread and the wine round and round, but they tasted quite different from common bread and common wine, and changed everybody that tasted them. Then they all rose up and danced, and secret things were brought out of some hiding place, and they played extraordinary games, and danced round and round and round in the moonlight, and sometimes people would suddenly disappear and never be heard of afterwards, and nobody knew what had happened to them. And they drank more of that curious wine, and they made images and worshipped them, and nurse showed me how the images were made one day when we were out for a walk, and we passed by a place where there was a lot of wet clay. So nurse asked me if I would like to know what those things were like that they made on the hill, and I said yes. Then she asked me if I would promise never to tell a living soul a word about it, and if I did I was to be thrown into the black pit with the dead people, and I said I wouldn't tell anybody, and she said the same thing again and again, and I promised. So she took my wooden spade and dug a big lump of clay and put it in my tin bucket, and told me to say if any one met us that I was going to make pies when I went home. Then we went on a little way till we came to a little brake growing right down into the road, and nurse stopped, and looked up the road and down it, and then peeped through the hedge into the field on the other side, and then she said, "Quick!" and we ran into the brake, and crept in and out among the bushes till we had gone a good way from the road. Then we sat down under a bush, and I wanted so much to know what nurse was going to make with the clay, but before she would begin she made me promise again not to say a word about it, and she went again and peeped through the bushes on every side, though the lane was so small and deep that hardly anybody ever went there. So we sat down, and nurse took the clay out of the bucket, and began to knead it with her hands, and do queer things with it, and turn it about. And she hid it under a big dock-leaf for a minute or two and then she brought it out again, and then she stood up and sat down, and walked round the clay in a peculiar manner, and all the time she was softly singing a sort of rhyme, and her face got very red. Then she sat down again, and took the clay in her hands and began to shape it into a doll, but not like the dolls I have at home, and she made the queerest doll I had ever seen, all out of the wet clay, and hid it under a bush to get dry and hard, and all the time she was making it she was singing these rhymes to herself, and her face got redder and redder. So we left the doll there, hidden away in the bushes where nobody would ever find it. And a few days later we went the same walk, and when we came to that narrow, dark part of the lane where the brake runs down to the bank, nurse made me promise all over again, and she looked about, just as she had done before, and we crept into the bushes till we got to the green place where the little clay man was hidden. I remember it all so well, though I was only eight, and it is eight years ago now as I am writing it down, but the sky was a deep violet blue, and in the middle of the brake where we were sitting there was a great elder tree covered with blossoms, and on the other side there was a clump of meadowsweet, and when I think of that day the smell of the meadowsweet and elder blossom seems to fill the room, and if I shut my eyes I can see the glaring blue sky, with little clouds very white floating across it, and nurse who went away long ago sitting opposite me and looking like the beautiful white lady in the wood. So we sat down and nurse took out the clay doll from the secret place where she had hidden it, and she said we must "pay our respects," and she would show me what to do, and I must watch her all the time. So she did all sorts of queer things with the little clay man, and I noticed she was all streaming with perspiration, though we had walked so slowly, and then she told me to "pay my respects," and I did everything she did because I liked her, and it was such an odd game. And she said that if one loved very much, the clay man was very good, if one did certain things with it, and if one hated very much, it was just as good, only one had to do different things, and we played with it a long time, and pretended all sorts of things. Nurse said her great-grandmother had told her all about these images, but what we did was no harm at all, only a game. But she told me a story about these images that frightened me very much, and that was what I remembered that night when I was lying awake in my room in the pale, empty darkness, thinking of what I had seen and the secret wood. Nurse said there was once a young lady of the high gentry, who lived in a great castle. And she was so beautiful that all the gentlemen wanted to marry her, because she was the loveliest lady that anybody had ever seen, and she was kind to everybody, and everybody thought she was very good. But though she was polite to all the gentlemen who wished to marry her, she put them off, and said she couldn't make up her mind, and she wasn't sure she wanted to marry anybody at all. And her father, who was a very great lord, was angry, though he was so fond of her, and he asked her why she wouldn't choose a bachelor out of all the handsome young men who came to the castle. But she only said she didn't love any of them very much, and she must wait, and if they pestered her, she said she would go and be a nun in a nunnery. So all the gentlemen said they would go away and wait for a year and a day, and when a year and a day were gone, they would come back again and ask her to say which one she would marry. So the day was appointed and they all went away; and the lady had promised that in a year and a day it would be her wedding day with one of them. But the truth was, that she was the queen of the people who danced on the hill on summer nights, and on the proper nights she would lock the door of her room, and she and her maid would steal out of the castle by a secret passage that only they knew of, and go away up to the hill in the wild land. And she knew more of the secret things than any one else, and more than any one knew before or after, because she would not tell anybody the most secret secrets. She knew how to do all the awful things, how to destroy young men, and how to put a curse on people, and other things that I could not understand. And her real name was the Lady Avelin, but the dancing people called her Cassap, which meant somebody very wise, in the old language. And she was whiter than any of them and taller, and her eyes shone in the dark like burning rubies; and she could sing songs that none of the others could sing, and when she sang they all fell down on their faces and worshipped her. And she could do what they called shib-show, which was a very wonderful enchantment. She would tell the great lord, her father, that she wanted to go into the woods to gather flowers, so he let her go, and she and her maid went into the woods where nobody came, and the maid would keep watch. Then the lady would lie down under the trees and begin to sing a particular song, and she stretched out her arms, and from every part of the wood great serpents would come, hissing and gliding in and out among the trees, and shooting out their forked tongues as they crawled up to the lady. And they all came to her, and twisted round her, round her body, and her arms, and her neck, till she was covered with writhing serpents, and there was only her head to be seen. And she whispered to them, and she sang to them, and they writhed round and round, faster and faster, till she told them to go. And they all went away directly, back to their holes, and on the lady's breast there would be a most curious, beautiful stone, shaped something like an egg, and coloured dark blue and yellow, and red, and green, marked like a serpent's scales. It was called a glame stone, and with it one could do all sorts of wonderful things, and nurse said her great-grandmother had seen a glame stone with her own eyes, and it was for all the world shiny and scaly like a snake. And the lady could do a lot of other things as well, but she was quite fixed that she would not be married. And there were a great many gentlemen who wanted to marry her, but there were five of them who were chief, and their names were Sir Simon, Sir John, Sir Oliver, Sir Richard, and Sir Rowland. All the others believed she spoke the truth, and that she would choose one of them to be her man when a year and a day was done; it was only Sir Simon, who was very crafty, who thought she was deceiving them all, and he vowed he would watch and try if he could find out anything. And though he was very wise he was very young, and he had a smooth, soft face like a girl's, and he pretended, as the rest did, that he would not come to the castle for a year and a day, and he said he was going away beyond the sea to foreign parts. But he really only went a very little way, and came back dressed like a servant girl, and so he got a place in the castle to wash the dishes. And he waited and watched, and he listened and said nothing, and he hid in dark places, and woke up at night and looked out, and he heard things and he saw things that he thought were very strange. And he was so sly that he told the girl that waited on the lady that he was really a young man, and that he had dressed up as a girl because he loved her so very much and wanted to be in the same house with her, and the girl was so pleased that she told him many things, and he was more than ever certain that the Lady Avelin was deceiving him and the others. And he was so clever, and told the servant so many lies, that one night he managed to hide in the Lady Avelin's room behind the curtains. And he stayed quite still and never moved, and at last the lady came. And she bent down under the bed, and raised up a stone, and there was a hollow place underneath, and out of it she took a waxen image, just like the clay one that I and nurse had made in the brake. And all the time her eyes were burning like rubies. And she took the little wax doll up in her arms and held it to her breast, and she whispered and she murmured, and she took it up and she laid it down again, and she held it high, and she held it low, and she laid it down again. And she said, "Happy is he that begat the bishop, that ordered the clerk, that married the man, that had the wife, that fashioned the hive, that harboured the bee, that gathered the wax that my own true love was made of." And she brought out of an aumbry a great golden bowl, and she brought out of a closet a great jar of wine, and she poured some of the wine into the bowl, and she laid her mannikin very gently in the wine, and washed it in the wine all over. Then she went to a cupboard and took a small round cake and laid it on the image's mouth, and then she bore it softly and covered it up. And Sir Simon, who was watching all the time, though he was terribly frightened, saw the lady bend down and stretch out her arms and whisper and sing, and then Sir Simon saw beside her a handsome young man, who kissed her on the lips. And they drank wine out of the golden bowl together, and they ate the cake together. But when the sun rose there was only the little wax doll, and the lady hid it again under the bed in the hollow place. So Sir Simon knew quite well what the lady was, and he waited and he watched, till the time she had said was nearly over, and in a week the year and a day would be done. And one night, when he was watching behind the curtains in her room, he saw her making more wax dolls. And she made five, and hid them away. And the next night she took one out, and held it up, and filled the golden bowl with water, and took the doll by the neck and held it under the water. Then she said—

> "Sir Dickon, Sir Dickon, your day is done,
>   You shall be drowned in the water wan."

And the next day news came to the castle that Sir Richard had been drowned at the ford. And at night she took another doll and tied a violet cord round its neck and hung it up on a nail. Then she said—

> "Sir Rowland, your life has ended its span,
>   High on a tree I see you hang."

And the next day news came to the castle that Sir Rowland had been hanged by robbers in the wood. And at night she took another doll, and drove her bodkin right into its heart. Then she said—

> "Sir Noll, Sir Noll, so cease your life,
>   Your heart pierced with the knife."

And the next day news came to the castle that Sir Oliver had fought in a tavern, and a stranger had stabbed him to the heart. And at night she took another doll, and held it to a fire of charcoal till it was melted. Then she said—

> "Sir John, return, and turn to clay,
>   In fire of fever you waste away."

And the next day news came to the castle that Sir John had died in a burning fever. So then Sir Simon went out of the castle and mounted his horse and rode away to the bishop and told him everything. And the bishop sent his men, and they took the Lady Avelin, and everything she had done was found out. So on the day after the year and a day, when she was to have been married, they carried her through the town in her smock, and they tied her to a great stake in the market-place, and burned her alive before the bishop with her wax image hung round her neck. And people said the wax man screamed in the burning of the flames. And I thought of this story again and again as I was lying awake in my bed, and I seemed to see the Lady Avelin in the market-place, with the yellow flames eating up her beautiful white body. And I thought of it so much that I seemed to get into the story myself, and I fancied I was the lady, and that they were coming to take me to be burnt with fire, with all the people in the town looking at me. And I wondered whether she cared, after all the strange things she had done, and whether it hurt very much to be burned at the stake. I tried again and again to forget nurse's stories, and to remember the secret I had seen that afternoon, and what was in the secret wood, but I could only see the dark and a glimmering in the dark, and then it went away, and I only saw myself running, and then a great moon came up white over a dark round hill. Then all the old stories came back again, and the queer rhymes that nurse used to sing to me; and there was one beginning "Halsy cumsy Helen musty," that she used to sing very softly when she wanted me to go to sleep. And I began to sing it to myself inside of my head, and I went to sleep.

The next morning I was very tired and sleepy, and could hardly do my lessons, and I was very glad when they were over and I had had my dinner, as I wanted to go out and be alone. It was a warm day, and I went to a nice turfy hill by the river, and sat down on my mother's old shawl that I had brought with me on purpose. The sky was grey, like the day before, but there was a kind of white gleam behind it, and from where I was sitting I could look down on the town, and it was all still and quiet and white, like a picture. I remembered that it was on that hill that nurse taught me to play an old game called "Troy Town," in which one had to dance, and wind in and out on a pattern in the grass, and then when one had danced and turned long enough the other person asks you questions, and you can't help answering whether you want to or not, and whatever you are told to do you feel you have to do it. Nurse said there used to be a lot of games like that that some people knew of, and there was one by which people could be turned into anything you liked, and an old man her great-grandmother had seen had known a girl who had been turned into a large snake. And there was another very ancient game of dancing and winding and turning, by which you could take a person out of himself and hide him away as long as you liked, and his body went walking about quite empty, without any sense in it. But I came to that hill because I wanted to think of what had happened the day before, and of the secret of the wood. From the place where I was sitting I could see beyond the town, into the opening I had found, where a little brook had led me into an unknown country. And I pretended I was following the brook over again, and I went all the way in my mind, and at last I found the wood, and crept into it under the bushes, and then in the dusk I saw something that made me feel as if I were filled with fire, as if I wanted to dance and sing and fly up into the air, because I was changed and wonderful. But what I saw was not changed at all, and had not grown old, and I wondered again and again how such things could happen, and whether nurse's stories were really true, because in the daytime in the open air everything seemed quite different from what it was at night, when I was frightened, and thought I was to be burned alive. I once told my father one of her little tales, which was about a ghost, and asked him if it was true, and he told me it was not true at all, and that only common, ignorant people believed in such rubbish. He was very angry with nurse for telling me the story, and scolded her, and after that I promised her I would never whisper a word of what she told me, and if I did I should be bitten by the great black snake that lived in the pool in the wood. And all alone on the hill I wondered what was true. I had seen something very amazing and very lovely, and I knew a story, and if I had really seen it, and not made it up out of the dark, and the black bough, and the bright shining that was mounting up to the sky from over the great round hill, but had really seen it in truth, then there were all kinds of wonderful and lovely and terrible things to think of, so I longed and trembled, and I burned and got cold. And I looked down on the town, so quiet and still, like a little white picture, and I thought over and over if it could be true. I was a long time before I could make up my mind to anything; there was such a strange fluttering at my heart that seemed to whisper to me all the time that I had not made it up out of my head, and yet it seemed quite impossible, and I knew my father and everybody would say it was dreadful rubbish. I never dreamed of telling him or anybody else a word about it, because I knew it would be of no use, and I should only get laughed at or scolded, so for a long time I was very quiet, and went about thinking and wondering; and at night I used to dream of amazing things, and sometimes I woke up in the early morning and held out my arms with a cry. And I was frightened, too, because there were dangers, and some awful thing would happen to me, unless I took great care, if the story were true. These old tales were always in my head, night and morning, and I went over them and told them to myself over and over again, and went for walks in the places where nurse had told them to me; and when I sat in the nursery by the fire in the evenings I used to fancy nurse was sitting in the other chair, and telling me some wonderful story in a low voice, for fear anybody should be listening. But she used to like best to tell me about things when we were right out in the country, far from the house, because she said she was telling me such secrets, and walls have ears. And if it was something more than ever secret, we had to hide in brakes or woods; and I used to think it was such fun creeping along a hedge, and going very softly, and then we would get behind the bushes or run into the wood all of a sudden, when we were sure that none was watching us; so we knew that we had our secrets quite all to ourselves, and nobody else at all knew anything about them. Now and then, when we had hidden ourselves as I have described, she used to show me all sorts of odd things. One day, I remember, we were in a hazel brake, overlooking the brook, and we were so snug and warm, as though it was April; the sun was quite hot, and the leaves were just coming out. Nurse said she would show me something funny that would make me laugh, and then she showed me, as she said, how one could turn a whole house upside down, without anybody being able to find out, and the pots and pans would jump about, and the china would be broken, and the chairs would tumble over of themselves. I tried it one day in the kitchen, and I found I could do it quite well, and a whole row of plates on the dresser fell off it, and cook's little work-table tilted up and turned right over "before her eyes," as she said, but she was so frightened and turned so white that I didn't do it again, as I liked her. And afterwards, in the hazel copse, when she had shown me how to make things tumble about, she showed me how to make rapping noises, and I learnt how to do that, too. Then she taught me rhymes to say on certain occasions, and peculiar marks to make on other occasions, and other things that her great-grandmother had taught her when she was a little girl herself. And these were all the things I was thinking about in those days after the strange walk when I thought I had seen a great secret, and I wished nurse were there for me to ask her about it, but she had gone away more than two years before, and nobody seemed to know what had become of her, or where she had gone. But I shall always remember those days if I live to be quite old, because all the time I felt so strange, wondering and doubting, and feeling quite sure at one time, and making up my mind, and then I would feel quite sure that such things couldn't happen really, and it began all over again. But I took great care not to do certain things that might be very dangerous. So I waited and wondered for a long time, and though I was not sure at all, I never dared to try to find out. But one day I became sure that all that nurse said was quite true, and I was all alone when I found it out. I trembled all over with joy and terror, and as fast as I could I ran into one of the old brakes where we used to go—it was the one by the lane, where nurse made the little clay man—and I ran into it, and I crept into it; and when I came to the place where the elder was, I covered up my face with my hands and lay down flat on the grass, and I stayed there for two hours without moving, whispering to myself delicious, terrible things, and saying some words over and over again. It was all true and wonderful and splendid, and when I remembered the story I knew and thought of what I had really seen, I got hot and I got cold, and the air seemed full of scent, and flowers, and singing. And first I wanted to make a little clay man, like the one nurse had made so long ago, and I had to invent plans and stratagems, and to look about, and to think of things beforehand, because nobody must dream of anything that I was doing or going to do, and I was too old to carry clay about in a tin bucket. At last I thought of a plan, and I brought the wet clay to the brake, and did everything that nurse had done, only I made a much finer image than the one she had made; and when it was finished I did everything that I could imagine and much more than she did, because it was the likeness of something far better. And a few days later, when I had done my lessons early, I went for the second time by the way of the little brook that had led me into a strange country. And I followed the brook, and went through the bushes, and beneath the low branches of trees, and up thorny thickets on the hill, and by dark woods full of creeping thorns, a long, long way. Then I crept through the dark tunnel where the brook had been and the ground was stony, till at last I came to the thicket that climbed up the hill, and though the leaves were coming out upon the trees, everything looked almost as black as it was on the first day that I went there. And the thicket was just the same, and I went up slowly till I came out on the big bare hill, and began to walk among the wonderful rocks. I saw the terrible voor again on everything, for though the sky was brighter, the ring of wild hills all around was still dark, and the hanging woods looked dark and dreadful, and the strange rocks were as grey as ever; and when I looked down on them from the great mound, sitting on the stone, I saw all their amazing circles and rounds within rounds, and I had to sit quite still and watch them as they began to turn about me, and each stone danced in its place, and they seemed to go round and round in a great whirl, as if one were in the middle of all the stars and heard them rushing through the air. So I went down among the rocks to dance with them and to sing extraordinary songs; and I went down through the other thicket, and drank from the bright stream in the close and secret valley, putting my lips down to the bubbling water; and then I went on till I came to the deep, brimming well among the glittering moss, and I sat down. I looked before me into the secret darkness of the valley, and behind me was the great high wall of grass, and all around me there were the hanging woods that made the valley such a secret place. I knew there was nobody here at all besides myself, and that no one could see me. So I took off my boots and stockings, and let my feet down into the water, saying the words that I knew. And it was not cold at all, as I expected, but warm and very pleasant, and when my feet were in it I felt as if they were in silk, or as if the nymph were kissing them. So when I had done, I said the other words and made the signs, and then I dried my feet with a towel I had brought on purpose, and put on my stockings and boots. Then I climbed up the steep wall, and went into the place where there are the hollows, and the two beautiful mounds, and the round ridges of land, and all the strange shapes. I did not go down into the hollow this time, but I turned at the end, and made out the figures quite plainly, as it was lighter, and I had remembered the story I had quite forgotten before, and in the story the two figures are called Adam and Eve, and only those who know the story understand what they mean. So I went on and on till I came to the secret wood which must not be described, and I crept into it by the way I had found. And when I had gone about halfway I stopped, and turned round, and got ready, and I bound the handkerchief tightly round my eyes, and made quite sure that I could not see at all, not a twig, nor the end of a leaf, nor the light of the sky, as it was an old red silk handkerchief with large yellow spots, that went round twice and covered my eyes, so that I could see nothing. Then I began to go on, step by step, very slowly. My heart beat faster and faster, and something rose in my throat that choked me and made me want to cry out, but I shut my lips, and went on. Boughs caught in my hair as I went, and great thorns tore me; but I went on to the end of the path. Then I stopped, and held out my arms and bowed, and I went round the first time, feeling with my hands, and there was nothing. I went round the second time, feeling with my hands, and there was nothing. Then I went round the third time, feeling with my hands, and the story was all true, and I wished that the years were gone by, and that I had not so long a time to wait before I was happy for ever and ever.

Nurse must have been a prophet like those we read of in the Bible. Everything that she said began to come true, and since then other things that she told me of have happened. That was how I came to know that her stories were true and that I had not made up the secret myself out of my own head. But there was another thing that happened that day. I went a second time to the secret place. It was at the deep brimming well, and when I was standing on the moss I bent over and looked in, and then I knew who the white lady was that I had seen come out of the water in the wood long ago when I was quite little. And I trembled all over, because that told me other things. Then I remembered how sometime after I had seen the white people in the wood, nurse asked me more about them, and I told her all over again, and she listened, and said nothing for a long, long time, and at last she said, "You will see her again." So I understood what had happened and what was to happen. And I understood about the nymphs; how I might meet them in all kinds of places, and they would always help me, and I must always look for them, and find them in all sorts of strange shapes and appearances. And without the nymphs I could never have found the secret, and without them none of the other things could happen. Nurse had told me all about them long ago, but she called them by another name, and I did not know what she meant, or what her tales of them were about, only that they were very queer. And there were two kinds, the bright and the dark, and both were very lovely and very wonderful, and some people saw only one kind, and some only the other, but some saw them both. But usually the dark appeared first, and the bright ones came afterwards, and there were extraordinary tales about them. It was a day or two after I had come home from the secret place that I first really knew the nymphs. Nurse had shown me how to call them, and I had tried, but I did not know what she meant, and so I thought it was all nonsense. But I made up my mind I would try again, so I went to the wood where the pool was, where I saw the white people, and I tried again. The dark nymph, Alanna, came, and she turned the pool of water into a pool of fire . . .

EPILOGUE

"That's a very queer story," said Cotgrave, handing back the green book to the recluse, Ambrose. "I see the drift of a good deal, but there are many things that I do not grasp at all. On the last page, for example, what does she mean by 'nymphs?' "

"Well, I think there are references throughout the manuscript to certain 'processes' which have been handed down by tradition from age to age. Some of these processes are just beginning to come within the purview of science, which has arrived at them—or rather at the steps which lead to them—by quite different paths. I have interpreted the reference to 'nymphs' as a reference to one of these processes."

"And you believe that there are such things?"

"Oh, I think so. Yes, I believe I could give you convincing evidence on that point. I am afraid you have neglected the study of alchemy? It is a pity, for the symbolism, at all events, is very beautiful, and moreover if you were acquainted with certain books on the subject, I could recall to your mind phrases which might explain a good deal in the manuscript that you have been reading."

"Yes; but I want to know whether you seriously think that there is any foundation of fact beneath these fancies. Is it not all a department of poetry; a curious dream with which man has indulged himself?"

"I can only say that it is no doubt better for the great mass of people to dismiss it all as a dream. But if you ask my veritable belief—that goes quite the other way. No; I should not say belief, but rather knowledge. I may tell you that I have known cases in which men have stumbled quite by accident on certain of these 'processes,' and have been astonished by wholly unexpected results. In the cases I am thinking of there could have been no possibility of 'suggestion' or sub-conscious action of any kind. One might as well suppose a schoolboy 'suggesting' the existence of Æschylus to himself, while he plods mechanically through the declensions.

"But you have noticed the obscurity," Ambrose went on, "and in this particular case it must have been dictated by instinct, since the writer never thought that her manuscripts would fall into other hands. But the practice is universal, and for most excellent reasons. Powerful and sovereign medicines, which are, of necessity, virulent poisons also, are kept in a locked cabinet. The child may find the key by chance, and drink herself dead; but in most cases the search is educational, and the phials contain precious elixirs for him who has patiently fashioned the key for himself."

"You do not care to go into details?"

"No, frankly, I do not. No, you must remain unconvinced. But you saw how the manuscript illustrates the talk we had last week?"

"Is this girl still alive?"

"No. I was one of those who found her. I knew the father well; he was a lawyer, and had always left her very much to herself. He thought of nothing but deeds and leases, and the news came to him as an awful surprise. She was missing one morning; I suppose it was about a year after she had written what you have read. The servants were called, and they told things, and put the only natural interpretation on them—a perfectly erroneous one.

"They discovered that green book somewhere in her room, and I found her in the place that she described with so much dread, lying on the ground before the image."

"It was an image?"

"Yes, it was hidden by the thorns and the thick undergrowth that had surrounded it. It was a wild, lonely country; but you know what it was like by her description, though of course you will understand that the colours have been heightened. A child's imagination always makes the heights higher and the depths deeper than they really are; and she had, unfortunately for herself, something more than imagination. One might say, perhaps, that the picture in her mind which she succeeded in a measure in putting into words, was the scene as it would have appeared to an imaginative artist. But it is a strange, desolate land."

"And she was dead?"

"Yes. She had poisoned herself—in time. No; there was not a word to be said against her in the ordinary sense. You may recollect a story I told you the other night about a lady who saw her child's fingers crushed by a window?"

"And what was this statue?"

"Well, it was of Roman workmanship, of a stone that with the centuries had not blackened, but had become white and luminous. The thicket had grown up about it and concealed it, and in the Middle Ages the followers of a very old tradition had known how to use it for their own purposes. In fact it had been incorporated into the monstrous mythology of the Sabbath. You will have noted that those to whom a sight of that shining whiteness had been vouchsafed by chance, or rather, perhaps, by apparent chance, were required to blindfold themselves on their second approach. That is very significant."

"And is it there still?"

"I sent for tools, and we hammered it into dust and fragments."

"The persistence of tradition never surprises me," Ambrose went on after a pause. "I could name many an English parish where such traditions as that girl had listened to in her childhood are still existent in occult but unabated vigour. No, for me, it is the 'story' not the 'sequel,' which is strange and awful, for I have always believed that wonder is of the soul."

For the Blood Is the Life

F. Marion Crawford

———◆———

W E HAD DINED AT SUNSET ON THE BROAD ROOF OF THE OLD TOWER, because it was cooler there during the great heat of summer. Besides, the little kitchen was built at one corner of the great square platform, which made it more convenient than if the dishes had to be carried down the steep stone steps broken in places and everywhere worn with age. The tower was one of those built all down the west coast of Calabria by the Emperor Charles V early in the sixteenth century, to keep off the Barbary pirates, when the unbelievers were allied with Francis I against the Emperor and the Church. They have gone to ruin, a few still stand intact, and mine is one of the largest. How it came into my possession ten years ago, and why I spend a part of each year in it, are matters which do not concern this tale. The tower stands in one of the loneliest spots in Southern Italy, at the extremity of a curving, rocky promontory, which forms a small but safe natural harbour at the southern extremity of the Gulf of Policastro, and just north of Cape Scalea, the birthplace of Judas Iscariot, according to the old local legend. The tower stands alone on this hooked spur of the rock, and there is not a house to be seen within three miles of it. When I go there I take a couple of sailors, one of whom is a fair cook, and when I am away it is in charge of a gnome-like little being who was once a miner and who attached himself to me long ago.

My friend, who sometimes visits me in my summer solitude, is an artist by profession, a Scandinavian by birth, and a cosmopolitan by force of circumstances. We had dined at sunset; the sunset glow had reddened and faded again, and the evening purple steeped the vast chain of the mountains that embrace the deep gulf to eastward and rear themselves higher and higher towards the south. It was hot, and we sat at the landward corner of the platform, waiting for the night breeze to come down from the lower hills. The colour sank out of the air, there was a little interval of deep-grey twilight, and a lamp sent a yellow streak from the open door of the kitchen, where the men were getting their supper.

Then the moon rose suddenly above the crest of the promontory, flooding the platform and lighting up every little spur of rock and knoll of grass below us, down to the edge of the motionless water. My friend lighted his pipe and sat looking at a spot on the hillside. I knew that he was looking at it, and for a long time past I had wondered whether he would ever see anything there that would fix his attention. I knew that spot well. It was clear that he was interested at last, though it was a long time before he spoke. Like most painters, he trusts to his own eyesight, as a lion trusts his strength and a stag his speed, and he is always disturbed when he cannot reconcile what he sees with what he believes that he ought to see.

"It's strange," he said. "Do you see that little mound just on this side of the boulder?"

"Yes," I said, and I guessed what was coming.

"It looks like a grave," observed Holger.

"Very true. It does look like a grave."

"Yes," continued my friend, his eyes still fixed on the spot. "But the strange thing is that I see the body lying on the top of it. Of course," continued Holger, turning his head on one side as artists do, "it must be an effect of light. In the first place, it is not a grave at all. Secondly, if it were, the body would be inside and not outside. Therefore, it's an effect of the moonlight. Don't you see it?"

"Perfectly; I always see it on moonlight nights."

"It doesn't seem it interest you much," said Holger.

"On the contrary, it does interest me, though I am used to it. You're not so far wrong, either. The mound is really a grave."

"Nonsense!" cried Holger incredulously. "I suppose you'll tell me that what I see lying on it is really a corpse!"

"No," I answered, "it's not. I know, because I have taken the trouble to go down and see."

"Then what is it?" asked Holger.

"It's nothing."

"You mean that it's an effect of light, I suppose?"

"Perhaps it is. But the inexplicable part of the matter is that it makes no difference whether the moon is rising or setting, or waxing or waning. If there's any moonlight at all, from east or west or overhead, so long as it shines on the grave you can see the outline of the body on top."

Holger stirred up his pipe with the point of his knife, and then used his finger for a stopper. When the tobacco burned well, he rose from his chair.

"If you don't mind," he said, "I'll go down and take a look at it."

He left me, crossed the roof, and disappeared down the dark steps. I did not move, but sat looking down until he came out of the tower below. I heard him humming an old Danish song as he crossed the open space in the bright moonlight, going straight to the mysterious mound. When he was ten paces from it, Holger stopped short, made two steps forward, and then three or four backward, and then stopped again. I know what that meant. He had reached the spot where the Thing ceased to be visible—where, as he would have said, the effect of light changed.

Then he went on till he reached the mound and stood upon it. I could see the Thing still, but it was no longer lying down; it was on its knees now, winding its white arms round Holger's body and looking up into his face. A cool breeze stirred my hair at that moment, as the night wind began to come down from the hills, but it felt like a breath from another world.

The Thing seemed to be trying to climb to its feet helping itself up by Holger's body while he stood upright, quite unconscious of it and apparently looking toward the tower, which is very picturesque when the moonlight falls upon it on that side.

"Come along!" I shouted. "Don't stay there all night!"

It seemed to me that he moved reluctantly as he stepped from the mound, or else with difficulty. That was it. The Thing's arms were still round his waist, but its feet could not leave the grave. As he came slowly forward it was drawn and lengthened like a wreath of mist, thin and white, till I saw distinctly that Holger shook himself, as a man does who feels a chill. At the same instant a little wail of pain came to me on the breeze—it might have been the cry of the small owl that lives amongst the rocks—and the misty presence floated swiftly back from Holger's advancing figure and lay once more at its length upon the mound.

Again I felt the cool breeze in my hair, and this time an icy thrill of dread ran down my spine. I remembered very well that I had once gone down there alone in the moon-light; that presently, being near, I had seen nothing; that, like Holger, I had gone and had stood upon the mound; and I remembered how when I came back, sure that there was nothing there, I had felt the sudden conviction that there was something after all if I would only look back, a temptation I had resisted as unworthy of a man of sense, until, to get rid of it, I had shaken myself just as Holger did.

And now I knew that those white, misty arms had been round me, too; I knew it in a flash, and I shuddered as I remembered that I had heard the night owl then, too. But it had not been the night owl. It was the cry of the Thing.

I refilled my pipe and poured out a cup of strong southern wine; in less than a minute Holger was seated beside me again.

"Of course there's nothing there," he said, "but it's creepy, all the same. Do you know, when I was coming back I was so sure that there was something behind me that I wanted to turn around and look? It was an effort not to."

He laughed a little, knocked the ashes out of his pipe, and poured himself out some wine. For a while neither of us spoke, and the moon rose higher and we both looked at the Thing that lay on the mound.

"You might make a story about that," said Holger after a long time.

"There is one," I answered. "If you're not sleepy, I'll tell it to you."

"Go ahead," said Holger, who likes stories.

Old Alario was dying up there in the village beyond the hill. You remember him, I have no doubt. They say that he made his money by selling sham jewelry in South America, and escaped with his gains when he was found out. Like all those fellows, if they bring anything back with them, he at once set to work to enlarge his house, and as there are no masons here, he sent all the way to Paola for two workmen. They were a rough-looking pair of scoundrels—a Neapolitan who had lost one eye and a Sicilian with an old scar half an inch deep across his left cheek. I often saw them, for on Sundays they used to come down here and fish off the rocks. When Alario caught the fever that killed him the masons were still at work. As he had agreed that part of their pay should be their board and lodging, he made them sleep in the house. His wife was dead, and he had an only son called Angelo, who was a much better sort than himself. Angelo was to marry the daughter of the richest man in the village, and, strange to say, though the marriage was arranged by their parents, the young people were said to be in love with each other.

For that matter, the whole village was in love with Angelo, and among the rest a wild, good-looking creature called Cristina, who was more like a gipsy than any girl I ever saw about here. She had very red lips and very black eyes, she was built like a greyhound, and had the tongue of the devil. But Angelo did not care a straw for her. He was rather a simpleminded fellow, quite different from his old scoundrel of a father, and under what I should call normal circumstances I really believe that he would never have looked at any girl except the nice plump little creature, with a fat dowry, whom his father meant him to marry. But things turned up which were neither normal nor natural.

On the other hand, a very handsome young shepherd from the hills above Maratea was in love with Cristina, who seems to have been quite indifferent to him. Cristina had no regular means of subsistence, but she was a good girl and willing to do any work or go on errands to any distance for the sake of a loaf of bread or a mess of beans, and permission to sleep under cover. She was especially glad when she could get something to do about the house of Angelo's father. There is no doctor in the village, and when the neighbours saw that old Alario was dying they sent Cristina to Scalea to fetch one. That was late in the afternoon, and if they had waited so long it was because the dying miser refused to allow any such extravagance while he was able to speak. But while Cristina was gone matters grew rapidly worse, the priest was brought to the bedside, and when he had done what he could he gave it as his opinion to the bystanders that the old man was dead, and left the house.

You know these people. They have a physical horror of death. Until the priest spoke, the room had been full of people. The words were hardly out of his mouth before it was empty. It was night now. They hurried down the dark steps and out into the street.

Angelo, as I have said, was away, Cristina had not come back—the simple woman-servant who had nursed the sick man fled with the rest, and the body was left alone in the flickering light of the earthen oil lamp.

Five minutes later two men looked in cautiously and crept forward toward the bed. They were the one-eyed Neapolitan mason and his Sicilian companion. They knew what they wanted. In a moment they had dragged from under the bed a small but heavy iron-bound box, and long before anyone thought of coming back to the dead man they had left the house and the village under cover of darkness. It was easy enough, for Alario's house is the last toward the gorge which leads down here, and the thieves merely went out by the back door, got over the stone wall, and had nothing to risk after that except that possibility of meeting some belated countryman, which was very small indeed, since few of the people use that path. They had a mattock and shovel, and they made their way without accident.

I am telling you this story as it must have happened, for, of course, there were no witnesses to this part of it. The men brought the box down by the gorge, intending to bury it on the beach in the wet sand, where it would have been much safer. But the paper would have rotted if they had been obliged to leave it there long, so they dug their hole down there, close to that boulder. Yes, just where the mound is now.

Cristina did not find the doctor in Scalea, for he had been sent for from a place up the valley, halfway to San Domenico. If she had found him we would have come on his mule by the upper road, which is smoother but much longer. But Cristina took the short cut by the rocks, which passes about fifty feet above the mound, and goes round that corner.

The men were digging when she passed, and she heard them at work. It would not have been like her to go by without finding out what the noise was, for she was never afraid of anything in her life, and, besides, the fishermen sometimes come ashore here at night to get a stone for an anchor or to gather sticks to make a little fire. The night was dark and Cristina probably came close to the two men before she could see what they were doing. She knew them, of course, and they knew her, and understood instantly that they were in her power. There was only one thing to be done for their safety, and they did it. They knocked her on the head, they dug the hole deep, and they buried her quickly with the iron-bound chest. They must have understood that their only chance of escaping suspicion lay in getting back to the village before their absence was noticed, for they returned immediately, and were found half an hour later gossiping quietly with the man who was making Alario's coffin. He was a crony of theirs, and had been working at the repairs in the old man's house. So far as I have been able to make out, the only persons who were supposed to know where Alario kept his treasure were Angelo and the one woman-servant I have mentioned. Angelo was away; it was the woman who discovered the theft.

It was easy enough to understand why no one else knew where the money was. The old man kept his door locked and the key in his pocket when he was out, and did not let the woman enter to clean the place unless he was there himself. The whole village knew that he had money somewhere, however, and the masons had probably discovered the whereabouts of the chest by climbing in at the window in his absence. If the old man had not been delirious until he lost consciousness he would have been in frightful agony of mind for his riches. The faithful woman-servant forgot their existence only for a few moments when she fled with the rest, overcome by the horror of death. Twenty minutes had not passed before she returned with the two hideous old hags who are always called in to prepare the dead for burial. Even then she had not at first the courage to go near the bed with them, but she made a pretence of dropping something, went down on her knees as if to find it, and looked under the bedstead. The walls of the room were newly whitewashed down to the floor and she saw at a glance that the chest was gone. It had been there in the afternoon, it had therefore been stolen in the short interval since she had left the room.

There are no carabineers stationed in the village; there is not so much as a municipal watchman, for there is no municipality. There never was such a place, I believe. Scalea is supposed to look after it in some mysterious way, and it takes a couple of hours to get anybody from there. As the old woman had lived in the village all her life, it did not even occur to her to apply to any civil authority for help. She simply set up a howl and ran through the village in the dark, screaming out that her dead master's house had been robbed. Many of the people looked out, but at first no one seemed inclined to help her. Most of them, judging her by themselves, whispered to each other that she had probably stolen the money herself. The first man to move was the father of the girl whom Angelo was to marry; having collected his household, all of whom felt a personal interest in the wealth which was to have come into the family, he declared it to be his opinion that the chest had been stolen by the two journeymen masons who lodged in the house. He headed a search for them, which naturally began in Alario's house and ended in the carpenter's workshop, where the thieves were found discussing a measure of wine with the carpenter over the half-finished coffin, by the light of one earthen lamp filled with oil and tallow. The search party at once accused the delinquents of the crime, and threatened to lock them up in the cellar till the carabineers could be fetched from Scalea. The two men looked at each other for one moment, and then without the slightest hesitation they put out the single light, seized the unfinished coffin between them, and using it as a sort of battering ram, dashed upon their assailants in the dark. In a few moments they were beyond pursuit.

That is the end of the first part of the story. The treasure had disappeared, and as no trace of it could be found the people supposed that the thieves had succeeded in carrying it off. The old man was buried, and when Angelo came back at last he had to borrow money to pay for the miserable funeral, and had some difficulty in doing so. He hardly needed to be told that in losing his inheritance he had lost his bride. In this part of the world marriages are made on strictly business principles, and if the promised cash is not forthcoming on the appointed day, the bride or the bridegroom whose parents have failed to produce it may as well take themselves off, for there will be no wedding. Poor Angelo knew that well enough. His father had been possessed of hardly any land, and now that the hard cash which he had brought from South America was gone, there was nothing left but debts for the building materials that were to have been used for enlarging and improving the old house. Angelo was beggared, and the nice plump little creature who was to have been his, turned up her nose at him in the most approved fashion. As for Cristina, it was several days before she was missed, for no one remembered that she had been sent to Scalea for the doctor, who had never come. She often disappeared in the same way for days together, when she could find a little work here and there at the distant farms among the hills. But when she did not come back at all, people began to wonder, and at last made up their minds that she had connived with the masons and had escaped with them.

* * *

I paused and emptied my glass.

"That sort of thing could not happen anywhere else," observed Holger, filling his everlasting pipe again. "It is wonderful what a natural charm there is about murder and sudden death in a romantic country like this. Deeds that would be simply brutal and disgusting anywhere else become dramatic and mysterious because this is Italy, and we are living in a genuine tower of Charles V built against Barbary pirates."

"There's something in that," I admitted. Holger is the most romantic man in the world inside of himself, but he always thinks it necessary to explain why he feels anything.

"I suppose the found the poor girl's body with the box," he said presently.

"As it seems to interest you," I answered, "I'll tell you the rest of the story."

The mood had risen by this time; the outline of the Thing on the mound was clearer to our eyes than before.

The village very soon settled down to its small dull life. No one missed old Alario, who had been away so much on his voyages to South America that he had never been a familiar figure in his native place. Angelo lived in the half-finished house, and because he had no money to pay the old woman-servant she would not stay with him, but once in a long time she would come and wash a shirt for him for old acquaintance' sake. Besides the house, he had inherited a small patch of ground at some distance from the village; he tried to cultivate it, but he had no heart in the work, for he knew he could never pay the taxes on it and on the house, which would certainly be confiscated by the Government, or seized for the debt of the building material, which the man who had supplied it refused to take back.

Angelo was very unhappy. So long as his father had been alive and rich, every girl in the village had been in love with him; but that was all changed now. It had been pleasant to be admired and courted, and invited to drink wine by fathers who had girls to marry. It was hard to be stared at coldly, and sometimes laughed at because he had been robbed of his inheritance. He cooked his miserable meals for himself, and from being sad became melancholy and morose.

At twilight, when the day's work was done, instead of hanging about in the open space before the church with young fellows of his own age, he took to wandering in lonely places on the outskirts of the village till it was quite dark. Then he slunk home and went to bed to save the expense of a light. But in those lonely twilight hours he began to have strange waking dreams. He was not always alone, for often when he sat on the stump of a tree, where the narrow path turns down the gorge, he was sure that a woman came up noiselessly over the rough stones, as if her feet were bare; and she stood under a clump of chestnut trees only half a dozen yards down the path, and beckoned to him without speaking. Though she was in the shadow he knew that her lips were red, and that when they parted a little and smiled at him she showed two small sharp teeth. He knew this at first rather than saw it, and he knew that it was Cristina, and that she was dead. Yet he was not afraid; he only wondered whether it was a dream, for he thought that if he had been awake he should have been frightened.

Besides, the dead woman had red lips, and that could only happen in a dream. Whenever he went near the gorge after sunset she was already there waiting for him, or else she very soon appeared, and he began to be sure of her blood-red mouth, but now each feature grew distinct, and the pale face looked at him with deep and hungry eyes.

It was the eyes that grew dim. Little by little he came to know that someday the dream would not end when he turned away to go home, but would lead him down the gorge out of which the vision rose. She was nearer now when she beckoned to him. Her cheeks were not livid like those of the dead, but pale with starvation, with the furious and unappeased physical hunger of her eyes that devoured him. They feasted on his soul and cast a spell over him, and at last they were close to his own and held him. He could not tell whether her breath was as hot as fire, or as cold as ice; he could not tell whether her red lips burned his or froze them, or whether her five fingers on his wrists seared scorching scars or bit his flesh like frost; he could not tell whether he was awake or asleep, whether she was alive or dead, but he knew that she loved him, she alone of all creatures, earthly or unearthly, and her spell had power over him.

When the moon rose high that night the shadow of that Thing was not alone down there upon the mound.

Angelo awoke in the cool dawn, drenched with dew and chilled through flesh, and blood, and bone. He opened his eyes to the faint grey light, and saw the stars were still shining overhead. He was very weak, and his heart was beating so slowly that he was almost like a man fainting. Slowly he turned his head on the mound, as on a pillow, but the other face was not there. Fear seized him suddenly, a fear unspeakable and unknown; he sprang to his feet and fled up the gorge, and he never looked behind him until he reached the door of the house on the outskirts of the village. Drearily he went to his work that day, and wearily the hours dragged themselves after the sun, till at last it touched the sea and sank, and the great sharp hills above Maratea turned purple against the dove-coloured eastern sky.

Angelo shouldered his heavy hoe and left the field. He felt less tired now than in the morning when he had begun to work, but he promised himself that he would go home without lingering by the gorge, and eat the best supper he could get himself, and sleep all night in his bed like a Christian man. Not again would he be tempted down the narrow way by a shadow with red lips and icy breath; not again would he dream that dream of terror and delight. He was near the village now; it was half an hour since the sun had set, and the cracked church bell sent little discordant echoes across the rocks and ravines to tell all good people that the day was done. Angelo stood still a moment where the path forked, where it led toward the village on the left, and down to the gorge on the right, where a clump of chestnut trees overhung the narrow way. He stood still a minute, lifting his battered hat from his head and gazing at the fast-fading sea westward, and his lips moved as he silently repeated the familiar evening prayer. His lips moved, but the words that followed them in his brain lost their meaning and turned into others, and ended in a name that he spoke aloud—Cristina! With the name, the tension of his will relaxed suddenly, reality went out and the dream took him again, and bore him on swiftly and surely like a man walking in his sleep, down, down, by the steep path in the gathering darkness. And as she glided beside him, Cristina whispered strange, sweet things in his ear, which somehow, if he had been awake, he knew that he could not quite have understood; but now they were the most wonderful words he had ever heard in his life. And she kissed him also, but not upon his mouth. He felt her sharp kisses upon his white throat, and he knew that her lips were red. So the wild dream sped on through twilight and darkness and moonrise, and all the glory of the summer's night. But in the chilly dawn he lay as one half dead upon the mound down there, recalling and not recalling, drained of his blood, yet strangely longing to give those red lips more. Then came the fear, the awful nameless panic, the mortal horror that guards the confines of the world we see not, neither know of as we know of other things, but which we feel when its icy chill freezes our bones and stirs our hair with the touch of a ghostly hand. Once more Angelo sprang from the mound and fled up the gorge in the breaking day, but his step was less sure this time, and he panted for breath as he ran; and when he came to the bright spring of water that rises halfway up the hillside, he dropped upon his knees and hands and plunged his whole face in and drank as he had never drunk before—for it was the thirst of the wounded man who has lain bleeding all night upon the battle-field.

She had him fast now, and he could not escape her, but would come to her every evening at dusk until she had drained him of his last drop of blood. It was in vain that when the day was done he tried to take another turning and to go home by a path that did not lead near the gorge. It was in vain that he made promises to himself each morning at dawn when he climbed the lonely way up from the shore to the village. It was all in vain, for when the sun sank burning into the sea, and the coolness of the evening stole out as from a hiding-place to delight the weary world, his feet turned toward the old way, and she was waiting for him in the shadow under the chestnut trees; and then all happened as before, and she fell to kissing his white throat even as she flitted lightly down the way, winding one arm about him. And as his blood failed, she grew more hungry and more thirsty every day, and every day when he awoke in the early dawn it was harder to rouse himself to the effort of climbing the steep path to the village; and when he went to his work his feet dragged painfully, and there was hardly strength in his arms to wield the heavy hoe. He scarcely spoke to anyone now, but the people said he was "consuming himself" for love of the girl he was to have married when he lost his inheritance; and they laughed heartily at the thought, for this is not a very romantic country. At this time, Antonio, the man who stays here to look after the tower, returned from a visit to his people, who live near Salerno. He had been away all the time since before Alario's death and knew nothing of what had happened. He has told me that he came back late in the afternoon and shut himself up in the tower to eat and sleep, for he was very tired. It was past midnight when he awoke, and when he looked out toward the mound, and he saw something, and he did not sleep again that night. When he went out again in the morning it was broad daylight, and there was nothing to be seen on the mound but loose stones and driven sand. Yet he did not go very near it; he went straight up the path to the village and directly to the house of the old priest.

"I have seen an evil thing this night," he said; "I have seen how the dead drink the blood of the living. And the blood is the life."

"Tell me what you have seen," said the priest in reply.

Antonio told him everything he had seen.

"You must bring your book and your holy water to-night," he added. "I will be here before sunset to go down with you, and if it pleases your reverence to sup with me while we wait, I will make ready."

"I will come," the priest answered, "for I have read in old books of these strange beings which are neither quick nor dead, and which lie ever fresh in their graves, stealing out in the dusk to taste life and blood."

Antonio cannot read, but he was glad to see that the priest understood the business; for, of course, the books must have been instructed him as to the best means of quieting the half-living Thing for ever.

So Antonio went away to his work, which consists largely in sitting on the shady side of the tower, when he is not perched upon a rock with a fishing-line catching nothing. But on that day he went twice to look at the mound in the bright sunlight, and he searched round and round it for some hole through which the being might get in and out; but he found none. When the sun began to sink and the air was cooler in the shadows, he went up to fetch the old priest, carrying a little wicker basket with him; and in this they placed a bottle of holy water, and the basin, and sprinkler, and the stole which the priest would need; and they came down and waited in the door of the tower till it should be dark. But while the light still lingered very grey and faint, they saw something moving, just there, two figures, a man's that walked, and a woman's that flitted beside him, and while her head lay on his shoulder she kissed his throat. The priest has told me that, too, and that his teeth chattered and he grasped Antonio's arm. The vision passed and disappeared into the shadow. Then Antonio got the leathern flask of strong liquor, which he kept for great occasions, and poured such a draught as made the old man feel almost young again; and gave the priest his stole to put on and the holy water to carry, and they went out together toward the spot where the work was to be done. Antonio says that in spite of the rum his own knees shook together, and the priest stumbled over his Latin. For when they were yet a few yards from the mound the flickering light of the lantern fell upon Angelo's white face, unconscious as if in sleep, and on his upturned throat, over which a very thin red line of blood trickled down into his collar; and the flickering light of the lantern played upon another face that looked up from the feast, upon two deep, dead eyes that saw in spite of death—upon parted lips, redder than life itself—upon two gleaming teeth on which glistened a rosy drop. Then the priest, good old man, shut his eyes tight and showered holy water before him, and his cracked voice rose almost to a scream; and then Antonio, who is no coward after all, raised his pick in one hand and the lantern in the other, as he sprang forward, not knowing what the end should be; and then he swears that he heard a woman's cry, and the Thing was gone, and Angelo lay alone on the mound unconscious, with the red line on his throat and the beads of deathly sweat on his cold forehead. They lifted him, half-dead as he was, and laid him on the ground close by; then Antonio went to work, and the priest helped him, thought he was old and could not do much; and they dug deep, and at last Antonio, standing in the grave, stooped down with his lantern to see what he might see.

His hair used to be dark brown, with grizzled streaks about the temples; in less than a month from that day he was as grey as a badger. He was a miner when he was young, and most of these fellows have seen ugly sights now and then, when accidents have happened, but he had never seen what he saw that night—that Thing which is neither alive nor dead, that Thing that will abide neither above ground nor in the grave. Antonio had brought something with him which the priest had not noticed—a sharp stake shaped from a piece of tough old driftwood. He had it with him now, and he had his heavy pick, and he had taken the lantern down into the grave. I don't think any power on earth could make him speak of what happened then, and the old priest was too frightened to look in. He says he heard Antonio breathing like a wild beast, and moving as if he were fighting with something almost as strong as himself; and he heard an evil sound also, with blows, as of something violently driven through flesh and bone; and then, the most awful sound of all—a woman's shriek, the unearthly scream of a woman neither dead nor alive, but buried deep for many days. And he, the poor old priest, could only rock himself as he knelt there in the sand, crying aloud his prayers and exorcisms to drown these dreadful sounds. Then suddenly a small iron-bound chest was thrown up and rolled over against the old man's knee, and in a moment more Antonio was beside him, his face as white as tallow in the flickering light of the lantern, shoveling the sand and pebbles into the grave with furious haste, and looking over the edge till the pit was half full; and the priest said that there was much fresh blood on Antonio's hands and on his clothes.

I had come to the end of my story. Holger finished his wine and leaned back in his chair.

"So Angelo got his own again," he said. "Did he marry the prim and plump young person to whom he had been betrothed?"

"No; he had been badly frightened. He went to South America, and has not been heard of since."

"And that poor thing's body is there still, I suppose," said Holger. "Is it quite dead yet, I wonder?"

I wonder, too. But whether it be dead or alive, I should hardly care to see it, even in broad daylight. Antonio is as grey as a badger, and he has never been quite the same man since that night.

Ancient Sorceries

Algernon Blackwood

———◆———

I

There are, it would appear, certain wholly unremarkable persons, with none of the characteristics that invite adventure, who yet once or twice in the course of their smooth lives undergo an experience so strange that the world catches its breath—and looks the other way! And it was cases of this kind, perhaps, more than any other, that fell into the widespread net of John Silence, the psychic doctor, and, appealing to his deep humanity, to his patience, and to his great qualities of spiritual sympathy, led often to the revelation of problems of the strangest complexity, and of the profoundest possible human interest.

Matters that seemed almost too curious and fantastic for belief he loved to trace to their hidden sources. To unravel a tangle in the very soul of things—and to release a suffering human soul in the process—was with him a veritable passion. And the knots he untied were, indeed, often passing strange.

The world, of course, asks for some plausible basis to which it can attach credence—something it can, at least, pretend to explain. The adventurous type it can understand: such people carry about with them an adequate explanation of their exciting lives, and their characters obviously drive them into the circumstances which produce the adventures. It expects nothing else from them, and is satisfied. But dull, ordinary folk have no right to out-of-the-way experiences, and the world having been led to expect otherwise, is disappointed with them, not to say shocked. Its complacent judgment has been rudely disturbed.

"Such a thing happen to *that* man!" it cries—"a commonplace person like that! It is too absurd! There must be something wrong!"

Yet there could be no question that something did actually happen to little Arthur Vezin, something of the curious nature he described to Dr. Silence. Outwardly, or inwardly, it happened beyond a doubt, and in spite of the jeers of his few friends who heard the tale, and observed wisely that "such a thing might perhaps have come to Iszard, that crack-brained Iszard, or to that odd fish Minski, but it could never have happened to commonplace little Vezin, who was fore-ordained to live and die according to scale."

But, whatever his method of death was, Vezin certainly did not "live according to scale" so far as this particular event in his otherwise uneventful life was concerned; and to hear him recount it, and watch his pale delicate features change, and hear his voice grow softer and more hushed as he proceeded, was to know the conviction that his halting words perhaps failed sometimes to convey. He lived the thing over again each time he told it. His whole personality became muffled in the recital. It subdued him more than ever, so that the tale became a lengthy apology for an experience that he deprecated. He appeared to excuse himself and ask your pardon for having dared to take part in so fantastic an episode. For little Vezin was a timid, gentle, sensitive soul, rarely able to assert himself, tender to man and beast, and almost constitutionally unable to say No, or to claim many things that should rightly have been his. His whole scheme of life seemed utterly remote from anything more exciting than missing a train or losing an umbrella on an omnibus. And when this curious event came upon him he was already more years beyond forty than his friends suspected or he cared to admit.

John Silence, who heard him speak of his experience more than once, said that he sometimes left out certain details and put in others; yet they were all obviously true. The whole scene was unforgettably cinematographed on to his mind. None of the details were imagined or invented. And when he told the story with them all complete, the effect was undeniable. His appealing brown eyes shone, and much of the charming personality, usually so carefully repressed, came forward and revealed itself. His modesty was always there, of course, but in the telling he forgot the present and allowed himself to appear almost vividly as he lived again in the past of his adventure.

He was on the way home when it happened, crossing northern France from some mountain trip or other where he buried himself solitary-wise every summer. He had nothing but an unregistered bag in the rack, and the train was jammed to suffocation, most of the passengers being unredeemed holiday English. He disliked them, not because they were his fellow-countrymen, but because they were noisy and obtrusive, obliterating with their big limbs and tweed clothing all the quieter tints of the day that brought him satisfaction and enabled him to melt into insignificance and forget that he was anybody. These English clashed about him like a brass band, making him feel vaguely that he ought to be more self-assertive and obstreperous, and that he did not claim insistently enough all kinds of things that he didn't want and that were really valueless, such as corner seats, windows up or down, and so forth.

So that he felt uncomfortable in the train, and wished the journey were over and he was back again living with his unmarried sister in Surbiton.

And when the train stopped for ten panting minutes at the little station in northern France, and he got out to stretch his legs on the platform, and saw to his dismay a further batch of the British Isles debouching from another train, it suddenly seemed impossible to him to continue the journey. Even *his* flabby soul revolted, and the idea of staying a night in the little town and going on next day by a slower, emptier train, flashed into his mind. The guard was already shouting "*en voiture*" and the corridor of his compartment was already packed when the thought came to him. And, for once, he acted with decision and rushed to snatch his bag.

Finding the corridor and steps impassable, he tapped at the window (for he had a corner seat) and begged the Frenchman who sat opposite to hand his luggage out to him, explaining in his wretched French that he intended to break the journey there. And this elderly Frenchman, he declared, gave him a look, half of warning, half of reproach, that to his dying day he could never forget; handed the bag through the window of the moving train; and at the same time poured into his ears a long sentence, spoken rapidly and low, of which he was able to comprehend only the last few words: "*à cause du sommeil et à cause des chats.*"

In reply to Dr. Silence, whose singular psychic acuteness at once seized upon this Frenchman as a vital point in the adventure, Vezin admitted that the man had impressed him favourably from the beginning, though without being able to explain why. They had sat facing one another during the four hours of the journey, and though no conversation had passed between them—Vezin was timid about his stuttering French—he confessed that his eyes were being continually drawn to his face, almost, he felt, to rudeness, and that each, by a dozen nameless little politenesses and attentions, had evinced the desire to be kind. The men liked each other and their personalities did not clash, or would not have clashed had they chanced to come to terms of acquaintance. The Frenchman, indeed, seemed to have exercised a silent protective influence over the insignificant little Englishman, and without words or gestures betrayed that he wished him well and would gladly have been of service to him.

"And this sentence that he hurled at you after the bag?" asked John Silence, smiling that peculiarly sympathetic smile that always melted the prejudices of his patient, "were you unable to follow it exactly?"

"It was so quick and low and vehement," explained Vezin, in his small voice, "that I missed practically the whole of it. I only caught the few words at the very end, because he spoke them so clearly, and his face was bent down out of the carriage window so near to mine."

"'*A cause du sommeil et à cause des chats*'?" repeated Dr. Silence, as though half speaking to himself.

"That's it exactly," said Vezin; "which, I take it, means something like 'because of sleep and because of the cats,' doesn't it?"

"Certainly, that's how I should translate it," the doctor observed shortly, evidently not wishing to interrupt more than necessary.

"And the rest of the sentence—all the first part I couldn't understand, I mean—was a warning not to do something—not to stop in the town, or at some particular place in the town, perhaps. That was the impression it made on me."

Then, of course, the train rushed off, and left Vezin standing on the platform alone and rather forlorn.

The little town climbed in straggling fashion up a sharp hill rising out of the plain at the back of the station, and was crowned by the twin towers of the ruined cathedral peeping over the summit. From the station itself it looked uninteresting and modern, but the fact was that the mediæval position lay out of sight just beyond the crest. And once he reached the top and entered the old streets, he stepped clean out of modern life into a bygone century. The noise and bustle of the crowded train seemed days away. The spirit of this silent hill-town, remote from tourists and motor-cars, dreaming its own quiet life under the autumn sun, rose up and cast its spell upon him. Long before he recognised this spell he acted under it. He walked softly, almost on tiptoe, down the winding narrow streets where the gables all but met over his head, and he entered the doorway of the solitary inn with a deprecating and modest demeanour that was in itself an apology for intruding upon the place and disturbing its dream.

At first, however, Vezin said, he noticed very little of all this. The attempt at analysis came much later. What struck him then was only the delightful contrast of the silence and peace after the dust and noisy rattle of the train. He felt soothed and stroked like a cat.

"Like a cat, you said?" interrupted John Silence, quickly catching him up.

"Yes. At the very start I felt that." He laughed apologetically. "I felt as though the warmth and the stillness and the comfort made me purr. It seemed to be the general mood of the whole place—then."

The inn, a rambling ancient house, the atmosphere of the old coaching days still about it, apparently did not welcome him too warmly. He felt he was only tolerated, he said. But it was cheap and comfortable, and the delicious cup of afternoon tea he ordered at once made him feel really very pleased with himself for leaving the train in this bold, original way. For to him it had seemed bold and original. He felt something of a dog. His room, too, soothed him with its dark panelling and low irregular ceiling, and the long sloping passage that led to it seemed the natural pathway to a real Chamber of Sleep—a little dim cubby hole out of the world where noise could not enter. It looked upon the courtyard at the back. It was all very charming, and made him think of himself as dressed in very soft velvet somehow, and the floors seemed padded, the walls provided with cushions. The sounds of the streets could not penetrate there. It was an atmosphere of absolute rest that surrounded him.

On engaging the two-franc room he had interviewed the only person who seemed to be about that sleepy afternoon, an elderly waiter with Dundreary whiskers and a drowsy courtesy, who had ambled lazily towards him across the stone yard; but on coming downstairs again for a little promenade in the town before dinner he encountered the proprietress herself. She was a large woman whose hands, feet, and features seemed to swim towards him out of a sea of person. They emerged, so to speak. But she had great dark, vivacious eyes that counteracted the bulk of her body, and betrayed the fact that in reality she was both vigorous and alert. When he first caught sight of her she was knitting in a low chair against the sunlight of the wall, and something at once made him see her as a great tabby cat, dozing, yet awake, heavily sleepy, and yet at the same time prepared for instantaneous action. A great mouser on the watch occurred to him.

She took him in with a single comprehensive glance that was polite without being cordial. Her neck, he noticed, was extraordinarily supple in spite of its proportions, for it turned so easily to follow him, and the head it carried bowed so very flexibly.

"But when she looked at me, you know," said Vezin, with that little apologetic smile in his brown eyes, and that faintly deprecating gesture of the shoulders that was characteristic of him, "the odd notion came to me that really she had intended to make quite a different movement, and that with a single bound she could have leaped at me across the width of that stone yard and pounced upon me like some huge cat upon a mouse."

He laughed a little soft laugh, and Dr. Silence made a note in his book without interrupting, while Vezin proceeded in a tone as though he feared he had already told too much and more than we could believe.

"Very soft, yet very active she was, for all her size and mass, and I felt she knew what I was doing even after I had passed and was behind her back. She spoke to me, and her voice was smooth and running. She asked if I had my luggage, and was comfortable in my room, and then added that dinner was at seven o'clock, and that they were very early people in this little country town. Clearly, she intended to convey that late hours were not encouraged."

Evidently, she contrived by voice and manner to give him the impression that here he would be "managed," that everything would be arranged and planned for him, and that he had nothing to do but fall into the groove and obey. No decided action or sharp personal effort would be looked for from him. It was the very reverse of the train. He walked quietly out into the street feeling soothed and peaceful. He realised that he was in a *milieu* that suited him and stroked him the right way. It was so much easier to be obedient. He began to purr again, and to feel that all the town purred with him.

About the streets of that little town he meandered gently, falling deeper and deeper into the spirit of repose that characterised it. With no special aim he wandered up and down, and to and fro. The September sunshine fell slantingly over the roofs. Down winding alleyways, fringed with tumbling gables and open casements, he caught fairy-like glimpses of the great plain below, and of the meadows and yellow copses lying like a dream-map in the haze. The spell of the past held very potently here, he felt.

The streets were full of picturesquely garbed men and women, all busy enough, going their respective ways; but no one took any notice of him or turned to stare at his obviously English appearance. He was even able to forget that with his tourist appearance he was a false note in a charming picture, and he melted more and more into the scene, feeling delightfully insignificant and unimportant and unselfconscious. It was like becoming part of a softly-coloured dream which he did not even realise to be a dream.

On the eastern side the hill fell away more sharply, and the plain below ran off rather suddenly into a sea of gathering shadows in which the little patches of woodland looked like islands and the stubble fields like deep water. Here he strolled along the old ramparts of ancient fortifications that once had been formidable, but now were only vision-like with their charming mingling of broken grey walls and wayward vine and ivy. From the broad coping on which he sat for a moment, level with the rounded tops of clipped plane trees, he saw the esplanade far below lying in shadow. Here and there a yellow sunbeam crept in and lay upon the fallen yellow leaves, and from the height he looked down and saw that the townsfolk were walking to and fro in the cool of the evening. He could just hear the sound of their slow footfalls, and the murmur of their voices floated up to him through the gaps between the trees. The figures looked like shadows as he caught glimpses of their quiet movements far below.

He sat there for some time pondering, bathed in the waves of murmurs and half-lost echoes that rose to his ears, muffled by the leaves of the plane trees. The whole town, and the little hill out of which it grew as naturally as an ancient wood, seemed to him like a being lying there half asleep on the plain and crooning to itself as it dozed.

And, presently, as he sat lazily melting into its dream, a sound of horns and strings and wood instruments rose to his ears, and the town band began to play at the far end of the crowded terrace below to the accompaniment of a very soft, deep-throated drum. Vezin was very sensitive to music, knew about it intelligently, and had even ventured, unknown to his friends, upon the composition of quiet melodies with low-running chords which he played to himself with the soft pedal when no one was about. And this music floating up through the trees from an invisible and doubt-less very picturesque band of the townspeople wholly charmed him. He recognised nothing that they played, and it sounded as though they were simply improvising without a conductor. No definitely marked time ran through the pieces, which ended and began oddly after the fashion of wind through an Æolian harp. It was part of the place and scene, just as the dying sunlight and faintly-breathing wind were part of the scene and hour, and the mellow notes of old-fashioned plaintive horns, pierced here and there by the sharper strings, all half smothered by the continuous booming of the deep drum, touched his soul with a curiously potent spell that was almost too engrossing to be quite pleasant.

There was a certain queer sense of bewitchment in it all. The music seemed to him oddly unartificial. It made him think of trees swept by the wind, of night breezes singing among wires and chimney-stacks, or in the rigging of invisible ships; or—and the simile leaped up in his thoughts with a sudden sharpness of suggestion—a chorus of animals, of wild creatures, somewhere in desolate places of the world, crying and singing as animals will, to the moon. He could fancy he heard the wailing, half-human cries of cats upon the tiles at night, rising and falling with weird intervals of sound, and this music, muffled by distance and the trees, made him think of a queer company of these creatures on some roof far away in the sky, uttering their solemn music to one another and the moon in chorus.

It was, he felt at the time, a singular image to occur to him, yet it expressed his sensation pictorially better than anything else. The instruments played such impossibly odd intervals, and the crescendos and diminuendos were so very suggestive of cat-land on the tiles at night, rising swiftly, dropping without warning to deep notes again, and all in such strange confusion of discords and accords. But, at the same time a plaintive sweetness resulted on the whole, and the discords of these half-broken instruments were so singular that they did not distress his musical soul like fiddles out of tune.

He listened a long time, wholly surrendering himself as his character was, and then strolled homewards in the dusk as the air grew chilly.

"There was nothing to alarm?" put in Dr. Silence briefly.

"Absolutely nothing," said Vezin; "but you know it was all so fantastical and charming that my imagination was profoundly impressed. Perhaps, too," he continued, gently explanatory, "it was this stirring of my imagination that caused other impressions; for, as I walked back, the spell of the place began to steal over me in a dozen ways, though all intelligible ways. But there were other things I could not account for in the least, even then."

"Incidents, you mean?"

"Hardly incidents, I think. A lot of vivid sensations crowded themselves upon my mind and I could trace them to no causes. It was just after sunset and the tumbled old buildings traced magical outlines against an opalescent sky of gold and red. The dusk was running down the twisted streets. All round the hill the plain pressed in like a dim sea, its level rising with the darkness. The spell of this kind of scene, you know, can be very moving, and it was so that night. Yet I felt that what came to me had nothing directly to do with the mystery and wonder of the scene."

"Not merely the subtle transformations of the spirit that come with beauty," put in the doctor, noticing his hesitation.

"Exactly," Vezin went on, duly encouraged and no longer so fearful of our smiles at his expense. "The impressions came from somewhere else. For instance, down the busy main street where men and women were bustling home from work, shopping at stalls and barrows, idly gossiping in groups, and all the rest of it, I saw that I aroused no interest and that no one turned to stare at me as a foreigner and stranger. I was utterly ignored, and my presence among them excited no special interest or attention.

"And then, quite suddenly, it dawned upon me with conviction that all the time this indifference and inattention were merely feigned. Everybody as a matter of fact was watching me closely. Every movement I made was known and observed. Ignoring me was all a pretence—an elaborate pretence."

He paused a moment and looked at us to see if we were smiling, and then continued, reassured—

"It is useless to ask me how I noticed this, because I simply cannot explain it. But the discovery gave me something of a shock. Before I got back to the inn, however, another curious thing rose up strongly in my mind and forced my recognition of it as true. And this, too, I may as well say at once, was equally inexplicable to me. I mean I can only give you the fact, as fact it was to me."

The little man left his chair and stood on the mat before the fire. His diffidence lessened from now onwards, as he lost himself again in the magic of the old adventure. His eyes shone a little already as he talked.

"Well," he went on, his soft voice rising somewhat with his excitement, "I was in a shop when it came to me first—though the idea must have been at work for a long time subconsciously to appear in so complete a form all at once. I was buying socks, I think," he laughed, "and struggling with my dreadful French, when it struck me that the woman in the shop did not care two pins whether I bought anything or not. She was indifferent whether she made a sale or did not make a sale. She was only pretending to sell.

"This sounds a very small and fanciful incident to build upon what follows. But really it was not small. I mean it was the spark that lit the line of powder and ran along to the big blaze in my mind.

"For the whole town, I suddenly realised, was something other than I so far saw it. The real activities and interests of the people were elsewhere and otherwise than appeared. Their true lives lay somewhere out of sight behind the scenes. Their busyness was but the outward semblance that masked their actual purposes. They bought and sold, and ate and drank, and walked about the streets, yet all the while the main stream of their existence lay somewhere beyond my ken, underground, in secret places. In the shops and at the stalls they did not care whether I purchased their articles or not; at the inn, they were indifferent to my staying or going; their life lay remote from my own, springing from hidden, mysterious sources, coursing out of sight, unknown. It was all a great elaborate pretence, assumed possibly for my benefit, or possibly for purposes of their own. But the main current of their energies ran elsewhere. I almost felt as an unwelcome foreign substance might be expected to feel when it has found its way into the human system and the whole body organises itself to eject it or to absorb it. The town was doing this very thing to me.

"This bizarre notion presented itself forcibly to my mind as I walked home to the inn, and I began busily to wonder wherein the true life of this town could lie and what were the actual interests and activities of its hidden life.

"And, now that my eyes were partly opened, I noticed other things too that puzzled me, first of which, I think, was the extraordinary silence of the whole place. Positively, the town was muffled. Although the streets were paved with cobbles the people moved about silently, softly, with padded feet, like cats. Nothing made noise. All was hushed, subdued, muted. The very voices were quiet, low-pitched like purring. Nothing clamorous, vehement or emphatic seemed able to live in the drowsy atmosphere of soft dreaming that soothed this little hill-town into its sleep. It was like the woman at the inn—an outward repose screening intense inner activity and purpose.

"Yet there was no sign of lethargy or sluggishness anywhere about it. The people were active and alert. Only a magical and uncanny softness lay over them all like a spell."

Vezin passed his hand across his eyes for a moment as though the memory had become very vivid. His voice had run off into a whisper so that we heard the last part with difficulty. He was telling a true thing obviously, yet something that he both liked and hated telling.

"I went back to the inn," he continued presently in a louder voice, "and dined. I felt a new strange world about me. My old world of reality receded. Here, whether I liked it or no, was something new and incomprehensible. I regretted having left the train so impulsively. An adventure was upon me, and I loathed adventures as foreign to my nature. Moreover, this was the beginning apparently of an adventure somewhere deep within me, in a region I could not check or measure, and a feeling of alarm mingled itself with my wonder—alarm for the stability of what I had for forty years recognised as my 'personality.'

"I went upstairs to bed, my mind teeming with thoughts that were unusual to me, and of rather a haunting description. By way of relief I kept thinking of that nice, prosaic noisy train and all those wholesome, blustering passengers. I almost wished I were with them again. But my dreams took me elsewhere. I dreamed of cats, and soft-moving creatures, and the silence of life in a dim muffled world beyond the senses."

II

Vezin stayed on from day to day, indefinitely, much longer than he had intended. He felt in a kind of dazed, somnolent condition. He did nothing in particular, but the place fascinated him and he could not decide to leave. Decisions were always very difficult for him and he sometimes wondered how he had ever brought himself to the point of leaving the train. It seemed as though some one else must have arranged it for him, and once or twice his thoughts ran to the swarthy Frenchman who had sat opposite. If only he could have understood that long sentence ending so strangely with "*à cause du sommeil et à cause des chats.*" He wondered what it all meant.

Meanwhile the hushed softness of the town held him prisoner and he sought in his muddling, gentle way to find out where the mystery lay, and what it was all about. But his limited French and his constitutional hatred of active investigation made it hard for him to buttonhole anybody and ask questions. He was content to observe, and watch, and remain negative.

The weather held on calm and hazy, and this just suited him. He wandered about the town till he knew every street and alley. The people suffered him to come and go without let or hindrance, though it became clearer to him every day that he was never free himself from observation. The town watched him as a cat watches a mouse. And he got no nearer to finding out what they were all so busy with or where the main stream of their activities lay. This remained hidden. The people were as soft and mysterious as cats.

But that he was continually under observation became more evident from day to day.

For instance, when he strolled to the end of the town and entered a little green public garden beneath the ramparts and seated himself upon one of the empty benches in the sun, he was quite alone—at first. Not another seat was occupied; the little park was empty, the paths deserted. Yet, within ten minutes of his coming, there must have been fully twenty persons scattered about him, some strolling aimlessly along the gravel walks, staring at the flowers, and others seated on the wooden benches enjoying the sun like himself. None of them appeared to take any notice of him; yet he understood quite well they had all come there to watch. They kept him under close observation. In the street they had seemed busy enough, hurrying upon various errands; yet these were suddenly all forgotten and they had nothing to do but loll and laze in the sun, their duties unremembered. Five minutes after he left, the garden was again deserted, the seats vacant. But in the crowded street it was the same thing again; he was never alone. He was ever in their thoughts.

By degrees, too, he began to see how it was he was so cleverly watched, yet without the appearance of it. The people did nothing *directly*. They behaved *obliquely*. He laughed in his mind as the thought thus clothed itself in words, but the phrase exactly described it. They looked at him from angles which naturally should have led their sight in another direction altogether. Their movements were oblique, too, so far as these concerned himself. The straight, direct thing was not their way evidently. They did nothing obviously. If he entered a shop to buy, the woman walked instantly away and busied herself with something at the farther end of the counter, though answering at once when he spoke, showing that she knew he was there and that this was only her way of attending to him. It was the fashion of the cat she followed. Even in the dining-room of the inn, the be-whiskered and courteous waiter, lithe and silent in all his movements, never seemed able to come straight to his table for an order or a dish. He came by zigzags, indirectly, vaguely, so that he appeared to be going to another table altogether, and only turned suddenly at the last moment, and was there beside him.

Vezin smiled curiously to himself as he described how he began to realise these things. Other tourists there were none in the hostel, but he recalled the figures of one or two old men, inhabitants, who took their *déjeuner* and dinner there, and remembered how fantastically they entered the room in similar fashion. First, they paused in the doorway, peering about the room, and then, after a temporary inspection, they came in, as it were, sideways, keeping close to the walls so that he wondered which table they were making for, and at the last minute making almost a little quick run to their particular seats. And again he thought of the ways and methods of cats.

Other small incidents, too, impressed him as all part of this queer, soft town with its muffled, indirect life, for the way some of the people appeared and disappeared with extraordinary swiftness puzzled him exceedingly. It may have been all perfectly natural, he knew, yet he could not make it out how the alleys swallowed them up and shot them forth in a second of time when there were no visible doorways or openings near enough to explain the phenomenon. Once he followed two elderly women who, he felt, had been particularly examining him from across the street—quite near the inn this was—and saw them turn the corner a few feet only in front of him. Yet when he sharply followed on their heels he saw nothing but an utterly deserted alley stretching in front of him with no sign of a living thing. And the only opening through which they could have escaped was a porch some fifty yards away, which not the swiftest human runner could have reached in time.

And in just such sudden fashion people appeared when he never expected them. Once when he heard a great noise of fighting going on behind a low wall, and hurried up to see what was going on, what should he see but a group of girls and women engaged in vociferous conversation which instantly hushed itself to the normal whispering note of the town when his head appeared over the wall. And even then none of them turned to look at him directly, but slunk off with the most unaccountable rapidity into doors and sheds across the yard. And their voices, he thought, had sounded so like, so strangely like, the angry snarling of fighting animals, almost of cats.

The whole spirit of the town, however, continued to evade him as something elusive, protean, screened from the outer world, and at the same time intensely, genuinely vital; and, since he now formed part of its life, this concealment puzzled and irritated him; more—it began rather to frighten him.

Out of the mists that slowly gathered about his ordinary surface thoughts, there rose again the idea that the inhabitants were waiting for him to declare himself, to take an attitude, to do this, or to do that; and that when he had done so they in their turn would at length make some direct response, accepting or rejecting him. Yet the vital matter concerning which his decision was awaited came no nearer to him.

Once or twice he purposely followed little processions or groups of the citizens in order to find out, if possible, on what purpose they were bent; but they always discovered him in time and dwindled away, each individual going his or her own way. It was always the same: he never could learn what their main interest was. The cathedral was ever empty, the old church of St. Martin, at the other end of the town, deserted. They shopped because they had to, and not because they wished to. The booths stood neglected, the stalls unvisited, the little cafés desolate. Yet the streets were always full, the townsfolk ever on the bustle.

"Can it be," he thought to himself, yet with a deprecating laugh that he should have dared to think anything so odd, "can it be that these people are people of the twilight, that they live only at night their real life, and come out honestly only with the dusk? That during the day they make a sham though brave pretence, and after the sun is down their true life begins? Have they the souls of night-things, and is the whole blessed town in the hands of the cats?"

The fancy somehow electrified him with little shocks of shrinking and dismay. Yet, though he affected to laugh, he knew that he was beginning to feel more than uneasy, and that strange forces were tugging with a thousand invisible cords at the very centre of his being. Something utterly remote from his ordinary life, something that had not waked for years, began faintly to stir in his soul, sending feelers abroad into his brain and heart, shaping queer thoughts and penetrating even into certain of his minor actions. Something exceedingly vital to himself, to his soul, hung in the balance.

And, always when he returned to the inn about the hour of sunset, he saw the figures of the townsfolk stealing through the dusk from their shop doors, moving sentry-wise to and fro at the corners of the streets, yet always vanishing silently like shadows at his near approach. And as the inn invariably closed its doors at ten o'clock he had never yet found the opportunity he rather half-heartedly sought to see for himself what account the town could give of itself at night.

"——à cause du sommeil et à cause des chats"—the words now rang in his ears more and more often, though still as yet without any definite meaning.

Moreover, something made him sleep like the dead.

III

It was, I think, on the fifth day—though in this detail his story sometimes varied—that he made a definite discovery which increased his alarm and brought him up to a rather sharp climax. Before that he had already noticed that a change was going forward and certain subtle transformations being brought about in his character which modified several of his minor habits. And he had affected to ignore them. Here, however, was something he could no longer ignore; and it startled him.

At the best of times he was never very positive, always negative rather, compliant and acquiescent; yet, when necessity arose he was capable of reasonably vigorous action and could take a strongish decision. The discovery he now made that brought him up with such a sharp turn was that this power had positively dwindled to nothing. He found it impossible to make up his mind. For, on this fifth day, he realised that he had stayed long enough in the town and that for reasons he could only vaguely define to himself it was wiser *and safer* that he should leave.

And he found that he could not leave!

This is difficult to describe in words, and it was more by gesture and the expression of his face that he conveyed to Dr. Silence the state of impotence he had reached. All this spying and watching, he said, had as it were spun a net about his feet so that he was trapped and powerless to escape; he felt like a fly that had blundered into the intricacies of a great web; he was caught, imprisoned, and could not get away. It was a distressing sensation. A numbness had crept over his will till it had become almost incapable of decision. The mere thought of vigorous action—action towards escape— began to terrify him. All the currents of his life had turned inwards upon himself, striving to bring to the surface something that lay buried almost beyond reach, deter- mined to force his recognition of something he had long forgotten—forgotten years upon years, centuries almost ago. It seemed as though a window deep within his being would presently open and reveal an entirely new world, yet somehow a world that was not unfamiliar. Beyond that, again, he fancied a great curtain hung; and when that too rolled up he would see still farther into this region and at last understand something of the secret life of these extraordinary people.

"Is this why they wait and watch?" he asked himself with rather a shaking heart, "for the time when I shall join them—or refuse to join them? Does the decision rest with me after all, and not with them?"

And it was at this point that the sinister character of the adventure first really declared itself, and he became genuinely alarmed. The stability of his rather fluid little personality was at stake, he felt, and something in his heart turned coward.

Why otherwise should he have suddenly taken to walking stealthily, silently, mak- ing as little sound as possible, for ever looking behind him? Why else should he have moved almost on tiptoe about the passages of the practically deserted inn, and when he was abroad have found himself deliberately taking advantage of what cover presented itself? And why, if he was not afraid, should the wisdom of staying indoors after sun- down have suddenly occurred to him as eminently desirable? Why, indeed?

And, when John Silence gently pressed him for an explanation of these tings, he admitted apologetically that he had none to give.

"It was simply that I feared something might happen to me unless I kept a sharp look-out. I felt afraid. It was instinctive," was all he could say. "I got the impression that the whole town was after me—wanted me for something; and that if it got me I should lose myself, or at least the Self I knew, in some unfamiliar state of conscious- ness. But I am not a psychologist, you know," he added meekly, "and I cannot define it better than that."

It was while lounging in the courtyard half an hour before the evening meal that Vezin made this discovery, and he at once went upstairs to his quiet room at the end of the winding passage to think it over alone. In the yard it was empty enough, true, but there was always the possibility that the big woman whom he dreaded would come out of some door, with her pretence of knitting, to sit and watch him. This had happened several times, and he could not endure the sight of her. He still remembered his original fancy, bizarre though it was, that she would spring upon him the moment his back was turned and land with one single crushing leap upon his neck. Of course it was nonsense, but then it haunted him, and once an idea begins to do that it ceases to be nonsense. It has clothed itself in reality.

He went upstairs accordingly. It was dusk, and the oil lamps had not yet been lit in the passages. He stumbled over the uneven surface of the ancient flooring, passing the dim outlines of doors along the corridor—doors that he had never once seen opened—rooms that seemed never occupied. He moved, as his habit now was, stealthily and on tiptoe.

Half-way down the last passage to his own chamber there was a sharp turn, and it was just here, while groping round the walls with outstretched hands, that his fingers touched something that was not wall—something that moved. It was soft and warm in texture, indescribably fragrant, and about the height of his shoulder; and he immediately thought of a furry, sweet-smelling kitten. The next minute he knew it was something quite different.

Instead of investigating, however,—his nerves must have been too overwrought for that, he said,—he shrank back as closely as possible against the wall on the other side. The thing, whatever it was, slipped past him with a sound of rustling, and retreating with light footsteps down the passage behind him, was gone. A breath of warm, scented air was wafted to his nostrils.

Vezin caught his breath for an instant and paused, stockstill, half leaning against the wall—and then almost ran down the remaining distance and entered his room with a rush, locking the door hurriedly behind him. Yet it was not fear that made him run: it was excitement, pleasurable excitement. His nerves were tingling, and a delicious glow made itself felt all over his body. In a flash it came to him that this was just what he had felt twenty-five years ago as a boy when he was in love for the first time. Warm currents of life ran all over him and mounted to his brain in a whirl of soft delight. His mood was suddenly become tender, melting, loving.

The room was quite dark, and he collapsed upon the sofa by the window, wondering what had happened to him and what it all meant. But the only thing he understood clearly in that instant was that something in him had swiftly, magically changed: he no longer wished to leave, or to argue with himself about leaving. The encounter in the passage-way had changed all that. The strange perfume of it still hung about him, bemusing his heart and mind. For he knew that it was a girl who had passed him, a girl's face that his fingers had brushed in the darkness, and he felt in some extraordinary way as though he had been actually kissed by her, kissed full upon the lips.

Trembling, he sat upon the sofa by the window and struggled to collect his thoughts. He was utterly unable to understand how the mere passing of a girl in the darkness of a narrow passage-way could communicate so electric a thrill to his whole being that he still shook with the sweetness of it. Yet, there it was! And he found it as useless to deny as to attempt analysis. Some ancient fire had entered his veins, and now ran coursing through his blood; and that he was forty-five instead of twenty did not matter one little jot. Out of all the inner turmoil and confusion emerged the one salient fact that the mere atmosphere, the merest casual touch, of this girl, unseen, unknown in the darkness, had been sufficient to stir dormant fires in the centre of his heart, and rouse his whole being from a state of feeble sluggishness to one of tearing and tumultuous excitement.

After a time, however, the number of Vezin's years began to assert their cumulative power; he grew calmer; and when a knock came at length upon his door and he heard the waiter's voice suggesting that dinner was nearly over, he pulled himself together and slowly made his way downstairs into the dining-room.

Every one looked up as he entered, for he was very late, but he took his customary seat in the far corner and began to eat. The trepidation was still in his nerves, but the fact that he had passed through the courtyard and hall without catching sight of a petticoat served to calm him a little. He ate so fast that he had almost caught up with the current stage of the table d'hôte, when a slight commotion in the room drew his attention.

His chair was so placed that the door and the greater portion of the long *salle à manger* were behind him, yet it was not necessary to turn round to know that the same person he had passed in the dark passage had now come into the room. He felt the presence long before he heard or saw any one. Then he became aware that the old men, the only other guests, were rising one by one in their places, and exchanging greetings with some one who passed among them from table to table. And when at length he turned with his heart beating furiously to ascertain for himself, he saw the form of a young girl, lithe and slim, moving down the centre of the room and making straight for his own table in the corner. She moved wonderfully, with sinuous grace, like a young panther, and her approach filled him with such delicious bewilderment that he was utterly unable to tell at first what her face was like, or discover what it was about the whole presentment of the creature that filled him anew with trepidation and delight.

"Ah, Ma'mselle est de retour!" he heard the old waiter murmur at his side, and he was just able to take in that she was the daughter of the proprietress, when she was upon him, and he heard her voice. She was addressing him. Something of red lips he saw and laughing white teeth, and stray wisps of fine dark hair about the temples; but all the rest was a dream in which his own emotion rose like a thick cloud before his eyes and prevented his seeing accurately, or knowing exactly what he did. He was aware that she greeted him with a charming little bow; that her beautiful large eyes looked searchingly into his own; that the perfume he had noticed in the dark passage again assailed his nostrils, and that she was bending a little towards him and leaning with one hand on the table at his side. She was quite close to him—that was the chief thing he knew—explaining that she had been asking after the comfort of her mother's guests, and was now introducing herself to the latest arrival—himself.

"M'sieur has already been here a few days," he heard the waiter say; and then her own voice, sweet as singing, replied—

"Ah, but M'sieur is not going to leave us just yet, I hope. My mother is too old to look after the comfort of our guests properly, but now I am here I will remedy all that." She laughed deliciously. "M'sieur shall be well looked after."

Vezin, struggling with his emotion and desire to be polite, half rose to acknowledge the pretty speech, and to stammer some sort of reply, but as he did so his hand by chance touched her own that was resting upon the table, and a shock that was for all the world like a shock of electricity, passed from her skin into his body. His soul wavered and shook deep within him. He caught her eyes fixed upon his own with a look of most curious intentness, and the next moment he knew that he had sat down wordless again on his chair, that the girl was already half-way across the room, and that he was trying to eat his salad with a dessert-spoon and a knife.

Longing for her return, and yet dreading it, he gulped down the remainder of his dinner, and then went at once to his bedroom to be alone with his thoughts. This time the passages were lighted, and he suffered no exciting contretemps; yet the winding corridor was dim with shadows, and the last portion, from the bend of the walls onwards, seemed longer than he had ever known it. It ran downhill like the pathway on a mountain side, and as he tiptoed softly down it he felt that by rights it ought to have led him clean out of the house into the heart of a great forest. The world was singing with him. Strange fancies filled his brain, and once in the room, with the door securely locked, he did not light the candles, but sat by the open window thinking long, long thoughts that came unbidden in troops to his mind.

IV

This part of the story he told to Dr. Silence, without special coaxing, it is true, yet with much stammering embarrassment. He could not in the least understand, he said, how the girl had managed to affect him so profoundly, and even before he had set eyes upon her. For her mere proximity in the darkness had been sufficient to set him on fire. He knew nothing of enchantments, and for years had been a stranger to anything approaching tender relations with any member of the opposite sex, for he was encased in shyness, and realised his overwhelming defects only too well. Yet this bewitching young creature came to him deliberately. Her manner was unmistakable, and she sought him out on every possible occasion. Chaste and sweet she was undoubtedly, yet frankly inviting; and she won him utterly with the first glance of her shining eyes, even if she had not already done so in the dark merely by the magic of her invisible presence.

"You felt she was altogether wholesome and good?" queried the doctor. "You had no reaction of any sort—for instance, of alarm?"

Vezin looked up sharply with one of his inimitable little apologetic smiles. It was some time before he replied. The mere memory of the adventure had suffused his shy face with blushes, and his brown eyes sought the floor again before he answered.

"I don't think I can quite say that," he explained presently. "I acknowledged certain qualms, sitting up in my room afterwards. A conviction grew upon me that there was something about her—how shall I express it?—well, something unholy. It is not impurity in any sense, physical or mental, that I mean, but something quite indefinable that gave me a vague sensation of the creeps. She drew me, and at the same time repelled me, more than—than—"

He hesitated, blushing furiously, and unable to finish the sentence.

"Nothing like it has ever come to me before or since," he concluded, with lame confusion. "I suppose it was, as you suggested just now, something of an enchantment. At any rate, it was strong enough to make me feel that I would stay in that awful little haunted town for years if only I could see her every day, hear her voice, watch her wonderful movements, and sometimes, perhaps, touch her hand."

"Can you explain to me what you felt was the source of her power?" John Silence asked, looking purposely anywhere but at the narrator.

"I am surprised that *you* should ask me such a question," answered Vezin, with the nearest approach to dignity he could manage. "I think no man can describe to another convincingly wherein lies the magic of the woman who ensnares him. I certainly cannot. I can only say this slip of a girl bewitched me, and the mere knowledge that she was living and sleeping in the same house filled me with an extraordinary sense of delight.

"But there's one thing I can tell you," he went on earnestly, his eyes aglow, "namely, that she seemed to sum up and synthesise in herself all the strange hidden forces that operated so mysteriously in the town and its inhabitants. She had the silken movements of the panther, going smoothly, silently to and fro, and the same indirect, oblique methods as the townsfolk, screening, like them, secret purposes of her own—purposes that I was sure had *me* for their objective. She kept me, to my terror and delight, ceaselessly under observation, yet so carelessly, so consummately, that another man less sensitive, if I may say so"—he made a deprecating gesture—"or less prepared by what had gone before, would never have noticed it at all. She was always still, always reposeful, yet she seemed to be everywhere at once, so that I never could escape from her. I was continually meeting the stare and laughter of her great eyes, in the corners of the rooms, in the passages, calmly looking at me through the windows, or in the busiest parts of the public streets."

Their intimacy, it seems, grew very rapidly after this first encounter which had so violently disturbed the little man's equilibrium. He was naturally very prim, and prim folk live mostly in so small a world that anything violently unusual may shake them clean out of it, and they therefore instinctively distrust originality. But Vezin began to forget his primness after awhile. The girl was always modestly behaved, and as her mother's representative she naturally had to do with the guests in the hotel. It was not out of the way that a spirit of camaraderie should spring up. Besides, she was young, she was charmingly pretty, she was French, and—she obviously liked him.

At the same time, there was something indescribable—a certain indefinable atmosphere of other places, other times—that made him try hard to remain on his guard, and sometimes made him catch his breath with a sudden start. It was all rather like a delirious dream, half delight, half dread, he confided in a whisper to Dr. Silence; and more than once he hardly knew quite what he was doing or saying, as though he were driven forward by impulses he scarcely recognised as his own.

And though the thought of leaving presented itself again and again to his mind, it was each time with less insistence, so that he stayed on from day to day, becoming more and more a part of the sleepy life of this dreamy mediæval town, losing more and more of his recognisable personality. Soon, he felt, the Curtain within would roll up with an awful rush, and he would find himself suddenly admitted into the secret purposes of the hidden life that lay behind it all. Only, by that time, he would have become transformed into an entirely different being.

And, meanwhile, he noticed various little signs of the intention to make his stay attractive to him: flowers in his bedroom, a more comfortable arm-chair in the corner, and even special little extra dishes on his private table in the dining-room. Conversations, too, with "Mademoiselle Ilsé" became more and more frequent and pleasant, and although they seldom travelled beyond the weather, or the details of the town, the girl, he noticed, was never in a hurry to bring them to an end, and often contrived to interject little odd sentences that he never properly understood, yet felt to be significant.

And it was these stray remarks, full of a meaning that evaded him, that pointed to some hidden purpose of her own and made him feel uneasy. They all had to do, he felt sure, with reasons for his staying on in the town indefinitely.

"And has M'sieur not even yet come to a decision?" she said softly in his ear, sitting beside him in the sunny yard before *déjeuner*, the acquaintance having progressed with significant rapidity. "Because, if it's so difficult, we must all try together to help him!"

The question startled him, following upon his own thoughts. It was spoken with a pretty laugh, and a stray bit of hair across one eye, as she turned and peered at him half roguishly. Possibly he did not quite understand the French of it, for her near presence always confused his small knowledge of the language distressingly. Yet the words, and her manner, and something else that lay behind it all in her mind, frightened him. It gave such point to his feeling that the town was waiting for him to make his mind up on some important matter.

At the same time, her voice, and the fact that she was there so close beside him in her soft dark dress, thrilled him inexpressibly.

"It is true I find it difficult to leave," he stammered, losing his way deliciously in the depths of her eyes, "and especially now that Mademoiselle Ilsé has come."

He was surprised at the success of his sentence, and quite delighted with the little gallantry of it. But at the same time he could have bitten his tongue off for having said it.

"Then after all you like our little town, or you would not be pleased to stay on," she said, ignoring the compliment.

"I am enchanted with it, and enchanted with you," he cried, feeling that his tongue was somehow slipping beyond the control of his brain. And he was on the verge of saying all manner of other things of the wildest description, when the girl sprang lightly up from her chair beside him, and made to go.

"It is *soupe à l'onion* to-day!" she cried, laughing back at him through the sunlight, "and I must go and see about it. Otherwise, you know, M'sieur will not enjoy his dinner, and then, perhaps, he will leave us!"

He watched her cross the courtyard, moving with all the grace and lightness of the feline race, and her simple black dress clothed her, he thought, exactly like the fur of the same supple species. She turned once to laugh at him from the porch with the glass door, and then stopped a moment to speak to her mother, who sat knitting as usual in her corner seat just inside the hall-way.

But how was it, then, that the moment his eye fell upon this ungainly woman, the pair of them appeared suddenly as other than they were? Whence came that transforming dignity and sense of power that enveloped them both as by magic? What was it about that massive woman that made her appear instantly regal, and set her on a throne in some dark and dreadful scenery, wielding a sceptre over the red glare of some tempestuous orgy? And why did this slender stripling of a girl, graceful as a willow, lithe as a young leopard, assume suddenly an air of sinister majesty, and move with flame and smoke about her head, and the darkness of night beneath her feet?

Vezin caught his breath and sat there transfixed. Then, almost simultaneously with its appearance, the queer notion vanished again, and the sunlight of day caught them both, and he heard her laughing to her mother about the *soupe à l'onion*, and saw her glancing back at him over her dear little shoulder with a smile that made him think of a dew-kissed rose bending lightly before summer airs.

And, indeed, the onion soup was particularly excellent that day, because he saw another cover laid at his small table and, with fluttering heart, heard the waiter murmur by way of explanation that "Ma'mselle Ilsé would honour M'sieur to-day at *déjeuner*, as her custom sometimes is with her mother's guests."

So actually she sat by him all through that delirious meal, talking quietly to him in easy French, seeing that he was well looked after, mixing the salad-dressing, and even helping him with her own hand. And, later in the afternoon, while he was smoking in the courtyard, longing for a sight of her as soon as her duties were done, she came again to his side, and when he rose to meet her, she stood facing him a moment, full of a perplexing sweet shyness before she spoke—

"My mother thinks you ought to know more of the beauties of our little town, and *I* think so too! Would M'sieur like me to be his guide, perhaps? I can show him everything, for our family has lived here for many generations."

She had him by the hand, indeed, before he could find a single word to express his pleasure, and led him, all unresisting, out into the street, yet in such a way that it seemed perfectly natural she should do so, and without the faintest suggestion of boldness or immodesty. Her face glowed with the pleasure and interest of it, and with her short dress and tumbled hair she looked every bit the charming child of seventeen that she was, innocent and playful, proud of her native town, and alive beyond her years to the sense of its ancient beauty.

So they went over the town together, and she showed him what she considered its chief interest: the tumble-down old house where her forebears had lived; the sombre, aristocratic-looking mansion where her mother's family dwelt for centuries, and the ancient market-place where several hundred years before the witches had been burnt by the score. She kept up a lively running stream of talk about it all, of which he understood not a fiftieth part as he trudged along by her side, cursing his forty-five years and feeling all the yearnings of his early manhood revive and jeer at him. And, as she talked, England and Surbiton seemed very far away indeed, almost in another age of the world's history. Her voice touched something immeasurably old in him, something that slept deep. It lulled the surface parts of his consciousness to sleep, allowing what was far more ancient to awaken. Like the town, with its elaborate pretence of modern active life, the upper layers of his being became dulled, soothed, muffled, and what lay underneath began to stir in its sleep. That big Curtain swayed a little to and fro. Presently it might lift altogether. . . .

He began to understand a little better at last. The mood of the town was reproducing itself in him. In proportion as his ordinary external self became muffled, that inner secret life, that was far more real and vital, asserted itself. And this girl was surely the high-priestess of it all, the chief instrument of its accomplishment. New thoughts, with new interpretations, flooded his mind as she walked beside him through the winding streets, while the picturesque old gabled town, softly coloured in the sunset, had never appeared to him so wholly wonderful and seductive.

And only one curious incident came to disturb and puzzle him, slight in itself, but utterly inexplicable, bringing white terror into the child's face and a scream to her laughing lips. He had merely pointed to a column of blue smoke that rose from the burning autumn leaves and made a picture against the red roofs, and had then run to the wall and called her to his side to watch the flames shooting here and there through the heap of rubbish. Yet, at the sight of it, as though taken by surprise, her face had altered dreadfully, and she had turned and run like the wind, calling out wild sentences to him as she

ran, of which he had not understood a single word, except that the fire apparently frightened her, and she wanted to get quickly away from it, and to get him away too.

Yet five minutes later she was as calm and happy again as though nothing had
happened to alarm or waken troubled thoughts in her, and they had both forgotten the
incident.

They were leaning over the ruined ramparts together listening to the weird music
of the band as he had heard it the first day of his arrival. It moved him again profoundly
as it had done before, and somehow he managed to find his tongue and his best French.
The girl leaned across the stones close beside him. No one was about. Driven by some
remorseless engine within he began to stammer something—he hardly knew what—
of his strange admiration for her. Almost at the first word she sprang lightly off the
wall and came up smiling in front of him, just touching his knees as he sat there. She
was hatless as usual, and the sun caught her hair and one side of her cheek and throat.

"Oh, I'm *so* glad!" she cried, clapping her little hands softly in his face, "so very
glad, because that means that if you like me you must also like what I do, and what I
belong to."

Already he regretted bitterly having lost control of himself. Something in the
phrasing of her sentence chilled him. He knew the fear of embarking upon an unknown
and dangerous sea.

"You will take part in our real life, I mean," she added softly, with an indescribable
coaxing of manner, as though she noticed his shrinking. "You will come back to us."

Already this slip of a child seemed to dominate him; he felt her power coming
over him more and more; something emanated from her that stole over his senses and
made him aware that her personality, for all its simple grace, held forces that were
stately, imposing, august. He saw her again moving through smoke and flame amid
broken and tempestuous scenery, alarmingly strong, her terrible mother by her side.
Dimly this shone through her smile and appearance of charming innocence.

"You will, I know," she repeated, holding him with her eyes.

They were quite alone up there on the ramparts, and the sensation that she was
overmastering him stirred a wild sensuousness in his blood. The mingled abandon
and reserve in her attracted him furiously, and all of him that was man rose up and
resisted the creeping influence, at the same time acclaiming it with the full delight of
his forgotten youth. An irresistible desire came to him to question her, to summon
what still remained to him of his own little personality in an effort to retain the right
to his normal self.

The girl had grown quiet again, and was now leaning on the broad wall close beside him, gazing out across the darkening plain, her elbows on the coping, motionless as a figure carved in stone. He took his courage in both hands.

"Tell me, Ilsé," he said, unconsciously imitating her own purring softness of voice, yet aware that he was utterly in earnest, "what is the meaning of this town, and what is this real life you speak of? And why is it that the people watch me from morning to night? Tell me what it all means? And, tell me," he added more quickly with passion in his voice, "what you really are—yourself?"

She turned her head and looked at him through half-closed eyelids, her growing inner excitement betraying itself by the faint colour that ran like a shadow across her face.

"It seems to me,"—he faltered oddly under her gaze—"that I have some right to know—"

Suddenly she opened her eyes to the full. "You love me, then?" she asked softly.

"I swear," he cried impetuously, moved as by the force of a rising tide, "I never felt before—I have never known any other girl who—"

"Then you *have* the right to know," she calmly interrupted his confused confession; "for love shares all secrets."

She paused, and a thrill like fire ran swiftly through him. Her words lifted him off the earth, and he felt a radiant happiness, followed almost the same instant in horrible contrast by the thought of death. He became aware that she had turned her eyes upon his own and was speaking again.

"The real life I speak of," she whispered, "is the old, old life within, the life of long ago, the life to which you, too, once belonged, and to which you still belong."

A faint wave of memory troubled the deeps of his soul as her low voice sank into him. What she was saying he knew instinctively to be true, even though he could not as yet understand its full purport. His present life seemed slipping from him as he listened, merging his personality in one that was far older and greater. It was this loss of his present self that brought to him the thought of death.

"You came here," she went on, "with the purpose of seeking it, and the people felt your presence and are waiting to know what you decide, whether you will leave them without having found it, or whether—"

Her eyes remained fixed upon his own, but her face began to change, growing larger and darker with an expression of age.

"It is their thoughts constantly playing about your soul that makes you feel they watch you. They do not watch you with their eyes. The purposes of their inner life are calling to you, seeking to claim you. You were all part of the same life long, long ago, and now they want you back again among them."

Vezin's timid heart sank with dread as he listened; but the girl's eyes held him with a net of joy so that he had no wish to escape. She fascinated him, as it were, clean out of his normal self.

"Alone, however, the people could never have caught and held you," she resumed. "The motive force was not strong enough; it has faded through all these years. But I"—she paused a moment and looked at him with complete confidence in her splendid eyes—"I possess the spell to conquer you and hold you: the spell of old love. I can win you back again and make you live the old life with me, for the force of the ancient tie between us, if I choose to use it, is irresistible. And I do choose to use it I still want you. And you, dear soul of my dim past"—she pressed closer to him so that her breath passed across his eyes, and her voice positively sang—"I mean to have you, for you love me and are utterly at my mercy."

Vezin heard, and yet did not hear; understood, yet did not understand. He had passed into a condition of exaltation. The world was beneath his feet, made of music and flowers, and he was flying somewhere far above it through the sunshine of pure delight. He was breathless and giddy with the wonder of her words. They intoxicated him. And, still, the terror of it all, the dreadful thought of death, pressed ever behind her sentences. For flames shot through her voice out of black smoke and licked at his soul.

And they communicated with one another, it seemed to him, by a process of swift telepathy, for his French could never have compassed all he said to her. Yet she understood perfectly, and what she said to him was like the recital of verses long since known. And the mingled pain and sweetness of it as he listened were almost more than his little soul could hold.

"Yet I came here wholly by chance—" he heard himself saying.

"No," she cried with passion, "you came here because I called to you. I have called to you for years, and you came with the whole force of the past behind you. You had to come, for I own you, and I claim you."

She rose again and moved closer, looking at him with a certain insolence in the face—the insolence of power.

The sun had set behind the towers of the old cathedral and the darkness rose up from the plain and enveloped them. The music of the band had ceased. The leaves of the plane trees hung motionless, but the chill of the autumn evening rose about them and made Vezin shiver. There was no sound but the sound of their voices and the occasional soft rustle of the girl's dress. He could hear the blood rushing in his ears. He scarcely realised where he was or what he was doing. Some terrible magic of the imagination drew him deeply down into the tombs of his own being, telling him in no unfaltering voice that her words shadowed forth the truth. And this simple little French maid, speaking beside him with so strange authority, he saw curiously alter into quite another being. As he stared into her eyes, the picture in his mind grew and lived, dressing itself vividly to his inner vision with a degree of reality he was compelled to acknowledge. As once before, he saw her tall and stately, moving through wild and broken scenery of forests and mountain caverns, the glare of flames behind her head and clouds of shifting smoke about her feet. Dark leaves encircled her hair, flying loosely in the wind, and her limbs shone through the merest rags of clothing. Others were about her too, and ardent eyes on all sides cast delirious glances upon her, but her own eyes were always for One only, one whom she held by the hand. For she was leading the dance in some tempestuous orgy to the music of chanting voices, and the dance she led circled about a great and awful Figure on a throne, brooding over the scene through lurid vapours, while innumerable other wild faces and forms crowded furiously about her in the dance. But the one she held by the hand he knew to be himself, and the monstrous shape upon the throne he knew to be her mother.

The vision rose within him, rushing to him down the long years of buried time, crying aloud to him with the voice of memory reawakened. . . . And then the scene faded away and he saw the clear circle of the girl's eyes gazing steadfastly into his own, and she became once more the pretty little daughter of the innkeeper, and he found his voice again.

"And you," he whispered tremblingly—"you child of visions and enchantment, how is it that you so bewitch me that I loved you even before I saw?"

She drew herself up beside him with an air of rare dignity.

"The call of the Past," she said; "and besides," she added proudly, "in the real life I am a princess—"

"A princess!" he cried.

"—and my mother is a queen!"

At this, little Vezin utterly lost his head. Delight tore at his heart and swept him into sheer ecstasy. To hear that sweet singing voice, and to see those adorable little lips utter such things, upset his balance beyond all hope of control. He took her in his arms and covered her unresisting face with kisses.

But even while he did so, and while the hot passion swept him, he felt that she was soft and loathsome, and that her answering kisses stained his very soul. . . . And when, presently, she had freed herself and vanished into the darkness, he stood there, leaning against the wall in a state of collapse, creeping with horror from the touch of her yielding body, and inwardly raging at the weakness that he already dimly realised must prove his undoing.

And from the shadows of the old buildings into which she disappeared there rose in the stillness of the night a singular, long-drawn cry, which at first he took for laughter, but which later he was sure he recognised as the almost human wailing of a cat.

V

For a long time Vezin leant there against the wall, alone with his surging thoughts and emotions. He understood at length that he had done the one thing necessary to call down upon him the whole force of this ancient Past. For in those passionate kisses he had acknowledged the tie of olden days, and had revived it. And the memory of that soft impalpable caress in the darkness of the inn corridor came back to him with a shudder. The girl had first mastered him, and then led him to the one act that was necessary for her purpose. He had been waylaid, after the lapse of centuries—caught, and conquered.

Dimly he realised this, and sought to make plans for his escape. But, for the moment at any rate, he was powerless to manage his thoughts or will, for the sweet, fantastic madness of the whole adventure mounted to his brain like a spell, and he gloried in the feeling that he was utterly enchanted and moving in a world so much larger and wilder than the one he had ever been accustomed to.

The moon, pale and enormous, was just rising over the sea-like plain, when at last he rose to go. Her slanting rays drew all the houses into new perspective, so that their roofs, already glistening with dew, seemed to stretch much higher into the sky than usual, and their gables and quaint old towers lay far away in its purple reaches.

The cathedral appeared unreal in a silver mist. He moved softly, keeping to the shadows; but the streets were all deserted and very silent; the doors were closed, the shutters fastened. Not a soul was astir. The hush of night lay over everything; it was like a town of the dead, a churchyard with gigantic and grotesque tombstones.

Wondering where all the busy life of the day had so utterly disappeared to, he made his way to a back door that entered the inn by means of the stables, thinking thus to reach his room unobserved. He reached the courtyard safely and crossed it by keeping close to the shadow of the wall. He sidled down it, mincing along on tiptoe, just as the old men did when they entered the *salle à manger*. He was horrified to find himself doing this instinctively. A strange impulse came to him, catching him somehow in the centre of his body—an impulse to drop upon all fours and run swiftly and silently. He glanced upwards and the idea came to him to leap up upon his window-sill overhead instead of going round by the stairs. This occurred to him as the easiest, and most natural way. It was like the beginning of some horrible transformation of himself into something else. He was fearfully strung up.

The moon was higher now, and the shadows very dark along the side of the street where he moved. He kept among the deepest of them, and reached the porch with the glass doors.

But here there was light; the inmates, unfortunately, were still about. Hoping to slip across the hall unobserved and reach the stairs, he opened the door carefully and stole in. Then he saw that the hall was not empty. A large dark thing lay against the wall on his left. At first he thought it must be household articles. Then it moved, and he thought it was an immense cat, distorted in some way by the play of light and shadow. Then it rose straight up before him and he saw that it was the proprietress.

What she had been doing in this position he could only venture a dreadful guess, but the moment she stood up and faced him he was aware of some terrible dignity clothing her about that instantly recalled the girl's strange saying that she was a queen. Huge and sinister she stood there under the little oil lamp; alone with him in the empty hall. Awe stirred in his heart, and the roots of some ancient fear. He felt that he must bow to her and make some kind of obeisance. The impulse was fierce and irresistible, as of long habit. He glanced quickly about him. There was no one there. Then he deliberately inclined his head towards her. He bowed.

"Enfin! M'sieur s'est donc décidé. C'est bien alors. J'en suis contente."

Her words came to him sonorously as through a great open space.

Then the great figure came suddenly across the flagged hall at him and seized his trembling hands. Some overpowering force moved with her and caught him.

"On pourrait faire un p'tit tour ensemble, n'est-ce pas? Nous y allons cette nuit et il faut s'exercer un peu d'avance pour cela. Ilsé, Ilsé, viens donc ici. Viens vite!"

And she whirled him round in the opening steps of some dance that seemed oddly and horribly familiar. They made no sound on the stones, this strangely assorted couple. It was all soft and stealthy. And presently, when the air seemed to thicken like smoke, and a red glare as of flame shot through it, he was aware that some one else had joined them and that his hand the mother had released was now tightly held by the daughter. Ilsé had come in answer to the call, and he saw her with leaves of vervain twined in her dark hair, clothed in tattered vestiges of some curious garment, beautiful as the night, and horribly, odiously, loathsomely seductive.

"To the Sabbath! to the Sabbath!" they cried. "On to the Witches' Sabbath!"

Up and down that narrow hall they danced, the women on each side of him, to the wildest measure he had ever imagined, yet which he dimly, dreadfully remembered, till the lamp on the wall flickered and went out, and they were left in total darkness. And the devil woke in his heart with a thousand vile suggestions and made him afraid.

Suddenly they released his hands and he heard the voice of the mother cry that it was time, and they must go. Which way they went he did not pause to see. He only realised that he was free, and he blundered through the darkness till he found the stairs and then tore up them to his room as though all hell was at his heels.

He flung himself on the sofa, with his face in his hands, and groaned. Swiftly reviewing a dozen ways of immediate escape, all equally impossible, he finally decided that the only thing to do for the moment was to sit quiet and wait. He must see what was going to happen. At least in the privacy of his own bedroom he would be fairly safe. The door was locked. He crossed over and softly opened the window which gave upon the courtyard and also permitted a partial view of the hall through the glass doors.

As he did so the hum and murmur of a great activity reached his ears from the streets beyond—the sound of footsteps and voices muffled by distance. He leaned out cautiously and listened. The moonlight was clear and strong now, but his own window was in shadow, the silver disc being still behind the house. It came to him irresistibly that the inhabitants of the town, who a little while before had all been invisible behind closed doors, were now issuing forth, busy upon some secret and unholy errand. He listened intently.

At first everything about him was silent, but soon he became aware of movements going on in the house itself. Rustlings and cheepings came to him across that still, moonlit yard. A concourse of living beings sent the hum of their activity into the night. Things were on the move everywhere. A biting, pungent odour rose through the air, coming he knew not whence. Presently his eyes became glued to the windows of the opposite wall where the moonshine fell in a soft blaze. The roof overhead, and behind him, was reflected clearly in the panes of glass, and he saw the outlines of dark bodies moving with long footsteps over the tiles and along the coping. They passed swiftly and silently, shaped like immense cats, in an endless procession across the pictured glass, and then appeared to leap down to a lower level where he lost sight of them. He just caught the soft thudding of their leaps. Sometimes their shadows fell upon the white wall opposite, and then he could not make out whether they were the shadows of human beings or of cats. They seemed to change swiftly from one to the other. The transformation looked horribly real, for they leaped like human beings, yet changed swiftly in the air immediately afterwards, and dropped like animals.

The yard, too, beneath him, was now alive with the creeping movements of dark forms all stealthily drawing towards the porch with the glass doors. They kept so closely to the wall that he could not determine their actual shape, but when he saw that they passed on to the great congregation that was gathering in the hall, he understood that these were the creatures whose leaping shadows he had first seen reflected in the window-panes opposite. They were coming from all parts of the town, reaching the appointed meeting-place across the roofs and tiles, and springing from level to level till they came to the yard.

Then a new sound caught his ear, and he saw that the windows all about him were being softly opened, and that to each window came a face. A moment later figures began dropping hurriedly down into the yard. And these figures, as they lowered themselves down from the windows, were human, he saw; but once safely in the yard they fell upon all fours and changed in the swiftest possible second into—cats—huge, silent cats. They ran in streams to join the main body in the hall beyond.

So, after all, the rooms in the house had not been empty and unoccupied.

Moreover, what he saw no longer filled him with amazement. For he remembered it all. It was familiar. It had all happened before just so, hundreds of times, and he himself had taken part in it and known the wild madness of it all. The outline of the old building changed, the yard grew larger, and he seemed to be staring down upon it from a much greater height through smoky vapours. And, as he looked, half remembering, the old pains of long ago, fierce and sweet, furiously assailed him, and the blood stirred horribly as he heard the Call of the Dance again in his heart and tasted the ancient magic of Ilsé whirling by his side.

Suddenly he started back. A great lithe cat had leaped softly up from the shadows below on to the sill close to his face, and was staring fixedly at him with the eyes of a human. "Come," it seemed to say, "come with us to the Dance! Change as of old! Transform yourself swiftly and come!" Only too well he understood the creature's soundless call.

It was gone again in a flash with scarcely a sound of its padded feet on the stones, and then others dropped by the score down the side of the house, past his very eyes, all changing as they fell and darting away rapidly, softly, towards the gathering point. And again he felt the dreadful desire to do likewise; to murmur the old incantation, and then drop upon hands and knees and run swiftly for the great flying leap into the air. Oh, how the passion of it rose within him like a flood, twisting his very entrails, sending his heart's desire flaming forth into the night for the old, old Dance of the Sorcerers at the Witches' Sabbath! The whirl of the stars was about him; once more he met the magic of the moon. The power of the wind, rushing from precipice and forest, leaping from cliff to cliff across the valleys, tore him away. . . . He heard the cries of the dancers and their wild laughter, and with this savage girl in his embrace he danced furiously about the dim Throne where sat the Figure with the sceptre of majesty. . . .

Then, suddenly, all became hushed and still, and the fever died down a little in his heart. The calm moonlight flooded a courtyard empty and deserted. They had started. The procession was off into the sky. And he was left behind—alone.

Vezin tiptoed softly across the room and unlocked the door. The murmur from the streets, growing momentarily as he advanced, met his ears. He made his way with the utmost caution down the corridor. At the head of the stairs he paused and listened. Below him, the hall where they had gathered was dark and still, but through opened doors and windows on the far side of the building came the sound of a great throng moving farther and farther into the distance.

He made his way down the creaking wooden stairs, dreading yet longing to meet some straggler who should point the way, but finding no one; across the dark hall, so lately thronged with living, moving things, and out through the opened front doors into the street. He could not believe that he was really left behind, really forgotten, that he had been purposely permitted to escape. It perplexed him.

Nervously he peered about him, and up and down the street; then, seeing nothing, advanced slowly down the pavement.

The whole town, as he went, showed itself empty and deserted, as though a great wind had blown everything alive out of it. The doors and windows of the houses stood open to the night; nothing stirred; moonlight and silence lay over all. The night lay about him like a cloak. The air, soft and cool, caressed his cheek like the touch of a great furry paw. He gained confidence and began to walk quickly, though still keeping to the shadowed side. Nowhere could he discover the faintest sign of the great unholy exodus he knew had just taken place. The moon sailed high over all in a sky, cloudless and serene.

Hardly realising where he was going, he crossed the open market-place and so came to the ramparts, whence he knew a pathway descended to the high road and along which he could make good his escape to one of the other little towns that lay to the northward, and so to the railway.

But first he paused and gazed out over the scene at his feet where the great plain lay like a silver map of some dream country. The still beauty of it entered his heart, increasing his sense of bewilderment and unreality. No air stirred, the leaves of the plane trees stood motionless, the near details were defined with the sharpness of day against dark shadows, and in the distance the fields and woods melted away into haze and shimmering mistiness.

But the breath caught in his throat and he stood stockstill as though transfixed when his gaze passed from the horizon and fell upon the near prospect in the depth of the valley at his feet. The whole lower slopes of the hill, that lay hid from the brightness of the moon, were aglow, and through the glare he saw countless moving forms, shifting thick and fast between the openings of the trees; while overhead, like leaves driven by the wind, he discerned flying shapes that hovered darkly one moment against the sky and then settled down with cries and weird singing through the branches into the region that was aflame.

Spellbound, he stood and stared for a time that he could not measure. And then, moved by one of the terrible impulses that seemed to control the whole adventure, he climbed swiftly upon the top of the broad coping, and balanced a moment where the valley gaped at his feet. But in that very instant, as he stood hovering, a sudden movement among the shadows of the houses caught his eye, and he turned to see the outline of a large animal dart swiftly across the open space behind him, and land with a flying leap upon the top of the wall a little lower down. It ran like the wind to his feet and then rose up beside him upon the ramparts. A shiver seemed to run through the moonlight, and his sight trembled for a second. His heart pulsed fearfully. Ilsé stood beside him, peering into his face.

Some dark substance, he saw, stained the girl's face and skin, shining in the moonlight as she stretched her hands towards him; she was dressed in wretched tattered garments that yet became her mightily; rue and vervain twined about her temples; her eyes glittered with unholy light. He only just controlled the wild impulse to take her in his arms and leap with her from their giddy perch into the valley below.

"See!" she cried, pointing with an arm on which the rags fluttered in the rising wind towards the forest aglow in the distance. "See where they await us! The woods are alive! Already the Great Ones are there, and the dance will soon begin! The salve is here! Anoint yourself and come!"

Though a moment before the sky was clear and cloudless, yet even while she spoke the face of the moon grew dark and the wind began to toss in the crests of the plane trees at his feet. Stray gusts brought the sounds of hoarse singing and crying from the lower slopes of the hill, and the pungent odour he had already noticed about the courtyard of the inn rose about him in the air.

"Transform, transform!" she cried again, her voice rising like a song. "Rub well your skin before you fly. Come! Come with me to the Sabbath, to the madness of its furious delight, to the sweet abandonment of its evil worship! See! the Great Ones are there, and the terrible Sacraments prepared. The Throne is occupied. Anoint and come! Anoint and come!"

She grew to the height of a tree beside him, leaping upon the wall with flaming eyes and hair strewn upon the night. He too began to change swiftly. Her hands touched the skin of his face and neck, streaking him with the burning salve that sent the old magic into his blood with the power before which fades all that is good.

A wild roar came up to his ears from the heart of the wood, and the girl, when she heard it, leaped upon the wall in the frenzy of her wicked joy.

"Satan is there!" she screamed, rushing upon him and striving to draw him with her to the edge of the wall. "Satan has come! The Sacraments call us! Come, with your dear apostate soul, and we will worship and dance till the moon dies and the world is forgotten!"

Just saving himself from the dreadful plunge, Vezin struggled to release himself from her grasp, while the passion tore at his reins and all but mastered him. He shrieked aloud, not knowing what he said, and then he shrieked again. It was the old impulses, the old awful habits instinctively finding voice; for though it seemed to him that he merely shrieked nonsense, the words he uttered really had meaning in them, and were intelligible. It was the ancient call. And it was heard below. It was answered.

The wind whistled at the skirts of his coat as the air round him darkened with many flying forms crowding upwards out of the valley. The crying of hoarse voices smote upon his ears, coming closer. Strokes of wind buffeted him, tearing him this way and that along the crumbling top of the stone wall; and Ilsé clung to him with her long shining arms, smooth and bare, holding him fast about the neck. But not Ilsé alone, for a dozen of them surrounded him, dropping out of the air. The pungent odour of the anointed bodies stifled him, exciting him to the old madness of the Sabbath, the dance of the witches and sorcerers doing honour to the personified Evil of the world.

"Anoint and away! Anoint and away!" they cried in wild chorus about him. "To the Dance that never dies! To the sweet and fearful fantasy of evil!"

Another moment and he would have yielded and gone, for his will turned soft and the flood of passionate memory all but overwhelmed him, when—so can a small thing alter the whole course of an adventure—he caught his foot upon a loose stone in the edge of the wall, and then fell with a sudden crash on to the ground below. But he fell towards the houses, in the open space of dust and cobble stones, and fortunately not into the gaping depth of the valley on the farther side.

And they, too, came in a tumbling heap about him, like flies upon a piece of food, but as they fell he was released for a moment from the power of their touch, and in that brief instant of freedom there flashed into his mind the sudden intuition that saved him. Before he could regain his feet he saw them scrabbling awkwardly back upon the wall, as though bat-like they could only fly by dropping from a height, and had no hold upon him in the open. Then, seeing them perched there in a row like cats upon a roof, all dark and singularly shapeless, their eyes like lamps, the sudden memory came back to him of Ilsé's terror at the sight of fire.

Quick as a flash he found his matches and lit the dead leaves that lay under the wall.

Dry and withered, they caught fire at once, and the wind carried the flame in a long line down the length of the wall, licking upwards as it ran; and with shrieks and wailings, the crowded row of forms upon the top melted away into the air on the other side, and were gone with a great rush and whirring of their bodies down into the heart of the haunted valley, leaving Vezin breathless and shaken in the middle of the deserted ground.

"Ilsé!" he called feebly; "Ilsé!" for his heart ached to think that she was really gone to the great Dance without him, and that he had lost the opportunity of its fearful joy. Yet at the same time his relief was so great, and he was so dazed and troubled in mind with the whole thing, that he hardly knew what he was saying, and only cried aloud in the fierce storm of his emotion. . . .

The fire under the wall ran its course, and the moonlight came out again, soft and clear, from its temporary eclipse. With one last shuddering look at the ruined ramparts, and a feeling of horrid wonder for the haunted valley beyond, where the shapes still crowded and flew, he turned his face towards the town and slowly made his way in the direction of the hotel.

And as he went, a great wailing of cries, and a sound of howling, followed him from the gleaming forest below, growing fainter and fainter with the bursts of wind as he disappeared between the houses.

VI

"It may seem rather abrupt to you, this sudden tame ending," said Arthur Vezin, glancing with flushed face and timid eyes at Dr. Silence sitting there with his notebook, "but the fact is—er—from that moment my memory seems to have failed rather. I have no distinct recollection of how I got home or what precisely I did.

"It appears I never went back to the inn at all. I only dimly recollect racing down a long white road in the moonlight, past woods and villages, still and deserted, and then the dawn came up, and I saw the towers of a biggish town and so came to a station.

"But, long before that, I remember pausing somewhere on the road and looking back to where the hill-town of my adventure stood up in the moonlight, and thinking how exactly like a great monstrous cat it lay there upon the plain, its huge front paws lying down the two main streets, and the twin and broken towers of the cathedral marking its torn ears against the sky. That picture stays in my mind with the utmost vividness to this day.

"Another thing remains in my mind from that escape—namely, the sudden sharp reminder that I had not paid my bill, and the decision I made, standing there on the dusty highroad, that the small baggage I had left behind would more than settle for my indebtedness.

"For the rest, I can only tell you that I got coffee and bread at a café on the outskirts of this town I had come to, and soon after found my way to the station and caught a train later in the day. That same evening I reached London."

"And how long altogether," asked John Silence quietly, "do you think you stayed in the town of the adventure?"

Vezin looked up sheepishly.

"I was coming to that," he resumed, with apologetic wrigglings of his body. "In London I found that I was a whole week out in my reckoning of time. I had stayed over a week in the town, and it ought to have been September 15th,—instead of which it was only September 10th!"

"So that, in reality, you had only stayed a night or two in the inn?" queried the doctor.

Vezin hesitated before replying. He shuffled upon the mat.

"I must have gained time somewhere," he said at length—"somewhere or somehow. I certainly had a week to my credit. I can't explain it. I can only give you the fact."

"And this happened to you last year, since when you have never been back to the place?"

"Last autumn, yes," murmured Vezin; "and I have never dared to go back. I think I never want to."

"And, tell me," asked Dr. Silence at length, when he saw that the little man had evidently come to the end of his words and had nothing more to say, "had you ever read up the subject of the old witchcraft practices during the Middle Ages, or been at all interested in the subject?"

"Never!" declared Vezin emphatically. "I had never given a thought to such matters so far as I know—"

"Or to the question of reincarnation, perhaps?"

"Never—before my adventure; but I have since," he replied significantly.

There was, however, something still on the man's mind that he wished to relieve himself of by confession, yet could with difficulty bring himself to mention; and it was only after the sympathetic tactfulness of the doctor had provided numerous openings that he at length availed himself of one of them, and stammered that he would like to show him the marks he still had on his neck where, he said, the girl had touched him with her anointed hands.

He took off his collar after infinite fumbling hesitation, and lowered his shirt a little for the doctor to see. And there, on the surface of the skin, lay a faint reddish line across the shoulder and extending a little way down the back towards the spine. It certainly indicated exactly the position an arm might have taken in the act of embracing. And on the other side of the neck, slightly higher up, was a similar mark, though not quite so clearly defined.

"That was where she held me that night on the ramparts," he whispered, a strange light coming and going in his eyes.

It was some weeks later when I again found occasion to consult John Silence concerning another extraordinary case that had come under my notice, and we fell to discussing Vezin's story. Since hearing it, the doctor had made investigations on his own account, and one of his secretaries had discovered that Vezin's ancestors had actually lived for generations in the very town where the adventure came to him. Two of them, both women, had been tried and convicted as witches, and had been burned alive at the stake. Moreover, it had not been difficult to prove that the very inn where Vezin stayed was built about 1700 upon the spot where the funeral pyres stood and the executions took place. The town was a sort of headquarters for all the sorcerers and witches of the entire region, and after conviction they were burnt there literally by scores.

"It seems strange," continued the doctor, "that Vezin should have remained ignorant of all this; but, on the other hand, it was not the kind of history that successive generations would have been anxious to keep alive, or to repeat to their children. Therefore I am inclined to think he still knows nothing about it.

"The whole adventure seems to have been a very vivid revival of the memories of an earlier life, caused by coming directly into contact with the living forces still intense enough to hang about the place, and, by a most singular chance too, with the very souls who had taken part with him in the events of that particular life. For the mother and daughter who impressed him so strangely must have been leading actors, with himself, in the scenes and practices of witchcraft which at that period dominated the imaginations of the whole country.

"One has only to read the histories of the times to know that these witches claimed the power of transforming themselves into various animals, both for the purposes of disguise and also to convey themselves swiftly to the scenes of their imaginary orgies. Lycanthropy, or the power to change themselves into wolves, was everywhere believed in, and the ability to transform themselves into cats by rubbing their bodies with a special salve or ointment provided by Satan himself, found equal credence. The witchcraft trials abound in evidences of such universal beliefs."

Dr. Silence quoted chapter and verse from many writers on the subject, and showed how every detail of Vezin's adventure had a basis in the practices of those dark days.

"But that the entire affair took place subjectively in the man's own consciousness, I have no doubt," he went on, in reply to my questions; "for my secretary who has been to the town to investigate, discovered his signature in the visitors' book, and proved by it that he had arrived on September 8th, and left suddenly without paying his bill. He left two days later, and they still were in possession of his dirty brown bag and some tourist clothes. I paid a few francs in settlement of his debt, and have sent his luggage on to him. The daughter was absent from home, but the proprietress, a large woman very much as he described her, told my secretary that he had seemed a very strange, absent-minded kind of gentleman, and after his disappearance she had feared for a long time that he had met with a violent end in the neighbouring forest where he used to roam about alone.

"I should like to have obtained a personal interview with the daughter so as to ascertain how much was subjective and how much actually took place with her as Vezin told it. For her dread of fire and the sight of burning must, of course, have been the intuitive memory of her former painful death at the stake, and have thus explained why he fancied more than once that he saw her through smoke and flame."

"And that mark on his skin, for instance?" I inquired.

"Merely the marks produced by hysterical brooding," he replied, "like the stigmata of the *religieuses*, and the bruises which appear on the bodies of hypnotised subjects who have been told to expect them. This is very common and easily explained. Only it seems curious that these marks should have remained so long in Vezin's case. Usually they disappear quickly."

"Obviously he is still thinking about it all, brooding, and living it all over again," I ventured.

"Probably. And this makes me fear that the end of his trouble is not yet. We shall hear of him again. It is a case, alas! I can do little to alleviate."

Dr. Silence spoke gravely and with sadness in his voice.

"And what do you make of the Frenchman in the train?" I asked further—"the man who warned him against the place, *à cause du sommeil et à cause des chats*? Surely a very singular incident?"

"A *very* singular incident indeed," he made answer slowly, "and one I can only explain on the basis of a highly improbable coincidence—"

"Namely?"

"That the man was one who had himself stayed in the town and undergone there a similar experience. I should like to find this man and ask him. But the crystal is useless here, for I have no slightest clue to go upon, and I can only conclude that some singular psychic affinity, some force still active in his being out of the same past life, drew him thus to the personality of Vezin, and enabled him to fear what might happen to him, and thus to warn him as he did.

"Yes," he presently continued, half talking to himself, "I suspect in this case that Vezin was swept into the vortex of forces arising out of the intense activities of a past life, and that he lived over again a scene in which he had often played a leading part centuries before. For strong actions set up forces that are so slow to exhaust themselves, they may be said in a sense never to die. In this case they were not vital enough to render the illusion complete, so that the little man found himself caught in a very distressing confusion of the present and the past; yet he was sufficiently sensitive to recognise that it was true, and to fight against the degradation of returning, even in memory, to a former and lower state of development.

"Ah yes!" he continued, crossing the floor to gaze at the darkening sky, and seemingly quite oblivious of my presence, "subliminal up-rushes of memory like this can be exceedingly painful, and sometimes exceedingly dangerous. I only trust that this gentle soul may soon escape from this obsession of a passionate and tempestuous past. But I doubt it, I doubt it."

His voice was hushed with sadness as he spoke, and when he turned back into the room again there was an expression of profound yearning upon his face, the yearning of a soul whose desire to help is sometimes greater than his power.

The House on the Borderland

From the Manuscript, discovered in 1877 by Messrs. Tonnison and Berreggnog, in the Ruins that lie to the South of the Village of Kraighten, in the West of Ireland. Set out here, with Notes.

William Hope Hodgson

———◆———

AUTHOR'S INTRODUCTION TO THE MANUSCRIPT

Many are the hours in which I have pondered upon the story that is set forth in the following pages. Once again, and in my post as Editor, I have been tempted to (if I may coin so ungracious a word) "literarise" it; but I trust that my instincts are not awry when they prompt me to leave the account, in simplicity, as it was handed to me.

And the MS. itself—You must picture me, when first it was given into my care, turning it over, curiously, and making a swift, jerky examination. A small book it is; but thick, and all, save the last few pages, filled with a quaint but legible hand-writing, and writ very close. I have the queer, faint, pit-water smell of it in my nostrils now as I write, and my fingers have subconscious memories of the soft, "cloggy" feel of the long-damp pages.

I recall, with just a slight effort, my first impression of the worded contents of the book—an impression of the fantastic, gathered from casual glances, and an unconcentrated attention.

Then, conceive of me comfortably a-seat for the evening, and the little, squat book and I, companions for some close, solitary hours. And the change that came upon my judgments! The emergence of a half-belief. From a *seeming* "fantasia" there grew, to reward my unbiassed concentration, a cogent, coherent scheme of ideas that gripped my interest more securely than the mere bones of the *account* or *story*, whichever it be, and I confess to an inclination to use the first term. I found a greater story within the lesser—and the paradox is no paradox.

I read, and, in reading, lifted the Curtains of the Impossible that blind the mind, and looked out into the unknown. Amid stiff, abrupt sentences I wandered; and, presently, I had no fault to charge against their abrupt tellings; for, better far than my own ambitious phrasing, is this mutilated story capable of bringing home all that the old Recluse, of the vanished house, had striven to tell.

Of the simple, stiffly given account of weird and extraordinary matters, I will say little. It lies before you. The inner story must be uncovered, personally, by each reader, according to ability and desire. And even should any fail to see, as now I see, the shadowed picture and conception of that to which one may well give the accepted titles of Heaven and Hell; yet can I promise certain thrills, merely taking the story as a story.

On final impression, and I will cease from troubling. I cannot but look at the account of the Celestial Globes as a striking illustration (how nearly had I said "proof"!) of the actuality of our thought and emotions among the Realities. For, without seeming to suggest the annihilation of the lasting reality of Matter, as the hub and framework of the Machine of Eternity, it enlightens one with conceptions of the existence of worlds of thought and emotion, working in conjunction with, and duly subject to, the scheme of the material creation.

William Hope Hodgson
"Glaneifon," Borth,
Cardiganshire,
December 17, 1907

GRIEF *

Fierce hunger reigns within my breast,
   I had not dreamt that this whole world,
      Crushed in the hand of God, could yield
Such bitter essence of unrest,
   Such pain as Sorrow now hath hurled
      Out of its dreadful heart, unsealed!

Each sobbing breath is but a cry,
   My heart-strokes knells of agony,
      And my whole brain has but one thought
That nevermore through life shall I
   (Save in the ache of memory)
      Touch hands with thee, who now art naught!

Through the whole void of night I search,
   So dumbly crying out to thee;
      But thou are *not*; and night's vast throne
Becomes an all stupendous church
   With star-bells knelling unto me
      Who in all space am most alone!

An hungered, to the shore I creep,
   Perchance some comfort waits on me
      From the old Sea's eternal heart;
But lo! from all the solemn deep,
   Far voices out of mystery
      Seem questioning why we are apart!

Where'er I go I am alone
   Who once, through thee, had all the world.
      My breast is one whole raging pain
For that which was, and now is flown
   Into the Blank where life is hurled
      Where all is not, nor is again!

*These stanzas I found, in pencil, upon a piece of foolscap gummed in behind the fly-leaf of the MS. They have all the appearance of having been written at an earlier date than the Manuscript.—ED.

I. THE FINDING OF THE MANUSCRIPT

Right away in the west of Ireland lies a tiny hamlet called Kraighten. It is situated, alone, at the base of a low hill. Far around there spreads a waste of bleak and totally inhospitable country; where, here and there at great intervals, one may come upon the ruins of some long desolate cottage—unthatched and stark. The whole land is bare and unpeopled, the very earth scarcely covering the rock that lies beneath it, and with which the country abounds, in places rising out of the soil in wave-shaped ridges.

Yet, in spite of its desolation, my friend Tonnison and I had elected to spend our vacation there. He had stumbled on the place by mere chance the year previously, during the course of a long walking tour, and discovered the possibilities for the angler in a small and unnamed river that runs past the outskirts of the little village.

I have said that the river is without name; I may add that no map that I have hitherto consulted has shown either village or stream. They seem to have entirely escaped observation: indeed, they might never exist for all that the average guide tells one. Possibly this can be partly accounted for by the fact that the nearest railway-station (Ardrahan) is some forty miles distant.

It was early one warm evening when my friend and I arrived in Kraighten. We had reached Ardrahan the previous night, sleeping there in rooms hired at the village post-office, and leaving in good time on the following morning, clinging insecurely to one of the typical jaunting cars.

It had taken us all day to accomplish our journey over some of the roughest tracks imaginable, with the result that we were thoroughly tired and somewhat bad tempered. However, the tent had to be erected and our goods stowed away before we could think of food or rest. And so we set to work, with the aid of our driver, and soon had the tent up upon a small patch of ground just outside the little village, and quite near to the river.

Then, having stored all our belongings, we dismissed the driver, as he had to make his way back as speedily as possible, and told him to come across to us at the end of a fortnight. We had brought sufficient provisions to last us for that space of time, and water we could get from the stream. Fuel we did not need, as we had included a small oil-stove among our outfit, and the weather was fine and warm.

It was Tonnison's idea to camp out instead of getting lodgings in one of the cottages. As he put it, there was no joke in sleeping in a room with a numerous family of healthy Irish in one corner, and the pig-sty in the other, while overhead a ragged colony of roosting fowls distributed their blessings impartially, and the whole place so full of peat smoke that it made a fellow sneeze his head off just to put it inside the doorway.

Tonnison had got the stove lit now and was busy cutting slices of bacon into the frying-pan; so I took the kettle and walked down to the river for water. On the way, I had to pass close to a little group of the village people, who eyed me curiously, but not in any unfriendly manner, though none of them ventured a word.

As I returned with my kettle filled, I went up to them and, after a friendly nod, to which they replied in like manner, I asked them casually about the fishing; but, instead of answering, they just shook their heads silently, and stared at me. I repeated the question, addressing more particularly a great, gaunt fellow at my elbow; yet again I received no answer. Then the man turned to a comrade and said something rapidly in a language that I did not understand; and, at once, the whole crowd of them fell to jabbering in what, after a few moments, I guessed to be pure Irish. At the same time they cast many glances in my direction. For a minute, perhaps, they spoke among themselves thus; then the man I had addressed faced round at me and said something. By the expression of his face I guessed that he, in turn, was questioning me; but now I had to shake my head, and indicate that I did not comprehend what it was they wanted to know: and so we stood looking at one another, until I heard Tonnison calling to me to hurry up with the kettle. Then, with a smile and a nod, I left them, and all in the little crowd smiled and nodded in return, though their faces still betrayed their puzzlement.

It was evident, I reflected as I went towards the tent, that the inhabitants of these few huts in the wilderness did not know a word of English; and when I told Tonnison, he remarked that he was aware of the fact, and, more, that it was not at all uncommon in that part of the country, where the people often lived and died in their isolated hamlets without ever coming in contact with the outside world.

"I wish we had got the driver to interpret for us before he left," I remarked, as we sat down to our meal. "It seems so strange for the people of this place not even to know what we've come for."

Tonnison grunted an assent, and thereafter was silent for a while.

Later, having satisfied our appetites somewhat, we began to talk, laying our plans for the morrow; then, after a smoke, we closed the flap of the tent, and prepared to turn in.

"I suppose there's no chance of those fellows outside taking anything?" I asked, as we rolled ourselves in our blankets.

Tonnison said that he did not think so, at least while we were about; and, as he went on to explain, we could lock up everything, except the tent, in the big chest that we had brought to hold our provisions. I agreed to this, and soon we were both asleep.

Next morning, early, we rose and went for a swim in the river; after which we dressed, and had breakfast. Then we roused out our fishing tackle, and overhauled it, by which time, our breakfasts having settled somewhat, we made all secure within the tent and strode off in the direction my friend had explored on his previous visit.

During the day we fished happily, working steadily up-stream, and by evening we had one of the prettiest creels of fish that I had seen for a long while. Returning to the village, we made a good feed off our day's spoil, after which, having selected a few of the finer fish for our breakfast, we presented the remainder to the group of villagers who had assembled at a respectful distance to watch our doings. They seemed wonderfully grateful, and heaped mountains of what I presumed to be Irish blessings upon our heads.

Thus we spent several days, having splendid sport, and first-rate appetites to do justice upon our prey. We were pleased to find how friendly the villagers were inclined to be, and that there was no evidence of their having ventured to meddle with our belongings during our absences.

It was on a Tuesday that we arrived in Kraighten, and it would be on the Sunday following that we made a great discovery. Hitherto we had always gone up-stream; on that day, however, we laid aside our rods, and, taking some provisions, set off for a long ramble in the opposite direction. The day was warm, and we trudged along leisurely enough, stopping about midday to eat our lunch upon a great flat rock near the riverbank. Afterward we sat and smoked awhile, resuming our walk only when we were tired of inaction.

For, perhaps, another hour we wandered onward, chatting quietly and comfortably on this and that matter, and on several occasions stopping while my companion—who is something of an artist—made rough sketches of striking bits of the wild scenery.

And then, without any warning whatsoever, the river we had followed so confidently, came to an abrupt end—vanishing into the earth.

"Good Lord!" I said, "who ever would have thought of this?"

And I stared in amazement; then I turned to Tonnison. He was looking, with a blank expression upon his face, at the place where the river disappeared.

In a moment he spoke.

"Let us go on a bit; it may reappear again—anyhow, it is worth investigating."

I agreed, and we went forward once more, though rather aimlessly; for we were not at all certain in which direction to prosecute our search. For perhaps a mile we moved onward; then Tonnison, who had been gazing about curiously, stopped and shaded his eyes.

"See!" he said, after a moment, "isn't that mist or something, over there to the right—away in a line with that great piece of rock?" And he indicated with his hand.

I stared, and, after a minute, seemed to see something, but could not be certain, and said so.

"Anyway," my friend replied, "we'll just go across and have a glance." And he started off in the direction he had suggested, I following. Presently, we came among bushes, and, after a time, out upon the top of a high, boulder-strewn bank, from which we looked down into a wilderness of bushes and trees.

"Seems as though we had come upon an oasis in this desert of stone," muttered Tonnison, as he gazed interestedly. Then he was silent, his eyes fixed; and I looked also; for up from somewhere about the centre of the wooded lowland there rose high into the quiet air a great column of haze-like spray, upon which the sun shone, causing innumerable rainbows.

"How beautiful!" I exclaimed.

"Yes," answered Tonnison, thoughtfully. "There must be a waterfall, or something, over there. Perhaps it's our river come to light again. Let's go and see."

Down the sloping bank we made our way, and entered among the trees and shrubberies. The bushes were matted, and the trees overhung us, so that the place was disagreeably gloomy; though not dark enough to hide from me the fact that many of the trees were fruit trees, and that, here and there, one could trace indistinctly, signs of a long departed cultivation. Thus it came to me that we were making our way through the riot of a great and ancient garden. I said as much to Tonnison, and he agreed that there certainly seemed reasonable grounds for my belief.

What a wild place it was, so dismal and somber! Somehow, as we went forward, a sense of the silent loneliness and desertion of the old garden grew upon me, and I felt shivery. One could imagine things lurking among the tangled bushes; while, in the very air of the place, there seemed something uncanny. I think Tonnison was conscious of this also, though he said nothing.

Suddenly, we came to a halt. Through the trees there had grown upon our ears a distant sound. Tonnison bent forward, listening. I could hear it more plainly now; it was continuous and harsh—a sort of droning roar, seeming to come from far away.

I experienced a queer, indescribable, little feeling of nervousness. What sort of place was it into which we had got? I looked at my companion, to see what he thought of the matter; and noted that there was only puzzlement in his face; and then, as I watched his features, an expression of comprehension crept over them, and he nodded his head.

"That's a waterfall," he exclaimed, with conviction. "I know the sound now." And he began to push vigorously through the bushes, in the direction of the noise.

As we went forward, the sound became plainer continually, showing that we were heading straight towards it. Steadily, the roaring grew louder and nearer, until it appeared, as I remarked to Tonnison, almost to come from under our feet—and still we were surrounded by the trees and shrubs.

"Take care!" Tonnison called to me. "Look where you're going." And then, suddenly, we came out from among the trees, on to a great open space, where, not six paces in front of us, yawned the mouth of a tremendous chasm, from the depths of which the noise appeared to rise, along with the continuous, mist-like spray that we had witnessed from the top of the distant bank.

For quite a minute we stood in silence, staring in bewilderment at the sight; then my friend went forward cautiously to the edge of the abyss. I followed, and, together, we looked down through a boil of spray at a monster cataract of frothing water that burst, spouting, from the side of the chasm, nearly a hundred feet below.

"Good Lord!" said Tonnison.

I was silent, and rather awed. The sight was so unexpectedly grand and eerie; though this latter quality came more upon me later.

Presently, I looked up and across to the further side of the chasm. There, I saw something towering up among the spray: it looked like a fragment of a great ruin, and I touched Tonnison on the shoulder. He glanced round, with a start, and I pointed towards the thing. His gaze followed my finger, and his eyes lighted up with a sudden flash of excitement, as the object came within his field of view.

"Come along," he shouted above the uproar. "We'll have a look at it. There's something queer about this place; I feel it in my bones." And he started off, round the edge of the crater-like abyss. As we neared this new thing, I saw that I had not been mistaken in my first impression. It was undoubtedly a portion of some ruined building; yet now I made out that it was not built upon the edge of the chasm itself, as I had at first supposed; but perched almost at the extreme end of a huge spur of rock that jutted out some fifty or sixty feet over the abyss. In fact, the jagged mass of ruin was literally suspended in mid-air.

Arriving opposite it, we walked out on to the projecting arm of rock, and I must confess to having felt an intolerable sense of terror as I looked down from that dizzy perch into the unknown depths below us—into the deeps from which there rose ever the thunder of the falling water and the shroud of rising spray.

Reaching the ruin, we clambered round it cautiously, and, on the further side, came upon a mass of fallen stones and rubble. The ruin itself seemed to me, as I proceeded now to examine it minutely, to be a portion of the outer wall of some prodigious structure, it was so thick and substantially built; yet what it was doing in such a position, I could by no means conjecture. Where was the rest of the house, or castle, or whatever there had been?

I went back to the outer side of the wall, and thence to the edge of the chasm, leaving Tonnison rooting systematically among the heap of stones and rubbish on the outer side. Then I commenced to examine the surface of the ground, near the edge of the abyss, to see whether there were not left other remnants of the building to which the fragment of ruin evidently belonged. But though I scrutinized the earth with the greatest care, I could see no signs of anything to show that there had ever been a building erected on the spot, and I grew more puzzled than ever.

Then, I heard a cry from Tonnison; he was shouting my name, excitedly, and without delay I hurried along the rocky promontory to the ruin. I wondered whether he had hurt himself, and then the thought came, that perhaps he had found something.

I reached the crumbled wall and climbed round. There I found Tonnison standing within a small excavation that he had made among the *débris*: he was brushing the dirt from something that looked like a book, much crumpled and dilapidated; and opening his mouth, every second or two, to bellow my name. As soon as he saw that I had come, he handed his prize to me, telling me to put it into my satchel so as to protect it from the damp, while he continued his explorations. This I did, first, however, running the pages through my fingers, and noting that they were closely filled with neat, old-fashioned writing which was quite legible, save in one portion, where many of the pages were almost destroyed, being muddied and crumpled, as though the book had been doubled back at that part. This, I found out from Tonnison, was actually as he had discovered it, and the damage was due, probably, to the fall of masonry upon the opened part. Curiously enough, the book was fairly dry, which I attributed to its having been so securely buried among the ruins.

Having put the volume away safely, I turned-to and gave Tonnison a hand with his self-imposed task of excavating; yet, though we put in over an hour's hard work, turning over the whole of the upheaped stones and rubbish, we came upon nothing more than some fragments of broken wood, that might have been parts of a desk or table; and so we gave up searching, and went back along the rock, once more to the safety of the land.

The next thing we did was to make a complete tour of the tremendous chasm, which we were able to observe was in the form of an almost perfect circle, save for where the ruin-crowned spur of rock jutted out, spoiling its symmetry.

The abyss was, as Tonnison put it, like nothing so much as a gigantic well or pit going sheer down into the bowels of the earth.

For some time longer, we continued to stare about us, and then, noticing that there was a clear space away to the north of the chasm, we bent our steps in that direction.

Here, distant from the mouth of the mighty pit by some hundreds of yards, we came upon a great lake of silent water—silent, that is, save in one place where there was a continuous bubbling and gurgling.

Now, being away from the noise of the spouting cataract, we were able to hear one another speak, without having to shout at the tops of our voices, and I asked Tonnison what he thought of the place—I told him that I didn't like it, and that the sooner we were out of it the better I should be pleased.

He nodded in reply, and glanced at the woods behind furtively. I asked him if he had seen or heard anything. He made no answer; but stood silent, as though listening, and I kept quiet also.

Suddenly, he spoke.

"Hark!" he said, sharply. I looked at him, and then away among the trees and bushes, holding my breath involuntarily. A minute came and went in strained silence; yet I could hear nothing, and I turned to Tonnison to say as much; and then, even as I opened my lips to speak, there came a strange wailing noise out of the wood on our left. . . . It appeared to float through the trees, and there was a rustle of stirring leaves, and then silence.

All at once, Tonnison spoke, and put his hand on my shoulder. "Let us get out of here," he said, and began to move slowly towards where the surrounding trees and bushes seemed thinnest. As I followed him, it came to me suddenly that the sun was low, and that there was a raw sense of chilliness in the air.

Tonnison said nothing further, but kept on steadily. We were among the trees now, and I glanced around, nervously; but saw nothing, save the quiet branches and trunks and the tangled bushes. Onwards we went, and no sound broke the silence, except the occasional snapping of a twig under our feet, as we moved forward. Yet, in spite of the quietness, I had a horrible feeling that we were not alone; and I kept so close to Tonnison that twice I kicked his heels clumsily, though he said nothing. A minute, and then another, and we reached the confines of the wood coming out at last upon the bare rockiness of the countryside. Only then was I able to shake off the haunting dread that had followed me among the trees.

Once, as we moved away, there seemed to come again a distant sound of wailing, and I said to myself that it was the wind—yet the evening was breathless.

Presently, Tonnison began to talk.

"Look you," he said with decision, "I would not spend the night in *that* place for all the wealth that the world holds. There is something unholy—diabolical—about it. It came to me all in a moment, just after you spoke. It seemed to me that the woods were full of vile things—you know!"

"Yes," I answered, and looked back towards the place; but it was hidden from us by a rise in the ground.

"There's the book," I said, and I put my hand into the satchel.

"You've got it safely?" he questioned, with a sudden access of anxiety.

"Yes," I replied.

"Perhaps," he continued, "we shall learn something from it when we get back to the tent. We had better hurry, too; we're a long way off still, and I don't fancy, now, being caught out here in the dark."

It was two hours later when we reached the tent; and, without delay, we set to work to prepare a meal; for we had eaten nothing since our lunch at midday.

Supper over, we cleared the things out of the way, and lit our pipes. Then Tonnison asked me to get the manuscript out of my satchel. This I did, and then, as we could not both read from it at the same time, he suggested that I should read the thing out loud. "And mind," he cautioned, knowing my propensities, "don't go skipping half the book."

Yet, had he but known what it contained, he would have realised how needless such advice was, for once at least. And there seated in the opening of our little tent, I began the strange tale of "The House on the Borderland" (for such was the title of the MS.); this is told in the following pages.

II. THE PLAIN OF SILENCE

I am an old man. I live here in this ancient house, surrounded by huge, unkempt gardens.

The peasantry, who inhabit the wilderness beyond, say that I am mad. That is because I will have nothing to do with them. I live here alone with my old sister, who is also my housekeeper. We keep no servants—I hate them. I have one friend, a dog; yes, I would sooner have old Pepper than the rest of Creation together. He, at least, understands me—and has sense enough to leave me alone when I am in my dark moods.

I have decided to start a kind of diary; it may enable me to record some of the thoughts and feelings that I cannot express to anyone; but, beyond this, I am anxious to make some record of the strange things that I have heard and seen, during many years of loneliness, in this weird old building.

For a couple of centuries, this house has had a reputation, a bad one, and, until I bought it, for more than eighty years no one had lived here; consequently, I got the old place at a ridiculously low figure.

I am not superstitious; but I have ceased to deny that things happen in this old house—things that I cannot explain; and, therefore, I must needs ease my mind, by writing down an account of them, to the best of my ability; though, should this, my diary, ever be read when I am gone, the readers will but shake their heads, and be the more convinced that I was mad.

This house, how ancient it is! though its age strikes one less, perhaps, than the quaintness of its structure, which is curious and fantastic to the last degree. Little curved towers and pinnacles, with outlines suggestive of leaping flames, predominate; while the body of the building is in the form of a circle.

I have heard that there is an old story, told amongst the country people, to the effect that the devil built the place. However, that is as may be. True or not, I neither know nor care, save as it may have helped to cheapen it, ere I came.

I must have been here some ten years before I saw sufficient to warrant any belief in the stories, current in the neighbourhood, about this house. It is true that I had, on at least a dozen occasions, seen, vaguely, things that puzzled me, and, perhaps, had felt more than I had seen. Then, as the years passed, bringing age upon me, I became often aware of something unseen, yet unmistakably present, in the empty rooms and corridors. Still, it was as I have said many years before I saw any real manifestations of the so-called supernatural.

It was not Hallowe'en. If I were telling a story for amusement's sake, I should probably place it on that night of nights; but this is a true record of my own experiences, and I would not put pen to paper to amuse anyone. No. It was after midnight on the morning of the twenty-first day of January. I was sitting reading, as is often my custom, in my study. Pepper lay, sleeping, near my chair.

Without warning, the flames of the two candles went low, and then shone with a ghastly green effulgence. I looked up, quickly, and as I did so I saw the lights sink into a dull, ruddy tint; so that the room glowed with a strange, heavy, crimson twilight that gave the shadows behind the chairs and tables a double depth of blackness; and wherever the light struck, it was as though luminous blood had been splashed over the room.

Down on the floor, I heard a faint, frightened whimper, and something pressed itself in between my two feet. It was Pepper, cowering under my dressing-gown. Pepper, usually as brave as a lion!

It was this movement of the dog's, I think, that gave me the first twinge of *real* fear. I had been considerably startled when the lights burnt first green and then red; but had been momentarily under the impression that the change was due to some influx of noxious gas into the room. Now, however, I saw that it was not so; for the candles burned with a steady flame, and showed no signs of going out, as would have been the case had the change been due to fumes in the atmosphere.

I did not move. I felt distinctly frightened; but could think of nothing better to do than wait. For perhaps a minute, I kept my glance about the room, nervously. Then I noticed that the lights had commenced to sink, very slowly; until presently they showed minute specks of red fire, like the gleamings of rubies in the darkness. Still, I sat watching; while a sort of dreamy indifference seemed to steal over me; banishing altogether the fear that had begun to grip me.

Away in the far end of the huge old-fashioned room, I became conscious of a faint glow. Steadily it grew, filling the room with gleams of quivering green light; then they sank quickly, and changed—even as the candle flames had done—into a deep, somber crimson that strengthened, and lit up the room with a flood of awful glory.

The light came from the end wall, and grew ever brighter until its intolerable glare caused my eyes acute pain, and, involuntarily, I closed them. It may have been a few seconds before I was able to open them. The first thing I noticed was that the light had decreased, greatly; so that it no longer tried my eyes. Then, as it grew still duller, I was aware, all at once, that, instead of looking at the redness, I was staring through it, and through the wall beyond.

Gradually, as I became more accustomed to the idea, I realised that I was looking out on to a vast plain, lit with the same gloomy twilight that pervaded the room. The immensity of this plain scarcely can be conceived. In no part could I perceive its confines. It seemed to broaden and spread out, so that the eye failed to perceive any limitations. Slowly, the details of the nearer portions began to grow clear; then, in a moment almost, the light died away, and the vision—if vision it were—faded and was gone.

Suddenly, I became conscious that I was no longer in the chair. Instead, I seemed to be hovering above it, and looking down at a dim something, huddled and silent. In a little while, a cold blast struck me, and I was outside in the night, floating, like a bubble, up through the darkness. As I moved, an icy coldness seemed to enfold me, so that I shivered.

After a time, I looked to right and left, and saw the intolerable blackness of the night, pierced by remote gleams of fire. Onward, outward, I drove. Once, I glanced behind, and saw the earth, a small crescent of blue light, receding away to my left. Further off, the sun, a splash of white flame, burned vividly against the dark.

An indefinite period passed. Then, for the last time, I saw the earth—an enduring globule of radiant blue, swimming in an eternity of ether. And there I, a fragile flake of soul dust, flickered silently across the void, from the distant blue, into the expanse of the unknown.

A great while seemed to pass over me, and now I could nowhere see anything. I had passed beyond the fixed stars and plunged into the huge blackness that waits beyond. All this time I had experienced little, save a sense of lightness and cold discomfort. Now however the atrocious darkness seemed to creep into my soul, and I became filled with fear and despair. What was going to become of me? Where was I going? Even as the thoughts were formed, there grew against the impalpable blackness that wrapped me a faint tinge of blood. It seemed extraordinarily remote, and mist-like; yet, at once, the feeling of oppression was lightened, and I no longer despaired.

Slowly, the distant redness became plainer and larger; until, as I drew nearer, it spread out into a great, sombre glare—dull and tremendous. Still, I fled onward, and, presently, I had come so close, that it seemed to stretch beneath me, like a great ocean of sombre red. I could see little, save that it appeared to spread out interminably in all directions.

In a further space, I found that I was descending upon it; and, soon, I sank into a great sea of sullen, red-hued clouds. Slowly, I emerged from these, and there, below me, I saw the stupendous plain, that I had seen from my room in this house that stands upon the borders of the Silences.

Presently, I landed, and stood, surrounded by a great waste of loneliness. The place was lit with a gloomy twilight that gave an impression of indescribable desolation.

Afar to my right, within the sky, there burnt a gigantic ring of dull-red fire, from the outer edge of which were projected huge, writhing flames, darted and jagged. The interior of this ring was black, black as the gloom of the outer night. I comprehended, at once, that it was from this extraordinary sun that the place derived its doleful light.

From that strange source of light, I glanced down again to my surroundings. Everywhere I looked, I saw nothing but the same flat weariness of interminable plain. Nowhere could I descry any signs of life; not even the ruins of some ancient habitation.

Gradually, I found that I was being borne forward, floating across the flat waste. For what seemed an eternity, I moved onward. I was unaware of any great sense of impatience; though some curiosity and a vast wonder were with me continually. Always, I saw around me the breadth of that enormous plain; and, always, I searched for some new thing to break its monotony; but there was no change—only loneliness, silence, and desert.

Presently, in a half-conscious manner, I noticed that there was a faint mistiness, ruddy in hue, lying over its surface. Still, when I looked more intently, I was unable to say that it was really mist; for it appeared to blend with the plain, giving it a peculiar unrealness, and conveying to the senses the idea of unsubstantiality.

Gradually, I began to weary with the sameness of the thing. Yet, it was a great time before I perceived any signs of the place, towards which I was being conveyed.

At first, I saw it, far ahead, like a long hillock on the surface of the Plain. Then, as I drew nearer, I perceived that I had been mistaken; for, instead of a low hill, I made out, now, a chain of great mountains, whose distant peaks towered up into the red gloom, until they were almost lost to sight.

III. THE HOUSE IN THE ARENA

And so, after a time, I came to the mountains. Then, the course of my journey was altered, and I began to move along their bases, until, all at once, I saw that I had come opposite to a vast rift, opening into the mountains. Through this, I was borne, moving at no great speed. On either side of me, huge, scarped walls of rock-like substance rose sheer. Far overhead, I discerned a thin ribbon of red, where the mouth of the chasm opened, among inaccessible peaks. Within, was gloom, deep and sombre, and chilly silence. For a while, I went onward steadily, and then, at last, I saw, ahead, a deep, red glow, that told me I was near upon the further opening of the gorge.

A minute came and went, and I was at the exit of the chasm, staring out upon an enormous amphitheatre of mountains. Yet, of the mountains, and the terrible grandeur of the place, I recked nothing; for I was confounded with amazement to behold, at a distance of several miles and occupying the centre of the arena, a stupendous structure built apparently of green jade. Yet, in itself, it was not the discovery of the building that had so astonished me; but the fact, which became every moment more apparent, that in no particular, save in colour and its enormous size, did the lonely structure vary from this house in which I live.

For a while, I continued to stare, fixedly. Even then, I could scarcely believe that I saw aright. In my mind, a question formed, reiterating incessantly: "What does it mean?" "What does it mean?" and I was unable to make answer, even out of the depths of my imagination. I seemed capable only of wonder and fear. For a time longer, I gazed, noting, continually, some fresh point of resemblance that attracted me. At last, wearied and sorely puzzled, I turned from it, to view the rest of the strange place on to which I had intruded.

Hitherto, I had been so engrossed in my scrutiny of the House, that I had given only a cursory glance round. Now, as I looked, I began to realise upon what sort of a place I had come. The arena, for so I have termed it, appeared a perfect circle of about ten to twelve miles in diameter, the House, as I have mentioned before, standing in the centre. The surface of the place, like to that of the Plain, had a peculiar, misty appearance, that was yet not mist.

From a rapid survey, my glance passed quickly upwards along the slopes of the circling mountains. How silent they were. I think that this same abominable stillness was more trying to me than anything that I had so far seen or imagined. I was looking up, now, at the great crags, towering so loftily. Up there, the impalpable redness gave a blurred appearance to everything.

And then, as I peered, curiously, a new terror came to me; for away up among the dim peaks to my right, I had descried a vast shape of blackness, giant-like. It grew upon my sight. It had an enormous ass-like head, with gigantic ears, and seemed to peer steadfastly down into the arena. There was that about the pose that gave me the impression of an eternal watchfulness—of having warded that dismal place, through unknown eternities. Slowly, the monster became plainer to me; and then, suddenly, my gaze sprang from it to something further off and higher among the crags. For a long minute, I gazed, fearfully. I was strangely conscious of something not altogether unfamiliar—as though something stirred in the back of my mind. The thing was black, and had four grotesque arms. The features showed indistinctly. Round the neck, I made out several light-coloured objects. Slowly, the details came to me, and I realised, coldly, that they were skulls. Further down the body was another circling belt, showing less dark against the black trunk. Then, even as I puzzled to know what the thing was, a memory slid into my mind, and straightway, I knew that I was looking at a monstrous representation of Kali, the Hindu goddess of death.

Other remembrances of my old student days drifted into my thoughts. My glance fell back upon the huge ass-headed Thing. Simultaneously, I recognised it for the ancient Egyptian god Set, or Seth, the Destroyer of Souls. With the knowledge, there came a great sweep of questioning— "Two of the—!" I stopped, and endeavoured to think. Things beyond my imagination peered into my frightened mind. I saw, obscurely. "The old gods of mythology!" I tried to comprehend to what it was all pointing. My gaze dwelt, flickeringly, between the two. "If—"

An idea came swiftly, and I turned, and glanced rapidly upwards, searching the gloomy crags, away to my left. Something loomed out under a great peak, a shape of greyness. I wondered I had not seen it earlier, and then remembered I had not yet viewed that portion. I saw it more plainly now. It was, as I have said, grey. It had a tremendous head; but no eyes. That part of its face was blank.

Now, I saw that there were other things up among the mountains. Further off, reclining on a lofty ledge, I made out a livid mass, irregular and ghoulish. It seemed without form, save for an unclean, half-animal face, that looked out, vilely, from somewhere about its middle. And then I saw others—there were hundreds of them. They seemed to grow out of the shadows. Several I recognised almost immediately as mythological deities; others were strange to me, utterly strange, beyond the power of a human mind to conceive.

On each side, I looked, and saw more, continually. The mountains were full of strange things—Beast-gods, and Horrors, so atrocious and bestial that possibility and decency deny any further attempt to describe them. And I—I was filled with a terrible sense of overwhelming horror and fear and repugnance; yet, spite of these, I wondered exceedingly. Was there then, after all, something in the old heathen worship, something more than the mere deifying of men, animals and elements? The thought gripped me—was there?

Later, a question repeated itself. What were they, those Beast-gods, and the others? At first, they had appeared to me, just sculptured Monster,s placed indiscriminately among the inaccessible peaks and precipices of the surrounding mountains. Now, as I scrutinized them with greater intentness, my mind began to reach out to fresh conclusions. There was something about them, an indescribable sort of silent vitality that suggested, to my broadening consciousness, a state of life-in-death—a something that was by no means life, as we understand it; but rather an inhuman form of existence, that well might be likened to a deathless trance—a condition in which it was possible to imagine their continuing, eternally. "Immortal!" the word rose in my thoughts unbidden; and, straightway, I grew to wondering whether this might be the immortality of the gods.

And then, in the midst of my wondering and musing, something happened. Until then, I had been staying just within the shadow of the exit of the great rift. Now, without volition on my part, I drifted out of the semi-darkness, and began to move slowly across the arena—towards the House. At this, I gave up all thoughts of those prodigious Shapes above me—and could only stare, frightenedly, at the tremendous structure towards which I was being conveyed so remorselessly. Yet, though I searched earnestly, I could discover nothing that I had not already seen, and so became gradually calmer.

Presently, I had reached a point more than halfway between the House and the gorge. All around was spread the stark loneliness of the place, and the unbroken silence. Steadily, I neared the great building. Then, all at once, something caught my vision, something that came round one of the huge buttresses of the House, and so into full view. It was a gigantic thing, and moved with a curious lope, going almost upright, after the manner of a man. It was quite unclothed, and had a remarkable luminous appearance. Yet it was the face that attracted and frightened me the most. It was the face of a swine.

Silently, intently, I watched this horrible creature, and forgot my fear, momentarily, in my interest in its movements. It was making its way, cumbrously, round the building, stopping as it came to each window to peer in and shake at the bars, with which—as in this house—they were protected; and whenever it came to a door, it would push at it, fingering the fastening, stealthily. Evidently, it was searching for an ingress into the House.

I had come now to within less than a quarter of a mile of the great structure, and still I was compelled forward. Abruptly, the Thing turned and gazed, hideously, in my direction. It opened its mouth, and, for the first time, the stillness of that abominable place was broken, by a deep, booming note that sent an added thrill of apprehension through me.

Then, immediately, I became aware that it was coming towards me, swiftly and silently. In an instant, it had covered half the distance that lay between. And still, I was borne helplessly to meet it. Only a hundred yards, and the brutish ferocity of the giant face numbed me with a feeling of unmitigated horror. I could have screamed, in the supremeness of my fear; and then, in the very moment of my extremity and despair, I became conscious that I was looking down upon the arena, from a rapidly-increasing height. I was rising, rising. In an inconceivably short while, I had reached an altitude of many hundred feet. Beneath me, the spot that I had just left, was occupied by the foul Swine-creature. It had gone down on all fours and was snuffing and rooting, like a veritable hog, at the surface of the arena. A moment and it rose to its feet, clutching upwards, with an expression of desire upon its face such as I have never seen in this world.

Continually, I mounted higher. A few minutes, it seemed, and I had risen above the great mountains—floating, alone, afar in the redness. At a tremendous distance below, the arena showed, dimly; with the mighty House looking no larger than a tiny spot of green. The Swine-thing was no longer visible.

Presently, I passed over the mountains, out above the huge breadth of the plain. Far away, on its surface, in the direction of the ring-shaped sun, there showed a confused blur. I looked towards it, indifferently. It reminded me, somewhat, of the first glimpse I had caught of the mountain-amphitheatre.

With a sense of weariness, I glanced upwards at the immense ring of fire. What a strange thing it was! Then, as I stared, out from the dark centre, there spurted a sudden flare of extraordinary vivid fire. Compared with the size of the black centre, it was as naught; yet, in itself, stupendous. With awakened interest, I watched it carefully, noting its strange boiling and glowing. Then, in a moment, the whole thing grew dim and unreal, and so passed out of sight. Much amazed, I glanced down to the Plain from which I was still rising. Thus, I received a fresh surprise. The Plain—everything had vanished, and only a sea of red mist was spread, far below me. Gradually, as I stared this grew remote, and died away into a dim far mystery of red, against an unfathomable night. Awhile, and even this had gone, and I was wrapped in an impalpable, lightless gloom.

IV. THE EARTH

Thus I was, and only the memory that I had lived through the dark, once before, served to sustain my thoughts. A great time passed—ages. And then a single star broke its way through the darkness. It was the first of one of the outlying clusters of this universe. Presently, it was far behind, and all about me shone the splendour of the countless stars. Later, years it seemed, I saw the sun, a clot of flame. Around it, I made out, presently, several remote specks of light—the planets of the Solar system. And so I saw the earth again, blue and unbelievably minute. It grew larger, and became defined.

A long space of time came and went, and then at last I entered into the shadow of the world—plunging headlong into the dim and holy earth night. Overhead were the old constellations, and there was a crescent moon. Then, as I neared the earth's surface, a dimness swept over me, and I appeared to sink into a black mist.

For a while, I knew nothing. I was unconscious. Gradually, I became aware of a faint, distant whining. It became plainer. A desperate feeling of agony possessed me. I struggled madly for breath, and tried to shout. A moment, and I got my breath more easily. I was conscious that something was licking my hand. Something damp swept across my face. I heard a panting, and then again the whining. It seemed to come to my ears, now, with a sense of familiarity, and I opened my eyes. All was dark; but the feeling of oppression had left me. I was seated, and something was whining piteously, and licking me. I felt strangely confused, and, instinctively, tried to ward off the thing that licked. My head was curiously vacant, and, for the moment, I seemed incapable of action or thought. Then, things came back to me, and I called "Pepper," faintly. I was answered by a joyful bark, and renewed and frantic caresses.

In a little while, I felt stronger, and put out my hand for the matches. I groped about, for a few moments, blindly; then my hands lit upon them, and I struck a light, and looked confusedly around. All about me, I saw the old, familiar things. And there I sat, full of dazed wonders, until the flame of the match burnt my finger, and I dropped it; while a hasty expression of pain and anger, escaped my lips, surprising me with the sound of my own voice.

After a moment, I struck another match, and, stumbling across the room, lit the candles. As I did so, I observed that they had not burned away, but had been put out.

As the flames shot up, I turned, and stared about the study; yet there was nothing unusual to see; and, suddenly, a gust of irritation took me. What had happened? I held my head, with both hands, and tried to remember. Ah! the great, silent Plain, and the ring-shaped sun of red fire. Where were they? Where had I seen them? How long ago? I felt dazed and muddled. Once or twice, I walked up and down the room, unsteadily. My memory seemed dulled, and, already, the thing I had witnessed came back to me with an effort.

I have a remembrance of cursing, peevishly, in my bewilderment. Suddenly, I turned faint and giddy, and had to grasp at the table for support. During a few moments, I held on, weakly; and then managed to totter sideways into a chair. After a little time, I felt somewhat better, and succeeded in reaching the cupboard where, usually, I keep brandy and biscuits. I poured myself out a little of the stimulant, and drank it off. Then, taking a handful of biscuits, I returned to my chair, and began to devour them, ravenously. I was vaguely surprised at my hunger. I felt as though I had eaten nothing for an uncountably long while.

As I ate, my glance roved about the room, taking in its various details, and still searching, though almost unconsciously, for something tangible upon which to take hold, among the invisible mysteries that encompassed me. "Surely," I thought, "there must be something—" And, in the same instant, my gaze dwelt upon the face of the clock in the opposite corner. Therewith, I stopped eating, and just stared. For, though its ticking indicated most certainly that it was still going, the hands were pointing to a little *before* the hour of midnight; whereas it was, as well I knew, considerably *after* that time when I had witnessed the first of the strange happenings I have just described.

For perhaps a moment, I was astounded and puzzled. Had the hour been the same as when I had last seen the clock, I should have concluded that the hands had stuck in one place, while the internal mechanism went on as usual; but that would, in no way, account for the hands having travelled backward. Then, even as I turned the matter over in my wearied brain, the thought flashed upon me that it was now close upon the morning of the twenty-second, and that I had been unconscious to the visible world through the greater portion of the last twenty-four hours. The thought occupied my attention for a full minute; then I commenced to eat again. I was still very hungry.

During breakfast, next morning, I inquired casually of my sister regarding the date, and found my surmise correct. I had, indeed, been absent—at least in spirit—for nearly a day and a night.

My sister asked me no questions; for it is not by any means the first time that I have kept to my study for a whole day, and sometimes a couple of days at a time, when I have been particularly engrossed in my books or work.

And so the days pass on, and I am still filled with a wonder to know the meaning of all that I saw on that memorable night. Yet, well I know that my curiosity is little likely to be satisfied.

V. THE THING IN THE PIT

This house is, as I have said before, surrounded by a huge estate, and wild and uncultivated gardens.

Away at the back, distant some three hundred yards, is a dark, deep ravine—spoken of as the "Pit," by the peasantry. At the bottom, runs a sluggish stream so overhung by trees, as scarcely to be seen from above.

In passing, I must explain that this river has a subterranean origin, emerging suddenly at the East end of the ravine, and disappearing, as abruptly, beneath the cliffs that form its Western extremity.

It was some months after my vision (if vision it were) of the great Plain, that my attention was particularly attracted to the Pit.

I happened, one day, to be walking along its Southern edge, when, suddenly, several pieces of rock and shale were dislodged from the face of the cliff, immediately beneath me, and fell, with a sullen crash, through the trees. I heard them splash in the river, at the bottom; and then silence. I should not have given this incident more than a passing thought, had not Pepper, at once, begun to bark savagely; nor would he be silent when I bade him, which is most unusual behaviour on his part.

Feeling that there must be someone or something in the Pit, I went back to the house, quickly, for a stick. When I returned, Pepper had ceased his barks and was growling and smelling, uneasily, along the top.

Whistling to him, to follow me, I started to descend, cautiously. The depth, to the bottom of the Pit, must be about a hundred and fifty feet, and some time, as well as considerable care, was expended before we reached the bottom in safety.

Once down, Pepper and I started to explore along the banks of the river. It was very dark there, due to the overhanging trees, and I moved warily, keeping my glance about me and my stick ready.

Pepper was quiet now, and kept close to me all the time. Thus, we searched right up one side of the river, without hearing or seeing anything. Then, we crossed over—by the simple method of jumping—and commenced to beat our way back through the under-brush.

We had accomplished, perhaps, half the distance, when I heard, again, the sound of falling stones on the other side—the side from which we had just come. One large rock came thundering down through the tree-tops, struck the opposite bank, and bounded into the river, driving a great jet of water right over us. At this, Pepper gave out a deep growl; then stopped, and pricked up his ears. I listened, also.

A second later, a loud, half-human, half-pig-like squeal sounded from among the trees, apparently about half-way up the South cliff. It was answered by a similar note from the bottom of the Pit. At this, Pepper gave a short, sharp bark, and, springing across the little river, disappeared into the bushes.

Immediately afterwards, I heard his barks increase in depth and number, and, in between, there sounded a noise of confused jabbering. This ceased, and, in the suc-ceeding silence, there rose a semi-human yell of agony. Almost immediately, Pepper gave a long-drawn howl of pain, and then the shrubs were violently agitated, and he came running out with his tail down, and glancing as he ran over his shoulder. As he reached me, I saw that he was bleeding from what appeared to be a great claw wound in the side, that had almost laid bare his ribs.

Seeing Pepper thus mutilated, a furious feeling of anger seized me, and, whirling my staff, I sprang across, and into the bushes from which Pepper had emerged. As I forced my way through, I thought I heard a sound of breathing. Next instant, I had burst into a little clear space, just in time to see something, livid white in colour, disap-pear among the bushes on the opposite side. With a shout, I ran towards it; but, though I struck and probed among the bushes with my stick, I neither saw nor heard any-thing further; and so returned to Pepper. There, after bathing his wound in the river, I bound my wetted handkerchief round his body; having done which, we retreated up the ravine and into the daylight again.

On reaching the house, my sister inquired what had happened to Pepper, and I told her he had been fighting with a wild cat, of which I had heard there were several about.

I felt it would be better not to tell her how it had really happened; though, to be sure, I scarcely knew, myself; but this I did know, that the thing I had seen run into the bushes was no wild cat. It was much too big, and had, so far as I had observed, a skin like a hog's, only of a dead, unhealthy white colour. And then—it had run upright, or nearly so, upon its hind feet, with a motion somewhat resembling that of a human being. This much I had noticed in my brief glimpse, and, truth to tell, I felt a good deal of uneasiness, besides curiosity as I turned the matter over in my mind.

It was in the morning that the above incident had occurred.

Then, it would be after dinner, as I sat reading, that, happening to look up suddenly, I saw something peering in over the window-ledge—the eyes and ears alone showing.

"A pig, by Jove!" I said, and rose to my feet. Thus, I saw the thing more completely; but it was no pig—God alone knows what it was. It reminded me, vaguely, of the hideous Thing that had haunted the great arena. It had a grotesquely human mouth and jaw; but with no chin of which to speak. The nose was prolonged into a snout; thus it was that with the little eyes and queer ears, gave it such an extraordinarily swine-like appearance. Of forehead there was little, and the whole face was of an unwholesome white colour.

For, perhaps a minute, I stood looking at the thing, with an ever growing feeling of disgust, and some fear. The mouth kept jabbering, inanely, and once emitted a half-swinish grunt. I think it was the eyes that attracted me the most; they seemed to glow, at times, with a horribly human intelligence, and kept flickering away from my face, over the details of the room, as though my stare disturbed it.

It appeared to be supporting itself, by two claw-like hands upon the window-sill. These claws, unlike the face, were of a clayey brown hue, and bore an indistinct resemblance to human hands, in that they had four fingers and a thumb; though these were webbed up to the first joint, much as are a duck's. Nails it had also, but so long and powerful that they were more like the talons of an eagle than aught else.

As I have said, before, I felt some fear; though almost of an impersonal kind. I may explain my feeling better by saying that it was more a sensation of abhorrence; such as one might expect to feel, if brought in contact with something superhumanly foul; something unholy—belonging to some hitherto undreamt of state of existence.

I cannot say that I grasped these various details of the brute at the time. I think they seemed to come back to me, afterwards, as though imprinted upon my brain. I imagined more than I saw as I looked at the thing, and the material details grew upon me later.

For, perhaps a minute, I stared at the creature; then as my nerves steadied a little, I shook off the vague alarm that held me, and took a step towards the window. Even as I did so, the thing ducked and vanished. I rushed to the door, and looked round hurriedly; but only the tangled bushes and shrubs met my gaze.

I ran back into the house, and, getting my gun, sallied out to search through the gardens. As I went, I asked myself whether the thing I had just seen was likely to be the same of which I had caught a glimpse in the morning. I inclined to think it was.

I would have taken Pepper with me; but judged it better to give his wound a chance to heal. Besides, if the creature I had just seen was, as I imagined, his antagonist of the morning, it was not likely that he would be of much use.

I began my search, systematically. I was determined, if it were possible, to find and put an end to that swine-thing. This was, at least, a material Horror!

At first, I searched, cautiously; with the thought of Pepper's wound in my mind; but, as the hours passed, and not a sign of anything living, showed in the great, lonely gardens, I became less apprehensive. I felt almost as though I would welcome the sight of it. Anything seemed better than this silence, with the ever-present feeling that the creature might be lurking in every bush I passed. Later, I grew careless of danger, to the extent of plunging right through the bushes, probing with my gun-barrel as I went.

At times, I shouted; but only the echoes answered back. I thought thus perhaps to frighten or stir the creature to showing itself; but only succeeded in bringing my sister Mary out, to know what was the matter. I told her, that I had seen the wildcat that had wounded Pepper, and that I was trying to hunt it out of the bushes. She seemed only half satisfied, and went back into the house, with an expression of doubt upon her face. I wondered whether she had seen or guessed anything. For the rest of the afternoon, I prosecuted the search, anxiously. I felt that I should be unable to sleep, with that bestial thing haunting the shrubberies, and yet, when evening fell, I had seen nothing. Then, as I turned homewards, I heard a short, unintelligible noise, among the bushes to my right. Instantly, I turned, and, aiming quickly, fired in the direction of the sound. Immediately afterwards, I heard something scuttling away among the bushes. It moved rapidly, and in a minute had gone out of hearing. After a few steps I ceased my pursuit, realising how futile it must be in the fast gathering gloom; and so, with a curious feeling of depression, I entered the house.

That night, after my sister had gone to bed, I went round to all the windows and doors on the ground floor; and saw to it that they were securely fastened. This precaution was scarcely necessary as regards the windows, as all of those on the lower storey are strongly barred; but with the doors—of which there are five—it was wisely thought, as not one was locked.

Having secured these, I went to my study; yet, somehow, for once, the place jarred upon me; it seemed so huge and echoey. For some time, I tried to read; but, at last, finding it impossible I carried my book down to the kitchen, where a large fire was burning, and sat there.

I dare say, I had read for a couple of hours, when, suddenly, I heard a sound that made me lower my book, and listen, intently. It was a noise of something rubbing and fumbling against the back door. Once the door creaked, loudly; as though force were being applied to it. During those few, short moments, I experienced an indescribable feeling of terror, such as I should have believed impossible. My hands shook; a cold sweat broke out on me, and I shivered, violently.

Gradually, I calmed. The stealthy movements outside had ceased.

Then, for an hour, I sat, silent, and watchful. All at once, the feeling of fear took me again. I felt, as I imagine an animal must, under the eye of a snake. Yet now I could hear nothing. Still, there was no doubting that some unexplained influence was at work.

Gradually, imperceptibly almost, something stole on my ear—a sound that resolved itself into a faint murmur. Quickly it developed and grew into a muffled but hideous chorus of bestial shrieks. It appeared to rise from the bowels of the earth.

I heard a thud, and realised, in a dull, half comprehending way that I had dropped my book. After that, I just sat; and thus the daylight found me, when it crept wanly in through the barred, high windows of the great kitchen.

With the dawning light, the feeling of stupor and fear left me; and I came more into possession of my senses.

Thereupon, I picked up my book, and crept to the door to listen. Not a sound broke the chilly silence. For some minutes I stood there; then, very gradually and cautiously, I drew back the bolt and opening the door peeped out.

My caution was unneeded. Nothing was to be seen, save the grey vista of dreary, tangled bushes and trees, extending to the distant plantation.

With a shiver, I closed the door, and made my way, quietly, up to bed.

VI. THE SWINE-THINGS

It was evening, a week later. My sister sat in the garden, knitting. I was walking up and down, reading. My gun leant up against the wall of the house; for, since the advent of that strange thing in the gardens, I had deemed it wise to take precautions. Yet, through the whole week, there had been nothing to alarm me, either by sight or sound; so that I was able to look back, calmly, to the incident; though still with a sense of unmitigated wonder and curiosity.

I was, as I have just said, walking up and down, and somewhat engrossed in my book. Suddenly, I heard a crash, away in the direction of the Pit. With a quick movement, I turned and saw a tremendous column of dust rising high into the evening air.

My sister had risen to her feet, with a sharp exclamation of surprise and fright.

Telling her to stay where she was, I snatched up my gun, and ran towards the Pit. As I neared it, I heard a dull, rumbling sound, that grew quickly into a roar, split with deeper crashes, and up from the Pit drove a fresh volume of dust.

The noise ceased, though the dust still rose, tumultuously.

I reached the edge, and looked down; but could see nothing, save a boil of dust clouds swirling hither and thither. The air was so full of the small particles, that they blinded and choked me; and, finally, I had to run out from the smother, to breathe.

Gradually, the suspended matter sank, and hung in a panoply over the mouth of the Pit.

I could only guess at what had happened.

That there had been a land-slip of some kind, I had little doubt; but the cause was beyond my knowledge; and yet, even then, I had half imaginings; for, already, the thought had come to me, of those falling rocks, and that Thing in the bottom of the Pit; but, in the first minutes of confusion, I failed to reach the natural conclusion, to which the catastrophe pointed.

Slowly, the dust subsided, until, presently, I was able to approach the edge, and look down.

For a while, I peered impotently, trying to see through the reek. At first, it was impossible to make out anything. Then, as I stared, I saw something below, to my left, that moved. I looked intently towards it, and, presently, made out another, and then another—three dim shapes that appeared to be climbing up the side of the Pit. I could see them only indistinctly. Even as I stared and wondered, I heard a rattle of stones, somewhere to my right. I glanced across; but could see nothing. I leant forward, and peered over, and down into the Pit, just beneath where I stood; and saw no further than a hideous, white swine-face, that had risen to within a couple of yards of my feet. Below it, I could make out several others. As the Thing saw me, it gave a sudden, uncouth squeal, which was answered from all parts of the Pit. At that, a gust of horror and fear took me, and, bending down, I discharged my gun right into its face. Straightway, the creature disappeared, with a clatter of loose earth and stones.

There was a momentary silence, to which, probably, I owe my life; for, during it, I heard a quick patter of many feet, and, turning sharply, saw a troop of the creatures coming towards me, at a run. Instantly, I raised my gun and fired at the foremost, who plunged headlong, with a hideous howling. Then, I turned to run. More than halfway from the house to the Pit, I saw my sister—she was coming towards me. I could not see her face, distinctly, as the dusk had fallen; but there was fear in her voice as she called to know why I was shooting.

"Run!" I shouted in reply. "Run for your life!"

Without more ado, she turned and fled—picking up her skirts with both hands. As I followed, I gave a glance behind. The brutes were running on their hind legs—at times dropping on all fours.

I think it must have been the terror in my voice, that spurred Mary to run so; for I feel convinced that she had not, as yet, seen those hell-creatures that pursued.

On we went, my sister leading.

Each moment, the nearing sounds of the footsteps, told me that the brutes were gaining on us, rapidly. Fortunately, I am accustomed to live, in some ways, an active life. As it was, the strain of the race was beginning to tell severely upon me.

Ahead, I could see the back door—luckily it was open. I was some half-dozen yards behind Mary, now, and my breath was sobbing in my throat. Then, something touched my shoulder. I wrenched my head round, quickly, and saw one of those monstrous, pallid faces close to mine. One of the creatures, having outrun its companions, had almost overtaken me. Even as I turned, it made a fresh grab. With a sudden effort, I sprang to one side, and, swinging my gun by the barrel, brought it crashing down upon the foul creature's head. The Thing dropped, with an almost human groan.

Even this short delay had been nearly sufficient to bring the rest of the brutes down upon me; so that, without an instant's waste of time, I turned and ran for the door.

Reaching it, I burst into the passage; then, turning quickly, slammed and bolted the door, just as the first of the creatures rushed against it, with a sudden shock.

My sister sat, gasping, in a chair. She seemed in a fainting condition; but I had no time then to spend on her. I had to make sure that all the doors were fastened. Fortunately they were. The one leading from my study into the gardens, was the last to which I went. I had just had time to note that it was secured, when I thought I heard a noise outside. I stood perfectly silent, and listened. Yes! Now I could distinctly hear a sound of whispering, and something slithered over the panels, with a rasping, scratchy noise. Evidently, some of the brutes were feeling with their claw-hands, about the door, to discover whether there were any means of ingress.

That the creatures should so soon have found the door was—to me—a proof of their reasoning capabilities. It assured me that they must not be regarded, by any means, as mere animals. I had felt something of this before, when that first Thing peered in through my window. Then, I had applied the term superhuman to it, with an almost instinctive knowledge that the creature was something different from the brute-beast. Something beyond human; yet in no good sense; but rather as something foul and hostile to the *great* and *good* in humanity. In a word, as something intelligent, and yet inhuman. The very thought of the creatures filled me with revulsion.

Now, I bethought me of my sister, and, going to the cupboard, I got out a flask of brandy, and a wineglass. Taking these, I went down to the kitchen, carrying a lighted candle with me. She was not sitting in the chair, but had fallen out, and was lying upon the floor, face downwards.

Very gently, I turned her over, and raised her head, somewhat. Then, I poured a little of the brandy between her lips. After a while, she shivered, slightly. A little later, she gave several gasps, and opened her eyes. In a dreamy, unrealising way, she looked at me. Then her eyes closed, slowly, and I gave her a little more of the brandy. For, perhaps a minute longer, she lay silent, breathing quickly. All at once, her eyes opened again, and it seemed to me, as I looked, that the pupils were dilated, as though fear had come with returning consciousness. Then, with a movement so unexpected that I started backwards, she sat up. Noticing that she seemed giddy, I put out my hand to steady her. At that, she gave a loud scream, and, scrambling to her feet, ran from the room.

For a moment, I stayed there—kneeling, and holding the brandy flask. I was utterly puzzled and astonished.

Could she be afraid of me? But no! Why should she? I could only conclude that her nerves were badly shaken, and that she was temporarily unhinged. Upstairs, I heard a door bang, loudly, and I knew that she had taken refuge in her room. I put the flask down on the table. My attention was distracted by a noise in the direction of the back door. I went towards it, and listened. It appeared to be shaken, as though some of the creatures struggled with it, silently; but it was far too strongly constructed and hung to be easily moved.

Out in the gardens, rose a continuous sound. It might have been mistaken, by a casual listener, for the grunting and squealing of a herd of pigs. But, as I stood there, it came to me that there was sense and meaning to all those swinish noises. Gradually, I seemed able to trace a semblance in it to human speech—glutinous and sticky, as though each articulation were made with difficulty: yet, nevertheless, I was becoming convinced that it was no mere medley of sounds; but a rapid interchange of ideas.

By this time, it had grown quite dark in the passages, and from these came all the varied cries and groans of which an old house is so full after nightfall. It is, no doubt, because things are then quieter, and one has more leisure to hear. Also, there may be something in the theory that the sudden change of temperature, at sundown, affects the structure of the house, somewhat—causing it to contract and settle, as it were, for the night. However, this is as may be; but, on that night in particular, I would gladly have been quit of so many eerie noises. It seemed to me, that each crack and creak was the coming of one of those Things along the dark corridors; though I knew in my heart that this could not be, for I had seen, myself, that all the doors were secure.

Gradually, however, these sounds grew on my nerves to such an extent that, were it only to punish my cowardice, I felt I must make the round of the basement again, and, if anything were there, face it. And then, I would go up to my study; for I knew sleep was out of the question, with the house surrounded by creatures, half beasts, half something else, and entirely unholy.

Taking the kitchen lamp down from its hook, I made my way from cellar to cellar, and room to room; through pantry and coal-hole—along passages, and into the hundred-and-one little blind alleys and hidden nooks that form the basement of the old house. Then, when I knew I had been in every corner and cranny large enough to conceal aught of any size, I made my way to the stairs.

With my foot on the first step, I paused. It seemed to me, I heard a movement, apparently from the buttery, which is to the left of the staircase. It had been one of the first places I searched, and yet, I felt certain my ears had not deceived me. My nerves were strung now, and, with hardly any hesitation, I stepped up to the door, holding the lamp above my head. In a glance, I saw that the place was empty, save for the heavy, stone slabs, supported by brick pillars; and I was about to leave it, convinced that I had been mistaken; when, in turning, my light was flashed back from two bright spots outside the window, and high up. For a few moments, I stood there, staring. Then they moved—revolving slowly, and throwing out alternate scintillations of green and red; at least, so it appeared to me. I knew then that they were eyes.

Slowly, I traced the shadowy outline of one of the Things. It appeared to be holding on to the bars of the window, and its attitude suggested climbing. I went nearer to the window, and held the light higher. There was no need to be afraid of the creature; the bars were strong, and there was little danger of its being able to move them. And then, suddenly, in spite of the knowledge that the brute could not reach to harm me, I had a return of the horrible sensation of fear, that had assailed me on that night, a week previously. It was the same feeling of helpless, shuddering fright. I realised, dimly, that the creature's eyes were looking into mine with a steady, compelling stare. I tried to turn away; but could not. I seemed, now, to see the window through a mist.

Then, I thought other eyes came and peered, and yet others; until a whole galaxy of malignant, staring orbs seemed to hold me in thrall.

My head began to swim, and throb violently. Then, I was aware of a feeling of acute physical pain in my left hand. It grew more severe, and forced, literally forced, my attention. With a tremendous effort, I glanced down; and, with that, the spell that had held me was broken. I realised, then, that I had, in my agitation, unconsciously caught hold of the hot lamp-glass, and burnt my hand, badly. I looked up to the window, again. The misty appearance had gone, and, now, I saw that it was crowded with dozens of bestial faces. With a sudden access of rage, I raised the lamp, and hurled it, full at the window. It struck the glass (smashing a pane), and passed between two of the bars, out into the garden, scattering burning oil as it went. I heard several loud cries of pain, and, as my sight became accustomed to the dark, I discovered that the creatures had left the window.

Pulling myself together, I groped for the door, and, having found it, made my way upstairs, stumbling at each step. I felt dazed, as though I had received a blow on the head. At the same time, my hand smarted badly, and I was full of a nervous, dull rage against those Things.

Reaching my study, I lit the candles. As they burnt up, their rays were reflected from the rack of firearms on the side wall. At the sight, I remembered that I had there a power, which, as I had proved earlier, seemed as fatal to those monsters as to more ordinary animals; and I determined I would take the offensive.

First of all, I bound up my hand; for the pain was fast becoming intolerable. After that, it seemed easier, and I crossed the room, to the riflestand. There, I selected a heavy rifle—an old and tried weapon; and, having procured ammunition, I made my way up into one of the small towers, with which the house is crowned.

From there, I found that I could see nothing. The gardens presented a dim blur of shadows—a little blacker, perhaps, where the trees stood. That was all, and I knew that it was useless to shoot down into all that darkness. The only thing to be done, was to wait for the moon to rise; then, I might be able to do a little execution.

In the meantime, I sat still, and kept my ears open. The gardens were comparatively quiet now, and only an occasional grunt or squeal came up to me. I did not like this silence; it made me wonder on what devilry the creatures were bent. Twice, I left the tower, and took a walk through the house; but everything was silent.

Once, I heard a noise, from the direction of the Pit, as though more earth had fallen. Following this, and lasting for some fifteen minutes, there was a commotion among the denizens of the gardens. This died away, and, after that all was again quiet.

About an hour later, the moon's light showed above the distant horizon. From where I sat, I could see it over the trees; but it was not until it rose clear of them, that I could make out any of the details in the gardens below. Even then, I could see none of the brutes; until, happening to crane forward, I saw several of them lying prone, up against the wall of the house. What they were doing, I could not make out. It was, however, a chance too good to be ignored; and, taking aim, I fired at the one directly beneath. There was a shrill scream, and, as the smoke cleared away, I saw that it had turned on its back, and was writhing, feebly. Then, it was quiet. The others had disappeared.

Immediately after this, I heard a loud squeal, in the direction of the Pit. It was answered, a hundred times, from every part of the garden. This gave me some notion of the number of the creatures, and I began to feel that the whole affair was becoming even more serious than I had imagined.

As I sat there, silent and watchful, the thought came to me—Why was all this? What were these Things? What did it mean? Then my thoughts flew back to that vision (though, even now, I doubt whether it was a vision) of the Plain of Silence. What did that mean? I wondered—And that Thing in the arena? Ugh! Lastly, I thought of the house I had seen in that far-away place. That house, so like this in every detail of external structure, that it might have been modeled from it; or this from that. I had never thought of that——

At this moment, there came another long squeal, from the Pit, followed, a second later, by a couple of shorter ones. At once, the garden was filled with answering cries. I stood up, quickly, and looked over the parapet. In the moonlight, it seemed as though the shrubberies were alive. They tossed hither and thither, as though shaken by a strong, irregular wind; while a continuous rustling, and a noise of scampering feet, rose up to me. Several times, I saw the moonlight gleam on running, white figures among the bushes, and, twice, I fired. The second time, my shot was answered by a short squeal of pain.

A minute later, the gardens lay silent. From the Pit, came a deep, hoarse Babel of swine-talk. At times, angry cries smote the air, and they would be answered by multitudinous gruntings. It occurred to me, that they were holding some kind of a council, perhaps to discuss the problem of entering the house. Also, I thought that they seemed much enraged, probably by my successful shots.

It occurred to me, that now would be a good time to make a final survey of our defences. This, I proceeded to do at once; visiting the whole of the basement again, and examining each of the doors. Luckily, they are all, like the back one, built of solid, iron-studded oak. Then, I went upstairs to the study. I was more anxious about this door. It is, palpably, of a more modern make than the others, and, though a stout piece of work, it has little of their ponderous strength.

I must explain here, that there is a small, raised lawn on this side of the house, upon which this door opens—the windows of the study being barred on this account. All the other entrances—excepting the great gateway, which is never opened—are in the lower storey.

VII. THE ATTACK

I spent some time, puzzling how to strengthen the study door. Finally, I went down to the kitchen, and, with some trouble, brought up several heavy pieces of timber. These, I wedged up, slantwise, against it, from the floor, nailing them top and bottom. For half-an-hour, I worked hard, and, at last, got it shored to my mind.

Then, feeling easier, I resumed my coat, which I had laid aside, and proceeded to attend to one or two matters before returning to the tower. It was whilst thus employed, that I heard a fumbling at the door, and the latch was tried. Keeping silence, I waited. Soon, I heard several of the creatures outside. They were grunting to one another, softly. Then, for a minute, there was quietness. Suddenly, there sounded a quick, low grunt, and the door creaked under a tremendous pressure. It would have burst inwards; but for the supports I had placed. The strain ceased, as quickly as it had begun, and there was more talk.

Presently, one of the Things squealed, softly, and I heard the sound of others approaching. There was a short confabulation; then again, silence; and I realised that they had called several more to assist. Feeling that now was the supreme moment, I stood ready, with my rifle presented. If the door gave, I would, at least, slay as many as possible.

Again came the low signal; and, once more, the door cracked, under a huge force. For, a minute perhaps, the pressure was kept up; and I waited, nervously; expecting each moment to see the door come down with a crash. But no; the struts held, and the attempt proved abortive. Then followed more of their horrible, grunting talk, and, whilst it lasted, I thought I distinguished the noise of fresh arrivals.

After a long discussion, during which the door was several times shaken, they became quiet once more, and I knew that they were going to make a third attempt to break it down. I was almost in despair. The props had been severely tried in the two previous attacks, and I was sorely afraid that this would prove too much for them.

At that moment, like an inspiration, a thought flashed into my troubled brain. Instantly, for it was no time to hesitate, I ran from the room, and up stair after stair. This time, it was not to one of the towers, that I went; but out on to the flat, leaded roof itself. Once there, I raced across to the parapet, that walls it round, and looked down. As I did so, I heard the short, grunted signal, and, even up there, caught the crying of the door under the assault.

There was not a moment to lose, and, leaning over, I aimed, quickly, and fired. The report rang sharply, and, almost blending with it, came the loud splud of the bullet striking its mark. From below, rose a shrill wail; and the door ceased its groaning. Then, as I took my weight from off the parapet, a huge piece of the stone coping slid from under me, and fell with a crash among the disorganised throng beneath. Several horrible shrieks quavered through the night air, and then I heard a sound of scampering feet. Cautiously, I looked over. In the moonlight, I could see the great copingstone, lying right across the threshold of the door. I thought I saw something under it—several things, white; but I could not be sure.

And so a few minutes passed.

As I stared, I saw something come round, out of the shadow of the house. It was one of the Things. It went up to the stone, silently, and bent down. I was unable to see what it did. In a minute it stood up. It had something in its talons, which it put to its mouth and tore at. . . .

For the moment, I did not realise. Then, slowly, I comprehended. The Thing was stooping again. It was horrible. I started to load my rifle. When I looked again, the monster was tugging at the stone—moving it to one side. I leant the rifle on the coping, and pulled the trigger. The brute collapsed, on its face, and kicked, slightly.

Simultaneously, almost, with the report, I heard another sound—that of breaking glass. Waiting, only to recharge my weapon, I ran from the roof, and down the first two flights of stairs.

Here, I paused to listen. As I did so, there came another tinkle of falling glass. It appeared to come from the floor below. Excitedly, I sprang down the steps, and, guided by the rattle of the window-sash, reached the door of one of the empty bedrooms, at the back of the house. I thrust it open. The room was but dimly illuminated by the moonlight; most of the light being blotted out by moving figures at the window. Even as I stood, one crawled through, into the room. Levelling my weapon, I fired point-blank at it—filling the room with a deafening bang. When the smoke cleared, I saw that the room was empty, and the window free. The room was much lighter. The night air blew in, coldly, through the shattered panes. Down below, in the night, I could hear a soft moaning, and a confused murmur of swine-voices.

Stepping to one side of the window, I reloaded, and then stood there, waiting. Presently, I heard a scuffling noise. From where I stood in the shadow, I could see, without being seen.

Nearer came the sounds, and then I saw something come up above the sill, and clutch at the broken window-frame. It caught a piece of the woodwork; and, now, I could make out that it was a hand and arm. A moment later, the face of one of the Swine-creatures rose into view. Then, before I could use my rifle, or do anything, there came a sharp crack—cr-a-c-k; and the window-frame gave way under the weight of the Thing. Next instant, a squashing thud, and a loud outcry, told me that it had fallen to the ground. With a savage hope that it had been killed, I went to the window. The moon had gone behind a cloud, so that I could see nothing; though a steady hum of jabbering, just beneath where I stood, indicated that there were several more of the brutes close at hand.

As I stood there, looking down, I marvelled how it had been possible for the creatures to climb so far; for the wall is comparatively smooth, while the distance to the ground must be, at least, eighty feet.

All at once, as I bent, peering, I saw something, indistinctly, that cut the grey shadow of the house-side, with a black line. It passed the window, to the left, at a distance of about two feet. Then, I remembered that it was a gutter-pipe, that had been put there some years ago, to carry off the rain water. I had forgotten about it. I could see, now, how the creatures had managed to reach the window. Even as the solution came to me, I heard a faint slithering, scratching noise, and knew that another of the brutes was coming. I waited some odd moments; then leant out of the window and felt the pipe. To my delight, I found that it was quite loose, and I managed, using the rifle-barrel as a crow-bar, to lever it out from the wall. I worked quickly. Then, taking hold with both bands, I wrenched the whole concern away, and hurled it down—with the Thing still clinging to it—into the garden.

For a few minutes longer, I waited there, listening; but, after the first general outcry, I heard nothing. I knew, now, that there was no more reason to fear an attack from this quarter. I had removed the only means of reaching the window, and, as none of the other windows had any adjacent water pipes, to tempt the climbing powers of the monsters, I began to feel more confident of escaping their clutches.

Leaving the room, I made my way down to the study. I was anxious to see how the door had withstood the test of that last assault. Entering, I lit two of the candles, and then turned to the door. One of the large props had been displaced, and, on that side, the door had been forced inward some six inches.

It was Providential that I had managed to drive the brutes away just when I did! And that coping-stone! I wondered, vaguely, how I had managed to dislodge it. I had not noticed it loose, as I took my shot; and then, as I stood up, it had slipped away from beneath me. . . . I felt that I owed the dismissal of the attacking force, more to its timely fall than to my rifle. Then the thought came, that I had better seize this chance to shore up the door, again. It was evident that the creatures had not returned since the fall of the coping-stone; but who was to say how long they would keep away?

There and then, I set-to, at repairing the door—working hard and anxiously. First, I went down to the basement, and, rummaging round, found several pieces of heavy oak planking. With these, I returned to the study, and, having removed the props, placed the planks up against the door. Then, I nailed the heads of the struts to these, and, driving them well home at the bottoms, nailed them again there.

Thus, I made the door stronger than ever; for now it was solid with the backing of boards, and would, I felt convinced, stand a heavier pressure than hitherto, without giving way.

After that, I lit the lamp which I had brought from the kitchen, and went down to have a look at the lower windows.

Now that I had seen an instance of the strength the creatures possessed, I felt considerable anxiety about the windows on the ground floor—in spite of the fact that they were so strongly barred.

I went first to the buttery, having a vivid remembrance of my late adventure there. The place was chilly, and the wind, soughing in through the broken glass, produced an eerie note. Apart from the general air of dismalness, the place was as I had left it the night before. Going up to the window, I examined the bars, closely; noting, as I did so, their comfortable thickness. Still, as I looked more intently, it seemed to me, that the middle bar was bent slightly from the straight; yet it was but trifling, and it might have been so for years. I had never, before, noticed them particularly.

I put my hand through the broken window, and shook the bar. It was as firm as a rock. Perhaps the creatures had tried to "start" it, and, finding it beyond their power, ceased from the effort. After that, I went round to each of the windows, in turn; examining them with careful attention; but nowhere else could I trace anything to show that there had been any tampering. Having finished my survey, I went back to the study, and poured myself out a little brandy. Then to the tower to watch.

VIII. AFTER THE ATTACK

It was now about three a.m., and, presently, the Eastern sky began to pale with the coming of dawn. Gradually, the day came, and, by its light, I scanned the gardens, earnestly; but nowhere could I see any signs of the brutes. I leant over, and glanced down to the foot of the wall, to see whether the body of the Thing I had shot the night before was still there. It was gone. I supposed that others of the monsters had removed it during the night.

Then, I went down on to the roof, and crossed over to the gap from which the coping-stone had fallen. Reaching it, I looked over. Yes, there was the stone, as I had seen it last; but there was no appearance of anything beneath it; nor could I see the creatures I had killed, after its fall. Evidently, they also had been taken away. I turned, and went down to my study. There, I sat down, wearily. I was thoroughly tired. It was quite light now; though the sun's rays were not, as yet, perceptibly hot. A clock chimed the hour of four. . . .

I awoke, with a start, and looked round, hurriedly. The clock in the corner, indicated that it was three o'clock. It was already afternoon. I must have slept for nearly eleven hours.

With a jerky movement, I sat forward in the chair, and listened. The house was perfectly silent. Slowly, I stood up, and yawned. I felt desperately tired, still, and sat down again; wondering what it was that had waked me.

It must have been the clock striking, I concluded, presently; and was commencing to doze off, when a sudden noise brought me back, once more, to life. It was the sound of a step, as of a person moving cautiously down the corridor, towards my study. In an instant, I was on my feet, and grasping my rifle. Noiselessly, I waited. Had the creatures broken in, whilst I slept? Even as I questioned, the steps reached my door, halted momentarily, and then continued down the passage. Silently, I tiptoed to the doorway, and peeped out. Then, I experienced such a feeling of relief, as must a reprieved criminal—it was my sister. She was going towards the stairs.

I stepped into the hall, and was about to call to her, when it occurred to me, that it was very queer she should have crept past my door, in that stealthy manner. I was puzzled, and, for one brief moment, the thought occupied my mind, that it was not she, but some fresh mystery of the house. Then, as I caught a glimpse of her old petticoat, the thought passed as quickly as it had come, and I half laughed. There could be no mistaking that ancient garment. Yet, I wondered what she was doing; and, remembering her condition of mind, on the previous day, I felt that it might be best to follow, quietly—taking care not to alarm her—and see what she was going to do. If she behaved rationally, well and good; if not, I should have to take steps to restrain her. I could run no unnecessary risks, under the danger that threatened us.

Quickly, I reached the head of the stairs, and paused a moment. Then, I heard a sound that sent me leaping down, at a mad rate—it was the rattle of bolts being unshot. That foolish sister of mine was actually unbarring the back door.

Just as her hand was on the last bolt, I reached her. She had not seen me, and, the first thing she knew, I had hold of her arm. She glanced up quickly, like a frightened animal, and screamed aloud.

"Come, Mary!" I said, sternly, "what's the meaning of this nonsense? Do you mean to tell me you don't understand the danger, that you try to throw our two lives away in this fashion!"

To this, she replied nothing; only trembled, violently, gasping and sobbing, as though in the last extremity of fear.

Through some minutes, I reasoned with her; pointing out the need for caution, and asking her to be brave. There was little to be afraid of now, I explained—and, I tried to believe that I spoke the truth—but she must be sensible, and not attempt to leave the house for a few days.

At last, I ceased, in despair. It was no use talking to her; she was, obviously, not quite herself for the time being. Finally, I told her she had better go to her room, if she could not behave rationally.

Still, she took not any notice. So, without more ado, I picked her up in my arms, and carried her there. At first, she screamed, wildly; but had relapsed into silent trembling, by the time I reached the stairs.

Arriving at her room, I laid her upon the bed. She lay there quietly enough, neither speaking nor sobbing—just shaking in a very ague of fear. I took a rug from a chair near by, and spread it over her. I could do nothing more for her, and so, crossed to where Pepper lay in a big basket. My sister had taken charge of him since his wound, to nurse him, for it had proved more severe than I had thought, and I was pleased to note that, in spite of her state of mind, she had looked after the old dog, carefully. Stooping, I spoke to him, and, in reply, he licked my hand, feebly. He was too ill to do more.

Then, going to the bed, I bent over my sister, and asked her how she felt; but she only shook the more, and, much as it pained me, I had to admit that my presence seemed to make her worse.

And so, I left her—locking the door, and pocketing the key. It seemed to be the only course to take.

The rest of the day, I spent between the tower and my study. For food, I brought up a loaf from the pantry, and on this, and some claret, I lived for that day.

What a long, weary day it was. If only I could have gone out into the gardens, as is my wont, I should have been content enough; but to be cooped in this silent house, with no companion, save a mad woman and a sick dog, was enough to prey upon the nerves of the hardiest. And out in the tangled shrubberies that surrounded the house, lurked—for all I could tell—those infernal Swine-creatures waiting their chance. Was ever a man in such straits?

Once, in the afternoon, and again, later, I went to visit my sister. The second time, I found her tending Pepper; but, at my approach, she slid over, unobtrusively, to the far corner, with a gesture that saddened me beyond belief. Poor girl! her fear cut me intolerably, and I would not intrude on her, unnecessarily. She would be better, I trusted, in a few days; meanwhile, I could do nothing; and I judged it still needful— hard as it seemed—to keep her confined to her room. One thing there was that I took for encouragement, she had eaten some of the food I had taken to her, on my first visit.

And so the day passed.

As the evening drew on, the air grew chilly, and I began to make preparations for passing a second night in the tower—taking up two additional rifles, and a heavy ulster. The rifles I loaded, and laid alongside my other; as I intended to make things warm for any of the creatures who might show, during the night. I had plenty of ammunition, and I thought to give the brutes such a lesson, as should show them the uselessness of attempting to force an entrance.

After that, I made the round of the house again; paying particular attention to the props that supported the study door. Then, feeling that I had done all that lay in my power to insure our safety, I returned to the tower; calling in on my sister and Pepper, for a final visit, on the way. Pepper was asleep; but woke, as I entered, and wagged his tail, in recognition. I thought he seemed slightly better. My sister was lying on the bed; though whether asleep or not, I was unable to tell; and thus I left them.

Reaching the tower, I made myself as comfortable as circumstances would permit, and settled down to watch through the night. Gradually, darkness fell, and soon the details of the gardens were merged into shadows. During the first few hours, I sat, alert, listening for any sound that might help to tell me if anything were stirring down below. It was far too dark for my eyes to be of much use.

Slowly, the hours passed; without anything unusual happening. And the moon rose, showing the gardens, apparently empty, and silent. And so, through the night, without disturbance or sound.

Towards morning, I began to grow stiff and cold, with my long vigil; also, I was getting very uneasy, concerning the continued quietness on the part of the creatures. I mistrusted it, and would sooner, far, have had them attack the house, openly. Then, at least, I should have known my danger, and been able to meet it; but to wait like this, through a whole night, picturing all kinds of unknown devilment, was to jeopardise one's sanity. Once or twice, the thought came to me, that, perhaps, they had gone; but, in my heart, I found it impossible to believe that it was so.

IX. IN THE CELLARS

At last, what with being tired and cold, and the uneasiness that possessed me, I resolved to take a walk through the house; first calling in at the study, for a glass of brandy to warm me. This, I did, and, while there, I examined the door, carefully; but found all as I had left it the night before.

The day was just breaking, as I left the tower; though it was still too dark in the house to be able to see without a light, and I took one of the study candles with me on my round. By the time I had finished the ground floor, the daylight was creeping in, wanly, through the barred windows. My search had shown me nothing fresh. Everything appeared to be in order, and I was on the point of extinguishing my candle, when the thought suggested itself to me to have another glance round the cellars. I had not, if I remember rightly, been into them since my hasty search on the evening of the attack.

For, perhaps, the half of a minute, I hesitated. I would have been very willing to forego the task—as, indeed, I am inclined to think any man well might—for of all the great, awe-inspiring rooms in this house, the cellars are the hugest and weirdest. Great, gloomy caverns of places, unlit by any ray of daylight. Yet, I would not shirk the work. I felt that to do so would smack of sheer cowardice. Besides, as I reassured myself, the cellars were really the most unlikely places in which to come across any-thing dangerous; considering that they can be entered, only through a heavy oaken door, the key of which, I carry always on my person.

It is in the smallest of these places that I keep my wine; a gloomy hole close to the foot of the cellar stairs; and beyond which, I have seldom proceeded. Indeed, save for the rummage round, already mentioned, I doubt whether I had ever, before, been right through the cellars.

As I unlocked the great door, at the top of the steps, I paused, nervously, a moment, at the strange, desolate smell that assailed my nostrils. Then, throwing the barrel of my weapon forward, I descended, slowly, into the darkness of the underground regions.

Reaching the bottom of the stairs, I stood for a minute, and listened. All was silent, save for a faint drip, drip of water, falling, drop by drop, somewhere to my left. As I stood, I noticed how quietly the candle burnt; never a flicker nor flare, so utterly windless was the place.

Quietly, I moved from cellar to cellar. I had but a very dim memory of their arrangement. The impressions left by my first search were blurred. I had recollections of a succession of great cellars, and of one, greater than the rest, the roof of which was upheld by pillars; beyond that my mind was hazy, and predominated by a sense of cold and darkness and shadows. Now, however, it was different; for, although nervous, I was sufficiently collected to be able to look about me, and note the structure and size of the different vaults I entered.

Of course, with the amount of light given by my candle, it was not possible to examine each place, minutely; but I was enabled to notice, as I went along, that the walls appeared to be built with wonderful precision and finish; while, here and there, an occasional, massive pillar shot up to support the vaulted roof.

Thus, I came, at last, to the great cellar that I remembered. It is reached, through a huge, arched entrance, on which I observed strange, fantastic carvings, which threw queer shadows under the light of my candle. As I stood, and examined these, thought-fully, it occurred to me how strange it was, that I should be so little acquainted with my own house. Yet, this may be easily understood, when one realises the size of this ancient pile, and the fact that only my old sister and I live in it, occupying a few of the rooms, such as our wants decide.

Holding the light high, I passed on into the cellar, and, keeping to the right, paced slowly up, until I reached the further end. I walked quietly, and looked cautiously about, as I went. But, so far as the light showed, I saw nothing unusual.

At the top, I turned to the left, still keeping to the wall, and so continued, until I had traversed the whole of the vast chamber. As I moved along, I noticed that the floor was composed of solid rock, in places covered with a damp mould, in others bare, or almost so, save for a thin coating of light-grey dust.

I had halted at the doorway. Now, however, I turned, and made my way up the centre of the place; passing among the pillars, and glancing to right and left, as I moved. About half way up the cellar, I stubbed my foot against something that gave out a metallic sound. Stooping quickly, I held the candle, and saw that the object I had kicked, was a large, metal ring. Bending lower, I cleared the dust from around it, and, presently, discovered that it was attached to a ponderous trap-door, black with age.

Feeling excited, and wondering to where it could lead, I laid my gun on the floor, and, sticking the candle in the trigger guard, took the ring in both hands, and pulled. The trap creaked loudly—the sound echoing, vaguely, through the huge place—and opened, heavily.

Propping the edge on my knee, I reached for the candle, and held it in the opening, moving it to right and left; but could see nothing. I was puzzled and surprised. There were no signs of steps, nor even the appearance of there ever having been any. Nothing; save an empty blackness. I might have been looking down into a bottomless, sideless well. Then, even as I stared, full of perplexity, I seemed to hear, far down, as though from untold depths, a faint whisper of sound. I bent my head, quickly, more into the opening, and listened, intently. It may have been fancy; but I could have sworn to hearing a soft titter, that grew into a hideous, chuckling, faint and distant. Startled, I leapt backward, letting the trap fall, with a hollow clang, that filled the place with echoes. Even then, I seemed to hear that mocking, suggestive laughter; but this, I knew, must be my imagination. The sound, I had heard, was far too slight to penetrate through the cumbrous trap.

For a full minute, I stood there, quivering—glancing, nervously, behind and before; but the great cellar was silent as a grave, and, gradually, I shook off the frightened sensation. With a calmer mind, I became again curious to know into what that trap opened; but could not, then, summon sufficient courage to make a further investigation. One thing I felt, however, was that the trap ought to be secured. This, I accomplished by placing upon it several large pieces of "dressed" stone, which I had noticed in my tour along the East wall.

Then, after a final scrutiny of the rest of the place, I retraced my way through the cellars, to the stairs, and so reached the daylight, with an infinite feeling of relief, that the uncomfortable task was accomplished.

X. THE TIME OF WAITING

The sun was now warm, and shining brightly, forming a wondrous contrast to the dark and dismal cellars; and it was with comparatively light feelings, that I made my way up to the tower, to survey the gardens. There, I found everything quiet, and, after a few minutes, went down to Mary's room.

Here, having knocked, and received a reply, I unlocked the door. My sister was sitting, quietly, on the bed; as though waiting. She seemed quite herself again, and made no attempt to move away, as I approached; yet, I observed that she scanned my face, anxiously, as though in doubt, and but half assured in her mind that there was nothing to fear from me.

To my questions, as to how she felt, she replied, sanely enough, that she was hungry, and would like to go down to prepare breakfast, if I did not mind. For a minute, I meditated whether it would be safe to let her out. Finally, I told her she might go, on condition that she promised not to attempt to leave the house, or meddle with any of the outer doors. At my mention of the doors, a sudden look of fright crossed her face; but she said nothing, save to give the required promise, and then left the room, silently.

Crossing the floor, I approached Pepper. He had waked as I entered; but, beyond a slight yelp of pleasure, and a soft rapping with his tail, had kept quiet. Now, as I patted him, he made an attempt to stand up, and succeeded, only to fall back on his side, with a little yowl of pain.

I spoke to him, and bade him lie still. I was greatly delighted with his improvement, and also with the natural kindness of my sister's heart, in taking such good care of him, in spite of her condition of mind. After a while, I left him, and went downstairs, to my study.

In a little time, Mary appeared, carrying a tray on which smoked a hot breakfast. As she entered the room, I saw her gaze fasten on the props that supported the study door; her lips tightened, and I thought she paled, slightly; but that was all. Putting the tray down at my elbow, she was leaving the room, quietly, when I called her back. She came, it seemed, a little timidly, as though startled; and I noted that her hand clutched at her apron, nervously.

"Come, Mary," I said. "Cheer up! Things look brighter. I've seen none of the creatures since yesterday morning, early."

She looked at me, in a curiously puzzled manner; as though not comprehending. Then, intelligence swept into her eyes, and fear; but she said nothing, beyond an unintelligible murmur of acquiescence. After that, I kept silence; it was evident that any reference to the Swine-things, was more than her shaken nerves could bear.

Breakfast over, I went up to the tower. Here, during the greater part of the day, I maintained a strict watch over the gardens. Once or twice, I went down to the basement, to see how my sister was getting along. Each time, I found her quiet, and curiously submissive. Indeed, on the last occasion, she even ventured to address me, on her own account, with regard to some household matter that needed attention. Though this was done with an almost extraordinary timidity, I hailed it with happiness, as being the first word, voluntarily spoken, since the critical moment, when I had caught her unbarring the back door, to go out among those waiting brutes. I wondered whether she was aware of her attempt, and how near a thing it had been; but refrained from questioning her, thinking it best to let well alone.

That night, I slept in a bed; the first time for two nights. In the morning, I rose early, and took a walk through the house. All was as it should be, and I went up to the tower, to have a look at the gardens. Here, again, I found perfect quietness.

At breakfast, when I met Mary, I was greatly pleased to see that she had sufficiently regained command over herself, to be able to greet me in a perfectly natural manner. She talked sensibly and quietly; only keeping carefully from any mention of the past couple of days. In this, I humored her, to the extent of not attempting to lead the conversation in that direction.

Earlier in the morning, I had been to see Pepper. He was mending, rapidly; and bade fair to be on his legs, in earnest, in another day or two. Before leaving the breakfast table, I made some reference to his improvement. In the short discussion that followed, I was surprised to gather, from my sister's remarks, that she was still under the impression that his wound had been given by the wild cat, of my invention. It made me feel almost ashamed of myself for deceiving her. Yet, the lie had been told to prevent her from being frightened. And then, I had been sure that she must have known the truth, later, when those brutes had attacked the house.

During the day, I kept on the alert; spending much of my time, as on the previous day, in the tower; but not a sign could I see of the Swine-creatures, nor hear any sound. Several times, the thought had come to me, that the Things had, at last, left us; but, up to this time, I had refused to entertain the idea, seriously; now, however, I began to feel that there was reason for hope. It would soon be three days since I had seen any of the Things; but still, I intended to use the utmost caution. For all that I could tell, this protracted silence might be a ruse to tempt me from the house—

perhaps right into their arms. The thought of such a contingency, was, alone, sufficient to make me circumspect.

So it was, that the fourth, fifth and sixth days went by, quietly, without my making any attempt to leave the house.

On the sixth day, I had the pleasure of seeing Pepper, once more, upon his feet; and, though still very weak, he managed to keep me company during the whole of that day.

XI. THE SEARCHING OF THE GARDENS

How slowly the time went; and never a thing to indicate that any of the brutes still infested the gardens.

It was on the ninth day that, finally, I decided to run the risk, if any there were, and sally out. With this purpose in view, I loaded one of the shot-guns, carefully—choosing it, as being more deadly than a rifle, at close quarters; and then, after a final scrutiny of the grounds, from the tower, I called Pepper to follow me, and made my way down to the basement.

At the door, I must confess to hesitating a moment. The thought of what might be awaiting me among the dark shrubberies, was by no means calculated to encourage my resolution. It was but a second, though, and then I had drawn the bolts, and was standing on the path outside the door.

Pepper followed, stopping at the doorstep to sniff, suspiciously; and carrying his nose up and down the jambs, as though following a scent. Then, suddenly, he turned, sharply, and started to run here and there, in semicircles and circles, all around the door; finally returning to the threshold. Here, he began again to nose about.

Hitherto, I had stood, watching the dog; yet, all the time, with half my gaze on the wild tangle of gardens, stretching round me. Now, I went towards him, and, bending down, examined the surface of the door, where he was smelling. I found that the wood was covered with a network of scratches, crossing and recrossing one another, in inextricable confusion. In addition to this, I noticed that the doorposts, themselves, were gnawed in places. Beyond these, I could find nothing; and so, standing up, I began to make the tour of the house wall.

Pepper, as soon as I walked away, left the door, and ran ahead, still nosing and sniffing as he went along. At times, he stopped to investigate. Here, it would be a bullet-hole in the pathway, or, perhaps, a powder stained wad. Anon, it might be a piece of torn sod, or a disturbed patch of weedy path; but, save for such trifles, he found nothing. I observed him, critically, as he went along, and could discover nothing of uneasiness, in his demeanour, to indicate that he felt the nearness of any of the creatures. By this, I was assured that the gardens were empty, at least for the present, of those hateful Things. Pepper could not be easily deceived, and it was a relief to feel that he would know, and give me timely warning, if there were any danger.

Reaching the place where I had shot that first creature, I stopped, and made a careful scrutiny; but could see nothing. From there, I went on to where the great coping-stone had fallen. It lay on its side, apparently just as it had been left when I shot the brute that was moving it. A couple of feet to the right of the nearer end, was a great dent in the ground; showing where it had struck. The other end was still within the indentation—half in, and half out. Going nearer, I looked at the stone, more closely. What a huge piece of masonry it was! And that creature had moved it, single-handed, in its attempt to reach what lay below.

I went round to the further end of the stone. Here, I found that it was possible to see under it, for a distance of nearly a couple of feet. Still, I could see nothing of the stricken creatures, and I felt much surprised. I had, as I have before said, guessed that the remains had been removed; yet, I could not conceive that it had been done so thoroughly as not to leave some certain sign, beneath the stone, indicative of their fate. I had seen several of the brutes struck down beneath it, with such force that they must have been literally driven into the earth; and now, not a vestige of them was to be seen—not even a bloodstain.

I felt more puzzled, than ever, as I turned the matter over in my mind; but could think of no plausible explanation; and so, finally, gave it up, as one of the many things that were unexplainable.

From there, I transferred my attention to the study door. I could see, now, even more plainly, the effects of the tremendous strain, to which it had been subjected; and I marvelled how, even with the support afforded by the props, it had withstood the attacks, so well. There were no marks of blows—indeed, none had been given—but the door had been literally riven from its hinges, by the application of enormous, silent force. One thing that I observed affected me profoundly—the head of one of the props had been driven right through a panel. This was, of itself, sufficient to show how huge an effort the creatures had made to break down the door, and how nearly they had succeeded.

Leaving, I continued my tour round the house, finding little else of interest; save at the back, where I came across the piece of piping I had torn from the wall, lying among the long grass underneath the broken window.

Then, I returned to the house, and, having re-bolted the back door, went up to the tower. Here, I spent the afternoon, reading, and occasionally glancing down into the gardens. I had determined, if the night passed quietly, to go as far as the Pit, on the morrow. Perhaps, I should be able to learn, then, something of what had happened. The day slipped away, and the night came, and went much as the last few nights had gone.

When I rose, the morning had broken, fine and clear; and I determined to put my project into action. During breakfast, I considered the matter, carefully; after which, I went to the study for my shot-gun. In addition, I loaded, and slipped into my pocket, a small, but heavy, pistol. I quite understood that, if there were any danger, it lay in the direction of the Pit, and I intended to be prepared.

Leaving the study, I went down to the back door, followed by Pepper. Once outside, I took a quick survey of the surrounding gardens, and then set off towards the Pit. On the way, I kept a sharp outlook, holding my gun, handily. Pepper was running ahead, I noticed, without any apparent hesitation. From this, I augured that there was no imminent danger to be apprehended, and I stepped out more quickly in his wake. He had reached the top of the Pit, now, and was nosing his way along the edge.

A minute later, I was beside him, looking down into the Pit. For a moment, I could scarcely believe that it was the same place, so greatly was it changed. The dark, wooded ravine of a fortnight ago, with a foliage-hidden stream, running sluggishly, at the bottom, existed no longer. Instead, my eyes showed me a ragged chasm, partly filled with a gloomy lake of turbid water. All one side of the ravine was stripped of underwood, showing the bare rock.

A little to my left, the side of the Pit appeared to have collapsed altogether, forming a deep V-shaped cleft in the face of the rocky cliff. This rift ran, from the upper edge of the ravine, nearly down to the water, and penetrated into the Pit side, to a distance of some forty feet. Its opening was, at least, six yards across; and, from this, it seemed to taper into about two. But, what attracted my attention, more than even the stupendous split itself, was a great hole, some distance down the cleft, and right in the angle of the V. It was clearly defined, and not unlike an arched doorway in shape; though, lying as it did in the shadow, I could not see it very distinctly.

The opposite side of the Pit, still retained its verdure; but so torn in places, and everywhere covered with dust and rubbish, that it was hardly distinguishable as such.

My first impression, that there had been a land slip, was, I began to see, not sufficient, of itself, to account for all the changes I witnessed. And the water——? I turned, suddenly; for I had become aware that, somewhere to my right, there was a noise of running water. I could see nothing; but, now that my attention had been caught, I distinguished, easily, that it came from somewhere at the East end of the Pit.

Slowly, I made my way in that direction; the sound growing plainer as I advanced, until in a little, I stood right above it. Even then, I could not perceive the cause, until I knelt down, and thrust my head over the cliff. Here, the noise came up to me, plainly; and I saw, below me, a torrent of clear water, issuing from a small fissure in the Pit side, and rushing down the rocks, into the lake beneath. A little further along the cliff, I saw another, and, beyond that again, two smaller ones. These, then, would help to account for the quantity of water in the Pit; and, if the fall of rock and earth had blocked the outlet of the stream at the bottom, there was little doubt but that it was contributing a very large share.

Yet, I puzzled my head to account for the generally *shaken* appearance of the place—these streamlets, and that huge cleft, further up the ravine! It seemed to me, that more than the land-slip was necessary to account for these. I could imagine an earthquake, or a great *explosion*, creating some such condition of affairs as existed; but, of these, there had been neither. Then, I stood up, quickly, remembering that crash, and the cloud of dust that had followed, directly, rushing high into the air. But I shook my head, unbelievingly. No! it must have been the noise of the falling rocks and earth, I had heard; of course, the dust would fly, naturally. Still, in spite of my reasoning, I had an uneasy feeling, that this theory did not satisfy my sense of the probable; and yet, was any other, that I could suggest, likely to be half so plausible? Pepper had been sitting on the grass, while I conducted my examination. Now, as I turned up the North side of the ravine, he rose and followed.

Slowly, and keeping a careful watch in all directions, I made the circuit of the Pit; but found little else, that I had not already seen. From the West end, I could see the four waterfalls, uninterruptedly. They were some considerable distance up from the surface of the lake—about fifty feet, I calculated.

For a little while longer, I loitered about; keeping my eyes and ears open, but still, without seeing or hearing anything suspicious. The whole place was wonderfully quiet; indeed, save for the continuous murmur of the water, at the top end, no sound, of any description, broke the silence.

All this while, Pepper had shown no signs of uneasiness. This seemed, to me, to indicate that, for the time being, at least, there was none of the Swine-creatures in the vicinity. So far as I could see, his attention appeared to have been taken, chiefly, with scratching and sniffing among the grass at the edge of the Pit. At times, he would leave the edge, and run along towards the house, as though following invisible tracks; but, in all cases, returning after a few minutes. I had little doubt but that he was really tracing out the footsteps of the Swine-things; and the very fact that each one seemed to lead him back to the Pit, appeared to me, a proof that the brutes had all returned whence they came.

At noon, I went home, for dinner. During the afternoon, I made a partial search of the gardens, accompanied by Pepper; but, without coming upon anything to indicate the presence of the creatures.

Once, as we made our way through the shrubberies, Pepper rushed in among some bushes, with a fierce yelp. At that, I jumped back, in sudden fright, and threw my gun forward, in readiness; only to laugh, nervously, as Pepper reappeared, chasing an unfortunate cat. Towards evening, I gave up the search, and returned to the house. All at once, as we were passing a great clump of bushes, on our right, Pepper disappeared, and I could hear him sniffing and growling among them, in a suspicious manner. With my gun-barrel, I parted the intervening shrubbery, and looked inside. There was nothing to be seen, save that many of the branches were bent down, and broken; as though some animal had made a lair there, at no very previous date. It was probably, I thought, one of the places occupied by some of the Swine-creatures, on the night of the attack.

Next day, I resumed my search through the gardens; but without result. By evening, I had been right through them, and now, I knew, beyond the possibility of doubt, that there were no longer any of the Things concealed about the place. Indeed, I have often thought since, that I was correct in my earlier surmise, that they had left soon after the attack.

XII. THE SUBTERRANEAN PIT

Another week came and went, during which I spent a great deal of my time about the Pit mouth. I had come to the conclusion a few days earlier, that the arched hole, in the angle of the great rift, was the place through which the Swine-things had made their exit, from some unholy place in the bowels of the world. How near the probable truth this went, I was to learn later.

It may be easily understood, that I was tremendously curious, though in a frightened way, to know to what infernal place that hole led; though, so far, the idea had not struck me, seriously, of making an investigation. I was far too much imbued with a sense of horror of the Swine-creatures, to think of venturing, willingly, where there was any chance of coming into contact with them.

Gradually, however, as time passed, this feeling grew insensibly less; so that when, a few days later, the thought occurred to me that it might be possible to clamber down and have a look into the hole, I was not so exceedingly averse to it, as might have been imagined. Still, I do not think, even then, that I really intended to try any such fool-hardy adventure. For all that I could tell, it might be certain death, to enter that doleful looking opening. And yet, such is the pertinacity of human curiosity, that, at last, my chief desire was but to discover what lay beyond that gloomy entrance.

Slowly, as the days slid by, my fear of the Swine-things became an emotion of the past—more an unpleasant, incredible memory, than aught else.

Thus, a day came, when, throwing thoughts and fancies adrift, I procured a rope from the house, and, having made it fast to a stout tree, at the top of the rift, and some little distance back from the Pit edge, let the other end down into the cleft, until it dangled right across the mouth of the dark hole.

Then, cautiously, and with many misgivings as to whether it was not a mad act that I was attempting, I climbed slowly down, using the rope as a support, until I reached the hole. Here, still holding on to the rope, I stood, and peered in. All was perfectly dark, and not a sound came to me. Yet, a moment later, it seemed that I could hear something. I held my breath, and listened; but all was silent as the grave, and I breathed freely once more. At the same instant, I heard the sound again. It was like a noise of labored breathing—deep and sharp-drawn. For a short second, I stood, petrified; not able to move. But now the sounds had ceased again, and I could hear nothing.

As I stood there, anxiously, my foot dislodged a pebble, which fell inward, into the dark, with a hollow chink. At once, the noise was taken up and repeated a score of times; each succeeding echo being fainter, and seeming to travel away from me, as though into remote distance. Then, as the silence fell again, I heard that stealthy breathing. For each respiration I made, I could hear an answering breath. The sounds appeared to be coming nearer; and then, I heard several others; but fainter and more distant. Why I did not grip the rope, and spring up out of danger, I cannot say. It was as though I had been paralysed. I broke out into a profuse sweat, and tried to moisten my lips with my tongue. My throat had gone suddenly dry, and I coughed, huskily. It came back to me, in a dozen, horrible, throaty tones, mockingly. I peered, helplessly, into the gloom; but still nothing showed. I had a strange, choky sensation, and again

I coughed, dryly. Again the echo took it up, rising and falling, grotesquely, and dying slowly into a muffled silence.

Then, suddenly, a thought came to me, and I held my breath. The other breathing stopped. I breathed again, and, once more, it re-commenced. But now, I no longer feared. I knew that the strange sounds were not made by any lurking Swine-creature; but were simply the echo of my own respirations.

Yet, I had received such a fright, that I was glad to scramble up the rift, and haul up the rope. I was far too shaken and nervous to think of entering that dark hole then, and so returned to the house. I felt more myself next morning; but even then, I could not summon up sufficient courage to explore the place.

All this time, the water in the Pit had been creeping slowly up, and now stood but a little below the opening. At the rate at which it was rising, it would be level with the floor in less than another week; and I realised that, unless I carried out my investigations soon, I should probably never do so at all; as the water would rise and rise, until the opening, itself, was submerged.

It may have been that this thought stirred me to act; but, whatever it was, a couple of days later, saw me standing at the top of the cleft, fully equipped for the task.

This time, I was resolved to conquer my shirking, and go right through with the matter. With this intention, I had brought, in addition to the rope, a bundle of candles, meaning to use them as a torch; also my double-barreled shot-gun. In my belt, I had a heavy horse-pistol, loaded with buck-shot.

As before, I fastened the rope to the tree. Then, having tied my gun across my shoulders, with a piece of stout cord, I lowered myself over the edge of the Pit. At this movement, Pepper, who had been eyeing my actions, watchfully, rose to his feet, and ran to me, with a half bark, half wail, it seemed to me, of warning. But I was resolved on my enterprise, and bade him lie down. I would much have liked to take him with me; but this was next to impossible, in the existing circumstances. As my face dropped level with the Pit edge, he licked me, right across the mouth; and then, seizing my sleeve between his teeth, began to pull back, strongly. It was very evident that he did not want me to go. Yet, having made up my mind, I had no intention of giving up the attempt; and, with a sharp word to Pepper, to release me, I continued my descent, leaving the poor old fellow at the top, barking and crying like a forsaken pup.

Carefully, I lowered myself from projection to projection. I knew that a slip might mean a wetting.

Reaching the entrance, I let go the rope, and untied the gun from my shoulders. Then, with a last look at the sky—which I noticed was clouding over, rapidly—I went forward a couple of paces, so as to be shielded from the wind, and lit one of the candles. Holding it above my head, and grasping my gun, firmly, I began to move on, slowly, throwing my glances in all directions.

For the first minute, I could hear the melancholy sound of Pepper's howling, coming down to me. Gradually, as I penetrated further into the darkness, it grew fainter; until, in a little while, I could hear nothing. The path tended downward somewhat, and to the left. Thence it kept on, still running to the left, until I found that it was leading me right in the direction of the house.

Very cautiously, I moved onward, stopping, every few steps, to listen. I had gone, perhaps, a hundred yards, when, suddenly, it seemed to me that I caught a faint sound, somewhere along the passage behind. With my heart thudding heavily, I listened. The noise grew plainer, and appeared to be approaching, rapidly. I could hear it distinctly, now. It was the soft padding of running feet. In the first moments of fright, I stood, irresolute; not knowing whether to go forward or backward. Then, with a sudden realisation of the best thing to do, I backed up to the rocky wall on my right, and, holding the candle above my head, waited—gun in hand—cursing my foolhardy curiosity, for bringing me into such a strait.

I had not long to wait, but a few seconds, before two eyes reflected back from the gloom, the rays of my candle. I raised my gun, using my right hand only, and aimed quickly. Even as I did so, something leapt out of the darkness, with a blustering bark of joy that woke the echoes, like thunder. It was Pepper. How he had contrived to scramble down the cleft, I could not conceive. As I brushed my hand, nervously, over his coat, I noticed that he was dripping; and concluded that he must have tried to follow me, and fallen into the water; from which he would not find it very difficult to climb.

Having waited a minute, or so, to steady myself, I proceeded along the way, Pepper following, quietly. I was curiously glad to have the old fellow with me. He was company, and, somehow, with him at my heels, I was less afraid. Also, I knew how quickly his keen ears would detect the presence of any unwelcome creature, should there be such, amid the darkness that wrapped us.

For some minutes we went slowly along; the path still leading straight towards the house. Soon, I concluded, we should be standing right beneath it, did the path but carry far enough. I led the way, cautiously, for another fifty yards, or so. Then, I stopped, and held the light high; and reason enough I had to be thankful that I did so; for there, not three paces forward, the path vanished, and, in place, showed a hollow blackness, that sent sudden fear through me.

Very cautiously, I crept forward, and peered down; but could see nothing. Then, I crossed to the left of the passage, to see whether there might be any continuation of the path. Here, right against the wall, I found that a narrow track, some three feet wide, led onward. Carefully, I stepped on to it; but had not gone far, before I regretted venturing thereon. For, after a few paces, the already narrow way, resolved itself into a mere ledge, with, on the one side the solid, unyielding rock, towering up, in a great wall, to the unseen roof, and, on the other, that yawning chasm. I could not help reflecting how helpless I was, should I be attacked there, with no room to turn, and where even the recoil of my weapon might be sufficient to drive me headlong into the depths below.

To my great relief, a little further on, the track suddenly broadened out again to its original breadth. Gradually, as I went onward, I noticed that the path trended steadily to the right, and so, after some minutes, I discovered that I was not going forward; but simply circling the huge abyss. I had, evidently, come to the end of the great passage.

Five minutes later, I stood on the spot from which I had started; having been completely round, what I guessed now to be a vast pit, the mouth of which must be at least a hundred yards across.

For some little time, I stood there, lost in perplexing thought. "What does it all mean?" was the cry that had begun to reiterate through my brain.

A sudden idea struck me, and I searched round for a piece of stone. Presently, I found a bit of rock, about the size of a small loaf. Sticking the candle upright in a crevice of the floor, I went back from the edge, somewhat, and, taking a short run, launched the stone forward into the chasm—my idea being to throw it far enough to keep it clear of the sides. Then, I stooped forward, and listened; but, though I kept perfectly quiet, for at least a full minute, no sound came back to me from out of the dark.

I knew, then, that the depth of the hole must be immense; for the stone, had it struck anything, was large enough to have set the echoes of that weird place, whispering for an indefinite period. Even as it was, the cavern had given back the sounds of my foot-falls, multitudinously. The place was awesome, and I would willingly have retraced my steps, and left the mysteries of its solitudes unsolved; only, to do so, meant admitting defeat.

Then, a thought came, to try to get a view of the abyss. It occurred to me that, if I placed my candles round the edge of the hole, I should be able to get, at least, some dim sight of the place.

I found, on counting, that I had brought fifteen candles, in the bundle—my first intention having been, as I have already said, to make a torch of the lot. These, I proceeded to place round the Pit mouth, with an interval of about twenty yards between each.

Having completed the circle, I stood in the passage, and endeavoured to get an idea of how the place looked. But I discovered, immediately, that they were totally insufficient for my purpose. They did little more than make the gloom visible. One thing they did, however, and that was, they confirmed my opinion of the size of the opening; and, although they showed me nothing that I wanted to see; yet the contrast they afforded to the heavy darkness, pleased me, curiously. It was as though fifteen tiny stars shone through the subterranean night.

Then, even as I stood, Pepper gave a sudden howl, that was taken up by the echoes, and repeated with ghastly variations, dying away, slowly. With a quick movement, I held aloft the one candle that I had kept, and glanced down at the dog; at the same moment, I seemed to hear a noise, like a diabolical chuckle, rise up from the hitherto, silent depths of the Pit. I started; then, I recollected that it was, probably, the echo of Pepper's howl.

Pepper had moved away from me, up the passage, a few steps; he was nosing along the rocky floor; and I thought I heard him lapping. I went towards him, holding the candle low. As I moved, I heard my boot go sop, sop; and the light was reflected from something that glistened, and crept past my feet, swiftly towards the Pit. I bent lower, and looked; then gave vent to an expression of surprise. From somewhere, higher up the path, a stream of water was running quickly in the direction of the great opening, and growing in size every second.

Again, Pepper gave vent to that deep-drawn howl, and, running at me, seized my coat, and attempted to drag me up the path towards the entrance. With a nervous gesture, I shook him off, and crossed quickly over to the left-hand wall. If anything were coming, I was going to have the wall at my back.

Then, as I stared anxiously up the pathway, my candle caught a gleam, far up the passage. At the same moment, I became conscious of a murmurous roar, that grew louder, and filled the whole cavern with deafening sound. From the Pit, came a deep, hollow echo, like the sob of a giant. Then, I had sprung to one side, on to the narrow ledge that ran round the abyss, and, turning, saw a great wall of foam sweep past me, and leap tumultuously into the waiting chasm. A cloud of spray burst over me, extinguishing my candle, and wetting me to the skin. I still held my gun. The three nearest candles went out; but the further ones gave only a short flicker. After the first rush, the flow of water eased down to a steady stream, maybe a foot in depth; though I could not see this, until I had procured one of the lighted candles, and, with it, started to reconnoitre. Pepper had, fortunately, followed me as I leapt for the ledge, and now, very much subdued, kept close behind.

A short examination showed me that the water reached right across the passage, and was running at a tremendous rate. Already, even as I stood there, it had deepened. I could make only a guess at what had happened. Evidently, the water in the ravine had broken into the passage, by some means. If that were the case, it would go on increasing in volume, until I should find it impossible to leave the place. The thought was frightening. It was evident that I must make my exit as hurriedly as possible.

Taking my gun by the stock, I sounded the water. It was a little under knee-deep. The noise it made, plunging down into the Pit, was deafening. Then, with a call to Pepper, I stepped out into the flood, using the gun as a staff. Instantly, the water boiled up over my knees, and nearly to the tops of my thighs, with the speed at which it was racing. For one short moment, I nearly lost my footing; but the thought of what lay behind, stimulated me to a fierce endeavour, and, step-by-step, I made headway.

Of Pepper, I knew nothing at first. I had all I could do to keep on my legs; and was overjoyed, when he appeared beside me. He was wading manfully along. He is a big dog, with longish thin legs, and I suppose the water had less grasp on them, than upon mine. Anyway, he managed a great deal better than I did; going ahead of me, like a guide, and wittingly—or otherwise—helping, somewhat, to break the force of the water. On we went, step by step, struggling and gasping, until somewhere about a hundred yards had been safely traversed. Then, whether it was because I was taking less care, or that there was a slippery place on the rocky floor, I cannot say; but, suddenly, I slipped, and fell on my face. Instantly, the water leapt over me in a cataract, hurling me down, towards that bottomless hole, at a frightful speed. Frantically I struggled; but it was impossible to get a footing. I was helpless, gasping and drowning. All at once, something gripped my coat, and brought me to a standstill. It was Pepper. Missing me, he must have raced back, through the dark turmoil, to find me, and then caught, and held me, until I was able to get to my feet.

I have a dim recollection of having seen, momentarily, the gleams of several lights; but, of this, I have never been quite sure. If my impressions are correct, I must have been washed down to the very brink of that awful chasm, before Pepper managed to bring me to a standstill. And the lights, of course, could only have been the distant flames of the candles, I had left burning. But, as I have said, I am not by any means sure. My eyes were full of water, and I had been badly shaken.

And there was I, without my helpful gun, without light, and sadly confused, with the water deepening; depending solely upon my old friend Pepper, to help me out of that hellish place.

I was facing the torrent. Naturally, it was the only way in which I could have sustained my position a moment; for even old Pepper could not have held me long against that terrific strain, without assistance, however blind, from me.

Perhaps a minute passed, during which it was touch and go with me; then, gradually I re-commenced my tortuous way up the passage. And so began the grimmest fight with death, from which ever I hope to emerge victorious. Slowly, furiously, almost hopelessly, I strove; and that faithful Pepper led me, dragged me, upward and onward, until, at last, ahead I saw a gleam of blessed light. It was the entrance. Only a few yards further, and I reached the opening, with the water surging and boiling hungrily around my loins.

And now I understood the cause of the catastrophe. It was raining heavily, literally in torrents. The surface of the lake was level with the bottom of the opening—nay! more than level, it was above it. Evidently, the rain had swollen the lake, and caused this premature rise; for, at the rate the ravine had been filling, it would not have reached the entrance for a couple more days.

Luckily, the rope by which I had descended, was streaming into the opening, upon the inrushing waters. Seizing the end, I knotted it securely round Pepper's body; then, summoning up the last remnant of my strength, I commenced to swarm up the side of the cliff. I reached the Pit edge, in the last stage of exhaustion. Yet, I had to make one more effort, and haul Pepper into safety.

Slowly and wearily, I hauled on the rope. Once or twice, it seemed that I should have to give up; for Pepper is a weighty dog, and I was utterly done. Yet, to let go, would have meant certain death to the old fellow, and the thought spurred me to greater exertions. I have but a very hazy remembrance of the end. I recall pulling, through moments that lagged strangely. I have also some recollection of seeing

Pepper's muzzle, appearing over the Pit edge, after what seemed an indefinite period of time. Then, all grew suddenly dark.

XIII. THE TRAP IN THE GREAT CELLAR

I suppose I must have swooned; for, the next thing I remember, I opened my eyes, and all was dusk. I was lying on my back, with one leg doubled under the other, and Pepper was licking my ears. I felt horribly stiff, and my leg was numb, from the knee, downwards. For a few minutes, I lay thus, in a dazed condition; then, slowly, I struggled to a sitting position, and looked about me.

It had stopped raining, but the trees still dripped, dismally. From the Pit, came a continuous murmur of running water. I felt cold and shivery. My clothes were sodden, and I ached all over. Very slowly, the life came back into my numbed leg, and, after a little, I essayed to stand up. This, I managed, at the second attempt; but I was very tottery, and peculiarly weak. It seemed to me, that I was going to be ill, and I made shift to stumble my way towards the house. My steps were erratic, and my head confused. At each step that I took, sharp pains shot through my limbs.

I had gone, perhaps, some thirty paces, when a cry from Pepper, drew my attention, and I turned, stiffly, towards him. The old dog was trying to follow me; but could come no further, owing to the rope, with which I had hauled him up, being still tied round his body, the other end not having been unfastened from the tree. For a moment, I fumbled with the knots, weakly; but they were wet and hard, and I could do nothing. Then, I remembered my knife, and, in a minute, the rope was cut.

How I reached the house, I scarcely know, and, of the days that followed, I remember still less. Of one thing, I am certain, that, had it not been for my sister's untiring love and nursing, I had not been writing at this moment.

When I recovered my senses, it was to find that I had been in bed for nearly two weeks. Yet another week passed, before I was strong enough to totter out, into the gardens. Even then, I was not able to walk so far as the Pit. I would have liked to ask my sister, how high the water had risen; but felt it was wiser not to mention the subject to her. Indeed, since then, I have made a rule never to speak to her about the strange things, that happen in this great, old house.

It was not until a couple of days later, that I managed to get across to the Pit. There, I found that, in my few weeks' absence, there had been wrought a wondrous change. Instead of the three-parts filled ravine, I looked out upon a great lake, whose placid surface, reflected the light, coldly. The water had risen to within half a dozen feet of the Pit edge. Only in one part was the lake disturbed, and that was above the place where, far down under the silent waters, yawned the entrance to the vast, underground Pit. Here, there was a continuous bubbling; and, occasionally, a curious sort of sobbing gurgle would find its way up from the depth. Beyond these, there was nothing to tell of the things that were hidden beneath. As I stood there, it came to me how wonderfully things had worked out. The entrance to the place whence the Swine-creatures had come, was sealed up, by a power that made me feel there was nothing more to fear from them. And yet, with the feeling, there was a sensation that, now, I should never learn anything further, of the place from which those dreadful Things had come. It was completely shut off and concealed from human curiosity forever.

Strange—in the knowledge of that underground hell-hole—how apposite has been the naming of the Pit. One wonders how it originated, and when. Naturally, one concludes that the shape and depth of the ravine would suggest the name "Pit." Yet, is it not possible that it has, all along, held a deeper significance, a hint—could one but have guessed—of the greater, more stupendous Pit that lies far down in the earth, beneath this old house? Under this house! Even now, the idea is strange and terrible to me. For I have proved, beyond doubt, that the Pit yawns right below the house, which is evidently supported, somewhere above the centre of it, upon a tremendous, arched roof, of solid rock.

It happened in this wise, that, having occasion to go down to the cellars, the thought occurred to me to pay a visit to the great vault, where the trap is situated; and see whether everything was as I had left it.

Reaching the place, I walked slowly up the centre, until I came to the trap. There it was, with the stones piled upon it, just as I had seen it last. I had a lantern with me, and the idea came to me, that now would be a good time to investigate whatever lay under the great, oak slab. Placing the lantern on the floor, I tumbled the stones off the trap, and, grasping the ring, pulled the door open. As I did so, the cellar became filled with the sound of a murmurous thunder, that rose from far below. At the same time, a damp wind blew up into my face, bringing with it a load of fine spray. Therewith, I dropped the trap, hurriedly, with a half frightened feeling of wonder.

For a moment, I stood puzzled. I was not particularly afraid. The haunting fear of the Swine-things had left me, long ago; but I was certainly nervous and astonished.

Then, a sudden thought possessed me, and I raised the ponderous door, with a feeling of excitement. Leaving it standing upon its end, I seized the lantern, and, kneeling down, thrust it into the opening. As I did so, the moist wind and spray drove in my eyes, making me unable to see, for a few moments. Even when my eyes were clear, I could distinguish nothing below me, save darkness, and whirling spray.

Seeing that it was useless to expect to make out anything, with the light so high, I felt in my pockets for a piece of twine, with which to lower it further into the opening. Even as I fumbled, the lantern slipped from my fingers, and hurtled down into the darkness. For a brief instant, I watched its fall, and saw the light shine on a tumult of white foam, some eighty or a hundred feet below me. Then it was gone. My sudden surmise was correct, and now, I knew the cause of the wet and noise. The great cellar was connected with the Pit, by means of the trap, which opened right above it; and the moisture, was the spray, rising from the water, falling into the depths.

In an instant, I had an explanation of certain things, that had hitherto puzzled me. Now, I could understand why the noises—on the first night of the invasion—had seemed to rise directly from under my feet. And the chuckle that had sounded when first I opened the trap! Evidently, some of the Swine-things must have been right beneath me.

Another thought struck me. Were the creatures all drowned? Would they drown? I remembered how unable I had been to find any traces to show that my shooting had been really fatal. Had they life, as we understand life, or were they ghouls? These thoughts flashed through my brain, as I stood in the dark, searching my pockets for matches. I had the box in my hand now, and, striking a light, I stepped to the trap door, and closed it. Then, I piled the stones back upon it; after which, I made my way out from the cellars.

And so, I suppose the water goes on, thundering down into that bottomless hell-pit. Sometimes, I have an inexplicable desire to go down to the great cellar, open the trap, and gaze into the impenetrable, spray-damp darkness. At times, the desire becomes almost overpowering, in its intensity. It is not mere curiosity, that prompts me; but more as though some unexplained influence were at work. Still, I never go; and intend to fight down the strange longing, and crush it; even as I would the unholy thought of self-destruction.

This idea of some intangible force being exerted, may seem reasonless. Yet, my instinct warns me, that it is not so. In these things, reason seems to me less to be trusted than instinct.

One thought there is, in closing, that impresses itself upon me, with ever growing insistence. It is, that I live in a very strange house; a very awful house. And I have begun to wonder whether I am doing wisely in staying here. Yet, if I left, where could I go, and still obtain the solitude, and the sense of her presence,* that alone make my old life bearable?

XIV. THE SEA OF SLEEP

For a considerable period after the last incident which I have narrated in my diary, I had serious thoughts of leaving this house, and might have done so; but for the great and wonderful thing, of which I am about to write.

How well I was advised, in my heart, when I stayed on here—spite of those visions and sights of unknown and unexplainable things; for, had I not stayed, then I had not seen again the face of her I loved. Yes, though few know it, none now save my sister Mary, I have loved and, ah! me—lost.

I would write down the story of those sweet, old days; but it would be like the tearing of old wounds; yet, after that which has happened, what need have I to care? For she has come to me out of the unknown. Strangely, she warned me; warned me passionately against this house; begged me to leave it; but admitted, when I questioned her, that she could not have come to me, had I been elsewhere. Yet, in spite of this, still she warned me, earnestly; telling me that it was a place, long ago given over to evil, and under the power of grim laws, of which none here have knowledge. And I—I just asked her, again, whether she would come to me elsewhere, and she could only stand, silent.

It was thus, that I came to the place of the Sea of Sleep—so she termed it, in her dear speech with me. I had stayed up, in my study, reading; and must have dozed over the book. Suddenly, I awoke and sat upright, with a start. For a moment, I looked round, with a puzzled sense of something unusual. There was a misty look about the room, giving a curious softness to each table and chair and furnishing.

Gradually, the mistiness increased; growing, as it were, out of nothing. Then, slowly, a soft, white light began to glow in the room. The flames of the candles shone through it, palely. I looked from side to side, and found that I could still see each piece of furniture; but in a strangely unreal way, more as though the ghost of each table and chair had taken the place of the solid article.

---

*An apparently unmeaning interpolation. I can find no previous reference in the MS. to this matter. It becomes clearer, however, in the light of succeeding incidents.—ED.

Gradually, as I looked, I saw them fade and fade; until, slowly, they resolved into nothingness. Now, I looked again at the candles. They shone wanly, and, even as I watched, grew more unreal, and so vanished. The room was filled, now, with a soft, yet luminous, white twilight, like a gentle mist of light. Beyond this, I could see nothing. Even the walls had vanished.

Presently, I became conscious that a faint, continuous sound, pulsed through the silence that wrapped me. I listened intently. It grew more distinct, until it appeared to me that I harked to the breathings of some great sea. I cannot tell how long a space passed thus; but, after a while, it seemed that I could see through the mistiness; and, slowly, I became aware that I was standing upon the shore of an immense and silent sea. This shore was smooth and long, vanishing to right and left of me, in extreme distances. In front, swam a still immensity of sleeping ocean. At times, it seemed to me that I caught a faint glimmer of light, under its surface; but of this, I could not be sure. Behind me, rose up, to an extraordinary height, gaunt, black cliffs. Overhead, the sky was of a uniform cold grey colour—the whole place being lit by a stupendous globe of pale fire, that swam a little above the far horizon, and shed a foam-like light above the quiet waters.

Beyond the gentle murmur of the sea, an intense stillness prevailed. For a long while, I stayed there, looking out across its strangeness. Then, as I stared, it seemed that a bubble of white foam floated up out of the depths, and then, even now I know not how it was, I was looking upon, nay, looking *into* the face of Her—aye! into her face—into her soul; and she looked back at me, with such a commingling of joy and sadness, that I ran towards her, blindly; crying strangely to her, in a very agony of remembrance, of terror, and of hope, to come to me. Yet, spite of my crying, she stayed out there upon the sea, and only shook her head, sorrowfully; but, in her eyes was the old earth-light of tenderness, that I had come to know, before all things, ere we were parted.

At her perverseness, I grew desperate, and essayed to wade out to her; yet, though I would, I could not. Something, some invisible barrier, held me back, and I was fain to stay where I was, and cry out to her in the fullness of my soul, "O, my Darling, my Darling—" but could say no more, for very intensity. And, at that, she came over, swiftly, and touched me, and it was as though heaven had opened. Yet, when I reached out my hands to her, she put me from her with tenderly stern hands, and I was abashed—"

NOTE.—Here, the writing becomes indecipherable, owing to the damaged condition of this part of the MS. Below, I print such fragments as are legible.—ED.

The Fragments

(The legible portions of the mutilated leaves.)

. . . through tears . . . noise of eternity in my ears, we parted. . . . She whom I love. O, my God . . . !

I was a great time dazed, and then I was alone in the blackness of the night. I knew that I journeyed back, once more, to the known universe. Presently, I emerged from that enormous darkness. I had come among the stars . . . vast time . . . the sun, far and remote.

I entered into the gulf that separates our system from the outer suns. As I sped across the dividing dark, I watched, steadily, the ever-growing brightness and size of our sun. Once, I glanced back to the stars, and saw them shift, as it were, in my wake, against the mighty background of night, so vast was the speed of my passing spirit.

I drew nigher to our system, and now I could see the shine of Jupiter. Later, I distinguished the cold, blue gleam of the earth-light. . . . I had a moment of bewilderment. All about the sun there seemed to be bright objects, moving in rapid orbits. Inward, nigh to the savage glory of the sun, there circled two darting points of light, and, further off, there flew a blue, shining speck, that I knew to be the earth. It circled the sun in a space that seemed to be no more than an earth-minute.

. . . nearer with great speed. I saw the radiances of Jupiter and Saturn, spinning, with incredible swiftness, in huge orbits. And ever I drew more nigh, and looked out upon this strange sight—the visible circling of the planets about the mother sun. It was as though time had been annihilated for me; so that a year was no more to my unfleshed spirit, than is a moment to an earth-bound soul.

The speed of the planets, appeared to increase; and, presently, I was watching the sun, all ringed about with hair-like circles of different coloured fire—the paths of the planets, hurtling at mighty speed, about the central flame. . . .

. . . the sun grew vast, as though it leapt to meet me. . . . And now I was within the circling of the outer planets, and flitting swiftly, towards the place where the earth, glimmering through the blue splendour of its orbit, as though a fiery mist, circled the sun at a monstrous speed. . . ."

NOTE.—The severest scrutiny has not enabled me to decipher more of the damaged portion of the MS. It commences to be legible again with the chapter entitled "The Noise in the Night."—ED.

XV. THE NOISE IN THE NIGHT

And now, I come to the strangest of all the strange happenings that have befallen me in this house of mysteries. It occurred quite lately—within the month; and I have little doubt but that what I saw was in reality the end of all things. However, to my story.

I do not know how it is; but, up to the present, I have never been able to write these things down, directly they happened. It is as though I have to wait a time, recovering my just balance, and digesting—as it were—the things I have heard or seen. No doubt, this is as it should be; for, by waiting, I see the incidents more truly, and write of them in a calmer and more judicial frame of mind. This by the way.

It is now the end of November. My story relates to what happened in the first week of the month.

It was night, about eleven o'clock. Pepper and I kept one another company in the study—that great, old room of mine, where I read and work. I was reading, curiously enough, the Bible. I have begun, in these later days, to take a growing interest in that great and ancient book. Suddenly, a distinct tremor shook the house, and there came a faint and distant, whirring buzz, that grew rapidly into a far, muffled screaming. It reminded me, in a queer, gigantic way, of the noise that a clock makes, when the catch is released, and it is allowed to run down. The sound appeared to come from some remote height—somewhere up in the night. There was no repetition of the shock. I looked across at Pepper. He was sleeping peacefully.

Gradually, the whirring noise decreased, and there came a long silence.

All at once, a glow lit up the end window, which protrudes far out from the side of the house, so that, from it, one may look both East and West. I felt puzzled, and, after a moment's hesitation, walked across the room, and pulled aside the blind. As I did so, I saw the Sun rise, from behind the horizon. It rose with a steady, perceptible movement. I could see it travel upwards. In a minute, it seemed, it had reached the tops of the trees, through which I had watched it. Up, up—It was broad daylight now. Behind me, I was conscious of a sharp, mosquito-like buzzing. I glanced round, and knew that it came from the clock. Even as I looked, it marked off an hour. The minute hand was moving round the dial, faster than an ordinary second-hand. The hour hand moved quickly from space to space. I had a numb sense of astonishment. A moment later, so it seemed, the two candles went out, almost together. I turned swiftly back to the window; for I had seen the shadow of the window-frames, traveling along the floor towards me, as though a great lamp had been carried up past the window.

I saw now, that the sun had risen high into the heavens, and was still visibly moving. It passed above the house, with an extraordinary sailing kind of motion. As the window came into shadow, I saw another extraordinary thing. The fine-weather clouds were not passing, easily, across the sky—they were scampering, as though a hundred-mile-an-hour wind blew. As they passed, they changed their shapes a thousand times a minute, as though writhing with a strange life; and so were gone. And, presently, others came, and whisked away likewise.

To the West, I saw the sun, drop with an incredible, smooth, swift motion. Eastward, the shadows of every seen thing crept towards the coming greyness. And the movement of the shadows was visible to me—a stealthy, writhing creep of the shadows of the wind-stirred trees. It was a strange sight.

Quickly, the room began to darken. The sun slid down to the horizon, and seemed, as it were, to disappear from my sight, almost with a jerk. Through the greyness of the swift evening, I saw the silver crescent of the moon, falling out of the Southern sky, towards the West. The evening seemed to merge into an almost instant night. Above me, the many constellations passed in a strange, "noiseless" circling, Westwards. The moon fell through that last thousand fathoms of the night-gulf, and there was only the starlight. . . .

About this time, the buzzing in the corner ceased; telling me that the clock had run down. A few minutes passed, and I saw the Eastward sky lighten. A grey, sullen morning spread through all the darkness, and hid the march of the stars. Overhead, there moved, with a heavy, everlasting rolling, a vast, seamless sky of grey clouds—a cloud-sky that would have seemed motionless, through all the length of an ordinary earth-day. The sun was hidden from me; but, from moment to moment, the world would brighten and darken, brighten and darken, beneath waves of subtle light and shadow. . . .

The light shifted ever Westward, and the night fell upon the earth. A vast rain seemed to come with it, and a wind of a most extraordinary loudness—as though the howling of a night-long gale, were packed into the space of no more than a minute.

This noise passed, almost immediately, and the clouds broke; so that, once more, I could see the sky. The stars were flying Westward, with astounding speed. It came to me now, for the first time, that, though the noise of the wind had passed, yet a constant "blurred" sound was in my ears. Now that I noticed it, I was aware that it had been with me all the time. It was the world-noise.

And then, even as I grasped at so much comprehension, there came the Eastward light. No more than a few heart-beats, and the sun rose, swiftly. Through the trees, I saw it, and then it was above the trees. Up—up, it soared and all the world was light. It passed, with a swift, steady swing to its highest altitude, and fell thence, Westward. I saw the day roll visibly over my head. A few light clouds flittered Northward, and vanished. The sun went down with one swift, clear plunge, and there was about me, for a few seconds, the darker growing grey of the gloaming.

Southward and Westward, the moon was sinking rapidly. The night had come, already. A minute it seemed, and the moon fell those remaining fathoms of dark sky. Another minute, or so, and the Eastward sky glowed with the coming dawn. The sun leapt upon me with a frightening abruptness, and soared ever more swiftly towards the zenith. Then, suddenly, a fresh thing came to my sight. A black thundercloud rushed up out of the South, and seemed to leap all the arc of the sky, in a single instant. As it came, I saw that its advancing edge flapped, like a monstrous black cloth in the heaven, twirling and undulating rapidly, with a horrid suggestiveness. In an instant, all the air was full of rain, and a hundred lightning flashes seemed to flood downwards, as it were in one great shower. In the same second of time, the world-noise was drowned in the roar of the wind, and then my ears ached, under the stunning impact of the thunder.

And, in the midst of this storm, the night came; and then, within the space of another minute, the storm had passed, and there was only the constant "blur" of the world-noise on my hearing. Overhead, the stars were sliding quickly Westward; and something, mayhaps the particular speed to which they had attained, brought home to me, for the first time, a keen realisation of the knowledge that it was the world that revolved. I seemed to see, suddenly, the world—a vast, dark mass—revolving visibly against the stars.

The dawn and the sun seemed to come together, so greatly had the speed of the world-revolution increased. The sun drove up, in one long, steady curve; passed its highest point, and swept down into the Western sky, and disappeared. I was scarcely conscious of evening, so brief was it. Then I was watching the flying constellations, and the Westward hastening moon. In but a space of seconds, so it seemed, it was sliding swiftly downward through the night-blue, and then was gone. And, almost directly, came the morning.

And now there seemed to come a strange acceleration. The sun made one clean, clear sweep through the sky, and disappeared behind the Westward horizon, and the night came and went with a like haste.

As the succeeding day, opened and closed upon the world, I was aware of a sweat of snow, suddenly upon the earth. The night came, and, almost immediately, the day. In the brief leap of the sun, I saw that the snow had vanished; and then, once more, it was night.

Thus matters were; and, even after the many incredible things that I have seen, I experienced all the time a most profound awe. To see the sun rise and set, within a space of time to be measured by seconds; to watch (after a little) the moon leap—a pale, and ever growing orb—up into the night sky, and glide, with a strange swiftness, through the vast arc of blue; and, presently, to see the sun follow, springing out of the Eastern sky, as though in chase; and then again the night, with the swift and ghostly passing of starry constellations, was all too much to view believingly. Yet, so it was— the day slipping from dawn to dusk, and the night sliding swiftly into day, ever rapidly and more rapidly.

The last three passages of the sun had shown me a snow-covered earth, which, at night, had seemed, for a few seconds, incredibly weird under the fast-shifting light of the soaring and falling moon. Now, however, for a little space, the sky was hidden, by a sea of swaying, leaden-white clouds, which lightened and blackened, alternately, with the passage of day and night.

The clouds rippled and vanished, and there was once more before me, the vision of the swiftly leaping sun, and nights that came and went like shadows.

Faster and faster, spun the world. And now each day and night was completed within the space of but a few seconds; and still the speed increased.

It was a little later, that I noticed that the sun had begun to have the suspicion of a trail of fire behind it. This was due, evidently, to the speed at which it, apparently, traversed the heavens. And, as the days sped, each one quicker than the last, the sun began to assume the appearance of a vast, flaming comet*, flaring across the sky at short, periodic intervals. At night, the moon presented, with much greater truth, a comet-like aspect; a pale, and singularly clear, fast traveling shape of fire, trailing streaks of cold flame. The stars showed now, merely as fine hairs of fire against the dark.

Once, I turned from the window, and glanced at Pepper. In the flash of a day, I saw that he slept, quietly, and I moved once more to my watching.

The sun was now bursting up from the Eastern horizon, like a stupendous rocket, seeming to occupy no more than a second or two in hurling from East to West. I could

---

*The Recluse uses this as an illustration, evidently in the sense of the popular conception of a comet.—ED.

no longer perceive the passage of clouds across the sky, which seemed to have darkened somewhat. The brief nights, appeared to have lost the proper darkness of night; so that the hair-like fire of the flying stars, showed but dimly. As the speed increased, the sun began to sway very slowly in the sky, from South to North, and then, slowly again, from North to South.

So, amid a strange confusion of mind, the hours passed.

All this while had Pepper slept. Presently, feeling lonely and distraught, I called to him, softly; but he took no notice. Again, I called, raising my voice slightly; still he moved not. I walked over to where he lay, and touched him with my foot, to rouse him. At the action, gentle though it was, he fell to pieces. That is what happened; he literally and actually crumbled into a mouldering heap of bones and dust.

For the space of, perhaps a minute, I stared down at the shapeless heap, that had once been Pepper. I stood, feeling stunned. What can have happened? I asked myself; not at once grasping the grim significance of that little hill of ash. Then, as I stirred the heap with my foot, it occurred to me that this could only happen in a great space of time. Years—and years.

Outside, the wearying, fluttering light held the world. Inside, I stood, trying to understand what it meant—what that little pile of dust and dry bones, on the carpet, meant. But I could not think, coherently.

I glanced away, round the room, and now, for the first time, noticed how dusty and old the place looked. Dust and dirt everywhere; piled in little heaps in the corners, and spread about upon the furniture. The very carpet, itself, was invisible beneath a coating of the same, all pervading, material. As I walked, little clouds of the stuff rose up from under my footsteps, and assailed my nostrils, with a dry, bitter odour that made me wheeze, huskily.

Suddenly, as my glance fell again upon Pepper's remains, I stood still, and gave voice to my confusion—questioning, aloud, whether the years were, indeed, passing; whether this, which I had taken to be a form of vision, was, in truth, a reality. I paused. A new thought had struck me. Quickly, but with steps which, for the first time, I noticed, tottered, I went across the room to the great pier-glass, and looked in. It was too covered with grime, to give back any reflection, and, with trembling hands, I began to rub off the dirt. Presently, I could see myself. The thought that had come to me, was confirmed. Instead of the great, hale man, who scarcely looked fifty, I was looking at a bent, decrepit man, whose shoulders stooped, and whose face was wrinkled with the years of a century. The hair—which a few short hours ago had been nearly coal black—was now silvery white. Only the eyes were bright. Gradually, I traced, in that ancient man, a faint resemblance to my self of other days.

I turned away, and tottered to the window. I knew, now, that I was old, and the knowledge seemed to confirm my trembling walk. For a little space, I stared moodily out into the blurred vista of changeful landscape. Even in that short time, a year passed, and, with a petulant gesture, I left the window. As I did so, I noticed that my hand shook with the palsy of old age; and a short sob choked its way through my lips.

For a little while, I paced, tremulously, between the window and the table; my gaze wandering hither and thither, uneasily. How dilapidated the room was. Everywhere lay the thick dust—thick, sleepy, and black. The fender was a shape of rust. The chains that held the brass clock-weights, had rusted through long ago, and now the weights lay on the floor beneath; themselves two cones of verdigris.

As I glanced about, it seemed to me that I could see the very furniture of the room rotting and decaying before my eyes. Nor was this fancy, on my part; for, all at once, the bookshelf, along the sidewall, collapsed, with a cracking and rending of rotten wood, precipitating its contents upon the floor, and filling the room with a smother of dusty atoms.

How tired I felt. As I walked, it seemed that I could hear my dry joints, creak and crack at every step. I wondered about my sister. Was she dead, as well as Pepper? All had happened so quickly and suddenly. This must be, indeed, the beginning of the end of all things! It occurred to me, to go to look for her; but I felt too weary. And then, she had been so queer about these happenings, of late. Of late! I repeated the words, and laughed, feebly—mirthlessly, as the realisation was borne in upon me that I spoke of a time, half a century gone. Half a century! It might have been twice as long!

I moved slowly to the window, and looked out once more across the world. I can best describe the passage of day and night, at this period, as a sort of gigantic, ponderous flicker. Moment by moment, the acceleration of time continued; so that, at nights now, I saw the moon, only as a swaying trail of palish fire, that varied from a mere line of light to a nebulous path, and then dwindled again, disappearing periodically.

The flicker of the days and nights quickened. The days had grown perceptibly darker, and a queer quality of dusk lay, as it were, in the atmosphere. The nights were so much lighter, that the stars were scarcely to be seen, saving here and there an occasional hair-like line of fire, that seemed to sway a little, with the moon.

Quicker, and ever quicker, ran the flicker of day and night; and, suddenly it seemed, I was aware that the flicker had died out, and, instead, there reigned a comparatively steady light, which was shed upon all the world, from an eternal river of flame that swung up and down, North and South, in stupendous, mighty swings.

The sky was now grown very much darker, and there was in the blue of it a heavy gloom, as though a vast blackness peered through it upon the earth. Yet, there was in it, also, a strange and awful clearness, and emptiness. Periodically, I had glimpses of a ghostly track of fire that swayed thin and darkly towards the sun-stream; vanished and reappeared. It was the scarcely visible moon-stream.

Looking out at the landscape, I was conscious again, of a blurring sort of "flitter," that came either from the light of the ponderous-swinging sun-stream, or was the result of the incredibly rapid changes of the earth's surface. And every few moments, so it seemed, the snow would lie suddenly upon the world, and vanish as abruptly, as though an invisible giant "flitted" a white sheet off and on the earth.

Time fled, and the weariness that was mine, grew insupportable. I turned from the window, and walked once across the room, the heavy dust deadening the sound of my footsteps. Each step that I took, seemed a greater effort than the one before. An intolerable ache, knew me in every joint and limb, as I trod my way, with a weary uncertainty.

By the opposite wall, I came to a weak pause, and wondered, dimly, what was my intent. I looked to my left, and saw my old chair. The thought of sitting in it brought a faint sense of comfort to my bewildered wretchedness. Yet, because I was so weary and old and tired, I would scarcely brace my mind to do anything but stand, and wish myself past those few yards. I rocked, as I stood. The floor, even, seemed a place for rest; but the dust lay so thick and sleepy and black. I turned, with a great effort of will, and made towards my chair. I reached it, with a groan of thankfulness. I sat down.

Everything about me appeared to be growing dim. It was all so strange and unthought of. Last night, I was a comparatively strong, though elderly man; and now, only a few hours later—! I looked at the little dust-heap, that had once been Pepper. Hours! and I laughed, a feeble, bitter laugh; a shrill, cackling laugh, that shocked my dimming senses.

For a while, I must have dozed. Then I opened my eyes, with a start. Somewhere across the room, there had been a muffled noise of something falling. I looked, and saw, vaguely, a cloud of dust hovering above a pile of *débris*. Nearer the door, something else tumbled, with a crash. It was one of the cupboards; but I was tired, and took little notice. I closed my eyes, and sat there in a state of drowsy, semi-unconsciousness. Once or twice—as though coming through thick mists—I heard noises, faintly. Then I must have slept.

XVI. THE AWAKENING

I awoke, with a start. For a moment, I wondered where I was. Then memory came to me. . . .

The room was still lit with that strange light—half-sun, half-moon, light. I felt refreshed, and the tired, weary ache had left me. I went slowly across to the window, and looked out. Overhead, the river of flame drove up and down, North and South, in a dancing semi-circle of fire. As a mighty sleigh in the loom of time it seemed—in a sudden fancy of mine—to be beating home the picks of the years. For, so vastly had the passage of time been accelerated, that there was no longer any sense of the sun passing from East to West. The only apparent movement was the North and South beat of the sun-stream, that had become so swift now, as to be better described as a *quiver*.

As I peered out, there came to me a sudden, inconsequent memory of that last journey among the Outer Worlds.* I remembered the sudden vision that had come to me, as I neared the Solar System, of the fast whirling planets about the sun—as though the governing quality of time had been held in abeyance, and the Machine of a Universe allowed to run down an eternity, in a few moments or hours. The memory passed, along with a, but partially comprehended, suggestion that I had been permitted a glimpse into further time spaces. I stared out again, seemingly, at the quake of the sun-stream. The speed seemed to increase, even as I looked. Several life-times came and went, as I watched.

Suddenly, it struck me, with a sort of grotesque seriousness, that I was still alive. I thought of Pepper, and wondered how it was that I had not followed his fate. He had reached the time of his dying, and had passed, probably through sheer length of years. And here was I, alive, hundreds of thousands of centuries after my rightful period of years.

For, a time, I mused, absently. "Yesterday—" I stopped, suddenly. Yesterday! There was no yesterday. The yesterday of which I spoke had been swallowed up in the abyss of years, ages gone. I grew dazed with much thinking.

Presently, I turned from the window, and glanced round the room. It seemed different—strangely, utterly different. Then, I knew what it was that made it appear so strange. It was bare: there was not a piece of furniture in the room; not even a solitary

---

* Evidently referring to something set forth in the missing and mutilated pages. See fragments, p. 577.—
ED.

fitting of any sort. Gradually, my amazement went, as I remembered, that this was but the inevitable end of that process of decay, which I had witnessed commencing, before my sleep. Thousands of years! Millions of years!

Over the floor was spread a deep layer of dust, that reached half way up to the window-seat. It had grown immeasurably, whilst I slept; and represented the dust of untold ages. Undoubtedly, atoms of the old, decayed furniture helped to swell its bulk; and, somewhere among it all, mouldered the long-ago-dead Pepper.

All at once, it occurred to me, that I had no recollection of wading knee-deep through all that dust, after I awoke. True, an incredible age of years had passed, since I approached the window; but that was evidently as nothing, compared with the count-less spaces of time that, I conceived, had vanished whilst I was sleeping. I remembered now, that I had fallen asleep, sitting in my old chair. Had it gone . . . ? I glanced towards where it had stood. Of course, there was no chair to be seen. I could not satisfy myself, whether it had disappeared, after my waking, or before. If it had mouldered under me, surely, I should have been waked by the collapse. Then I remembered that the thick dust, which covered the floor, would have been sufficient to soften my fall; so that it was quite possible, I had slept upon the dust for a million years or more.

As these thoughts wandered through my brain, I glanced again, casually, to where the chair had stood. Then, for the first time, I noticed that there were no marks, in the dust, of my footprints, between it and the window. But then, ages of years had passed, since I had awaked—tens of thousands of years!

My look rested, thoughtfully, again upon the place where once had stood my chair. Suddenly, I passed from abstraction to intentness; for there, in its standing place, I made out a long undulation, rounded off with the heavy dust. Yet it was not so much hidden, but that I could tell what had caused it. I knew—and shivered at the knowledge—that it was a human body, ages-dead, lying there, beneath the place where I had slept. It was lying on its right side, its back turned towards me. I could make out and trace each curve and outline, softened, and moulded, as it were, in the black dust. In a vague sort of way, I tried to account for its presence there. Slowly, I began to grow bewildered, as the thought came to me that it lay just about where I must have fallen when the chair collapsed.

Gradually, an idea began to form itself within my brain; a thought that shook my spirit. It seemed hideous and insupportable; yet it grew upon me, steadily, until it became a conviction. The body under that coating, that shroud of dust, was neither more nor less than my own dead shell. I did not attempt to prove it. I knew it now, and wondered I had not known it all along. I was a bodyless thing.

Awhile, I stood, trying to adjust my thoughts to this new problem. In time—how many thousands of years, I know not—I attained to some degree of quietude—sufficient to enable me to pay attention to what was transpiring around me.

Now, I saw that the elongated mound had sunk, collapsed, level with the rest of the spreading dust. And fresh atoms, impalpable, had settled above that mixture of grave-powder, which the æons had ground. A long while, I stood, turned from the window. Gradually, I grew more collected, while the world slipped across the centuries into the future.

Presently, I began a survey of the room. Now, I saw that time was beginning its destructive work, even on this strange old building. That it had stood through all the years was, it seemed to me, proof that it was something different from any other house. I do not think, somehow, that I had thought of its decaying. Though, why, I could not have said. It was not until I had meditated upon the matter, for some considerable time, that I fully realised that the extraordinary space of time through which it had stood, was sufficient to have utterly pulverized the very stones of which it was built, had they been taken from any earthly quarry. Yes, it was undoubtedly mouldering now. All the plaster had gone from the walls; even as the woodwork of the room had gone, many ages before.

While I stood, in contemplation, a piece of glass, from one of the small, diamond-shaped panes, dropped, with a dull tap, amid the dust upon the sill behind me, and crumbled into a little heap of powder. As I turned from contemplating it, I saw light between a couple of the stones that formed the outer wall. Evidently, the mortar was falling away. . . .

After awhile, I turned once more to the window, and peered out. I discovered, now, that the speed of time had become enormous. The lateral quiver of the sun-stream, had grown so swift as to cause the dancing semi-circle of flame to merge into, and disappear in, a sheet of fire that covered half the Southern sky from East to West.

From the sky, I glanced down to the gardens. They were just a blur of a palish, dirty green. I had a feeling that they stood higher, than in the old days; a feeling that they were nearer my window, as though they had risen, bodily. Yet, they were still a long way below me; for the rock, over the mouth of the pit, on which this house stands, arches up to a great height.

It was later, that I noticed a change in the constant colour of the gardens. The pale, dirty green was growing ever paler and paler, towards white. At last, after a great space, they became greyish-white, and stayed thus for a very long time. Finally, however, the greyness began to fade, even as had the green, into a dead white. And this remained, constant and unchanged. And by this I knew that, at last, snow lay upon all the Northern world.

And so, by millions of years, time winged onward through eternity, to the end—the end, of which, in the old-earth days, I had thought remotely, and in hazily speculative fashion. And now, it was approaching in a manner of which none had ever dreamed.

I recollect that, about this time, I began to have a lively, though morbid, curiosity, as to what would happen when the end came—but I seemed strangely without imaginings.

All this while, the steady process of decay was continuing. The few remaining pieces of glass, had long ago vanished; and, every now and then, a soft thud, and a little cloud of rising dust, would tell of some fragment of fallen mortar or stone.

I looked up again, to the fiery sheet that quaked in the heavens above me and far down into the Southern sky. As I looked, the impression was borne in upon me, that it had lost some of its first brilliancy—that it was duller, deeper hued.

I glanced down, once more, to the blurred white of the world-scape. Sometimes, my look returned to the burning sheet of dulling flame, that was, and yet hid, the sun. At times, I glanced behind me, into the growing dusk of the great, silent room, with its æon-carpet of sleeping dust. . . .

So, I watched through the fleeting ages, lost in soul-wearing thoughts and wonderings, and possessed with a new weariness.

XVII. THE SLOWING ROTATION

It might have been a million years later, that I perceived, beyond possibility of doubt, that the fiery sheet that lit the world, was indeed darkening.

Another vast space went by, and the whole enormous flame had sunk to a deep, copper colour. Gradually, it darkened, from copper to copper-red, and from this, at times, to a deep, heavy, purplish tint, with, in it, a strange loom of blood.

Although the light was decreasing, I could perceive no diminishment in the apparent speed of the sun. It still spread itself in that dazzling veil of speed.

The world, so much of it as I could see, had assumed a dreadful shade of gloom, as though, in very deed, the last day of the worlds approached.

The sun was dying; of that there could be little doubt; and still the earth whirled onward, through space and all the æons. At this time, I remember, an extraordinary sense of bewilderment took me. I found myself, later, wandering, mentally, amid an odd chaos of fragmentary modern theories and the old Biblical story of the world's ending.

Then, for the first time, there flashed across me, the memory that the sun, with its system of planets, was, and had been, traveling through space at an incredible speed. Abruptly, the question rose—*Where?* For a very great time, I pondered this matter; but, finally, with a certain sense of the futility of my puzzlings, I let my thoughts wander to other things. I grew to wondering, how much longer the house would stand. Also, I queried, to myself, whether I should be doomed to stay, bodiless, upon the earth, through the dark-time that I knew was coming. From these thoughts, I fell again to speculations upon the possible direction of the sun's journey through space. . . . And so another great while passed.

Gradually, as time fled, I began to feel the chill of a great winter. Then, I remembered that, with the sun dying, the cold must be, necessarily, extraordinarily intense. Slowly, slowly, as the æons slipped into eternity, the earth sank into a heavier and redder gloom. The dull flame in the firmament took on a deeper tint, very sombre and turbid.

Then, at last, it was borne upon me that there was a change. The fiery, gloomy curtain of flame that hung quaking overhead, and down away into the Southern sky, began to thin and contract; and, in it, as one sees the fast vibrations of a jarred harpstring, I saw once more the sun-stream quivering, giddily, North and South.

Slowly, the likeness to a sheet of fire, disappeared, and I saw, plainly, the slowing beat of the sun-stream. Yet, even then, the speed of its swing was inconceivably swift. And all the time, the brightness of the fiery arc grew ever duller. Underneath, the world loomed dimly—an indistinct, ghostly region.

Overhead, the river of flame swayed slower, and even slower; until, at last, it swung to the North and South in great, ponderous beats, that lasted through seconds. A long space went by, and now each sway of the great belt lasted nigh a minute; so that, after a great while, I ceased to distinguish it as a visible movement; and the streaming fire ran in a steady river of dull flame, across the deadly-looking sky.

An indefinite period passed, and it seemed that the arc of fire became less sharply defined. It appeared to me to grow more attenuated, and I thought blackish streaks showed, occasionally. Presently, as I watched, the smooth onward-flow ceased; and I was able to perceive that there came a momentary, but regular, darkening of the world. This grew until, once more, night descended, in short, but periodic, intervals upon the wearying earth.

Longer and longer became the nights, and the days equalled them; so that, at last, the day and the night grew to the duration of seconds in length, and the sun showed, once more, like an almost invisible, coppery-red coloured ball, within the glowing mistiness of its flight. Corresponding to the dark lines, showing at times in its trail, there were now distinctly to be seen on the half-visible sun itself, great, dark belts.

Year after year flashed into the past, and the days and nights spread into minutes. The sun had ceased to have the appearance of a tail; and now rose and set—a tremendous globe of a glowing copper-bronze hue; in parts ringed with blood-red bands; in others, with the dusky ones, that I have already mentioned. These circles—both red and black—were of varying thicknesses. For a time, I was at a loss to account for their presence. Then it occurred to me, that it was scarcely likely that the sun would cool evenly all over; and that these markings were due, probably, to differences in temperature of the various areas; the red representing those parts where the heat was still fervent, and the black those portions which were already comparatively cool.

It struck me, as a peculiar thing, that the sun should cool in evenly defined rings; until I remembered that, possibly, they were but isolated patches, to which the enormous rotatory speed of the sun had imparted a belt-like appearance. The sun, itself, was very much greater than the sun I had known in the old-world days; and, from this, I argued that it was considerably nearer.

At nights, the moon* still showed; but small and remote; and the light she reflected was so dull and weak that she seemed little more than the small, dim ghost of the olden moon, that I had known.

Gradually, the days and nights lengthened out, until they equalled a space somewhat less than one of the old-earth hours; the sun rising and setting like a great, ruddy bronze disk, crossed with ink-black bars. About this time, I found myself, able once more, to see the gardens, with clearness. For the world had now grown very still, and changeless. Yet, I am not correct in saying, "gardens"; for there were no gardens—nothing that I knew or recognised. In place thereof, I looked out upon a vast plain, stretching away into distance. A little to my left, there was a low range

---

* No further mention is made of the moon. From what is said here, it is evident that our satellite had greatly increased its distance from the earth. Possibly, at a later age it may even have broken loose from our attraction. I cannot but regret that no light is shed on this point.—Ed.

of hills. Everywhere, there was a uniform, white covering of snow, in places rising into hummocks and ridges.

It was only now, that I recognized how really great had been the snowfall. In places it was vastly deep, as was witnessed by a great, upleaping, wave-shaped hill, away to my right; though it is not impossible, that this was due, in part, to some rise in the surface of the ground. Strangely enough, the range of low hills to my left—already mentioned—was not entirely covered with the universal snow; instead, I could see their bare, dark sides showing in several places. And everywhere and always there reigned an incredible death-silence and desolation. The immutable, awful quiet of a dying world.

All this time, the days and nights were lengthening, perceptibly. Already, each day occupied, maybe, some two hours from dawn to dusk. At night, I had been surprised to find that there were very few stars overhead, and these small, though of an extraordinary brightness; which I attributed to the peculiar, but clear, blackness of the night-time.

Away to the North, I could discern a nebulous sort of mistiness; not unlike, in appearance, a small portion of the Milky Way. It might have been an extremely remote star-cluster; or—the thought came to me suddenly—perhaps it was the sidereal universe that I had known, and now left far behind, forever—a small, dimly glowing mist of stars, far in the depths of space.

Still, the days and nights lengthened, slowly. Each time, the sun rose duller than it had set. And the dark belts increased in breadth.

About this time, there happened a fresh thing. The sun, earth, and sky were suddenly darkened, and, apparently, blotted out for a brief space. I had a sense, a certain awareness (I could learn little by sight), that the earth was enduring a very great fall of snow. Then, in an instant, the veil that had obscured everything, vanished, and I looked out, once more. A marvellous sight met my gaze. The hollow in which this house, with its gardens, stands, was brimmed with snow.* It lipped over the sill of my window. Everywhere, it lay, a great level stretch of white, which caught and reflected, gloomily, the sombre, coppery glows of the dying sun. The world had become a shadowless plain, from horizon to horizon.

* Conceivably, frozen air.—ED.

I glanced up at the sun. It shone with an extraordinary, dull clearness. I saw it, now, as one who, until then, had seen it, only through a partially obscuring medium. All about it, the sky had become black, with a clear, deep blackness, frightful in its nearness, and its unmeasured deep, and its utter unfriendliness. For a great time, I looked into it, newly, and shaken and fearful. It was so near. Had I been a child, I might have expressed some of my sensation and distress, by saying that the sky had lost its roof.

Later, I turned, and peered about me, into the room. Everywhere, it was covered with a thin shroud of the all-pervading white. I could see it but dimly, by reason of the somber light that now lit the world. It appeared to cling to the ruined walls; and the thick, soft dust of the years, that covered the floor knee-deep, was nowhere visible. The snow must have blown in through the open framework of the windows. Yet, in no place had it drifted; but lay everywhere about the great, old room, smooth and level. Moreover, there had been no wind these many thousand years. But there was the snow,* as I have told.

And all the earth was silent. And there was a cold, such as no living man can ever have known.

The earth was now illuminated, by day, with a most doleful light, beyond my power to describe. It seemed as though I looked at the great plain, through the medium of a bronze-tinted sea.

It was evident that the earth's rotatory movement was departing, steadily.

The end came, all at once. The night had been the longest yet; and when the dying sun showed, at last, above the world's edge, I had grown so wearied of the dark, that I greeted it as a friend. It rose steadily, until about twenty degrees above the horizon. Then, it stopped suddenly, and, after a strange retrograde movement, hung motionless—a great shield in the sky.** Only the circular rim of the sun showed bright—only this, and one thin streak of light near the equator.

Gradually, even this thread of light died out; and now, all that was left of our great and glorious sun, was a vast dead disk, rimmed with a thin circle of bronze-red light.

---

* See previous footnote. This would explain the snow (?) within the room.—ED.

** I am confounded that neither here, nor later on, does the Recluse make any further mention of the continued north and south movement (apparent, of course,) of the sun from solstice to solstice.—ED.

XVIII. THE GREEN STAR

The world was held in a savage gloom—cold and intolerable. Outside, all was quiet—quiet! From the dark room behind me, came the occasional, soft thud* of falling matter—fragments of rotting stone. So time passed, and night grasped the world, wrapping it in wrappings of impenetrable blackness.

There was no night-sky, as we know it. Even the few straggling stars had vanished, conclusively. I might have been in a shuttered room, without a light; for all that I could see. Only, in the impalpableness of gloom, opposite, burnt that vast, encircling hair of dull fire. Beyond this, there was no ray in all the vastitude of night that surrounded me; save that, far in the North, that soft, mist-like glow still shone.

Silently, years moved on. What period of time passed, I shall never know. It seemed to me, waiting there, that eternities came and went, stealthily; and still I watched. I could see only the glow of the sun's edge, at times; for now, it had commenced to come and go—lighting up a while, and again becoming extinguished.

All at once, during one of these periods of life, a sudden flame cut across the night—a quick glare that lit up the dead earth, shortly; giving me a glimpse of its flat lonesomeness. The light appeared to come from the sun—shooting out from somewhere near its centre, diagonally. A moment, I gazed, startled. Then the leaping flame sank, and the gloom fell again. But now it was not so dark; and the sun was belted by a thin line of vivid, white light. I stared, intently. Had a volcano broken out on the sun? Yet, I negatived the thought, as soon as formed. I felt that the light had been far too intensely white, and large, for such a cause.

Another idea there was, that suggested itself to me. It was, that one of the inner planets had fallen into the sun—becoming incandescent, under that impact. This theory appealed to me, as being more plausible, and accounting more satisfactorily for the extraordinary size and brilliance of the blaze, that had lit up the dead world, so unexpectedly.

Full of interest and emotion, I stared, across the darkness, at that line of white fire, cutting the night. One thing it told to me, unmistakably: the sun was yet rotating at an

---

* At this time the sound-carrying atmosphere must have been either incredibly attenuated, or—more probably—nonexistent. In the light of this, it cannot be supposed that these, or any other, noises would have been apparent to living ears—to hearing, as we, in the material body, understand that sense. —ED.

enormous speed.* Thus, I knew that the years were still fleeting at an incalculable rate; though so far as the earth was concerned, life, and light, and time, were things belonging to a period lost in the long gone ages.

After that one burst of flame, the light had shown, only as an encircling band of bright fire. Now, however, as I watched, it began slowly to sink into a ruddy tint, and, later, to a dark, copper-red colour; much as the sun had done. Presently, it sank to a deeper hue; and, in a still further space of time, it began to fluctuate; having periods of glowing, and anon, dying. Thus, after a great while, it disappeared.

Long before this, the smouldering edge of the sun had deadened into blackness. And so, in that supremely future time, the world, dark and intensely silent, rode on its gloomy orbit around the ponderous mass of the dead sun.

My thoughts, at this period, can be scarcely described. At first, they were chaotic and wanting in coherence. But, later, as the ages came and went, my soul seemed to imbibe the very essence of the oppressive solitude and dreariness, that held the earth.

With this feeling, there came a wonderful clearness of thought, and I realised, despairingly, that the world might wander for ever, through that enormous night. For a while, the unwholesome idea filled me, with a sensation of overbearing desolation; so that I could have cried like a child. In time, however, this feeling grew, almost insensibly, less, and an unreasoning hope possessed me. Patiently, I waited.

From time to time, the noise of dropping particles, behind in the room, came dully to my ears. Once, I heard a loud crash, and turned, instinctively, to look; forgetting, for the moment, the impenetrable night in which every detail was submerged. In a while, my gaze sought the heavens; turning, unconsciously, towards the North. Yes, the nebulous glow still showed. Indeed, I could have almost imagined that it looked somewhat plainer. For a long time, I kept my gaze fixed upon it; feeling, in my lonely soul, that its soft haze was, in some way, a tie with the past. Strange, the trifles from which one can suck comfort! And yet, had I but known—But I shall come to that in its proper time.

For a very long space, I watched, without experiencing any of the desire for sleep, that would so soon have visited me in the old-earth days. How I should have welcomed it; if only to have passed the time, away from my perplexities and thoughts.

---

* I can only suppose that the time of the earth's yearly journey had ceased to bear its present *relative* proportion to the period of the sun's rotation.—ED.

Several times, the comfortless sound of some great piece of masonry falling, disturbed my meditations; and, once, it seemed I could hear whispering in the room, behind me. Yet it was utterly useless to try to see anything. Such blackness, as existed, scarcely can be conceived. It was palpable, and hideously brutal to the sense; as though something dead, pressed up against me—something soft, and icily cold.

Under all this, there grew up within my mind, a great and overwhelming distress of uneasiness, that left me, but to drop me into an uncomfortable brooding. I felt that I must fight against it; and, presently, hoping to distract my thoughts, I turned to the window, and looked up towards the North, in search of the nebulous whiteness, which, still, I believed to be the far and misty glowing of the universe we had left. Even as I raised my eyes, I was thrilled with a feeling of wonder; for, now, the hazy light had resolved into a single, great star, of vivid green.

As I stared, astonished, the thought flashed into my mind, that the earth must be traveling towards the star; not away, as I had imagined. Next, that it could not be the universe the earth had left; but, possibly, an outlying star, belonging to some vast starcluster, hidden in the enormous depths of space. With a sense of commingled awe and curiosity, I watched it, wondering what new thing was to be revealed to me.

For a while, vague thoughts and speculations occupied me, during which my gaze dwelt insatiably upon that one spot of light, in the otherwise pit-like darkness. Hope grew up within me, banishing the oppression of despair, that had seemed to stifle me. Wherever the earth was traveling, it was, at least, going once more towards the realms of light. Light! One must spend an eternity wrapped in soundless night, to understand the full horror of being without it.

Slowly, but surely, the star grew upon my vision, until, in time, it shone as brightly as had the planet Jupiter, in the old-earth days. With increased size, its colour became more impressive; reminding me of a huge emerald, scintillating rays of fire across the world.

Years fled away in silence, and the green star grew into a great splash of flame in the sky. A little later, I saw a thing that filled me with amazement. It was the ghostly outline of a vast crescent, in the night; a gigantic new moon, seeming to be growing out of the surrounding gloom. Utterly bemused, I stared at it. It appeared to be quite close—comparatively; and I puzzled to understand how the earth had come so near to it, without my having seen it before.

The light, thrown by the star, grew stronger; and, presently, I was aware that it was possible to see the earth-scape again; though indistinctly. Awhile, I stared, trying to make out whether I could distinguish any detail of the world's surface, but I found the light insufficient. In a little, I gave up the attempt, and glanced once more towards the star. Even in the short space, that my attention had been diverted, it had increased considerably, and seemed now, to my bewildered sight, about a quarter of the size of the full moon. The light it threw, was extraordinarily powerful; yet its colour was so abominably unfamiliar, that such of the world as I could see, showed unreal; more as though I looked out upon a landscape of shadow, than aught else.

All this time, the great crescent was increasing in brightness, and began, now, to shine with a perceptible shade of green. Steadily, the star increased in size and brilliancy, until it showed, fully as large as half a full moon; and, as it grew greater and brighter, so did the vast crescent throw out more and more light, though of an ever deepening hue of green. Under the combined blaze of their radiances, the wilderness that stretched before me, became steadily more visible. Soon, I seemed able to stare across the whole world, which now appeared, beneath the strange light, terrible in its cold and awful, flat dreariness.

It was a little later, that my attention was drawn to the fact, that the great star of green flame, was slowly sinking out of the North, towards the East. At first, I could scarcely believe that I saw aright; but soon there could be no doubt that it was so. Gradually, it sank, and, as it fell, the vast crescent of glowing green, began to dwindle and dwindle, until it became a mere arc of light, against the livid coloured sky. Later it vanished, disappearing in the self-same spot from which I had seen it slowly emerge.

By this time, the star had come to within some thirty degrees of the hidden horizon. In size it could now have rivalled the moon at its full; though, even yet, I could not distinguish its disk. This fact led me to conceive that it was, still, an extraordinary distance away; and, this being so, I knew that its size must be huge, beyond the conception of man to understand or imagine.

Suddenly, as I watched, the lower edge of the star vanished—cut by a straight, dark line. A minute—or a century—passed, and it dipped lower, until the half of it had disappeared from sight. Far away out on the great plain, I saw a monstrous shadow blotting it out, and advancing swiftly. Only a third of the star was visible now. Then, like a flash, the solution of this extraordinary phenomenon revealed itself to me. The star was sinking behind the enormous mass of the dead sun. Or rather, the sun—obedient to its attraction—was rising towards it,* with the earth following in its trail. As these thoughts

---

* A careful reading of the MS. suggests that, either the sun is traveling on an orbit of great eccentricity, or else that it was approaching the green star on a lessening orbit. And at this moment, I conceive it to be finally torn directly from its oblique course, by the gravitational pull of the immense star.—ED.

expanded in my mind, the star vanished; being completely hidden by the tremendous bulk of the sun. Over the earth there fell, once more, the brooding night.

With the darkness, came an intolerable feeling of loneliness and dread. For the first time, I thought of the Pit, and its inmates. After that, there rose in my memory the still more terrible Thing, that had haunted the shores of the Sea of Sleep, and lurked in the shadows of this old building. Where were they? I wondered—and shivered with miserable thoughts. For a time, fear held me, and I prayed, wildly and incoherently, for some ray of light with which to dispel the cold blackness that enveloped the world.

How long I waited, it is impossible to say—certainly for a very great period. Then, all at once, I saw a loom of light shine out ahead. Gradually, it became more distinct. Suddenly, a ray of vivid green, flashed across the darkness. At the same moment, I saw a thin line of livid flame, far in the night. An instant, it seemed, and it had grown into a great clot of fire; beneath which, the world lay bathed in a blaze of emerald green light. Steadily it grew, until, presently, the whole of the green star had come into sight again. But now, it could be scarcely called a star; for it had increased to vast proportions, being incomparably greater than the sun had been in the olden time.

"Then, as I stared, I became aware that I could see the edge of the lifeless sun, glowing like a great crescent-moon. Slowly, its lighted surface, broadened out to me, until half of its diameter was visible; and the star began to drop away on my right. Time passed, and the earth moved on, slowly traversing the tremendous face of the dead sun."*

Gradually, as the earth travelled forward, the star fell still more to the right; until, at last, it shone on the back of the house, sending a flood of broken rays, in through the skeleton-like walls. Glancing upwards, I saw that much of the ceiling had vanished, enabling me to see that the upper storeys were even more decayed. The roof had, evidently, gone entirely; and I could see the green effulgence of the Star-light shining in, slantingly.

XIX. THE END OF THE SOLAR SYSTEM

From the abutment, where once had been the windows, through which I had watched that first, fatal dawn, I could see that the sun was hugely greater, than it had been,

---

* It will be noticed here that the earth was "*slowly* traversing the tremendous face of the dead sun." No explanation is given of this, and we must conclude, either that the speed of time had slowed, or else that the earth was actually progressing on its orbit at a rate, slow, when measured by existing standards. A careful study of the MS., however, leads me to conclude that the speed of time had been steadily decreasing for a very considerable period.—ED.

when first the Star lit the world. So great was it, that its lower edge seemed almost to touch the far horizon. Even as I watched, I imagined that it drew closer. The radiance of green that lit the frozen earth, grew steadily brighter.

Thus, for a long space, things were. Then, on a sudden, I saw that the sun was changing shape, and growing smaller, just as the moon would have done in past time. In a while, only a third of the illuminated part was turned towards the earth. The Star bore away on the left.

Gradually, as the world moved on, the Star shone upon the front of the house, once more; while the sun showed, only as a great bow of green fire. An instant, it seemed, and the sun had vanished. The Star was still fully visible. Then the earth moved into the black shadow of the sun, and all was night—Night, black, starless, and intolerable.

Filled with tumultuous thoughts, I watched across the night—waiting. Years, it may have been, and then, in the dark house behind me, the clotted stillness of the world was broken. I seemed to hear a soft padding of many feet, and a faint, inarticulate whisper of sound, grew on my sense. I looked round into the blackness, and saw a multitude of eyes. As I stared, they increased, and appeared to come towards me. For an instant, I stood, unable to move. Then a hideous swine-noise* rose up into the night; and, at that, I leapt from the window, out on to the frozen world. I have a confused notion of having run awhile; and, after that, I just waited—waited. Several times, I heard shrieks; but always as though from a distance. Except for these sounds, I had no idea of the whereabouts of the house. Time moved onward. I was conscious of little, save a sensation of cold and hopelessness and fear.

An age, it seemed, and there came a glow, that told of the coming light. It grew, tardily. Then—with a loom of unearthly glory—the first ray from the Green Star, struck over the edge of the dark sun, and lit the world. It fell upon a great, ruined structure, some two hundred yards away. It was the house. Staring, I saw a fearsome sight—over its walls crawled a legion of unholy things, almost covering the old building, from tottering towers to base. I could see them, plainly; they were the Swine-creatures.

The world moved out into the light of the Star, and I saw that, now, it seemed to stretch across a quarter of the heavens. The glory of its livid light was so tremendous, that it appeared to fill the sky with quivering flames. Then, I saw the sun. It was so close that half of its diameter lay below the horizon; and, as the world circled across its face, it seemed to tower right up into the sky, a stupendous dome of emerald coloured

* See footnote, page 593.

fire. From time to time, I glanced towards the house; but the Swine-things seemed unaware of my proximity.

Years appeared to pass, slowly. The earth had almost reached the centre of the sun's disk. The light from the Green *Sun*—as now it must be called—shone through the interstices, that gapped the mouldered walls of the old house, giving them the appearance of being wrapped in green flames. The Swine-creatures still crawled about the walls.

Suddenly, there rose a loud roar of swine-voices, and, up from the centre of the roofless house, shot a vast column of blood-red flame. I saw the little, twisted towers and turrets flash into fire; yet still preserving their twisted crookedness. The beams of the Green Sun, beat upon the house, and intermingled with its lurid glows; so that it appeared a blazing furnace of red and green fire.

Fascinated, I watched, until an overwhelming sense of coming danger, drew my attention. I glanced up, and, at once, it was borne upon me, that the sun was closer; so close, in fact, that it seemed to overhang the world. Then—I know not how—I was caught up into strange heights—floating like a bubble in the awful effulgence.

Far below me, I saw the earth, with the burning house leaping into an ever grow-ing mountain of flame, round about it, the ground appeared to be glowing; and, in places, heavy wreaths of yellow smoke ascended from the earth. It seemed as though the world were becoming ignited from that one plague-spot of fire. Faintly, I could see the Swine-things. They appeared quite unharmed. Then the ground seemed to cave in, suddenly, and the house, with its load of foul creatures, disappeared into the depths of the earth, sending a strange, blood coloured cloud into the heights. I remembered the hell Pit under the house.

In a while, I looked round. The huge bulk of the sun, rose high above me. The distance between it and the earth, grew rapidly less. Suddenly, the earth appeared to shoot forward. In a moment, it had traversed the space between it and the sun. I heard no sound; but, out from the sun's face, gushed an ever-growing tongue of dazzling flame. It *seemed* to leap, almost to the distant Green Sun—shearing through the emer-ald light, a very cataract of blinding fire. It reached its limit, and sank; and, on the sun, glowed a vast splash of burning white—the grave of the earth.

The sun was very close to me, now. Presently, I found that I was rising higher; until, at last, I rode above it, in the emptiness. The Green Sun was now so huge that its breadth seemed to fill up all the sky, ahead. I looked down, and noted that the sun was passing directly beneath me.

A year may have gone by—or a century—and I was left, suspended, alone. The sun showed far in front—a black, circular mass, against the molten splendor of the great, Green Orb. Near one edge, I observed that a lurid glow had appeared, marking the place where the earth had fallen. By this, I knew that the long-dead sun was still revolving; though with great slowness.

Afar to my right, I seemed to catch, at times, a faint glow of whitish light. For a great time, I was uncertain whether to put this down to fancy or not. Thus, for a while, I stared, with fresh wonderings; until, at last, I knew that it was no imaginary thing; but a reality. It grew brighter; and, presently, there slid out of the green, a pale globe of softest white. It came nearer, and I saw that it was apparently surrounded by a robe of gently glowing clouds. Time passed. . . .

I glanced towards the diminishing sun. It showed, only as a dark blot on the face of the Green Sun. As I watched, I saw it grow smaller, steadily, as though rushing towards the superior orb, at an immense speed. Intently, I stared. What would happen? I was conscious of extraordinary emotions, as I realised that it would strike the Green Sun. It grew no bigger than a pea, and I looked, with my whole soul, to witness the final end of our System—that system which had borne the world through so many æons, with its multitudinous sorrows and joys; and now—

Suddenly, something crossed my vision, cutting from sight all vestige of the spectacle I watched with such soul-interest. What happened to the dead sun, I did not see; but I have no reason—in the light of that which I saw afterwards—to disbelieve that it fell into the strange fire of the Green Sun, and so perished.

And then, suddenly, an extraordinary question rose in my mind, whether this stupendous globe of green fire might not be the vast *Central* Sun—the great sun, round which our universe and countless others revolve. I felt confused. I thought of the probable end of the dead sun, and another suggestion came, dumbly—Do the dead stars make the Green Sun their grave? The idea appealed to me with no sense of grotesqueness; but rather as something both possible and probable.

XX. THE CELESTIAL GLOBES

For a while, many thoughts crowded my mind, so that I was unable to do aught, save stare, blindly, before me. I seemed whelmed in a sea of doubt and wonder and sorrowful remembrance.

It was later, that I came out of my bewilderment. I looked about, dazedly. Thus, I saw so extraordinary a sight that, for a while, I could scarcely believe I was not still wrapped in the visionary tumult of my own thoughts. Out of the reigning green, had grown a boundless river of softly shimmering globes—each one enfolded in a wondrous fleece of pure cloud. They reached, both above and below me, to an unknown distance; and, not only hid the shining of the Green Sun; but supplied, in place thereof, a tender glow of light, that suffused itself around me, like unto nothing I have ever seen, before or since.

In a little, I noticed that there was about these spheres, a sort of transparency, almost as though they were formed of clouded crystal, within which burned a radiance—gentle and subdued. They moved on, past me, continually, floating onward at no great speed; but rather as though they had eternity before them. A great while, I watched, and could perceive no end to them. At times, I seemed to distinguish faces, amid the cloudiness; but strangely indistinct, as though partly real, and partly formed of the mistiness through which they showed.

For a long time, I waited, passively, with a sense of growing content. I had no longer that feeling of unutterable loneliness; but felt, rather, that I was less alone, than I had been for kalpas of years. This feeling of contentment, increased, so that I would have been satisfied to float in company with those celestial globules, for ever.

Ages slipped by, and I saw the shadowy faces, with increased frequency, also with greater plainness. Whether this was due to my soul having become more attuned to its surroundings, I cannot tell—probably it was so. But, however this may be, I am assured now, only of the fact that I became steadily more conscious of a new mystery about me, telling me that I had, indeed, penetrated within the borderland of some unthought of region—some subtle, intangible place, or form, of existence.

The enormous stream of luminous spheres continued to pass me, at an unvarying rate—countless millions; and still they came, showing no signs of ending, nor even diminishing.

Then, as I was borne, silently, upon the unbuoying ether, I felt a sudden, irresistible, forward movement, towards one of the passing globes. An instant, and I was beside it. Then, I slid through, into the interior, without experiencing the least resistance, of any description. For a short while, I could see nothing; and waited, curiously.

All at once, I became aware that a sound broke the inconceivable stillness. It was like the murmur of a great sea at calm—a sea breathing in its sleep. Gradually, the mist that obscured my sight, began to thin away; and so, in time, my vision dwelt once again upon the silent surface of the Sea of Sleep.

For a little, I gazed, and could scarcely believe I saw aright. I glanced round. There was the great globe of pale fire, swimming, as I had seen it before, a short distance above the dim horizon. To my left, far across the sea, I discovered, presently, a faint line, as of thin haze, which I guessed to be the shore, where my Love and I had met, during those wonderful periods of soul-wandering, that had been granted to me in the old earth-days.

Another, a troubled, memory came to me—of the Formless Thing that had haunted the shores of the Sea of Sleep. The guardian of that silent, echoless place. These, and other, details, I remembered, and knew, without doubt that I was looking out upon that same sea. With the assurance, I was filled with an overwhelming feeling of surprise, and joy, and shaken expectancy, conceiving it possible that I was about to see my Love, again. Intently, I gazed around; but could catch no sight of her. At that, for a little, I felt hopeless. Fervently, I prayed, and ever peered, anxiously. . . . How still was the sea!

Down, far beneath me, I could see the many trails of changeful fire, that had drawn my attention, formerly. Vaguely, I wondered what caused them; also, I remembered that I had intended to ask my dear One about them, as well as many other matters—and I had been forced to leave her, before the half that I had wished to say, was said.

My thoughts came back with a leap. I was conscious that something had touched me. I turned quickly. God, Thou wert indeed gracious—it was She! She looked up into my eyes, with an eager longing, and I looked down to her, with all my soul. I should like to have held her; but the glorious purity of her face, kept me afar. Then, out of the winding mist, she put her dear arms. Her whisper came to me, soft as the rustle of a passing cloud. "Dearest!" she said. That was all; but I had heard, and, in a moment I held her to me—as I prayed—forever.

In a little, she spoke of many things, and I listened. Willingly, would I have done so through all the ages that are to come. At times, I whispered back, and my whispers brought to her spirit face, once more, an indescribably delicate tint—the bloom of love. Later, I spoke more freely, and to each word she listened, and made answer, delightfully; so that, already, I was in Paradise.

She and I; and nothing, save the silent, spacious void to see us; and only the quiet waters of the Sea of Sleep to hear us.

Long before, the floating multitude of cloud-enfolded spheres had vanished into nothingness. Thus, we looked upon the face of the slumberous deeps, and were alone. Alone, God, I would be thus alone in the hereafter, and yet be never lonely! I had her, and, greater than this, she had me. Aye, æon-aged me; and on this thought, and some others, I hope to exist through the few remaining years that may yet lie between us.

XXI. THE DARK SUN

How long our souls lay in the arms of joy, I cannot say; but, all at once, I was waked from my happiness, by a diminution of the pale and gentle light that lit the Sea of Sleep. I turned towards the huge, white orb, with a premonition of coming trouble. One side of it was curving inward, as though a convex, black shadow were sweeping across it. My memory went back. It was thus, that the darkness had come, before our last parting. I turned towards my Love, inquiringly. With a sudden knowledge of woe, I noticed how wan and unreal she had grown, even in that brief space. Her voice seemed to come to me from a distance. The touch of her hands was no more than the gentle pressure of a summer wind, and grew less perceptible.

Already, quite half of the immense globe was shrouded. A feeling of desperation seized me. Was she about to leave me? Would she have to go, as she had gone before? I questioned her, anxiously, frightenedly; and she, nestling closer, explained, in that strange, faraway voice, that it was imperative she should leave me, before the Sun of Darkness—as she termed it—blotted out the light. At this confirmation of my fears, I was overcome with despair; and could only look, voicelessly, across the quiet plains of the silent sea.

How swiftly the darkness spread across the face of the White Orb. Yet, in reality, the time must have been long, beyond human comprehension.

At last, only a crescent of pale fire, lit the, now dim, Sea of Sleep. All this while, she had held me; but, with so soft a caress, that I had been scarcely conscious of it. We waited there, together, she and I; dumb, for very sorrow. In the dimming light, her face showed, shadowy—blending into the dusky mistiness that encircled us.

Then, when a thin, curved line of soft light was all that lit the sea, she released me—pushing me from her, tenderly. Her voice sounded in my ears, "I may not stay longer, Dear One." It ended in a sob.

She seemed to float away from me, and became invisible. Her voice came to me, out of the shadows, faintly; apparently from a great distance:—

"A little while—" It died away, remotely. In a breath, the Sea of Sleep darkened into night. Far to my left, I seemed to see, for a brief instant, a soft glow. It vanished, and, in the same moment, I became aware that I was no longer above the still sea; but once more suspended in infinite space, with the Green Sun—now eclipsed by a vast, dark sphere—before me.

Utterly bewildered, I stared, almost unseeingly, at the ring of green flames, leaping above the dark edge. Even in the chaos of my thoughts, I wondered, dully, at their extraordinary shapes. A multitude of questions assailed me. I thought more of her, I had so lately seen, than of the sight before me. My grief, and thoughts of the future, filled me. Was I doomed to be separated from her, always? Even in the old earth-days, she had been mine, only for a little while; then she had left me, as I thought, forever. Since then, I had seen her but these times, upon the Sea of Sleep.

A feeling of fierce resentment filled me, and miserable questionings. Why could I not have gone with my Love? What reason to keep us apart? Why had I to wait alone, while she slumbered through the years, on the still bosom of the Sea of Sleep? The Sea of Sleep! My thoughts turned, inconsequently, out of their channel of bitterness, to fresh, desperate questionings. Where was it? Where was it? I seemed to have but just parted from my Love, upon its quiet surface, and it had gone, utterly. It could not be far away! And the White Orb which I had seen hidden in the shadow of the Sun of Darkness! My sight dwelt upon the Green Sun—eclipsed. What had eclipsed it? Was there a vast, dead star circling it? Was the *Central* Sun—as I had come to regard it—a double star? The thought had come, almost unbidden; yet why should it not be so?

My thoughts went back to the White Orb. Strange, that it should have been—I stopped. An idea had come, suddenly. The White Orb and the Green Sun! Were they one and the same? My imagination wandered backwards, and I remembered the luminous globe to which I had been so unaccountably attracted. It was curious that I should have forgotten it, even momentarily. Where were the others? I reverted again to the globe I had entered. I thought, for a time, and matters became clearer. I conceived that, by entering that impalpable globule, I had passed, at once, into some further, and, until then, invisible dimension; There, the Green Sun was still visible; but as a stupendous sphere of pale, white light—almost as though its ghost showed, and not its material part.

A long time, I mused on the subject. I remembered how, on entering the sphere, I had, immediately, lost all sight of the others. For a still further period, I continued to revolve the different details in my mind.

In a while, my thoughts turned to other things. I came more into the present, and began to look about me, seeingly. For the first time, I perceived that innumerable rays, of a subtle, violet hue, pierced the strange semi-darkness, in all directions. They radiated from the fiery rim of the Green Sun. They seemed to grow upon my vision, so that, in a little, I saw that they were countless. The night was filled with them—spreading outward from the Green Sun, fan-wise. I concluded that I was enabled to see them, by reason of the Sun's glory being cut off by the eclipse. They reached right out into space, and vanished.

Gradually, as I looked, I became aware that fine points of intensely brilliant light, traversed the rays. Many of them seemed to travel from the Green Sun, into distance. Others came out of the void, towards the Sun; but, one and all, each kept strictly to the ray in which it travelled. Their speed was inconceivably great; and it was only when they neared the Green Sun, or as they left it, that I could see them as separate specks of light. Further from the sun, they became thin lines of vivid fire within the violet.

The discovery of these rays, and the moving sparks, interested me, extraordinarily. To where did they lead, in such countless profusion? I thought of the worlds in space. . . . And those sparks! Messengers! Possibly, the idea was fantastic; but I was not conscious of its being so. Messengers! Messengers from the Central Sun!

An idea evolved itself, slowly. Was the Green Sun the abode of some vast Intelligence? The thought was bewildering. Visions of the Unnamable rose, vaguely. Had I, indeed, come upon the dwelling-place of the Eternal? For a time, I repelled the thought, dumbly. It was too stupendous. Yet. . . .

Huge, vague thoughts had birth within me. I felt, suddenly, terribly naked. And an awful Nearness, shook me.

And Heaven! . . . Was that an illusion?

My thoughts came and went, erratically. The Sea of Sleep—and she! Heaven . . . . I came back, with a bound, to the present. Somewhere, out of the void behind me, there rushed an immense, dark body—huge and silent. It was a dead star, hurling onward to the burying place of the stars. It drove between me and the Central Suns—blotting them out from my vision, and plunging me into an impenetrable night.

An age, and I saw again the violet rays. A great while later—æons it must have been—a circular glow grew in the sky, ahead, and I saw the edge of the receding star, show darkly against it. Thus, I knew that it was nearing the Central Suns. Presently, I saw the bright ring of the Green Sun, show plainly against the night. The star had passed into the shadow of the Dead Sun. After that, I just waited. The strange years went slowly, and ever, I watched, intently.

The thing I had expected, came at last—suddenly, awfully. A vast flare of dazzling light. A streaming burst of white flame across the dark void. For an indefinite while, it soared outwards—a gigantic mushroom of fire. It ceased to grow. Then, as time went by, it began to sink backward, slowly. I saw, now, that it came from a huge, glowing spot near the centre of the Dark Sun. Mighty flames, still soared outward from this. Yet, spite of its size, the grave of the star was no more than the shining of Jupiter upon the face of an ocean, when compared with the inconceivable mass of the Dead Sun.

I may remark here, once more, that no words will ever convey to the imagination, the enormous bulk of the two Central Suns.

XXII. THE DARK NEBULA

Years melted into the past, centuries, æons. The light of the incandescent star, sank to a furious red.

It was later, that I saw the dark nebula—at first, an impalpable cloud, away to my right. It grew, steadily, to a clot of blackness in the night. How long I watched, it is impossible to say; for time, as we count it, was a thing of the past. It came closer, a shapeless monstrosity of darkness—tremendous. It seemed to slip across the night, sleepily—a very hell-fog. Slowly, it slid nearer, and passed into the void, between me and the Central Suns. It was as though a curtain had been drawn before my vision. A strange tremor of fear took me, and a fresh sense of wonder.

The green twilight that had reigned for so many millions of years, had now given place to impenetrable gloom. Motionless, I peered about me. A century fled, and it seemed to me that I detected occasional dull glows of red, passing me at intervals.

Earnestly, I gazed, and, presently, seemed to see circular masses, that showed muddily red, within the clouded blackness. They appeared to be growing out of the nebulous murk. Awhile, and they became plainer to my accustomed vision. I could see them, now, with a fair amount of distinctness—ruddy-tinged spheres, similar, in size, to the luminous globes that I had seen, so long previously.

They floated past me, continually. Gradually, a peculiar uneasiness seized me. I became aware of a growing feeling of repugnance and dread. It was directed against those passing orbs, and seemed born of intuitive knowledge, rather than of any real cause or reason.

Some of the passing globes were brighter than others; and, it was from one of these, that a face looked, suddenly. A face, human in its outline; but so tortured with woe, that I stared, aghast. I had not thought there was such sorrow, as I saw there. I was conscious of an added sense of pain, on perceiving that the eyes, which glared so wildly, were sightless. A while longer, I saw it; then it had passed on, into the surrounding gloom. After this, I saw others—all wearing that look of hopeless sorrow; and blind.

A long time went by, and I became aware that I was nearer to the orbs, than I had been. At this, I grew uneasy; though I was less in fear of those strange globules, than I had been, before seeing their sorrowful inhabitants; for sympathy had tempered my fear.

Later, there was no doubt but that I was being carried closer to the red spheres, and, presently, I floated among them. In awhile, I perceived one bearing down upon me. I was helpless to move from its path. In a minute, it seemed, it was upon me, and I was submerged in a deep red mist. This cleared, and I stared, confusedly, across the immense breadth of the Plain of Silence. It appeared just as I had first seen it. I was moving forward, steadily, across its surface. Away ahead, shone the vast, blood-red ring* that lit the place. All around, was spread the extraordinary desolation of stillness, that had so impressed me during my previous wanderings across its starkness.

Presently, I saw, rising up into the ruddy gloom, the distant peaks of the mighty amphitheatre of mountains, where, untold ages before, I had been shown my first glimpse of the terrors that underlie many things; and where, vast and silent, watched by a thousand mute gods, stands the replica of this house of mysteries—this house that I had seen swallowed up in that hell-fire, ere the earth had kissed the sun, and vanished for ever.

Though I could see the crests of the mountain-amphitheatre, yet it was a great while before their lower portions became visible. Possibly, this was due to the strange, ruddy haze, that seemed to cling to the surface of the Plain. However, be this as it may, I saw them at last.

In a still further space of time, I had come so close to the mountains, that they appeared to overhang me. Presently, I saw the great rift, open before me, and I drifted into it, without volition on my part.

Later, I came out upon the breadth of the enormous arena. There, at an apparent distance of some five miles, stood the House, huge, monstrous and silent—lying in the very centre of that stupendous amphitheatre. So far as I could see, it had not altered in

* Without doubt, the flame-edged mass of the Dead Central Sun, seen from another dimension.—ED.

any way; but looked as though it were only yesterday that I had seen it. Around, the grim, dark mountains frowned down upon me from their lofty silences.

Far to my right, away up among inaccessible peaks, loomed the enormous bulk of the great Ass-god. Higher, I saw the hideous form of the dread goddess, rising up through the red gloom, thousands of fathoms above me. To the left, I made out the monstrous Eyeless-Thing, grey and inscrutable. Further off, reclining on its lofty ledge, the livid Ghoul-Shape showed—a splash of sinister colour, among the dark mountains.

Slowly, I moved out across the great arena—floating. As I went, I made out the dim forms of many of the other lurking Horrors that peopled those supreme heights.

Gradually, I neared the House, and my thoughts flashed back across the abyss of years. I remembered the dread Spectre of the Place. A short while passed, and I saw that I was being wafted directly towards the enormous mass of that silent building.

About this time, I became aware, in an indifferent sort of way, of a growing sense of numbness, that robbed me of the fear, which I should otherwise have felt, on approaching that awesome Pile. As it was, I viewed it, calmly—much as a man views calamity through the haze of his tobacco smoke.

In a little while, I had come so close to the House, as to be able to distinguish many of the details about it. The longer I looked, the more was I confirmed in my long-ago impressions of its entire similitude to this strange house. Save in its enormous size, I could find nothing unlike.

Suddenly, as I stared, a great feeling of amazement filled me. I had come opposite to that part, where the outer door, leading into the study, is situated. There, lying right across the threshold, lay a great length of coping stone, identical—save in size and colour—with the piece I had dislodged in my fight with the Pit-creatures.

I floated nearer, and my astonishment increased, as I noted that the door was broken partly from its hinges, precisely in the manner that my study door had been forced inward, by the assaults of the Swine-things. The sight started a train of thoughts, and I began to trace, dimly, that the attack on *this* house, might have a far deeper significance than I had, hitherto, imagined. I remembered how, long ago, in the old earth-days, I had half suspected that, in some unexplainable manner, this house, in which I live, was *en rapport*—to use a recognized term—with that other tremendous structure, away in the midst of that incomparable Plain.

Now, however, it began to be borne upon me, that I had but vaguely conceived what the realisation of my suspicion meant. I began to understand, with a more than human clearness, that the attack I had repelled, was, in some extraordinary manner, connected with an attack upon that strange edifice.

With a curious inconsequence, my thoughts abruptly left the matter; to dwell, wonderingly, upon the peculiar material, out of which the House was constructed. It was—as I have mentioned, earlier—of a deep, green colour. Yet, now that I had come so close to it, I perceived that it fluctuated at times, though slightly—glowing and fading, much as do the fumes of phosphorus, when rubbed upon the hand, in the dark.

Presently, my attention was distracted from this, by coming to the great entrance. Here, for the first time, I was afraid; for, all in a moment, the huge doors swung back, and I drifted in between them, helplessly. Inside, all was blackness, impalpable. In an instant, I had crossed the threshold, and the great doors closed, silently, shutting me in that lightless place.

For a while, I seemed to hang, motionless; suspended amid the darkness. Then, I became conscious that I was moving again; where, I could not tell. Suddenly, far down beneath me, I seemed to hear a murmurous noise of Swine-laughter. It sank away, and the succeeding silence appeared clogged with horror.

Then a door opened somewhere ahead; a white haze of light filtered through, and I floated slowly into a room, that seemed strangely familiar. All at once, there came a bewildering, screaming noise, that deafened me. I saw a blurred vista of visions, flaming before my sight. My senses were dazed, through the space of an eternal moment. Then, my power of seeing, came back to me. The dizzy, hazy feeling passed, and I saw, clearly.

XXIII. PEPPER

I was seated in my chair, back again in this old study. My glance wandered round the room. For a minute, it had a strange, quivery appearance—unreal and unsubstantial. This disappeared, and I saw that nothing was altered in any way. I looked towards the end window—the blind was up.

I rose to my feet, shakily. As I did so, a slight noise, in the direction of the door, attracted my attention. I glanced towards it. For a short instant, it appeared to me that it was being closed, gently. I stared, and saw that I must have been mistaken—it seemed closely shut.

With a succession of efforts, I trod my way to the window, and looked out. The sun was just rising, lighting up the tangled wilderness of gardens. For, perhaps, a minute, I stood, and stared. I passed my hand, confusedly, across my forehead.

Presently, amid the chaos of my senses, a sudden thought came to me; I turned, quickly, and called to Pepper. There was no answer, and I stumbled across the room, in a quick access of fear. As I went, I tried to frame his name; but my lips were numb. I reached the table, and stooped down to him, with a catching at my heart. He was lying in the shadow of the table, and I had not been able to see him, distinctly, from the window. Now, as I stooped, I took my breath, shortly. There was no Pepper; instead, I was reaching towards an elongated, little heap of grey, ash-like dust. . . .

I must have remained, in that half-stooped position, for some minutes. I was dazed—stunned. Pepper had really passed into the land of shadows.

XXIV. THE FOOTSTEPS IN THE GARDEN

Pepper is dead! Even now, at times, I seem scarcely able to realise that this is so. It is many weeks, since I came back from that strange and terrible journey through space and time. Sometimes, in my sleep, I dream about it, and go through, in imagination, the whole of that fearsome happening. When I wake, my thoughts dwell upon it. That Sun—those Suns, were they indeed the great Central Suns, round which the whole universe, of the unknown heavens, revolves? Who shall say? And the bright globules, floating forever in the light of the Green Sun! And the Sea of Sleep on which they float! How unbelievable it all is. If it were not for Pepper, I should, even after the many extraordinary things that I have witnessed, be inclined to imagine that it was but a gigantic dream. Then, there is that dreadful, dark nebula (with its multitudes of red spheres) moving always within the shadow of the Dark Sun, sweeping along on its stupendous orbit, wrapped eternally in gloom. And the faces that peered out at me! God, do they, and does such a thing really exist? . . . There is still that little heap of grey ash, on my study floor. I will not have it touched.

At times, when I am calmer, I have wondered what became of the outer planets of the Solar System. It has occurred to me, that they may have broken loose from the sun's attraction, and whirled away into space. This is, of course, only a surmise. There are so many things, about which I wonder.

Now that I am writing, let me record that I am certain, there is something horrible about to happen. Last night, a thing occurred, which has filled me with an even greater terror, than did the Pit fear. I will write it down now, and, if anything more happens, endeavor to make a note of it, at once. I have a feeling, that there is more in this last affair, than in all those others. I am shaky and nervous, even now, as I write. Somehow, I think death is not very far away. Not that I fear death—as death is understood. Yet, there is that in the air, which bids me fear—an intangible, cold horror. I felt it last night. It was thus:—

Last night, I was sitting here in my study, writing. The door, leading into the garden, was half open. At times, the metallic rattle of a dog's chain, sounded faintly. It belongs to the dog I have bought, since Pepper's death. I will not have him in the house—not after Pepper. Still, I have felt it better to have a dog about the place. They are wonderful creatures.

I was much engrossed in my work, and the time passed, quickly. Suddenly, I heard a soft noise on the path, outside in the garden—pad, pad, pad, it went, with a stealthy, curious sound. I sat upright, with a quick movement, and looked out through the opened door. Again the noise came—pad, pad, pad. It appeared to be approaching. With a slight feeling of nervousness, I stared into the gardens; but the night hid everything.

Then the dog gave a long howl, and I started. For a minute, perhaps, I peered, intently; but could hear nothing. After a little, I picked up the pen, which I had laid down, and recommenced my work. The nervous feeling had gone; for I imagined that the sound I had heard, was nothing more than the dog walking round his kennel, at the length of his chain.

A quarter of an hour may have passed; then, all at once, the dog howled again, and with such a plaintively sorrowful note, that I jumped to my feet, dropping my pen, and inking the page on which I was at work.

"Curse that dog!" I muttered, noting what I had done. Then, even as I said the words, there sounded again that queer—pad, pad, pad. It was horribly close—almost by the door, I thought. I knew, now, that it could not be the dog; his chain would not allow him to come so near.

The dog's growl came again, and I noted, subconsciously, the taint of fear in it.

Outside, on the window-sill, I could see Tip, my sister's pet cat. As I looked, it sprang to its feet, its tail swelling, visibly. For an instant it stood thus; seeming to stare, fixedly, at something, in the direction of the door. Then, quickly, it began to back along the sill; until, reaching the wall at the end, it could go no further. There it stood, rigid, as though frozen in an attitude of extraordinary terror.

Frightened, and puzzled, I seized a stick from the corner, and went towards the door, silently; taking one of the candles with me. I had come to within a few paces of it, when, suddenly, a peculiar sense of fear thrilled through me—a fear, palpitant and real; whence, I knew not, nor why. So great was the feeling of terror, that I wasted no time; but retreated straightway—walking backward, and keeping my gaze, fearfully, on the door. I would have given much, to rush at it, fling it to, and shoot the bolts; for I have had it repaired and strengthened, so that, now, it is far stronger than ever it has been. Like Tip, I continued my, almost unconscious, progress backwards, until the wall brought me up. At that, I started, nervously, and glanced round, apprehensively. As I did so, my eyes dwelt, momentarily, on the rack of firearms, and I took a step towards them; but stopped, with a curious feeling that they would be needless. Outside, in the gardens, the dog moaned, strangely.

Suddenly, from the cat, there came a fierce, long screech. I glanced, jerkily, in its direction—Something, luminous and ghostly, encircled it, and grew upon my vision. It resolved into a glowing hand, transparent, with a lambent, greenish flame flickering over it. The cat gave a last, awful caterwaul, and I saw it smoke and blaze. My breath came with a gasp, and I leant against the wall. Over *that* part of the window there spread a smudge, green and fantastic. It hid the thing from me, though the glare of fire shone through, dully. A stench of burning, stole into the room.

Pad, pad, pad—Something passed down the garden path, and a faint, mouldy odor seemed to come in through the open door, and mingle with the burnt smell.

The dog had been silent for a few moments. Now, I heard him yowl, sharply, as though in pain. Then, he was quiet, save for an occasional, subdued whimper of fear.

A minute went by; then the gate on the West side of the gardens, slammed, distantly. After that, nothing; not even the dog's whine.

I must have stood there some minutes. Then a fragment of courage stole into my heart, and I made a frightened rush at the door, dashed it to, and bolted it. After that, for a full half-hour, I sat, helpless—staring before me, rigidly.

Slowly, my life came back into me, and I made my way, shakily, up-stairs to bed.

That is all.

XXV. THE THING FROM THE ARENA

This morning, early, I went through the gardens; but found everything as usual. Near the door, I examined the path, for footprints; yet, here again, there was nothing to tell me whether, or not, I dreamed last night.

It was only when I came to speak to the dog, that I discovered tangible proof, that something did happen. When I went to his kennel, he kept inside, crouching up in one corner, and I had to coax him, to get him out. When, finally, he consented to come, it was in a strangely cowed and subdued manner. As I patted him, my attention was attracted to a greenish patch, on his left flank. On examining it, I found, that the fur and skin had been apparently, burnt off; for the flesh showed, raw and scorched. The shape of the mark was curious, reminding me of the imprint of a large talon or hand.

I stood up, thoughtful. My gaze wandered towards the study window. The rays of the rising sun, shimmered on the smoky patch in the lower corner, causing it to fluctuate from green to red, oddly. Ah! that was undoubtedly another proof; and, suddenly, the horrible Thing I saw last night, rose in my mind. I looked at the dog, again. I knew the cause, now, of that hateful looking wound on his side—I knew, also, that, what I had seen last night, had been a real happening. And a great discomfort filled me. Pepper! Tip! And now this poor animal. . . ! I glanced at the dog again, and noticed that he was licking at his wound.

"Poor brute!" I muttered, and bent to pat his head. At that, he got upon his feet, nosing and licking my hand, wistfully.

Presently, I left him, having other matters to which to attend.

After dinner, I went to see him, again. He seemed quiet, and disinclined to leave his kennel. From my sister, I have learnt that he has refused all food today. She appeared a little puzzled, when she told me; though quite unsuspicious of anything of which to be afraid.

The day has passed, uneventfully enough. After tea, I went, again, to have a look at the dog. He seemed moody, and somewhat restless; yet persisted in remaining in his kennel. Before locking up, for the night, I moved his kennel out, away from the wall, so that I shall be able to watch it from the small window, tonight. The thought came to me, to bring him into the house for the night; but consideration has decided me, to let him remain out. I cannot say that the house is, in any degree, less to be feared than the gardens. Pepper was in the house, and yet. . . .

It is now two o'clock. Since eight, I have watched the kennel, from the small, side window in my study. Yet, nothing has occurred, and I am too tired to watch longer. I will go to bed. . . .

During the night, I was restless. This is unusual for me; but, towards morning, I obtained a few hours' sleep.

I rose early, and, after breakfast, visited the dog. He was quiet; but morose, and refused to leave his kennel. I wish there was some horse doctor near here; I would have the poor brute looked to. All day, he has taken no food; but has shown an evident desire for water—lapping it up, greedily. I was relieved to observe this.

The evening has come, and I am in my study. I intend to follow my plan of last night, and watch the kennel. The door, leading into the garden, is bolted, securely. I am consciously glad there are bars to the windows. . . .

Night:—Midnight has gone. The dog has been silent, up to the present. Through the side window, on my left, I can make out, dimly, the outlines of the kennel. For the first time, the dog moves, and I hear the rattle of his chain. I look out, quickly. As I stare, the dog moves again, restlessly, and I see a small patch of luminous light, shine from the interior of the kennel. It vanishes; then the dog stirs again, and, once more, the gleam comes. I am puzzled. The dog is quiet, and I can see the luminous thing, plainly. It shows distinctly. There is something familiar about the shape of it. For a moment, I wonder; then it comes to me, that it is not unlike the four fingers and thumb of a hand. Like a hand! And I remember the contour of that fearsome wound on the dog's side. It must be the wound I see. It is luminous at night—Why? The minutes pass. My mind is filled with this fresh thing. . . .

Suddenly, I hear a sound, out in the gardens. How it thrills through me. It is approaching. Pad, pad, pad. A prickly sensation traverses my spine, and seems to creep across my scalp. The dog moves in his kennel, and whimpers, frightenedly. He must have turned round; for, now, I can no longer see the outline of his shining wound.

Outside, the gardens are silent, once more, and I listen, fearfully. A minute passes, and another; then I hear the padding sound, again. It is quite close, and appears to be coming down the gravelled path. The noise is curiously measured and deliberate. It ceases outside the door; and I rise to my feet, and stand motionless. From the door, comes a slight sound—the latch is being slowly raised. A singing noise is in my ears, and I have a sense of pressure about the head——

The latch drops, with a sharp click, into the catch. The noise startles me afresh; jarring, horribly, on my tense nerves. After that, I stand, for a long while, amid an ever growing quietness. All at once, my knees begin to tremble, and I have to sit, quickly.

An uncertain period of time passes, and, gradually, I begin to shake off the feeling of terror, that has possessed me. Yet, still I sit. I seem to have lost the power of movement. I am strangely tired, and inclined to doze. My eyes open and close, and, presently, I find myself falling asleep, and waking, in fits and starts.

It is some time later, that I am sleepily aware that one of the candles is guttering. When I wake again, it has gone out, and the room is very dim, under the light of the one remaining flame. The semi-darkness troubles me little. I have lost that awful sense of dread, and my only desire seems to be to sleep—sleep.

Suddenly, although there is no noise, I am awake—wide awake. I am acutely conscious of the nearness of some mystery, of some overwhelming Presence. The very air seems pregnant with terror. I sit huddled, and just listen, intently. Still, there is no sound. Nature, herself, seems dead. Then, the oppressive stillness is broken by a little eldritch scream of wind, that sweeps round the house, and dies away, remotely.

I let my gaze wander across the half-lighted room. By the great clock in the far corner, is a dark, tall shadow. For a short instant, I stare, frightenedly. Then, I see that it is nothing, and am, momentarily, relieved.

In the time that follows, the thought flashes through my brain, why not leave this house—this house of mystery and terror? Then, as though in answer, there sweeps up, across my sight, a vision of the wondrous Sea of Sleep—the Sea of Sleep where she and I have been allowed to meet, after the years of separation and sorrow; and I know that I shall stay on here, whatever happens.

Through the side window, I note the sombre blackness of the night. My glance wanders away, and round the room; resting on one shadowy object and another. Suddenly, I turn, and look at the window on my right; as I do so, I breathe quickly, and bend forward, with a frightened gaze at something outside the window, but close to the bars. I am looking at a vast, misty swine-face, over which fluctuates a flamboyant flame, of a greenish hue. It is the Thing from the arena. The quivering mouth seems to drip with a continual, phosphorescent slaver. The eyes are staring straight into the room, with an inscrutable expression. Thus, I sit rigidly—frozen.

The Thing has begun to move. It is turning, slowly, in my direction. Its face is coming round towards me. It sees me. Two huge, inhumanly human, eyes are looking through the dimness at me. I am cold with fear; yet, even now, I am keenly conscious, and note, in an irrelevant way, that the distant stars are blotted out by the mass of the giant face.

A fresh horror has come to me. I am rising from my chair, without the least intention. I am on my feet, and something is impelling me towards the door that leads out into the gardens. I wish to stop; but cannot. Some immutable power is opposed to my will, and I go slowly forward, unwilling and resistant. My glance flies round the room, helplessly, and stops at the window. The great swine-face has disappeared, and I hear, again, that stealthy pad, pad, pad. It stops outside the door—the door towards which I am being compelled. . . .

There succeeds a short, intense silence; then there comes a sound. It is the rattle of the latch, being slowly lifted. At that, I am filled with desperation. I will not go forward another step. I make a vast effort to return; but it is, as though I press back, upon an invisible wall. I groan out loud, in the agony of my fear, and the sound of my voice is frightening. Again comes that rattle, and I shiver, clammily. I try—aye, fight and struggle, to hold back, *back*; but it is no use. . . .

I am at the door, and, in a mechanical way, I watch my hand go forward, to undo the topmost bolt. It does so, entirely without my volition. Even as I reach up towards the bolt, the door is violently shaken, and I get a sickly whiff of mouldy air, which seems to drive in through the interstices of the doorway. I draw the bolt back, slowly, fighting, dumbly, the while. It comes out of its socket, with a click, and I begin to shake, aguishly. There are two more; one at the bottom of the door; the other, a massive affair, is placed about the middle.

For, perhaps a minute, I stand, with my arms hanging slackly, by my sides. The influence to meddle with the fastenings of the door, seems to have gone. All at once, there comes the sudden rattle of iron, at my feet. I glance down, quickly, and realise, with an unspeakable terror, that my foot is pushing back the lower bolt. An awful sense of helplessness assails me. . . . The bolt comes out of its hold, with a slight, ringing sound and I stagger on my feet, grasping at the great, central bolt, for support. A minute passes, an eternity; then another . . . . My God, help me! I am being forced to work upon the last fastening. *I will not!* Better to die, than open to the Terror, that is on the other side of the door. Is there no escape? . . . God help me, I have jerked the bolt half out of its socket! My lips emit a hoarse scream of terror; the bolt is three parts drawn, now, and still my unconscious hands work towards my doom. Only a fraction of steel, between my soul and *That*. Twice, I scream out in the supreme agony of my fear; then, with a mad effort, I tear my hands away. My eyes seem blinded. A great blackness is falling upon me. Nature has come to my rescue. I feel my knees giving. There is a loud, quick thudding upon the door, and I am falling, falling. . . .

I must have lain there, at least a couple of hours. As I recover, I am aware that the other candle has burnt out, and the room is in an almost total darkness. I cannot rise to my feet, for I am cold, and filled with a terrible cramp. Yet my brain is clear, and there is no longer the strain of that unholy influence.

Cautiously, I get upon my knees, and feel for the central bolt. I find it, and push it securely back into its socket; then the one at the bottom of the door. By this time, I am able to rise to my feet, and so manage to secure the fastening at the top. After that, I go down upon my knees, again, and creep away among the furniture, in the direction of the stairs. By doing this, I am safe from observation from the window.

I reach the opposite door, and, as I leave the study, cast one nervous glance over my shoulder, towards the window. Out in the night, I seem to catch a glimpse of something impalpable; but it may be only a fancy. Then, I am in the passage, and on the stairs.

Reaching my bedroom, I clamber into bed, all clothed as I am, and pull the bed-clothes over me. There, after awhile, I begin to regain a little confidence. It is impossible to sleep; but I am grateful for the added warmth of the bedclothes. Presently, I try to think over the happenings of the past night; but, though I cannot sleep, I find that it is useless, to attempt consecutive thought. My brain seems curiously blank.

Towards morning, I begin to toss, uneasily. I cannot rest, and, after awhile, I get out of bed, and pace the floor. The wintry dawn is beginning to creep through the windows, and shows the bare discomfort of the old room. Strange, that, through all these years, it has never occurred to me how dismal the place really is. And so a time passes.

From somewhere down stairs, a sound comes up to me. I go to the bedroom door, and listen. It is Mary, bustling about the great, old kitchen, getting the break-fast ready. I feel little interest. I am not hungry. My thoughts, however; continue to dwell upon her. How little the weird happenings in this house seem to trouble her. Except in the incident of the Pit creatures, she has seemed unconscious of anything unusual occurring. She is old, like myself; yet how little we have to do with one another. Is it because we have nothing in common; or only that, being old, we care less for society, than quietness? These and other matters pass through my mind, as I meditate; and help to distract my attention, for a while, from the oppressive thoughts of the night.

After a time, I go to the window, and, opening it, look out. The sun is now above the horizon, and the air, though cold, is sweet and crisp. Gradually, my brain clears, and a sense of security, for the time being, comes to me. Somewhat happier, I go down stairs, and out into the garden, to have a look at the dog.

As I approach the kennel, I am greeted by the same mouldy stench that assailed me at the door last night. Shaking off a momentary sense of fear, I call to the dog; but he takes no heed, and, after calling once more, I throw a small stone into the kennel. At this, he moves, uneasily, and I shout his name, again; but do not go closer. Presently, my sister comes out, and joins me, in trying to coax him from the kennel.

In a little the poor beast rises, and shambles out lurching queerly. In the daylight he stands swaying from side to side, and blinking stupidly. I look and note that the horrid wound is larger, much larger, and seems to have a whitish, fungoid appearance. My sister moves to fondle him; but I detain her, and explain that I think it will be better not to go too near him for a few days; as it is impossible to tell what may be the matter with him; and it is well to be cautious.

A minute later, she leaves me; coming back with a basin of odd scraps of food. This she places on the ground, near the dog, and I push it into his reach, with the aid of a branch, broken from one of the shrubs. Yet, though the meat should be tempting, he takes no notice of it; but retires to his kennel. There is still water in his drinking vessel, so, after a few moments' talk, we go back to the house. I can see that my sister is much puzzled as to what is the matter with the animal; yet it would be madness, even to hint the truth to her.

The day slips away, uneventfully; and night comes on. I have determined to repeat my experiment of last night. I cannot say that it is wisdom; yet my mind is made up. Still, however, I have taken precautions; for I have driven stout nails in at the back of each of the three bolts, that secure the door, opening from the study into the gardens. This will, at least, prevent a recurrence of the danger I ran last night.

From ten to about two-thirty, I watch; but nothing occurs; and, finally, I stumble off to bed, where I am soon asleep.

XXVI. THE LUMINOUS SPECK

I awake suddenly. It is still dark. I turn over, once or twice, in my endeavors to sleep again; but I cannot sleep. My head is aching, slightly; and, by turns I am hot and cold. In a little, I give up the attempt, and stretch out my hand, for the matches. I will light my candle, and read, awhile; perhaps, I shall be able to sleep, after a time. For a few moments, I grope; then my hand touches the box; but, as I open it, I am startled, to see a phosphorescent speck of fire, shining amid the darkness. I put out my other hand, and touch it. It is on my wrist. With a feeling of vague alarm, I strike a light, hurriedly, and look; but can see nothing, save a tiny scratch.

"Fancy!" I mutter, with a half sigh of relief. Then the match burns my finger, and I drop it, quickly. As I fumble for another, the thing shines out again. I know, now, that it is no fancy. This time, I light the candle, and examine the place, more closely. There is a slight, greenish discolouration round the scratch. I am puzzled and worried. Then a thought comes to me. I remember the morning after the Thing appeared. I remember that the dog licked my hand. It was this one, with the scratch on it; though I have not been even conscious of the abasement, until now. A horrible fear has come to me. It creeps into my brain—the dog's wound, shines at night. With a dazed feeling, I sit down on the side of the bed, and try to think; but cannot. My brain seems numbed with the sheer horror of this new fear.

Time moves on, unheeded. Once, I rouse up, and try to persuade myself that I am mistaken; but it is no use. In my heart, I have no doubt.

Hour after hour, I sit in the darkness and silence, and shiver, hopelessly. . . .

The day has come and gone, and it is night again.

This morning, early, I shot the dog, and buried it, away among the bushes. My sister is startled and frightened; but I am desperate. Besides, it is better so. The foul growth had almost hidden its left side. And I—the place on my wrist has enlarged, perceptibly. Several times, I have caught myself muttering prayers—little things learnt as a child. God, Almighty God, help me! I shall go mad.

Six days, and I have eaten nothing. It is night. I am sitting in my chair. Ah, God! I wonder have any ever felt the horror of life that I have come to know? I am swathed in terror. I feel ever the burning of this dread growth. It has covered all my right arm and side, and is beginning to creep up my neck. Tomorrow, it will eat into my face. I shall become a terrible mass of living corruption. There is no escape. Yet, a thought has come to me, born of a sight of the gun-rack, on the other side of the room. I have looked again—with the strangest of feelings. The thought grows upon me. God, Thou knowest, Thou must know, that death is better, aye, better a thousand times than *This*. This! Jesus, forgive me, but I cannot live, cannot, cannot! I dare not! I am beyond *all* help—there is nothing else left. It will, at least, spare me that final horror. . . .

I think I must have been dozing. I am very weak, and oh! so miserable, so miserable and tired—tired. The rustle of the paper, tries my brain. My hearing seems preternaturally sharp. I will sit awhile and think. . . .

"Hush! I hear something, down—down in the cellars. It is a creaking sound. My God, it is the opening of the great, oak trap. What can be doing that? The scratching of my pen deafens me. . . . I must listen. . . . There are steps on the stairs; strange padding steps, that come up and nearer. . . . Jesus, be merciful to me, an old man. There is something fumbling at the door-handle. O God, help me now! Jesus—The door is opening—slowly. Somethi—"

That is all.

XXVII. CONCLUSION

I put down the Manuscript, and glanced across at Tonnison: he was sitting, staring out into the dark. I waited a minute; then I spoke.

"Well?" I said.

He turned, slowly, and looked at me. His thoughts seemed to have gone out of him into a great distance.

"Was he mad?" I asked, and indicated the MS., with a half nod.

Tonnison stared at me, unseeingly, a moment; then, his wits came back to him, and, suddenly, he comprehended my question.

"No!" he said.

I opened my lips, to offer a contradictory opinion; for my sense of the saneness of things, would not allow me to take the story literally; then I shut them again, without saying anything. Somehow, the certainty in Tonnison's voice affected my doubts. I felt, all at once, less assured; though I was by no means convinced as yet.

After a few moments' silence, Tonnison rose, stiffly, and began to undress. He seemed disinclined to talk; so I said nothing; but followed his example. I was weary; though still full of the story I had just read.

Somehow, as I rolled into my blankets, there crept into my mind a memory of the old gardens, as we had seen them. I remembered the odd fear that the place had conjured up in our hearts; and it grew upon me, with conviction, that Tonnison was right.

It was very late when we rose—nearly midday; for the greater part of the night had been spent in reading the MS.

Tonnison was grumpy, and I felt out of sorts. It was a somewhat dismal day, and there was a touch of chilliness in the air. There was no mention of going out fishing, on either of our parts. We got dinner, and, after that, just sat and smoked in silence.

Note.—From the unfinished word, it is possible, on the MS., to trace a faint line of ink, which suggests that the pen has trailed away over the paper; possibly, through fright and weakness.—Ed.

Presently, Tonnison asked for the Manuscript: I handed it to him, and he spent most of the afternoon in reading it through by himself.

It was while he was thus employed, that a thought came to me:—

"What do you say to having another look at—?" I nodded my head down stream.

Tonnison looked up. "Nothing!" he said, abruptly; and, somehow, I was less annoyed, than relieved, at his answer.

After that, I left him alone.

A little before tea-time, he looked up at me, curiously.

"Sorry, old chap, if I was a bit short with you just now;" (just now, indeed! he had not spoken for the last three hours) "but I would not go there again," and he indicated with his head, "for anything that you could offer me. Ugh!" and he put down that history of a man's terror and hope and despair.

The next morning, we rose early, and went for our accustomed swim: we had partly shaken off the depression of the previous day; and so, took our rods when we had finished breakfast, and spent the day at our favourite sport.

After that day, we enjoyed our holiday to the utmost; though both of us looked forward to the time when our driver should come; for we were tremendously anxious to inquire of him, and through him among the people of the tiny hamlet, whether any of them could give us information about that strange garden, lying away by itself in the heart of an almost unknown tract of country.

At last, the day came, on which we expected the driver to come across for us. He arrived early, while we were still abed; and, the first thing we knew, he was at the opening of the tent, inquiring whether we had had good sport. We replied in the affirmative; and then, both together, almost in the same breath, we asked the question that was uppermost in our minds:—Did he know anything about an old garden, and a great pit, and a lake, situated some miles away, down the river; also, had he ever heard of a great house thereabouts?

No, he did not, and had not; yet, stay, he had heard a rumour, once upon a time, of a great, old house standing alone out in the wilderness; but, if he remembered rightly, it was a place given over to the fairies; or, if that had not been so, he was certain that there had been something "quare" about it; and, anyway, he had heard nothing of it for a very long while—not since he was quite a gossoon. No, he could not remember anything particular about it; indeed, he did not know he remembered anything "at all, at all" until we questioned him.

"Look here," said Tonnison, finding that this was about all that he could tell us, "just take a walk round the village, while we dress, and find out something, if you can."

With a nondescript salute, the man departed on his errand; while we made haste to get into our clothes; after which, we began to prepare breakfast.

We were just sitting down to it, when he returned.

"It's all in bed the lazy divvils is, sor," he said, with a repetition of the salute, and an appreciative eye to the good things spread out on our provision chest, which we utilized as a table.

"Oh, well, sit down," replied my friend, "and have something to eat with us." Which the man did without delay.

After breakfast, Tonnison sent him off again on the same errand, while we sat and smoked. He was away some three-quarters of an hour, and, when he returned, it was evident that he had found out something. It appeared that he had got into conversation with an ancient man of the village, who, probably, knew more—though it was little enough—of the strange house, than any other person living.

The substance of this knowledge was, that, in the "ancient man's" youth—and goodness knows how long back that was—there had stood a great house in the centre of the gardens, where now was left only that fragment of ruin. This house had been empty for a great while; years before his—the ancient man's—birth. It was a place shunned by the people of the village, as it had been shunned by their fathers before them. There were many things said about it, and all were of evil. No one ever went near it, either by day or night. In the village it was a synonym of all that is unholy and dreadful.

And then, one day, a man, a stranger, had ridden through the village, and turned off down the river, in the direction of the House, as it was always termed by the villagers. Some hours afterwards, he had ridden back, taking the track by which he had come, towards Ardrahan. Then, for three months or so, nothing was heard. At the end of that time, he reappeared; but now, he was accompanied by an elderly woman, and a large number of donkeys, laden with various articles. They had passed through the village without stopping, and gone straight down the bank of the river, in the direction of the House.

Since that time, no one, save the man whom they had chartered to bring over monthly supplies of necessaries from Ardrahan, had ever seen either of them: and him, none had ever induced to talk; evidently, he had been well paid for his trouble.

The years had moved onwards, uneventfully enough, in that little hamlet; the man making his monthly journeys, regularly.

One day, he had appeared as usual on his customary errand. He had passed through the village without exchanging more than a surly nod with the inhabitants and gone on towards the House. Usually, it was evening before he made the return journey. On this occasion, however, he had reappeared in the village, a few hours later, in an extraordinary state of excitement, and with the astounding information, that the House had disappeared bodily, and that a stupendous pit now yawned in the place where it had stood.

This news, it appears, so excited the curiosity of the villagers, that they overcame their fears, and marched *en masse* to the place. There, they found everything, just as described by the carrier.

This was all that we could learn. Of the author of the MS., who he was, and whence he came, we shall never know.

His identity is, as he seems to have desired, buried forever.

That same day, we left the lonely village of Kraighten. We have never been there since.

Sometimes, in my dreams, I see that enormous pit, surrounded, as it is, on all sides by wild trees and bushes. And the noise of the water rises upwards, and blends—in my sleep—with other and lower noises; while, over all, hangs the eternal shroud of spray.

The Snout

Edward Lucas White

───◆───

I

I was not so much conning the specimens in the Zoölogical Garden as idly basking in the agreeable morning sunshine and relishing at leisure the perfect weather. So I saw him the instant he turned the corner of the building. At first, I thought I recognized him, then I hesitated. At first he seemed to know me and to be just about to greet me; then he saw past me into the cage. His eyes bulged; his mouth opened into a long egg-shaped oval, till you might almost have said that his jaw dropped; he made an inarticulate sound, partly a grunt, partly the ghost of a howl, and collapsed in a limp heap on the gravel. I had not seen a human being since I passed the gate, some distance away. No one came when I called. So I dragged him to the grass by a bench, untied his faded, shiny cravat, took off his frayed collar and unbuttoned his soiled neckband. Then I peeled his coat off him, rolled it up, and put it under his knees as he lay on his back. I tried to find some water, but could see none. So I sat down on the bench near him. There he lay, his legs and body on the grass, his head in the dry gutter, his arms on the pebbles of the path. I was sure I knew him, but I could not recall when or where we had encountered each other before. Presently he answered to my rough and ready treatment and opened his eyes, blinking at me heavily. He drew up his arms to his shoulders and sighed.

"Queer," he muttered, "I come here because of you and I meet you."

Still I could not remember him and he had revived enough to read my face. He sat up.

"Don't try to stand up!" I warned him.

He did not need the admonition, but clung to the end of the bench, his head bowed wagglingly over his arms.

"Don't you remember," he asked thickly. "You said I had a pretty good smattering of an education on everything except Natural History and Ancient History. I'm hoping for a job in a few days, and I thought I'd put in the time and keep out of mischief brushing up. So I started on Natural History first and—"

He broke off and glared up at me. I remembered him now. I should have recognized him the moment I saw him, for he was daily in my mind. But his luxuriant hair, his tanned skin and above all his changed expression, a sort of look of acquired cosmopolitanism, had baffled me.

"Natural History!" he repeated, in a hoarse whisper. His fingers digging in the slats of the bench he wrenched himself round to face the cage.

"Hell!" he screamed. "There it is yet!"

He held on by the end iron-arm of the bench, shaking, almost sobbing.

"What's wrong with you?" I queried. "What do think you see in that cage?"

"Do you see anything in that cage?" he demanded in reply.

"Certainly," I told him.

"Then for God's sake," he pleaded. "What do you see?"

I told him briefly.

"Good Lord," he ejaculated. "Are we both crazy?"

"Nothing crazy about either of us," I assured him. "What we see in the cage is what is in the cage."

"Is there such a critter as that, honest?" he pressed me. I gave him a pretty full account of the animal, its habits and relationships.

"Well," he said, weakly, "I suppose you're telling the truth. If there is such a critter let's get where I can't see it."

I helped him to his feet and assisted him to a bench altogether out of sight of that building. He put on his collar and knotted his cravat. While I had held it I had noticed that, through its greasy condition, it showed plainly having been a very expensive cravat. His clothes I remarked were seedy, but had been of the very best when new.

"Let's find a drinking fountain," he suggested, "I can walk now." We found one not far away and at no great distance from it a shaded bench facing an agreeable view. I offered him a cigarette and we smoked. I meant to let him do most of the talking.

"Do you know," he began presently. "Things you said to me run in my head more than anything anybody ever said to me. I suppose it's because you're a sort of philosopher and student of human nature and what you say is true. For instance, you said that criminals would get off clear three times out of four, if they just kept their mouths shut, but they have to confide in some one, even against all reason. That's just the way with me now."

"You aren't a criminal," I interrupted him. "You lost your temper and made a fool of yourself just once. If you'd been a criminal and had done what you did, you'd have likely enough got off, because you'd have calculated how to do it. As it was you put yourself in a position where everything was against you and you had no chance. We were all sorry for you."

"You most of all," he amplified. "You treated me bully."

"But we were all sorry for you," I repeated, "and all the jury too, and the judge. You're no criminal."

"How do you know," he demanded defiantly, "what I have done since I got out?"

"You've grown a pretty good head of hair," I commented.

"I've had time," he said. "I've been all over the world and blown in ten thousand dollars."

"And never seen—" I began.

He interrupted me at the third word.

"Don't say it," he shuddered. "I never had, nor heard of one. But I wasn't after caged animals while I had any money left. I didn't remember your advice and your other talk till I was broke. Now, it's just as you said, I've just got to tell you. That's the criminal in me, I suppose."

"You're no criminal," I repeated soothingly.

"Hell," he snarled, "a year in the pen makes a man a criminal, if he never was before."

"Not necessarily," I encouraged him.

"It's pretty sure to," he sighed. "They treated me mighty well and put me to bookkeeping, and I got my full good-conduct allowance. But I met professionals, and they never forget a man."

"Now it don't make any difference what I did when I got out, nor what I tried to do nor how I met Rivvin, nor how he put Thwaite after me.. No, nor how Thwaite got hold of me, nor what he said to me, nor anything, right up to the very night, till after we had started."

He looked me in the eye. His attitude became alert. I could see him warming to his narrative. In fact, when after very little rumination he began it, his early self dropped from him with his boyhood dialect and the jargon of his late associates. He was all the easy cosmopolitan telling his tale with conscious zest.

II

As if it had been broad day Thwaite drove the car at a terrific pace for nearly an hour. Then he stopped it while Rivvin put out every lamp. We had not met or over-taken anything, but when we started again through the moist, starless blackness it was too much for my nerves. Thwaite was as cool as if he could see. I could not so much as guess at him in front of me, but I could feel his self-confidence in every quiver of the car. It was one of those super-expensive makes which are, on any gear, at any speed, on any grade, as noiseless as a puma. Thwaite never hesitated in the gloom; he kept straight or swerved, crept or darted, whizzed or crawled for nearly an hour more. Then he turned sharp to the left and uphill. I could feel and smell the soaked, hang-ing boughs close above and about me, the wet foliage on them, and the deep sodden earth mold that squelched under the tires. We climbed steeply, came to a level and then backed and went forward a length or so a half dozen times, turning. Then we stopped dead. Thwaite moved things that clicked or thumped and presently said:

"Now I'll demonstrate how a man can fill his gasoline tank in the pitch dark if he knows the touch system."

After some more time he said:

"Rivvin, go bury this."

Rivvin swore, but went. Thwaite climbed in beside me. When Rivvin returned he climbed in on the other side of me. He lit his pipe, Thwaite lit a cigar and looked at his watch. After I had lit too, Thwaite said:

"We've plenty of time to talk here and all you have to do is to listen. I'll begin at the beginning. When old Hiram Eversleigh died—"

"You don't mean—" I interrupted him.

"Shut up!" he snapped, "and keep your mouth shut. You'll have your say when I've done."

I shut up.

"When old man Eversleigh died," he resumed, "the income of the fortune was divided equally among his sons. You know what the others did with their shares: palaces in New York and London and Paris, chateaux on the Breton Coast, deer and grouse moors in Scotland, steam yachts and all the rest of it, the same as they have kept it up ever since. At first Vortigern Eversleigh went in for all that sort of thing harder than any one of his brothers. But when his wife died, more than forty years ago, he stopped all that at once. He sold everything else, bought this place, put the wall round it and built that infinity of structures inside. You've seen the pinnacles and roofs of them, and that's all anybody I ever talked to has ever seen of them since they were finished about five years after his wife's death. You've seen the two gate-houses and you know each is big even for a millionaire's mansion. You can judge of the size and extent of the complication of buildings that make up the castle or mansion-house or whatever you choose to call it. There Vortigern Eversleigh lived. Not once did he ever leave it that I can learn of. There he died. Since his death, full twenty years ago, his share of the Eversleigh income has been paid to his heir. No one has ever seen that heir. From what I'll tell you presently you'll see as I have that the heir is probably not a woman. But nobody knows anything about him, he has never been outside these miles of wall. Yet not one of the greedy, selfish Eversleigh grandsons and grand-daughters, and sons-in-law and daughters-in-law, has ever objected to the payment to that heir of the full entire portion of Vortigern Eversleigh, and that portion has been two hundred thousand dollars a month, paid in gold on the first banking day of each month. I found that out for sure, for there have been disputes about the division of Wulfstan Eversleigh's share and of Cedric Eversleigh's share and I made certain from the papers in the suits. All that money, or the value of it, has been either reinvested or spent inside that park wall. Not much has been reinvested. I got on the track of the heir's purchases. He buys musical instruments any quantity and at any price. Those were the first things I made sure of. And artists' materials, paints, brushes, canvas, tools, woods, clay, marble, tons of clay and great blocks of superfine-grained marble. He's no magpie collecting expensive trash for a whim; he knows what he wants and why; he has taste. He buys horses and saddlery and carriages, furniture and carpets and tapestries, pictures, all landscapes, never any figure pictures, he buys photographs of pictures by the ten thousand, and he buys fine porcelains, rare vases, table silver, ornaments of Venetian glass, silver and gold filigree, jewelry, watches, chains, gems, pearls, rubies, emeralds and—diamonds; diamonds!"

Thwaite's voice shook with excitement, though he kept it soft and even.

"Oh, I did two years investigating," he went on, "I know. People blabbed. But not any of the servants or grooms or gardeners. Not a word could I get, at first or second or third hand, from them or any of their relatives or friends. They keep dumb. They know which side their bread is buttered on. But some of the discharged tradesmen's assistants told all I wanted to know and I got it straight, though not direct. No one from outside ever gets into that place beyond the big paved courtyards of the gate-houses. Every bit of supplies for all that regiment of servants goes into the brownstone gate-house. The outer gates open and the wagon or whatever it is drives under the archway. There it halts. The outer gates shut and the inner gates open. It drives into the courtyard. Then the Major-domo (I suppose that wouldn't be too big a name for him) makes his selections. The inner gates of the other gateway open and the wagon drives under the archway and halts. The inner gates close fast and the outer gates open. That's the way with every wagon and only one enters at a time. Everything is carried through the gate-house to the smaller inner courtyard and loaded on the wagons of the estate to be driven up to the mansion.

"Everything like furniture, for instance, comes into the courtyard of the green-stone gate-house. There a sort of auditor verifies the inventory and receipts for the goods before two witnesses from the dealers and two for the estate. The consignment may be kept a day or a month; it may be returned intact or kept entire; any difference is settled for at once upon return of what is rejected. So with jewelry. I had luck. I found out for certain that more than a million dollars worth of diamonds alone have gone into this place in the last ten years and stayed there."

Thwaite paused dramatically. I never said a word and we sat there in the rear seat of that stationary auto, the leather creaking as we breathed, Rivvin sucking at his pipe, and the leaves dripping above us; not another sound.

"It's all in there," Thwaite began again. "The biggest stack of loot in North America. And this is going to be the biggest and most successful burglary ever per-petrated on this continent. And no one will ever be convicted for it or so much as suspected of it. Mark my words."

"I do," I broke in, "and I don't feel a bit better than when we started. You promised to explain and you said I'd be as eager and confident as you and Rivvin. I acknowledge the bait, admitting all you say is true, and it doesn't seem likely. But do you suppose any recluse millionaire eccentric is going to live unguarded? If he is careless himself his household are the reverse. By what you tell of the gate-houses there are precau-tions enough. Diamonds are tempting if you like, but so is the bullion in the mint. By your account all this accumulation of treasure you imagine is as safe where it is as the gold reserve in the United States Treasury. You scare me, you don't reassure me."

"Keep your head," Thwaite interrupted. "I'm no fool. I've spent years on this scheme. After I was sure of the prize I made sure of the means. There are precautions a-many, but not enough. How simple to put a watchman's cottage every hundred yards on the other side of the road across from the wall? They haven't done it. How simple to light the road and the outside of the wall? They haven't done that. Nor have they thought of any one of the twenty other simple outside precautions. The park's big enough to be lonely. And outside the wall is all dark, lonely road and unfenced, empty woods like this. They're overconfident. They think their wall and their gate-houses are enough. And they are not. They think their outside precautions are perfect. They are not. I know. I've been over that wall ten times, twenty times, fifty times. I've risked it and I have risked man-traps and spring guns and alarm wires. There aren't any. There isn't any night patrol, nor any regular day patrol, only casual gardeners and such. I know. I made sure of it by crawling all over the place on my belly like an Iroquois Indian in one of Cooper's novels. They are so confident of the potency of their wall that they haven't so much as a watch dog, nor any dog of any kind."

I was certainly startled. "No dog!" I exclaimed. "Are you sure?"

"Dead sure!" Thwaite returned, triumphantly, "And sure there never has been a dog on the place."

"How could you be sure of that?" I cavilled.

"I'm coming to that," Thwaite went on, "I could not get anybody that ever belonged to the place to talk, but I managed to arrange to overhear two of them talking to each other; and more than once, too. Most of what they said was no use to me, but I overheard scraps I could piece together. There's a cross-wall that divides the park. In the smaller division, into which the lodge gates lead, are the homes of all the caretakers and servants, of the overseers and manager and of the estate doctor; for there is an estate doctor. He has two assistants, young men, frequently changed. He is married like most of the retinue. There is a sort of village of them inside the outer wall, outside the inner cross-wall. Some of them have been there thirty-five years. When they get too old they are pensioned off and sent away, somewhere; far off, for I could not get a clue to any pensioner.

"The valets or keepers, whichever they are, and there are many of them, to relieve each other, are all unmarried except two or three of the most trusted. The rest are all brought over from England and shipped back usually after four or five years of service. The men I overheard were two of these, an old hand soon to finish his enlistment, as he called it, and go home, and the lad he was training to take his place. All these specials have plenty of time off to spend outside. They'd sit over their beer for two or three hours at a time, chatting on, Appleshaw giving points to Kitworth or Kitworth asking questions. I learnt from them about the cross-wall."

"Never's been a woman t' other side of it since it was built," Appleshaw said. "I shouldn't have thought it," Kitworth ruminated.

"Can you imagine a woman," Appleshaw asked, "standin' him?"

"No," Kitworth admitted, "I hardly can. But some women'll stand more 'n a man."

"Anyhow," Appleshaw added, "he can't abide the sight of a woman."

"Odd," said Kitworth, "I've heard his kind are all the other way."

"They are, as we know," Appleshaw replied, "havin' watched 'em; but he ain't. He can't endure 'em."

"I suppose it's the same way about dogs," Kit-worth reflected.

"No dog'd ever get used to him," Appleshaw agreed, "and he's that afraid of dogs, they're not allowed inside the place anywhere. Never's been one here since he was born, I'm told. No, nor any cat, either, not one even."

Another time I heard Appleshaw say:

"He built the museums, and the pavilion and the towers, the rest was built before he grew up."

Generally I could not hear much of Kitworth's utterances, he talked so low. I once heard Appleshaw reply:

"Sometimes nights and nights he'll be quiet as anybody, lights out early and sleep sound for all we know. Again he'll be up all night, every window blazin', or up late, till after midnight. Whoever's on duty sees the night out, nobody else's business, unless they send an alarm for help, and that ain't often; not twice a year. Mostly he's as quiet as you or me, as long as he's obeyed.

"His temper's short though. Now he'll fly into a rage if he's not answered quick; again he'll storm if the watchers come near him uncalled."

Of long inaudible whispers I caught fragments.

Once:

"Oh, then he'll have no one near. You can hear him sobbing like a child. When he's worst you'll hear him, still nights, howlin' and screamin' like a lost soul."

Again:

"Clean-fleshed as a child and no more hairy than you or me." Again:

"Fiddle? No violinist can beat him. I've listened hours. It makes you think of your sins. An' then it'll change an' you remember your first sweetheart, an' spring rains and flowers, an' when you was a child on your mother's knee. It tears your heart out."

The two phrases that seemed to mean most were: "He won't stan' any interference."

And:

"Never a lock touched till daylight after he's once locked in."

"Now what do you think?" Thwaite asked me.

"It sounds," I said, "as if the place were a one-patient asylum for a lunatic with long lucid intervals."

"Something like that," Thwaite answered, "but there seems to be more in it than that. I can't make all the things I hear fit." Appleshaw said one thing that runs in my head:

"Seein' him in the suds give me a turn."

And Kitworth said once:

"It was the bright colors alongside of it that made my blood run cold."

And Appleshaw said more than once, in varying words, but always with the same meaning tone:

"You'll never get over bein' afraid of him. But you'll respect him more and more, you'll almost love him. You won't fear him for his looks, but for his awful wisdom. He's that wise, no man is more so."

Once Kitworth answered:

"I don't envy Sturry locked in there with him."

"Sturry nor none of us that's his most trusted man for the time bein' is not to be envied," Appleshaw agreed. "But you'll come to it, as I have, if you're the man I take you for."

"That's about all I got from listening," Thwaite went on, "the rest I got from watching and scouting. I made sure of the building they call the Pavilion, that's his usual home. But sometimes he spends his nights in one or the other of the towers, they stand all by themselves. Sometimes the lights are all out after ten o'clock or even nine; then again they're on till after midnight. Sometimes they come on late, two o'clock or three. I have heard music too, violin music, as Appleshaw described it, and organ music, too; but no howling. He is certainly a lunatic, judging by the statuary."

"Statuary?" I queried.

"Yes," Thwaite said, "statuary. Big figures and groups, all crazy men with heads like elephants or American eagles, perfectly crazy statuary. But all well-done. They stand all about the park. The little, square building between the Pavilion and the green tower is his sculpture studio."

"You seem to know the place mighty well," I said.

"I do," Thwaite assented, "I've gotten to know it well. At first I tried nights like this. Then I dared starlight. Then I dared even moonlight. I've never had a scare. I've sat on the front steps of the Pavilion at one o'clock of starlight night and never been challenged. I even tried staying in all day, hiding in some bushes, hoping to see him."

"Ever see him?" I inquired.

"Never," Thwaite answered, "I've heard him though. He rides horseback after dark. I've watched the horse being led up and down in front of the Pavilion, till it got too dark to see it from where I was hid. I've heard it pass me in the dark. But I could never get the horse against the sky to see what was on it. Hiding and getting downhill of a road, close to it, don't go together."

"You didn't see him the day you spent there?" I insisted.

"No," Thwaite said, "I didn't. I was disappointed too. For a big auto purred up to the Pavilion entrance and stood under the porte cochère. But when it spun round the park there was nobody in it, only the chauffeur in front and a pet monkey on the back seat."

"A pet monkey!" I exclaimed.

"Yes," he said. "You know how a dog, a Newfoundland, or a terrier, will sit up in an auto and look grand and superior and enjoy himself? Well, that monkey sat there just like that turning his head one way and the other taking in the view."

"What was he like?" I asked.

"Sort of dog-faced ape," Thwaite told me, "more like a mastiff."

Rivvin grunted.

"This isn't business," Thwaite went on, "we've got to get down to business. The point is the wall is their only guard, there's no dog, perhaps because of the pet monkey as much as anything else. They lock Mr. Eversleigh up every night with only one valet to take care of him. They never interfere whatever noise they hear or light they see, unless the alarm is sent out and I have located the alarm wires you are to cut. That's all. Do you go?"

Rivvin was sitting close to me, half on me. I could feel his great muscles and the butt of his pistol against my hip.

"I come with you," I said.

"Of your own accord?" Thwaite insisted. The butt of that pistol moved as Rivvin breathed.

"I come of my own accord," I said.

III

Afoot Thwaite led as confidently as he had driven the car. It was the stillest, pitchiest night I ever experienced, without light, air, sound or smell to guide anyone: through that fog Thwaite sped like a man moving about his own bedroom, never for a second at a loss.

"Here's the place," he said at the wall, and guided my hand to feel the ring-bolt in the grass at its foot. Rivvin made a back for him and I scrambled up on the two. Tip-toe on Thwaite's shoulders I could just finger the coping.

"Stand on my head, you fool!" he whispered.

I clutched the coping. Once astraddle of it I let down one end of the silk ladder. "Fast!" breathed Thwaite from below.

I drew it taut and went down. The first sweep of my fingers in the grass found the other ring-bolt. I made the ladder fast and gave it the signal twitches. Rivvin came over first, then Thwaite. Through the park he led evenly. When he halted he caught me by the elbow and asked:

"Can you see any lights?"

"Not a light," I told him.

"Same here," he said, "there are no lights. Every window is dark. We're in luck." He led again for a while. Stopping he said only:

"Here's where you shin up. Cut every wire, but don't waste time cutting any twice."

The details of his directions were exact. I found every handhold and foothold as he had schooled me. But I needed all my nerve. I realized that no heavyweight like Rivvin or Thwaite could have done it. When I came down I was limp and tottery.

"Just one swallow!" Thwaite said, putting a flask to my lips. Then we went on. The night was so black and the fog so thick that I saw no loom of the building till we were against its wall.

"Here's where you go in," Thwaite directed.

Doubly I understood why I was with them. Neither could have squeezed through that aperture in the stone. I barely managed it. Inside, instead of the sliding crash I had dreaded, I landed with a mere crunch, the coal in that bin was not anthracite. Likewise the bin under the window was for soft-coal. I blessed my luck and felt encouraged. The window I got open without too much work. Rivvin and Thwaite slid in. We crunched downhill four or five steps and stood on a firm floor. Rivvin flashed his electric candle boldly round. We were between a suite of trim coal-bins and a battery of serried furnaces. There was no door at either end of the open space in which we stood. I had a momentary vision of the alternate windows and coal-chutes above the bins, of two big panels of shiny, colored tiling, of clear brick-work, fresh-painted, jetty iron and dazzling-white brass-ringed asbestos, of a black vacancy between two furnaces. Toward that I half heard, half felt Rivvin turn. During the rest of our adventure he led, Thwaite followed and I mostly tagged or groped after Thwaite, often judging of their position or movement by that combination of senses which is neither hearing nor touch, though partly both.

Rivvin's torch flashed again. We were in a cement-floored, brick-walled passage, with a door at each end and on the side facing us doors in a bewildering row. In the darkness that came after the flash I followed the others to the right. Well through the doorway we stood still, breathing and listening. When Rivvin illuminated our environment we saw about us thousands of bottles, all set aslant, neck down, in tiers of racks that reached to the ceiling. Edging between them we made the circuit of the cellar, but found no sign of any door save that by which we had entered. A whispered growl from Rivvin, a nudge from Thwaite and we went back the full length of the passage. Again we found ourselves in a wine vault, the duplicate of that we had left, and with the same peculiarity.

Our curiosity overcame any prudence. Rivvin, instead of flashing his torch at intervals, kept the light steady, and we scrutinized, examined and whispered our astonishment. As in its fellow there was not in all this vault any spare space, the aisles were narrow, the racks reached the girders supporting the flat arches, every rack was so full that a holder empty of its bottle was scarcely findable. And there was not in all that great cellar, there was not among all those tens of thousands of bottles a magnum, or a quart or even a pint. They were all splits. We handled a number and all had the same label. I know now what the device was, from seeing it so often and so much larger afterwards, but there it seemed a picture of a skirt-dancer leading an alligator by a dog chain. There was no name of any wine or liquor on any bottle, but each label had a red number, 17, or 45 or 328, above the picture, and under it:

"Bottled for Hengist Eversleigh."

"We know his name now," Thwaite whispered.

Back in the passage Rivvin took the first door to the left. It brought us to an easy stone stair between walls, which turned twice to the left at broad landings.

When we trod a softer footing we stood a long time breathing cautiously and listening. Presently Rivvin flashed his light. It showed to our left a carpeted stair, the dull red carpet bulging up over thick pads and held down by brass stair-rods; the polished quartered oak of the molded door-jamb or end of wainscot beyond it; the floor-covering of brownish-yellow or yellowish-brown linoleum or something similar, made to look like inlaid wood; and the feet, legs and thighs of a big stocky man. The light shone but the fraction of a second, yet it showed plain his knee-breeches, tight stockings on his big calves, and bright buckles at his knees and on his low shoes.

There was no loud sound, but the blurred brushy noise of a mute struggle. I backed against a window-sill and could back no further. All I could hear was the shuffling, rasping sounds of the fight, and panting that became a sort of gurgle.

Again the light flashed and stayed full bright. I saw that it was Thwaite struggling with the man, and that one of his big hands was on Thwaite's throat. Thwaite had him round the neck and his face was against Thwaite's chest. His hair was brownish. Rivvin's slung-shot crunched horribly on his skull. Instantly the light went out.

Thwaite, radiating heat like a stove, stood gasping close by me. I heard no other noise after the body thudded on the floor except that on the carpeted stair I seemed to hear light treads, as it were of a big dog or of a frightened child, padding away upward.

"Did you hear anything?" I whispered.

Rivvin punched me.

After Thwaite was breathing naturally, he turned on his torch and Rivvin did the same. The dead man was oldish, over fifty I should judge, tall, large in all his dimensions, and spare, though heavy. His clothing was a gold-laced livery of green velvet, with green velvet knee breeches, green silk stockings and green leather pumps. The four buckles were gold.

Thwaite startled me by speaking out loud.

"I take it, Rivvin," he said, "this is the trusted valet. He would have yelled if there had been anybody to call. Either we have this building to ourselves or we have no one to deal with except Mr. Hengist Eversleigh."

Rivvin grunted.

"If he is here," Thwaite went on, "he's trying to send the alarm over the cut wires, or he's frightened and hiding. Let's find him and finish him, if he's here, and then find his diamonds. Anyway let's find those diamonds."

Rivvin grunted.

Swiftly they led from room to room and floor to floor. Not a door resisted. We had been curious and astonished in the wine-vaults; above we were electrified and numb. We were in a palace of wonders, among such a profusion of valuables that even Rivvin, after the second or third opportunity, ceased any attempt to pocket or bag anything. We came upon nothing living, found no door locked and apparently made the tour of the entire building.

When they halted, I halted. We were delirious with amazement, frantic with inquisitiveness, frenzied with curiosity, incredulous, hysterical, dazed and quivering.

Thwaite spoke in the dark.

"I'm going to see this place plain, all over it, if I die for it."

They flashed their torches. We were right beside the body of the murdered footman. Rivvin and Thwaite did not seem to mind the corpse. They waved their torches until one fell on an electric-light button.

"Hope those wires are underground," Thwaite remarked. He pushed the button and the electric lights came on full and strong. We were apparently at the foot of the back stairs, in a sort of lobby, an expanded passage-way out of which opened several doors.

We all three regarded the knobs of those doors. As we had half seen by flash-light on every door everywhere each door had two knobs, one like any door-knob, the other about half way between it and the floor. Rivvin opened one which proved to lead into a broom closet. He tried the knobs, Thwaite and I watching too. The lock and latch were at the upper knob, but controlled by either knob indifferently. They tried another door, but my eyes would roam to the dead body.

Rivvin and Thwaite paid no more attention to it than if it had not been there. I had never seen but one killed man before and neither wanted to be reminded of that one nor relished the sight of this one. I stared down the blackness of the stone stair up which we had come or glanced into the dimness of the padded stairway.

Then Rivvin, feeling inside the open door, found the button and turned on the lights. It was a biggish dining-room, the four corners cut off by inset glass-framed shelved closets, full of china and glassware. The furniture was oak.

"Servants dining-room," Thwaite commented.

Turning on the lights in each we went through a series of rooms; a sort of sitting-room, with card-tables and checker-boards; a library walled with bookcases and open book-shelves, its two stout oak tables littered with magazines and newspapers; a billiard room with three tables, a billiard-table, a pool-table and one for bagatelle; a sort of lounging room, all leather-covered sofas and deep armchairs; an entry with hat-hooks and umbrella-stands, the outer door dark oak with a great deal of stained glass set in and around it.

"All servants' rooms," Thwaite commented. "Every bit of the furniture is natural man-size. Let's go on."

Back we went along a passage and into a big kitchen beyond the dining-room. "Never mind the pantries till we come down again," Thwaite commanded. "Let's go upstairs. We'll do the banqueting-hall after those bedrooms, and the writing rooms and study last. I want a real sight of those pictures."

They passed the dead flunkey as if he had not been there at all. On the floor above Thwaite touched Rivvins' elbow.

"I forgot these," he said.

We inspected a medium-sized sitting-room with a round center-table, an armchair drawn up by it, and in the armchair a magazine and a sort of wadded smoking-jacket. Next this room was a bedroom and a bathroom.

"Mr. Footman's quarters," Thwaite remarked, staring unconcernedly at a photograph of a dumpy young woman and two small children, set on the bureau. "All man-size furniture here, too."

Rivvin nodded.

Up the second flight of that back-stair we went again. It ended in a squarish hallway or lobby or room with nothing in it but two settees. It had two doors.

Rivvin pushed one open, felt up and down for the electric button and found it.

We all three gasped; we almost shouted. We had had glimpses of this gallery before, but the flood of light from a thousand bulbs under inverted trough-reflectors dazzled us; the pictures fairly petrified us.

The glare terrified me.

"Surely we are crazy," I objected, "to make all this illumination. It's certain to give the alarm."

"Alarm nothing," Thwaite snapped. "Haven't I watched these buildings night after night. I told you he is never disturbed at any hour, lights or no lights."

My feeble protest thus brushed away I became absorbed, like the others, in those incredible paintings. Rivvin was merely stupidly dazed in uncomprehending wonder, Thwaite keenly speculative, questing for a clue to the origin of their peculiarities, I totally bewildered at the perfection of their execution, shivering at their uncanniness.

The gallery was all of ninety feet long, nearly thirty wide and high. Apparently it had a glass roof above the rectangle of reflectors. The pictures covered all four walls, except the little door at either end. None was very small and several were very large. A few were landscapes, but all had figures in them, most were crowded with figures.

Those figures!

They were human figures, but not one had a human head. The heads were invariably those of birds, animals or fishes, generally of animals, some of common animals, many of creatures I had seen pictures of or had heard of, some of imaginary creatures like dragons or griffons, more than half of the heads either of animals I knew nothing of or which had been invented by the painter.

Close to me when the lights blazed out was a sea picture, blurred grayish foggy weather and a heavy ground-swell; a strange other-world open boat with fish heaped in the bottom of it and standing among them four human figures in shining boots like rubber boots and wet, shiny, loose coats like oilskins, only the boots and skins were red as claret, and the four figures had hyenas' heads. One was steering and the others were hauling at a net. Caught in the net was a sort of merman, but different from the pictures of mermaids. His shape was all human except the head and hands and feet; every bit of him was covered with fish-scales all rainbowy. He had flat broad fins in place of hands and feet and his head was the head of a fat hog. He was thrashing about in the net in an agony of impotent effort. Queer as the picture was it had a compelling impression of reality, as if the scene were actually happening before our eyes.

Next it was a picnic in a little meadow by a pond between woods with mountains behind it higher up. Every one of the picnickers about the white table-cloth spread on the grass had the head of a different animal, one of a sheep, one of a camel, and the rest of animals like deer, not one of them known to me.

Then next to that was a fight of two compound creatures shaped like centaurs, only they had bulls' bodies, with human torsos growing out of them, where the necks ought to be, the arms scaly snakes with open-mouthed, biting heads in place of hands; and instead of human heads roosters' heads, bills open and pecking. Under the creatures in place of bulls' hoofs were yellow roosters' legs, stouter than chickens' legs and with short thick toes, and long sharp spurs like game roosters'. Yet these fantastic chimeras appeared altogether alive and their movements looked natural, yes that's the word, natural.

Every picture was as complete a staggerer as these first three. Every one was signed in the lower left hand corner in neat smallish letters of bright gold paint:

HENGIST EVERSLEIGH

and a date.

"Mr. Hengist Eversleigh is a lunatic that's certain," Thwaite commented, "but he unquestionably knows how to paint."

There must have been more than fifty pictures in that gallery, maybe as many as seventy-five, and every one a nightmare.

Beyond was a shorter gallery of the same width, end on to the side of the first, and beyond that the duplicate of the first; the three taking up three sides of the building. The fourth side was a studio, the size of the second gallery; it had a great skylight of glass tilted sideways all along over one whole wall. It was white-washed, very plain and empty-looking, with two easels, a big one and a little one.

On the little one was a picture of some vegetables and five or six little fairies, as it were, with children's bodies and mice's heads, nibbling at a carrot.

On the big one was a canvas mostly blank. One side of it had a palm-tree in splashy, thick slaps of paint and under it three big crabs with cocoanuts in their claws. A man's feet and legs showed beside them and the rest was unfinished.

The three galleries had fully three hundred paintings, for the smaller gallery contained only small canvases. Besides being impressed with the grotesqueness of the subjects and the perfection of the drawing and coloring, two things struck me as to the pictures collectively.

First, there was not represented in any one of all those paintings any figure of a woman or any female shape of any kind. The beast-headed figures were all, whether clothed or nude, figures of men. The animals, as far as I could see, were all males.

Secondly, nearly half of the pictures were modifications, or parallels or emulations (I could hardly say travesties or imitations), of well-known pictures by great artists, paintings I had seen in public galleries or knew from engravings or photographs or reproductions in books or magazines.

There was a picture like Washington crossing the Delaware and another like Washington saying farewell to his generals. There was a batch of Napoleon pictures; after the paintings of Napoleon at Austerlitz, at Friedland, giving the eagles to his regiments, on the morning of Waterloo, coming down the steps at Fontainebleau, and on the deck of the ship going to St. Helena. There were dozens of other pictures of generals or kings or emperors reviewing victorious armies; two or three of Lincoln. One that hit me hardest, obviously after some picture I had never seen or heard of, of the ghost of Lincoln, far larger than a life-size man, towering above the surviving notabilities of his time on the grandstand reviewing the homecoming Federal army marching through Washington.

In every one of these pictures, the dominant figure, whether it stood for Lincoln, Napoleon, Washington, or some other general or ruler; whatever uniform or regalia clothed its human shape, had the same head. The heads of the fighting men in all these pictures were those of dogs, all alike in any one picture, but differing from one to another; terriers or wolf-hounds or mastiffs or what not. The heads of any men not soldiers were those of oxen or sheep or horses or some other mild sort of animal. The head of the dominant figure I then took to be invented, legendary, fabulous—oh, that's not the word I want."

"Mythological?" I suggested, the only interruption I interjected into his entire narrative.

Yes, mythological, he returned. I thought it was a mythological creature. The long-jawed head, like a hound's; the little pointed yellow beard under the chin; the black, naked ears, like a hairless dog's ears and yet not doggy, either; the ridge of hair on top of the skull; the triangular shape of the whole head; the close-set, small, beady, terribly knowing eyes; the brilliant patches of color on either side of the muzzle; all these made a piercing impression of individuality and yet seemed not so much actual as mythological.

It takes a great deal longer to tell what we saw on that third floor than it took to see it. All round the galleries under the pictures were cases of drawers, solidly built in one length like a counter and about as high. Thwaite went down one side of the gallery and Rivvin down the other, pulling them out and slamming them shut again. All I saw held photographs of pictures. But Rivvin and Thwaite were taking no chances and looked into every drawer. I had plenty of time to gaze about me and circulated at a sort of cantering trot around the green-velvet miniature sofas and settees placed back to back down the middle of the floor-space. It seemed to me that Mr. Hengist Eversleigh was a great master of figure and landscape drawing, color, light and perspective.

As we went down the duplicate staircase at the other corner from where we came up Thwaite said:

"Now for those bedrooms."

By the stair we found another valet's or footman's apartment, sitting-room, bed-room and bathroom, just like the one by the other stair. And there were four more between them, under the studio and over the lounging-rooms.

On the east and west sides of the building were "the" bedrooms, twelve apart-ments, six on each side; each of the twelve made up of a bedroom, a dressing-room and a bathroom.

The beds were about three feet long, and proportionately narrow and low. The furniture, bureaus, tables, chairs, chests-of-drawers and the rest, harmonized with the dimensions of the beds, except the cheval-glasses and wall-mirrors which reached the ceilings. The bathtubs were almost pools, about nine feet by six and all of three feet deep, each a single block of porcelain.

The shapes and sizes and styles of the furniture were duplicated all through, but the colors varied, so that the twelve suites were in twelve colors; black, white, gray and brown, and light and dark yellow, red, green and blue; wall coverings, hangings, carpets and rugs all to match in each suite. The panels of the walls had the same picture, however, repeated over and over, two, four or six times to a room and in every suite alike.

This picture was the design I had failed to make out on the labels of the bottles. It was set as a medallion in each panel of the blue or red walls, or whatever other color they were. The background of the picture was a vague sort of palish sky and blurred, hazy clouds above tropical-looking foliage. The chief figure was an angel, in flowing white robes, floating on silvery-plumed wings widespread. The angel's face was a human face, the only human face in any picture in that palace, the face of a grave, gentle, rather girlish young man.

The creature the angel was leading was a huge, bulky crocodile, with a gold collar about its neck, and a gold chain from that, not to the angel's hand, but to a gold fetter about his wrist.

Under each picture was a verse of four lines, always the same.

> Let not your baser nature drag you down.
>   Utter no whimper, not one sigh or moan,
> Hopeless of respite, solace, palm or crown
>   Live out your life unflinching and alone.

I saw it so often I shall never forget it.

The bathrooms were luxurious in the extreme, a needle-bath, a shower-bath, two basins of different sizes in each, besides the sunk pool-tub. The dressing-rooms has each a variety of wardrobes. One or two we opened, finding in each several suits of little clothes, as if for a boy under six years old. One closet had shelf above shelf of small shoes, not much over four inches long.

"Evidently," Thwaite remarked, "Hengist Eversleigh is a dwarf, whatever else he is." Rivvin left the wardrobes and closets alone after the first few.

Each bedroom had in it nothing but the bed and on each side of it a sort of wine-cooler, like a pail with a lid, but bigger, set on three short legs so that its top was level with the bed. We opened most of them; every one we opened was filled with ice, bedded in which were several half-pint bottles. Every one of the twelve beds had the covers carefully turned down. Not one showed any sign of having been occupied. The wine-coolers were solid silver but we left them where they were. As Thwaite remarked, it would have taken two full-sized freight cars to contain the silver we had seen.

In the dressing-rooms the articles like brushes and combs on the bureaus were all of gold, and most set with jewels. Rivvin began to fill a bag with those entirely of metal, but even he made no attempt to tear the backs off the brushes or to waste energy on any other breakage. By the time we had scanned the twelve suites Rivvin could barely carry his bag.

The front room on the south side of the building was a library full of small, showily-bound books in glass-fronted cases all the way to the ceiling, covering every wall except where the two doors and six windows opened. There were small, narrow tables, the height of those in the dressing-rooms. There were magazines on them and papers. Thwaite opened a bookcase and I another and we looked at three or four books. Each had in it a book-plate with the device of the angel and the crocodile.

Rivvin did not find the electric button in the main hallway and we went down the great broad, curving stair by our electric candles. Rivvin turned to the left and we found ourselves in the banquet hall as Thwaite had called it, a room all of forty by thirty and gorgeous beyond any description.

The diminutive table, not three feet square, was a slab of crystal-white glass set on silver- covered legs. The tiny armchair, the only chair in the big room, was solid silver, with a crimson cushion loose in it.

The sideboards and glass-fronted closets paralyzed us. One had fine china and cut glass; wonderful china and glass. But four held a table service of gold, all of pure gold; forks, knives, spoons, plates, bowls, platters, cups, everything; all miniature, but a profusion of everything. We hefted the pieces. They were gold. All the pieces were normal in shape except that instead of wine-glasses, goblets and tumblers were things like broad gravy-boats on stems or short feet, all lopsided, with one projecting edge like the mouth of a pitcher, only broader and flatter. There were dozens of these. Rivvin filled two bags with what two bags would hold. The three bags were all we three could carry, must have been over a hundred and fifty pounds apiece.

"We'll have to make two trips to the wall," Thwaite said. "You brought six bags, didn't you, Rivvin?"

Rivvin grunted.

At the foot of the grand staircase Rivvin found the electric button and flooded the magnificent stairway with light.

The stair itself was all white marble, the rails yellow marble, and the paneling of the dado malachite. But the main feature was the painting above the landing. This was the most amazing of all the paintings we had come upon.

I remembered something like it, an advertisement of a root-beer or talcum powder, or some other proprietary article, representing all the nations of the earth and their rulers in the foreground congratulating the orator.

This picture was about twenty feet wide and higher than its width. There was a throne, a carved and jeweled throne, set on an eminence. There was a wide view on either side of the throne, and all filled with human figures with animal heads, an infinite throng, all facing the throne. Nearest it were figures that seemed meant for all the presidents and kings and queens and emperors of the world. I recognized the robes or uniforms of some of them. Some had heads taken from their national coat of arms, like the heads of the Austrian and Russian eagles. All these figures were paying homage to the figure that stood before the throne; the same monster we had seen in place of Lincoln or Washington or Napoleon in the paintings upstairs.

He stood proudly with one foot on a massive crocodile. He was dressed in a sort of revolutionary uniform, low shoes, with gold buckles, white stockings and knee-breeches, a red waistcoat, and a bright blue coat. His head was the same beast-head of the other pictures, triangular and strange, which I then though mythological.

Above and behind the throne floated on outspread silver wings the white-robed angel with the Sir Galahad face.

Rivvin shut off the lights almost instantly, but even in the few breaths while I looked I saw it all.

The three sacks of swag we put down by the front door.

The room opposite the banquet-hall was a music room, with an organ and a piano, both with keys and keyboards far smaller than usual; great cases of music books; an array of brass instruments and cellos and more than a hundred violin cases. Thwaite opened one or two.

"These'd be enough to make our fortune," he said. "If we could get away with them."

Beyond the music-room was the study. It had in it four desks, miniature in size and the old-fashioned model with drawers below, a lid to turn down and form a writing surface, and a sort of bookcase above with a peaked top. All were carved and on the lids in the carving we read:

JOURNAL

MUSIC

CRITICISM

BUSINESS

Thwaite opened the desk marked business and pulled open the drawers. In pigeon-holes of the desk were bundles of new, clean greenbacks and treasury notes of higher denominations; five each of fives, tens, twenties, fifties and hundreds. Thwaite tossed one bundle of each to me and Rivvin and pocketed the rest.

He bulged.

One drawer had a division down the middle. One half was full of ten-dollar gold pieces, the other half of twenties.

"I've heard of misers," said Thwaite, "but this beats hell. Think of that crazy dwarf, a prisoner in this palace, running his hands through this and gloating over the cash he can never use.

Rivvin loaded a bag with the coin and when he had them all he could barely lift the bag. Leaving it where it lay before the desk he strode the length of the room and tried the door at the end.

It was fast.

Instantly Rivvin and Thwaite were like two terriers after a rat.

"This is where the diamonds are," Thwaite declared, "and Mr. Hengist Eversleigh is in there with them."

He and Rivvin conferred a while together.

"You kneel low," Thwaite whispered. "Duck when you open it. He'll fire over you. Then you've got him. See?"

Rivvin tip-toed to the door, knelt and tried key after key in the lock.

There were at least twenty bulbs in the chandelier of that room and the light beat down on him. His red neck dew-lapped over the low collar of his lavenderish shirt, his great broad back showed vast and powerful.

On the other side of the doorway Thwaite stood, his finger at the electric button.

Each had his slung-shot in his left hand. They had spun the cylinders of their revolvers and stuck them in their belts in front before Rivvin began work on the lock.

I heard a click.

Rivvin put up his hand.

The lights went out.

In the black dark we stood, stood until I could almost see the outlines of the windows; less black against the intenser blackness.

Soon I heard another click, and the grate of an opened door.

Then a kind of snarl, a thump like a blow, a sort of strangling gasp, and the cushiony sounds of a struggle.

Thwaite turned on the lights.

Rivvin was in the act of staggering up from his knees. I saw a pair of small, pink hands, the fingers intertwined, locked behind Rivvin's neck. They slipped apart as I caught sight of them.

I had a vision of small feet in little patent leather silver-buckled low-shoes, of green socks, of diminutive legs in white trousers flashing right and left in front of Rivvin, as if he held by the throat a struggling child.

Next I saw that his arms were thrown up, wide apart.

He collapsed and fell back his full length with a dull crash.

Then I saw the snout!

Saw the wolf-jaws vised on his throat!

Saw the blood welling round the dazzling white fangs, and recognized the reality of the sinister head I had seen over and over in his pictures.

Rivvin made the fish-out-of-water contortions of a man being killed.

Thwaite brought his slung-shot down on the beast-head skull.

The blow was enough to crush in a steel cylinder. The beast wrinkled its snout and shook its head from side to side, worrying like a bull-dog at Rivvin's throat.

Again Thwaite struck and again and again. At each blow the portentous head oscillated viciously. The awful thing about it to me was the two blue bosses on each side of the muzzle, like enamel, shiny and hard looking; and the hideous welt of red, like fresh sealing-wax, down between them and along the snout.

Rivvin's struggles grew weaker as the great teeth tore at his throat. He was dead before Thwaite's repeated blows drove in the splintered skull and the clenched jaws relaxed, the snout crinkling and contracting as the dog-teeth slid from their hold.

Thwaite gave the monster two or three more blows, touched Rivvin and fairly dashed out of the room, shouting.

"You stay here!"

I heard the sound of prying and sawing. There alone I looked but once at the dead cracksman. The thing that had killed him was the size of a four to six year old child, but more stockily built, looked entirely human up to the neck, and was dressed in a coat of bright dark blue, a vest of crimson velvet, and white duck trousers. As I looked the muzzle wriggled for the last time, the jaws fell apart and the carcass rolled sideways. It was the very duplicate in miniature of the figure in the big picture on the staircase landing.

Thwaite came dashing back. Without any sign of any qualm he searched Rivvin and tossed me two or three bundles of greenbacks.

He stood up.

He laughed.

"Curiosity," he said, "will be the death of me." Then he stripped the clothing from the dead monster, kneeling by it.

The beast-hair stopped at the shirt collar. Below that the skin was human, as was the shape, the shape of a forty-year-old man, strong and vigorous and well-made, only dwarfed to the smallness of a child.

Across the hairy breast was tatooed in blue,

HENGIST EVERSLEIGH.

"Hell," said Thwaite.

He stood up and went to the fatal door. Inside he found the electric button. The room was small and lined with cases of little drawers, tier on tier, rows of brass knobs on mahogany.

Thwaite opened one.

It was velvet lined and grooved like a jeweler's tray and contained rings, the settings apparently emeralds.

Thwaite dumped them into one of the empty bags he had taken from Rivvin's corpse. The next case was of similar drawers of rings set with rubies. The first of these Thwaite dumped in with the emeralds.

But then he flew round the room pulling out drawers and slamming them shut, until he came upon trays of unset diamonds. These he emptied into his sack to the last of them, then diamond rings on them, other jewelry set with diamonds, then rubies and emeralds till the sack was full.

He tied its neck, had me open a second sack and was dumping drawer after drawer into that when suddenly he stopped.

His nose worked, worked horridly like that of the dead monster.

I thought he was going crazy and was beginning to laugh nervously, was on the verge of hysterics when he said:

"Smell! Try what you smell." I sniffed. "I smell smoke," I said.

"So do I," he agreed. "This place is afire."

"And we locked in!" I exclaimed.

"Locked in?" he sneered. "Bosh. I broke open the front door the instant I was sure they were dead. Come! Drop that empty bag. This is no time for haggling."

We had to step between the two corpses. Rivvin was horridly dead. The colors had all faded from the snout. The muzzle was all mouse-color.

When we had hold of the bag of coin, Thwaite turned off the electric lights and we struggled out with that and the bag of jewels, and went out into the hallway full of smoke.

"We can carry only these," Thwaite warned me. "We'll have to leave the rest."

I shouldered the bag of coin, and followed him down the steps, across a gravel road, and, oh the relief of treading turf and feeling the fog all about me.

At the wall Thwaite turned and looked back.

"No chance to try for those other bags," he said.

In fact the red glow was visible at that distance and was fast becoming a glare. I heard shouts.

We got the bags over the wall and reached the car. Thwaite cranked up at once and we were off.

How we went I could not guess, nor in what directions, nor even how long. Ours was the only vehicle on the roads we darted along.

When the dawn light was near enough for me to see Thwaite stopped the car. He turned to me.

"Get out!" he said.

"What?" I asked.

He shoved his pistol muzzle in my face. "You've fifty thousand dollars in bank bills in your pockets," he said. "It's a half a mile down that road to a railway station. Do you understand English? Get out!"

I got out.

The car shot forward into the morning fog and was gone.

IV

He was silent a long time.

"What did you do then?" I asked.

"Headed for New York," he said, "and got on a drunk. When I came round I had barely eleven thousand dollars. I headed for Cook's office and bargained for a ten thousand dollar tour of the world, the most places and the longest time they'd give for the money; the whole cost on them. I not to need a cent after I started."

"What date was that?" I asked.

He meditated and gave me some approximate indications rather rambling and roundabout. "What did you do after you left Cook's?" I asked.

"I put a hundred dollars in a savings bank," he said. "Bought a lot of clothes and things and started.

"I kept pretty sober all round the world because the only way to get full was by being treated and I had no cash to treat back with.

"When I landed in New York I thought I was all right for life. But no sooner did I have my hundred and odd dollars in my pockets than I got full again. I don't seem able to keep sober."

"Are you sober now?" I asked.

"Sure," he asserted.

He seemed to shed his cosmopolitan vocabulary the moment he came back to everyday matters.

"Let's see you write what I tell you on this," I suggested, handing him a fountain-pen and a torn envelope, turned inside out.

Word by word after my dictation he wrote.

Until you hear from me again

Yours truly,

No Name.

I took the paper from him and studied the handwriting. "How long were you on that spree?" I asked.

"Which?" he twinkled.

"Before you came to and had but eleven thousand dollars left," I explained. "I don't know," he said, "I didn't know anything I had been doing."

"I can tell you one thing you did," I said.

"What?" he queried.

"You put four packets, each of one hundred hundred-dollar bills, in a thin manila clasp-envelope, directed it to a New York lawyer and mailed the envelope to him with no letter in it, only a half sheet of dirty paper with nothing on it except: 'Keep this for me until I ask for it,' and the signature you have just written."

"Honest?" he enunciated incredulously. "Fact!" I said.

"Then you believe what I've told you," he exclaimed joyfully.

"Not a bit I don't," I asseverated.

"How's that?" he asked.

"If you were drunk enough," I explained, "to risk forty thousand dollars in that crazy way, you were drunk enough to dream all the complicated nightmare you have spun out to me."

"If I did," he argued, "how did I get the fifty thousand odd dollars?"

"I'm willing to suppose you got it with no more dishonesty on your part," I told him, "than if you had come by it as you described."

"It makes me mad you won't believe me," he said.

"I don't," I finished.

He gloomed in silence. Presently he said: "I can stand looking at him now," and led the way to the cage where the big blue-nosed mandril chattered his inarticulate bestialities and scratched himself intermittently.

He stared at the brute.

"And you don't believe me?" he regretted.

"No, I don't," I repeated, "and I'm not going to. The thing's incredible."

"Couldn't there be a mongrel, a hybrid?" he suggested.

"Put that out of your head," I told him, "the whole thing's incredible."

"Suppose she'd seen a critter like this," he persisted, "just at the wrong time?"

"Bosh!" I said. "Old wives' tales! Superstition! Impossibility!"

"His head," he declared, "was just like that." He shuddered.

"Somebody put drops in some of your drink," I suggested. "Anyhow, let's talk about something else. Come and have lunch with me."

Over the lunch I asked him:

"What city did you like best of all you saw?"

"Paris for mine," he grinned, "Paris forever."

"I tell you what I advise you to do," I said.

"What's that?" he asked, his eyes bright on mine. "Let me buy you an annuity with your forty thousand," I explained, "an annuity payable in Paris. There's enough interest already to pay your way to Paris and leave you some cash till the first quarterly payment comes due."

"You wouldn't feel yourself defrauding the Eversleighs?" he questioned.

"If I'm defrauding any people," I said, "I don't know who they are."

"How about the fire?" he insisted. "I'll bet you heard of it. Don't the dates agree?"

"The dates agree," I admitted. "And the servants were all dismissed, the remaining buildings and walls torn down and the place cut up and sold in portions just about as it would have been if your story were true."

"There now!" he ejaculated. "You do believe me!"

"I do not!" I insisted. "And the proof is that I'm ready to carry out my annuity plan for you."

"I agree," he said, and stood up from the lunch table.

"Where are we going now?" he inquired as we left the restaurant.

"Just you come with me," I told him, "and ask no questions."

I piloted him to the Museum of Archæology and led him circuitously to what I meant for an experiment on him. I dwelt on other subjects nearby and waited for him to see it himself.

He saw.

He grabbed me by the arm. "That's him!" he whispered. "Not the size, but his very expression, in all his pictures." He pointed to that magnificent, enigmatical black-diorite twelfth-dynasty statue which represents neither Anubis nor Seth, but some nameless cynocephalus god.

"That's him," he repeated. "Look at the awful wisdom of him." I said nothing.

"And you brought me here!" he cried. "You meant me to see this! You do believe!"

"No," I maintained. "I do not believe."

V

After I waved a farewell to him from the pier I never saw him again.

We had an extensive correspondence six months later when he wanted his annuity exchanged for a joint-life annuity for himself and his bride. I arranged it for him with less difficulty than I had anticipated. His letter of thanks, explaining that a French wife was so great an economy that the shrinkage in his income was more than made up for, was the last I heard from him.

As he died more than a year ago and his widow is already married, this story can do him no harm. If the Eversleighs were defrauded they will never feel it and my conscience, at least, gives me no twinges.

The Hoard of the Gibbelins

Lord Dunsany

———•———

THE GIBBELINS EAT, AS IS WELL KNOWN, NOTHING LESS GOOD THAN man. Their evil tower is joined to Terra Cognita, to the lands we know, by a bridge. Their hoard is beyond reason; avarice has no use for it; they have a separate cellar for emeralds and a separate cellar for sapphires; they have filled a hole with gold and dig it up when they need it. And the only use that is known for their ridiculous wealth is to attract to their larder a continual supply of food. In times of famine they have even been known to scatter rubies abroad, a little trail of them to some city of Man, and sure enough their larders would soon be full again.

Their tower stands on the other side of that river known to Homer— ὁ ῥόος ἀχεανοῖο as he called it—which surrounds the world. And where the river is narrow and fordable the tower was built by the Gibbelins' gluttonous sires, for they liked to see burglars rowing easily to their steps. Some nourishment that common soil has not the huge trees drained there with their colossal roots from both banks of the river.

There the Gibbelins lived and discreditably fed.

Alderic, Knight of the Order of the City and the Assault, hereditary Guardian of the King's Peace of Mind, a man not unremembered among the makers of myth, pondered so long upon the Gibbelins' hoard that by now he deemed it his. Alas that I should say of so perilous a venture, undertaken at dead of night by a valorous man, that its motive was sheer avarice! Yet upon avarice only the Gibbelins relied to keep their larders full, and once in every hundred years sent spies into the cities of men to see how avarice did, and always the spies returned again to the tower saying that all was well.

It may be thought that, as the years went on and men came by fearful ends on that tower's wall, fewer and fewer would come to the Gibbelins' table: but the Gibbelins found otherwise.

Not in the folly and frivolity of his youth did Alderic come to the tower, but he studied carefully for several years the manner in which burglars met their doom when they went in search of the treasure that he considered his. *In every case they had entered by the door.*

He consulted those who gave advice on this quest; he noted every detail and cheerfully paid their fees, and determined to do nothing that they advised, for what were their clients now? No more than examples of the savoury art, mere half-forgotten memories of a meal; and many, perhaps, no longer even that.

These were the requisites for the quest that these men used to advise: a horse, a boat, mail armour, and at least three men-at-arms. Some said, "Blow the horn at the tower door"; others said, "Do not touch it."

Alderic thus decided: he would take no horse down to the river's edge, he would not row along it in a boat, and he would go alone and by way of the Forest Unpassable.

How pass, you may say, by the unpassable? This was his plan: there was a dragon he knew of who if peasants' prayers are heeded deserved to die, not alone because of the number of maidens he cruelly slew, but because he was bad for the crops; he ravaged the very land and was the bane of a dukedom.

Now Alderic determined to go up against him. So he took horse and spear and pricked till he met the dragon, and the dragon came out against him breathing bitter smoke. And to him Alderic shouted, "Hath foul dragon ever slain true knight?" And well the dragon knew that this had never been, and he hung his head and was silent, for he was glutted with blood. "Then," said the knight, "if thou would'st ever taste maiden's blood again thou shalt be my trusty steed, and if not, by this spear there shall befall thee all that the troubadours tell of the dooms of thy breed."

And the dragon did not open his ravening mouth, nor rush upon the knight, breathing out fire; for well he knew the fate of those that did these things, but he consented to the terms imposed, and swore to the knight to become his trusty steed.

It was on a saddle upon this dragon's back that Alderic afterwards sailed above the unpassable forest, even above the tops of those measureless trees, children of wonder. But first he pondered that subtle plan of his which was more profound than merely to avoid all that had been done before; and he commanded a blacksmith, and the blacksmith made him a pickaxe.

Now there was great rejoicing at the rumour of Alderic's quest, for all folk knew that he was a cautious man, and they deemed that he would succeed and enrich the world, and they rubbed their hands in the cities at the thought of largesse; and there was joy among all men in Alderic's country, except perchance among the lenders of money, who feared they would soon be paid. And there was rejoicing also because men hoped that when the Gibbelins were robbed of their hoard, they would shatter their high-built bridge and break the golden chains that bound them to the world, and drift back, they and their tower, to the moon, from which they had come and to which they rightly belonged. There was little love for the Gibbelins, though all men envied their hoard.

So they all cheered, that day when he mounted his dragon, as though he was already a conqueror, and what pleased them more than the good that they hoped he would do to the world was that he scattered gold as he rode away; for he would not need it, he said, if he found the Gibbelins' hoard, and he would not need it more if he smoked on the Gibbelins' table.

When they heard that he had rejected the advice of those that gave it, some said that the knight was mad, and others said he was greater than those that gave the advice, but none appreciated the worth of his plan.

He reasoned thus: for centuries men had been well advised and had gone by the cleverest way, while the Gibbelins came to expect them to come by boat and to look for them at the door whenever their larder was empty, even as a man looketh for a snipe in the marsh; but how, said Alderic, if a snipe should sit in the top of a tree, and would men find him there? Assuredly never! So Alderic decided to swim the river and not to go by the door, but to pick his way into the tower through the stone. Moreover, it was in his mind to work below the level of the ocean, the river (as Homer knew) that girdles the world, so that as soon as he made a hole in the wall the water should pour in, confounding the Gibbelins, and flooding the cellars, rumoured to be twenty feet in depth, and therein he would dive for emeralds as a diver dives for pearls.

And on the day that I tell of he galloped away from his home scattering largesse of gold, as I have said, and passed through many kingdoms, the dragon snapping at maidens as he went, but being unable to eat them because of the bit in his mouth, and earning no gentler reward than a spurthurst where he was softest. And so they came to the swart arboreal precipice of the unpassable forest. The dragon rose at it with a rattle of wings. Many a fanner near the edge of the world saw him up there where yet the twilight lingered, a faint, black, wavering line; and mistaking him for a row of geese going inland from the ocean, went into their houses cheerily rubbing their hands and saying that winter was coming, and that we should soon have snow. Soon even there the twilight faded away, and when they descended at the edge of the world it was night and the moon was shining. Ocean, the ancient river, narrow and shallow there, flowed by and made no murmur. Whether the Gibbelins banqueted or whether they watched by the door, they also made no murmur. And Alderic dismounted and took his armour off, and saying one prayer to his lady, swam with his pickaxe. He did not part from his sword, for fear that he meet with a Gibbelin. Landed the other side, he began to work at once, and all went well with him. Nothing put out its head from any window, and all were lighted so that nothing within could see him in the dark. The blows of his pickaxe were dulled in the deep walls. All night he worked, no sound came to molest him, and at dawn the last rock swerved and tumbled inwards, and the river poured in after. Then Alderic took a stone, and went to the bottom step, and hurled the stone at the door; he heard the echoes roll into the tower, then he ran back and dived through the hole in the wall.

He was in the emerald-cellar. There was no light in the lofty vault above him, but, diving through twenty feet of water, he felt the floor all rough with emeralds, and open coffers full of them. By a faint ray of the moon he saw that the water was green with them, and, easily filling a satchel, he rose again to the surface; and there were the Gibbelins waist-deep in the water, with torches in their hands! And, without saying a word, *or even smiling*, they neatly hanged him on the outer wall—and the tale is one of those that have not a happy ending.

The House of Sounds

M. P. Shiel

———◆———

E caddi come l'uom cui sonno piglia.
Dante

A GOOD MANY YEARS AGO, WHEN A YOUNG MAN, A STUDENT IN PARIS, I knew the great Carot, and witnessed by his side several of those cases of mind-malady, in the analysis of which he was such a master. I remember one little maid of the Marais, who, until the age of nine, did not differ from her play-mates; but one night, lying abed, she whispered into her mother's ear: "Mama, can you not hear the sound of the world?" It appears that her geography had just taught her that our globe reels with an enormous velocity, on an orbit about the sun; and that this sound of the world of hers was merely a murmur in the ear, heard in the silence of night, and attributed by her fancy to the song of this high motion. Within six months she was as mad as a March-hare.

I mentioned the incident to my friend, Haco Harfager, then occupying with me an old mansion in St. Germain, shut in by a wall and a jungle of shrubbery. He listened with singular interest, and during a good while sat wrapped in gloom.

Another case which I gave made a great impression upon my friend: A young man, a toy-maker of St. Antoine, suffering from consumption—but sober, indus-trious—returning one gloaming to his garret, happened to purchase one of those factious journals which circulate by lamplight over the Boulevards. This simple act was the beginning of his doom. He had never been a reader: knew little of the reel and turmoil of the world. But the next night he purchased another journal. Soon he acquired a knowledge of politics, the huge movements, the tumult of life. And this interest grew absorbing. Till late into the night, every night, he lay poring over the roar of action, the printed passion. He would awake sick, but brisk of spirit—and bought a morning paper. And the more his teeth gnashed, the less they ate. He grew negligent, irregular at work, turning on his bed through the day. Rags overtook him. As the grand grew upon his frail soul, so every lesser interest failed him. There came a day when he no more cared for his own life; and another day when he tore the hairs from his head.

As to this man, the great Carot said to me:

"Really, one does not know whether to chuckle or to weep over such a business. Observe, for one thing, how diversely men are made! There are minds precisely so sensitive as a thread of melted lead: *every* breath will fret and trouble them: and how about the hurricane? For such this scheme is clearly no fit habitation, but a Machine of Death, a baleful Immense. *Too* cruel to some is the rushing shriek of Being—they *cannot* stand the world. Let each look well to his own little shred of existence, I say, and leave the monstrous Automaton alone! Here, in this poor toy-maker you have a case of the ear: it is only the neurosis, Oxyecoia. Splendid was that Greek myth of 'the Harpies'—by *them* was this creature snatched away—or say, caught by a limb in the wheels of the universe, and so perished. It is quite a ravishing exit—translation in a chariot of flame. Only remember the first seized was *the pinna*—he bent *ear* to the howl of the world, and ended by himself howling. Between chaos and our shoes swings, I assure you, the thinnest film! I knew a man who had this aural peculiarity: that every sound brought him some knowledge of the matter causing the sound: a rod, for instance, of mixed copper and tin striking upon a rod of mixed copper and lead, conveyed to him not merely the proportion of each metal in each rod, but some knowledge of the essential meaning and spirit, as it were, of copper, of tin, of iron and of lead. Him also did the Harpies snatch aloft!"

I have mentioned that I related some of these cases to my friend, Hafarger: and I was astonished at the obvious pains which he gave himself to his interest, his gaping nostrils. . . .

From first days when we happened to attend the same seminary in Stockholm, an intimacy accompanied by ordinary signs of friendship. Harfager was the shyest, most isolated, of beings. Though our joint housekeeping (brought about by a chance meeting at a midnight *séance*) had now lasted some months, I knew nothing of his plans. Through the day we read together, he rapt back into the past, I engrossed with the present; late at night we reclined on sofas within the vast cave of an old hearthplace *Louis Onze*, and smoked over the dying flame in a silence. Occasionally a *soirée* or lecture might draw me from the house; except once, I never understood that Harfager left it. On that occasion I was hurrying through the Rue St. Honoré, where a rush of traffic rattles over the old pavers retained there, when I came upon him. In this tumult he stood in a listening attitude; and for a moment did not know me.

Even as a boy I had seen in my friend the genuine patrician—not that his personality gave an impression of loftiness or opulence: on the contrary. He did, however, suggest an incalculable *ancientness*; and I have I have known no nobleman who bore in his expression the assurance of the essential Prince, whose pale blossom is of yesterday, and will perish to-morrow, but whose root shoots through the ages. This much I knew of Harfager; also that on one or other of his islands north of Zetland lived his mother and an aunt; that he was somewhat deaf; but liable to a thousand torments or delights at certain sounds, the whine of a door, the note of a bird. . . .

He was somewhat under middle height; and inclined to portliness. His nose rose highly aquiline from that sort of brow called "the musical"—that is, with temples which incline *outward* to the cheek-bones, making breadth for the base of the brain; while the direction of the heavy-lidded eyes, and of the eyebrows, was a downward *droop* from the nose of their outer ends. He wore a thin chin-beard. But the feature of his face were the ears, which were nearly circular, very small and flat, without that outer curve called "the helix." I came to understand that this had long been a trait of his race. Over the whole wan face of my friend was engraved an air of woeful inability, utter gravity of sorrow: one said "Sardanapalus," frail last of the race of Nimrod.

After a year I found it necessary to mention to Harfager my intention of leaving Paris, as we reclined one night in our nooks within the fireplace. He replied to my tidings with a polite "Indeed!" and continued to gloat over the gate; but after an hour turned to me and observed: "Well, it seems to be a hard world."

Truisms uttered with just such a tone of discovery I occasionally heard from him; but his earnest gaze, his despondency, now astonished me.

"Apropos of what?" I asked.

"My friend, do not leave me!" He spread his arms.

I learned that he was the object of a devilish malice; that he was the prey of a hellish temptation. That a lure, a becking hand, a lurking lust, which it was the effort of his life to escape (and to which he was especially liable in solitude) perpetually enticed him; and that so it had been almost from the day when, at time age of five, he had been sent by his father from his desolate home in the ocean.

And whose was this malice?

He told me his mother's and aunt's.

And what was this temptation?

He said it was the temptation to go back—to hurry with the frenzy of hunger—back to that home.

I demanded with what motives, and in what way, the malice of his mother and aunt manifested itself. He answered that there was, he fancied, no definite motive, but only a fated malevolence, involuntary and fated; and that the respect in which it manifested itself was the prayers and commands with which they plagued him to go again to the hold of his ancestors.

All this I could in not understand, and said so. In what consisted this magnetism, and this peril, of his home? To this Harfager did not reply, but rising from his seat, disappeared behind the hearth-curtains, and left the apartment. When he returned, it was with a quarto tome bound in hide, which proved to be Hugh Gascoigne's "Chronicle of Norse Families" in English black-letter. The passage to which he pointed I read as follows:

> Now of these two brothers the older, Harold, being of seemly personage and prowess, did go a pilgimage into Danemark, wherein he repaired again home to Hjaltland (Zetland), and with him fetched the amiable Thronda for his wife, who was a daughter of the sank (blood) royal of Danemark. And his younger brother, Sweyn, that was sad and debonair, but far surpassed the other in cunning, received him with all good cheer.
>
> But eftsoons (soon after) fell Sweyn sick for all his love that he had of Thronda, his brother's wife. And while the worthy Harold ministered about the bed where Sweyne lay sick, lo, Sweyn fastened on him with a violent stroke with a sword, and with no longer tarring enclosed his hands in bonds, and cast him in the bottom of a deep hold. And because Harold would not deprive himself of the governance of Thronda his wife, Sweyn cut off both his ear[s], and put out one of his eyes, and after divers such torments was ready to slay him. But on a day the valiant Harold, breaking his bonds, and embracing his adversary, did by the sleight of wrestling overthrow him, and escaped. Notwithstanding, he faltered when he came to the Somburgh Head not far from the Castle, and albeit that he was swift-foot, could no farther run, by reason that he was faint with the long plagues of his brother. And whilst he there lay in a swoon, did Sweyne come upon him, and when he had stricken him with a dart, cast him from Somburgh Head into the sea.

Not long hereafterward did the lady Thronda (thoogh she knew not
the manner of her lord's death, nor, verily, if he was dead or alive) receive
Sweyn into favour, and with great gaudying and blowing of beamous
(trumpets) did become his wife. And right so they two went thence to
sojourn in far parts.

Now, it befell that Sweyn was minded by a dream to have built a great
mansion in Hjaltland for the home-coming of the lady Thronda; wherefore
he called to him a cunning Master-workman, and sent him to England to
gather men for the building of this lusty House, while he himself remained
with his lady at Rome. Then came this architect to London, but passing
thence to Hjaltland was drowned, he and his feers (mates), all and some.
And after two years, which was the time assigned, Sweyn Harfager sent a
letter to Hjaltlande to understand how his great House did: for he knew not
the drowning of the Architect: and soon after he received answer that the
House *did well*, and was building on the Isle of Rayba; but that was not the
Isle where Sweyn had appointed the building to be; and he was afeard, and
near fell down dead for dread, because in the letter, he saw before him the
manner of writing of his brother Harold. And he said in this form: "Surely
Harold is alive, else be this a letter writ with ghost hand." And he was wo
many days, seeing that this was a deadly stroke.

Thereafter, he took himself back to Hjaltland to know how the matter was, and there the old Castle on Somburg Head was break down to the
earth. Then Sweyne was wode-wroth, and cried: "Jhesu mercy, where is all
the great house of my fathers gone? alas! this wicked day of destiny." And
one of the people told him that a host of workmen from far parts had break
it down. And he said: "Who hath bid them?" but that could none answer.
Then he said again: "nis (is not) my brother Harold alive? for I have behold
his writing"; and that, too, none could answer. So he went to Rayba, and
saw there a great House stand, and when he looked on it, he said: "This,
sooth, was y-built by my brother Harold, be he dead, or be he on-live." And
there he dwelt, and his lady, and his son's sons until now: for that the House
is ruthless and without pity; wherefore 'tis said that up on all who dwell
there falleth a wicked madness and a lecherous anguish; and that by way
of the ears do they drinck the cup of the furie of the earless Harold, till the
time of the House be ended.

After I had read the narrative half-aloud, I smiled, saying: "This, Harfager, is very tolerable romance on the part of the good Gascoigne, but has the look of indifferent history."

"It is, nevertheless, *history*," he replied.

"You believe that?"

"The house still stands solidly on Rayba."

"But you believe that mediæval ghosts superintended the building of their family mansions?"

"Gascoigne nowhere says that," he answered: "for to be 'stricken with a darte,' is not necessarily to die; nor, if he did say it, have I any knowledge on the subject."

"And what, Harfager, is the nature of that 'wicked madness,' that 'lecherous anguish,' of which Gascoigne speaks?"

"Do you ask me?"—he spread his arms—"what do I know? I know nothing! I was banished from the place at the age of five. Yet the cry of it still rings in my mind. And have I not *told* you of anguishes—even in myself—of inherited longing and loathing. . . ."

Anyway, I *had* to go to Heidelberg just then; so I said I would compromise by making my absence short, and rejoin him in a few weeks for me. I took his moody silence to mean assent; and soon afterwards left him.

But I was detained; and when I got back to our old house found it empty. Harfager was gone.

It was only after twelve years that a letter was forwarded me—a rather wild letter, an awfully long one—in the writing of my friend. It was dated at Rayba. From the writing I understood that it had been dashed off *with furious haste*, so I was the more astonished at the very trivial nature of the contents. On the first half page he spoke of our old friendship, and asked if I would see his mother, who was dying; the rest of the epistle consisted of an analysis of his mother's family-tree, the apparent aim being to show that she was a genuine Harfager, and a distant cousin of his father. He then went on to comment on the great prolificness of his race, stating that since the fourteenth century, over *four millions* of its members had lived; three only of them, he believed, being now left. That settled, the letter ended.

Influenced by this, I travelled northward; reached Caithness; passed the stormy Orkneys; reached Lerwick; and from Unst, the most bleak and northerly of the Zetlands, contrived, by dint of bribes, to pit the weather-worthiness of a lug-sailed "sixern" (identical with the "lang-schips" of the Vikings) against a flowing sea and an ugly sky. The trip, I was told, was at such a season of some risk. It was the sombre December of those seas; and the weather, they said, although never cold, is seldom other than tempestuous. A mist now lay over the billows, enclosing our boat in a dome of doleful gloaming; and there was a ghostly something in the look of the silent sea and brooding sky which produced upon my nerves the mood of a journey out of nature, a cruise beyond the world. Occasionally, however, we ran past one of those solitary "skerries," or sea-stacks, whose craggy sea-walls, disintegrated by the struggles of the Gulf Stream with the North Sea, had a look of awful ruin and havoc. But I only noticed three of these: for before the dun day had well run half its course, sudden darkness was upon us; and with it one of those storms, of which the winter of this semi-Arctic sea is one succession. During the haggard glimpses of the following day the rain did not stop; but before darkness had quite fallen, my skipper (who talked continuously to a mate of seal-maidens, and water-horses, and *grüles*), paused to point me out a mound of gloomier grey on the weather-bow, which, he said, should be Rayba.

Rayba, he said, was the centre of quite a system of those *rösts* (dangerous eddies) and cross-currents, which the tidal wave hurls with complicated swirlings among all of the islands: but at Rayba they ran with more than usual angriness, owing to the row of sea-crags which garrisoned the land around: approach was therefore at all times difficult, and at night foolhardy. With a running sea, however, we came sufficiently close to see the mane of foam which railed round the coast-wall. Its shock, according to the captain, had often more than all the efficiency of artillery, tossing tons of rock to heights of six hundred feet upon the island.

When the sun next pried above the horizon, we had closely approached the coast; and it was then that for the first time the impression of some *spinning* motion of the island (due probably to the swirling movement of the water) was produced upon me. We affected a landing at a *voe*, or sea-arm, on the west coast; the east, though the point of my aim, was out of the question on account of the swell. Here I found two *skeoes* (or sheds), thatched with feal, five or six seamen, who gained a livelihood by trading for the groceries of the great house on the east; and, taking one of them for a guide, I began the climb of the island.

Now, during the night in the boat, I had been aware of a booming in the ears for which even the roar of the sea round the coast seemed insufficient to account; and this now, as we went on, became sufficiently augmented—and with it, once more, the conviction within me of *spinning* motions. Rayba I found discovered to be a land of precipices of granite and flaggy gneiss; at about the centre, however, we came upon a tableland, sloping from west to east, and covered by lots of lochs, which sullenly flowed into one another. I could see no shore eastward to this chain of waters, and by dint of shouting to my leader, and bending ear to his shoutings, I came to know that there *was* no such shore—I say *shout*, for nothing less could have sounded through the steady bellowing as of ten thousand bisons that now resounded on every side. A certain trembling, too, of the earth became distinct. In vain, meantime, did the eye in its dreary survey seek a tree or shrub—for no kind of vegetation, save peat, could brave for a day the perennial tempest of this benighted island. Darkness, half an hour after noon, commenced to fall upon us: and it was soon afterwards that my guide, pointing down a defile near the eastern coast, hurriedly started back the way he had come. I bawled a question after him, as he went: but at this point the voice of mortals had ceased to be in the least audible.

Down this defile, with a sinking of the heart, and a most singular sickness of giddiness, I passed; and, on reaching its end, emerged upon a ledge of rock which shuddered to the immediate onsets of the sea—though all this part of the island was, besides, in the grip of an ague not due to the great guns of the sea. Hugging a crag of cliff for steadiness from the gusts, I gazed forth upon a scene not less eerily dismal than some drear district of the dreams of Dante. Three "skerries," flanked by stacks as fantastic and twisted as a witch's finger, and giving a home to hosts of osprey and scart, seal and walrus, lay at some fathoms distance; and from its rush among them, the sea in blanched, tumultuous, but inaudible wrath, like an army with banners, ranted toward the land. Letting go my crag, I staggered some distance to the left: and now all at once an amphitheatre opened before me, and there broke upon my view a panorama of such appalling majesty as had never entered my heart to fancy.

"An amphitheatre," I said: but it was rather the form of a Norman door that I saw. Fancy such a door, half a mile wide, flat on the ground, the rounded part farthest from the sea; and all round it let a wall of rock tower perpendicular forty yards: and now down this rounded door shape, and *over its whole extent*, let a roaring ocean roll its tonnage in hoary fury—and the stupor with which I looked, and then the shrinking, and then the instinct of flight, will find comprehension.

This was the disemboguement of the lochs of Rayba.

And within the curve of this Norman cataract, robed in the world of its smokes and far-excursive surfs, stood a fabric of brass.

The last beam of the day had now nearly passed; but I could still see through the mist which had bleakly nimbused it as in tears, that the building was low in proportion to the hugeness of its circumference; that it was roofed with a dome; and that about it ran two rows of Norman windows, the upper smaller than the lower. Certain indications led me to infer that the house had been founded upon a bed of rock which lay, circular and detached, within the curve of the cataract; but this nowhere emerged above the flood: for the whole floor which I had before me dashed one reeking deep river to the beachless sea—passage to the mansion being made possible by a massive causeway-bridge, with arches, all bearded with sea-weed.

Descending from my ledge, I passed along it, now drenched in spray; and as I came nearer, could see that this house, too, was to half its height more thickly bearded than an old hull with barnacles and every variety of bright sea-weed; also—what was very surprising—that from many spots near the top of the brazen wall ponderous chains, dropping beards, reached out in rays: so that the fabric had the aspect of a many-anchored ark. But without pausing to look closely, I pushed forward, and rushing through the smooth waterfall which poured all round from the roof, by one of its many porches I entered the dwelling.

Darkness now was around me—and sound. I seemed to stand in the very centre of some yelling planet, the low resembling the sounding of many thousands of cannon, purchased by strange crashing and breaking uproars. And a madness descended on me; I was near to tears. "Here," I said, "is the place of weeping; not elsewhere is the vale of sighing." However, I passed forward through a succession of halls, and was wondering where to go next, when a hideous figure, with a lamp in his hand, stalked rapidly towards me. I shrank from him! It seemed the skeleton of a lank man wrapped in a winding-sheet till the light of one tiny eye, and a film of skin over a portion of the face reassured one. Of ears he showed no sign. His name, I afterwards learned, was Aith; and his appearance was explained by his pretence (true or false) that he had once suffered *burning*, almost to the cinder-stage, but had somehow recovered. With an expression of malice, and agitated gestures, he led the way to a chamber on the upper stage, where, having struck light to a taper, he made signs toward a spread table, and left me.

For a long time I sat in solitude, conscious of the shaking of the mansion, though every sense was swallowed up and confounded in the one impression of sound. Water, water, was the world—a nightmare on my breast, a tingling on my nerves, a sense of being infinitely drowned and buried in boundless deluges; and when the feeling of giddiness, too, increased, I sprang up and paced—but suddenly stopped, angry, I scarce knew why, with myself. I had, in fact, caught myself walking with a certain *hurry*, not usual with me, not natural to me. So I forced myself to stand and take note of the hall.

It was large, and damp with mists, so that its tattered, but rich, furniture looked lost in it, its centre occupied by a tomb bearing the name of a Harfager of the fourteenth century, and its walls old panels of oak. Having drearily seen these things, I waited on with an intolerable consciousness of solitude; but a little after midnight the tapestry parted, and Harfager with a rapid stalk walked in.

In twelve years my friend had grown old. He showed, it is true, a tendency to portliness: yet, to a knowing eye, he was in reality tabid, ill-nourished. And his neck stuck forward from his chest; and the lower part of his back had quite a forward bend of age; and his hair floated about his face and shoulders in a wildness of awful whiteness, while a white chin-beard hung to his chest. His dress was a robe of bauge, which, as he went, waved aflaunt from his bare and hairy shins, and he was shod in those soft slippers called *rivlins*.

To my astonishment, he spoke. When I passionately shouted that I could gather no fragment of sound from his moving mouth, he clapped both his palms to his ears, and then anew besieged mine: but again without result: and now, with an angry throw of the hand, he caught up his taper, and walked from the apartment.

There was something strikingly unnatural in his manner—something which reminded me of the skeleton, Aith: an excess of zeal, a fever, a rage, a *loudness*, an eagerness of gait, a great extravagance of gesture. His hand constantly dashed the whiffs of hair from his face which, though of the saffron of death, had red eyes—thick-lidded eyes, fixed in a downward and sideward gaze. When he came back to me, it was with a leaf a folio of ivory, and a piece of graphite, hanging from the cord tied round his garment; and he rapidly wrote a petition that, if not too tired, I would take part with him in the funeral of his mother.

I shouted assent.

Once more he clapped palms to his ears; then wrote: "Do not shout: no whisper in any part of the building is inaudible to me."

I remembered that, in early life, he had been slightly *deaf*.

We passed together through many apartments, he shading the taper with his hand—a necessary action, for, as I quickly discovered, in no nook of the quivering building was the air in a state of rest, but was fo rever commoved by a curious agitation, a faint windiness, like an echo of tempests, which communicated a universal nervousness to the curtains. Everywhere I met the same past grandeur, present raggedness and decay. In many of the rooms were tombs; one was a museum thronged with bronzes, but broken, grown with fungoids, dripping with moisture—it was as if the mansion, in ardour of travail, sweated; and a miasma of decomposition tainted all the air.

I followed Harfager through the maze of his way with some difficulty, for he went headlong—only once stopping, when with a face ungainly wild over the glare of the light, he tossed up his fingers, and gave out a single word: from the form of his lips I guessed the word "*Hark!*"

Presently we entered a very long chamber, in which, on chairs beside a bed, lay a coffin, flanked by a file of candles. The coffin was very deep, and had this singularity—that the foot-piece was absent, so that the soles of the corpse could be seen as we approached. I saw, too, three upright rods secured to a side of the coffin, each rod fitted at its top with a little silver bell of the sort called *morrice*, pendent from a flexible spring. At the head of the bed, Aith, with an air of irascibility, was stamping to and fro with a narrow area.

Harfager deposited the taper upon a stone table, and stood poring with a crazy intentness over the body. I, too, stood and looked at death so grim and rigorous as I think I never saw. The coffin looked angrily full of tangled grey locks, the lady being of great age, bony and hook-nosed; and her face shook with solemn constancy to the quivering of the building. I noticed that over the body had been set fixed three bridges, like the bridge of a violin, their sides fitting into groves in the coffin's sides, and their tops of a shape to fit the slope of the two coffin-lids when closed. One of these bridges passed over the knees of the dead lady; another bridged her stomach; the third her neck. In each of them was a hole, and across each of the three holes passed a string from the morrice-bell above it—the three holes being thus divided by the three tight strings into six semi-circles. Before I could guess the significance of all this, Harfager closed the folding coffin-lids, which had little holes for the passage of the three strings. He then turned the key in the lock, and uttered a word which I took to be, "come."

Aith now took hold of the handle at the coffin's head; and out of the dark part of the hall a lady in black walked forward. She was very tall, pallid, of imposing aspect; and from the curvature of the nose, and her circular ears, I guessed her the lady Swertha, aunt of Harfager. Her eyes were red—if with crying I could not tell.

Harfager and I taking each a handle near the coffin-foot, and the lady bearing before us one of the black candlesticks, the obsequies began. When I got to the doorway, I noticed in a corner there were two more coffins, engraved with the names of Harfager and his aunt. Thence we wound our way down a wide stairway winding to a lower floor; and descending thence still lower by narrow brass steps, came to a portal of metal, where the lady, depositing the candlestick, left us.

The chamber of death into which we now bore the body had for its outer wall the brazen outer wall of the whole house at a spot where this approached the cataract, and was no doubt profoundly drowned in the world of surge without: so that the earthquake there was urgent. On every side the place was piled with coffins, ranged high and wide upon shelves; and the huge rush and scampering which ensued on our entrance proved it was the paradise of troops of rats. As it was inconceivable that these could have eaten a way through sixteen brazen feet—for even the floor here was brazen—I assumed that some fruitful pair must have found in the house, on its building, an ark from the waters. Even this guess, though, seemed wild; and Harfager afterwards confided to me his suspicion that they had for some reason been *placed* there by the original builder.

We deposited our load upon a stone bench in the centre; whereupon Aith made haste to be away. Harfager then repeatedly walked from end to end of the place, scrutinising with many a stoop and peer and upward stretch the shelves and their props. Could he, I was led to wonder, have any doubts as to their soundness? Damp, in fact, and decay pervaded everything. A bit of which I touched crumbled to dust under my thumb.

He presently beckoned to me, and with yet one halt and "*Hark!*" from him, we passed through the house to my chamber; where, left alone, I paced long about, agitated with a strange anger; then tumbled to an agony of slumber.

In the far interior of the mansion even the bleared day of this land of bleakness never rose upon our gloom; but I was able to regulate my gettings-up by a clock which stood in my chamber; or I was called by Harfager, with whom in a short time, I renewed more than all our former friendship. That I should say *more* is curious: but so it *was*: and this was proved by the fact that we grew to take, and to excuse, freedoms of speech and manner which, as two persons of more than usual reserve, we had once never dreamed of permitting to ourselves in respect of each other. Down corridors that vanished either way in darkness and length of perspective remoteness we linked ourselves in perambulations of purposeless urgency. Once, for example, in our pacings of aimless haste down passages that vanished in shadow and length of perspective remoteness, he wrote that my step was very slow. I replied that it was just such a step as suited my then mood. He wrote: "You have developed an tendency to *fret*." I was very offended, and said: "Certainly there are more fingers than one in the world which that ring will fit!"

Another day he was no less than rude to me for seeking to reveal to him the secret of the unhuman keenness of his hearing—and of mine! For I, too, to my dismay, began, as time passed, to catch hints of shouted sounds. The cause might he found, I asserted, in a fervour of the auditory nerve, which, if the cataract were absent, the roar of the ocean, and the perpetual tempest about us, might be sufficient to bring about; in his own ear-interior, I said, must be inflamed to an exquisite pitch of fever; and I named the disease to him as the "Paracusis Wilisü." When he frowned dissent, I, quite undeterred, proceeded to relate the case (that had occurred within my own experience) of a very deaf lady who could hear the drop of a pin in a railway-train*; and now he made me the reply: "Of ignorant persons I am accustomed to consider the mere scientist the most ignorant!"

But I, for my part, regarded it as merely far-fetched that he should pretend to be in the dark as to the morbid state of his hearing! He himself, indeed, confessed to me his own, Aith's, and the lady Swertha's proneness to paroxysms of *vertigo*. I was startled! for I had myself shortly previously roused out of sleep by feelings of reeling and nausea, and an assurance that the room flew furiously round with me. The impression passed away, and I attributed it, perhaps hastily, to some disturbance in the nerve-endings of the "labyrinth," or inner ear. In Harfager, however, the conviction of whirling motions in the house, in the world, got to so horrible a degree of certainty, that its effects sometimes resembled those of lunacy or energumenal possession. Never, he said, was the sensation of giddiness altogether dead in him; seldom the sensation that he gazed with stretched-out arms over the brink of abysms voids which wooed his half-consenting foot. Once, as we walked, he was hurled, as by unearthly powers, to the ground; and there for an hour sprawled, bathed in sweat, with distraught bedazzlement and amaze in his stare, while watched the racing walls. He was constantly racked, moreover, with the consciousness of sounds so peculiar in their character, that I could account for them on no other supposition than that of a *tinnitùs* infinitely sick. Through the roar there sometimes visited him, he told me, the lullaby of some bird, from the burden of whose song he had the consciousness that she derived from a very remote country, was of the whiteness of foam, and crested with a comb of mauve. Or else he knew aware of accumulated human tones, distant yet articulate, busily contending in volubility, and in the end melting into a medley of

---

* Such cases are known to many medical men. The concussion on the deaf nerve is the cause of the acquired sensitiveness; nor is there any limit to that sensitiveness when the tumult is immensely augmented.

musical movements. Or, anon, he was shocked by an infinite and imminent crashing, like the monstrous racket of the crackling of a cosmos of crockery round his ears. He told me, moreover, that he could frequently see, rather than hear, the parti-coloured wheels of a mazy sphere-music deep, deep, within the black dark of the cataract's roar. These impressions, which I protested *must* be purely entotic, had sometimes a pleasing effect upon him, and he would stand long to listen with a lifted hand to their seduction: others again inflamed him to a mad angry madness. I guessed that they were the cause of those "*Harks*!" that at intervals of about an hour did not fail to break from him. But in truth I was wrong: and it was with a thrill of dismay that I shortly came to know the truth.

For, as once we were once passing by an iron door on the lower floor, he stopped, and for some minutes stood, listening with a leer most keen and cunning. Presently the cry "*Hark*!" escaped him; and he then turned to me and wrote up the tablet: "Did you did not hear?" I heard nothing but the roar; and he howled into my ear in sounds now audible to me as an echo caught far off in dreams: "You shall see."

He took up the candlestick; produced from the pocket of his robe a key; unlocked the iron door; and we passed into a room very loftily domed in proportion to its area, and empty, save that a pair of steps lay against its wall, and that in the centre of its marble floor was a pool, like a Roman "impluvium," only round like the room—a pool evidently profound in depth, full of a thick and inky fluid. I was very perturbed by its present aspect, for as the candle burned upon its surface, I observed that this had been quite recently *disturbed*, in a style for which the shivering of the house could not account, since *ripples* of slime were now rounding out from its middle to its brink. When I glanced at Harfager for explanation; he gave me a signal to wait; and now for about an hour, with his hands behind his back, paced the chamber; but then paused and we two stood together by the pool's margin, gazing into the water. Suddenly his clutch tightened on my arm, and I saw, with a touch of horror, a tiny ball, probably of lead, but daubed blood-red by some chemical, fall from the roof, and sink into the middle of the pool. It hissed on contact with the water a whiff of mist.

"In the name of all that is sinister," I whispered, "what thing is this?"

Again he made me a busy and confident signal to wait, moved the ladder-steps toward the pool, handed me the taper. When I had mounted, holding high the light, I saw hanging out of the fogs in dome a globe of old copper, lengthened into balloon-shape by a neck, at the end of which I could spy a tiny hole. Painted over the globe was barely visible in red print-letters:

HAFARGER-HOUS: 1388–188

I was down quicker than I went up!

"But the meaning?" I panted.

"Did you see the writing?"

"Yes. The meaning?"

He wrote: "By comparing Gascoigne with Thrunster, I find that the mansion was *built* around 1389."

"But the last figures?"

"After the last 8," he replied, "there is another figure not quite obliterated by a tarnish-spot."

"What figure?" I asked.

"It cannot be read but may be surmised. The year 1888 is now all but passed. It can only be the figure 9."

"Oh, you are depraved in mind!" I cried, very irritated; "you assume—you *state*—in a manner which no mind trained to base its conclusions on facts can bear with patience."

"And you are irrational," he wrote. "You know, I suppose, the formula of Archimedes by which, the diameter of a globe being known, its volume also is know. Now, the diameter of the globe in the dome I know to be four and a half feet; and the diameter of the leaden balls about a third of an inch. Supposing, then, that 1389 was the year in which the globe was full of balls, you may readily calculate that not many fellows of the four million and odd which have since dropped at the rate of one an hour are now left within. The fall of balls *cannot* persist another year. The figure 9 is therefore forced upon us."

"But you assume, Harfager!" I cried: "Oh, believe me, my friend, this is the very wantonness of wickedness! By what algebra of despair do you know that each ball represents one of your house, or that the last date was intended to correspond with the stoppage of the horologe. And, even if so, what is the significance of it? It can have no *significance*!"

"Do you want to madden me?" he shouted. Then furiously writing: "I swear that I know nothing of its significance! But is it not evident to you that the thing is a big hour-glass, intended to count the hours, not of a day, but of a cycle; and of a cycle of five hundred years?"

"But the whole contrivance," I passionately cried, "is a baleful phantasm of our brains! How is the fall of the balls regulated? Ah, my friend, you wander—your mind is debauched in this brawl of waters."

"I have not ascertained," he replied, "by what internal works, or clammy medium, or spiral coil, dependent probably for its action upon the vibration of the mansion, the balls are retarded in their fall: that was a matter well within the skill of the mediæval mechanic, the inventor of the clock; but this at least is clear, that one element of their retardation is the smallness of the aperture through which they have to pass; that this element, by known laws of statics, will cease to operate when no more than three balls remain; and that, consequently, the last three will fall at almost the same instant."

"In Heaven's name!" I exclaimed, careless now what folly I poured out, "but your mother is dead, Harfager! Do you deny that there remain but you and the lady Swertha?"

A glance of disdain was all the answer he then gave me as to this.

But he confessed to me a day later that the leaden drops were a constant sorrow to his ears; that from hour to hour his life was a keen waiting for their fall; that even from his brief sleeps he infallibly started awake at each descent; that in whatever reach of the mansion he chanced to be, they found him out with a crashing *loudness*; and that each drop tweaked him with a twinge of anguish within the ear. I was therefore shocked at his declaration that these droppings had now become to as the life of life to him; had acquired an entwining so close with the tone of his mind, that their ceasing might even mean for him the reeling of Reason: at which confession he sobbed, with his face buried, as he leant upon a column. When this paroxysm was past, I asked him if it was out of the question that he should once and for all cast off the fascination of the horologe, and escape with me from the place. He wrote in mysterious reply: "A *three*-fold cord is not easily broken." I started, asking—"How three-fold?" He wrote with a bitter smile: "To be in love with pain—to pine after aching—is not that a wicked madness?" "A lecherous anguish!" "You have seen my aunt's face," he proceeded; "your eyes were dim if you did not see in it an impious calm, the glee of a blasphemous patience, a grin behind her daring smile." He then spoke of a prospect at the terror of which his whole soul trembled, yet which sometimes laughed in his heart in the form of a *hope*. It was the prospect of any considerable increase in the volume of sound about his ears. At *that*, he said, the brain must totter. On the night of my arrival the noise of my boots, and since then, my voice occasionally raised voice, had produced acute pain in him. To such an ear, I understood him to say, the luxury of torture involved in a large sound-increase around was an allurement from which no human virtue could turn: and when I said that I could not even conceive such an increase, much less the means by which it could be effected, he brought out from the archives of the mansion some annals kept by the heads of the family. From these it appeared that the tempests that ever lacerated the latitude of Rayba did not fail to give place, at intervals of some years, to one mammoth madness, one Samson among the merry men, and Sirius among the suns. At such periods the rains descended—and the floods came—even as in the first world-deluge; those *rösts*, or eddies, which ever encircled Rayba, spurning the bands of lateral space, burst aloft into a whirl of water-spouts, to dance about the little land, upon which, converging, some of them discharged their waters: and the locks which flowed to the cataract thus redoubled their volume, and crashed with redoubled roar. Harfager said that it was miraculous that for eighteen years no such great event had transacted itself at Rayba.

"And what," I asked, "in addition toe the dropping balls, and the prospect of an increase of sound, it the third strand of that '*three-fold cord*' of which you have spoken?"

For answer he led me to a circular hall which, he said, he had ascertained to be the center of the circular mansion. It was a very large hall—so large as I think I never saw—so large that the amount of wall lighted at any one time by the candle seemed nearly flat: and nearly the whole of its area, from floor to roof, was occupied by a column of brass, the space between wall and cylinder being only such as to admit of a stretched-out arm.

"This column," Hafarger wrote, "goes up to the dome and passes beyond it; it goes down to the lower floor, and passes through that; it goes down thence to the brazen flooring of the vaults, and *passes through that* into the bedrock. Under each floor it spreads out, helping to support the floor. What is the precise quality of the impression which I have made upon your mind by this description?"

"I do not know!" I answered, turning from him: "ask me none of your enigmas, Harfager: I feel a giddiness. . . ."

"But answer me," he said: "consider *the strangeness* of that brazen lowest floor, which I have discovered to be some six feet thick, and whose under-surface, I have reason to think, is somewhat *above* the bed-rock; remember that the fabric is at no point *fastened* to the column; think of the *chains* that ray out from the outer wall, apparently *anchoring* the house to the ground. Tell me, what impression have I *now* made?"

"And is it for *this* you wait?" I cried. Yet there may have been no malevolent intention! You jump at conclusions! Any fixed building in such a land and spot as this would at any time be liable to be broken up by some sovereign tempest! What if it was the intention of the builder that in such a case the chains should break, and the building, by yielding, be saved?"

"You have no lack of charity at least," he replied; and we returned to the book we then read together.

He had not wholly lost the old habit of study, although he could no longer get himself to *sit* to read; so with a volume (often tossed down) he would stamp about within the region of the lamplight; or I, unconscious of my voice, might read to him. By a whim of his mood the few books which now lay within the limits of his patience had all for their motive something of the *picaresque*, or the foppishly speculative: Quevedo's "Tacaño"; or the system of Tycho Brahe; above all, George Hakewill's "Power and Providence of God." One day, however, as I read, he interrupted me with the sentence, *à propos* of nothing: "What I cannot understand is that you, a scientist, should believe that the physical life ceases with the ceasing of breathing"—and from that moment the tone of our reading changed. For he led me to the crypts of the library in the lowest part of the building, and hour after hour, with a *furore* of triumph, overwhelmed me with books proving the length of life after "death." What, he asked, was my opinion of Baron Verulam's account of the dead man who was heard to utter words of prayer? or of the bounding bowels of the dead convict? On my expressing unbelief, he seemed surprised, and reminded me of the writhings of dead cobras, of the long beatings of a frog's heart after "death." "She is not dead," he quoted, "but *sleepeth*." The idea of Bacon and Paracelsus that the principle of life resides in the spirit or fluid was proof to him that such fluid could not, from its very nature, undergo any *sudden* annihilation, while the organs which it pervades remain. When I asked him what limit he, then, set to the persistence of "life" in the "dead," he answered that when decay had so far advanced that the nerves could no longer be called nerves, or when the brain had been disconnected at the neck from the body, as by rats gnawing, then the king of terrors was king verily. With an indiscretion strange to me before my residence at Rayba, I now blurted out the question whether all this could be referring to his mother? For a while he stood thoughtful, then wrote: "Even if I had I not reason to believe that my own and Swertha's life in some way hung upon the final cessation of hers, I should still have taken precautions to ascertain the march of the destroyer on her frame: as it is, I shall not lack even the exactest information." He then explained that the rats which ran riot in the place of death would in their time do their full work upon her; but would be unable to reach the region of the throat without first gnawing their way through the three strings stretched across the holes of the bridges within the coffin, and thus, one by one, liberating the three morrisco-bells to a tinkling.

The winter solstice had gone; another year began. I was sleeping in a deep sleep by night when Harfager came into my chamber, and shook me. His face was ghastly in the taper's glare. A change within a short time had taken place upon him. He was hardly the same. He was like some poor wight into whose surprised eyes in the night—have pried into the eyes of Affright.

He said that he was aware of strainings and creakings, which gave him the feeling of being suspended in airy spaces by a thread which must break to his weight; and he begged me, for God's sake, to accompany him to the coffins. We passed together through the house, he craven, haggard, his gate now laggard, into the chamber of the dead, where he stole to and fro examining the shelves. Out of the footless coffin of the dowager trembling on its bench I saw a water-rat crawl; and as Harfager passed beneath one of the shortest of the shelves which bore one coffin, it suddenly dropped from a height with to dust at his feet. He screamed the cry of a frighted creature; tottered to my support; and I bore him back to the upper parts of the palace.

He sat, with his face buried, in a corner of a small chamber, doddering, overtaken, as it were, with the extremity of age, no longer marking with his "*Hark*!" the fall of the leaden drops. To my remonstrances he answered only with the moan, "so soon!" Whenever I looked for him, I found him there, his manhood now collapsed in an ague. I do not think that during this time he slept.

On the second night, as I was approaching him, he sprang suddenly upright with the outcry: "The first bell is tinkling!"

And he had screamed it when, from some long way off, a faint wail, which at its origin must have been a fierce shriek, reached my now feverish ears. Harfager, for his part, clapped his palms to his ears, and dashed from his place, I following in hot chase through the black breadth of the mansion: till we came to a chamber containing a candelabrum, and arrased in faded red. On the floor in swoon lay the lady Swertha, her dark-grey hair in disarray wrapping her like an angry sea; tufts of it scattered, torn from the roots; and on her throat prints of strangling fingers. We bore her to the bed in an alcove; and, having discovered some tincture in a cabinet, I administered it between her fixed teeth. In her rapt countenance I saw that death was not; and, as I found something appalling in her aspect, shortly afterwards left her to Harfager.

When I next saw him his manner had undergone a kind of change which I can only describe as gruesome. It resembled the officious self-importance seen in a person of weak intellect who spurs himself with the thought, "to business! the time is short!" while his walk sickened me with a hint of *ataxie locomotrice*. When I asked him as to his aunt, as to the meaning of the marks of violence on her body, bending ear to his deep and unctuous tone, I could hear: "An attempt has been made upon her the skeleton, Aith."

He seemed not share my astonishment at this thing! nor could give me any clear answer as to his reason for retaining such a servant, or as to the origin of Aith's service. Aith, he told me, had been admitted into the palace during the period of his own absence in youth, and he knew little of him beyond the fact that he was extraordinarily strong. *Whence* he had come, or how, no person except the lady Swertha was aware: and she, it seems, feared, or at least persistently flinched from admitting him into the mystery. He added that, as a matter of fact, the lady, from the day of his coming back to Rayba, had with some object imposed upon herself a dumbness on all subjects, which he had never once known her to break through, except by an occasional note.

With an ataxic strenuousness, with the airs of a drunken man constraining himself to ordered action, Harfager now set himself to the doing of a host of trivial things: he collected chronicles and arranged them in order of date; he docketed or ticketed packets of documents; he insisted upon my assistance in turning the faces of paintings to the wall. He was, however, now constantly stopped by bursts of vertigo, six times in a single hour being hurled to the ground, while blood frequently guttered from his ears. He complained to me in a tone of piteous wail of the wooing of a silver *piccolo* that continually seduced him. As he bent, sweating, over his momentous nothings, his hands fluttered like aspen. I noted the movements of his whimpering lips, the rheum of his sunken eyes: sudden dotage had come upon his youth.

On a day he threw it utterly off, and was young anew. He entered my room; roused me from my dreams; I observed the lunacy of bliss in his eyes, heard his hiss in my ear:

"Up! The *storm*!"

Ah! I had known it—in the nightmare of the night. I felt it in the air of the room. It had come. I saw it lurid by the lamplight on the hell of Harfager's face.

A glee burst at once into birth within me, as I sprang from my couch, glancing at the clock: it was eight—in the morning. Harfager, with the naked stalk of some maniac prophet, had already taken himself away; and I started out after him. A deepening was clearly felt in the quivering of the edifice; anon for a second it stopped still, as if, breathlessly, to listen; its air was troubled with a vague gustiness. Occasionally there came to me as it were the noising of some far-off lamentation and voice in Ramah, but whether this was in my ear or the screaming of the gale, I could not tell; or again I could hear one clear chord of an organ's vaunt. About noon I spied Harfager, lamp in hand, running along a corridor, with naked soles. As we met he looked at me, but hardly with recognition, and passed by; stopped, however, and ran back to howl into my ear the question: "Would you *see*?" He then beckoned before me, and I followed to a very small window in the outer wall, closed with a slab of brass. As he lifted a latch, the slab dashed inward with instant impetuosity and tossed him a long way, while the breath of the tempest, braying through the brazen tube with a brutal bravura, caught and pinned me upon a corner of a wall, and all down the corridor a long crashing racket of crowds of pictures and couches followed. I nevertheless managed to push my way on the belly to the opening. Hence the sea should have been visible; but my senses were met by nothing but a vision of tumbled tenebrousness, and a general impression of the letter O. The sun of Rayba had gone out. In a moment of opportunity our two forces got the shutter again.

"Come!"—he had obtained a fresh glimmer, and beckoned before me—"let us see how the dead fare in the great desolation": and we ran, but had hardly got to the middle of the stairway, when I was thrilled by the consciousness of some great shock, the bass of a dull thud, which nothing save the thumping to the floor of the whole lump of the coffins could have caused. I looked for Harfager, and for a moment only saw his heels skedaddling, panic-hounded, his ears stopped ears, his mouth round! Then, indeed, fear reached me—a tremor in the audacity of my heart, a thought that at any rate I must desert him in his extremity, and work out my own salvation. Yet it was with a hesitancy that I turned to search him for the last farewell—a hesitancy which I felt not to be unselfish, but selfish, and unhealthy. I rambled through the night, seeking light, and having happened upon a lamp, proceeded to hunt for Harfager. Several hours went by in this way, during which I could not doubt from the state of the air in the house that the violence about me was being wildly heightened. Sounds as of screams—unreal, like the shriekings of demons—now reached my ears. As the time of night came on, I began to detect in the greatly augmented baritone of the cataract a fresh character—a shrillness—the whistle of rapture—a malice—the menace of a rabies blind and deaf. It must have been at about the hour of six that I found Harfager. He sat in an obscure room, with his head bowed down, his hands on his knees, his face was covered with hair, and blood from the ears. The right sleeve of his robe had been rent away in some renewed attempt, I imagine, to manipulate a window, and the rather crushed arm hung lank from the shoulder. For some time I stood and eyed him mouthing his mumblings; but now that I had found him uttered nothing as to my departure. Presently he looked sharply up with the call "*Hark*!"—then with impatience, "Hark! Hark!"—then with a shout, "The second bell!" And *again*, in an immediate sequence upon his shout, there sounded a wail, vague yet real, through the house. Harfager at the instant dropped reeling with giddiness; but I, snatching up a lamp, dashed out, shivering, but eager. For some while the wild wailing went on (either actually, or by reflex action of my ear); and as I ran for the lady's apartment, I saw, opposite to it the open door of an armoury, into which I passed, caught up a battle-axe, and was not about to dart in to her aid, when Aith, with a blazing eye, shied out of her chamber. I cast up my axe, and, shouting, dashed forward to down him: but by some chance the lamp fell from me, and before I knew anything more, the axe sprang from my grasp, and I was cast far backward by some grim vigour. There was, however, enough light shining out of the chamber to show that the skeleton had darted into a door of the armoury, so I instantly slammed and locked the door near me by which I had procured the axe, and hurrying to the other, secured it, too. Aith was thus a prisoner. I entered the lady's chamber. She lay over the bed in the alcove, and to my bent ear grossly croaked the ruckle of death. A glance at the mangled throat convincing me that her last moments were come, I settled her on the bed, curtained her within the loosened festoons of the hangings of black, and turned from the cursedness of her aspect. On an *escritoire* near I noticed a note, intended apparently for Harfager: "I mean to defy, and fly; not from fear, but for the light of the defiance itself. *Can* you come?" Taking a flame from the candelabrum, I left her to her loneliness, and throes of her death.

I had passed some way backward when I was startled by a queer sound—a crash—resembling the crash of a tamboureen; and as I could hear it pretty clearly, and from a distance, this meant some prodigious energy. In two minutes it again broke out, and thenceforth at regular intervals—with an effect of pain upon me; and the conviction grew gradually within me that Aith had unhung two of the old brass shields from their pegs, and holding them by their handles, and dash them viciously together, thus expressed the frenzy that had now overtaken him. When I found my way back to Harfager, very anguish now stamping in him about the chamber; he shook his head like a tormented horse, brushing and barring from his hearing each crash of the brass shields. "Ah, when—when—" he hoarsely groaned into my ear, "will that ruckle cease in her throat? I will myself, I tell you—*with my own hand*—oh God. . . ." Since the morning his auditory fever (as indeed my own also) appeared to have increased in steady proportion with the roaring and screeching chaos round; and the death-struggle in the lady's throat bitterly filled for him the intervals of the grisly cymbaling of Aith. He presently sent twinkling fingers into the air, and with arms cast out, darted into the darkness.

And again I sought him, and long again in vain. As the hours passed, and the day deepened toward its baleful midnight, the cry of the now redoubled cataract, mixed with the mass and majesty of the now climactic tempest, took on too intentional a *shriek* to be longer tolerable to any reason. My own mind escaped my sway, and went its way; for here, in the hot-bed of fever, I was fevered. I wandered from chamber to chamber, precipitate, dizzy on the upbuoyance of a joy. "As a man upon whom sleep seizes," so had I fallen. Even yet, as I passed near the region of the armoury, the rapturous shields of Aith did not fail to smash faintly upon my ear. Harfager I did not see, for he, too, was doubtless roaming a hurtling Ahasuerus round the world of the house. However, at about midnight, observing light shining from a door on the lower stage, I entered and saw him there—the chamber of the dropping horologe. He sat hugging himself on the ladder-steps, gazing at the gloomy pool. The final lights of the riot of the day seemed dying in his eyes; and he gave me no glance as I ran in. His hands, his bare arm, were all washed with new-shed blood; but of this, too, he looked unconscious; his mouth was hanging open to his pantings. As I eyed him, he suddenly leapt high, smiting hands with the yell, "The last bell tinkling!" and ran out raving. He therefore did not see (though he may have understood by hearing) the thing which, with cowering awe, I now saw: for a ball slipped from the horologe with a hiss and mist of smoke into the pool; and while the clock once ticked another: and while the clock yet ticked, another! and the smoke of the first had not perfectly thinned, when the smoke of the third, mixing with it, floated toward the dome. Understanding that the sands of the mansion were run, I, too, throwing up my arms, rushed from the spot; but was suddenly stopped in my flight by the sense of some stupendous destiny emptying its vials upon the edifice; and was quickly made aware by a crackling racket, like musketry, above, and the downpour of a world of waters, that some water-spout, in the waltz and whirl, had hurled its broken summit upon us, and burst through the dome. At that moment I beheld Harfager running toward me, his hands buried in his hair; and, as he raced past, I caught him, crying: "Harfager, save yourself! the very fountains, Hafarger—by the grand God, man"—I hissed it into his inmost ear—"*the very fountains of the Great Deep* . . .!" He glared at me and went on his way while I, whisking myself into a room, closed the door. Here for some time with weak knees I waited, I waited; but the eagerness of my frenzy pressed me, and I again stepped out, to find the corridors everywhere thigh-deep with water; while rags of the storm, bragging through the whole in the dome, were now blustering about the house. My light was at once puffed out, but I was surprised by the presence of *another* light—most ghostly, gloomy, bluish—mild, yet wild—which now gloated everywhere through the house. I was staring in wonder at this when a gust of auguster passion galloped up the mansion; and, with it, I was made aware of the *snap* of something somewhere. There was a minute's infinite waiting—and then—quick—ever quicker—came the throb, snap, pop, in spacious succession, of the anchoring chains of the mansion before the hurried shoulder of the hurricane. And *again* a second of breathless stillness—and then—deliberately—its hour came—the house moved. My flesh worked like the flesh of worms which squirm. Slowly moved and stopped—then was a sweep—and a swirl—and a pause! then a swirl—and a sweep—and a pause!— then steady labour on the brazen axis, as the labourer tramps by the harrow; then a heightening of zest—then intensity—then the final liveliness of flight. And now once again, as, staggering and plunging I spun, the notion of escape for a moment came to me, but this time I shook an impious fist. "No, but God, no, no," I gasped, "I will no more go from here: there waltzing let me pass, in this carnival of the vortices, anarchy of the thunders!"—and I ran staggering. But memory gropes in a greying gloaming as to all that followed. I struggled up the stairway, now flowing a river, and for a good while ran plunging, full of wild rantings, about, amid the downfall of roofs now, save three rafters, having been snatched by the wind away, and in the blush of that bluish moonshine the tapestries were flapping and trailing wildly out after the flying place, like the streaming hair of some ranting fakir stung reeling by the tarantulas of distraction. At one point, where the largest of the porticoes protruded, the mansion began at every revolution to bump with grum shudderings against some obstruction: it bumped, and while the lips said one-two-three it three times bumped again. It was the mænadism of mass! Swift—still swifter—in ague of flurry it raced, every portico a sail to the gale, racking its great frame to fragments. I, running by the door of a room littered with the ruins of a fallen wall, saw through that livid moonlight Harfager sitting on a tomb— a drum by him, upon which, with a club in his bloody fist, he feebly but persistingly, beat. The speed of the leaning house had now attained the *sleeping* stage, that last pitch of the spinning-top; and now all at once Harfager dashed away mat of hair which wrapped his face, sprang, stretched his arms, and began to spin—giddily—in the same direction as the mansion—nor less sleep-embathed—with lifted hair, with quivering cheeks. . . . From such a sight I shied with retching; and, staggering, plunging, pres- ently found myself on the lower floor opposite a porch, where an outer door chancing to crash before me, the breath of the tempest smote freshly upon me. On this impulse, partly of madness, more of sanity, spurred in my soul; and I spurted out of the doorway, to be whirled far out into the limbo without.

The river at once rushed me deep-drenched toward the sea—though even there, in the depth of the whirlpool, a shrill din like the splitting of a world, reached my ears. It had hardly passed when my body butted in its course upon one of the arches, cushioned with seaweed, of the not all-demolished causeway. Nor had I utterly lost consciousness. A clutch freed my head from the drench; and in the end I heaved myself to the level of the summit. Hence to the ledge of rock by which I had come, the bridge being intact, I rowed myself on my face under the thumps of wind, and under a rushing of rain, like a shimmering of silk, through the air. Noticing the same wild shining about me which had blushed through the broken dome into the mansion, I glanced backward—and the whole northern heaven, to the zenith, shone one ocean of variegated glories—the *aurora borealis*, which was being fairly blushed and flustered by the gale. At the augustness of which sight, I was touched to a gush of tears. And with them, the dream broke! the infatuation passed! a palm seemed to skin back from my brain the films and media of delusion; and on my knees I threw my hands to heaven in thankfulness for the marvel of my rescue from all the temptation, and the tribulation, and the breakage, of Rayba.

The Last Kiss

Maurice Level

———◆———

"FORGIVE ME. . . . FORGIVE ME."

His voice was less assured as he replied:

"Get up, dry your eyes. I, too, have a good deal to reproach myself with."

"No, no," she sobbed. He shook his head.

"I ought never to have left you; you loved me. Just at first after it all happened . . . when I could still feel the fire of the vitriol burning my face, when I began to realize that I should never see again, that all my life I should be a thing of horror, of Death, certainly I wasn't able to think of it like that. It isn't possible to resign oneself all at once to such a fate. . . . But living in this eternal darkness, a man's thoughts pierce far below the surface and grow quiet like those of a person falling asleep, and gradually calm comes. To-day, no longer able to use my eyes, I see with my imagination. I see again our little house, our peaceful days, and your smile. I see your poor little face the night I said that last good-bye. The judge couldn't imagine any of that, could he? And it was only fair to try to explain, for they thought only of your action, the action that made me into . . . what I am. They were going to send you to prison where you would slowly have faded. . . . No years of such punishment for you could have given me back my eyes. . . . When you saw me go into the witness-box you were afraid, weren't you? You believed that I would charge you, have you condemned? No, I could never have done that, never . . ."

She was still crying, her face buried in her hands.

"How good you are! . . ."

"I am just . . ."

In a voice that came in jerks she repeated:

"I repent, I repent; I have done the most awful thing to you that a woman could do, and you—you begged for my acquittal! And now you can even find words of pity for me! What can I do to prove my sorrow? Oh, you are wonderful . . . wonderful . . ."

He let her go on talking and weeping; his head thrown back, his hands on the arms of his chair, he listened apparently without emotion. When she was calm again, he asked:

"What are you going to do now?"

"I don't know. . . . I shall rest for a few days. . . . I am so tired. . . . Then I shall go back to work. I shall try to find a place in a shop or as a mannequin."

His voice was a little stifled as he asked:

"You are still as pretty as ever?"

She did not reply.

"I want to know if you are as pretty as you used to be?"

She remained silent. "With a slight shiver, he murmured: "It is dark now, isn't it? Turn on the light. Though I can no longer see, I like to feel that there is light around me. . . . Where are you? . . . Near the mantelpiece? . . . Stretch out your hand. You will find the switch there."

No sense even of light could penetrate his eyelids, but from the sudden sound of horror she stifled, he knew that the lamp was on. For the first time she was able to see the result of her work, the terrifying face streaked with white swellings, seamed with red furrows, a narrow black band round the eyes. While he had pleaded for her in court, she had crouched on her seat weeping, not daring to look at him; now, before this abominable thing, she grew sick with a kind of disgust. But it was without any anger that he murmured:

"I am very different from the man you knew in the old days—I horrify you now, don't I? You shrink from me? . . ."

She tried to keep her voice steady.

"Certainly not. I am here, in the same place. . . ."

"Yes, now . . . and I want you to come still nearer. If you knew how the thought of your hands tempt me in my darkness. How I should love to feel their softness once again. But I dare not. . . . And yet that is what I wanted to ask you: to let me feel your hand for a minute in mine. We, the blind, can get such marvelous memories from just a touch."

Turning her head away, she held out her arm. Caressing her fingers, he murmured:

"Ah, how good. Don't tremble. Let me try to imagine we are lovers again just as we used to be . . . but you are not wearing my ring. Why? I have not taken yours off. Do you remember? You said, 'It is our wedding-ring.' Why have you taken it off?"

"I dare not wear it. . . ."

"You must put it on again. You will wear it? Promise me."

She stammered:

"I promise you."

He was silent for a little while; then in a calmer voice:

"It must be quite dark now. How cold I am! If you only knew how cold it feels when one is blind. Your hands are warm; mine are frozen. I have not yet developed the fuller sense of touch. It takes time, they say. . . . At present I am like a little child learning."

She let her fingers remain in his, sighing:

"Oh, *Mon Dieu . . . Mon Dieu . . .*"

Speaking like a man in a dream, he went on:

"How glad I am that you came. I wondered whether you would, and I felt I wanted to keep you with me for a long, long time: always. . . . But that wouldn't be possible. Life with me would be too sad. You see, little one, when people have memories like ours, they must be careful not to spoil them, and it must be horrible to look at me now, isn't it?"

She tried to protest; what might have been a smile passed over his face.

"Why lie? I remember I once saw a man whose mistress had thrown vitriol over him. His face was not human. Women turned their heads away as they passed, while he, not being able to see and so not knowing, went on talking to the people who were shrinking away from him. I must be, I am like that poor wretch, am I not? Even you who knew me as I used to be, you tremble with disgust; I can feel it. For a long time you will be haunted by the remembrance of my face . . . it will come in between you and everything else. . . . How the thought hurts . . . but don't let us go on talking about me. . . . You said just now that you were going back to work. Tell me your plans; come nearer, I don't hear as well as I used to. . . . Well?"

Their two armchairs were almost touching. She was silent. He sighed:

"Ah, I can smell your scent! How I have longed for it. I bought a bottle of the perfume you always used, but on me it didn't smell the same. From you it comes mixed with the scent of your skin and hair. Come nearer, let me drink it in. . . . You are going away, you will never come back again; let me draw in for the last time as much of you as I can. . . . You shiver . . . am I then so horrible?"

She stammered:

"No . . . it is cold . . ."

"Why are you so lightly dressed? I don't believe you brought a cloak. In November, too. It must be damp and dreary in the streets. How you tremble! How warm and comfortable it was in our little home . . . do you remember? You used to lay your face on my shoulder, and I used to hold you close to me. Who would want to sleep in my arms now? Come nearer. Give me your hand. . . . There. . . . What did you think when your lawyer told you I had asked to see you?"

"I thought I ought to come."

"Do you still love me? . . ."

Her voice was only a breath:

"Yes. . . ."

Very slowly, his voice full of supplication, he said:

"I want to kiss you for the last time. I know it will be almost torture for you. . . . Afterwards I won't ask anything more. You can go. . . . May I? . . . Will you let me? . . ."

Involuntarily she shrank back; then, moved by shame and pity, not daring to refuse a joy to the poor wretch, she laid her head on his shoulder, held up her mouth and shut her eyes. He pressed her gently to him, silent, prolonging the happy moment. She opened her eyes, and seeing the terrible face so near, almost touching her own, for the second time she shivered with disgust and would have drawn sharply away. But he pressed her closer to him, passionately.

"You would go away so soon? . . . Stay a little longer. . . . You haven't seen enough of me. . . . Look at me . . . and give me your mouth again . . . more of it than that. . . . It is horrible, isn't it?"

She moaned:

"You hurt me. . . ."

"Oh, no," he sneered, "I frighten you."

She struggled.

"You hurt me! You hurt me!"

In a low voice he said:

"Sh-h. No noise; be quiet. I've got you now and I'll keep you. For how many days have I waited for this moment. . . . Keep still, I say, keep still! No nonsense! You know I am much stronger than you."

He seized both her hands in one of his, took a little bottle from the pocket of his coat, drew out the stopper with his teeth, and went on in the same quiet voice:

"Yes, it is vitriol; bend your head . . . there, . . . You will see; we are going to be incomparable lovers, made for each other . . . Ah, you tremble? Do you understand now why I had you acquitted, and why I made you come here to-day? Your pretty face will be exactly like mine. You will be a monstrous thing, and like me, blind! . . . Ah, yes, it hurts, hurts terribly."

She opened her mouth to implore. He ordered:

"No! Not that! Shut your mouth! I don't want to kill you, that would make it too easy for you."

Gripping her in the bend of his arm, he pressed his hand on her mouth and poured the acid slowly over her forehead, her eyes, her cheeks. She struggled desperately, but he held her too firmly and kept on pouring as he talked:

"There . . . a little more . . . you bite, but that's nothing. . . . It hurts, doesn't it? It is Hell. . . ."

Suddenly he flung her away, crying:

"I am burning myself."

She fell writhing on the floor. Already her face was nothing but a red rag.

Then he straightened himself, stumbled over her, felt about the wall to find the switch, and put out the light. And round them, as in them, was a great Darkness. . . .

The Bad Lands

John Metcalfe

———◆———

I T IS NOW PERHAPS FIFTEEN YEARS AGO THAT BRENT ORMEROD, SEEKING THE rest and change of scene that should help him to slay the demon neurosis, arrived in Todd towards the close of a mid-October day. A decrepit fly bore him to the one hotel, where his rooms were duly engaged, and it is this vision of himself sitting in the appalling vehicle that makes him think it was October or thereabouts, for he distinctly remembers the determined settling down of the dusk that forced him to drive when he would have preferred to follow his luggage on foot.

He decided immediately that five o'clock was an unsuitable time to arrive in Todd. The atmosphere, as it were, was not receptive. There was a certain repellent quality about the frore autumn air, and something peculiarly shocking in the way in which desultory little winds would spring up in darkening streets to send the fallen leaves scurrying about in hateful, furtive whirlpools.

Dinner, too, at the hotel hardly brought the consolation he had counted on. The meal itself was unexceptionable, and the room cheerful and sufficiently well filled for that time of year, yet one trivial circumstance was enough to send him upstairs with his temper ruffled and his nerves on edge. They had put him to a table with a one-eyed man, and that night the blank eye haunted all his dreams.

But for the first eight or nine days at Todd things went fairly well with him. He took frequent cold baths and regular exercise and made a point of coming back to the hotel so physically tired that to get into bed was usually to drop immediately into sleep. He wrote back to his sister Joan, at Kensington, that his nerves were already much improved and that only another fortnight seemed needed to complete the cure. "Altogether a highly satisfactory week."

Those who have been to Todd remember it as a quiet, secretive watering-place, couched watchfully in a fold of a long range of low hills along the Norfolk coast. It has been pronounced "restful" by those in high authority, for time there has a way of passing dreamily as if the days, too, were being blown past like the lazy clouds on the wings of wandering breezes. At the back, the look of the land is somehow strangely forbidding, and it is wiser to keep to the shore and the more neighbouring villages. Salterton, for instance, has been found quite safe and normal.

There are long stretches of sand dunes to the west, and by their side a nine-hole golf-course. Here, at the time of Brent's visit, stood an old and crumbling tower, an enigmatic structure which he found interesting from its sheer futility. Behind it an inexplicable road seemed to lead with great decision most uncomfortably to nowhere. . . . Todd, he thought, was in many ways a nice spot, but he detected in it a tendency to grow on one unpleasantly.

He came to this conclusion at the end of the ninth day, for it was then that he became aware of a peculiar uneasiness, an indescribable *malaise*.

This feeling of disquiet he at first found himself quite unable to explain or analyse. His nerves he had thought greatly improved since he had left Kensington, and his general health was good. He decided, however, that perhaps yet more exercise was necessary, and so he walked along the links and the sand dunes to the queer tower and the inexplicable road that lay behind it three times a day instead of twice.

His discomfort rapidly increased. He would become conscious, as he set out for his walk, of a strange sinking at his heart and of a peculiar moral disturbance which was very difficult to describe. These sensations attained their maximum when he had reached his goal upon the dunes, and he suffered then what something seemed to tell him was very near the pangs of spiritual dissolution.

It was on the eleventh day that some faint hint of the meaning of these peculiar symptoms crossed his mind. For the first time he asked himself why it was that of all the many rambles he had taken in Todd since his arrival each one seemed inevitably to bring him to the same place—the yellow sand dunes with the mysterious looking tower in the background. Something in the bland foolishness of the structure seemed to have magnetised him, and in the unaccountable excitement which the sight of it invariably produced, he had found himself endowing it with almost human characteristics.

With its white nightcap dome and its sides of pale yellow stucco it might seem at one moment to be something extravagantly ridiculous, a figure of fun at which one should laugh and point. Then, as likely as not, its character would change a little, and it would take on the abashed and crestfallen look of a jester whose best joke has fallen deadly flat, while finally, perhaps, it would develop with startling rapidity into a jovial old gentleman laughing madly at Ormerod from the middle distance out of infinite funds of merriment.

Now Brent was well aware of the dangers of an obsession such as this, and he immediately resolved to rob the tower of its unwholesome fascination by simply walking straight up to it, past it, and onwards along the road that stretched behind it.

It was on the morning of one of the last October days that he set out from the hotel with this intention in his mind. He reached the dunes at about ten, and plodded with some difficulty across them in the direction of the tower. As he neared it his accustomed sensations became painfully apparent, and presently increased to such a pitch that it was all he could do to continue on his way.

He remembered being struck again with the peculiar character of the winding road that stretched before him into a hazy distance where everything seemed to melt and swim in shadowy vagueness. On his left the gate stood open, to his right the grotesque form of the tower threatened. . . .

Now he had reached it, and its shadow fell straight across his path. He did not halt to examine it, but strode forward through the open gate and entered upon the winding road. At the same moment he was astonished to notice that the painful clutch at his heart was immediately lifted, and that with it, too, all the indescribable uneasiness which he had characterised to himself as "moral" had utterly disappeared.

He had walked on for some little distance before another rather remarkable fact struck his attention. The country was no longer vague; rather, it was peculiarly distinct, and he was able to see for long distances over what seemed considerable stretches of park-like land, grey, indeed, in tone and somehow sad with a most poignant melancholy, yet superficially, at least, well cultivated and in some parts richly timbered. He looked behind him to catch a glimpse of Todd and of the sea, but was surprised to find that in that direction the whole landscape was become astonishingly indistinct and shadowy.

It was not long before the mournful aspect of the country about him began so to depress him and work upon his nerves that he debated with himself the advisability of returning at once to the hotel. He found that the ordinary, insignificant things about him were becoming charged with sinister suggestion and that the scenery on all sides was rapidly developing an unpleasant tendency to the *macabre*. Moreover his watch told him that it was now half-past eleven— and lunch was at one. Almost hastily he turned about and began to descend the winding road.

It was about an hour later that he again reached the tower and saw the familiar dunes stretching once more before him. For some reason or other he seemed to have found the way back much longer and more difficult than the outward journey, and it was with a feeling of distinct relief that he actually passed through the gate and set his face towards Todd.

He did not go out again that afternoon, but sat smoking and thinking in the hotel. In the lounge he spoke to a man who sat in a chair beside him.

"What a queer place that is all at the back there behind the dunes!"

His companion's only comment was a somewhat drowsy grunt.

"Behind the tower," pursued Ormerod, "the funny tower at the other end of the links. The most God-forsaken, dismal place you can imagine. And simply miles of it!"

The other, roused to coherence much against his will, turned slowly round. "Don't know it," he said. "There's a large farm where you say, and the other side of that is a river, and then you come to Harkaby or somewhere."

He closed his eyes and Ormerod was left to ponder the many difficulties of his remarks.

At dinner he found a more sympathetic listener. Mr. Stanton-Boyle had been in Todd a week when Brent arrived, and his sensitive, young-old face with the eager eyes and the quick, nervous contraction of the brows had caught the newcomer's attention from the first. Up to now, indeed, they had only exchanged commonplaces, but tonight each seemed more disposed towards intimacy. Ormerod began.

"I suppose you've walked around the country at the back here a good deal?" he said.

"No," replied the other. "I never go there now. I went there once or twice and that was enough."

"Why?"

"Oh, it gets on my nerves, that's all. Do you get any golf here?"

The conversation passed to other subjects, and it was not until both were smoking together over liqueur brandies in the lounge that it returned to the same theme. And then they came to a remarkable conclusion.

"The country at the back of this place," said Brent's companion, "is somehow abominable. It ought to be blown up or something. I don't say it was always like that. Last year, for instance, I don't remember noticing it at all. I fancy it may have been depressing enough, but it was not—not abominable. It's gone abominable since then, particularly to the south-west!"

They said goodnight after agreeing to compare notes on Todd, S.W., and Ormerod had a most desolating dream wherein he walked up and up into a strange dim country, full of sighs and whisperings and crowding, sombre trees, where hollow breezes blew fitfully, and a queer house set with lofty pine shone out white against a lurid sky. . . .

On the next day he walked again past the tower and through the gate and along the winding road. As he left Todd behind him and began the slow ascent among the hills he became conscious of some strange influence that hung over the country like a brooding spirit. The clearness of the preceding day was absent; instead, all seemed nebulous and indistinct, and the sad landscape dropped behind and below him in the numb, unreal recession of a dream.

It was about four o'clock, and as he slowly ascended into the mournful tracts the greyness of the late autumn day was deepening into dusk. All the morning, clouds had been gathering in the west, and now the dull ache of the damp sky gave the uneasy sense of impending rain. Here a fitful wind blew the gold flame of a sear leaf athwart the November gloom, and out along the horizon great leaden masses were marching out to sea.

A terrible sense of loneliness fell upon the solitary walker trudging up into the sighing country, and even the sight of scattered habitations, visible here and there among the shadows, seemed only to intensify his feeling of dream and unreality. Everywhere the uplands strained in the moist wind, and the lines of gaunt firs that marched against the horizon gloom pointed ever out to sea. The wan crowding on of the weeping heavens, the settled pack of those leaning firs, and the fitful scurry of the leaves in the chill blast down the lane smote upon his spirit as something unutterably sad and terrible. On his right a skinny black thorn shot up hard and wiry towards the dull, grey sky; there ahead trees in a wood fluttered ragged, yellow flags against the dimness.

A human figure appeared before him, and presently he saw that it was a man, apparently a labourer. He carried tools upon his shoulders, and his head was bent so that it was only when Ormerod addressed him that he looked up and showed a withered countenance. "What is the name of all this place?" said Brent, with a wide sweep of his arm.

"This," said the labourer, in a voice so thin and tired that it seemed almost like the cold breath of the wind that drove beside them, "is Hayes-in-the-Up. Of course, though, it'll be a mile further on for you before you get to Fennington." He pointed in the direction from which he had just come, turned his sunken eyes again for a moment upon Ormerod, and then quickly faded down the descending path.

Brent looked after him wondering, but as he swept his gaze about him much of his wonder vanished. All around, the wan country seemed to rock giddily beneath those lowering skies, so heavy with the rain that never fell; all around, the sailing uplands seemed to heave and yearn under the sad tooting of the damp November wind. Oh, he could well imagine that the men of this weary, twilight region would be worn and old before their time, with its sinister stare in their eyes and its haggard gloom abroad in their pinched faces!

Thinking thus, he walked on steadily, and it was not long before certain words of the man he had met rose with uneasy suggestion to the surface of his mind. What, he asked himself, was Fennington? Somehow he did not think that the name stood for another village; rather, the word seemed to connect itself ominously with the dream he had had some little time ago. He shuddered, and had not walked many paces further before he found that his instinct was correct.

Opposite him, across a shallow valley, stood that white house, dimly set in giant pine. Here the winds seemed almost visible as they strove in those lofty trees and the constant rush by of the weeping sky behind made all the view seem to tear giddily through some unreal, watery medium. A striking resemblance of the pines to palm-trees and a queer effect of light which brought the white façade shaking bright against the sailing cloud-banks gave the whole a strangely exotic look.

Gazing at it across the little valley, Ormerod felt somehow that this, indeed, was the centre and hub of the wicked country, the very kernel and essence of this sad, unwholesome land that he saw flung wide in weariness about him. This abomination was it that magnetised him, that attracted him from afar with fatal fascination, and threatened him with untold disaster. Almost sobbing, he descended his side of the valley and then rose again to meet the house.

Park-like land surrounded the building, and from the smooth turf arose the pines and some clusters of shrubs. Amongst these Ormerod walked carefully till he was suddenly so near that he could look into a small room through its open window whilst he sheltered in a large yew whose dusky skirts swept the ground.

The room seemed strangely bare and deserted. A small table was pushed to one side, and dust lay thick upon it. Nearer Ormerod a chair or two appeared, and, opposite, a great black mantelpiece glowered in much gloom. In the centre of the floor was set the object that seemed to dominate the whole.

This was a large and cumbrous spinning-wheel of forbidding mien. It glistened foully in the dim light, and its many moulded points pricked the air in very awful fashion. Waiting there in the close stillness, the watcher fancied he could see the treadle stir. Quickly, with beating heart, beset by sudden dread, he turned away, retraced his steps among the sheltering shrubs, and descended to the valley bottom.

He climbed up the other side, and was glad to walk rapidly away down the winding path till, on turning his head, it was no longer possible to see the evil house he had just left.

It must have been near six o'clock when, on approaching the gate and tower, weary from his walk and anxious to reach the familiar and reassuring atmosphere of the hotel, he came suddenly upon a man walking through the darkness in the same direction as himself. It was Stanton-Boyle.

Ormerod quickly overtook him and spoke. "You have no idea," he said, "how glad I am to see you. We can walk back together now."

As they strolled to the hotel Brent described his walk, and he saw the other trembling.

Presently Stanton-Boyle looked at him earnestly and spoke. "I've been there too," he said, "and I feel just as you do about it. I feel that that place Fennington is the centre of the rottenness. I looked through the window, too, and saw the spinning-wheel and—" He stopped suddenly.

"No," he went on quietly a moment later, "I won't tell you what else I saw!"

"It ought to be destroyed!" shouted Ormerod. A curious excitement tingled in his blood. His voice was loud, so that people passing them in the street turned and gazed after them. His eyes were very bright. He went on, pulling Stanton-Boyle's arm impressively. "I shall destroy it!" he said. "I shall burn it and I shall most assuredly smash that old spinning-wheel and break off its horrid spiky points!" He had a vague sense of saying curious and unusual things, but this increased rather than moderated his unaccountable elation.

Stanton-Boyle seemed somewhat abnormal too. He seemed to be gliding along the pavement with altogether unexampled smoothness and nobility as he turned his glowing eyes on Brent. "Destroy it!" he said. "Burn it! Before it is too late and it destroys you. Do this and you will be an unutterably brave man!"

When they reached the hotel Ormerod found a telegram awaiting him from Joan. He had not written to her for some time and she had grown anxious and was coming down herself on the following day. He must act quickly, before she came, for her mind in this matter would be unsympathetic. That night as he parted from Stanton-Boyle his eyes blazed in a high resolve. "Tomorrow," he said, as he shook the other's hand, "I shall attempt it."

The following morning found the neurotic as good as his word. He carried matches and a tin of oil. His usually pale cheeks were flushed and his eyes sparkled strangely. Those who saw him leave the hotel remembered afterwards how his limbs had trembled and his speech halted. Stanton-Boyle, who was to see him off at the tower, reflected these symptoms in a less degree. Both men were observed to set out arm-in-arm engaged in earnest conversation.

At about noon Stanton-Boyle returned. He had walked with Ormerod to the sand dunes, and there left him to continue on his strange mission alone. He had seen him pass the tower, strike the fatal gate in the slanting morning sun, and then dwindle up the winding path till he was no more than an intense, pathetic dot along that way of mystery.

As he returned he was aware of companionship along the street. He looked round and noticed a policeman strolling in much abstraction some fifty yards behind him. Again at the hotel-entrance he turned about. The same figure in blue uniform was visible, admiring the houses opposite from the shade of an adjacent lamp-post. Stanton-Boyle frowned and withdrew to lunch.

At half-past two Joan arrived. She inquired nervously for Ormerod, and was once addressed by Stanton-Boyle, who had waited for her in the entrance hall as desired by Brent. "Mr. Ormerod," he told her, "is out. He is very sorry. Will you allow me the impropriety of introducing myself? My name is Stanton-Boyle. . . ."

Joan tore open the note which had been left for her by Ormerod. She seemed to find the contents unsatisfactory, for she proceeded to catechise Stanton-Boyle upon her brother's health and general habit of life at Todd. Following this she left the hotel hastily after ascertaining the direction from which Ormerod might be expected to return.

Stanton-Boyle waited. The moments passed, heavy, anxious, weighted with the sense of coming trouble. He sat and smoked. Discreet and muffled noises from within the hotel seemed full somehow of uneasy suggestion and foreboding. Outside, the street looked very gloomy in the November darkness. Something, assuredly, would happen directly.

It came, suddenly. A sound of tramping feet and excited cries that grew rapidly in volume and woke strange echoes in the reserved autumnal roads. Presently the tumult lessened abruptly, and only broken, fitful shouts and staccato ejaculations stabbed the silence. Stanton-Boyle jumped to his feet and walked hurriedly to the entrance hall.

Here there were cries and hustlings and presently strong odours and much suppressed excitement. He saw Joan talking very quickly to the manager of the hotel. She seemed to be developing a Point-of-View, and it was evident that it was not the manager's. For some time the press of people prevented him from discovering the cause of the commotion, but here and there he could make out detached sentences: "Tried to set old Hackney's farm on fire—" "But they'd seen him before and another man too, so—" "Asleep in the barn several times."

Before long, all but the hotel residents had dispersed, and in the centre of the considerable confusion which still remained, it was now possible to see Ormerod supported by two policemen. A third hovered in the background with a large notebook. As Stanton-Boyle gazed, Brent lifted his bowed head so that their eyes met. "I have done it," he said. "I smashed it up. I brought back one of its points in my pocket. . . . Overcoat, left hand . . . as a proof." Having pronounced which words Mr. Ormerod fainted very quietly.

For some time there was much disturbance. The necessary arrangements for the temporary pacification of the Law and of the Hotel had to be carried through, and after that Ormerod had to be got to bed. It was only after the initial excitement had in large measure abated that Stanton-Boyle ventured to discuss the matter over the after-dinner coffee. He had recognised one of the three policemen as the man whom he had noticed in the morning, and had found it well to retire from observation until he and his companions had left the hotel. Now, however, he felt at liberty to explain his theories of the situation to such as chose to listen.

He held forth with peculiar vehemence and with appropriate gestures. He spoke of a new kind of *terre-mauvaise*, of strange regions, connected, indeed, with definite geographical limits upon the earth, yet somehow apart from them and beyond them. "The relation," he said, "is rather one of parallelism and correspondence than of actual connection. I honestly believe that these regions do exist, and are quite as 'real' in their way as the ordinary world we know. We might say they consist in a special and separated set of stimuli to which only certain minds in certain conditions are able to respond. Such a district seems to be superimposed upon the country to the south-west of this place."

A laugh arose. "You won't get the magistrate to believe that," said someone. "Why, all where you speak of past that gate by the dunes is just old Hackney's farm and nothing else."

"Of course," said another. "It was one of old Hackney's barns he was setting alight, I understand. I was speaking to one of the policemen about it. He said that fellow Ormerod had always been fossicking around there, and had gone to sleep in the barn twice. I expect it's all bad dreams."

A third spoke derisively. "Surely," he said, "you don't really expect us to believe in your Bad Lands. It's like Jack-in-the-Beanstalk."

"All right!" said Stanton-Boyle. "Have it your own way! I know my use of the term 'Bad Lands' may be called incorrect, because it usually means that bit in the States, you know—but that's a detail. I tell you I've run up against things like this before. There was the case of Dolly Wishart, but no, I won't say anything about that—you wouldn't believe it."

The group around looked at him oddly. Suddenly there was a stir, and a man appeared in the doorway. He carried Ormerod's overcoat.

"This may settle the matter," he said. "I heard him say he'd put something in the pocket. He said—"

Stanton-Boyle interrupted him excitedly. "Why, yes," he said. "I'd forgotten that. What I was telling you about—the spinning-wheel. It will be interesting to see if—" He stopped and fumbled in the pockets. In another moment he brought out something which he held in his extended hand for all to see.

It was part of the handle of a patent separator—an object familiar enough to any who held even meagre acquaintance with the life of farms, and upon it could still be discerned the branded letters G. P. H.

"George Philip Hackney," interpreted the unbelievers with many smiles.

The Death-Mask

Mrs. H. D. Everett

———◆———

YES, THAT IS A PORTRAIT OF MY WIFE. IT IS CONSIDERED TO BE A GOOD likeness. But of course she was older-looking towards the last."

Enderby and I were on our way to the smoking-room after dinner, and the picture hung on the staircase. We had been chums at school a quarter of a century ago, and later on at college; but I had spent the last decade out of England. I returned to find my friend a widower of four years' standing. And a good job too, I thought to myself when I heard of it, for I had no great liking for the late Gloriana. Probably the sentiment, or want of sentiment, had been mutual: she did not smile on me, but I doubt if she smiled on any of poor Tom Enderby's bachelor cronies. The picture was certainly like her. She was a fine woman, with aquiline features and a cold eye. The artist had done the features justice—and the eye, which seemed to keep a steely watch on all the comings and goings of the house out of which she had died.

We made only a brief pause before the portrait, and then went on. The smoking-room was an apartment built out at the back of the house by a former owner, and shut off by double doors to serve as a nursery. Mrs. Enderby had no family, and she disliked the smell of tobacco. So the big room was made over to Tom's pipes and cigars; and if Tom's friends wanted to smoke, they must smoke there or not at all. I remembered the room and the rule, but I was not prepared to find it still existing. I had expected to light my after dinner cigar over the dessert dishes, now there was no presiding lady to consider.

We were soon installed in a couple of deep-cushioned chairs before a good fire. I thought Enderby breathed more freely when he closed the double doors behind us, shutting off the dull formal house, and the staircase and the picture. But he was not looking well; there hung about him an unmistakable air of depression. Could he be fretting after Gloriana? Perhaps during their married years, he had fallen into the way of depending on a woman to care for him. It is pleasant enough when the woman is the right sort; but I shouldn't myself have fancied being cared for by the late Mrs. Enderby. And, if the fretting was a fact, it would be easy to find a remedy. Evelyn has a couple of pretty sisters, and we would have him over to stay at our place.

"You must run down and see us," I said presently, pursuing this idea. "I want to introduce you to my wife. Can you come next week? "

His face lit up with real pleasure.

"I should like it of all things," he said heartily. "But a qualification came after. The cloud settled back over him and he sighed. "That is, if I can get away."

"Why, what is to hinder you? "

"It may not seem much to stay for, but I—I have got in the way of stopping here—to keep things together." He did not look at me, but leaned over to the fender to knock the ash off his cigar.

"Tell you what, Tom, you are getting hipped living by yourself. Why don't you sell the house, or let it off just as it is, and try a complete change?"

"I can't sell it. I'm only the tenant for life. It was my wife's."

"Well, I suppose there is nothing to prevent you letting it? Or if you can't let it, you might shut it up."

"There is nothing *legal* to prevent me—!" The emphasis was too fine to attract notice, but I remembered it after.

"Then, my dear fellow, why not? Knock about a bit, and see the world. But, to my thinking, the best thing you could do would be to marry again."

He shook his head drearily.

"Of course it is a delicate matter to urge upon a widower. But you have paid the utmost ceremonial respect. Four years, you know. The greatest stickler for propriety would deem it ample.

"It isn't that. Dick, I—I've a great mind to tell you rather a queer story." He puffed hard at his smoke, and stared into the red coals in the pauses. "But I don't know what you'd think of it. Or think of me."

"Try me," I said. "I'll give you my opinion after. And you know I'm safe to confide in."

"I sometimes think I should feel better if I told it. It's—it's queer enough to be laughable. But it hasn't been any laughing matter to me."

He threw the stump of his cigar into the fire, and turned to me. And then I saw how pale he was, and that a dew of perspiration was breaking out on his white face.

"I was very much of your opinion, Dick: I thought I should be happier if I married again. And I went so far as to get engaged. But the engagement was broken off, and I am going to tell you why.

"My wife was some time ailing before she died, and the doctors were in consultation. But I did not know how serious her complaint was till the last. Then they told me there was no hope, as coma had set in. But it was possible, even probable, that there would be a revival of consciousness before death, and for this I was to hold myself ready.

"I daresay you will write me down a coward, but I dreaded the revival: I was ready to pray that she might pass away in her sleep. I knew she held exalted views about the marriage tie, and I felt sure if there were any last words she would exact a pledge. I could not at such a moment refuse to promise, and I did not want to be tied. You will recollect that she was my senior. I was about to be left a widower in middle life, and in the natural course of things I had a good many years before me. You see?"

"My dear fellow, I don't think a promise so extorted ought to bind you. It isn't fair—!"

"Wait and hear me. I was sitting here, miserable enough, as you may suppose, when the doctor came to fetch me to her room. Mrs. Enderby was conscious and had asked for me, but he particularly begged me not to agitate her in any way, lest pain should return. She was lying stretched out in the bed, looking already like a corpse.

"'Tom,' she said, 'they tell me I am dying, and there is something I want you to promise.'

"I groaned in spirit. It was all up with me, I thought. But she went on.

"'When I am dead and in my coffin, I want you to cover my face with your own hands. Promise me this.'

"It was not in the very least what I expected. Of course I promised.

"'I want you to cover my face with a particular handkerchief on which I set a value. When the time comes, open the cabinet to the right of the window, and you will find it in the third drawer from the top. You cannot mistake it, for it is the only thing in the drawer.'

"That was every word she said, if you believe me, Dick. She just sighed and shut her eyes as if she was going to sleep, and she never spoke again. Three or four days later they came again to ask me if I wished to take a last look, as the undertaker's men were about to close the coffin.

"I felt a great reluctance, but it was necessary I should go. She looked as if made of wax, and was colder than ice to touch. I opened the cabinet, and there, just as she said, was a large handkerchief of very fine cambric, lying by itself. It was embroidered with a monogram device in all four corners, and was not of a sort I had ever seen her use. I spread it out and laid it over the dead face; and then what happened was rather curious. It seemed to draw down over the features and cling to them, to nose and mouth and forehead and the shut eyes, till it became a perfect mask. My nerves were shaken, I suppose; I was seized with horror, and flung back the covering sheet, hastily quitting the room. And the coffin was closed that night.

"Well, she was buried, and I put up a monument which the neighbourhood considered handsome. As you see, I was bound by no pledge to abstain from marriage; and, though I knew what would have been her wish, I saw no reason why I should regard it. And, some months after, a family of the name of Ashcroft came to live at The Leasowes, and they had a pretty daughter.

"I took a fancy to Lucy Ashcroft the first time I saw her, and it was soon apparent that she was well inclined to me. She was a gentle, yielding little thing; not the superior style of woman. Not at all like—"

(I made no comment, but I could well understand that in his new matrimonial venture Tom would prefer a contrast.)

"—But I thought I had a very good chance of happiness with her; and I grew fond of her; very fond of her indeed. Her people were of the hospitable sort, and they encouraged me to go to The Leasowes, dropping in when I felt inclined: it did not seem as if they would be likely to put obstacles in our way. Matters progressed, and I made up my mind one evening to walk over there and declare myself. I had been up to town the day before, and came back with a ring in my pocket: rather a fanciful design of double hearts, but I thought Lucy would think it pretty, and would let me put it on her finger. I went up to change into dinner things, making myself as spruce as possible, and coming to the conclusion before the glass that I was not such a bad figure of a man after all, and that there was not much grey in my hair. Ay, Dick, you may smile: it is a good bit greyer now.

"I had taken out a clean handkerchief, and thrown the one carried through the day away crumpled on the floor. I don't know what made me turn to look at it as it lay there, but, once it caught my eye, I stood staring at it as if spell-bound. The handkerchief was moving—Dick, I swear it—rapidly altering in shape, puffing up here and there as if blown by wind, spreading and moulding itself into the features of a face.

And what face should it be but that death-mask of Gloriana, which I had covered in the coffin eleven months before!

"To say I was horror-stricken conveys little of the feeling that possessed me. I snatched up the rag of cambric and flung it on the fire, and it was nothing but a rag in my hand, and in another moment no more than blackened tinder on the bar of the grate. There was no face below."

"Of course not," I said. "It was a mere hallucination. You were cheated by an excited fancy."

"You may be sure I told myself all that, and more; and I went downstairs and tried to pull myself together with a dram. But I was curiously upset, and, for that night at least, I found it impossible to play the wooer. The recollection of the death-mask was too vivid; it would have come between me and Lucy's lips.

"The effect wore off, however. In a day or two I was bold again, and as much disposed to smile at my folly as you are at this moment. I proposed, and Lucy accepted me; and I put on the ring. Ashcroft *père* was graciously pleased to approve of the settlements I offered, and Ashcroft *mère* promised to regard me as a son. And during the first forty-eight hours of our engagement, there was not a cloud to mar the blue.

"I proposed on a Monday, and on Wednesday I went again to dine and spend the evening with just their family party. Lucy and I found our way afterwards into the back drawing-room, which seemed to be made over to us by tacit understanding. Any way, we had it to ourselves; and as Lucy sat on the settee, busy with her work, I was privileged to sit beside her, close enough to watch the careful stitches she was setting, under which the pattern grew.

"She was embroidering a square of fine linen to serve as a tea-cloth, and it was intended for a present to a friend; she was anxious, she told me, to finish it in the next few days, ready for despatch. But I was somewhat impatient of her engrossment in the work; I wanted her to look at me while we talked, and to be permitted to hold her hand. I was making plans for a tour we would take together after Easter; arguing that eight weeks spent in preparation was enough for any reasonable bride. Lucy was easily entreated; she laid aside the linen square on the table at her elbow. I held her fingers captive, but her eyes wandered from my face, as she was still deliciously shy.

"All at once she exclaimed. Her work was moving, there was growing to be a face in it: did I not see?

"I saw, indeed. It was the Gloriana death-mask, forming there as it had formed in my handkerchief at home: the marked nose and chin, the severe mouth, the mould of forehead, almost complete. I snatched it up and dropped it over the back of the couch. 'It did look like a face,' I allowed. 'Put never mind it, darling; I want you to attend to me.' Something of this sort I said, I hardly know what, for my blood was running cold. Lucy pouted; she wanted to dwell on the marvel, and my impatient action had displeased her. I went on talking wildly, being afraid of pauses, but the psychological moment had gone by. I felt I did not carry her with me as before: she hesitated over my persuasions; the forecast of a Sicilian honeymoon had ceased to charm. By-and-bye she suggested that Mrs. Ashcroft would expect us to rejoin the circle in the other room. And perhaps I would pick up her work for her—still with a slight air of offence.

"I walked round the settee to recover the luckless piece of linen; but she turned also, looking over the back, so at the same instant we both saw.

"There again was the Face, rigid and severe; and now the corners of the cloth were tucked under, completing the form of the head. And that was not all. Some white drapery had been improvised and extended beyond it on the floor, presenting the complete figure laid out straight and stiff, ready for the grave. Lucy's alarm was excusable. She shrieked aloud, shriek upon shriek, and immediately an indignant family of Ashcrofts rushed in through the half-drawn portifères which divided the two rooms, demanding the cause of her distress.

"Meanwhile I had fallen upon the puffed-out form, and destroyed it. Lucy's embroidery composed the head; the figure was ingeniously contrived out of a large Turkish bath-sheet, brought in from one of the bedrooms, no one knew how or when. I held up the things protesting their innocence, while the family were stabbing me through and through with looks of indignation, and Lucy was sobbing in her, mother's arms. She might have been foolish, she allowed; it did seem ridiculous now she saw what it was. But at the moment it was too dreadful: it looked so like—so like! And here a fresh sob choked her into silence.

"Peace was restored at last, but plainly the Ashcrofts doubted me. The genial father stiffened, and Mrs. Ashcroft administered indirect reproofs. She hated practical joking, so she informed me; she might be wrong, and no doubt she was old-fashioned, but she had been brought up to consider it in the highest degree ill-bred. And perhaps I had not considered how sensitive Lucy was, and how easily alarmed. She hoped I would take warning for the future, and that nothing of this kind would occur again.

"Practical joking—oh, ye gods! As if it was likely that I, alone with the girl of my heart, would waste the precious hour in building up effigies of sham corpses on the floor! And Lucy ought to have known that the accusation was absurd, as I had never for a moment left her side. She did take my part when more composed; but the mystery remained, beyond explanation of hers or mine.

"As for the future, I could not think of that without a failing heart. If the Power arrayed against us were in truth what my superstition feared, I might as well give up hope at once, for I knew there would be no relenting. I could see the whole absurdity of the thing as well as you do now; but, if you put yourself in my place, Dick, you will be forced to confess that it was tragic too.

"I did not see Lucy the next day, as I was bound to go again to town; but we had planned to meet and ride together on the Friday morning. I was to be at The Leasowes at a certain hour, and you may be sure I was punctual. Her horse had already been brought round, and the groom was leading it up and down. I had hardly dismounted when she came down the steps of the porch; and I noticed at once a new look on her face, a harder set about that red mouth of hers which was so soft and kissable. But she let me put her up on the saddle and settle her foot in the stirrup, and she was the bearer of a gracious message from her mother. I was expected to return to lunch, and Mrs. Ashcroft begged us to be punctual, as a friend who had stayed the night with them, would be leaving immediately after.

" 'You will be pleased to meet her, I think,' said Lucy, leaning forward to pat her horse. 'I find she knows you very well. It is Miss Kingsworthy.'

"Now Miss Kingsworthy was a school-friend of Gloriana's, who used now and then to visit us here. I was not aware that she and the Ashcrofts were acquainted; but, as I have said, they had only recently come into the neighbourhood as tenants of The Leasowes. I had no opportunity to express pleasure or the reverse, for Lucy was riding on, and putting her horse to a brisk pace. It was some time before she drew rein, and again admitted conversation. We were descending a steep hill, and the groom was following at a discreet distance behind, far enough to be out of earshot.

"Lucy looked very pretty on horseback; but this is by the way. The mannish hat suited her, and so did the habit fitting closely to her shape.

" 'Tom,' she said; and again I noticed that new hardness in her face. 'Tom, Miss Kingsworthy tells me your wife did not wish you to marry again, and she made you promise her that you would not. Miss Kingsworthy was quite astonished to hear that you and I were engaged. Is this true?'

"I was able to tell her it was not: that my wife had never asked, and I had never given her, any such pledge. I allowed she disliked second marriages—in certain cases, and perhaps she had made some remark to that effect to Miss Kingsworthy; it was not unlikely. And then I appealed to her. Surely she would not let a mischief-maker's tittle-tattle come between her and me?

"I thought her profile looked less obdurate, but she would not let her eyes meet mine as she answered:

"'Of course not, if that was all. And I doubt if I would have heeded it, only that it seemed to fit in with—something else. Tom, it was very horrible, what we saw on Wednesday evening. And—and—don't be angry, but I asked Miss Kingsworthy what your wife was like. I did not tell her why I wanted to know.'

"'What has that to do with it?' I demanded—stoutly enough; but, alas! I was too well aware.

"'She told me Mrs. Enderby was handsome, but she had very marked features, and was severe-looking when she did not smile. A high forehead, a Roman nose, and a decided chin. Tom, the face in the cloth was just like that. Did you not see?'

"Of course I protested.

"'My darling, what nonsense! I saw it looked a little like a face, but I pulled it to pieces at once because you were frightened. Why, Lucy, I shall have you turning into a spiritualist if you take up these fancies.'

"'No,' she said, 'I do not want to be anything foolish. I have thought it over, and if it happens only once I have made up my mind to believe it a mistake and to forget. But if it comes again—if it goes on coming—!' Here she shuddered and turned white. 'Oh Tom, I could not—I could not!'

"That was the ultimatum. She liked me as much as ever; she even owned to a warmer feeling; but she was not going to marry a haunted man. Well, I suppose I cannot blame her. I might have given the same advice in another fellow's case, though in my own I felt it hard.

"I am close to the end now, so I shall need to tax your patience very little longer. A single chance remained. Gloriana's power, whatever its nature and however derived, might have been so spent in the previous efforts that she could effect no more. I clung to this shred of hope, and did my best to play the part of the light-hearted lover, the sort of companion Lucy expected, who would shape himself to her mood; but I was conscious that I played it ill.

"The ride was a lengthy business. Lucy's horse cast a shoe, and it was impossible to change the saddle on to the groom's hack or my own mare, as neither of them had been trained to the habit. We were bound to return at a foot-pace, and did not reach The Leasowes until two o'clock. Lunch was over: Mrs. Ashcroft had set out for the station driving Miss Kingsworthy; but some cutlets were keeping hot for us, so we were informed, and could be served immediately.

"We went at once into the dining-room, as Lucy was hungry; and she took off her hat and laid it on a side-table: she said the close fit of it made her head ache. The cutlets had been misrepresented: they were lukewarm; but Lucy made a good meal off them and the fruit-tart which followed, very much at her leisure. Heaven knows I would not have grudged her so much as a mouthful; but that luncheon was an ordeal I cannot readily forget.

"The servant absented himself, having seen us served; and then my troubles began. The tablecloth seemed alive at the corner which was between us; it rose in waves as if puffed up by wind, though the window was fast shut against any wandering airs. I tried to seem unconscious; tried to talk as if no horror of apprehension was filling all my mind, while I was flattening out the bewitched damask with a grasp I hardly dared relax. Lucy rose at last, saying she must change her dress. Occupied with the cloth, it had not occurred to me to look round, or keep watch on what might be going on in another part of the room. The hat on the side-table had been tilted over sideways, and in that position it was made to crown another presentation of the Face. What it was made of this time I cannot say; probably a serviette, as several lay about. The linen material, of whatever sort, was again moulded into the perfect form; but this time the mouth showed humour, and appeared to relax in a grim smile.

"Lucy shrieked, and dropped into my arms in a swoon: a real genuine fainting-fit, out of which she was brought round with difficulty, after summoned help of doctors.

"I hung about miserably till her safety was assured, and then went as miserably home. Next morning I received a cutting little note from my mother-in-law elect, in which she returned the ring, and informed me the engagement must be considered at an end.

"Well, Dick, you know now why I do not marry. And what have you to say?"

Seaton's Aunt

Walter de la Mare

———◆———

I HAD HEARD RUMOURS OF SEATON'S AUNT LONG BEFORE I ACTUALLY encountered her. Seaton, in the hush of confidence, or at any little show of toleration on our part, would remark, "My aunt," or "My old aunt, you know," as if his relative might be a kind of cement to an entente cordiale.

He had an unusual quantity of pocket-money; or, at any rate, it was bestowed on him in unusually large amounts; and he spent it freely, though none of us would have described him as an "awfully generous chap." "Hullo, Seaton," he would say, "the old Begum?" At the beginning of term, too, he used to bring back surprising and exotic dainties in a box with a trick padlock that accompanied him from his first appearance at Gummidge's in a billycock hat to the rather abrupt conclusion of his school-days.

From a boy's point of view he looked distastefully foreign, with his yellow skin, and slow chocolate-coloured eyes, and lean weak figure. Merely for his looks he was treated by most of us true-blue Englishmen with condescension, hostility, or contempt. We used to call him "Pongo," but without any better excuse for the nickname than his skin. He was, that is, in one sense of the term what he assuredly was not in the other sense, a sport.

Seaton and I were never in any sense intimate at school, our orbits only intersected in class. I kept instinctively aloof from him. I felt vaguely he was a sneak, and remained quite unmollified by advances on his side, which, in a boy's barbarous fashion, unless it suited me to be magnanimous, I haughtily ignored.

We were both of us quick-footed, and at Prisoner's Base used occasionally to hide together. And so I best remember Seaton—his narrow watchful face in the dusk of summer evening; his peculiar crouch, and his inarticulate whisperings and mumblings. Otherwise he played all games slackly and limply; used to stand and feed at his locker with a crony or two until his "tuck" gave out; or waste his money on some outlandish fancy or other. He bought, for instance, a silver bangle, which he wore above his left elbow, until some of the fellows showed their masterly contempt of the practice by dropping it nearly red-hot down his neck.

It needed, therefore, a rather peculiar taste, a rather rare kind of schoolboy courage and indifference to criticism, to be much associated with him. And I had neither the taste nor the courage. None the less, he did make advances, and on one memorable occasion went to the length of bestowing on me a whole pot of some outlandish mulberry-coloured jelly that had been duplicated in his term's supplies. In the exuberance of my gratitude I promised to spend the next half-term holiday with him at his aunt's house.

I had clean forgotten my promise when, two or three days before the holiday, he came up and triumphantly reminded me of it.

"Well, to tell you the honest truth, Seaton, old chap—" I began graciously; but he cut me short.

"My aunt expects you," he said; "she is very glad you are coming. She's sure to be quite decent to *you*, Withers."

I looked at him in some astonishment; the emphasis was unexpected. It seemed to suggest an aunt not hitherto hinted at, and a friendly feeling on Seaton's side that was more disconcerting than welcome.

We reached his home partly by train, partly by a lift in an empty farm-cart, and partly by walking. It was a whole-day holiday, and we were to sleep the night; he lent me extraordinary night-gear, I remember. The village street was unusually wide, and was fed from a green by two converging roads, with an inn, and a high green sign at the corner. About a hundred yards down the street was a chemist's shop—Mr. Tanner's. We descended the two steps into his dusky and odorous interior to buy, I remember, some rat poison. A little beyond the chemist's was the forge. You then walked along a very narrow path, under a fairly high wall, nodding here and there with weeds and tufts of grass, and so came to the iron garden-gates, and saw the high flat house behind its huge sycamore. A coach-house stood on the left of the house, and on the right a gate led into a kind of rambling orchard. The lawn lay away over to the left again, and at the bottom (for the whole garden sloped gently to a sluggish and rushy pond-like stream) was a meadow.

We arrived at noon, and entered the gates out of the hot dust beneath the glitter of the dark-curtained windows. Seaton led me at once through the little garden-gate to show me his tadpole pond, swarming with what, being myself not the least bit of a naturalist, I considered the most horrible creatures—of all shapes, consistencies, and sizes, but with whom Seaton seemed to be on the most intimate of terms. I can see his absorbed face now as he sat on his heels and fished the slimy things out in his sallow palms. Wearying at last of his pets, we loitered about awhile in an aimless fashion. Seaton seemed to be listening, or at any rate waiting, for something to happen or for some one to come. But nothing did happen and no one came.

That was just like Seaton. Anyhow, the first view I got of his aunt was when, at the summons of a distant gong, we turned from the garden, very hungry and thirsty, to go into luncheon. We were approaching the house when Seaton suddenly came to a standstill. Indeed, I have always had the impression that he plucked at my sleeve. Something, at least, seemed to catch me back, as it were, as he cried, "Look out, there she is!"

She was standing in an upper window which opened wide on a hinge, and at first sight she looked an excessively tall and overwhelming figure. This, however, was mainly because the window reached all but to the floor of her bedroom. She was in reality rather an under-sized woman, in spite of her long face and big head. She must have stood, I think, unusually still, with eyes fixed on us, though this impression may be due to Seaton's sudden warning and to my consciousness of the cautious and sub-dued air that had fallen on him at sight of her. I know that without the least reason in the world I felt a kind of guiltiness, as if I had been "caught." There was a silvery star pattern sprinkled on her black silk dress, and even from the ground I could see the immense coils of her hair and the rings on her left hand which was held fingering the small jet buttons of her bodice. She watched our united advance without stirring, until, imperceptibly, her eyes raised and lost themselves in the distance, so that it was out of an assumed reverie that she appeared suddenly to awaken to our presence beneath her when we drew close to the house.

"So this is your friend, Mr. Smithers, I suppose?" she said, bobbing to me.

"Withers, aunt," said Seaton.

"It's much the same," she said, with eyes fixed on me. "Come in, Mr. Withers, and bring him along with you."

She continued to gaze at me—at least, I think she did so. I know that the fixity of her scrutiny and her ironical "Mr." made me feel peculiarly uncomfortable. But she was extremely kind and attentive to me, though perhaps her kindness and attention showed up more vividly against her complete neglect of Seaton. Only one remark that I have any recollection of she made to him: "When I look on my nephew, Mr.

Smithers, I realise that dust we are, and dust shall become. You are hot, dirty, and incorrigible, Arthur."

She sat at the head of the table, Seaton at the foot, and I, before a wide waste of damask tablecloth, between them. It was an old and rather close dining-room, with windows thrown wide to the green garden and a wonderful cascade of fading roses. Miss Seaton's great chair faced this window, so that its rose-reflected light shone full on her yellowish face, and on just such chocolate eyes as my schoolfellow's, except that hers were more than half-covered by unusually long and heavy lids.

There she sat, eating, with those sluggish eyes fixed for the most part on my face; above them stood the deep-lined fork between her eyebrows; and above that the wide expanse of a remarkable brow beneath its strange steep bank of hair. The lunch was copious, and consisted, I remember, of all such dishes as are generally considered mischievous and too good for the schoolboy digestion—lobster mayonnaise, cold game sausages, an immense veal and ham pie farced with eggs and numberless delicious flavours; besides sauces, kickshaws, creams, and sweetmeats. We even had wine, a half-glass of old darkish sherry each.

Miss Seaton enjoyed and indulged an enormous appetite. Her example and a natural schoolboy voracity soon overcame my nervousness of her, even to the extent of allowing me to enjoy to the best of my bent so rare a "spread." Seaton was singularly modest; the greater part of his meal consisted of almonds and raisins, which he nibbled surreptitiously and as if he found difficulty in swallowing them.

I don't mean that Miss Seaton "conversed" with me. She merely scattered trenchant remarks and now and then twinkled a baited question over my head. But her face was like a dense and involved accompaniment to her talk. She presently dropped the "Mr.," to my intense relief, and called me now Withers, or Wither, now Smithers, and even once towards the close of the meal distinctly Johnson, though how on earth my name suggested it, or whose face mine had reanimated in memory, I cannot conceive.

"And is Arthur a good boy at school, Mr. Wither?" was one of her many questions. "Does he please his masters? Is he first in his class? What does the reverend Dr. Gummidge think of him, eh?"

I knew she was jeering at him, but her face was adamant against the least flicker of sarcasm or facetiousness. I gazed fixedly at a blushing crescent of lobster.

"I think you're eighth, aren't you, Seaton?"

Seaton moved his small pupils towards his aunt. But she continued to gaze with a kind of concentrated detachment at me.

"Arthur will never make a brilliant scholar, I fear," she said, lifting a dexterously-burdened fork to her wide mouth. . . .

After luncheon she preceded me up to my bedroom. It was a jolly little bedroom, with a brass fender and rugs and a polished floor, on which it was possible, I afterwards found, to play "snow-shoes." Over the washstand was a little black-framed water-colour drawing, depicting a large eye with an extremely fishlike intensity in the spark of light on the dark pupil; and in "illuminated" lettering beneath was printed very minutely, "Thou God Seest ME," followed by a long looped monogram, "S.S.," in the corner. The other pictures were all of the sea: brigs on blue water; a schooner overtopping chalk cliffs; a rocky island of prodigious steepness, with two tiny sailors dragging a monstrous boat up a shelf of beach.

"This is the room, Withers, my brother William died in when a boy. Admire the view!"

I looked out of the window across the tree-tops. It was a day hot with sunshine over the green fields, and the cattle were standing swishing their tails in the shallow water. But the view at the moment was only exaggeratedly vivid because I was horribly dreading that she would presently enquire after my luggage, and I had not brought even a toothbrush. I need have had no fear. Hers was not that highly-civilised type of mind that is stuffed with sharp material details. Nor could her ample presence be described as in the least motherly.

"I would never consent to question a schoolfellow behind my nephew's back," she said, standing in the middle of the room, "but tell me, Smithers, why is Arthur so unpopular? You, I understand, are his only close friend." She stood in a dazzle of sun, and out of it her eyes regarded me with such leaden penetration beneath their thick lids that I doubt if my face concealed the least thought from her. "But there, there," she added very suavely, stooping her head a little, "don't trouble to answer me. I never extort an answer. Boys are queer fish. Brains might perhaps have suggested his washing his hands before luncheon; but—not my choice, Smithers. God forbid! And now, perhaps, you would like to go into the garden again. I cannot actually see from here, but I should not be surprised if Arthur is now skulking behind that hedge."

He was. I saw his head come out and take a rapid glance at the windows.

"Join him, Mr. Smithers; we shall meet again, I hope, at the tea-table. The afternoon I spend in retirement."

Whether or not, Seaton and I had not been long engaged with the aid of two green switches in riding round and round a lumbering old gray horse we found in the meadow, before a rather bunched-up figure appeared, walking along the field-path on the other side of the water, with a magenta parasol studiously lowered in our direction throughout her slow progress, as if that were the magnetic needle and we the fixed pole. Seaton at once lost all nerve in his riding. At the next lurch of the old mare's heels he toppled over into the grass, and I slid off the sleek broad back to join him where he stood, rubbing his shoulder and sourly watching the rather pompous figure till it was out of sight.

"Was that your aunt, Seaton?" I enquired; but not till then.

He nodded.

"Why didn't she take any notice of us, then?"

"She never does."

"Why not?"

"Oh, she knows all right, without; that's the dam awful part of it." Seaton was about the only fellow at Gummidge's who ever had the ostentation to use bad language. He had suffered for it, too. But it wasn't, I think, bravado. I believe he really felt certain things more intensely than most of the other fellows, and they were generally things that fortunate and average people do not feel at all—the peculiar quality, for instance, of the British schoolboy's imagination.

"I tell you, Withers," he went on moodily, slinking across the meadow with his hands covered up in his pockets, "she sees everything. And what she doesn't see she knows without."

"But how?" I said, not because I was much interested, but because the afternoon was so hot and tiresome and purposeless, and it seemed more of a bore to remain silent. Seaton turned gloomily and spoke in a very low voice.

"Don't appear to be talking of her, if you wouldn't mind. It's—because she's in league with the devil." He nodded his head and stooped to pick up a round flat pebble. "I tell you," he said, still stooping, "you fellows don't realise what it is. I know I'm a bit close and all that. But so would you be if you had that old hag listening to every thought you think."

I looked at him, then turned and surveyed one by one the windows of the house.

"Where's your *pater*?" I said awkwardly.

"Dead, ages and ages ago, and my mother too. She's not my aunt by rights."

"What is she, then?"

"I mean she's not my mother's sister, because my grandmother married twice; and she's one of the first lot. I don't know what you call her, but anyhow she's not my real aunt."

"She gives you plenty of pocket-money."

Seaton looked steadfastly at me out of his flat eyes. "She can't give me what's mine. When I come of age half of the whole lot will be mine; and what's more"—he turned his back on the house—"I'll make her hand over every blessed shilling of it."

I put my hands in my pockets and stared at Seaton. "Is it much?"

He nodded.

"Who told you?" He got suddenly very angry; a darkish red came into his cheeks, his eyes glistened, but he made no answer, and we loitered listlessly about the garden until it was time for tea. . . .

Seaton's aunt was wearing an extraordinary kind of lace jacket when we sidled sheepishly into the drawing-room together. She greeted me with a heavy and protracted smile, and bade me bring a chair close to the little table.

"I hope Arthur has made you feel at home," she said as she handed me my cup in her crooked hand. "He don't talk much to me; but then I'm an old woman. You must come again, Wither, and draw him out of his shell. You old snail!" She wagged her head at Seaton, who sat munching cake and watching her intently.

"And we must correspond, perhaps." She nearly shut her eyes at me. "You must write and tell me everything behind the creature's back." I confess I found her rather disquieting company. The evening drew on. Lamps were brought by a man with a nondescript face and very quiet footsteps. Seaton was told to bring out the chess-men. And we played a game, she and I, with her big chin thrust over the board at every move as she gloated over the pieces and occasionally croaked "Check!" after which she would sit back inscrutably staring at me. But the game was never finished. She simply hemmed me defencelessly in with a cloud of men that held me impotent, and yet one and all refused to administer to my poor flustered old king a merciful *coup de grâce*.

"There," she said, as the clock struck ten—"a drawn game, Withers. We are very evenly matched. A very creditable defence, Withers. You know your room. There's supper on a tray in the dining-room. Don't let the creature over-eat himself. The gong will sound three-quarters of an hour before a punctual breakfast." She held out her cheek to Seaton, and he kissed it with obvious perfunctoriness. With me she shook hands.

"An excellent game," she said cordially, "but my memory is poor, and"—she swept the pieces helter-skelter into the box—"the result will never be known." She raised her great head far back. "Eh?"

It was a kind of challenge, and I could only murmur: "Oh, I was absolutely in a hole, you know!" when she burst out laughing and waved us both out of the room.

Seaton and I stood and ate our supper, with one candlestick to light us, in a corner of the dining-room. "Well, and how would you like it?" he said very softly, after cautiously poking his head round the doorway.

"Like what?"

"Being spied on—every blessed thing you do and think?"

"I shouldn't like it at all," I said, "if she does."

"And yet you let her smash you up at chess!"

"I didn't let her!" I said indignantly.

"Well, you funked it, then."

"And I didn't funk it either," I said; "she's so jolly clever with her knights." Seaton stared fixedly at the candle. "You wait, that's all," he said slowly. And we went upstairs to bed.

I had not been long in bed, I think, when I was cautiously awakened by a touch on my shoulder. And there was Seaton's face in the candlelight and his eyes looking into mine.

"What's up?" I said, rising quickly to my elbow.

"Don't scurry," he whispered, "or she'll hear. I'm sorry for waking you, but I didn't think you'd be asleep so soon."

"Why, what's the time, then?" Seaton wore, what was then rather unusual, a night-suit, and he hauled his big silver watch out of the pocket in his jacket.

"It's a quarter to twelve. I never get to sleep before twelve—not here."

"What do you do, then?"

"Oh, I read and listen."

"Listen?"

Seaton stared into his candle-flame as if he were listening even then. "You can't guess what it is. All you read in ghost stories, that's all rot. You can't see much, Withers, but you know all the same."

"Know what?"

"Why, that they're there."

"Who's there?" I asked fretfully, glancing at the door.

"Why, in the house. It swarms with 'em. Just you stand still and listen outside my bed-room door in the middle of the night. I have, dozens of times; they're all over the place."

"Look here, Seaton," I said, "you asked me to come here, and I didn't mind chucking up a leave just to oblige you and because I'd promised; but don't get talking a lot of rot, that's all, or you'll know the difference when we get back."

"Don't fret," he said coldly, turning away. "I shan't be at school long. And what's more, you're here now, and there isn't anybody else to talk to. I'll chance the other."

"Look here, Seaton," I said, "you may think you're going to scare me with a lot of stuff about voices and all that. But I'll just thank you to clear out; and you may please yourself about pottering about all night."

He made no answer; he was standing by the dressing-table looking across his candle into the looking-glass; he turned and stared slowly round the walls.

"Even this room's nothing more than a coffin. I suppose she told you—'It's all exactly the same as when my brother William died'—trust her for that! And good luck to him, say I. Look at that." He raised his candle close to the little water-colour I have mentioned. "There's hundreds of eyes like that in the house; and even if God does see you, he takes precious good care you don't see Him. And it's just the same with them. I tell you what, Withers, I'm getting sick of all this. I shan't stand it much longer."

The house was silent within and without, and even in the yellowish radiance of the candle a faint silver showed through the open window on my blind. I slipped off the bedclothes, wide awake, and sat irresolute on the bedside.

"I know you're only guying me," I said angrily, "but why is the house full of— what you say? Why do you hear—what you *do* hear? Tell me that, you silly fool!"

Seaton sat down on a chair and rested his candlestick on his knee. He blinked at me calmly. "She brings them," he said, with lifted eyebrows.

"Who? Your aunt?"

He nodded.

"How?"

"I told you," he answered pettishly. "She's in league. You don't know. She as good as killed my mother; I know that. But it's not only her by a long chalk. She just sucks you dry. I know. And that's what she'll do for me; because I'm like her—like my mother, I mean. She simply hates to see me alive. I wouldn't be like that old she-wolf for a million pounds. And so"—he broke off, with a comprehensive wave of his candlestick— "they're always here. Ah, my boy, wait till she's dead! She'll hear something then, I can tell you. It's all very well now, but wait till then! I wouldn't be in her shoes when she has to clear out—for something. Don't you go and believe I care for ghosts, or whatever you like to call them. We're all in the same box. We're all under her thumb."

He was looking almost nonchalantly at the ceiling at the moment, when I saw his face change, saw his eyes suddenly drop like shot birds and fix themselves on the cranny of the door he had just left ajar. Even from where I sat I could see his colour change; he went greenish. He crouched without stirring, simply fixed. And I, scarcely daring to breathe, sat with creeping skin, simply watching him. His hands relaxed, and he gave a kind of sigh.

"Was that one?" I whispered, with a timid show of jauntiness. He looked round, opened his mouth, and nodded. "What?" I said. He jerked his thumb with meaningful eyes, and I knew that he meant that his aunt had been there listening at our door cranny.

"Look here, Seaton," I said once more, wriggling to my feet. "You may think I'm a jolly noodle; just as you please. But your aunt has been civil to me and all that, and I don't believe a word you say about her, that's all, and never did. Every fellow's a bit off his pluck at night, and you may think it a fine sport to try your rubbish on me. I heard your aunt come upstairs before I fell asleep. And I'll bet you a level tanner she's in bed now. What's more, you can keep your blessed ghosts to yourself. It's a guilty conscience, I should think."

Seaton looked at me curiously, without answering for a moment. "I'm not a liar, Withers; but I'm not going to quarrel either. You're the only chap I care a button for; or, at any rate, you're the only chap that's ever come here; and it's something to tell a fellow what you feel. I don't care a fig for fifty thousand ghosts, although I swear on my solemn oath that I know they're here. But she"—he turned deliberately—"you laid a tanner she's in bed, Withers; well, I know different. She's never in bed much of the night, and I'll prove it, too, just to show you I'm not such a nolly as you think I am. Come on!"

"Come on where?"

"Why, to see."

I hesitated. He opened a large cupboard and took out a small dark dressing-gown and a kind of shawl-jacket. He threw the jacket on the bed and put on the gown. His dusky face was colourless, and I could see by the way he fumbled at the sleeves he was shivering. But it was no good showing the white feather now. So I threw the tasselled shawl over my shoulders and, leaving our candle brightly burning on the chair, we went out together and stood in the corridor. "Now then, listen!" Seaton whispered.

We stood leaning over the staircase. It was like leaning over a well, so still and chill the air was all around us. But presently, as I suppose happens in most old houses, began to echo and answer in my ears a medley of infinite small stirrings and whisperings. Now out of the distance an old timber would relax its fibers, or a scurry die away behind the perishing wainscot. But amid and behind such sounds as these I seemed to begin to be conscious, as it were, of the lightest of footfalls, sounds as faint as the vanishing remembrance of voices in a dream. Seaton was all in obscurity except his face; out of that his eyes gleamed darkly, watching me.

"You'd hear, too, in time, my fine soldier," he muttered. "Come on!"

He descended the stairs, slipping his lean fingers lightly along the balusters. He turned to the right at the loop, and I followed him barefooted along a thickly-carpeted corridor. At the end stood a door ajar. And from here we very stealthily and in complete blackness ascended five narrow stairs. Seaton, with immense caution, slowly pushed open a door and we stood together looking into a great pool of duskiness, out of which, lit by the feeble clearness of a night-light, rose a vast bed. A heap of clothes lay on the floor; beside them two slippers dozed, with noses each to each, two yards apart. Somewhere a little clock ticked huskily. There was a rather close smell of lavender and eau de Cologne, mingled with the fragrance of ancient sachets, soap, and drugs. Yet it was a scent even more peculiarly commingled than that.

And the bed! I stared warily in; it was mounded gigantically, and it was empty.

Seaton turned a vague pale face, all shadows: "What did I say?" he muttered. "Who's—who's the fool now, I say? How are we going to get back without meeting her, I say? Answer me that! Oh, I wish to goodness you hadn't come here, Withers."

He stood visibly shivering in his skimpy gown, and could hardly speak for his teeth chattering. And very distinctly, in the hush that followed his whisper, I heard approaching a faint unhurried voluminous rustle. Seaton clutched my arm, dragged me to the right across the room to a large cupboard, and drew the door close to on us. And, presently, as with bursting lungs I peeped out into the long, low, curtained bedroom, waddled in that wonderful great head and body. I can see her now, all patched and lined with shadow, her tied-up hair (she must have had enormous quantities of it for so old a woman), her heavy lids above those flat, slow, vigilant eyes. She just passed across my ken in the vague dusk; but the bed was out of sight.

We waited on and on, listening to the clock's muffled ticking. Not the ghost of a sound rose up from the great bed. Either she lay archly listening or slept a sleep serener than an infant's. And when, it seemed, we had been hours in hiding and were cramped, chilled, and half suffocated, we crept out on all fours, with terror knocking at our ribs, and so down the five narrow stairs and back to the little candle-lit blue-and-gold bedroom.

Once there, Seaton gave in. He sat livid on a chair with closed eyes.

"Here," I said, shaking his arm, "I'm going to bed; I've had enough of this foolery; I'm going to bed." His lids quivered, but he made no answer. I poured out some water into my basin and, with that cold pictured azure eye fixed on us, bespattered Seaton's sallow face and forehead and dabbled his hair. He presently sighed and opened fish-like eyes.

"Come on!" I said. "Don't get shamming, there's a good chap. Get on my back, if you like, and I'll carry you into your bedroom."

He waved me away and stood up. So, with my candle in one hand, I took him under the arm and walked him along according to his direction down the corridor. His was a much dingier room than mine, and littered with boxes, paper, cages, and clothes. I huddled him into bed and turned to go. And suddenly, I can hardly explain it now, a kind of cold and deadly terror swept over me. I almost ran out of the room, with eyes fixed rigidly in front of me, blew out my candle, and buried my head under the bedclothes.

When I awoke, roused by a long-continued tapping at my door, sunlight was raying in on cornice and bedpost, and birds were singing in the garden. I got up, ashamed of the night's folly, dressed quickly, and went downstairs. The breakfast-room was sweet with flowers and fruit and honey. Seaton's aunt was standing in the garden beside the open French window, feeding a great flutter of birds. I watched her for a moment, unseen. Her face was set in a deep reverie beneath the shadow of a big loose sunhat. It was deeply lined, crooked, and, in a way I can't describe, fixedly vacant and strange. I coughed, and she turned at once with a prodigious smile to inquire how I had slept. And in that mysterious way by which we learn each other's secret thoughts without a sentence spoken I knew that she had followed every word and movement of the night before, and was triumphing over my affected innocence and ridiculing my friendly and too easy advances.

We returned to school, Seaton and I, lavishly laden, and by rail all the way. I made no reference to the obscure talk we had had, and resolutely refused to meet his eyes or to take up the hints he let fall. I was relieved—and yet I was sorry—to be going back, and strode on as fast as I could from the station, with Seaton almost trotting at my heels. But he insisted on buying more fruit and sweets—my share of which I accepted with a very bad grace. It was uncomfortably like a bribe; and, after all, I had no quarrel with his rum old aunt, and hadn't really believed half the stuff he had told me.

I saw as little of him as I could after that. He never referred to our visit or resumed his confidences, though in class I would sometimes catch his eye fixed on mine, full of a mute understanding, which I easily affected not to understand. He left Gummidge's, as I have said, rather abruptly, though I never heard of anything to his discredit. And I did not see him or have any news of him again till by chance we met one summer's afternoon in the Strand.

He was dressed rather oddly in a coat too large for him and a bright silky tie. But we instantly recognised one another under the awning of a cheap jeweler's shop. He immediately attached himself to me and dragged me off, not too cheerfully, to lunch with him at an Italian restaurant near by. He chattered about our old school, which he remembered only with dislike and disgust; told me cold-bloodedly of the disastrous fate of one or two of the old fellows who had been among his chief tormentors; insisted on an expensive wine and the whole gamut of the "rich" menu; and finally informed me, with a good deal of niggling, that he had come up to town to buy an engagement-ring.

And of course: "How is your aunt?" I enquired at last.

He seemed to have been awaiting the question. It fell like a stone into a deep pool, so many expressions flitted across his long un-English face.

"She's aged a good deal," he said softly, and broke off.

"She's been very decent," he continued presently after, and paused again. "In a way." He eyed me fleetingly. "I dare say you heard that she—that is, that we—had lost a good deal of money."

"No," I said.

"Oh, yes!" said Seaton, and paused again.

And somehow, poor fellow, I knew in the clink and clatter of glass and voices that he had lied to me; that he did not possess, and never had possessed, a penny beyond what his aunt had squandered on his too ample allowance of pocket-money.

"And the ghosts?" I enquired quizzically.

He grew instantly solemn, and, though it may have been my fancy, slightly yellowed. But "You are making game of me, Withers," was all he said.

He asked for my address, and I rather reluctantly gave him my card.

"Look here, Withers," he said, as we stood in the sunlight on the thronging kerb, saying good-bye, "here I am, and it's all very well; I'm not perhaps as fanciful as I was. But you are practically the only friend I have on earth—except Alice. . . . And there—to make a clean breast of it, I'm not sure that my aunt cares much about my getting married. She doesn't say so, of course. You know her well enough for that." He looked sidelong at the rattling gaudy traffic.

"What I was going to say is this. Would you mind coming down? You needn't stay the night unless you please, though, of course, you know you would be awfully welcome. But I should like you to meet my—to meet Alice; and then, perhaps, you might tell me your honest opinion of—of the other too."

I vaguely demurred. He pressed me. And we parted with a half promise that I would come. He waved his ball-topped cane at me and ran off in his long jacket after a 'bus.

A letter arrived soon after, in his small weak handwriting, giving me full particulars regarding route and trains. And without the least curiosity, even, perhaps with some little annoyance that chance should have thrown us together again, I accepted his invitation and arrived one hazy midday at his out-of-the-way station to find him sitting on a low seat under a clump of double hollyhocks, awaiting me.

His face looked absent and singularly listless; but he seemed, none the less, pleased to see me.

We walked up the village street, past the little dingy apothecary's and the empty forge, and, as on my first visit, skirted the house together, and, instead of entering by the front door, made our way down the green path into the garden at the back. A pale haze of cloud muffled the sun; the garden lay in a grey shimmer—its old trees, its snap-dragoned faintly glittering walls. But there seemed now an air of neglect where before all had been neat and methodical. There was a patch of shallowly-dug soil and a worn-down spade leaning against a tree. There was an old broken wheelbarrow. The goddess of neglect was there.

"You ain't much of a gardener, Seaton," I said, with a sigh of ease.

"I think, do you know, I like it best like this," said Seaton. "We haven't any gardener now, of course. Can't afford it." He stood staring at his little dark square of freshly-turned earth. "And it always seems to me," he went on ruminatingly, "that, after all, we are nothing better than interlopers on the earth, disfiguring and staining wherever we go. I know it's shocking blasphemy to say so, but then it's different here, you see. We are farther away."

"To tell you the truth, Seaton, I *don't* quite see," I said; "but it isn't a new philosophy, is it? Anyhow, it's a precious beastly one."

"It's only what I think," he replied, with all his odd old stubborn meekness.

We wandered on together, talking little, and still with that expression of uneasy vigilance on Seaton's face. He pulled out his watch as we stood gazing idly over the green meadow and the dark motionless bulrushes.

"I think, perhaps, it's nearly time for lunch," he said. "Would you like to come in?"

We turned and walked slowly towards the house, across whose windows I confess my own eyes, too, went restlessly wandering in search of its rather disconcerting inmate. There was a pathetic look of draggledness, of want of means and care, rust and overgrowth and faded paint. Seaton's aunt, a little to my relief, did not share our meal. Seaton carved the cold meat, and dispatched a heaped-up plate by the elderly servant for his aunt's private consumption. We talked little and in half-suppressed tones, and sipped a bottle of Madeira which Seaton had rather heedfully fetched out of the great mahogany sideboard.

I played him a dull and effortless game of chess, yawning between the moves he generally made almost at haphazard, and with attention elsewhere engaged. About five o'clock came the sound of a distant ring, and Seaton jumped up, overturning the board, and so ending a game that else might have fatuously continued to this day. He effusively excused himself, and after some little while returned with a slim, dark, rather sallow girl of about nineteen, in a white gown and hat, to whom I was presented with some little nervousness as "his dear old friend and schoolfellow."

We talked on in the pale afternoon light, still, as it seemed to me, and even in spite of real effort to be clear and gay, in a half-suppressed, lack-lustre fashion. We all seemed, if it were not my fancy, to be expectant, to be rather anxiously awaiting an arrival, the appearance of someone who all but filled our collective consciousness. Seaton talked least of all, and in a restless interjectory way, as he continually fidgeted from chair to chair. At last he proposed a stroll in the garden before the sun should have quite gone down.

Alice walked between us. Her hair and eyes were conspicuously dark against the whiteness of her gown. She carried herself not ungracefully, and yet without the least movement of her arms or body, and answered us both without turning her head. There was a curious provocative reserve in that impassive and rather long face, a half-unconscious strength of character.

And yet somehow I knew—I believe we all knew—that this walk, this discussion of their future plans was a futility. I had nothing to base such a cynicism on, except only a vague sense of oppression, the foreboding remembrance of the inert invincible power in the background, to whom optimistic plans and love-making and youth are as chaff and thistledown. We came back, silent, in the last light. Seaton's aunt was there—under an old brass lamp. Her hair was as barbarously massed and curled as ever. Her eye-lids,

I think, hung even a little heavier in age over their slow-moving inscrutable pupils. We filed in softly out of the evening, and I made my bow.

"In this short interval, Mr. Withers," she remarked amiably, "you have put off youth, put on the man. Dear me, how sad it is to see the young days vanishing! Sit down. My nephew tells me you met by chance—or act of Providence, shall we call it?—and in my beloved Strand! You, I understand, are to be best man—yes, best man, or am I divulging secrets?" She surveyed Arthur and Alice with overwhelming graciousness. They sat apart on two low chairs and smiled in return.

"And Arthur—how do you think Arthur is looking?"

"I think he looks very much in need of a change," I said deliberately.

"A change! Indeed?" She all but shut her eyes at me and with an exaggerated sentimentality shook her head. "My dear Mr. Withers! Are we not *all* in need of a change in this fleeting, fleeting world?" She mused over the remark like a connoisseur. "And you," she continued, turning abruptly to Alice, "I hope you pointed out to Mr. Withers all my pretty bits?"

"We walked round the garden," said Alice, looking out of the window. "It's a very beautiful evening."

"Is it?" said the old lady, starting up violently. "Then on this very beautiful evening we will go in to supper. Mr. Withers, your arm; Arthur, bring your bride."

I can scarcely describe with what curious ruminations I led the way into the faded, heavy-aired dining-room, with this indefinable old creature leaning weightily on my arm—the large flat bracelet on the yellow-laced wrist. She fumed a little, breathed rather heavily, as if with an effort of mind rather than of body; for she had grown much stouter and yet little more proportionate. And to talk into that great white face, so close to mine, was a queer experience in the dim light of the corridor, and even in the twinkling crystal of the candles. She was naïve—appallingly naïve; she was sudden and superficial; she was even arch; and all these in the brief, rather puffy passage from one room to the other, with these two tongue-tied children bringing up the rear. The meal was tremendous. I have never seen such a monstrous salad. But the dishes were greasy and over-spiced, and were indifferently cooked. One thing only was quite unchanged—my hostess's appetite was as Gargantuan as ever. The old solid candelabra that lighted us stood before her high-backed chair. Seaton sat a little removed, with his plate almost in darkness.

And throughout this prodigious meal his aunt talked, mainly to me, mainly at Seaton, with an occasional satirical courtesy to Alice and muttered explosions of directions to the servant. She had aged, and yet, if it be not nonsense to say so, seemed no older. I suppose to the Pyramids a decade is but as the rustling down of a handful of dust. And she reminded me of some such unshakable prehistoricism. She certainly was an amazing talker—racy, extravagant, with a delivery that was perfectly overwhelming. As for Seaton—her flashes of silence were for him. On her enormous volubility would suddenly fall a hush: acid sarcasm would be left implied; and she would sit softly moving her great head, with eyes fixed full in a dreamy smile; but with her whole attention, one could see, slowly, joyously absorbing his mute discomfiture.

She confided in us her views on a theme vaguely occupying at the moment, I suppose, all our minds. "We have barbarous institutions, and so must put up, I suppose, with a never-ending procession of fools—of fools *ad infinitum*. Marriage, Mr. Withers, was instituted in the privacy of a garden; *sub rosa*, as it were. Civilization flaunts it in the glare of day. The dull marry the poor; the rich the effete; and so our New Jerusalem is peopled with naturals, plain and coloured, at either end. I detest folly; I detest still more (if I must be frank, dear Arthur) mere cleverness. Mankind has simply become a tailless host of uninstinctive animals. We should never have taken to Evolution, Mr. Withers. 'Natural Selection!'—little gods and fishes!—the deaf for the dumb. We should have used our brains—intellectual pride, the ecclesiastics call it. And by brains I mean—what do I mean, Alice?—I mean, my dear child," and she laid two gross fingers on Alice's narrow sleeve. "I mean courage. Consider it, Arthur. I read that the scientific world is once more beginning to be afraid of spiritual agencies. Spiritual agencies that tap, and actually float, bless their hearts! I think just one more of those mulberries—thank you.

"They talk about 'blind Love,'" she ran inconsequently on as she helped herself, with eyes fixed on the dish, "but why blind? I think, do you know, from weeping over its rickets. After all, it is we plain women that triumph, Mr. Withers, beyond the mockery of time. Alice, now! Fleeting, fleeting is youth, my child! What's that you were confiding to your plate, Arthur? Satirical boy! He laughs at his old aunt: nay, but thou didst laugh. He detests all sentiment. He whispers the most acid asides. Come, my love, we will leave these cynics; we will go and commiserate with each other on our sex. The choice of two evils, Mr. Smithers!" I opened the door, and she swept out as if borne on a torrent of unintelligible indignation; and Arthur and I were left in the clear four-flamed light alone.

For a while we sat in silence. He shook his head at my cigarette-case, and I lit a cigarette. Presently he fidgeted in his chair and poked his head forward into the light. He paused to rise and shut again the shut door.

"How long will you be?" he said, standing by the table.

I laughed.

"Oh, it's not that!" he said, in some confusion. "Of course, I like to be with her. But it's not that only. The truth is, Withers, I don't care about leaving her too long with my aunt."

I hesitated. He looked at me questioningly.

"Look here, Seaton," I said, "you know well enough that I don't want to interfere in your affairs, or to offer advice where it is not wanted. But don't you think perhaps you may not treat your aunt quite in the right way? As one gets old, you know, a little give and take. I have an old godmother, or something. She talks, too. . . . A little allowance: it does no harm. But, hang it all, I'm no talker."

He sat down with his hands in his pockets and still with his eyes fixed almost incredulously on mine. "How?" he said.

"Well, my dear fellow, if I'm any judge—mind, I don't say that I am—but I can't help thinking she thinks you don't care for her; and perhaps takes your silence for—for bad temper. She has been very decent to you, hasn't she?"

"'Decent'? My God!" said Seaton.

I smoked on in silence; but he still continued to look at me with that peculiar concentration I remembered of old.

"I don't think, perhaps, Withers," he began presently, "I don't think you quite understand. Perhaps you are not quite our kind. You always did, just like the other fellows, guy me at school. You laughed at me that night you came to stay here—about the voices and all that. But I don't mind being laughed at—because I know."

"Know what?" It was the same old system of dull question and evasive answer.

"I mean I know that what we see and hear is only the smallest fraction of what is. I know she lives quite out of this. She *talks* to you; but it's all make-believe. It's all a 'parlour game.' She's not really with you; only pitting her outside wits against yours and enjoying the fooling. She's living on inside, on what you're rotten without. That's what it is—a cannibal feast. She's a spider. It doesn't much matter what you call it. It means the same kind of thing. I tell you, Withers, she hates me; and you can scarcely dream what that hatred means. I used to think I had an inkling of the reason. It's oceans deeper than that. It just lies behind: herself against myself. Why, after all, how much do we really understand of anything? We don't even know our own histories, and not a tenth, not a tenth of the reasons. What has life been to me?—nothing but a trap. And when one is set free, it only begins again. I thought you might understand; but you are on a different level: that's all."

"What on earth are you talking about?" I said, half contemptuously, in spite of myself.

"I mean what I say," he said gutturally. "All this outside's only make-believe— but there! what's the good of talking? So far as this is concerned I'm as good as done. You wait."

Seaton blew out three of the candles and, leaving the vacant room in semi-darkness, we groped our way along the corridor to the drawing-room. There a full moon stood shining in at the long garden windows. Alice sat stooping at the door, with her hands clasped, looking out, alone.

"Where is she?" Seaton asked in a low tone.

Alice looked up; their eyes met in a kind of instantaneous understanding, and the door immediately afterwards opened behind us.

"*Such* a moon!" said a voice that, once heard, remained unforgettably on the ear. "A night for lovers, Mr. Withers, if ever there was one. Get a shawl, my dear Arthur, and take Alice for a little promenade. I dare say we old cronies will manage to keep awake. Hasten, hasten, Romeo! My poor, poor Alice, how laggard a lover!"

Seaton returned with a shawl. They drifted out into the moonlight. My companion gazed after them till they were out of hearing, turned to me gravely, and suddenly twisted her white face into such a convulsion of contemptuous amusement that I could only stare blankly in reply.

"Dear innocent children!" she said, with inimitable unctuousness. "Well, well, Mr. Withers, we poor seasoned old creatures must move with the times. Do you sing?"

I scouted the idea.

"Then you must listen to my playing. Chess"—she clasped her forehead with both cramped hands—"chess is now completely beyond my poor wits."

She sat down at the piano and ran her fingers in a flourish over the keys. "What shall it be? How shall we capture them, those passionate hearts? That first fine careless rapture? Poetry itself." She gazed softly into the garden a moment, and presently, with a shake of her body, began to play the opening bars of Beethoven's "Moonlight" Sonata. The piano was old and woolly. She played without music. The lamplight was rather dim. The moonbeams from the window lay across the keys. Her head was in shadow. And whether it was simply due to her personality or to some really occult skill in her playing I cannot say: I only know that she gravely and deliberately set herself to satirise the beautiful music. It brooded on the air, disillusioned, charged with mockery and bitterness. I stood at the window; far down the path I could see the white figure glimmering in that pool of colourless light. A few faint stars shone; and still that amazing woman behind me dragged out of the unwilling keys her wonderful grotesquerie of youth and love and beauty. It came to an end. I knew the player was watching me. "Please, please, go on!" I murmured, without turning. "Please go on playing, Miss Seaton."

No answer was returned to my rather fluttering sarcasm, but I knew in some indefinite way that I was being acutely scrutinised, when suddenly there followed a procession of quiet, plaintive chords which broke at last softly into the hymn, *A Few More Years Shall Roll*.

I confess it held me spellbound. There is a wistful strained, plangent pathos in the tune; but beneath those masterly old hands it cried softly and bitterly the solitude and desperate estrangement of the world. Arthur and his lady-love vanished from my thoughts. No one could put into a rather hackneyed old hymn-tune such an appeal who had never known the meaning of the words. Their meaning, anyhow, isn't commonplace. I turned very cautiously and glanced at the musician. She was leaning forward a little over the keys, so that at the approach of my cautious glance she had but to turn her face into the thin flood of moonlight for every feature to become distinctly visible. And so, with the tune abruptly terminated, we steadfastly regarded one another, and she broke into a chuckle of laughter.

"Not quite so seasoned as I supposed, Mr. Withers. I see you are a real lover of music. To me it is too painful. It evokes too much thought. . . ."

I could scarcely see her little glittering eyes under their penthouse lids.

"And now," she broke off crisply, "tell me, as a man of the world, what do you think of my new niece?"

I was not a man of the world, nor was I much flattered in my stiff and dullish way of looking at things by being called one; and I could answer her without the least hesitation.

"I don't think, Miss Seaton, I'm much of a judge of character. She's very charming."

"A brunette?"

"I think I prefer dark women."

"And why? Consider, Mr. Withers; dark hair, dark eyes, dark cloud, dark night, dark vision, dark death, dark grave, dark dark!"

Perhaps the climax would have rather thrilled Seaton, but I was too thick-skinned. "I don't know much about all that," I answered rather pompously. "Broad daylight's difficult enough for most of us."

"Ah," she said, with a sly inward burst of satirical laughter.

"And I suppose," I went on, perhaps a little nettled, "it isn't the actual darkness one admires, its the contrast of the skin, and the colour of the eyes, and—and their shining. Just as," I went blundering on, too late to turn back, "just as you only see the stars in the dark. It would be a long day without any evening. As for death and the grave, I don't suppose we shall much notice that." Arthur and his sweetheart were slowly returning along the dewy path. "I believe in making the best of things."

"How very interesting!" came the smooth answer. "I see you are a philosopher, Mr. Withers. H'm! 'As for death and the grave, I don't suppose we shall much notice that.' Very interesting. . . . And I'm sure," she added in a particularly suave voice, "I profoundly hope so." She rose slowly from her stool. "You will take pity on me again, I hope. You and I would get on famously—kindred spirits—elective affinities. And, of course, now that my nephew's going to leave me, now that his affections are centred on another, I shall be a very lonely old woman. . . . Shall I not, Arthur?"

Seaton blinked stupidly. "I didn't hear what you said, Aunt."

"I was telling our old friend, Arthur, that when you are gone I shall be a very lonely old woman."

"Oh, I don't think so," he said in a strange voice.

"He means, Mr. Withers, he means, my dear child," she said, sweeping her eyes over Alice, "he means that I shall have memory for company—heavenly memory—the ghosts of other days. Sentimental boy! And did you enjoy our music, Alice? Did I really stir that youthful heart? . . . O, O, O," continued the horrible old creature, "you billers and cooers, I have been listening to such flatteries, such confessions! Beware, beware, Arthur, there's many a slip." She rolled her little eyes at me, she shrugged her shoulders at Alice, and gazed an instant stonily into her nephew's face.

I held out my hand. "Good night, good night!" she cried. "'He that fights and runs away.' Ah, good night, Mr. Withers; come again soon!" She thrust out her cheek at Alice, and we all three filed slowly out of the room.

Black shadow darkened the porch and half the spreading sycamore. We walked without speaking up the dusty village street. Here and there a crimson window glowed. At the fork of the high-road I said good-bye. But I had taken hardly more than a dozen paces when a sudden impulse seized me.

"Seaton!" I called.

He turned in the moonlight.

"You have my address; if by any chance, you know, you should care to spend a week or two in town between this and the—the Day, we should be delighted to see you."

"Thank you, Withers, thank you," he said in a low voice.

"I dare say"—I waved my stick gallantly to Alice—"I dare say you will be doing some shopping; we could all meet," I added, laughing.

"Thank you, thank you, Withers—immensely," he repeated.

And so we parted.

But they were out of the jog-trot of my prosaic life. And being of a stolid and incurious nature, I left Seaton and his marriage, and even his aunt, to themselves in my memory, and scarcely gave a thought to them until one day I was walking up the Strand again, and passed the flashing gloaming of the covered-in jeweller's shop where I had accidentally encountered my old schoolfellow in the summer. It was one of those still close autumnal days after a rainy night. I cannot say why, but a vivid recollection returned to my mind of our meeting and of how suppressed Seaton had seemed, and of how vainly he had endeavoured to appear assured and eager. He must be married by now, and had doubtless returned from his honeymoon. And I had clean forgotten my manners, had sent not a word of congratulation, nor—as I might very well have done, and as I knew he would have been immensely pleased at my doing—the ghost of a wedding-present.

On the other hand, I pleaded with myself, I had had no invitation. I paused at the corner of Trafalgar Square, and at the bidding of one of those caprices that seize occasionally on even an unimaginative mind, I suddenly ran after a green 'bus that was passing, and found myself bound on a visit I had not in the least foreseen.

All the colours of autumn were over the village when I arrived. A beautiful late afternoon sunlight bathed thatch and meadow. But it was close and hot. A child, two dogs, a very old woman with a heavy basket I encountered. One or two incurious tradesmen looked idly up as I passed by. It was all so rural and so still, my whimsical impulse had so much flagged, that for a while I hesitated to venture under the shadow of the sycamore-tree to enquire after the happy pair. I deliberately passed by the faint-blue gates and continued my walk under the high green and tufted wall. Hollyhocks had attained their topmost bud and seeded in the little cottage gardens beyond; the Michaelmas daisies were in flower; a sweet warm aromatic smell of fading leaves was in the air. Beyond the cottages lay a field where cattle were grazing, and beyond that I came to a little churchyard. Then the road wound on, pathless and houseless, among gorse and bracken. I turned impatiently and walked quickly back to the house and rang the bell.

The rather colourless elderly woman who answered my enquiry informed me that Miss Seaton was at home, as if only taciturnity forbade her adding, "But she doesn't want to see *you*."

"Might I, do you think, have Mr. Arthur's address?" I said.

She looked at me with quiet astonishment, as if waiting for an explanation. Not the faintest of smiles came into her thin face.

"I will tell Miss Seaton," she said after a pause. "Please walk in."

She showed me into the dingy undusted drawing-room, filled with evening sunshine and the green-dyed light that penetrated the leaves overhanging the long French windows. I sat down and waited on and on, occasionally aware of a creaking footfall overhead. At last the door opened a little, and the great face I had once known peered round at me. For it was enormously changed; mainly, I think, because the old eyes had rather suddenly failed, and so a kind of stillness and darkness lay over its calm and wrinkled pallor.

"Who is it?" she asked.

I explained myself and told her the occasion of my visit.

She came in and shut the door carefully after her and, though the fumbling was scarcely perceptible, groped her way to a chair. She had on an old dressing-gown, like a cassock, of a patterned cinnamon colour.

"What is it you want?" she said, seating herself and lifting her blank face to mine.

"Might I just have Arthur's address?" I said deferentially. "I am so sorry to have disturbed you."

"H'm. You have come to see my nephew?"

"Not necessarily to see him, only to hear how he is, and, of course, Mrs. Seaton too. I am afraid my silence must have appeared. . . ."

"He hasn't noticed your silence," croaked the old voice out of the great mask; "besides, there isn't any Mrs. Seaton."

"Ah, then," I answered, after a momentary pause, "I have not seemed so black as I painted myself! And how is Miss Outram?"

"She's gone into Yorkshire," answered Seaton's aunt.

"And Arthur too?"

She did not reply, but simply sat blinking at me with lifted chin, as if listening, but certainly not for what I might have to say. I began to feel rather at a loss.

"You were no close friend of my nephew's, Mr. Smithers?" she said presently.

"No," I answered, welcoming the cue, "and yet, do you know, Miss Seaton, he is one of the very few of my old schoolfellows I have come across in the last few years, and I suppose as one gets older one begins to value old associations. . . ." My voice seemed to trail off into a vacuum. "I thought Miss Outram," I hastily began again, "a particularly charming girl. I hope they are both quite well."

Still the old face solemnly blinked at me in silence.

"You must find it very lonely, Miss Seaton, with Arthur away?"

"I was never lonely in my life," she said sourly. "I don't look to flesh and blood for my company. When you've got to be my age, Mr. Smithers (which God forbid), you'll find life a very different affair from what you seem to think it is now. You won't seek company then, I'll be bound. It's thrust on you." Her face edged round into the clear green light, and her eyes, as it were, groped over my vacant, disconcerted face. "I dare say, now," she said, composing her mouth, "I dare say my nephew told you a good many tarradiddles in his time. Oh, yes, a good many, eh? He was always a liar. What, now, did he say of me? Tell me, now." She leant forward as far as she could, trembling, with an ingratiating smile.

"I think he is rather superstitious," I said coldly, "but, honestly, I have a very poor memory, Miss Seaton."

"Why?" she said. "*I* haven't."

"The engagement hasn't been broken off, I hope."

"Well, between you and me," she said, shrinking up and with an immensely confidential grimace, "it has."

"I'm sure I'm very sorry to hear it. And where is Arthur?"

"Eh?"

"Where is Arthur?"

We faced each other mutely among the dead old bygone furniture. Past all my scrutiny was that large, flat, grey, cryptic countenance. And then, suddenly, our eyes for the first time, really met. In some indescribable way out of that thick-lidded obscurity a far small something stooped and looked out at me for a mere instant of time that seemed of almost intolerable protraction. Involuntarily I blinked and shook my head. She muttered something with great rapidity, but quite inarticulately; rose and hobbled to the door. I thought I heard, mingled in broken mutterings, something about tea.

"Please, please, don't trouble," I began, but could say no more, for the door was already shut between us. I stood and looked out on the long-neglected garden. I could just see the bright greenness of Seaton's old tadpole pond. I wandered about the room. Dusk began to gather, the last birds in that dense shadowiness of trees had ceased to sing. And not a sound was to be heard in the house. I waited on and on, vainly speculating. I even attempted to ring the bell; but the wire was broken, and only jangled loosely at my efforts.

I hesitated, unwilling to call or to venture out, and yet more unwilling to linger on, waiting for a tea that promised to be an exceedingly comfortless supper. And as darkness drew down, a feeling of the utmost unease and disquietude came over me. All my talks with Seaton returned on me with a suddenly enriched meaning. I recalled again his face as we had stood hanging over the staircase, listening in the small hours to the inexplicable stirrings of the night. There were no candles in the room; every minute the autumnal darkness deepened. I cautiously opened the door and listened, and with some little dismay withdrew, for I was uncertain of my way out. I even tried the garden, but was confronted under a veritable thicket of foliage by a padlocked gate. It would be a little too ignominious to be caught scaling a friend's garden fence!

Cautiously returning into the still and musty drawing-room, I took out my watch and gave the incredible old woman ten minutes in which to reappear. And when that tedious ten minutes had ticked by I could scarcely distinguish its hands. I determined to wait no longer, drew open the door, and, trusting to my sense of direction, groped my way through the corridor that I vaguely remembered led to the front of the house.

I mounted three or four stairs and, lifting a heavy curtain, found myself facing the starry fanlight of the porch. Hence I glanced into the gloom of the dining-room. My fingers were on the latch of the outer door when I heard a faint stirring in the darkness above the hall. I looked up and became conscious of, rather than saw, the huddled old figure looking down on me.

There was an immense hushed pause. Then, "Arthur, Arthur," whispered an inexpressively peevish, rasping voice, "is that you? Is that you, Arthur?"

I can scarcely say why, but the question horribly startled me. No conceivable answer occurred to me. With head craned back, hand clenched on my umbrella, I continued to stare up into the gloom, in this fatuous confrontation.

"Oh, oh," the voice croaked. "It is you, is it? *That* disgusting man! . . . Go away out. Go away out."

Hesitating no longer, I caught open the door and, slamming it behind me, ran out into the garden, under the gigantic old sycamore, and so out at the open gate.

I found myself half up the village street before I stopped running. The local butcher was sitting in his shop reading a piece of newspaper by the light of a small oil-lamp. I crossed the road and enquired the way to the station. And after he had with minute and needless care directed me, I asked casually if Mr. Arthur Seaton still lived with his aunt at the big house just beyond the village. He poked his head in at the little parlour door.

"Here's a gentleman enquiring after young Mr. Seaton, Millie," he said. "He's dead, ain't he?"

"Why, yes, bless you," replied a cheerful voice from within. "Dead and buried these three months or more—young Mr. Seaton. And just before he was to be married, don't you remember, Bob?"

I saw a fair young woman's face peer over the muslin of the little door at me.

"Thank you," I replied, "then I go straight on?"

"That's it, sir; past the pond, bear up the hill a bit to the left, and then there's the station lights before your eyes."

We looked intelligently into each other's faces in the beam of the smoky lamp. But not one of the many questions in my mind could I put into words.

And again I paused irresolutely a few paces further on. It was not, I fancy, merely a foolish apprehension of what the raw-boned butcher might "think" that prevented my going back to see if I could find Seaton's grave in the benighted churchyard. There was precious little use in pottering about in the muddy dark merely to find where he was buried. And yet I felt a little uneasy. My rather horrible thought was that, so far as I was concerned—one of his esteemed few friends—he had never been much better than "buried" in my mind.

Where Their Fire Is Not Quenched

May Sinclair

————◆————

THERE WAS NOBODY IN THE ORCHARD. HARRIOTT LEIGH WENT OUT, carefully, through the iron gate into the field. She had made the latch slip into its notch without a sound.

The path slanted widely up the field from the orchard gate to the site under the elder tree. George Waring waited for her there.

Years afterwards, when she thought of George Waring she smelt the sweet, hot, wine-scent of the elder flowers. Years afterwards, when she smelt elder flowers she saw George Waring, with his beautiful, gentle face, like a poet's or a musician's, his black-blue eyes, and sleek, olive-brown hair. He was a naval lieutenant.

Yesterday he had asked her to marry him and she had consented. But her father hadn't, and she had come to tell him that and say good-bye before he left her. His ship was to sail the next day.

He was eager and excited. He couldn't believe that anything could stop their happiness, that anything he didn't want to happen could happen.

"Well?" he said.

"He's a perfect beast, George. He won't let us. He says we're too young."

"I was twenty last August," he said, aggrieved.

"And I shall be seventeen in September."

"And this is June. We're quite old, really. How long does he mean us to wait?"

"Three years."

"Three years before we can be engaged even—Why, we might be dead."

She put her arms round him to make him feel safe. They kissed; and the sweet, hot, wine-scent of the elder flowers mixed with their kisses. They stood, pressed close together, under the elder tree.

Across the yellow fields of charlock they heard the village clock strike seven.

Up in the house a gong clanged.

"Darling, I must go," she said.

"Oh stay—Stay *five* minutes."

He pressed her close. It lasted five minutes, and five more. Then he was running fast down the road to the station, while Harriott went along the field-path, slowly, struggling with her tears.

"He'll be back in three months," she said. "I can live through three months."

But he never came back. There was something wrong with the engines of his ship, the *Alexandra*. Three weeks later she went down in the Mediterranean, and George with her.

Harriott said she didn't care how soon she died now. She was quite sure it would be soon, because she couldn't live without him.

Five years passed.

The two lines of beech trees stretched on and on, the whole length of the Park, a broad green drive between. When you came to the middle they branched off right and left in the form of a cross, and at the end of the right arm there was a white stucco pavilion with pillars and a three-cornered pediment like a Greek temple. At the end of the left arm, the west entrance to the Park, double gates and a side door.

Harriott, on her stone seat at the back of the pavilion, could see Stephen Philpotts the very minute he came through the side door.

He had asked her to wait for him there. It was the place he always chose to read his poems aloud in. The poems were a pretext. She knew what he was going to say. And she knew what she would answer.

There were elder bushes in flower at the back of the pavilion, and Harriott thought of George Waring. She told herself that George was nearer to her now than he could ever have been, living. If she married Stephen she would not be unfaithful, because she loved him with another part of herself. It was not as though Stephen were taking George's place. She loved Stephen with her soul, in an unearthly way.

But her body quivered like a stretched wire when the door opened and the young man came towards her down the drive under the beech trees.

She loved him; she loved his slenderness, his darkness and sallow whiteness, his black eyes lighting up with the intellectual flame, the way his black hair swept back from his forehead, the way he walked, tiptoe, as if his feet were lifted with wings.

He sat down beside her. She could see his hands tremble. She felt that her moment was coming; it had come.

"I wanted to see you alone because there's something I must say to you. I don't quite know how to begin. . . ."

Her lips parted. She panted lightly.

"You've heard me speak of Sybill Foster?"

Her voice came stammering, "N-no, Stephen. Did you?"

"Well, I didn't mean to, till I knew it was all right. I only heard yesterday."

"Heard what?"

"Why, that she'll have me. Oh, Harriott—do you know what it's like to be ter-ribly happy?"

She knew. She had known just now, the moment before he told her. She sat there, stone-cold and stiff, listening to his raptures, listening to her own voice saying she was glad.

Ten years passed.

Harriott Leigh sat waiting in the drawing-room of a small house in Maida Vale. She lived there ever since her father's death two years before.

She was restless. She kept on looking at the clock to see if it was four, the hour that Oscar Wade had appointed. She was not sure that he would some, after she had sent him away yesterday.

She now asked herself, why, when she had sent him away yesterday, she had let him come to-day. Her motives were not altogether clear. If she really meant what she had said then, she oughtn't to let him come to her again. Never again.

She had shown him plainly what she meant. She could see herself, sitting very straight in her chair, uplifted by a passionate integrity, while he stood before her, hang-ing his head, ashamed and beaten; she could feel again the throb in her voice as she kept on saying that she couldn't, she couldn't; he must see that she couldn't; that no, nothing would make her change her mind; she couldn't forget he had a wife; that he must think of Muriel.

To which he had answered savagely: "I needn't. That's all over. We only live together for the look of the thing."

And she, serenely, with great dignity: "And for the look of the thing, Oscar, we must leave off seeing each other. Please go."

"Do you mean it?"

"Yes. We must never see each other again."

And he had gone then, ashamed and beaten.

She could see him, squaring his broad shoulders to meet the blow. And she was sorry for him. She told herself she had been unnecessarily hard. Why shouldn't they see each other again, now he understood where they must draw the line? Until yesterday the line had never been very clearly drawn. Today she meant to ask him to forget what he had said to her. Once it was forgotten, they could go on being friends as if nothing had happened.

It was four o'clock. Half-past. Five. She had finished tea and given him up when, between the half-hour and six o'clock, he came.

He came as he had come a dozen times, with his measured, deliberate, thoughtful tread, carrying himself well braced, with a sort of held-in arrogance, his great shoulders heaving. He was a man of about forty, broad and tall, lean-flanked and short-necked, his straight, handsome features showing small and even in the big square face and in the flush that swamped it. The close-clipped, reddish-brown moustache bristled forwards from the push-out upper lip. His small, flat eyes shone, reddish-brown, eager and animal.

She liked to think of him when he was not there, but always at the first sight of him she felt a slight shock. Physically, he was very far from her admired ideal. So different from George Waring and Stephen Philpotts.

He sat down, facing her.

There was an embarrassed silence, broken by Oscar Wade.

"Well, Harriott, you said I could come." He seemed to be throwing the responsibility on her.

"So I suppose you've forgiven me?" he said.

"Oh, yes, Oscar, I've forgiven you."

He said she'd better show it by coming to dine with him somewhere that evening. She could give no reason to herself for going. She simply went.

He took her to a restaurant in Soho. Oscar Wade dined well, even extravagantly, giving each dish its importance. She liked his extravagance. He had none of the mean virtues.

It was over. His flushed, embarrassed silence told her what he was thinking. But when he had seen her home, he left her at her garden gate. He had thought better of it.

She was not sure whether she were glad or sorry. She had had her moment of righteous exaltation and she had enjoyed it. But there was no joy in the weeks that followed it. She had given up Oscar Wade because she didn't want him very much; and now she wanted him furiously, perversely, because she had given him up. Though he had no resemblance to her ideal, she couldn't live without him.

She dined with him again and again, till she knew Schnebler's Restaurant by heart, the white panelled walls picked out with gold; the white pillars, and the curling gold fronds of their capitals; the thick crimson velvet cushions, that clung to her skirts; the glitter of silver and glass on the innumerable white circles of the tables. And the faces of the diners, red, white, pink, brown, grey and sallow, distorted and excited; the curled mouths that twisted as they ate; the convoluted electric bulbs pointing, pointing down at them, under the red, crinkled shades. All shimmering in a thick air that the red light stained as wine stains water.

And Oscar's face, flushed with his dinner. Always, when he leaned back from the table and brooded in silence she knew what he was thinking. His heavy eyelids would lift; she would find his eyes fixed on hers, wondering, considering.

She knew now what the end would be. She thought of George Waring, and Stephen Philpotts, and of her life, cheated. She hadn't chosen Oscar, she hadn't really wanted him; but now he had forced himself on her she couldn't afford to let him go. Since George died no man had loved her, no other man ever would.

And she was sorry for him when she thought of him going from her, beaten and ashamed.

She was certain, before he was, of the end. Only she didn't know when and where and how it would come. That was what Oscar knew.

It came at the close of one of their evenings when they had dined in a private sitting-room. He said he couldn't stand the heat and noise of the public restaurant.

She went before him, up a steep, red-carpeted stair to a white door on the second landing.

From time to time they repeated the furtive, hidden adventure. Sometimes she met him in the room above Schnebler's. Sometimes, when her maid was out, she received him at her house in Maida Vale. But that was dangerous, not to be risked too often.

Oscar declared himself unspeakably happy. Harriott was not quite sure. This was love, the thing she had never had, that she had dreamed of, hungered and thirsted for; but now she had it she was not satisfied. Always she looked for something just beyond it, some mystic, heavenly rapture, always beginning to come, that never came. There was something about Oscar that repelled her. But because she had taken him for her lover, she couldn't bring herself to admit that it was a certain coarseness. She looked another way and pretended it wasn't there. To justify herself, she fixed her mind on his good qualities, his generosity, his strength, the way he had built up his engineering business. She made him take her over his works, and show her his great dynamos. She made him lend her the books he read. But always, when she tried to talk to him, he let her see that *that* wasn't what she was there for.

"My dear girl, we haven't time," he said. "It's waste of our priceless moments."

She persisted. "There's something wrong about it all if we can't talk to each other."

He was irritated. "Woman never seem to consider that a man can get all the talk he wants from other men. What's wrong is our meeting in this unsatisfactory way. We ought to live together. It's the only sane thing. I would, only I don't want to break up Muriel's home and make her miserable."

"I thought you said she wouldn't care."

"My dear, she cares for her home and her position and the children. You forget the children."

Yes. She had forgotten the children. She had forgotten Muriel. She had left off thinking of Oscar as a man with a wife and children and a home.

He had a plan. His mother-in-law was coming to stay with Muriel in October and he would get away. He would go to Paris, and Harriott should come to him there. He could say he went on business. No need to lie about it; he *had* business in Paris.

He engaged rooms in an hotel in the rue de Rivoli. They spent two weeks there.

For three days Oscar was madly in love with Harriott and Harriott with him. As she lay awake she would turn on the light and look at him as he slept at her side. Sleep made him beautiful and innocent; it laid a fine, smooth tissue over his coarseness; it made his mouth gentle; it entirely hid his eyes.

In six days reaction had set in. At the end of the tenth day, Harriott, returning with Oscar from Montmartre, burst into a fit of crying. When questioned, she answered wildly that the Hotel Saint Pierre was too hideously ugly; it was getting on her nerves. Mercifully Oscar explained her state as fatigue following excitement. She tried hard to believe that she was miserable because her love was purer and more spiritual than Oscar's; but all the time she knew perfectly well she had cried from pure boredom. She was in love with Oscar, and Oscar bored her. Oscar was in love with her, and she bored him. At close quarters, day in and day out, each was revealed to the other as an incredible bore.

At the end of the second week she began to doubt whether she had ever been really in love with him.

Her passion returned for a little while after they got back to London. Freed from the unnatural strain which Paris had put on them, they persuaded themselves that their romantic temperaments were better fitted to the old life of casual adventure.

Then, gradually, the sense of danger began to wake in them. They lived in perpetual fear, face to face with all the chances of discovery. They tormented themselves and each other by imagining possibilities that they would never have considered in their first fine moments. It was as though they were beginning to ask themselves if it were, after all, worth while running such awful risks, for all they go out of it. Oscar still swore that if he had been free he would have married her. He pointed out that his intentions at any rate were regular. But she asked herself: Would I marry *him*? Marriage would be the Hotel Saint Pierre all over again, without any possibility of escape. But, if she wouldn't marry him, was she in love with him? That was the test. Perhaps it was a good thing he wasn't free. Then she told herself that these doubts were morbid, and that the question wouldn't arise.

One evening Oscar called to see her. He had come to tell her that Muriel was ill.

"Seriously ill?"

"I'm afraid so. It's pleurisy. May turn to pneumonia. We shall know one way or another in the next few days."

A terrible fear seized upon Harriott. Muriel might die of her pleurisy; and if Muriel died, she would have to marry Oscar. He was looking at her queerly, as if he knew what she was thinking, and she could see that the same thought had occurred to him and that he was frightened too.

Muriel got well again; but their danger had enlightened them. Muriel's life was now inconceivably precious to them both; she stood between them and that permanent union, which they dreaded and yet would not have the courage to refuse.

After enlightenment the rupture.

It came from Oscar, one evening when he sat with her in her drawing-room.

"Harriott," he said, "do you know I'm thinking seriously of settling down?"

"How do you mean, settling down?"

"Patching it up with Muriel, poor girl. . . . Has it never occurred to you that this little affair of ours can't go on forever?"

"You don't want it to go on?"

"I don't want to have any humbug about it. For God's sake, let's be straight. If it's done, it's done. Let's end it decently."

"I see. You want to get rid of me."

"That's a beastly way of putting it."

"Is there any way that isn't beastly? The whole thing's beastly. I should have thought you'd have stuck to it now you've made it what you wanted. When I haven't an ideal, I haven't a single illusion, when you've destroyed everything you didn't want."

"What didn't I want?"

"The clean, beautiful pan of it. The part *I* wanted."

"My part at least was real. It was cleaner and more beautiful than all that putrid stuff you wrapped it up in. You were a hypocrite, Harriott, and I wasn't. You're a hypocrite now if you say you weren't happy with me."

"I was never really happy. Never for one moment. There was always something I missed. Something you didn't give me. Perhaps you couldn't."

"No. I wasn't spiritual enough," he sneered.

"You were not. And you made me what you were."

"Oh, I noticed that you were always very spiritual *after* you'd got what you wanted."

"What I wanted?" she cried. "Oh, my God—"

"If you ever knew what you wanted."

"What—I—wanted," she repeated, drawing out her bitterness.

"Come," he said, "why not be honest? Face facts. I was awfully gone on you. You were awfully gone on me—once. We got tired of each other and it's over. But at least you might own we had a good time while it lasted."

"A good time?"

"Good enough for me."

"For you, because for you love only means one thing. Everything that's high and noble in it you dragged down to that, till there's nothing left for us but that. *That's* what you made of love."

Twenty years passed.

It was Oscar who died first, three years after the rupture. He did it suddenly one evening, falling down in a fit of apoplexy.

His death was an immense relief to Harriott. Perfect security had been impossible as long as he was alive. But now there wasn't a living soul who knew her secret.

Stilt, in the first moment of shock Harriott told herself that Oscar dead would be nearer to her than ever. She forgot how tittle she had wanted him to be near her, alive. And long before the twenty years had passed she had contrived to persuade herself that he had never been near to her at all. It was incredible that she had ever known such a person as Oscar Wade. As for their affair, she couldn't think of Harriott Leigh as the sort of woman to whom such a thing could happen. Schnebler's and the Hotel Saint Pierre ceased to figure among prominent images of her past. Her memories, if she had allowed herself to remember, would have clashed disagreeably with the reputation for sanctity which she had now acquired.

For Harriott at fifty-two was the friend and helper of the Reverend Clement Farmer, Vicar of St. Mary the Virgin's, Maida Vale. She worked as a deaconess in his parish, wearing the uniform of a deaconess, the semi-religious gown, the cloak, the bonnet and veil, the cross and rosary, the holy smile. She was also secretary to the Maida Vale and Kilburn Home for Fallen Girls.

Her moments of excitement came when Clement Farmer, the lean, austere likeness of Stephen Philpotts, in his cassock and lace-bordered surplice, issued from the vestry, when he mounted the pulpit, when he stood before the altar rails and lifted up his arms in the Benediction; her moments of ecstasy when she received the Sacrament from his hands. And she had moments of calm happiness when his study door closed on their communion. All these moments were saturated with a solemn holiness.

And they were insignificant compared with the moment of her dying.

She lay dozing in her white bed under the black crucifix with the ivory Christ. The basins and medicine bottles had been cleared from the table by her pillow; it was spread for the last rites. The priest moved quietly about the room, arranging the candles, the Prayer Book and the Holy Sacrament. Then he drew a chair to her bedside and watched with her, waiting for her to come up out of her doze.

She woke suddenly. Her eyes were fixed upon him. She had a flash of lucidity. She was dying, and her dying made her supremely important to Clement Farmer.

"Are you ready?" he asked.

"Not yet. I think I'm afraid. Make me not afraid."

He rose and tit the two candles on the altar. He took down the crucifix from the wall and stood it against the foot-rail of the bed.

She sighed. That was not what she had wanted.

"You will not be afraid now," he said.

"I'm not afraid of the hereafter. I suppose you get used to it. Only it may be terrible just at first."

"Our first state will depend very much on what we are thinking of at our last hour."

"There'll be my—confession," she said.

"And after it you will receive the Sacrament. Then you will have your mind fixed firmly upon God and your Redeemer. . . . Do you feel able to make your confession now, Sister? Everything is ready."

Her mind went back over her past and found Oscar Wade there. She wondered: Should she confess to him about Oscar Wade? One moment she thought it was possible; the next she knew that she couldn't. She could not. It wasn't necessary. For twenty years he had not been part of her life. No. She wouldn't confess about Oscar Wade. She had been guilty of other sins.

She made a careful selection.

"I have cared too much for the beauty of this world. . . . I have failed in charity to my poor girls. Because of my intense repugnance to their sin . . . I have thought, often, about—people I love, when I should have been thinking about God."

After that she received the Sacrament.

"Now," he said, "there is nothing to be afraid of."

"I won't be afraid if—if you would hold my hand."

He held it. And she lay still a long time, with her eyes shut. Then he heard her murmuring something. He stopped close.

"This—is—dying. I thought it would be horrible. And it's bliss . . . Bliss."

The priest's hand slackened, as if at the bidding of some wonder. She gave a weak cry.

"Oh—don't let me go."

His grasp tightened.

"Try," he said, "to think about God. Keep on looking at the crucifix."

"If I look," she whispered, "you won't let go my hand?"

"I will not let you go."

He held it till it was wrenched from him in the last agony.

She lingered for some hours in the room where these things had happened.

Its aspects was familiar and yet unfamiliar, and slightly repugnant to her. The altar, the crucifix, the lighted candles, suggested some tremendous and awful experience the details of which she was not able to recall. She seemed to remember that they had been connected in some way with the sheeted body on the bed; but the nature of the connection was not clear, and she did not associate the dead body with herself. When the nurse came in and laid it out, she saw that it was the body of a middle-aged woman. Her own living body was that of a young woman of about thirty-two.

Her mind had no past and no future, no sharp-edged, coherent memories, and no idea of anything to be done next.

Then, suddenly, the room began to come apart before her eyes, to split into shafts of floor and furniture and ceiling that shifted and were thrown by their commotion into different planes. They leaned slanting at every possible angle; they crossed and overlaid each other with a transparent mingling of dislocated perspectives, like reflections fallen on an interior seen behind glass.

The bed and the sheeted body slid away somewhere out of sight. She was standing by the door that still remained in position.

She opened it and found herself in the street, outside a building of yellowish-grey brick and freestone, with a tall slated spire. Her mind came together with a palpable click of recognition. This object was the Church of St. Mary the Virgin, Maida Vale. She could hear the droning of the organ. She opened the door and slipped in.

She had gone back into a definite space and time, and recovered a certain limited section of coherent memory. She remembered the rows of pitch-pine benches, with their Gothic peaks and mouldings; the stone-coloured walls and pillars with their chocolate stencilling; the hanging rings of lights along the aisles of the nave; the high altar with its lighted candles, and the polished brass cross, twinkling. These things were somehow permanent and real, adjusted to the image that now took possession of her.

She knew what she had come there for. The service was over. The choir had gone from the chancel; the sacristan moved before the altar, putting out the candles. She walked up the middle aisle to a seat that she knew under the pulpit. She knelt down and covered her face with her hands. Peeping sideways through her fingers, she could see the door of the vestry on her left at the end of the north aisle. She watched it steadily.

Up in the organ loft the organist drew out the Recessional, slowly and softly, to its end in the two solemn, vibrating chords.

The vestry door opened and Clement Farmer came out, dressed in his black cassock. He passed before her, close, close outside the bench where she knelt.

He paused at the opening. He was waiting for her. There was something he had to say.

She stood up and went towards him. He still waited. He didn't move to make way for her. She came close, closer than she had ever come to him, so close that his features grew indistinct. She bent her head back, peering short-sightedly, and found herself looking into Oscar Wade's face.

He stood still, horribly still, and close, barring her passage.

She drew back; his heaving shoulders followed her. He leaned forward, covering her with his eyes. She opened her mouth to scream and no sound came.

She was afraid to move lest he should move with her. The heaving of his shoulders terrified her.

One by one the lights in the side aisles were going out. The lights in the middle aisle would go next. They had gone. If she didn't get away she would be shut up with him there, in the appalling darkness.

She turned and moved towards the north aisle, groping, steadying herself by the book ledge.

When she looked back, Oscar Wade was not there.

Then she remembered that Oscar Wade was dead. Therefore, what she had seen was not Oscar; it was his ghost. He was dead; dead seventeen years ago. She was safe from him for ever.

When she came out on the steps of the church she saw that the road it stood in had changed. It was not the road she remembered. The pavement on this side was raised slightly and covered in. It ran under a succession of arches. It was a long gallery walled with glittering shop windows on one side; on the other a line of tall grey columns divided it from the street.

She was going along the arcades of the rue de Rivoli. Ahead of her she could see the edge of an immense grey pillar jutting out. That was the porch of the Hotel Saint Pierre. The revolving glass doors swung forward to receive her; she crossed the grey, sultry vestibule under the pillared arches. She knew it. She knew the porter's shining, wine-coloured, mahogany pen on her left, and the shining, wine-coloured, mahogany barrier of the clerk's bureau on her night; she made straight for the great grey carpeted staircases; she climbed the endless flights that turned round and round the caged-in shaft of the well, past the latticed doors of the lift, and came up on to a landing that she knew, and into the long, ash-grey, foreign corridor lit by a dull window at one end.

It was there that the horror of the place came on her. She had no longer any memory of St. Mary's Church, so that she was unaware of her backward course through time. All space and time were here.

She remembered she had to go to the left, the left.

But there was something there; where the corridor turned by the window; at the end of all the corridors. If she went the other way she would escape it.

The corridor stopped there. A blank wall. She was driven back past the stairhead to the left.

At the corner, by the window, she turned down another long ash-grey corridor on her right, and to the right again where the night-light spluttered on the table-flap at the turn.

This third corridor was dark and secret and depraved. She knew the soiled walls, and the warped door at the end. There was a sharp-pointed streak of light at the top. She could see the number on it now, 107.

Something had happened there. If she went in it would happen again.

Oscar Wade was in the room waiting for her behind the closed door. She felt him moving about in there. She leaned forward, her ear to the key-hole, and listened. She could hear the measured, deliberate, thoughtful footsteps. They were coming from the bed to the door.

She turned and ran; her knees gave way under her; she sank and ran on, down the long grey corridors and the stairs, quick and blind, a hunted beast seeking for cover, hearing his feet coming after her.

The revolving doors caught her and pushed her out into the street.

The strange quality of her state was this, that it had no time. She remembered dimly that there had once been a thing called time; but she had forgotten altogether what it was like. She was aware of things happening and about to happen; she fixed them by the place they occupied, and measured their duration by the space she went through.

So now she thought: If I could only go back and get to the place where it hadn't happened.

To get back farther—

She was walking now on a white road that went between broad grass borders. To the right and left were the long raking lines of the hills, curve after curve, shimmering in a thin mist.

The road dropped to the green valley. It mounted the humped bridge over the river. Beyond it she saw the twin gables of the grey house pricked up over the high, grey garden wall. The tall iron gate stood in front of it between the ball-topped stone pillars.

And now she was in a large, low-ceilinged room with drawn blinds. She was standing before the wide double bed. It was her father's bed. The dead body, stretched out in the middle under the drawn white sheet, was her father's body.

The outline of the sheet sank from the peak of the upturned toes to the shin bone, and from the high bridge of the nose to the chin.

She lifted the sheet and folded it back across the breast of the dead man. The face she saw then was Oscar Wade's face, stilled and smoothed in the innocence of sleep, the supreme innocence of death. She stared at it, fascinated, in a cold, pitiless joy.

Oscar was dead.

She remembered how he used to lie like that beside her in the room in the Hotel Saint Pierre, on his back with his hands folded on his waist, his mouth half open, his big chest rising and falling. If he was dead, it would never happen again. She would be safe.

The dead face frightened her, and she was about to cover it up again when she was aware of a light heaving, a rhythmical rise and fall. As she drew the sheet up tighter, the hands under it began to struggle convulsively, the broad ends of the fingers appeared above the edge, clutching it to keep it down. The mouth opened; the eyes opened; the whole face stared back at her in a look of agony and horror.

Then the body drew itself forwards from the hips and sat up, its eyes peering into her eyes; he and she remained for an instant motionless, each held there by the other's fear.

Suddenly she broke away, turned and ran, out of the room, out of the house.

She stood at the gate, looking up and down the road, not knowing by which way she must go to escape Oscar. To the right, over the bridge and up the hill and across the downs she would come to the arcades of the rue de Rivoli and the dreadful grey corridors of the hotel. To the left the road went through the village.

If she could get further back she would be safe, out of Oscar's reach. Standing by her father's death-bed she had been young, but not young enough. She must get back to the place where she was younger still, to the Park and the green drive under the beech trees and the white pavilion at the cross. She knew how to find it. At the end of the village the high road ran right and left, east and west, under the Park walls; the south gate stood there at the top looking down the narrow street.

She ran towards it through the village, past the long grey barns of Goodyer's farm, pat the grocer's shop, past the yellow front and blue sign of the "Queen's Head," past the post office, with its one black window blinking under its vine, past the church and the yew-trees in the churchyard, to where the south gate made a delicate black pattern on the green grass.

These things appeared insubstantial, drawn back behind a sheet of air that shimmered over them like thin glass. They opened out, floated pat and away from her; and instead of the high road and park walls she saw a London street of dingy white façades and instead of the south gate the swinging glass doors of Schnebler's Restaurant.

The glass doors swung open and she passed into the restaurant. The scene beat on her with the hard impact of reality: the white and gold panels, the white pillars and their curling gold capitals, the white circles of the tables, glittering, the flushed faces of the diners, moving mechanically.

She was driven forward by some irresistible compulsion to a table in the corner, where a man sat alone. The table napkin he was using hid his mouth, and jaw, and chest; and she was not sure of the upper part of the face above the straight, drawn edge. It dropped; and she saw Oscar Wade's face. She came to him, dragged, without power to resist; she sat down beside him, and he leaned to her over the table; she could feel the warmth of his red, congested face; the smell of wine floated towards her on his thick whisper.

"I knew you would come."

She ate and drank with him in silence, nibbling and sipping slowly, staving off the abominable moment it would end in.

At last they got up and faced each other. His long bulk stood before her, above her; she could almost feel the vibration of its power.

"Come," he said. "Come."

And she went before him, slowly, slipping out through the maze of the tables, hearing behind her Oscar's measured, deliberate, thoughtful tread. The steep, red-carpeted staircase rose up before her.

She swerved from it, but he turned her back.

"You know the way," he said.

At the top of the flight she found the white door of the room she knew. She knew the long windows guarded by drawn muslin blinds; the gilt looking-glass over the chimney-piece that reflected Oscar's head and shoulders grotesquely between two white porcelain babies and bulbous limbs and garlanded loins, she knew the sprawling stain on the drab carpet by the table, the shabby, infamous couch behind the screen.

They moved about the room, turning and turning in it like beasts in a cage, uneasy, inimical, avoiding each other.

At last they stood still, he at the window, she at the door, the length of the room between.

"It's no good your getting away like that," he said. "There couldn't be any other end to it—to what we did."

"But that *was* ended."

"Ended there, but not here."

"Ended for ever. We've done with it for ever."

"We haven't. We've got to begin again. And go on. And go on."

"Oh, no. No. Anything but that."

"There isn't anything else."

"We can't. We can't. Don't you remember how it bored us?"

"Remember? Do you suppose I'd touch you if I could help it. . . . That's what we're here for. We must. We must."

"No. No. I shall get away—now."

She turned to the door to open it.

"You can't," he said. "The door's locked."

"Oscar—what did you do that for?"

"We always did it. Don't you remember?"

She turned to the door again and shook it; she beat on it with her hands.

"It's no use, Harriott. If you got out now you'd only have to come back again. You might stave it off for an hour or so, but what's that in an immortality?"

"Immortality?"

"That's what we're in for."

"Time enough to talk about immortality when we're dead. . . . Ah—"

They were being drawn towards each other across the room, moving slowly, like figures in some monstrous and appalling dance, their heads thrown back over their shoulders, their faces turned from the horrible approach. Their arms rose slowly, heavy with intolerable reluctance; they stretched them out towards each other, aching, as if they held up an overpowering weight. Their feet dragged and were drawn.

Suddenly her knees sank under her; she shut her eyes; all her being went down before him in darkness and terror.

It was over. She had got away, she was going back, back, to the green drive of the Park, between the beech trees, where Oscar had never been, where he would never find her. When she passed through the south gate her memory became suddenly young and clean. She forgot the rue de Rivoli and the Hotel Saint Pierre; she forgot Schnebler's Restaurant and the room at the top of the stairs. She was back in her youth. She was

Harriott Leigh going to wait for Stephen Philpotts in the pavilion opposite the west gate. She could feel herself, a slender figure moving fast over the grass between the lines of the great beech trees. The freshness of her youth was upon her.

She came to heart of the drive where it branched right and left in the form of a cross. At the end of the right arm the white Greek temple, with its pediment and pillars, gleamed against the wood.

She was sitting on their seat at the back of the pavilion, watching the side door that Stephen would come in by.

The door was pushed open; he came towards her, light and young, skimming between the beech trees with his eager, tiptoeing stride. She rose up to meet him. She gave a cry.

"Stephen!"

It had been Stephen. She had seen him coming. But the man who stood before her between the pillars of the pavilion was Oscar Wade.

And now she was waiting along the field-path that slanted from the orchard door to the stile; further and further back, to where young George Waring waited for her under the elder tree. The smell of the elder flowers came to her over the field. She could feel on her lips and in all her body the sweet, innocent excitement of her youth.

"George, oh, George?"

As she went along the field-path she had seen him. But the man who stood waiting for her under the elder tree was Oscar Wade.

"I told you it's no use getting away, Harriott. Every path brings you back to me. You'll find me at every turn."

"But how did you get *here*?"

"As I got into the pavilion. As I got into your father's room, on to his death-bed. Because I *was* there. I am in all your memories."

"My memories are innocent. How could you take my father's place, and Stephen's, and George Waring's? You?"

"Because I did take them."

"Never. My love for *them* was innocent."

"Your love for me was part of it. You think the past affects the future. Has it never struck you that the future may affect the past? In your innocence there was the beginning of your sin. You *were* what you *were to be*.

"I shall get away," she said.

"And, this time, I shall go with you."

The stile, the elder tree, and the field floated away from her. She was going under the beech trees down the Park drive towards the south gate and the village, slinking close to the right-hand row of trees. She was aware that Oscar Wade was going with her under the left-hand row, keeping even with her, step by step, and tree by tree. And presently there was grey pavement under her feet and a row of grey pillars on her right hand. They were walking side by side down the rue de Rivoli towards the hotel.

They were sitting together now on the edge of the dingy white bed. Their arms hung by their sides, heavy and limp, their heads drooped, averted. Their passion weighed on them with the unbearable, unescapable boredom of immortality.

"Oscar—how long will it last?"

"I can't tell you. I don't know whether this is one moment of eternity, or the eternity of one moment."

"It must end some time," she said. "Life doesn't go on for ever. We shall die."

"Die? We *have* died. Don't you know what this is? Don't you know where you are? This is death. We're dead, Harriott. We're in hell."

"Yes. There can't be anything worse than this."

"This isn't the worst. We're not quite dead yet, as long as we've life in us to turn and run and get away from each other; as long as we can escape into our memories. But when you've got back to the farthest memory of all and there's nothing beyond it—when there's no memory but this—

"In the last hell we shall not run away any longer; we shall find no more roads, no more passages, no more open doors. We shall have no need to look for each other.

"In the last death we shall be shut up in this room, behind that locked door, together. We shall lie here together, for ever and ever, joined so fast that even God can't put us asunder. We shall be one flesh and one spirit, one sin repeated for ever, and ever; spirit loathing flesh, flesh loathing spirit; you and I loathing each other."

"Why? Why?" she cried.

"Because that's all that's left us. That's what you made of love."

The darkness came down swamping, it blotted out the room. She was walking along a garden path between high borders of phlox and larkspur and lupin. They were taller than she was, their flowers swayed and nodded above her head. She tugged at the tall stems and had no strength to break them. She was a little thing.

She said to herself then that she was safe. She had gone back so far that she was a child again; she had the blank innocence of childhood. To be a child, to go small under the heads of the lupins, to be blank and innocent, without memory, was to be safe.

The walk led her out through a yew hedge on to a bright green lawn. In the middle of the lawn there was a shallow round pond in a ring of rockery cushioned with small flowers, yellow and white and purple. Gold-fish swam in the olive brown water. She would be safe when she saw the gold-fish swimming towards her. The old one with the white scales would come up first, pushing up his nose, making bubbles in the water.

At the bottom of the lawn there was a privet hedge cut by a broad path that went through the orchard. She knew what she would find there; her mother was in the orchard. She would lift her up in her arms to play with the hard red balls of the apples that hung from the tree. She had got back to the farthest memory of all; there was nothing beyond it.

There would be an iron gate in the wall of the orchard. It would lead into a field.

Something was different here, something that frightened her. An ash-grey door instead of an iron gate.

She pushed it open and came into the last corridor of the Hotel Saint Pierre.

A Night in Malnéant

Clark Ashton Smith

———◆———

MY SOJOURN IN THE CITY OF MALNÉANT OCCURRED DURING A PERIOD of my life no less dim and dubious than that city itself and the misty regions lying there about. I have no precise recollection of its locality, nor can I remember exactly when and how I came to visit it. But I had heard vaguely that such a place was situated along my route; and when I came to the fog-enfolded river that flows beside its walls, and heard beyond the river the mortuary tolling of many bells, I surmised that I was approaching Malnéant.

On reaching the gray, colossal bridge that crosses the river, I could have continued at will on other roads leading to remoter cities: but it seemed to me that I might as well enter Malnéant as any other place. And so it was that I set foot on the bridge of shadowy arches, under which the black waters flowed in stealthy division and were joined again in a silence as of Styx and Acheron.

That period of my life, I have said, was dim and dubious: all the more so, mayhap, because of my need for forgetfulness, my persistent and at times partially rewarded search for oblivion. And that which I needed to forget above all was the death of the lady Mariel, and the fact that I myself had slain her as surely as if I had done the deed with my own hand. For she had loved me with an affection deeper and purer and more stable than mine; and my changeable temper, my fits of cruel indifference or ferocious irritability, had broken her gentle heart. So it was that she had sought the anodyne of a lethal poison; and after she was laid to rest in the somber vaults of her ancestors, I had become a wanderer, followed and forever tortured by a belated remorse. For months, or years, I am uncertain which, I roamed from old-world city to city, heeding little where I went if only wine and the other agents of oblivion were available. . . . And thus I came, some while in my indefinite journeying, to the dim environs of Malnéant.

The sun (if ever there was a sun above this region) had been lost for I knew not how long in a sky of leaden vapors; the day was drear and sullen at best. But now, by the thickening of the shadows and the mist, I felt that evening must be near; and the bells I had heard, however heavy and sepulchral their tolling, gave at least the assurance of prospective shelter for the night. So I crossed the long bridge and entered the grimly yawning gate with a quickening of my footsteps even if with no alacrity of spirit.

The dusk had gathered behind the gray walls, but there were few lights in the city. Few people were abroad, and these went upon their way with a sort of solemn haste, as if on some funereal errand that would admit of no delay. The streets were narrow, the houses high, with overhanging balconies and heavily curtained or shuttered windows. All was very silent, except for the bells, which tolled recurrently, sometimes faint and far off, and sometimes with a loud and startling clangor that seemed to come almost from overhead.

As I plunged among the shadowy mansions, along the streets from which a visible twilight issued to envelop me, it seemed that I was going farther and farther away from my memories at every step. For this reason I did not at once inquire my way to a tavern but was content to lose myself more and more in the gray labyrinth of buildings, which grew vaguer and vaguer amid the ever-mounting darkness and fog, as if they were about to dissolve in oblivion.

I think that my soul would have been almost at peace with itself, if it had not been for the reiterant ringing of the bells, which were like all bells that toll for the repose of the dead, and therefore set me to remembering those that had rung for Mariel. But whenever they ceased, my thoughts would drift back with an indolent ease, a recovered security, to the all-surrounding vagueness . . .

I had no idea how far I had gone in Malnéant, nor how long I had roamed among those houses that hardly seemed as if they could be peopled by any but the sleeping or the dead. At last, however, I became aware that I was very tired, and bethought me of food and wine and a lodging for the night. But nowhere in my wanderings had I noticed the sign-board of an inn; so I resolved to ask the next passer-by for the desired direction.

As I have said before, there were few people abroad. Now, when I made up my mind to address one of them, it appeared that there was no one at all; and I walked onward through street after street in my futile search for a living face.

At length I met two women, clothed in gray that was cold and dim as the folds of the fog, and veiled withal, who were hurrying along with the same funereal intentness

I had perceived in all other denizens of that city. I made bold to accost them, asking if they could direct me to an inn.

Scarcely pausing or even turning their heads, they answered: "We cannot tell you. We are shroud-weavers, and we have been busy making a shroud for the lady Mariel."

Now, at that name, which of all names in the world was the one I should least have expected or cared to hear, an unspeakable chill invaded my heart, and a dreadful dismay smote me like the breath of the tomb. It was indeed strange that in this dim city, so far in time and space from all I had fled to escape, a woman should have recently died who was also named Mariel. The coincidence appeared so sinister, that an odd fear of the streets through which I had wandered was born suddenly in my soul. The name had evoked, with a more irrevocable fatality than the tolling of the bells, all that I had vainly wished to forget; and my memories were like living coals in my heart.

As I went onward, with paces that had become more hurried, more feverish than those of the people of Malnéant, I met two men, who were likewise dressed from head to foot in gray; and I asked of them the same question I had asked of the shroud-weavers.

"We cannot tell you," they replied. "We are coffin-makers, and we have been busy making a coffin for the lady Mariel."

As they spoke, and hastened on, the bells rang out again, this time very near at hand, with a more dismal and sepulchral menace in their leaden tolling. And everything about me, the tall and misty houses, the dark, indefinite streets, the rare and wraith-like figures, became as if part of the obscure confusion and fear and bafflement of a nightmare. Moment by moment, the coincidence on which I had stumbled appeared all too bizarre for belief, and I was troubled now by the monstrous and absurd idea that the Mariel I knew had only just died, and that this fantastic city was in some unsurmisable manner connected with her death. But this, of course, my reason rejected summarily, and I kept repeating to myself: "The Mariel of whom they speak is another Mariel." And it irritated me beyond all measure that a thought so enormous and ludicrous should return when my logic had dismissed it.

I met no more people of whom to inquire my way. But at length, as I fought with my shadowy perplexity and my burning memories, I found that I had paused beneath the weather-beaten sign of an inn, on which the lettering had been half effaced by time and the brown lichens. The building was obviously very old, like all the houses in Malnéant; its upper stories were lost in the swirling fog, except for a few furtive lights that glowed obscurely down; and a vague and musty odor of antiquity came forth to greet me as I mounted the steps and tried to open the ponderous door. But the door had been locked or bolted; so I began to pound upon it with my fists to attract the attention of those within.

After much delay, the door was opened slowly and grudgingly, and a cadaverous-looking individual peered forth, frowning with portentous gravity as he saw me.

"What do you desire?" he queried, in tones that were both brusk and solemn.

"A room for the night, and wine," I requested.

"We cannot accommodate you. All the rooms are occupied by people who have come to attend the obsequies of the lady Mariel; and all the wine in the house has been requisitioned for their use. You will have to go elsewhere."

He closed the door quickly upon me with the last words.

I turned to resume my wanderings, and all that had troubled me before was now intensified a hundredfold. The gray mists and the grayer houses were full of the menace of memory: they were like traitorous tombs from which the cadavers of dead hours poured forth to assail me with envenomed fangs and talons. I cursed the hour when I had entered Malnéant, for it seemed to me now that in so doing I had merely completed a funereal, sinister circle through time, and had returned to the day of Mariel's death. And certainly, all my recollections of Mariel, of her final agony and her entombment, had assumed the frightful vitality of present things. But my reason still maintained, of course, that the Mariel who lay dead somewhere in Malnéant, and for whom all these obsequial preparations were being made, was not the lady whom I had loved, but another.

After threading streets that were even darker and narrower than those before traversed, I found a second inn, bearing a similar weather-beaten sign, and in all other respects very much like the first. The door was barred, and I knocked thereon with trepidation and was in no manner surprised when a second individual with a cadaverous face informed me in tones of sepulchral solemnity:

"We cannot accommodate you. All the rooms have been taken by musicians and mourners who will serve at the obsequies of the lady Mariel; and all the wine has been reserved for their use."

Now I began to dread the city about me with a manifold fear: for apparently the whole business of the people in Malnéant consisted of preparations for the funeral of this lady Mariel. And it began to be obvious that I must walk the streets of the city all night because of these same preparations. All at once, an overwhelming weariness was mingled with my nightmare terror and perplexity.

I had not long continued my peregrinations, after leaving the second inn, when the bells were tolled once more. For the first time, I found it possible to identify their source: they were in the spires of a great cathedral which loomed immediately before me through the fog. Some people were entering the cathedral, and a curiosity, which I knew to be both morbid and perilous, prompted me to follow them. Here, I somehow felt, I should be able to learn more regarding the mystery that tormented me.

All was dim within, and the light of many tapers scarcely served to illumine the vast nave and altar. Masses were being said by priests in black whose faces I could not see distinctly; and to me, their chanting was like words in a dream; and I could hear nothing, and nothing was plainly visible in all the place, except a bier of opulent fabrics on which there lay a motionless form in white. Flowers of many hues had been strewn upon the bier, and their fragrance filled the air with a drowsy languor, with an ano-dyne that seemed to drug my heart and brain. Such flowers had been cast on the bier of Mariel; and even thus, at her funeral, I had been overcome by a momentary dulling of the senses because of their perfume.

Dimly I became aware that someone was at my elbow. With eyes still intent on the bier, I asked:

"Who is it that lies yonder, for whom these masses are being said and these bells are rung?" And a slow, sepulchral voice replied:

"It is the lady Mariel, who died yesterday and who will be interred tomorrow in the vaults of her ancestors. If you wish, you may go forward and gaze upon her."

So I went down the cathedral aisle, even to the side of the bier, whose opulent fab-rics trailed on the cold flags. And the face of her who lay thereon, with a tranquil smile upon the lips, and tender shadows upon the shut eyelids, was the face of the Mariel I had loved and of none other. The tides of time were frozen in their flowing; and all that was or had been or could be, all of the world that existed aside from her, became as fad-ing shadows; and even as once before (was it eons or instants ago?) my soul was locked in the marble hell of its supreme grief and regret. I could not move, I could not cry out nor even weep, for my very tears were turned to ice. And now I knew with a terrible certitude that this one event, the death of the lady Mariel, had drawn apart from all other happenings, had broken away from the sequence of time and had found for itself a setting of appropriate gloom and solemnity; or perhaps had even built around itself the whole enormous maze of that spectral city, in which to abide my destined return among the mists of a deceptive oblivion.

At length, with an awful effort of will, I turned my eyes away; and leaving the cathedral with steps that were both hurried and leaden, I sought to find an egress from the dismal labyrinth of Malnéant to the gate by which I had entered. But this was by no means easy, and I must have roamed for hours in alleys blind and stifling as tombs, and along the tortuous, self-reverting thoroughfares, ere I came to a familiar street and was able henceforward to direct my paces with something of surety. And a dull and sunless daylight was dawning behind the mists when I crossed the bridge and came again to the road that would lead me away from that fatal city.

Since then, I have wandered long and in many places. But never again have I cared to revisit those old-world realms of fog and mist, for fear that I should come once more to Malnéant, and find that its people are still busied with their preparations for the obsequies of the lady Mariel.

Original Sources

Benson, E. F. "The Man Who Went Too Far," *The Pall Mall Magazine*, June 1904.

Bierce, Ambrose. "The Death of Halpin Frayser," *The Collected Works of Ambrose Bierce*, Volume III. New York: Nealy Publishing Company, 1910.

Blackwood, Algernon. "Ancient Sorceries," *John Silence: Physician Extraordinary*. London: Everleigh Nash, 1908.

Brown, Charles Brockden. "Carwin, The Biloquist," *Carwin, the Biloquist and Other American Tales*. London: Henry Colburn and Company, 1822.

Cram, Ralph Adams. "The Dead Valley," *Black Spirits and White*. Chicago: Stone & Kimball, 1895.

Crawford, F. Marion. "For the Blood Is the Life," *Wandering Ghosts*. New York: The Macmillan Company, 1911.

de la Mare, Walter. "Seaton's Aunt," *The London Mercury*, Apr. 1922.

Doyle, Arthur Conan. "Lot No. 249," *Harper's*, Sept. 1892.

Dunsany, Lord. "The Hoard of the Gibbelins," *The Book of Wonder*. New York: Boni & Liveright, 1918.

Erckmann-Chatrian. "The Waters of Death," *Library of the World's Best Mystery & Detective Stories*, edited by Julian Hawthorne. New York: The Review of Reviews Company, 1908.

Everett, H. D. "The Death-Mask," *The Death-Mask and Other Ghosts*. London: Philip J. Allan, 1920.

Forster, E. M. "The Story of a Panic," *The Celestial Omnibus and Other Stories*. London: Sidgwick & Jackson Ltd., 1912.

Freeman, Mary E. Wilkins. "The Southwest Chamber," *The Wind in the Rose-Bush*. New York: Doubleday, Page & Company, 1903.

Gautier, Théophile. "Clarimonde," *Stories*. London: T. C. & E. C. Jack, 1908.

Hawthorne, Nathaniel. "Ethan Brand," *Little Masterpieces*, edited by Bliss Perry. New York: Doubleday, Page & Co., 1921.

Hearn, Lafcadio. "The Ghostly Kiss," *Fantastics and Other Fancies*. Boston: Houghton Mifflin Company, 1919.

Hodgson, William Hope. *The House on the Borderland*. London: Chapman and Hall Ltd., 1908.

Hoffmann, E. T. A. "The Sandman," *Tales from the German*, translated by John Oxenford and C. A. Feiling. London: Chaptman and Hal Ltd., 1844.

Housman, Clemence. *The Were-Wolf*. London: John Lane, 1896.

Jacobs, W. W. "The Monkey's Paw," *The Lady of the Barge*. London: Harper & Brothers, 1902.

James, M. R. "The Treasure of Abbot Thomas," *Ghost Stories of an Antiquary*. London: Edward Arnold, 1905.

Kipling, Rudyard. "The Phantom 'Rickshaw," *The Phantom 'Rickshaw and Other Tales*. New York: John W. Lovell Company, 1890.

Level, Maurice. "The Last Kiss," *Tales of Mystery and Horror*. New York: Robert M. McBride & Co., 1920.

Machen, Arthur. "The White People," *The House of Souls*. New York: Alfred A. Knopf, 1922.

Marryatt, H. B. "The Were-Wolf," *Great Ghost Stories*, edited by Joseph Lewis French. New York: Dodd, Mead & Company, 1918.

Maupassant, Guy de. "On the River," *The Collected Novels and Stories of Guy de Maupassant*. New York: Alfred A. Knopf, 1922.

Mérimée, Prosper. "The Venus of Ille," *The Writings of Prosper Mérimée*. New York: Croscup & Holby Company, 1905.

Metcalfe, John. "The Bad Lands," *The Smoking Leg and Other Stories*. New York: Doubleday, Page & Company, 1926.

O'Brien, Fitz-James. "What Was It?" *The Poems and Stories of Fitz-James O'Brien*. Boston: James R. Osgood and Company, 1881.

Poe, Edgar Allan. "Ligeia," *The Works of the Late Edgar Allan Poe*. New York: J. S. Redfield, 1850.

Polidori, John. *The Vampyre*. London: Sherwood, Neely, and Jones, 1819.

Scott, Sir Walter. "The Tapestried Chamber," *The Talisman, The Two Drovers, My Aunt Margaret's Mirror, The Tapestried Chamber, The Laird's Jock*. New York: D. Appleton and Company, 1869.

Shiel, M. P. "The House of Sounds," *The Pale Ape and Other Pulses*. London: T. Werner Laurie, 1911

Sinclair, May. "Where Their Fire Is Not Quenched," *The English Review*, Oct. 1922.

Smith, Clark Ashton. "A Night in Malnéant," *The Double Shadow and Other Fantasies*. Auburn, CA: Auburn Journal Press, 1933. Reprinted with the permission of CASiana Enterprises, The Literary Estate of Clark Ashton Smith.

Wells, H. G. "The Red Room," *Thirty Strange Stories*. London: Harper & Brothers, 1898.

White, Edward Lucas. "The Snout," *Lukundoo and Other Stories*. New York: George H. Doran Company, 1927.